Atlas

The Story of Pa Salt

Also by Lucinda Riley

The Hothouse Flower
The Girl on the Cliff
The Light Behind the Window
The Midnight Rose
The Italian Girl
The Angel Tree
The Olive Tree
The Love Letter
The Butterfly Room
The Murders at Fleat House

The Seven Sisters Series
The Seven Sisters
The Storm Sister
The Shadow Sister
The Pearl Sister
The Moon Sister
The Sun Sister
The Missing Sister

Atlas

The Story of Pa Salt

By Lucinda Riley
&
Harry Whittaker

BLUE
BOX
PRESS

Atlas: The Story of Pa Salt
By Lucinda Riley

Copyright 2023 Lucinda Riley Limited
ISBN: 978-1-957568-18-8

Published by Blue Box Press, an imprint of Evil Eye Concepts,
Incorporated

Dedication

Lucinda dedicates this novel to her readers across the globe.

I dedicate it to my mother, Lucinda, who inspired me in every way—
H.W.

Foreword

Dear Reader,

Allow me to introduce myself. My name is Harry, and I am Lucinda Riley's eldest son. I suspect not, but perhaps it surprised you to see two names on the cover of this long-awaited novel.

Just before the release of *The Missing Sister* in 2021, Lucinda announced that there was to be a surprise eighth and final instalment in the Seven Sisters series, which would tell the tale of the enigmatic Pa Salt. In her Author's Note at the end of the seventh book, she wrote: 'It's been in my head for eight years, and I can't wait to finally get it down on paper.'

Tragically, Mum died in June 2021 following an oesophageal cancer diagnosis in 2017. Perhaps you are speculating that she never had the chance to pen anything. But fate works in mysterious ways. In 2016, Mum was flown over to Hollywood by a production company who were interested in acquiring the film rights to the Seven Sisters. As such, the team were desperate to know how she saw the series ending—four books ahead of schedule.

The process forced Mum to assemble her fragmented thoughts in a document. She wrote thirty pages of script dialogue for the potential producers, which take place at the climax of the series' narrative. I'm sure I don't need to persuade you that those pages were predictably magnificent; packed with drama, suspense…and an enormous surprise.

In addition to this, fans of the series will know that Pa Salt cameos in each book. Mum kept a timeline of the character's movements across the decades, forming a comprehensive spotter's guide. In these ways, Lucinda got more 'down on paper' than she ever gave herself credit for.

In 2018, Mum and I created the Guardian Angels series for children, and co-authored four books. During this time, she asked me to complete the Seven Sisters series if the worst were to happen. Our conversations will always remain private, but I wish to stress that I was a fail-safe put in place in case of the unthinkable. And unthinkable it was. I don't believe that Mum ever really considered that she would actually die, and neither did I. Several times, she somehow defied the laws of science and nature to bounce back from the brink. But then, Mum was always a little bit magic.

After her death, there was no question that I would keep my word. Many people have asked about the pressure of the task. Ultimately, *Atlas* promises to reveal secrets that have kept readers guessing for a decade. However, I've always seen the process as a tribute. I've completed the task for my best friend and my hero. In that way, there's been no pressure at all, and it's proved to be a labour of love. I predict that some will naturally obsess over which plot elements are Mum's and which are mine, but I don't think that's important. Put simply, the story is the story. And I know you will be emotionally satisfied at the end of this book. Mum has made sure of that.

Arguably Lucinda's greatest achievement is that no one has correctly identified the secret driving force behind the series—and there have been thousands of theories. *Atlas* will reward those who have loved the novels since the beginning, but there is a new story to tell, too (although it's always been there, hidden quietly amongst the first 4,500 pages). Perhaps all I'm doing is removing the smokescreen…

Working on *Atlas: The Story of Pa Salt* has been the challenge and privilege of a lifetime. It is Lucinda Riley's parting gift, and I am so excited to deliver it.

Harry Whittaker, 2023

There are more things in heaven and earth,
Horatio, than are dreamt of in your philosophy.

William Shakespeare

Cast of Characters

Prologue

Tobolsk, Siberia, 1925

As the bitter wind whipped up a flurry of snow before them, the two young boys pulled their thinning fur coats tightly around their faces.

'Come on!' cried the elder of the pair. Although he had just turned eleven, his voice already possessed a gruff, husky quality. 'That's enough. Let's get back home.'

The younger boy—only seven—picked up the pile of firewood they had been collecting and ran after the older boy, who was already striding away.

When they were halfway home, the children became aware of a faint cheeping noise coming from the trees. The older boy stopped in his tracks.

'Do you hear that?' he asked.

'Yes,' replied the small boy. His arms were aching from the weight of the wood, and although they had been still for just a moment, he had started to shiver. 'Can we get home, please? I'm tired.'

'Don't whine,' the older boy snapped. 'I'm going to investigate.' He made his way to the base of a nearby birch and knelt down. Reluctantly, the smaller boy followed behind.

Before them, wriggling helplessly on the hard ground, was a baby sparrow no bigger than a rouble.

'He's fallen from the nest,' the older boy sighed. 'Or, I wonder…listen.' The pair stood still in the snow, and eventually heard a high-pitched call from above. 'Aha! That's a cuckoo.'

'The bird from the clock?'

'Yes. But they are not friendly creatures. The cuckoo lays its eggs in the nests of other birds. Then, when the chick hatches, it pushes the other babies out.' He sniffed. 'That's what's happened here.'

'Oh no.' The smaller boy bent down and used his little finger to gently stroke the bird's head. 'It's all right, friend, we're here now.' He looked up at his companion. 'Maybe if we climb the tree, we can put him back.' The boy attempted to spot the nest. 'It must be very high up.' Suddenly, there was a sickening crunch from the forest floor. He looked down to see that the older boy had crushed the chick under his boot.

'What have you done?' the small boy cried in horror.

'The mother wouldn't have accepted it. Best to kill it now.'

'But…you don't know that.' Tears began to prick the boy's brown eyes. 'We could have tried.'

The elder of the pair put his hand up to dismiss the protestations. 'There is no point in trying when something is doomed to failure. That is simply a waste of time.' He continued down the hill. 'Come on. Let's get back.'

The younger boy bent down to look at the lifeless chick. 'I'm sorry about my brother,' he sobbed. 'He is in pain. He didn't mean to do this.'

The Diary of Atlas

1928–29

1

The diary is a present from Monsieur and Madame Paul Landowski. They say that because I don't speak, yet they know that I can write, it would be a good idea if I tried to note down things that I think. At first, they thought I was just plain stupid, that I had lost my wits, which in many ways I have. Or more accurately, perhaps I have just exhausted them, having lived by them for so long. They are very tired, and so am I.

The reason they know that I at least have some sense left is because they asked me to write. To begin with, they tried to make me write my name, age and where I had come from, but I learnt long ago that writing such things on paper can get you into trouble, and trouble is something I want no more of ever again. So, I sat at the table in the kitchen and copied out a piece of poetry that Papa had taught me. Of course, it was one that would not betray where I came from before I arrived under a hedge in their garden. Nor was it one of my favourites, but I felt the words suited my mood, and were enough to show this kind couple— whom fate had thrown in my path when death was knocking at my door—that I could communicate. So I wrote:

Tonight I've watched
the moon and then
the Pleiades
go down

*The night is now
half-gone; youth
goes; I am
in bed alone*

I wrote it in French, English and German, none of which was the language I'd used since I'd been old enough to talk (which I can, of course, but just like words on paper, anything spoken— especially in haste—can be used as currency). I admit to enjoying the look of surprise on Madame Landowski's face as she read what I'd written, even if it wasn't helpful to her in discovering who I was, or who I belonged to. Elsa the maid had a look in her eye which suggested that I should be posted back to where I had come from as soon as possible when she slammed down a bowl of food in front of me.

Not speaking is no hardship. It is over a year since I left the home I had known for as long as I could remember. In that time, I've only used my voice when absolutely necessary.

From where I am writing this, I can look out of the tiny attic window. Earlier, I watched the Landowski children come up the path. They had been to school and looked very smart in their uniforms—Françoise in white gloves and a straw hat they call a boater, and her brothers in white shirts and blazers. Even if I hear Monsieur Landowski complaining often about his lack of money, the big house, his lovely garden and the beautiful dresses that the ladies of the house wear tell me he must be very rich indeed.

I've also chewed my pencil, a habit Papa tried to prevent me from continuing by putting all sorts of terrible flavours on the end of it. He once told me the day's flavour tasted quite nice but was poison, so if I put it anywhere near my mouth, I would die. Yet still, as I thought about the translation he'd given me to decipher, into my mouth the pencil had gone. I'd heard a scream as he'd seen me, and I'd been taken outside by the scruff of the neck and my mouth packed with snow, which I then had to spit out. I didn't die, but I've often wondered since whether it was just a harsh ruse to shock me into stopping or whether the snow and the spitting had saved me.

Even though I do my best to remember him, it is so many years since I last saw him and he is fading from my mind...

Perhaps it is for the best. Yes, best in every way that I forget everything that has gone before. Then, if they torture me, I will have nothing to tell them. And if Monsieur or Madame Landowski think that I shall write things down in the diary they have so kindly given me, trusting to the little lock with a key that I can keep in my leather pouch, then they are sorely mistaken.

'A diary is a place in which you can write down anything you feel or think,' Madame Landowski had explained gently. 'It is also a place of privacy, for your eyes only. I promise that we shall never look.'

I had nodded profusely, then smiled my gratitude with my eyes, before running upstairs to my attic bedroom. I do not believe her. I know from experience how both locks and promises can be so easily broken.

I promise on your beloved mother's life that I shall return for you... Pray for me, wait for me...

I am shaking my head, trying to lose the memory of Papa's last words to me. Yet somehow, even though others I wish to recall float like dandelion seeds away from my brain's grasp the minute I try to harness them, that sentence will not budge whatever I do.

Still, the diary is leather-bound, and full of the thinnest of paper. It must have cost the Landowskis at least a franc (which is what they call their money here), and it was, I think, a gesture made to help me, so I shall use it. Besides, even though I have learnt not to talk, I often wondered on my long journey whether I might forget how to write. Having no paper or pencil with me, one of the ways I'd get through those freezing winter nights was to recite passages of poetry in my head, then imagine writing the letters in 'my mind's eye'.

I very much like that phrase—Papa had called it the window to our imagination and when I wasn't reciting poetry, I would often disappear into that cavernous place that Papa said contained no boundaries. It was as large as you wished it to be. Small-minded men, he'd added, had, by definition, a limited imagination.

And even if the kind Landowskis were proving to be my

human saviours, tending to the outer me, I still needed to disappear inside myself, screw my eyes up tight and think thoughts that could never be written down because I could never trust another human being again.

Therefore, I thought, *what the Landowskis would get if any of them ever read this*—and part of me was sure that they would try, just out of curiosity if nothing else—*is a diary that began on the day that I had already said my last prayers.*

In fact, maybe I had never said them; I had been so delirious with fever, starvation and exhaustion that perhaps I dreamt it—but anyway, it was the day that I had gazed into the most beautiful female face I had ever seen.

As I wrote an abridged, factual paragraph on how the beautiful lady had taken me in, whispered words of endearment and allowed me to sleep indoors for the first time in heaven knows how long, I thought about how sad she had looked the last time I'd seen her. I had since discovered her name was Izabela— Bel for short. She and Landowski's atelier assistant, Monsieur Brouilly (who'd asked me to call him Laurent, not that in my current state of dumbness I'd call him anything at all), had fallen madly in love. And that night, when she looked sad, she had come to say goodbye. Not just to me, but to him too.

Even though I was very young, I had actually read quite a lot about love. After Papa had left, I'd worked my way through his bookshelf and learnt some extraordinary things about the ways of grown-ups. At first, I had presumed that the physical act which was being described must make the story a comedy in some ways, but then when it had been repeated by authors I knew were definitely not humourists, I'd realised that it must be true. Now *that* was something I definitely wouldn't be writing about in my diary!

A small chuckle escaped my lips and I slapped my hands to my mouth. It felt so strange, because a chuckle was an expression of some level of happiness. The physical body's natural response.

'Goodness!' I whispered. It was odd to hear my own voice, which seemed deeper than the last time I'd uttered a word. No one would hear me up here in the attic; both the maids were downstairs scrubbing, polishing and working through the endless laundry that hung on the ropes tethered at the back of the house. Anyway, even if they couldn't hear me up here, it was a habit I mustn't get into, this happiness thing, because if I could chuckle, then it meant I had a voice and could definitely speak. I tried to think of things to make me sad, which really did feel very odd, given that the only way I seemed to—against all the odds—have made it to France was by disappearing into my imagination and thinking happy thoughts. I thought about the two maids, who I could always hear chattering through the thin wall that separated us at night. They complained that their pay was terrible, the hours too long, their mattresses lumpy and their attic bedroom freezing in winter. I wanted to hammer on the thin wall and shout that they should feel so lucky that there was a wall separating me and them, that the family did not all live together in a single room, that they *had* wages, however bad they were. And as for saying that their rooms were cold in winter...well, I had studied the climate of France, and even though Paris, which I'd discovered we were on the very edges of, was in the north, the thought of a couple of degrees below zero being a problem made me want to chuckle all over again.

I finished the first paragraph in my brand-new 'official' diary and read it back to myself, pretending that I was Monsieur Landowski who was reading it, with his funny little beard and big bushy moustache.

I live in Boulogne-Billancourt. I have been taken in by the kind Landowski family. Their names are Monsieur and Madame Paul and Amélie Landowski, and their children are Nadine (20), Jean-Max (17), Marcel (13) and Françoise (11). They are all very kind to me. They tell me I have been very ill and it will take time to get my strength back up. The maids are named Elsa and Antoinette, and the cook is Berthe. She is always offering me more and more of her beautiful patisserie, to fatten me up, she says. The first time she gave me a full plate, I ate every morsel on it and then I was violently sick five minutes later. When the doctor came to see me, he told Berthe that my stomach had shrunk through malnutrition and she must give me smaller plates of food, or I could get very sick again and die. I think this upset Berthe but I hope that now I am almost eating properly again, I am also appreciating her cooking. There's a member of staff I have not yet met, but who the family talk about a lot. Her name is Madame Evelyn Gelsen, and she is the housekeeper. She is on holiday at the moment, visiting her son who lives in Lyon.

I am worried that I am costing this kind family money, what with all the food I now eat, plus the doctor having to come out and visit me. I know how expensive doctors can be. I have no money and no occupation and I can't see a way of paying them back, which of course they will expect and is the right thing to do. I am not sure how long I will be allowed to stay here, but I try to enjoy every day in their beautiful home. I thank the Lord for their kindness and pray for them every night.

My teeth crunched down on the end of the pencil as I nodded with satisfaction. I had made the language simplistic, adding the odd basic spelling mistake just to make me look like I was a normal ten-year-old boy. It wouldn't do to let them know what kind of education I had once received. After Papa had left, I'd done my best to keep up my lessons as he'd urged me to do, but without him as my guide, things in that department had suffered rather.

Pulling out a beautiful sheet of clean white paper from the drawer in the old desk—and to me, having a drawer and a writing space all of my own was beyond any luxury I'd ever imagined—I began to write a letter.

Landowski Atelier
Rue Moisson Desroches
Boulogne-Billancourt
7th August 1928

Dear Monsieur and Madame Landowski,
I wish to say thank you to you both for your gift. It is the most beautiful diary I've ever owned and I will write in it every day, as you asked me.
Also, thank you for having me.

I was just about to add the polite 'Yours' and my name before I stopped myself. I folded the paper neatly in two and then four, and wrote their names on the front of it. I would put it on the silver dish that held the post tomorrow.

Even if I had not reached the place I had set out for, I was near enough. Compared to the distance I'd already completed, it was the equivalent to a stroll along the Rue Moisson Desroches and back. But I did not want to leave yet. As the doctor had said to Berthe, I needed to build up my strength, not just in my body, but in my mind. Even if the doctor could not see into it, I could have told him that the worst thing wasn't the physical punishment I'd taken, but the fear that clawed inside me still. Both the maids, probably because they'd got bored of complaining about everyone else in the house, had told me that I cried out in the night, waking them up. On my long journey, I had become so used to it and so exhausted besides, that I'd been able to fall straight back to sleep, but here, being rested and warm in my own bed had made me soft. Often, I couldn't return to sleep after the nightmares had come. I wasn't even sure that 'nightmares' was the correct way to describe them. So often it was my cruel mind making me relive things that had really happened to me.

Standing up and walking over to my bed, diary in hand, I climbed under the sheet and the blanket I did not need because the weather at present was *stifling*. I took the diary and rammed it down the inside of my pyjama bottoms, so it sat snugly against my inner thigh. Then I removed the leather pouch that hung from my neck and put it in the same place against my other thigh. If my long journey had taught me anything, it was where the safest hiding places were for such precious things.

I lay back on the mattress—another thing Elsa and Antoinette had complained about, yet to me it was like sleeping on a cloud of angels' wings—closed my eyes, said a quick prayer for Papa and my mama, wherever in heaven she might be, and tried to drift into sleep.

A thought was nagging at me as I did so. As much as I hated to admit it, there was another reason for me writing my thank you letter to the Landowskis: even though I knew I must continue my journey, I was not quite ready to give up the most wonderful feeling of all—safety.

2

'So, what do you think of him, young man?' Monsieur Landowski asked me as I looked into the eyes of our Lord, just one of which was almost as big as I was. He had just finished perfecting the head of what in Brazil they called the *Cristo Redentor*, and who I would call Jesus Christ. I had been told by Monsieur Laurent Brouilly that the statue would stand on top of a mountain in a city called Rio de Janeiro. It would be thirty metres tall by the time all the pieces had been put together. I had seen the miniature versions of the finished sculpture and knew that the Brazilian (and French) Christ would stand with his arms wide open, embracing the city beneath him. It was clever how, from a distance, you might just think it was a cross. How they would get the statue up the mountain and assemble it had been a matter of great discussion and worry over the past few weeks. Monsieur Landowski seemed to have many heads to worry about, because he was also working on the sculpture of a Chinese man called Sun Yat-sen, and was fretting over the eyes. He was a perfectionist, I thought.

During the long, hot summer days, I had been drawn to Monsieur Landowski's atelier, creeping in and hiding behind the many boulders that sat on the floor, waiting to be shaped into a form. The workshop was usually busy with apprentices and assistants who, like Laurent, were there to learn from the great master. Most of them ignored me, although Mademoiselle Margarida always gave me a smile when she arrived in the morning. She was a great friend of Bel, so I knew she was one of the trustworthy ones.

Monsieur espied me in the atelier one day and, like any father, reproached me for not asking permission before I entered. I shook my head and put my arms out in front of me, backing away towards the door, then the kind monsieur relented and beckoned me towards him.

'Brouilly here tells me you like to watch us at work. Is this true?'

I nodded.

'Well then, there is no need to hide. As long as you swear never to touch anything, you are welcome here, boy. I only wish my own children showed as much interest as you in my profession.'

Since that moment, I had been allowed to sit at the trestle table with a piece of unwanted soapstone, and provided with my own set of tools.

'Watch and learn, boy, watch and learn,' Landowski had advised. And I had. Not that it made any difference to my own methods, banging the hammer onto the chisel upon my piece of rock. No matter how I tried to shape it into the simplest of forms, I always ended up with a pile of rubble in front of me.

'So, boy, what do you think?' asked Monsieur Landowski, gesturing to the head of the *Cristo*. I nodded vigorously, as always feeling guilty that this kind man who had taken me in still tried to elicit a vocal response from me. He deserved to receive one just due to his perseverance, but I knew that as soon as I opened my mouth to talk, I'd be in danger.

Madame Landowski, now knowing I could write and understand what was being said to me, had handed me a pile of scrap paper.

'So, if I ask you a question, you can write the reply, yes?'

I'd nodded. From then on, communication had been very simple.

In answer to Monsieur Landowski's question, I took my pencil from my shorts pocket, wrote one word that took up almost the entire page, and handed it to him.

He chuckled as he read it.

'"Magnifique", eh? Well, thank you, young sir, and let us only hope that your response is the one the *Cristo* will receive when he stands proudly atop Corcovado Mountain on the other side of the world. *If* we can ever get him there…'

'Have faith, sir,' countered Laurent from behind me. 'Bel tells me that preparations for the use of the funicular railway are well underway.'

'Does she indeed?' Monsieur Landowski raised one of his bushy grey eyebrows. 'You seem to know more than I do. Heitor da Silva Costa keeps telling me we will discuss how to ship my sculpture over and then erect it, but the conversation never seems to take place. Is it lunchtime yet? I need some wine to calm my nerves. I am beginning to feel that this *Cristo* project may be the end of my career. I was a fool for ever saying yes to such madness.'

'I'll fetch the meal,' Laurent responded, and headed for the tiny kitchen, every detail of which I would always remember as being my first safe haven since I'd left home all those months ago. I smiled as I watched Laurent open a bottle of wine. As I often did when I was awake early, I'd crept down to the atelier at dawn just to be amongst the beauty it contained. I'd sit there and think about how Papa would have laughed that out of all the places I could have ended up, such as the Renault factory only a few kilometres from here, I'd arrived instead in a place that he himself would have called an artistic temple. I just knew that it would please him somehow.

This morning, as I'd sat amongst the boulders and looked up into the *Cristo*'s gentle face, I'd heard a noise from the room behind the curtain where we ate our food. Tiptoeing over to it and peering behind, I had seen a pair of feet sticking out from under the table. It transpired the sound was the gentle snoring of Laurent. Since Bel had gone back to Brazil, I'd noticed he often seemed the worse for drink in the morning, his eyes red and bleary, and his skin sallow and grey as if he might have to go and heave up the contents of his stomach at any moment. (And I had had *a lot* of experience in knowing when a man or a woman had sailed well past normal boundaries.)

As I watched him now pour a healthy glass for himself, I worried for his liver, which Papa had said was most affected by drink. But it wasn't just Laurent's liver I was concerned about; it was his heart too. Even though I understood that it was impossible for the organ itself to be physically broken by love, something inside the man *had*. Maybe one day I would understand the wish to drown away pain with alcohol.

'*Santé!*' the two men said as they clinked their glasses together. As they sat at the table, I made myself useful in the kitchen, collecting the bread, cheese and bulbous red tomatoes the lady down the road grew in her garden.

I knew this because I had watched Evelyn, the housekeeper, appear in the kitchen with a box laden with vegetables. As she was not a thin lady, and well into middle age, I'd run across the room to take the box from her and place it on the side.

'Goodness, today is a hot one,' she'd panted as she'd sat down heavily on one of the wooden chairs. I'd fetched her a glass of water before she'd even asked for it, and taking some paper and a pencil out of my pocket, I wrote down a question for her.

'Why don't I send the maids?' she read, then eyed me. 'Because, little boy, neither of those two would know a rotten peach from a perfect one. They're both city girls, with not a notion of fresh fruits and vegetables.'

Taking the paper back from her, I'd written another sentence.

Next time you go, I will come with you to carry the box.

'That is most kind of you, young man, and if this weather keeps up, I might just hold you to it.'

The weather did keep up and I did go and help her. On the way along the street, she chatted away about her son, telling me proudly he was at university studying to become an engineer.

'He'll make something of himself one day, you'll see,' she added as we'd picked our way through the vegetables displayed at the stall, me holding the box for those that passed her muster. Out of everyone in the Landowski household, Evelyn was my favourite person, even though I'd been dreading her return, having heard the maids' chatter through the walls about when 'the dragon' would be back. I'd been introduced to her as 'the boy with no name who can't speak'. (It had been Marcel, the Landowskis' thirteen-year-old son, who had said that. I knew he regarded me with suspicion, which I totally understood—my sudden arrival into any family would have ruffled a few feathers.) Yet Evelyn had simply shaken my outstretched hand and given me a warm smile.

'The more the merrier, that's what I say. What's the point of having a great big house like this and not filling every room?' Then she'd given me a wink and later that day, seeing me eyeing the leftover tarte tatin from lunch, had cut a slice for me.

It was odd, really, how a middle-aged lady and I could forge some kind of secret and most definitely unspoken (on my part, anyway) bond, but I knew we had. I'd noted a familiar look in her eyes which told me she had suffered deeply. Perhaps she recognised something similar in me too.

I had decided that the only way to make sure everyone in the house found no way of complaining about me was to either make myself invisible (to Landowski's children and, to a lesser extent, Monsieur and Madame Landowski) or very available to those in need, which basically comprised the servants. Evelyn, Berthe, Elsa and Antoinette had what I think they realised now to be a useful little helper at hand any time they needed. At home, it had often been me that had cleared up the tiny space that housed us. Even as a very young boy, I had always had an urge to make sure everything was in its place. Papa had noted that I liked order, not chaos, and had joked that I'd make someone a very good wife one day. In my old home, it had been impossible because every activity had happened in the one room, but here at the Landowski house, the very orderliness of it thrilled me. Perhaps my favourite job of all was helping Elsa and Antoinette take sheets and clothes from the line after they had blown dry in the sunshine. Both maids had laughed at my need to make sure each corner met perfectly, and I could not help but stick my nose into whichever item of laundry I was unpegging to breathe in its clean scent, which to me was the most beautiful of any perfume.

Anyway, after I had chopped the tomatoes as precisely as I folded the laundry, I went to join Monsieur Landowski and Laurent at the table. I watched them break the fresh baguette and cut a slice of cheese, and it was only when Monsieur Landowski indicated I should do the same that I shared in the feast too. Papa had always told me how wonderful French food tasted, and he was right. However, after my bouts of sickness when I had stuffed anything I was given at top speed down my gullet as if it was the last meal I was ever offered, I proceeded to eat like the gentleman I'd been brought up to be rather than a savage, as Berthe had once said within my hearing.

Still the chatter was of the *Cristo* and Sun Yat-sen's eyeballs, but I didn't mind. I understood that Monsieur Landowski was a true creative—he had won the gold medal in the Olympic art competition in the summer and was apparently renowned for his gifts around the world. What I admired the most about him was the way that fame hadn't changed him. Or at least, I imagined it hadn't, because he worked every hour he could, often missing supper, which Madame Landowski scolded him for because his children needed to see him and so did she. His attention to detail and the fact he strove for perfection, when he could easily have had Laurent finish his work for him, inspired me. Whatever in this world I was meant to do or be, I promised myself that I would always give all I had to it.

'And what about you, boy? Boy?'

Yet again, I pulled myself out of my thoughts. It was a place that I had become so used to inhabiting that having people showing any interest in me took some getting used to.

'You weren't listening, were you?'

Making an apology with my eyes, I shook my head.

'I asked you whether you thought that Sun Yat-sen's eyes were yet right? I showed you the photograph of him, remember?'

I picked up my pencil, thinking carefully about my answer before I wrote it. I'd always been taught to tell the truth, but I needed to be diplomatic as well. I wrote the words I needed to, then passed the book to him.

Almost, sir.

I watched Landowski take a sip of his wine, then throw back his head and laugh.

'Spot on, boy, spot on. So, this afternoon, I will have another go.'

When the two men had had their fill, I cleared away the leftover bread and cheese. Then I brewed the coffee for them, the way I knew Monsieur Landowski liked it. Whilst I was doing so, I stuffed the remains of the bread and cheese into my shorts pocket. This was one habit I was yet to break—one never knew when one's supply of food might be cut off. After I'd served them the coffee, I nodded and returned to my attic. I stowed the bread and cheese in the drawer in the desk. More often than not, whatever leftovers I put there would be secretly thrown away the next morning in the bin outside. But as I said, one never knew.

After a wash of my hands and a brush of my hair, I went downstairs to begin my afternoon round of being useful. Today it involved polishing silver, which, because of my precision and patience, even Evelyn had said I was good at. I glowed with the pride of someone starved of compliments for so long. The glow hadn't lasted long, though, because she'd stopped at the door and turned round as Elsa and Antoinette were replacing the knives and forks in their velvet beds.

'Perhaps you could both learn from the young man's skills,' she'd said, then walked out, leaving Elsa and Antoinette to glare at me. But as they were both lazy and impatient, they'd been happy to hand over the polishing. I loved sitting in the peace of the big dining room at the mahogany table, which always glowed with a shiny sheen, my hands busy and my mind free to roam wherever it pleased.

The main thought on my mind now, and almost every day since my body and senses had begun to recover, was how I could make money. However kind the Landowskis were, I knew that I was at their mercy. Even tonight, it could be that they would tell me that for whatever reason my time with them was up. Once again, I'd be cast out onto an unfamiliar street, vulnerable and alone. Instinctively, my fingers went to the leather pouch that I wore under my shirt. Just the touch of it and its familiar shape comforted me, even if I knew what it contained was not mine to sell. The fact it had survived the journey was a miracle in itself, yet its presence was a blessing and a curse. It alone held the reason why I was currently in Paris, living under the roof of strangers.

Having finished polishing the silver teapot, I decided there was only one person in the house I trusted enough to ask advice. Evelyn lived in what the family called 'the cottage', but in reality was a two-roomed extension to the main house. As Evelyn had said to me, at least it had its own private bathroom facilities, and most importantly, its own front door. I had not yet seen inside it, but tonight after supper, I would pluck up my courage and knock on that door.

I watched through the dining room window as Evelyn made her way to the cottage—she always left once the main course had been served, leaving her two maids in charge of the dessert and then the washing-up. I ate my supper and listened to the family chatter. Nadine, the oldest sister, wasn't yet married and spent much of her time leaving the house with an easel, brushes and a palette. I had never seen any of her paintings, but I knew she also designed the backgrounds for theatre stages. I had never seen a play on a stage, and of course couldn't speak to her to ask her about her work. As she spent so little time in the house and seemed very wrapped up in her own life, she took little notice of me, offering me the occasional smile if we crossed paths early in the morning. Then there was Marcel, who'd stopped me in my tracks one day, then puffed out his chest, put his hands on his hips and told me he didn't like me. Which, of course, was silly because he didn't know me, but I had heard him calling me a 'bootlicker' to his younger sister Françoise, because I helped in the kitchen before supper. I understood how he felt; his parents taking in a young ragamuffin who'd been found in their garden and refused to speak would have made anyone suspicious.

However, I forgave him everything from the moment I'd first heard the sound of beautiful music coming from a room downstairs and drifting into the kitchen. I'd stopped what I was doing and stood there, entranced. Even though Papa had played me what he could on his violin, I'd never actually heard the sound that piano keys could make when they were expertly handled by a human being. And it was glorious. Since then, I had become slightly obsessed with Marcel's fingers, wondering how they managed to cross the piano keys so fast and in such perfect order. I'd had to train myself to avert my eyes. One day I would pluck up the courage to ask him if I could watch him play. However he acted towards me, I thought him a magician.

His older brother Jean-Max seemed indifferent to me, being on the cusp of adulthood. I knew little about what he did when left the house, but he did once try to show me how to play the game of boules: the national pastime of France. This involved throwing balls at the gravel in the back courtyard, and I picked it up pretty easily.

Then there was Françoise, the Landowskis' youngest daughter, who was not much older than me. She had been friendly when I'd first arrived, though very shy. I was gratified when she'd wordlessly given me a sweet in the garden, some kind of sugar on a stick, and we'd sat side by side licking our respective treats and watching the bees collect their nectar. She joined Marcel in his piano practice, and enjoyed painting like Nadine. I'd often see her sitting at an easel facing the house. I had no idea if she was good or not, because I'd never seen anything she'd painted, but I suspected that a lovely pastoral view of a field and a river that hung along the downstairs hallway was hers. We were never to become great friends, of course—it must be quite boring for anyone to spend time with someone they cannot conduct a conversation with—but she often smiled at me and I could feel the sympathy in her eyes. On the odd occasion—normally Sunday, when Monsieur Landowski was free—the family would play boules or decide to go for a picnic together. I was always asked to join, but declined, out of respect for their family time, and because I'd learnt the hard way what resentment could do.

After supper, I helped Elsa and Antoinette with the dishes, and once they had gone upstairs to bed, I slipped out of the kitchen door and scurried around the back of the house, so that no one would see my departure.

Standing in front of Evelyn's front door, my heart knocked hard in my chest. Was this a mistake? Should I simply go back the way I had come and forget all about it?

'No,' I whispered under my breath. I had to trust someone at some point. The instincts that had kept me alive for as long as they had were telling me that it was the right thing to do.

My hand shook as it reached out for the door and I gave a timid knock. There was no response—of course there wasn't, no one who wasn't standing immediately on the other side of the piece of wood could have heard me. So I knocked louder. Within a few seconds, I saw the drawn curtain being lifted from the window, and then the door was opened.

'Well, what have we here?' Evelyn said as she smiled at me. 'Come in, come in. It's not often I get visitors knocking at my door, and that's for sure,' she chuckled.

I stepped into perhaps the cosiest room I'd ever seen. Even though I'd been told it had once been a garage for Monsieur Landowski's car and was simply a cement square, everywhere I looked there was something of beauty. Two upholstered chairs sat facing the centre of the room and brightly coloured embroidered quilts were draped over them. Family portraits and still-lifes dotted the walls, and an arrangement of flowers sat proudly on the clean mahogany table by the window. There was a small door which I presumed led to the bedroom and facilities, and a pile of books sat on a shelf above a dresser filled with china cups and glasses.

'Now then, sit down,' Evelyn said, pointing to one of the chairs and removing some kind of needle-point from her own. 'Can I get you some lemonade? It's my own recipe.'

I nodded eagerly. I'd never had lemonade before coming to France, and I couldn't get enough of it now. I watched her walk over to the dresser and take down two glasses. She poured the milky yellow liquid from a pitcher full of ice.

'There,' she said as she sat down, her large bulk just about fitting into the chair. '*Santé!*' She lifted her glass.

I lifted mine too but said nothing, as usual.

'So,' Evelyn said, 'what can I do for you?'

I'd already written down what I wanted to ask and drew out the paper from my pocket to hand it to her.

She read the words, then looked at me.

'How can you earn some money? That is what you are here to ask me?'

I nodded.

'Well, young man, I am not sure if I know. I'd have to think about it. But why is it you feel you need to earn money?'

I indicated she should turn the paper over.

'"In case the kind Landowskis decide they no longer have room for me,"' she read out loud. 'Well, given the monsieur's success and the amount of commissions he's getting, it's very doubtful they'd have to move to a smaller house. So, they are always going to have room for you here. But I think I know what you mean. You are frightened because they might one day decide to simply turn you out, is that it?'

I nodded vigorously.

'And you would just be another young, starving orphan on the streets of Paris. Which brings me to a very important question: are you an orphan? Yes or no will do.'

I shook my head as vigorously as I'd nodded it.

'Where are your parents?'

She handed the paper back to me and I wrote the words down.

I do not know.

'I see. I thought that they might have been lost in the Great War, but that ended in 1918, so you're perhaps too young for that to be the case.'

I shrugged, trying not to let my expression change. The problem with kindness was that it meant you let your guard down, and I knew I mustn't do that, whatever the cost. I watched as she gazed at me silently.

'I know you can talk if you want to, young man. That Brazilian lady who was here told us all that you said thank you to her in perfect French the night she found you. The question is, why won't you? The only answer I can think of—unless you have been struck dumb since, which I doubt very much—is that you are too scared to trust anyone. Would I be right?'

Now I was really torn… I wanted to say yes, she was absolutely right, and to throw myself into those comforting arms, to be held and to tell her everything, but I knew that still…*still* I could not. I indicated I needed the paper, and I wrote some words then handed it back to her.

I had a fever. I cannot remember speaking to Bel.

Evelyn read the words, then smiled at me. 'I understand, young man. I know you're lying, but whatever trauma it is that you've experienced has stopped you trusting. Perhaps one day, when we have known each other for a little longer, I will tell you something of my life. I was a nurse at the front during the Great War. The suffering I saw there…I will never forget it. And yes, I will be honest, for a time it made me lose my faith—and trust—in human nature. And also in God. Do you believe in God?'

I nodded my head slightly less vigorously. Partly because I did not know whether she was still a religious woman after her lapse of faith, and partly because I wasn't sure.

'I think that perhaps you are at the same point I was then. It took me a good long time to trust to anything again. Do you know what it was that brought back my faith and trust? Love. Love for my beloved boy. And that made everything right. Of course, love comes from God, or whatever you wish to call the spirit that joins all us humans in an invisible web to Him. Even if we sometimes feel that he's deserted us, He never has. Anyway, I really don't have an answer to your question, I'm afraid. There are many young boys like you on the streets of Paris, who manage to survive in ways I really don't wish to think about. But… Goodness, I wish you could at least trust me with your name. I promise you that Monsieur and Madame Landowski are good, kind people and would never just throw you out of their home.'

I indicated I needed the paper again and once I'd written on it, I passed it back.

Then what will they do with me?

'Well, if you could speak, they would allow you to live here in their house indefinitely and send you to school like their other children. But as it stands…'—she shrugged—'that is an impossibility, isn't it? It is doubtful any school will take a boy who is dumb, no matter what level of education he's had. I would guess from what I know of you that you are educated and would like to continue to be so. Is that true?'

I gave what I thought was a good impression of a French shrug, which everyone in the house seemed expert in executing.

'The one thing I don't like is liars, young man,' Evelyn

reprimanded me suddenly. 'I know you have your reasons for staying silent, but you can at least be truthful. Do you or do you not wish to continue your education?'

I nodded reluctantly.

Evelyn slapped her thigh. 'Well, there we have it. You must make up your mind whether you are prepared to start speaking, at which point your future in the Landowski household will be much safer. You would be a normal child who could go to a normal school and I know that they would continue to welcome you into their family. Now'—Evelyn yawned—'I have an early start tomorrow, but I've enjoyed this evening, and your company. Please feel free to knock on my door whenever you wish.'

I stood up immediately, nodding my thanks as I walked towards the door, and Evelyn stood up to follow me. Just as I was about to turn the knob, I felt a gentle pair of hands on my shoulders, which turned me round and then wrapped around my waist as she pulled me to her.

'A little bit of love is all you need, *chéri*. Goodnight now.'

3

Today the fire was lit in the dining room before supper. It is very exciting to see one, although I do not understand why everyone is complaining of the cold. The family is all in good health and very busy. Monsieur Landowski is fretting about the transportation of his precious Cristo sculpture to Rio de Janeiro. He also has Sun Yat-sen still to finish. I try to help out around the house as much as I can and I hope I am found to be useful and not a burden. I am very happy with my new set of winter clothes, which have been passed down from Marcel. The fabric the shirt, shorts and sweater are made from feels so fine and soft against my skin. Madame Landowski has kindly decided that even if I cannot go to school at the moment because I am mute, I should still have an education. She has set me some mathematics questions as well as a spelling test. I work hard to get the answers right. I am happy and grateful to be with kind people in this lovely house.

I set down my pen and closed and locked my diary, hoping that any prying eyes could not find fault with anything I said inside it. Then I reached underneath the drawer for the small sheaf of papers that I cut to the same size as the diary pages. These are the papers on which I document my *real* thoughts. At first, I wrote the diary merely to please those who had given it to me, in case they ever asked me whether I had used it. But I found that the fact I could not speak my thoughts and feelings was becoming more and more of a hardship, and setting down those thoughts and feelings was a necessary relief, an outlet. One day, I decided, when I was no longer living with the Landowskis, I could slot these sheets into the relevant section, which would give a much more honest picture of my life.

I think it was Evelyn who made it harder to think about leaving, because since she asked me to come and visit her whenever I wished to, I had. And I honestly believed that she had some kind of maternal feeling for me, which felt real and true. Many times over the past few weeks, as I've sat with her in her cosy room, I've listened to her chattering away about her life, which, as I suspected, has contained much suffering. Her husband and eldest son had never returned from the Great War. I had learnt a lot about the conflict since living in the Landowski household. But then, as I was born in 1918, it was a war I'd missed. Listening to Evelyn tell me of the enormous amount of men who had died on the battlefield when they were forced to go in 'over the top', screaming in pain, because pieces of them had been blown off, made me shudder.

'What upsets me most is the fact that my beloved Anton and Jacques died alone with no one to comfort them.'

I had watched Evelyn's eyes fill with tears and had reached out my hand to her. What I really wanted to do was to say words like, 'I'm so sorry. It must be so hard for you. I too have lost everyone I loved…'

She explained that this was why she was so proud and protective of the one son she had left. If she lost him, she would lose her mind. I wanted to tell her that I lost my mind, but to my surprise, it was slowly returning.

It was becoming harder and harder to be mute, especially as I knew very well that if I spoke, I would be off to school. And above all, I wanted to continue my education. Then again, I would be asked questions about my circumstances which I simply could not answer. Or I'd have to lie, and these good people who had taken me into their home, clothed and fed me, deserved better.

'Come in, come in!' Evelyn said as I pushed open her front door. I knew she had a bad leg, which I thought hurt more than she cared to say. I wasn't the only one that was concerned for their position in the Landowski household.

'Make the cocoa, will you, young man? Everything's ready for you,' she added.

I did so, breathing in the wonderful smell of chocolate, which I am sure I had tasted at some point in my past, but now couldn't get enough of here. Cocoa time with Evelyn was fast becoming my favourite moment of the day.

I took the two mugs and placed one of them on the table beside Evelyn, and the other upon the fireplace where the little fire was burning merrily in the grate. Sitting down, I waved my hand across my face, feeling almost dizzy from the heat.

'You came from a very cold land, didn't you?' Evelyn eyed me beadily and I knew she was on the prowl for information when I might be taken off guard.

I picked up my cocoa and sipped it to prove that I could tolerate a hot drink in my hot body, even though I was desperate to take off my woollen jumper.

'Ah, one day you will answer me,' she smiled, 'but for now you remain an enigma.'

I looked at her quizzically. 'Enigma' was a word I'd never heard before but it sounded interesting.

'Enigma means that no one is sure who you really are,' she explained. 'Which makes you interesting, for a time at least. Then, perhaps, it becomes rather boring.'

Ouch! Now that really hurt.

'Anyway…forgive me for my frustration. It is only because I worry for you. Monsieur and Madame Landowski's patience may at some point run out. I heard them talking the other day when I was dusting in the drawing room. They are thinking of sending you to a psychiatrist. Do you know what that is?'

I shook my head.

'It is—or they are—doctors of the mind. They ask you questions and decide on your mental state and the reasons for it. For example, if you have some mental disorder, it would mean that you need to be placed in a hospital of some kind.'

My eyes flew wide in horror. I knew exactly what she meant. One of our neighbours back home, whom we'd often heard shouting and screaming and once seen wandering naked down the main street of our town, had been taken away to what they called a 'sanatorium'. They are terrible places, apparently. Full of men and women screaming and shouting, or sitting there staring, as if they are already dead.

'Please, I shouldn't have said that to you,' said Evelyn now. 'We all know that you are not mad, and, in fact, hide just how clever you are. The reason they were thinking of sending you to a psychiatrist was to find out what it is you feel unable to communicate with us all when we know that you can.'

As always, I shook my head firmly. They all knew my answer to that question was that I had a fever and that I couldn't remember speaking to Bel. Which wasn't really a lie.

'They are trying to help you, my dear, not harm you. Please, do not look so terrified. See,' Evelyn said as she reached for a brown parcel sitting next to her chair, 'this is for you, for the winter.'

I took the brown parcel from her hands, and it felt like my birthday. It was a long time since I'd had a parcel of any kind to open. I almost wanted to savour it, but Evelyn encouraged me to tear the paper open. Inside was a colourful striped scarf and woollen hat.

'Try them on then, young man. See if they fit.'

Even though I was hot as a furnace, I did so. The scarf fitted me perfectly—how could it not? But the woollen hat was slightly too big, and the first time I pulled it on, it fell over my eyes.

'Give it to me,' Evelyn said, and I watched her fold back the front of the hat. 'There. That'll do it. What do you think?'

That I might die of heat stroke if I keep them on any longer...

I nodded enthusiastically, then stood up, walked over to her and gave her a hug. When I pulled away, I realised my eyes were full of tears.

'Aw now, silly boy, you know how much I love my knitting. I made hundreds of those for our boys at the front,' she added.

I turned round to walk back to my chair, the words 'thank you' hovering on my lips, but I held them tight together. Taking off my hat and scarf, I folded them and reverently placed them back in their brown paper.

'Now then, it's time for both you and me to be in our beds,' she said, looking up at the clock that sat on the mantelpiece above the fire. 'But first I must tell you that today I had some wonderful news.' I saw her indicate a letter sitting behind the clock. 'That there is from my son Louis. He is coming to visit me on my day off. Now, what do you think of that?'

I nodded enthusiastically, but inside I realised that a little bit of me was jealous of this magnificent Louis, who could do no wrong in his mother's eyes. I thought I might hate him.

'I'd like you to come across and meet him. He will take me out for lunch in the village, and we shall be back at half past three. Why don't you come and say hello at four?'

I nodded, and tried not to look as sulky as I felt. Giving her a small wave and a big smile as I tapped my package, I left her room. I curled up in bed that night, feeling unsettled about this competitor for Evelyn's affections arriving, and what she had said about the psychiatrist man that the Landowskis might make me visit.

I didn't sleep well that night.

On Sunday afternoon, I washed my face in the bowl of water provided for me every day by one of the maids. Up here on the attic floor, we didn't have 'facilities' (which was another thing that Elsa and Antoinette complained about, because they had to go downstairs in the night to do their business). I brushed my hair and decided I would not wear a woollen jumper, because the chances were that if her son was here, Evelyn would have lit the most roaring of fires. Downstairs, I let myself out of the kitchen door and began my normal walk towards her front door. Then a sound made me stop dead in my tracks. I listened to it and closed my eyes, a smile appearing on my lips because they just couldn't help but do anything else. I knew the piece of music too, and that it was being played by not quite a master like my father, but someone who had trained for many years.

Gathering myself together as the music stopped, I put one foot in front of the other and arrived at Evelyn's front door and knocked upon it. Immediately it was opened by a tall thin man, whom I knew was nineteen.

'Hello there,' he said with a smile. 'You must be the young waif that has joined the household since I last visited.'

He ushered me inside and my eyes darted around the room for the instrument he had just been playing. The violin was sitting in the chair I normally sat in, and I couldn't help but stare at it.

'Hello,' Evelyn said. 'This is Louis, my son.'

I nodded, but still my eyes could not leave that simple piece of wood that had been magically transformed from a tree into an instrument that could make the most glorious sounds on God's earth. In my opinion, anyway.

'You heard my son play?' Evelyn had not missed the way I was staring at the instrument.

I nodded, every bit of me wanting to reach for it and put it snugly under my chin, lift the bow and draw the notes from it.

'Would you like to hold it?'

I looked up at Louis, who reminded me of his mother in male form, with the same sweet smile. I nodded vehemently. He handed it to me and I took it as reverently as if I was holding the golden fleece. Then, almost automatically, I put the instrument under my chin.

'So you play,' said Louis.

It wasn't a question, but a statement.

I nodded again.

'Then let's hear you,' he said, reaching for the bow and handing it to me. Having heard him play, I knew the instrument was perfectly tuned, but I buzzed the bow across the strings anyway, trying to get the feel of it. It was heavier than the one Papa and I had played, more solid somehow, and I wondered whether I would be able to draw those notes out. It was such a very long time since I had last held a violin in my hands. Closing my eyes, I did what Papa had always taught me and began to caress the strings. I wasn't even sure before I began what it was I would play, but the beautiful notes of Bach's 'Allemande' from *Violin Partita* began to pour out of me. I was taken by surprise when the sound came to an end, and then there was silence. And clapping.

'Well, that was the last thing I was expecting,' I heard Evelyn say, as she flapped herself with her fan.

'You, monsieur…' Louis began, 'you are, well, quite remarkable. *That* was quite remarkable for a boy of your age. Tell me, where did you learn to play?'

I was not going to put the violin down while it was in my hands to find my scrap paper, so I just shrugged at him, hoping he'd ask me to play something else.

'I told you, Louis, he does not speak.'

'What he lacks in the vocal cord department is made up for by the sounds he makes with a violin.' Louis smiled at his mother, then turned to me. 'You are exceptional, really, for one so young. Here, let me take it from you and come and sit down and have a cup of tea.'

As Louis approached me, there was part of me that simply wanted to clasp the violin to my chest, then turn tail and run.

'Do not worry, young man,' said Evelyn. 'Now I know that you can play so beautifully, I will be encouraging you to do so as often as possible. The violin was my husband's, you see. He also played beautifully. So the violin lives here with me, under my bed. You may put it back for me,' Evelyn said gently as she pointed to the case, which was lying on the floor. As Louis made tea, I put the violin tenderly into its nest. The name of the maker was printed on the inside of the top of the box. It was one I'd never heard of, but no matter. The sound quality may not have been as good as my papa's, but it would do. Any violin would do. Evelyn did not ask me to put the case away, so it sat next to me as we all drank tea and I listened to Louis talk to his mother about the course he was studying.

'Perhaps one day I will be designing the next new Renault

car,' he said.

'Well, apart from being proud of you if you did, you know how much I would like that; you will live close by, rather than so far away in Lyon.'

'It is not for long—only another eighteen months before I graduate, then I shall write letters to all the car companies and see which one decides that they need me and my skills.'

'Even as a small boy, Louis was obsessed with cars,' Evelyn explained to me. 'There were not that many on the road in those days, but Louis would draw what he imagined to be a modern vehicle, and do you know, they are very close in design to what the car companies are now producing. Of course, such things are only for the rich…'

'Ah, but soon they won't be, *Maman*. One day, every family will have one, including me.'

'Well, there is nothing wrong with having dreams, is there?' Evelyn replied kindly. 'Now then, young man, are you able to finish up this cake, or shall Louis put it in the tin for tomorrow?'

I decided I had space for more and I took the last slice from the plate.

'So, what is it that you are passionate about?' Louis asked me.

I pulled out my scrap paper and wrote three words:

Food!

Violin.

Books.

I added *reading* in brackets, and then handed him the note.

'I see.' Louis grinned at me after he'd read it. 'I've certainly seen the first two in action today. Did you speak once?'

Not wanting to look as though I was thinking to pause, I decided to tell the truth and nodded.

'May I ask what happened to turn you mute?'

I simply shrugged and shook my head.

'Now then, it isn't our place to ask, is it?' Evelyn interrupted. 'He'll tell us when he's ready, won't you?'

I nodded, then hung my head in sorrow. Even if I couldn't use my voice, my acting skills were coming along a treat.

'Why don't you stoke the fire, Louis? The nights really are starting to draw in.' Evelyn gave a sudden shiver. 'I don't like the winter, do you, young man?'

I shook my head vehemently.

'But at least Christmas brings in the light to our homes and our hearts and it is something to look forward to. Do you like Christmas?'

I stared at her, then closed my eyes as a memory of a day when the fire had been burning brightly, and the smallest of presents had been handed out amongst us after church, came to me. There had been meat for our supper and some special delicacies that had been made. I had enjoyed it, even though it appeared in my memory like a picture in a book, as if it didn't belong to me.

'I do hope I can afford the fare to get up and see you, *Maman*. I will save as hard as I can,' said Louis.

'I know you will, *chéri*. Of course,' Evelyn added, addressing me too, 'it is the busiest time of my year here. Monsieur Landowski likes to throw parties for his friends, so perhaps it might be better if we leave it until after Christmas when the train fares might be cheaper.'

'Maybe, but we shall see. Now, I hate to say it but I must be on my way.'

'Of course,' Evelyn agreed, even though I could see the sadness in her eyes. 'Let me pack you some food for the journey.'

'*Maman*, stay where you are, please,' Louis said, indicating she should not rise from her chair. 'The lunch we ate was enormous, and I am stuffed with enough cake to see me home without starving, I promise. *Maman* likes to feed people, as you may have noticed,' he said as an aside to me.

I stood up because I did not want to be in the way of what was obviously a sad parting for mother and son. I hugged Evelyn, then shook Louis's hand.

'It's very nice to meet you and thank you for keeping *Maman* company. She needs a chick to cluck over, don't you?' Louis smiled.

'You know me too well.' Evelyn chuckled. 'Goodbye, young man, see you tomorrow.'

'And perhaps next time I'm visiting, you will have a name we can call you,' said Louis as I moved towards the door.

I walked back to the house, thinking about what Louis had said. It was something that I'd considered many times since I had become mute. The fact was that I would never give my real name to anyone again, ever. That meant that I could choose any I wished. Not that it could be better than my real name, but it was interesting to think what I would call myself. The problem was that once you *had* a name, even if it was the most terrible one in the world, it belonged to you. And often it was the first thing that people would know about you. So to try and unstick yourself from whatever it was was far more difficult than it sounded. I had whispered many to myself over the last few weeks, because I simply didn't like the fact that people struggled with knowing how to address me. It would help them if I had a name, and it was easy enough to write down. Yet the right name just would not put itself forward, however hard I tried.

Having cut a healthy slice of baguette and layered jam into the centre of it (the family fended for themselves on Sunday evening), I took myself upstairs to my attic room and sat on the bed, watching night fall from my small window. Then I went to my diary to add a couple of lines to my earlier paragraph.

I have just played the violin for the first time in a very long while. It was the most wonderful experience to feel the bow in my hands again and to be able to pull sounds from the instrument…

My pencil hung in mid-air, as I realised that I had just found the perfect name.

4

'So, at last the statue is finished.' Monsieur Landowski thumped his workbench in relief. 'But now the crazy Brazilian needs me to make a scale model of his Christ's head and hands. The head will be nearly four metres high, so it will only just fit into the studio. The fingers will almost reach the rafters. All of us here in the atelier will, in the most literal sense, experience Christ's hand upon us,' he joked. 'Then, so da Silva Costa tells me, once I have finished this, he will carve my creations up like joints of beef in order to ship them over to Rio de Janeiro. Never before have I worked liked this. But,' he sighed, 'perhaps I should trust to his madness.'

'Perhaps you have no choice,' agreed Laurent.

'Well, it pays the bills, Brouilly, although I can accept no more commissions until Our Lord's head and hands are gone from my atelier. There would simply be no room. So, we begin. Bring me the casts you made of the two ladies' hands some months ago. I must have something to work with.'

I watched Laurent go to the storeroom to retrieve the casts, and decided it was time to slip away. I could feel the tension of both men. I went outside the atelier and sat on the stone bench, looking up at what was a beautiful clear night sky. I shivered suddenly, glad for the first time of my woollen jumper. There would be a frost tonight, but I didn't think snow would follow.

And I should know. I turned my head to look at the right place in the sky, knowing that, now it was November, it was the time of year when those who had guided me here to my new home would appear in the Northern Hemisphere. I had seen them a few times already, when they'd been twinkling weakly, and were often obscured by clouds, but tonight…

I jumped as I always did when I heard footsteps approaching, and tried to make out who it was. Laurent's familiar shape appeared and he sat down next to me as I continued to gaze up into the heavens.

'You like stars?' he asked.

I gave him a smile and a nod.

'There is the belt of Orion.' Laurent pointed up into the night sky. 'And close by are the Seven Sisters in a cluster together. With their parents, Atlas and Pleione, watching over them.'

I followed his fingers as he traced the lines between the stars, not daring to look at him or he would see my surprise.

'My father was interested in astronomy, and kept a telescope in one of the attic rooms on the top floor of our chateau,' Laurent explained. 'Sometimes, he would take it up to the roof on clear nights and teach me about the stars. I once saw a shooting star, and thought it the most magical thing I had ever seen.' He looked down and inspected my face closely. 'Do you have parents?'

I kept my gaze trained on the stars, pretending not to have heard him.

'Ah, well, I must be going.' He patted me on the head. 'Goodnight.'

I watched him walk off and realised it was the nearest I'd come (after the violin episode at least) to actually speaking. Of all the stars he could have named in all the constellations… I knew they were famous, but somehow I'd always felt as though they were *my* secret, and I wasn't sure whether I liked the fact that anyone else found them special too.

Just look for the Seven Sisters of the Pleiades, my son. They'll always be there somewhere, watching over you and protecting you when I cannot…

I knew all of their stories inside out. When I was far smaller than I am now, I would listen to my papa as he told me of their ancient wonder. I knew that they were not just creatures of Greek mythology, but of many legends across the world, and in my mind, they had been real: seven women, watching over me. Whilst other children learnt of angels that would wrap their downy wings around them, Maia, Alcyone, Asterope, Celaeno, Taygete, Electra and Merope were all like mothers to me. I felt very lucky to have seven of them, because even if one wasn't shining as brightly on a particular night, others were. Each had different qualities, different strengths. I sometimes thought that if you put them all together, perhaps you'd have the perfect woman, like the Holy Mother. And even if I was—or had to be—grown-up these days, the fantasy of the sisters being real and coming to my rescue when I needed them did not disappear, because I wouldn't let it. I looked up at them again, then stood up from the bench and ran all the way up to my attic room to peer out of the window. And yes... YES! They were visible from here too.

That night, I think that perhaps I had the best night's rest I'd had for as long as I could remember, knowing that my guardians were there, shining down on me protectively.

Word had spread throughout the house that I could play the violin.

'They want to hear you play,' Evelyn said. 'And you will do so this Sunday.'

I gave a pout, which was more out of fear than annoyance. It was one thing playing for Evelyn, who was a housekeeper, but another playing for the Landowski family, especially with Marcel being such a talented pianist.

'Don't worry, you can use this to practise,' Evelyn said as she handed me the violin. 'Come over during the day when everyone is busy. Not that you need to rehearse, my dear, but perhaps it might make you feel better if you do. Do you know many pieces off by heart?'

I nodded.

'Then you must choose at least two or three,' she advised,

although I couldn't work out why. So, over the next few days, I came into Evelyn's little house whilst she was working next door, made sure all the windows were closed in case of prying ears, and played all my favourite pieces through. Evelyn had been right: I was rusty, and my fingers had lost some of their nimbleness, possibly due to what they had endured on my journey here. After much careful thought, I selected three pieces. The first, because it sounded very impressive, but was actually fairly simple to play. The next because it was a hard technical piece, just in case any member of the family had enough knowledge of violin playing to judge my skill. And the last because it was probably my favourite piece of violin music ever, and I loved playing it.

The 'performance' was to happen before lunch on Sunday. Even the servants had been invited to come and listen. I'm sure the Landowskis were just being kind by trying to ensure I felt special, but it made me feel as though I was being tested in some way, which I didn't like at all. Whatever their reasons, and I was sure it *was* out of kindness, I knew that I had no choice but to perform for them. It was really quite frightening as I'd only ever played in front of my old household before, and apart from Papa, no one else's opinion had really mattered. But this was a famous sculptor and his talented family, of whom some had serious musical knowledge.

I didn't sleep well the night before, tossing and turning and only wishing that I could run downstairs and into Evelyn's little house, so that I could practise and practise until the violin was an extension of my hands, which was how Papa had said it should be.

I spent Sunday morning playing until my fingers had nearly dropped off, then Evelyn came to find me and told me to go up and change. In the kitchen, she'd given me what she called a 'lick and a spit', which meant wetting my hair and brushing it back, as well as running her flannel over my face.

'There now, all done. You're ready.' She smiled at me, then pulled me to her. 'Just remember how proud I am of you.' Then she let me go and I saw tears in her eyes.

I was welcomed into the drawing room, where the family were gathered around a fireplace with a very big fire burning inside it. They all had glasses of wine, and I was ushered in to stand in front of them.

'Now then, boy, no need to be nervous, eh? Just play whenever you're ready,' said Monsieur Landowski.

I put the violin under my chin and moved it around until it was comfortable. Then I closed my eyes and asked all those who Papa had told me were protecting me—including him—to gather around me. Then I lifted my bow and began to play.

When I'd finished the last piece, there came what I felt was a dreadful silence. All my confidence had disappeared into my toes. What did Papa know? The housekeeper and her engineer son? I felt a red flush of embarrassment starting to creep up my cheeks and I wanted to run away and cry. My hearing must have disappeared for a bit in my misery, for eventually I came to, and heard the clapping. Even Marcel was looking animated and impressed.

'Bravo, young man! Bravo,' said Monsieur Landowski. 'I only wish that you could tell us where you learnt to play like that. Or will you tell us?' he added, with an almost desperate look on his face.

'Seriously, you are very, very good, especially for your age,' said Marcel, managing to give me a compliment and patronise me at the same time.

'Well done,' said Madame Landowski, patting me on the shoulder, and giving me one of her small warm smiles. 'Now,' she added as a bell tinkled from the hall, 'we must go in for lunch.'

There was much talk over the hors d'oeuvres of my incredible prowess, then the family amused themselves over the main course by asking me questions that I had to answer with a nod or shake of the head. Even though there was part of me that felt uncomfortable because they were treating my unknown life as a mere game, I knew none of them meant any harm. If I didn't wish to answer one of their questions, I merely had to do neither.

'We must find you some lessons, young man,' said Landowski. 'I have a friend at the *conservatoire*. Rachmaninoff would know a good teacher.'

'Papa, the *conservatoire* does not take on students until they are much older,' interjected Marcel.

'Ah, but this is not any pupil, and our young friend has

exceptional talent. Age of any kind is no barrier to talent. I will see what I can do,' said Monsieur Landowski with a wink. I saw Marcel pout.

Just before everyone stood up after dessert, I made a decision. I wanted desperately to give Monsieur Landowski in particular a gift for all he had done for me. So I took some paper and wrote a few words. As everyone was leaving the table, I put a hand out to stop Monsieur Landowski passing. Then, my hands shaking slightly, I handed him the paper. I watched him as he read the four words.

'Well, well, well,' he chuckled, 'after your performance earlier, it is as if it was meant to be. Do I presume that this is a nickname because of your talent?'

I nodded.

'Very well, then I will inform the family. Thank you for trusting us with this. I understand how difficult it is for you.'

I walked out into the hall, then ran upstairs to my attic room. I stood in front of the mirror and faced myself. Then I opened my mouth to speak the words.

'My name is Bo.'

A violin teacher had been found for me apparently, and I was to go to Paris after Christmas to play for him. I couldn't decide whether I was more excited about playing for a proper violinist, or because I would be taken into the city by Evelyn.

'Paris,' I mouthed as I lay under my covers. Evelyn had ordered the maids to provide me with a thicker woollen blanket, and snuggling in bed, warm under the covers, had now become one of the highlights of my day. I was also filled with this funny sensation in my tummy, which I remembered feeling before when I was much younger and my heart wasn't filled up with fear. It was as if a little bubble was rising up from my tummy into my chest, making my lips curl into a smile. The word for the feeling was, I thought, *excitement*. It was something I almost dared not feel because that then led to feeling happy, and I didn't want to get too happy because if I did, something awful might happen, like the Landowskis deciding they didn't want me under their roof anymore, and then it would be even harder to face the misery of being alone, penniless and starving again. The violin had saved me, made me even more 'intriguing', as Monsieur Landowski had said the day after to Laurent in the atelier (I'd had to look up the word 'intriguing' because it was missing from my vocabulary).

So if I wanted to stay, I had to carry on being as intriguing as I possibly could, as well as being useful, which, actually, was all very exhausting. Plans for Christmas were well underway too, with lots of secret whisperings about presents. This had worried me a lot, because, of course, I had no money to buy anything for anybody, and I was terrified that they, being the kind family that they were, would give me gifts. I had consulted with Evelyn about this on one of my nightly visits.

She'd read, *How do I get money for presents?* then looked at me and I could see she was thinking about it.

'I could loan you a few cents to buy a little gift for everyone, but I know that you would refuse to take it and that the Landowskis may wonder where the money had come from...if you know what I mean,' she'd said as she rolled her eyes. I think she meant that they might suspect me of stealing, which would not be the right thing to endear me to them at all.

She told me to put on the cocoa while she was thinking about it, and I did so. By the time I placed her mug beside her, I could see she had a plan.

'You know you spend all that time trying to chisel stones into shapes in the atelier?'

I nodded, but then took my paper and wrote, *But I'm very bad at it.*

'Well, who could be good, except a genius like Monsieur Landowski? But you have had practice at making shapes, so I was thinking that maybe you should try an easier form of material like wood, and see if you can carve each of the family a little something for their Christmas present. That would please Monsieur Landowski, for he would feel that the months you have spent watching and learning had given you a useful gift.'

I nodded very eagerly, because even though Evelyn would often say she wasn't educated, she did sometimes come up with the best ideas.

So, I went off and found myself some wood from the pile in the barn, and each morning before everyone was up, I would sit at the trestle table and practise. Evelyn had also been right about choosing wood instead of rock. It was like learning to play the tin whistle rather than a flute. And besides, I had watched others do it in my old home.

My old home...that was how I was beginning to think about it now.

So, in the three weeks before Christmas, I managed to carve each member of the family what I hoped was a thoughtful thing that they may appreciate. Monsieur Landowski's took the longest, for I wanted to carve him a wooden replica of his beloved *Cristo* statue. In fact, I spent as much time on that as I did all the other carvings put together.

He had suffered a difficult time in the last few weeks when the architect of the *Cristo* had said that the only way to ship what I called 'Christ's overcoat' (the concrete that would support him and his innards) was to chop it up into bits. From what I had overheard, on the long journey from France to Rio, there would be less chance of a part of him cracking. Monsieur Landowski had fretted terribly because he felt he should go with his precious Christ to watch over him, but it was such a long journey there and back—time he felt he couldn't spare because Sun Yat-sen and his eyeballs were still not finished to his satisfaction.

Of course, I had thought of the perfect solution for everyone: Laurent should go as nursemaid to the *Cristo*. Not only would this mean that Monsieur Landowski could stay here, but that Laurent could perhaps see his love in Rio...which might make him happier and stop him spending his nights on the streets of Montparnasse (a place I was desperate to see, even though Monsieur Landowski spent many moments complaining it was full of would-be artists, beggars and thieves). I was about to suggest this, when luckily Laurent managed to find his brain and suggest it himself. Monsieur Landowski was not sure at first, because it was quite true to say that recently, Laurent had not been at his most reliable. But after swearing over and over that he would sleep in the hold with the pieces of the *Cristo* if necessary, and not touch a drop of alcohol whilst the *Cristo* was in his care, everyone decided it was for the best. The look of anticipation in Laurent's eyes was beautiful to watch and I really hoped that one day I would be lucky enough to experience this love thing that lit him up from inside as he thought of seeing my beautiful angel Bel again.

Pleasure and pain, I thought as I carefully wrapped my own carving of the *Cristo* in the brown paper Evelyn had given me for my presents.

'You are not perfect, but at least you are whole.' I smiled at him as I folded the paper over his not exactly symmetrical face.

Once I'd finished wrapping all the carvings, I stowed them in my chest of drawers. Then, seeing that night-time was falling, I walked down the stairs and tiptoed into the drawing room to look at the fir tree that had been brought in earlier, for today it was Christmas Eve. I had watched as every member of the family had put pine cones hung by ribbon on its branches, and we had all placed a pair of our shoes under the tree for Père Noël to fill with presents. Monsieur Landowski had told me it was a very old French tradition, which the grown-ups enjoyed doing as well. Then they had attached candles to the branches' ends, and as dusk fell, lit them. It was the prettiest thing I had ever seen, especially now in the dark.

'Still looking at it, boy?'

The voice of the person I had just been thinking of made me jump and I turned to see Monsieur Landowski, who had not graduated to calling me by my new alias.

'I always think of Tchaikovsky's music when I look at the tree on Christmas Eve. Do you know the score from *The Nutcracker*?'

I used my hand to indicate that yes, I did, but not well. Papa had been less of an enthusiast of Tchaikovsky, complaining that he wrote his music to please his audience rather than writing his scores on a more technical level.

'I bet you didn't know that it was when Tchaikovsky was in Paris that he had an instrument called the celesta, which is also called a bell piano, because of the sound it makes. That inspired his "Dance of the Sugar Plum Fairy", and he returned to Russia with renewed energy for his composition.'

I did not know this and I nodded eagerly, wanting the conversation to continue.

'Can you play the *Overture*?'

I gave him another shrug to indicate a maybe—because of course I could play it once upon a time, but I would need to practise.

'Maybe this will help you remember. I was coming upstairs to find you and give it to you. I thought it might embarrass you if I handed it to you in front of the family,' he added.

In the dim light of the tree, I saw him produce a violin case from behind his back and offer it to me.

'My parents gave it to me as a child, but I am afraid I never showed much aptitude for it. Nevertheless I kept it, as one does with presents from one's parents. Sentimental value…you know.'

I did know, and for an instant I was caught between the sadness of everything I'd been forced to leave behind in my flight and the impending joy of what Monsieur Landowski was offering me.

'There, it is better in a talented pair of hands like yours than sitting atop my wardrobe, gathering dust.'

I opened my mouth automatically, so completely overwhelmed with his generosity and the possibilities that became open to me with my own violin, that I almost spoke. I looked at it resting in the palms of my hands and kissed it, then I went to him and gave him an uncomfortable hug. After a few seconds, he pulled me back from him by the shoulders.

'Perhaps, boy, one day you will really be able to trust me and say the words of gratitude that hang on your lips. For now, merry Christmas.'

I nodded eagerly in return and watched him as he left the room.

Upstairs, knowing the maids were still down in the kitchen, drinking some liquor that smelt like petroleum fluid and singing songs that didn't sound much like carols to me, I put the violin case on my bed and opened it, my heart beating fast against my chest. There inside lay a violin which had been made for a small person like me and its original owner. It would be much easier to handle than the adult version Evelyn had kindly lent me. Drawing it out, I could see the signs of age upon it—the odd scratch on the walnut sheen, and dust covering the strings.

Sitting down, I removed it reverently from its case and held it up to my mouth and blew, watching the dust motes free themselves from their prison and dance around my bedroom. I would open my window and release them tomorrow. Then I took my handkerchief from my pocket and wiped the strings. I removed the bow, then placed the violin under my chin. It could not have felt more comfortable if it had tried. Then I lifted the bow, closed my eyes and played.

My heart danced out of my chest to join the dust motes as I heard the mellow sound of a well-made violin. Yes, the strings needed some adjustment after years of neglect, but that was simple. Inspired by Monsieur Landowski's story about *The Nutcracker*, I played the first few bars of the *Overture*. And then I chuckled out loud, and danced around my room, playing a jolly folk song I'd often played at home when things had been more difficult than usual. Panting with emotion, I felt suddenly faint and had to lie down on my bed, as my head steadied and I drank some water from the flask in the cupboard next to me.

To think that this time last year, I'd believed that I'd never see another Christmas, yet here I was with a happy ending, just like Clara when she realises all she had seen was a dream. Or perhaps it was a new beginning.

I gave one last flashy stroke of the bow across...*my* instrument, then put it back and stowed it under the bedsheets at the bottom so my toes could reach out and touch the case.

Settling down onto my pillows, I smiled and said, 'I am Bo, and I *will* have a happy ending.'

5

After what was a very jolly time in the Landowski household, especially the party on New Year's Eve when Monsieur Landowski invited many of his artistic friends, I was counting down the days until my audition with my possible violin tutor. No one had cared to mention his name, and neither did I care, for if he was employed at the *conservatoire* that Rachmaninoff had been to, he could not be anything but impressive.

I spent as much time as I could practising, so often that I'd been given a scolding by the maids who'd told me my 'screeching' on that 'thing' meant they both had their pillows up over their heads and, anyway, it was 'past midnight'!

I had apologised profusely as I checked my clock and realised that they were right; I had lost all track of time.

The great day came and Evelyn bustled into my room to offer me a grey blazer of Marcel's to put over my shirt and woollen jumper.

'Right, now we must be leaving. The bus runs to its own timetable, not the one that's pinned to the stop.'

She chattered on as we walked down the road and into the village, but I wasn't really with her, even when she began walking up and down in frustration, talking to the other waiting passengers about the unreliability of our buses, and how ridiculous it was that Boulogne-Billancourt manufactured both cars and planes yet couldn't run a bus on time. I was in a different place, seeing the notes in my head, trying to remember all those years back what Papa had taught me about 'living the music' and feeling its soul. Even as we drove towards Paris, the city Papa had told me so much about, I closed my eyes knowing there would be another time to see it and take in its beauty, but for now, all that mattered was the violin that sat on my knee and the notes it would play.

'Come on, young man, keep up,' Evelyn reprimanded me because I insisted on holding my violin with both hands tight across my chest, so she couldn't hold mine. I noticed there were a lot of people on the wide pavements, and some trees, and…yes! A building that was instantly recognisable! The Eiffel Tower. I could still see it as Evelyn came to a standstill.

'Here we are, fourteen Rue de Madrid. So, in we go.'

I looked up at the large sandstone building that spanned almost the whole length of the street, and counted three stories of tall windows, with what looked to be smaller attic levels on the top of them. A brass plaque announced that this was indeed the famous Conservatoire de Paris.

Even though she said we were going in, I had to wait until she'd renewed her lipstick and tidied the hair that sat outside of her best hat. Inside was a grand waiting room lined with portraits of old composers. In the middle of the polished wooden floor was a woman at a round reception desk, who Evelyn immediately went to speak to. Light poured in through windows facing the street outside and what looked to be a large park at the back.

I was very pleased when the stern-looking lady on the reception finally nodded and told us to report to room four on the second floor. She pointed us towards what appeared to be a cage that you might put a bear in, and as I veered off for the stairs that were next to it, Evelyn pulled me towards the cage and pressed a button on its side.

'If you think I'm walking up two flights of stairs when there is a lift available, you must be mad.'

I wanted to ask her what a 'lift' was, but then I saw another box drop down inside it and the word made sense. Still, even though it looked exciting, I was taking no chances. I pointed to the stairs and began to take them two at a time. There was no sign of Evelyn when I arrived beside another cage that was the same as the one on the ground floor, and I suspected the worst, but then suddenly I heard a whirring and the box inside popped out of the ground. The door opened, and there was Evelyn, pulling back the front of the cage and stepping out as safely as anything.

'So, you've never seen one of those before, eh?' she asked me.

I shook my head, still marvelling at the miracle.

'Maybe you'll join me in it on the way down. That will give you something to look forward to, whatever happens. Now then, we need to find room four.' Evelyn headed towards a corridor, from which I could hear the sound of different instruments being played from behind closed doors. We stopped in front of room number four, and Evelyn tapped briskly on the door. There was no answer. Giving a good few seconds, she tapped again.

'No one at home.' She shrugged, then turned the doorknob as slowly and quietly as she could, and pushed it until there was room for her head—or should I say her hat—to peer around inside it.

'No, nobody there. We'll just have to wait, won't we?'

So, wait we did, and I know that people exaggerate when they say something was the happiest or the worst or the longest moment of their life, but really, however long it was I spent outside room four, waiting for the person who would tell me whether I was good enough for him to teach me, really felt very slow indeed. Even more annoyingly, I could still see the lift from here, and each time it whirred upwards and released its passenger, I'd imagine that *this* was the person who would decree my fate. However, each time they either walked the other way or straight past us.

'Oh really,' Evelyn said, and I could see she was shifting her weight from one leg to the other because it hurt her to stand, 'whoever this teacher is, his manners are downright rude.'

Finally, just as she was muttering about leaving and that there had obviously been some mistake, a door along the corridor opened. Then a young, slim man with very white skin and dark hair appeared. He walked towards us, looking what I decided was a little bit drunk, and stopped in front of us.

'Please forgive me, I taught a lesson with a pupil before you, then decided to take a brief rest. I'm afraid I fell asleep.' He stuck out his hand to Evelyn and she reluctantly released hers.

'Madame, petit monsieur, please forgive me,' he said. 'These are long days I work here and sleep is something that often deserts me at night. Now then, madame, now that you have delivered your precious cargo to me, why don't you go downstairs in the lift and wait in the entrance hall where there is a comfortable chair? Tell Violetta that Ivan asks her to get you a pot of tea or coffee, whichever may be your pleasure.'

Looking relieved but a little bit reluctant to leave me with what she obviously considered to be quite a strange man, her feet won, and she nodded.

'Once you have finished, you are to come straight down, do you understand, Bo?'

I nodded.

'You know he is mute?' she added to Monsieur Ivan.

'Yes, but it is the music that will speak for him, isn't that right?' he said to me.

Without further comment, he opened the door and ushered me inside.

Even when I was writing my diary later that evening—and then my secret diary straight afterwards, of which this is part—I had only vague memories of the time I spent with Monsieur Ivan. I know that first he made me play what he called my 'party pieces', then he produced a score to test my sight reading, then he took out his own violin and played a string of scales and arpeggios, which I had to follow. That really did seem to happen very fast. After that, he ushered me to a small, wooden table with chairs around it and told me to sit down.

As he pulled a chair in, he swore and looked at his finger. Then, he said something else and I realised he was speaking in Russian.

'So, I have a splinter, which I will have to pull out tonight at home. The smallest things can cause the greatest pain, don't you agree?'

I nodded, because whether I did or didn't, it would have made no difference. I wanted to please this man, more than any other I'd wanted to please since Papa had left.

'How do we communicate if you won't speak?'

Already prepared, I pulled out my scrap paper from my pocket, along with my pencil.

'Your name is Bo?'

Yes, I wrote.

'How old are you?'

Ten.

'Where are your parents?'

My mother is dead and I do not know where my father is.

'Where are you from originally?'

I do not know.

'I don't believe you, petit monsieur, and I have my suspicions already, but you hardly know me, and all us émigrés do not like to give up personal information easily, correct?'

Yes, I wrote, moved that he understood and did not think me strange like everyone else.

'Who taught you to play the violin?'

Papa.

'How long ago is it since you last took a lesson?'

I tried to think back but I couldn't be sure, so I wrote:

Three or four years.

'I have never met one so young with so much skill. It is quite remarkable, really. Your musicality comes naturally, which hides the flaws in your technical prowess. I was impressed that your nerves did not get the better of you, although I imagine that this chance to be taught at the *conservatoire* means everything to you?'

Yes, I wrote.

'Hmmm…'

I watched him as he put his hand to his chin and moved it up and down and to both sides as he thought about whether I was worth teaching.

'As you can imagine, I have many parents coming to me with their child geniuses, children who have had the best violins and suburban teachers, and are forced into hours of practice. Even if they are technically far more brilliant than you, I often feel that their soul is not in the music they play. In other words, they are performing monkeys, simply an extension of their parents' egos.

With you, this is definitely not the case, partly because you are an orphan and do not have parents, and your guardian is a man who hardly needs a child that does not belong to him to impress his friends when he *himself* is so impressive. So…even if there are flaws in the way you play and—no disrespect meant to your papa, but I would guess that he was not a professional?'

I shook my head, feeling as if I *was* being disrespectful, whatever Monsieur Ivan said.

'Do not look so sad, petit monsieur, really. I can see he taught you with love. And in turn, he found a talent that was much greater than his own that he wished to nurture. What school are you at, at present?'

None. I cannot speak so I cannot go.

'Even though it is none of my business, that is not good. I know you can speak, not just because I have been told so, but in the instinctive way you have stopped yourself replying to me since we have been talking. I think that you are surrounded by good, kind people and whatever terrible things have happened to you in the past, which have left you so damaged you dare not communicate, I hope for your sake there will be a time when you will. But no matter, I say that only as someone who has suffered much too, since I left Russia. So much suffering, so many wars in only fifteen years of humanity… You—and I—are both the result of it. One word of advice, my young friend: do not let those bad people win, all right? They have taken so much from you—your past, your family. Do not let them take your future too.'

Embarrassingly, my eyes filled with tears. I nodded slowly and then reached for my handkerchief.

'Ah, I have made you cry, I apologise. I can be too free with my words. The good news is that if you have no school, it will be far easier to slot you into my timetable. Now then, let me see…'

I watched him pull out a slim diary from his jacket pocket and turn the pages over, which weren't many, because it was only January.

'So, we shall begin with two lessons a week. I can make eleven o'clock on a Tuesday, and two o'clock on a Friday. We shall see how we go, but I have a good feeling about you. Really, I do. So, I shall take you down to your nursemaid. She seems like a kind woman,' he stated as he left the room and walked towards the lift.

I nodded.

Then I remembered, and hastily wrote some words.

How much for each lesson?

'I shall speak to Monsieur Landowski, but we émigrés must help each other, mustn't we?'

He slapped me on the back so hard that I nearly fell into the box inside the cage. He pulled the door closed, pressed a button and down we went. I wondered if it was how birds felt when they flew, but I doubted it somehow. Still, it was fun and I looked forward to doing it twice a week in the future. *If* Monsieur Landowski and Monsieur Ivan could agree on a price.

'Madame, your boy was a triumph! I shall be taking him for certain, at eleven o'clock on a Tuesday, and two o'clock on a Friday. Tell Monsieur Landowski I shall telephone him to talk about the details. Safe travels home,' he said. Then with a wink and a smile, Monsieur Ivan walked back towards the lift.

Merry

In transit: Dublin to Nice

June 2008

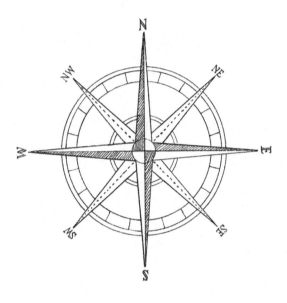

6

I closed the pages of the old, leather-bound diary and stared through the window of the jet. My intention to sleep had vanished after reading the letter, which pointed me to the journal that now sat on my lap. The man who claimed to be my father—Atlas— wrote with such deep regret.

I cannot voice or begin to explain the love I have felt for you since I knew of your imminent arrival. Nor can I tell you in this letter the lengths I took to find you and your mother, who were both lost to me so cruelly before you were born...

The emotional weight of the past few weeks descended upon me, and I felt my eyes fill with tears. At that moment, I wished for nothing more than an embrace from Jock, my husband, who seemed to have been taken from me at the point when I needed him most.

'If only you were here.' I dabbed my eyes with one of the silk napkins that had been placed in the side pocket of the luxurious leather seat. 'But you'd be loving this five-star treatment, that's for certain.'

The letter from Atlas had promised his diary would contain the answers to my true heritage, but it was absolutely enormous. After reading the first section, I was nowhere nearer to understanding his story or how I fit in to it. Whoever my 'father' was, he'd clearly led quite the life. Even though the opening part of the diary had been written by a ten-year-old child, the voice was filled with maturity and wisdom, as if the young boy was inhabited by an old soul.

I shook my head, noting the pattern of the last few weeks was repeating itself. Every time I seemed to be getting close to the truth of my past, further mysteries were thrown up. Why was the boy pretending to be mute? Why did he feel that he could not reveal his true name? And what on earth had led to him being discovered, orphaned, under a hedge in the middle of Paris? If anything, it seemed that Atlas's diary had begun too late for me to understand the full picture.

Mind you, I thought, if you're going to land on anyone's doorstep, the famed sculptor behind one of the new Seven Wonders of the World—*Christ the Redeemer*—wasn't a bad person to end up with.

I sighed, feeling somewhat odd that Atlas had entrusted me, the apparent biological daughter he had never met, with the story of his life before allowing his beloved adopted children to read it. They were, of course, the ones who had known and loved their 'Pa Salt' so very much. Surely they deserved to discover his secrets first?

I tried to quell the flutters in my stomach as I contemplated the nature of my situation. Here I was, jetting out to join a bunch of total strangers on a superyacht pilgrimage to lay a wreath for a man that I, as of yet, felt no connection to. Yes, I'd very briefly met a couple of them, but it wasn't enough to quell my nerves. I didn't even know if the other women were aware that I was seemingly genetically related to their adoptive father. That, coupled with the fact Atlas had decreed that I should be the first to read his diary, had the potential to make the sisters feel resentful.

I tried to comfort myself with the knowledge that it had been the family who had attempted to track *me* down, rather than the other way around.

'They want you there, Merry,' I told myself.

Of course, the greatest source of comfort came from the knowledge that I was flying towards my own children, Jack and Mary-Kate, who were already aboard the *Titan*. I knew just how thrilled they would be by my decision to join them on the cruise. Even if the six sisters turned out to be total lunatics, at least my kin would be there to protect me, and to keep me sane throughout the trip. Apparently, the cruise was due to take six days in total—three days to sail the *Titan* from Nice to Delos and lay the wreath, and three days to return. Plus, if it all became too much, I could 'abandon ship' on the nearby island of Mykonos, which boasted an international airport.

There was a knock on the panel doors, which had been pulled in from either side of the cabin to form a partition between front and back.

'Oh—hello?' I said, pulled away from my thoughts.

The panel slid open, and the tall, tanned figure of Georg Hoffman appeared. Still dressed immaculately in his dark suit, it appeared that he had not even loosened his tie during the course of the three-hour flight.

'Good evening, Merry. Or should I say good morning…' His eyes moved to the blanket and pillow which had been handed to me by the steward, both unused on a neighbouring seat. 'Ah. I take it you did not get much rest. Did you…open the package?'

'I did, Georg. I read the letter and, of course, had to start the diary. It's hugely long…as I'm sure you know.'

A hint of a smile appeared on Georg's moustachioed face. 'I have carried it with me for a long time, but I swear to you, I have never once turned its pages. It was not mine to read.'

'So you're telling me that you honestly have no idea about the history of Atlas?'

'Ah, no. I did not say that. Only that I have not read the diary.' Georg hesitated. 'I know… I *knew* Atlas—your father—very well. He was both the bravest and the kindest man I've ever had the privilege of meeting.'

'How long until we land?'

'The pilot has just let me know that we'll be starting our descent into Nice in a few moments' time. Then we have a car arranged that will take us directly to the port where the *Titan* is docked.'

I looked out of the cabin window. 'It's still dark, Georg. What time is it?'

He checked his watch and raised his eyebrows. 'Just approaching half past three here in France. I apologise, I appreciate what a whirlwind this must be for you.'

'You can say that again. I still don't know whether this is the right thing to be doing. I mean, do the other daughters know that…well…according to everything I've learnt…that I'm his biological daughter?'

Georg lowered his eyes. 'No. I…they assume you are referred to as "the missing sister" due to the fact that it was Atlas's intention to adopt you, but he was unsuccessful in doing so. I must confess that, as odd as it may sound, they are even unaware of his true name. As you know, he has simply always been referred to by his daughters as "Pa Salt".'

'*Jesus, Mary and Joseph*, Georg.' I rested my brow in between my thumb and index finger. 'Although I recall that when I met her, Tiggy had worked out the anagram.' I looked back at him. 'That's one of them, at least!' I said with a dollop of sarcasm.

Georg nodded. 'You must understand, Merry, I am but an employee. Even though I knew your father for nearly my entire life, and counted him as a dear friend, it is my duty to follow his orders, even in death.'

'And yet, you seem to know all about me, Georg. You knew where to find me. You know that I am, apparently, Atlas's descendant. And you say all of this has come to light in the last few weeks?'

'I…yes.' Georg shifted uncomfortably.

'So, given the fact that Atlas has been dead for a year now, where on earth did you get all of your information from? Who told you about the ring I was found with?' The exhaustion and frustration of the last few weeks was beginning to spill out. 'And what about Argideen House? How did you discover that's where I was born?'

Georg removed his pocket square and began to dab his brow. 'Merry, these are excellent questions, and ones that I promise will be answered. But not by me.'

His response was not quite to my satisfaction.

'I mean, and no offence intended to any of the sisters here, but did they never question why this strange man decided to adopt six girls and name them after the Seven Sisters? And that their surname, D'Aplièse, is an anagram of "Pleiades"?'

'Many times. As you'll see when you meet them, each of the girls is as intelligent as the man who raised them. They simply took his word that they were named after his favourite star cluster, and that their surname was a further reflection of his love for the heavens. They did not realise the connection—that they were so called because they were the daughters of Atlas.'

I closed my eyes, the prospect of walking into my own hand-crafted fairy tale aboard the *Titan* becoming less and less appealing.

'How far into the journal did you read?'

'Not far. Atlas is just a little boy. He's been taken in by the sculptor and his family.'

Georg nodded. 'I see. There is much to learn. I promise you, Merry, the more you read, the clearer the picture will become. You will understand who he was, who you are…and why he adopted the six girls.'

'Well, that's just the thing, Georg. I don't know if it's right that I'm the first to read it. As you yourself said, the other six girls were raised by Atlas. They loved him. I didn't even know him. I think that the others should have access to it before I do.'

'I…understand, Merry. This must be a very difficult situation for you. But please know, it was Atlas's wish for you to learn his story as soon as we were able to find you. Because it is your story too. His whole life, he lived with the guilt of you believing he had abandoned you, which could not be further from the truth. It just happens that…events have collided, as, for some reason, they always seem to. I could not have predicted that we would be able to locate you at the exact time the other sisters were planning to lay a wreath to mark the anniversary of his death.' The smile returned to Georg's face. 'One could say the stars have aligned.'

'Well, you might see it that way. I feel more like they're ricocheting than aligning. The letter says that my mother disappeared, and that Atlas didn't even know whether she lived or died. So I'm guessing he wouldn't be knowing anything about me being abandoned on Father O'Brien's doorstep?'

Georg shook his head. 'No. Once again, I can only advise

that you read the diary. For the other sisters to understand why they were adopted, they must first understand who you are.'

'Have you heard of the Parable of the Prodigal Son, Georg?'

'I am familiar with the term, but I must admit that—'

'In the gospel of Luke, Jesus tells of a son who asks his father for his inheritance, then squanders it recklessly by living a life of luxury and indulgence. When he runs out of money, he returns to his father and apologises, but instead of being angry, his daddy is overjoyed at his return, and throws a feast in his honour. But you know the most relevant part of the story, Georg? The brother of the prodigal son is not at all thrilled at his return. For that brother stayed loyally at his father's side throughout the years, and received no reward for it. I don't want to be the prodigal daughter, if you catch my drift.'

Georg furrowed his brow, flustered by my firm stance. 'Merry, please understand that the girls could not be more excited to welcome you into their family, if that is what you so choose. They know how much their father longed to find the missing sister, and I assure you that you will be shown nothing but love by Atlas's daughters. I believe you have already encountered Tiggy, and Star too. Did you feel anything but love and excitement from either?'

I reached over to my left and opened a cream leather compartment that contained bottles of water. I took one, and cracked it open. 'From Tiggy, no. It's a large part of the reason I'm sat here on this plane. But Star was pretending to be a Lady Sabrina something or other to extract information from me. The point is, Georg, I know better than most the bitterness that a dispute in a family can cause. What if some of the sisters are happy to know that "Pa Salt" has a daughter by blood, and others aren't?' I cast my mind back to the recent revelation that I shared a grandmother, Nuala, with the man that had originally caused me to flee Ireland, Bobby Noiro. 'I mean, from my conversations with Mary-Kate I understand that there's a global supermodel, Electra, who hasn't always been known for having the most...gentle of personalities.' I took a large glug of water.

'I assure you, Merry, each of the sisters has been on their own personal journey of self-discovery during the past year. It has been my great privilege to watch each mature into a magnificent human being. They all…' I observed Georg swallow hard, clearly fighting his emotion. 'They have all come to a realisation that reaches most of us far too late in life…that it is far too short.'

I sighed and rubbed my eyes. 'You've said what a great and wise man Atlas was. Well, if I have received any of that wisdom through genetic inheritance, perhaps I need to exercise some of it now, in his absence. As you say, Georg, it was Atlas's wish that I should read his story as soon as I was found. Which I shall do. But I would like you to make six copies of the diary for the other girls. So that we may read about our father simultaneously.'

Georg looked at me, and behind his gaze I noted the cogs turning in his brain. For whatever reason, he was determined to follow Atlas's wishes to the letter. What wasn't he telling me?

'Yes…yes, that might be a good idea. It is your choice to make, Merry.'

'Although I imagine finding a photocopying shop at four a.m. in the South of France might prove to be somewhat of a challenge.'

'Ah, fear not. The *Titan* is fully equipped with every modern convenience. There is a dedicated office on board with computers, and several industrial printers. For this I am grateful, as the diary contains…'—Georg paused to consider his next word— '…personal information. I could not risk it falling into the wrong hands.'

'A whole office on board the boat? My goodness. I would have thought that the whole point of a superyacht was to relax and unwind from the stresses of everyday life! Well, I say "everyday", but if you own a superyacht, then Lord knows what the "everyday" entails anyway. Tell me, Georg—what did Atlas do to accrue so much money?'

Georg shrugged, and pointed to the beaten leather journal resting on my lap. 'The answers lie within.'

There was another knock on the panel, and the steward peered through the gap.

'I'm so sorry to interrupt, but the captain has asked for you to prepare for landing. Would you mind putting your seat belts on? We'll be touching down in Nice in just a few minutes.'

'Yes, of course, thank you.' Georg nodded at him. 'Well then, perhaps you will temporarily return the diary to my care, and I will arrange for six copies to be made once we board the *Titan*.' I handed him the journal, but kept the letter. He gave me a large smile. 'There is nothing to be afraid of, Merry. I promise you that.'

'Thank you, Georg. I'll see you when we're on the ground.'

He returned through the partition, and I looked out of my window once more. As the jet descended, I watched the light from the barely risen sun dance on the ripples of the azure-blue Mediterranean Sea. I hoped it was a little warmer than the Atlantic water on Inchydoney Beach in West Cork. I sat back in my seat and closed my eyes, wondering just how that little boy found orphaned under a hedge in the city of Paris would one day go on to create me.

7

The Titan

Ally stared up at the polished mahogany ceiling that adorned all of the cabins on board the *Titan*. The very term 'cabin' amused her, as she was used to bunking in the closest possible quarters with burly, sweaty men on twenty-six-foot Contessas. The bedrooms on board the *Titan* were more akin to the Presidential Suite at the Grand Hotel in Oslo. The vessel was in an immaculate state, too. Even though the boat hadn't been used by the family for the best part of a year, it was still crewed by Pa's loyal staff, who continued to maintain the highest standards. Ally assumed that they were paid by the trust which Pa had established before his death. Like so much about the world of Pa Salt, things just…happened, and Ally hardly ever questioned them.

A ray of sunlight snuck its way through a crack in the curtains and landed on Ally's face. She wondered how much longer she had before Bear's cries from the cot at the end of the bed signalled the start of her day.

She'd be surprised if she'd even managed half an hour's sleep last night. Even though the gentle lap of the Mediterranean Sea in June caused very little rocking, she was so attuned to the feel of the water beneath her vessel that she sensed every small wave hit the boat. That, coupled with the cacophony of thoughts running through her mind, was hardly a perfect combination for rest. The bare bones of the situation in which she found herself were fraught enough, with her sisters and their partners gathered to formally pay their respects to their father. But for Ally, there was so much more she had to reconcile.

It had been her, after all, who had seen the *Titan* off the coast of Delos soon after Pa had died. She remembered so vividly lying on the deck of Theo's sunseeker, *Neptune*, when he excitedly told her that his friend had spotted a Benetti superyacht from his catamaran, with a name she might recognise. Her stomach had fluttered with nervousness at the thought of having to introduce Theo to Pa. But, knowing already that she was totally in love, she had seen little point in delaying the inevitable. Ally had duly radioed the *Titan*, expecting to hear the measured tones of Captain Hans, but received no response. In fact, it appeared that whoever was skippering the yacht had made the decision to speed away from Ally at full blast.

'Looks like your father's running away from you,' Theo had said.

When Georg and Ma had informed the sisters that in the event of his death, Pa had requested a private burial at sea (so as not to distress his daughters), Ally had simply assumed that she had stumbled upon the funeral. In fact, she had even suffered guilt at disrupting her father's final wishes. However, given recent events, she was starting to question the narrative that had been relayed to her.

She recalled that the *Titan* was not the only vessel anchored off the coast of Delos that day. When Theo's friend had radioed to report its presence, he had mentioned that there was a second 'floating palace' alongside: the *Olympus*, the boat of the infamous Kreeg Eszu, owner of Lightning Communications. Stranger still had been the reports of the business tycoon's death that very day, which had made headlines across the world. His body had washed ashore in an apparent suicide. Ally suddenly felt nauseous. Why had she not examined this more closely?

That wasn't the only odd thing that seemingly linked Pa Salt to Kreeg Eszu. Merry's coordinates—which had been engraved on the armillary sphere, and recently discovered by the sisters— pointed to Argideen House in Ireland's West Cork. Troublingly,

Ally had just learnt from Jack that the property was owned by an 'Eszu'. Although the building had apparently long since been abandoned, that was the last registered name.

What Ally had dismissed as a bizarre coincidence for the past year was suddenly beginning to enter the realm of the mysterious. It was no secret that Kreeg's son, Zed, had an infatuation with the D'Aplièse sisters which bordered on obsession. The way he had lured a teenage Maia into his arms with his good looks and oily charm, only to abandon her at the time she needed him most, still set Ally's teeth on edge. She had often thought that it was almost as if Zed had purposefully set out to hurt her sister. Ally did not question whether the way 'the Creep', as she caustically referred to him, had moved on to Electra had been planned. No doubt Zed had calculated that if there was one of Maia's sisters who would accept him as a lover after the way she had been treated, it would be Electra. For a predator of his nature, the vulnerability induced by a lifestyle of drink and drugs must have been too tempting to ignore. It made sense that he would set his sights upon Tiggy, too. Her inclination to see the inherent good in everyone, coupled with her tendency to drift towards the realm of the spiritual, had, in the past, allowed her to be taken advantage of. Ally was eternally grateful that Tiggy had not been conned by Zed's advances and had instead found the wonderful Charlie Kinnaird.

Ally was sure that Pa had never mentioned the Eszu name. In fact, it had been one of the first things she had asked Maia on her return to their family home, Atlantis, one year ago.

'I'm sure there's no link,' Maia had insisted. 'They didn't even know each other, did they? Delos is simply a very beautiful island that many boats head for.' Ally was beginning to worry that Maia's swift response was due to little more than denial at the unique awfulness of her particular situation. Ally chastised herself for failing to question the presence of the *Olympus*. At the end of the day, what did any of the sisters know about Pa's life beyond his house and his yacht? Growing up, they had encountered so few of his friends and business associates. It certainly wasn't beyond the realms of possibility that Pa Salt and Kreeg Eszu had met before.

Ally closed her eyes, hoping she could force an hour or two's sleep. As she often did when anxious, she imagined her father's deep, soothing voice. Her mind drifted back to Atlantis, where as a little girl she had watched Pa glide across the waters of Lake Geneva on his Laser at weekends. The way the sleek craft cut through the lake on calm days, creating barely a ripple on the glassy water as it did so, seemed to sum up Pa himself. He had always been such a pillar of strength and power, and yet seemed to slip through the world with a grace and poise that all those around him admired deeply.

One autumnal weekend, Pa had spied Ally watching his boat longingly from the shore, and had brought the Laser alongside the wooden jetty that protruded from the garden.

'Hello, my *petite princesse*. It's freezing cold out here. I think Maia's reading in the drawing room. Wouldn't you like to go and join her in the warm?'

'No, Pa. I love to watch you on the boat.'

'Ah.' He gave Ally a characteristically warm smile, which never failed to improve her mood no matter what problems that day had thrown up. 'Well then, perhaps you would be my first officer?'

'Ma says it's too dangerous.'

'Then it is a good job she is busy helping Claudia prepare tonight's dinner,' he said with a wink. Pa lifted Ally from the jetty with his muscular arms, making her feel as light as a feather, and sat her on his lap. 'Now, you will have seen that when the boat turns, it tilts to one side. When I need to go the other way, I must move to the other side of the boat, whilst ducking under this sail.'

'Yes, Pa!' Ally had replied enthusiastically.

'Excellent.' He began to remove his own orange life jacket and tie it around Ally. Naturally, it had totally enveloped her, and Pa chuckled as he fastened the straps as tightly as possible.

'What about you, Pa?'

'Oh, don't you worry about me, little one. The wind is light, and we're going to move very slowly. Do you see this small dip in the boat here?' He indicated a shallow groove in the white hull. 'I think it is Ally-sized, don't you?'

Ally nodded, and took the cue to position herself in the centre of the boat.

'All you have to do is look forward, and hold out your arms

to help you balance. We're going to do a big circle that will bring us back here to the jetty, which means I'm only going to lean out to the left. That's this side. See?' Ally nodded, anticipation coursing through her little body. 'All right then.' He lifted his leg from the jetty, and the Laser began to drift. Pa grabbed the large black handle that Ally had observed as the primary method for steering the craft.

'We're not moving, Pa!' Ally had said, somewhat disappointed.

'Not everything is in the sailor's control, Ally. We must wait for a breeze.'

As if on cue, Ally felt a surge pull the Laser away from the jetty. The wind began to rush through her thick auburn hair, and her heart quickened.

'Off we go!' Pa had cried.

Ally remembered the exhilaration of being so close to the water, the Laser moving through the still lake powered by nothing but the air that surrounded them. She looked back at the magnificent fairy-tale castle that was Atlantis. The snow-capped mountains rose steeply behind the pale pink house, and Ally felt lucky to live in such a magical place.

'I'm going to increase the turn now,' Pa said. 'That means the boat is going to lean a little more towards me. Remember to put your arms out to help.' Ally did so. 'Perfect, Ally, perfect!' Pa had beamed as Ally seamlessly adapted to the change in angle and elevation.

The sun glinted off the surface of the glassy water, and Ally allowed herself to close her eyes. That day, for the first time, she had felt a freedom which had returned whenever she took to the water. As Pa had skilfully glided the Laser in towards the jetty, and ensured Ally had climbed off safely, the smile on his daughter's face had told him everything.

'So, my *petite princesse*, you feel it too…there is nothing quite like being out on the open lake. It is the best place on earth to think.'

'Is that why you are out here so often?'

He chuckled warmly. 'Perhaps it is not a coincidence, no. Things rarely are.' His gaze left Ally's and ventured out across the lake. Sometimes, Pa's eyes clouded over, and Ally felt as though his mind was taking him to another place. 'Coincidence means only that there is a connection waiting to be discovered, after all.' Pa looked back at Ally. 'I'm sorry, little one… It just makes me very happy to know that you have the same love for sailing as your pa.'

'Do you think I could have some lessons?' Ally chirped.

'Hmm. I think this can be arranged. As long as you can fit them in alongside your tuition on the flute.' He gave her another wink.

'Of course, Pa! Do you think one day I will be as good as you?'

'Oh no, Ally. I think you will be better. Now, go inside and warm up. And don't tell Ma about our little trip!'

'I won't, Pa,' Ally replied, disentangling herself from the life jacket. She sprinted down the jetty towards the turreted shell of Atlantis.

The noise of Bear gurgling brought Ally out of her dream. She rubbed her eyes, glad that she'd at last managed a little rest, rolled out of bed and walked over to the cot. The sight of his mother caused Bear to lift out his arms and produce a small squeal of delight.

'Good morning to you too,' Ally said, lifting her son out of his bed. 'Are we hungry today, sir? I'm afraid the breakfast menu is a little sparse.' She expertly unbuttoned her pyjama top one-handed and Bear suckled happily, while Ally looked out of her cabin window.

She couldn't help but feel a perfect storm of guilt brewing inside her. It was undeniably lovely to see Jack again. The sight of him striding across the sun deck last night was enough to confirm that her feelings for him not only existed, but were deep. Yet here she was, about to sail to the exact spot where one year previously she'd been so overwhelmingly happy with Theo. If only he had been able to be here with her, this trip would have been so much easier. She wasn't given to self-indulgence, but Ally was acutely aware that she was the only one of the sisters who didn't have someone to confide in, or take strength from. Although she was genuinely happy to see her siblings and their partners on board the

Titan, it did rub salt into the wound still only too fresh from Theo's cruel early death.

Even Electra's bagged herself a human rights lawyer, Ally thought, knowing that her derision came from a place of sisterly love, not bitterness.

She looked down at Bear, who had Theo's soft eyes and hints of his unruly brown hair.

What a mess. Ally thought she'd probably blown any chance of a future relationship with Jack by failing to mention her son. The quizzical look on his face when she had introduced him to Bear last night was enough to tell her it had not been the right thing to do. 'He probably thinks I'm a total lunatic, Bear. First, I turn up in Provence incognito in order to secretly mine him for information about his family, and just when he's forgiven me for that, I text him for days on end and totally fail to tell him about you. And if *he* thinks I'm bananas, then goodness only knows what his mother will make of me!'

Ally checked her watch. It was approaching five a.m. Merry would be boarding very soon, as long as Georg had managed to convince her to get on the plane. The last thing that she had heard from Jack was that 'the missing sister' was not remotely interested in joining them for this cruise. Although, from the look on his face as he left, Georg may very well have dragged her onto the jet kicking and screaming. The sight of him leaving in such a panic for Dublin yesterday afternoon had only had the effect of unsettling Ally further. She had very rarely seen him rattled.

Ally groaned in frustration. Sometimes she wished she could do with Georg what she did with her crew a few days before any regatta—take them out and get them roaring drunk. In her career, she had found that there was little better way to build a bond of trust than drinking copious amounts of alcohol and sharing stories and secrets together.

Fat chance of that happening, she thought.

Bear gave a contented mewl, and Ally went to place him back in his cot. Then she crossed over to the en-suite bathroom, turned on the shower, and began mentally preparing to meet her missing sister. She thought how strange it would be to physically see her, standing before her eyes. The mysterious child that Pa had always said he had never found. The six sisters had searched the globe to find her, and Ally hoped that Pa, wherever he was, was enormously proud of what his girls had managed to achieve. Of course, the mystery of why Merry was 'missing' in the first place had yet to be solved. Had something gone awry with her adoption process? Why had Pa been so set upon that one girl?

As Ally luxuriated under the hot water and the superb pressure of the shower—which never ceased to amaze her, given the fact that they were at sea—she tried to work out when Merry might have first entered Pa's life. She was now fifty-nine years old. Pa had died aged eighty-nine last year, meaning that he would have been around thirty when he tried to adopt her. Considering that he had found Maia when he was approaching sixty, Ally began to wonder what had happened to Merry that had prevented Pa from attempting to adopt again for over twenty-five years.

However, Merry's age certainly made Ally feel a little better about the fact that she was rapidly developing strong feelings for her son, Jack. She allowed herself a small chuckle at the oddity of the situation.

And I thought our family couldn't get any weirder.

8

Merry

The car that had whisked us from the airport to the Port de Nice was as extravagant as the jet itself. I had to admit that even if I was hesitant about the trip, I was certainly enjoying the luxury. I'd wound all of the windows down and was enjoying the fresh smell of the pines in the air. The sun was barely up, but I could already feel that the day was going to be sweltering.

As it was so early, the limousine was able to drive right down to the dock. Every square inch of water was occupied by a boat, each more unashamedly opulent than the last. Mere inches separated the enormous vessels, which had been reversed with great skill into unimaginably small gaps. I shuddered to think of the cost of a repair to a scraped hull. All of the boats seemed to have their own team working on them, polishing, sweeping, laying tables for breakfast… To me, it all felt incredibly claustrophobic. Perhaps it's because I was so used to the wide, open space of the vineyards in the Gibbston Valley, or more recently, the rolling green fields of West Cork.

'You know, Georg, if I had all this money, I'd buy somewhere enormous in the middle of nowhere, not come here to sit crammed in like sardines. You'd never get any peace and quiet.'

'I am inclined to agree with you. It seems to me that most people in this port spend their entire summers moored, rarely leaving for sea. For the majority, these yachts are symbols of status—nothing more.'

'Well, isn't that just what the *Titan* is?'

'No. I must disagree with you on that. To Atlas, the *Titan* was a place of safety.'

'Safety?' I eyed him.

'That is correct. If ever he needed to…escape from…the stresses and pressures of life, he knew that he could board his yacht, along with his daughters, and sail to anywhere in the world.'

I noted the way the word 'escape' had hung on Georg's lips. The limo came to a stop at the end of the dock.

'So, which one is it then? I have to say, any will do. I'm not fussy.' My door was opened for me by the driver, who proceeded to remove my bag from the boot. Thank goodness I was supposed to be in the middle of a world tour. It meant that my suitcase was mightily well equipped. Before I knew it, another man in a navy polo shirt had taken the case from the driver. 'Is it this one? Right at the end?' I pointed towards the last yacht on the dock.

'No, Merry.' Georg replied. The young man who had taken my bag walked straight past what I had assumed was the *Titan* and was carrying it down a wooden jetty which protruded into the water. 'The *Titan* is actually anchored out in the bay. A very short ride on a tender will take us there.' Georg pointed out beyond the end of the dock towards one boat that made the others look like bath toys.

'Jesus!' I couldn't deny it looked absolutely magnificent. I counted no fewer than four levels, and the enormous radio tower with satellite dishes galore clearly marked it out from every other vessel in the vicinity. 'I mean, Jack and Mary-Kate had told me how enormous it was…but I…wow. Maybe I'll take back my comment about being crammed in like sardines.' Georg smiled at me.

'Good morning, sir,' said the young man who had taken my suitcase a moment before. 'Was that the only luggage?'

'Yes, thank you,' Georg replied.

'Very good. The captain has brought the tender here himself.' The young man looked at me. 'If you would just follow me down to the end of the jetty, madame.'

I did so, and there waiting for us aboard the tender was a handsome, tanned man, with salt and pepper hair and tortoiseshell glasses.

'I must say, you're very well dressed for so early in the morning,' I said.

'I confess, normally I would have sent Victor here to retrieve you, but you are an incredibly special passenger. It is my pleasure to personally escort you on board. My name is Hans Gaia.' He extended his hand to me, shaking it before helping me aboard the tender. 'I skipper the *Titan*.'

'Thank you very much, Hans. Sorry if I'm a disappointment. I haven't slept in forty-eight hours.'

'I assure you, Mrs McDougal, you are anything but a disappointment. It is a great honour to welcome you aboard. I knew your father for many years, and he was very good to me. I know how happy he would be to finally see you on his ocean home.'

'Well…I…thank you again for getting up so early.'

'Good morning, Mr Hoffman. Welcome back.' He nodded to Georg.

'Thank you, Hans.'

'Well then, if we're all accounted for, let's get back to the yacht. Victor, remove the line.' The deckhand loosened the loop from the concrete piling, and joined us in the tender. 'It will be just a few moments, Mrs McDougal.'

'Is anybody else awake?'

'Not to my knowledge, no. Victor, did you notice anyone up and about?'

'No, Captain.'

I felt a surge of relief. In all honesty, the welcome from Captain Hans had been intense enough, and he was just the man who steered the boat. One thing was for certain: whoever Atlas had been, he clearly engendered fierce loyalty in all those he employed. I wasn't sure I could face an immediate 'family reunion' as soon as I set foot on board. All I wanted was a bed to get my head down for a few hours.

'I will arrange for the six copies of the diary to be made when we're on board,' Georg assured me as we skimmed the short distance across the still water.

'Thanks, Georg. No rush. I just want to sleep if I'm honest.'

Once Victor had unloaded the bag, and Captain Hans had helped me aboard, I was led up the steps to the aft deck and then into the main salon, where Georg showed me a bedroom plan pinned to an enormous cork board.

'Let us see…deck two, suite one. Excellent. You have been placed right next to your children. They will be in the two cabins immediately to your right.'

'Blimey, Georg, there's a lot of names on here… Have all the sisters brought their partners?'

'Yes, you are correct. As you can imagine, this trip carries a significant emotional weight, and the girls collectively decided that it would be best for each to have a significant other.'

'Do…do all the sisters have a *significant other*?' I raised my eyebrow, the overly protective mother in me thinking immediately of Jack. I knew full well that his primary motivation for coming on this cruise was a certain young auburn-haired woman.

'All apart from Ally, the second sister. But she is here with her young son, Bear.' The fact that I was so tired meant that an unchecked look of surprise registered on my face.

'Are you all right, Merry?'

'Oh yes, fine. Are there many children on board?'

'Two others. Valentina, the daughter of Maia's partner, Floriano, and Rory, who is the son of Mouse—Star's partner. I should mention too that young Rory is deaf, though he can lipread incredibly well.'

'My, what a busy boat. I think you're all going to have to be sympathetic to me on the name front.'

'I don't doubt for a moment that everyone shall be. Shall I show you to your room?'

'Yes, thank you, I…' The salon suddenly began to spin a little, and a familiar swimming sensation descended. It dawned on me that in addition to the lack of sleep, the last thing I'd consumed was an Irish coffee in Belfast yesterday afternoon. 'May I just grab a little air, Georg? I feel light-headed.'

'Of course, take my arm.'

Georg led me out onto the sun deck, and sat me on some

enormous cushions which formed a large seating area at the rear.

'Let me find you some bottled water. I'm sorry, as it's early, there aren't so many staff around. Will you be all right for a moment?'

'I'm sure I will be.' Georg left at a quickened pace. I tried to control my breathing and slow my heart rate, which was thumping so aggressively I thought it might explode out of my chest. I really did feel completely overwhelmed, just as I'd feared. The thought of being stranded in the middle of the ocean with these strangers, their partners and all those associated with them, not to mention the revelations I had been tasked with delivering, was all too much. As I closed my eyes, I heard another sound over my deep inhalations—the rhythm of feet padding along the deck. I opened my eyes expecting to see Georg sprinting towards me with a bottle of Evian, but instead a man who I had never met before stood in front of me. He was tall with rippling muscles, which were on full display in his close-fitting running gear. From the grey that peppered his tightly curled hair, I would have placed him in his late thirties.

'Oh, hey there,' he said, in an American accent.

'Hi,' I replied meekly.

'You doing okay? You look a little, uh…peaky.'

'Oh, yes, I'm okay. Georg has just run to grab me some water.'

'Georg…that's the lawyer, right?'

'Yes. Didn't you know?'

'Sorry, allow me to introduce myself. I'm Miles. I'm here with Electra.'

'That's the lady who models, isn't it?'

'That's right. You must be Mary.'

'I am, yes. But most people call me Merry.'

'Here, take a gulp of this.' Miles presented me with a bottle of liquid that was such a vivid blue that it could have been chemical. 'It's Gatorade. I figured stocks of it here on the boat might be a little lacking, so I made sure to bring a whole bunch over from the States.'

I took a swig of the cool, sweet liquid. It didn't taste as terrifying as it looked.

'Thank you.'

'No problem. I tend to get up super early and exercise. I was going to visit one of the treadmills in the on-board gym, but this place is so enormous, and with no one else around, it seemed a shame to waste the sunrise. A few laps of each deck and I'll be ready to start my day.'

'Cheers to that,' I said, taking another large glug of the Gatorade. 'Sorry, I'm probably draining your precious supply.'

'Not at all. You must have had quite the twenty-four hours.'

'You could say that, Miles, yes.'

'Well, I know just how excited Electra is to meet you. As is everybody else on board, quite frankly. Hey, you're more in demand than the global supermodel.' He gave me a wide smile.

'If I can be honest with you, Miles, that's what I'm worried about.'

'I can understand. I know our situations aren't really comparable, but this is all new to me too. I've only known Electra for a matter of weeks. I was a little surprised that she asked me to come along. To tell you the truth, I've been full of nerves for days.'

'What do you do for a job? Are you an actor? Or a photographer or something?'

'No, ma'am, nothing quite as exciting as that, I'm afraid. I'm a lawyer.'

I berated myself for making an assumption based on the fact he was dating the supermodel. In fact, there was something about Miles that had an incredibly calming effect on me. I was struggling to work out whether my head was clearing due to the Gatorade or the presence of this polite, down-to-earth man who was showing me some sympathy.

'So, how did you and Electra meet?'

Miles looked out at the ocean. 'Oh, we had, uh…mutual interests. Our paths crossed at a farm in Arizona. By the way, it was a real pleasure to meet your kids last night, Merry. Jack and Mary-Kate were the life and soul at dinner. I was glad to have them there, they did a wonderful job of making sure the conversation never ran dry. It could have been a little awkward, you know? Lots of strangers, such an emotional time for the sisters…'

'That'll be my two. If there's one thing that people from Down Under can do, it's talk.'

'That's true! CeCe's girlfriend—uh, Chrissie I think her name is—is from Australia. She's exactly the same.'

'Right, so you're from America, Chrissie's from Australia… Does anyone else hale from an exotic location which I should know about?'

'Well, it depends on your definition of "exotic"… Maia's partner Floriano and his daughter Valentina are from Brazil. But all of the sisters have an amazing story to tell. Their father—*your* father—left clues for them to discover after he'd died. The guy had the coordinates of all their birthplaces engraved on this sculpture thing in their family garden—they call it an armillary sphere. It turns out that he adopted children from all corners of the globe…'

'Gosh. He led quite the life, that's for certain.'

'As have you, from the sounds of things. Jack and Mary-Kate have been telling us about your journey over the last few weeks. Merry, I'm so sorry to hear of all you've been through. I don't know how you've coped. The sisters following you around the globe must have frightened the life out of you. I think you're an incredibly strong person to be standing here on this yacht. Your kids do too. They wouldn't stop singing your praises last night.'

I don't know quite what it was, but there was something about Miles's calm sincerity that brought tears to my eyes.

'Thank you, Miles. That's very generous of you to say.'

'And Merry… I haven't known them long, but these are good people. I know a little something or two about character. I work in human rights, you see, so I've had to learn to be a pretty good judge on that side of things when it comes to my job. I promise that you're safe here, and everyone is really excited to get to know you.'

'I just hope I…live up to expectations.' The feeling of being overwhelmed returned.

'My perspective on it is that they've known you their whole life. Well, at least, they've known of your existence. Apparently, your dad would mention you frequently. He always said that you were lost to him, and he never found you. So they're just all real thrilled that they've managed to get you here, and fulfil his life-long wish.'

'Miles, you're a lawyer, so you understand the sensitivities that exist within families, particularly after the death of a loved one.'

'I most certainly do, yes.'

'You'll already have noted that I'm a fair bit older than the other girls.'

'I…would never have noticed, but I've obviously heard from the others.'

'You *are* a lawyer, Miles. That was very tactful. Anyway, I imagine that given your profession, you can keep a secret?'

Miles chuckled and nodded at me. 'Oh yes. I have a fair few which will go with me to the grave.'

'Well, there'll be no need for that thankfully, but I would appreciate your perspective on something.'

He took a moment to look me square in the eye. 'You can count on my discretion.'

I reached into my handbag and pulled out the letter from Atlas. 'Would you read this, Miles?'

'Of course. You're sure you want me to?'

'I need an outside opinion that's not Georg's. It's a note from my father to me. It seems to confirm, that I'm his…you can read it yourself.' Miles did so, and I studied his face as he scanned it. Soon Miles was the one with tears in his eyes.

'Excuse me,' he said, handing back the letter. 'That was pretty powerful stuff.'

'Yes.'

'If you don't mind me asking, what are you so worried about? The fact that this means you're his biological daughter?'

'Yes! And the fact that he's entrusted me with his life story before the others.'

Miles took a moment to formulate his response. 'I can understand that. Well, I can't speak for everyone, but think about it from their perspective—you're an answer to a fundamental question. Their whole life, they've wondered why their mysterious father made it his mission to adopt these girls from around the globe. If he lost his wife and daughter when he was much younger, perhaps that goes some way to explaining it?'

I leant back into the pillows and considered his perspective. 'I suppose I hadn't thought of it like that.'

'Anyhow, Jack and Mary-Kate have done the heavy lifting. Everyone loves them so much that they're already practically part of the furniture.'

'I can well imagine. Thank you, Miles.'

'Don't sweat it. And if things get a little too intense over the next few days and you need an outside perspective to talk things through with, just let me know.'

I heard the sound of running feet once more, and turned to see Georg emerging from the salon, brandishing a bottle of water.

'I apologise, Merry. I had to venture down into the kitchen. It turns out that obtaining a law degree from the Universität Basel is a less complex process than searching the chief steward's pantries.'

'That's quite all right, Georg. Miles managed to save me with his blue concoction here.' I held the Gatorade aloft.

'I'll put a small charge on your bill at the end of your stay, madame,' Miles replied with a wink. 'Well, I'll let you get settled, Merry. I've got another few laps to jog before Electra's up and I'm on the coffee run.' He stood up, and nodded at Georg. 'And remember my offer. I'm always here. Deck three, suite four, I believe.' Miles laughed, and I gave him a wave before he turned to continue his circuit of the *Titan*.

'I'm sorry, Merry, I didn't realise anyone was up.'

'Not at all, Georg. It was nice to meet him. He was a very reassuring presence.'

'Yes. He has overcome a lot in his life. I do believe him to be the perfect companion for Electra. Anyway, are you feeling a little better?'

'Yes, thank you, Georg. Certainly well enough to make it to my bedroom, anyway.'

'Take my arm. I'll show you downstairs. Victor has ensured that your luggage is waiting for you.'

I hung on to Georg as we ventured through the bowels of the enormous vessel. I don't know whether it was my delirious state or the fact that every corridor was lined with the same dark brown wood—polished to the extent that every surface was akin to a mirror—but I felt like I was traversing an M. C. Escher painting. En route to my quarters, we passed by numerous staff, who were waking to prepare for the journey ahead. Some were in polo shirts, some in short-sleeved white shirts adorned with epaulettes. Georg mumbled something about 'deck crew' and 'interior crew', but I wasn't paying a great deal of attention. One thing connected all the uniforms, however—every shirt was embroidered with the name *Titan*, and immediately below, stitched in rich gold, was the image of an armillary sphere. Several staircases and hallways later, Georg signalled to a door on the second deck.

'This is your room,' he whispered. 'Mary-Kate and Jack are just here, to your right.' He opened the cabin door.

'That's grand, Georg. Now, is there anything I have to be up for, before I collapse on the bed and depart from the land of the living for a few hours?'

'Not at all, Merry. Please take all the rest you need. Of course, we'll shortly be departing from Nice, and I should warn you that the engines can be somewhat…intrusive,' he said sheepishly.

'That's all right, Georg, I think I'm tired enough to sleep through anything. I imagine you'll be wanting some kip yourself, but if you wouldn't mind asking someone to alert my children to the fact their mother has made it on board, that would be wonderful.'

'No problem, I shall see to it, along with the preparation of the diaries. Goodnight, Merry.'

'Good morning, more like.' I sighed wearily, entering the room and gently shutting the door behind me. I wasn't at all surprised to find that the cabin was akin to a five-star hotel. In fact, it might even have been nicer than the suite I'd recently stayed in at Claridge's in London. My suitcase had been placed next to the bed, but I lacked the energy to open it up and attempt to find any suitable nightwear. Instead, I kicked off my shoes, pushed the towels (beautifully hand-crafted into little elephants) to the floor, and flopped onto the mattress. Pulling the covers tight around me, I closed my eyes and slept.

9

Maia stretched and yawned as she surveyed the empty breakfast table. She checked her watch: 10.50 a.m. The plan was for everyone to meet here on the sun deck at eleven, but from the looks of things, she'd be dining on her own. Approximately an hour ago the *Titan*'s engines had roared into gear, and the journey to Delos, and Pa, had begun. However, she suspected the amount of wine drunk last night was probably enough to ensure that the noise wouldn't rouse those who had indulged a little too heavily. Maia hadn't touched a drop, of course. Thankfully, everyone had all too easily accepted the party line of 'keeping a clear head for the next few days'.

Initially, Maia had been worried that she wouldn't have the comfort of the odd glass of Provençal rosé to help her through the cruise, but after last night, she didn't think she'd miss it too much. In fact, she had felt enormously content at how wonderfully everyone had gelled at dinner. Deep down, Maia had been dreading this trip for months, along with, she suspected, most of the other passengers. She and her sisters had made an enormous amount of progress in the last year, each learning to adapt to life without the guiding light of Pa Salt. The eldest D'Aplièse sister feared that this journey would only serve as a reminder of the enormous loss she and her siblings had suffered. Even arriving at the dock yesterday had proved difficult, as the

Titan had always been a symbol of the family reuniting for the summer; a place of safety to unwind and catch up. But, as she sipped on her water, Maia admitted to herself that last night had almost been, dare she say…fun?

In all honesty, it was the presence of the 'partners' who had made the evening such a joyous affair. Quite the eclectic cast had been assembled for the voyage, which surely Pa would have approved of. There was the hardworking Doctor Charlie Kinnaird, who did a wonderful job of grounding her spiritual sister Tiggy. Electra had Miles, a calm, sagacious man, who saw her not as a global superstar, but as the vulnerable yet passionate woman she was. Chrissie was able to give as good as she got from CeCe (although Maia was glad that she didn't have to live under that particularly noisy roof). Even the socially reticent Mouse had last night revealed himself to be a pillar of eloquence and humility. Together with his charming son, Rory, the pair had given the quiet Star the confidence she needed to flourish.

Then, of course, there was Ally. Maia could only imagine the added pain that her sister had been forced to endure over the last year, following the loss of her beloved Theo. She so admired her sister's strength and resilience, rising to the challenge of motherhood under the most difficult of circumstances… Something that she herself had once failed to do.

'Morning, Maia,' said Tiggy, as she crossed the deck and pulled out a seat opposite her.

'Good morning, Tigs.' Tiggy ran her hands through her thick chestnut hair, which almost seemed to sparkle in the sunlight.

'What a beautiful day,' she said.

Maia thought just how well her sister looked. Tiggy had always had a natural grace and ease about her, but Pa's death one year ago seemed to have affected her more than anyone. Now, with the steadfast Charlie by her side, and her dream job repopulating the Highlands with wildcats, a smile seemed to have permanently returned to Tiggy's lips.

'Looks like it'll be a quieter breakfast than expected, I'm afraid,' sighed Maia.

'Oh, I wouldn't be so sure. There are definite rumblings below deck. Charlie's just in the on-board office. He's reviewing a report on some bloodwork or something. I'm glad I'm not a doctor, it doesn't seem like you're entitled to a minute's peace! Where are your two, anyway?'

'Floriano's just gone to find Valentina. In the end the crew had to make up a spare cabin for her and little Rory to share last night. They insisted on it. Rory's begun to teach Valentina how to sign, and in return, she's instructing him in Portuguese...' Maia and Tiggy both giggled. 'They're like brother and sister.'

Tiggy raised her eyebrows, before turning to check the sun deck was still unoccupied.

'Now then, speaking of brothers and sisters, Maia...' Tiggy glanced down at Maia's belly, then gave her an enormous grin.

Maia exhaled, shook her head, and smiled at her younger sister.

'Normally, in this situation, I should be offended that you're making a comment on my weight. But because it's you, I suspect that's not the reason you ask.'

Tiggy squealed with excitement. 'I knew it! Have you told them yet?'

'Shhh... I've told Floriano, yes. But not Valentina. How do you always know, Tiggy?'

Tiggy shrugged, and looked incredibly satisfied.

'No, come on. I've always let you off the hook on this front, ever since we were children. I'll never forget the time when you told me that Madeleine the cat was going to have exactly six kittens. And, sure enough, later that evening, six mewling babies appeared. And we've all heard the story from Ally about Bear's birth. She swears that neither of them would be here without you and Angelina. Tell me, what do you see that others can't?'

Tiggy looked out at the ocean to the rear of the *Titan*, where the yacht's enormous motor was creating a path of choppy white water. 'It's an ancestral gift,' she said. 'I'm a *bruja*.'

'Hang on, you're a witch?' Maia asked.

Tiggy laughed. 'Ah, yes, I should have thought about the fact that you're a translator. No, Maia. I'm not a witch. To be a *bruja* is to be a part of a spiritual lineage.'

Maia looked sheepish. 'Sorry, Tiggy, I didn't mean to say the wrong thing, it's just the way my brain works.'

'You should be sorry! Now, listen up as I explain, or I'll hit you over the head with my broom.' Tiggy pointed to the water. 'When you look at the ocean there, you can see the blue, and the swell, and the waves. But that's only part of the story. You can't see below the waterline, where the *Titan* is creating a current. To the sea life—the fish, the plants—that current is a force beyond their control, from a place they do not understand.' Tiggy closed her eyes, as if visualising the thing she was trying to describe. 'It's like that up here too. All around us are energies and forces which most people don't question or can't comprehend. But I can see some of it.' Tiggy reopened her eyes and looked at Maia. 'It's not, like, magic or anything. Everything is here for us to see. It's just that I know how to look.'

'You're incredible, Tiggy. So, the question is…can you see whether you're going to be an auntie to a niece or a nephew?'

Tiggy raised an eyebrow at her sister. 'I suggest a nice neutral colour for the room,' she replied with a wink.

A smiling blonde steward emerged from the upper lounge. Maia shot Tiggy a look, and Tiggy responded by miming the zipping of her lips. Neither sister had met the steward before now. In fact, more often than not, the interior staff would change every season on the *Titan*, with a new crew of young 'yachties' appearing each year.

'Good morning, Miss D'Aplièse, and…Miss D'Aplièse. Can I get either of you a coffee? Or perhaps some juice?' she enquired timidly. Maia felt for her. Working on superyachts, she imagined the usual clientele weren't always the most easy-going of individuals. She moved to reassure her.

'Please, it's Maia and Tiggy, and yes, thank you. I'd love a latte, please,' replied Maia.

'And for me too, thank you,' added Tiggy. 'With oat milk, please!'

'Lovely, I'll get those for you now. And Chef has asked if you plan to go ahead with breakfast for everyone at eleven?'

'Absolutely, please feel free to start bringing things up. I'm sure the smell of bacon and coffee will be enough to lure the rest from the depths. And if it's not, we'll go and round them up,' Maia promised.

'Great,' replied the steward, before heading back inside.

Maia inhaled deeply. 'You know, it does feel a little alien to me to experience such wealth and luxury now. I feel a bit embarrassed by it, if I'm honest.'

'I know what you mean. Personally, I'm much more at home in a tarpaulin hide in the middle of a woodland glen,' agreed Tiggy.

'Well, I'm not so sure about that. I don't know if I could survive too long without the Brazilian heat. In any case, I suppose we must all remember to keep giving back to the world whenever we can. I've actually started visiting a *favela* in Rio every week to tutor children in English and Spanish.'

'Wow, Maia, that's fantastic. It's where your life began after all,' said Tiggy gently.

'It is, yes. I feel very passionately about offering any help I can to improve their future prospects. I think it's unlikely an enigmatic billionaire is likely to come and save them, as was the case with us.'

'No. Pa certainly provided all of us with a lifeline. How different our stories would have been had he not plucked each of us from around the globe.' Tiggy shook her head, then looked back at her sister. 'I miss him so much, Maia. I feel like I've lost my anchor. Whatever problem I was facing, he'd know exactly what to say to make me feel better. I imagine it's the same for you?'

'Yes. For all of us, I think.'

'The irony is that we need him now more than ever, and he's not here to help us.'

'Not physically, no. But, in a way, I think he is with us,' Maia replied.

Tiggy looked at her sister. 'Maia, are you about to offer some spiritual wisdom to the *bruja* herself?'

'I wouldn't go that far, but look what we did—we found the missing sister. We couldn't have done that without him guiding us.'

'He'd be so happy she's coming.' Tiggy smiled.

'He would be, yes.'

'It's just…' Tiggy put her head in her hands. 'You know what I was saying before, about being able to feel the different energies that influence our lives?'

'Yes…'

'Please don't think I'm mad,' Tiggy said pleadingly.

'I promise I don't think that, Tiggy. I never have.'

'Okay. Well, usually, when someone is about to die, I can sense it. I've always been able to. Just as I can feel new life too, like the one growing inside you at the moment.' Maia nodded sincerely at her sister. 'Then, after people I've known in my life have passed on, I've always been able to…to say goodbye to them. I mean, to their spirit or life force or whatever you want to call it, before they go. It's always been very comforting for me. And, I think, for them too.'

'I understand.'

'But Maia, I never felt it with Pa. I didn't sense that he was about to leave us, and I certainly haven't been able to feel him since. That's really why I've found the last year so difficult. I haven't been able to say goodbye to him.'

'Gosh. I'm so sorry, Tiggy, that must be incredibly difficult.'

'Yes. He was everything to me—to all of us—and I can't believe that he hasn't come to see me one final time.' Tiggy dropped her head and began examining her hands, as she often did when contemplating matters beyond the physical world.

Maia struggled to know what to say to her sister. 'Perhaps it's because he knows just how much it would upset you, Tiggy?'

'Maybe,' she replied. 'I'd begun to think that maybe he had sent me Charlie, and *that* was his goodbye.'

'That sounds very Pa,' Maia offered.

'Yes. But then these last few weeks, I've started to feel unsettled again.'

'Is everything all right with Charlie?'

'Oh, absolutely. I just mean that I've begun to feel very anxious about Pa all of a sudden. Which is not something I expected given the fact that he died a year ago.'

'No, I can imagine. But Tiggy, I think it's only natural, given what we're here to do. I'm sure all of us have felt something similar.'

Tiggy thought for a moment. 'Yes. I'm sure you're right. Sorry, Maia, I didn't mean to go all serious and *bruja* on you there.

Particularly after last night—what a hoot that turned out to be!'

'Gosh, I know. Jack and Mary-Kate are so lovely.'

'Absolutely. Speaking of which, do we know if Georg made it back with Merry last night?'

'Something tells me he did, yes. There are two extra places at the table. Last night we were sixteen, and this morning we are eighteen.'

'Gosh. I can't believe everyone's finally going to meet the missing sister. After all these years…she was just a story. And this morning she'll be sipping orange juice with us.'

'Poor Merry. She's been through so much, Tiggy. I can't believe Georg has managed to get her aboard. We must make sure we go above and beyond to look out for her over the next few days.'

'Agreed. She really does have a beautiful soul, Maia. Even though I only met her briefly in Dublin, I know she's going to fit in incredibly well.'

There was a brief silence as the pair reflected on the significance of the new passenger. Eventually, Maia spoke. 'It was quite funny to see Georg run off the boat yesterday, wasn't it? I don't think I've ever seen him break a sweat. He really was absolutely desperate for Merry to make the trip. I mean, I know we all were, but I think we all know how to take no for an answer,' Maia mused.

Tiggy looked off into the distance again. 'I don't think letting her go was an option for him, Maia.' She grinned. 'Do you know, I have the strangest feeling that—'

Tiggy was interrupted by voices coming from the salon.

'My daddy says that the *Ore Brasil* is a boat which is even bigger than this one,' Valentina told Rory proudly.

'Wooow… Do you know what the *Titanic* is?' Rory countered. The pair emerged onto the deck, followed by Floriano.

'Okay, okay, I do not think we need to talk about that ship now, young sir.' Floriano grinned at Maia and raised his eyebrows.

'*Bom dia*, Maia!'

'*Bom dia*, Valentina. *Apenas Inglês, por favor.* Only English on this trip.'

'Okay…'

'Thank you, Valentina,' Tiggy said. 'Some of us aren't as clever as you. Or as pretty!'

'Oh please, Auntie Tiggy, this one's head does not need to grow any bigger…' Floriano said, lifting Valentina up and tickling her.

'Any sign of the others, Floriano?' Maia enquired.

Rory chipped in. 'We went and knocked on everyone's doors, didn't we, Valentina? Then we had a race around the boat, and we found Ma with Ally and Bear at the front. They're all coming. Are we having sausages for breakfast?'

'Oh, I'm sure Chef will send up some sausages, Rory. Good choice. Is that your favourite thing to eat for breakfast?' asked Tiggy.

'I dare say they are, aren't they, old man?' Mouse's voice boomed from the salon, and he emerged, holding Star's hand.

'Morning, Star! Morning, Daddy!'

'Hello, Rory. Morning, everyone.' Star gave a little wave to the table. 'I ran into Mary-Kate on the way up. She said that she and Jack are going to go in and see their mum—and to go ahead and start breakfast without them,' she informed the table.

'Of course. Are you nervous, Star?' asked Maia.

'Yes. To tell you the truth, my tummy's been doing somersaults all morning. Obviously, the last time we spoke I was "in character" executing Orlando's stupid scheme. I feel awful about the whole thing.'

'Seriously, Star, don't worry. When I met Merry in Dublin, she gave the impression all was forgiven,' Tiggy reassured her.

'I'm sure it is,' added Maia, taking Star's hand. 'This is a big moment.' She looked around the table. 'The six sisters are about to become seven.'

10

Merry

Even though I'd only slept for six hours, it was deep and restorative. In the Gibbston valley, where our house sat in the middle of vast vineyards, the nights were entirely silent. The only downside to the peace was that it often meant I slept terribly when I wasn't in my own bed. In hotels, I'd found that even the slightest footstep in the corridor outside was enough to bring me round. But aboard the *Titan*, I'd easily sunk into a heavy slumber. In fact, it only dawned on me once I had rolled out of bed and approached the cabin window that we were in transit. Not even the engines had disturbed me. I unlatched the glass circlet from the porthole and stretched it out as far as it would allow—at least ten centimetres. I breathed in the warm, salty air coming off the Mediterranean Sea, and it served to further invigorate me. After Jock had died, I had promised myself an adventure and, well, I was certainly having one. No, it wasn't quite the world tour I had imagined, but here I was on a superyacht on a quest to discover my true heritage. Yes, today was going to be…unpredictable, but my chat with Miles, combined with a good few hours' rest, meant that I was feeling altogether more positive.

I picked up my phone from the bedside table and found two texts, one from Jack and one from Mary-Kate. Both had asked me to let them know when I was awake. I replied, telling them that they'd be welcome in half an hour after I'd hopped in the shower.

After a wash and a shampoo, I salvaged a clean linen dress from my suitcase and dug out a hairdryer. Staring at myself in the mirror, I thought of the charcoal drawing that Georg had shown me last night. There was no denying it, the woman in the portrait could have been me. I wondered what my birth mother's story was, and what had motivated her to leave me on Father O'Brien's doorstep all those years ago. I simply couldn't imagine what possible situation could ever have driven me to do that to Jack or MK. A shiver ran down my spine at the thought.

A few minutes after I'd shut off the hairdryer, there was a familiar knock at the door—the same knock that had rapped on my bedroom door more than a quarter of a century ago when my son had had a nightmare, and wanted to join Jock and me in the bed.

'Come in, Jack,' I called. The door opened, and his wavy blond hair, piercing blue eyes and effortlessly cheerful face appeared.

'Hello, Mum! Welcome aboard the good ship *Titan*!' he beamed.

'Mum! You made it! It's so good to see you!' Mary-Kate followed in behind, adorned in a bikini and kaftan.

I embraced them simultaneously, and held them both for a long time. Even though we were floating in the middle of a vast sea in another hemisphere, in that moment, I was home again.

'I'm happy to see you too, Mary-Kate. You have no idea. Here, come and sit down.' I gestured to the two armchairs that were positioned on either side of the coffee table, and perched myself on the end of the bed.

'So, Mum…what changed your mind? Ally told us that Georg rushed off the boat last night to go and kidnap you. Assuming he didn't actually bundle you into a burlap sack, what did he say to you to get you here?'

'It was my old friend Ambrose, really. You know how much I trust him. He's known me for longer than anyone else alive. He told me I should come. And I listened.'

'Well, you're like a celebrity on board. Even more so than the *actual* celebrity. Do you even know about Electra, Mum? She's only one of the biggest stars on the planet right now. She did this speech at the Concert for Africa right after Obama, and—'

'Yes, yes, I might've read something about that back in NZ.' I turned to my son. 'And how's young Ally, Jack?'

'Oh, yeah. She's good.'

I held his gaze.

'Well, yeah, she, uh, has a baby.'

'I heard a little whisper about that from Georg earlier on,' I said. 'And how do you feel about it? It's a little odd she wouldn't say anything.'

'The baby's not a problem. He's a lovely little fella, his name's Bear.'

Mary-Kate nudged Jack in the arm. 'She's definitely single, though, Mum. You should see the two of them together. It's adorable!'

'Ah, come on, MK. She only lost Bear's dad a year ago. If I had to guess, she didn't tell me about her baby because she didn't want to hurt my feelings, that's all. I'll survive. Anyway, I'm hardly the main event here, Mum! Are you ready to come and *meet the family*?'

I inhaled deeply. 'You know, there's actually a couple of things I've recently come to learn that I'd like to talk to you about. Particularly before all these grand introductions.'

Sensing my trepidation, Mary-Kate rose and sat next to me on the bed, putting her hand on mine. 'Of course, Mum.'

I walked over to my handbag, and produced Atlas's letter, alongside the charcoal drawing.

'Bloody hell, Mum. It's so much to take in. Particularly after all you've been through in the last few weeks. How are you feeling?' Jack asked gently, his arm around my shoulder.

'Sick, at first. But better now, after a good sleep. I also met a man called Miles…'

'Electra's boyfriend?'

'That's it. And he was very reassuring. Georg's making copies of this diary to give to everyone, so they can all read it simultaneously.'

'You're really this Pa Salt's biological daughter then?' Mary-Kate asked.

'So it would seem. Atlas is my father. And your grandfather.' A silence hung in the air.

'Oh yeah, of course! Although you two are, like, actually, properly, officially related to him,' said MK, referencing the fact my daughter was herself adopted. She ran her hands through her long blonde hair. 'This is nuts!'

'Christ, no wonder Georg was so desperate to get you on board, Mum. You're…we're Pa Salt's flesh and blood,' stumbled Jack.

'Has all this been, you know, verified?' asked Mary-Kate.

'Do you mean DNA tests? That might be a little hard to organise, given where we are and what we're here to do.'

'Well, I wouldn't imagine there's much need for that anyway. That woman in the charcoal drawing is the spit of you, Mum. I guess you've got no information on what happened to her?' Jack enquired.

'I do not. I'm hoping that the diary will provide some answers.'

'Yeah. I hope it'll tell us a bit more about Argideen House in Cork, too.'

Mary-Kate pointed to the ceiling. 'What about everyone up there? How d'you reckon they'll take it?'

'I don't know. It's important to remember that I didn't seek to be here. Those women searched the world to find me, quite literally.' I looked around the grand cabin, taking in its ornate chandelier and bespoke walnut headboard. 'I've no wish to claim any of *this* from them either.'

Jack looked crestfallen. 'I'll be honest, Mum. I think revealing to Ally that I'm her secret nephew might just trump her failing to tell me she had a baby son.'

'Oh, don't be daft, Jack. Ally was adopted. She's the daughter of a musician from Norway. There's absolutely no blood relationship there whatsoever,' Mary-Kate reminded him firmly.

'Anyway, that's hardly the takeaway here. Are you all right, Mum? Is there anything we can do to support you?'

'Oh, you know, steal a lifeboat if the other six decide to throw me overboard.'

'For what it's worth, I think there's very little chance of that happening,' said Mary-Kate, putting a reassuring hand on my back. 'They're all pretty lovely. What's your plan, by the way? Are you just going to go right up and tell them?'

'I think I have to,' I sighed. 'Keeping any sort of information to myself doesn't seem fair. As I've said to everyone, this Atlas is a stranger to me. But he's everything to them.'

'You know, Mum, you're amazing. Everything you've been through—are still *going* through—and you're putting others first.'

'Thank you, Mary-Kate. And hey, your dad always made me promise that I was to have a whirlwind adventure if anything ever happened to him. And here we are.' The three of us joined hands, and sat together for a moment. 'And it's what Dad would have done, too. He was about the most selfless individual on God's green earth. Lord knows, we know exactly what they're going through up there. So, if I—if *we*—can help these six young women at the most difficult moment of their lives, then we will.' I squeezed Jack and Mary-Kate's hands tight. 'Are people just milling around?'

'No, actually. Everyone's sat up there for a late breakfast. We said we'd join them after we'd had a chance to come and see you.'

'Well then.' I took a deep breath, slapped my knees and stood up. 'Let's go and say hello.'

Jack and Mary-Kate led me back up through the *Titan*. With my two children forming a miniature phalanx around me, I felt comforted. Whatever was about to happen, they were here to protect me.

The yacht's central staircase took us through great lounges, dining areas and the office space that Georg had mentioned to me when I was on the jet. Now I was rested, I could truly appreciate what a floating fortress the ship actually was.

After ascending no fewer than three flights, we reached the top of the *Titan* which was comprised of a small salon, encased in lightly tinted glass. Some of the panes had been slid back, allowing the bright French sun to pour in.

'Are you ready, Mum? It's just through here,' Jack said, giving me one of his reassuring grins.

My heart began to thump a little harder as I heard a cacophony of voices. *This is what it must have felt like to be fed to the lions*, I thought. In amongst the crowd, I heard Georg's measured tones, and it provided me with the confidence I needed to step over the threshold. Mary-Kate took my hand and gave it a squeeze, as the three of us passed through the door.

The table was completely full, and a sea of faces greeted me.

Jack spoke first. 'Morning, everyone! I just wanted to introduce you to my mum, Mary. You might have heard of her before now...' There was an odd silence. I'm sure it must have only been a few seconds, but for me the pause was stretched out into what seemed like an eternity. It felt like the crowd was absorbing me, taking me in, as if my presence was somehow difficult to comprehend. A couple of the women looked at each other and smiled. The others just stared at me, with eyes wide and lips slightly apart, as if they were overwhelmed. In any case, it seemed that no one was exactly sure of what to say, so I broke the tension.

'Hi there. Everyone calls me Merry, as in Merry Christmas. So you can be after calling me that if you want to, so.' My nerves ensured that I had immediately slipped back into my West Cork brogue.

A woman with thick, auburn hair, who had been bouncing a baby on her lap, was the first to stand up. There were no prizes for guessing which sister she was. Her fair skin and wide eyes were captivating, her delicate eyebrows and high cheekbones enhancing her beauty. I could certainly see why Jack was entranced.

'Merry. Hello...I...we, all of us...are just so very pleased to have you on board.'

'Thank you. It's lovely that you've gone to so much trouble to get me here.'

At that moment, another woman, this one with deep brown eyes and flowing dark hair, began to clap. Almost instantly, the entire table joined her in the applause. Soon, the table was on its feet, and I couldn't help but laugh at the enthusiastic response. I noted Georg, stood at the head, giving me a nod. Was that a tear in his eye? Surely not… Certainly, every face was adorned with a smile, and the genuine warmth radiating from the assembled mass was really quite heartening.

A tall woman made her way towards me. I estimated that she was in her mid-sixties. She was elegant, with strong, aquiline features.

'Hello, Merry. My name is Marina. The girls—forgive me, that is what I call them—know me as "Ma". I looked after them when they were growing up. I cannot tell you what a privilege for us it is that you have joined us. You have made a lot of people incredibly happy, and many hearts full, *chérie.*'

'Is that a French accent you have there?'

'Ah, you have a delicate ear! I am French, but perhaps you know I live in Switzerland.'

'Of course. I've heard all about your wonderful home on the shores of Lake Geneva.'

'*Oui, chérie*! You must come and visit us!' I couldn't help but giggle at this lady's enthusiasm.

'Come on, Ma! Don't scare her away, for God's sake. She'll be jumping overboard and swimming for shore if you carry on like that.' The words came from a statuesque woman with beautiful ebony skin and a tangled, tightly curled mane. She was so strikingly beautiful that I myself was nearly lost for words. 'Hey. I'm Electra. It's an honour to meet you.' Her yellow-gold eyes looked into mine, and it was obvious that this was the supermodel.

'Ah, of course. I've seen you on the television! In fact, were you in an advert for a perfume recently?'

Electra chuckled and shook her head. 'Probably. I'm sorry that my face was trying to flog you something on your TV before we had a chance to meet in person.'

'Well, I can confirm you're as lovely in person as you were on my screen!'

'You're very sweet. Hey, this is my sister, CeCe.' Electra indicated a stocky woman with hazel-flecked almond eyes, whose hair was shaved into a boyish crop.

'Hey, Merry. Can I just say, I think you have a great name.'

'Oh, thank you. So do you! CeCe, wasn't it?'

'That's right, short for Celaeno. It's a bit less of a mouthful. You can blame my dad for that one.'

Behind CeCe was the willowy blonde who reminded me of Mary-Kate. We had met before at Claridge's, of course, under different pretences. I locked eyes with her.

'Hello, Merry,' she said meekly. 'I—'

'Goodness me!' I exclaimed. 'If it isn't the one and only Lady Sabrina Vaughan. Funny to see you here. How's the viscount?' The poor girl's pale face immediately adopted a rouge hue.

'I'm just so terribly sorry about that, Merry. It was the stupid idea of my silly friend, Orlando. He's a little eccentric. On all fronts.'

'Oh, she's being far too kind. He certainly is very silly. I have the misfortune of being his brother,' chimed a well-spoken English man from the breakfast table.

'I never should have gone along with it.' The blonde woman put out her hand. 'If we can start again, I'm Star. Technically, it's short for—'

'Asterope,' I accepted her handshake. 'You're all named after the Seven Sisters of the Pleiades. It's beautiful.'

'Yes, you're absolutely right! Gosh, normally that takes a fair bit of explaining,' Star said.

'Ah, well, you're in luck with me. I did my dissertation on Orion's pursuit of Merope. And don't worry, Lady Sabrina. All is forgiven. It's nice to meet the *real* Star.'

Another familiar face was lined up behind Star. 'Hello again, Merry,' said the gentle Tiggy. 'It's so lovely to see you.' She approached me and we hugged. When we had met in Dublin, it had been her soft-spoken manner that had convinced me that this family wasn't out to harm my own.

'Hello, Tiggy. It's nice to see you again,' I replied.

She held my gaze, and looked deep into my eyes. 'Wow. I can't believe you're here. It would mean so much to our father. Thank you.'

If it had been any of the others, this moment would have felt quite uncomfortable, but Tiggy's calming aura prevailed, and just like before, I felt somehow connected to her. The way she was looking at me—it was as though we both somehow shared a secret that the others did not.

'I think that just leaves us,' said Ally. 'I'm Ally, and this is my older sister, Maia. We've spoken on the phone a few times.'

'Hello, Ally, Jack's told me all about you.' I looked for the blush, and it arrived immediately. 'It's lovely to meet you too, Maia.'

'We just couldn't be more thrilled, Merry.' Maia's voice cracked a little. 'Sorry, it's a big moment for us.'

'I can only imagine. You must all be going through such a difficult time. But it's so lovely that you're all here together.' I addressed everyone, including those still sat at the table. 'Growing up, I actually had a lot of siblings. But I didn't see them for so many years.'

'I reckon you must be starving, Merry. Come and get some grub!' exclaimed a woman whose skin was nut-brown, the same colour as CeCe's. 'I'm Chrissie, by the way. It's a pleasure to meet ya!'

'Lovely to meet you, too. It's nice to have a fellow Antipodean on board!'

'I know, right? Although with that accent, obviously we never managed to get you sounding like a local…'

I took a seat in between Mary-Kate and Jack. The table was piled high with plates of pastries, and metal lids were lifted on sausages, bacon, eggs and all manner of freshly prepared treats. During breakfast, I was introduced to a doctor, who was the heir to an enormous country estate in Scotland, a Brazilian author, the well-spoken English gentleman who was restoring a house, and just for good measure, I learnt that Chrissie was a former elite swimmer, who had lost her leg in an accident.

'This is Miles, Merry,' Electra said, gesturing to the man sitting next to her.

'Actually, we've already had the pleasure of meeting when Georg brought me aboard this morning.'

'Oh. You didn't mention it, Miles,' said Electra, flashing him a fierce look.

'You never asked.' He returned Electra's gaze with a wide smile and a wink. I noted the disarming effect it had. 'Anyway, did you manage to sleep well, Merry?'

'Wonderfully, thank you.' My head was spinning by the time I'd finally managed to clear my plate. 'Goodness me, if you don't mind me saying, it's like one of those old Agatha Christie novels, with all of the interesting characters assembled here.'

'*Murder on the* Titan,' chuckled the well-spoken Mouse.

Star tutted and rolled her eyes. 'You're certainly in no danger of that, Merry.'

'I'm just amazed that Georg managed to convince you to join us in the first place,' CeCe said.

I glanced at the man himself, sat at the head of the table. His eyes were fixed on me, anticipating my response.

'Well…he told me just how much effort you girls had put in to find me, and what a horrible time you were going through. He was very persuasive,' I offered.

'Yes, he certainly can be when he wants to be. He is an attorney after all. Right, Georg?' teased Electra.

'As you know, I am here to carry out your father's wishes, even though he is not with us. I recognised that when we had confirmed who Merry was, your father would have stopped at nothing to bring her on board,' Georg replied coolly.

CeCe addressed me again. 'There must have been something he said to you that changed your mind, though, right? Because we all understood that you didn't want to come—'

'CeCe,' Ally interrupted.

'No, I mean, understandably, you didn't want to come. Hell, I certainly wouldn't be too keen if I'd been pursued around the globe by a bunch of total strangers who claimed that I was their *missing sister*!' I wasn't sure if it was CeCe's intention, but an unspoken tension had descended on the table 'What changed?' she continued. 'That's all I'm asking.' I looked to Georg again. He was scanning the table, observing the assembled faces as the line of questioning continued.

'Please forgive CeCe, she's never been particularly good at filtering what comes out of her mouth, have you, Cee?' Star gave her sister an earnest look which caused CeCe to take a pause.

'Sorry. Am I being rude? I probably am. I apologise, Merry. It's just…'

'What? Please don't worry about upsetting me. You can ask

me whatever you like,' I reassured her.

'I think Georg's been hiding something from us,' CeCe ventured.

Almost comically, the entire table turned to look at the man sat at the head.

'Rory! Come along, old boy. I think you promised to take me up to have a look at the bridge, didn't you?' Mouse interjected tactfully. 'Would you like to come too, Valentina? I'm sure that if we're very nice, Captain Hans might let us have a go at steering.' The two children were blissfully unaware of the uneasy atmosphere that had rapidly developed, and bounced off behind Mouse, who I assumed must have been very happy to get away from the table himself.

'Please continue, CeCe. What do you mean, "hiding something"?' Georg eventually replied.

'What do you think I mean, Georg? You have coordinates carved into Pa's armillary sphere without our knowledge. They've been there for ages, apparently. Next, you go missing in action for the last few weeks, just as soon as you've got us all running around the globe trying to locate the missing sister. We've heard from Maia and Ally about your mysterious phone calls, too. Then, yesterday, you practically sprint off the *Titan* for Dublin to go and drag poor Merry on board a boat which she's already made clear she doesn't wish to be on!' A stunned silence followed.

Mary-Kate put a reassuring hand on my knee as we waited for Georg's response.

'My goodness. Thank you for your honesty, CeCe. Is this how you all feel? That I am in some way withholding information from you?'

'Oh, please, Georg. You're always withholding information from us,' Electra joined in. 'Pa's death, for one thing. You made sure not to tell us until after he'd had his private funeral. Then there's the armillary sphere, the coordinates, the letters from Pa. You've always known more than we do, even though we're supposed to be his daughters. We've just accepted it.'

Marina—Ma—spoke next. '*Chérie*, please. Do not be angry at Georg. I have never known an individual so dedicated to their profession, and so loyal to one person. Believe me, he has grown to love each of you as much as I myself do.'

'Thank you, Marina. But it's all right. I quite understand the frustration,' Georg sighed.

'Georg, please don't feel that you have to justify yourself in any way,' Ally said calmly. 'This is such an emotional time for us all, and we really must do our best to honour Pa by behaving as he would want us to. Particularly given the fact that we are joined by our missing sister.' She gestured to me, and I tried to give her my best sympathetic smile. The truth was, though, that the butterflies in my stomach had begun to flap.

'I'm sorry, Ally. I don't mean to sound frustrated. It's just that, sometimes, I feel like we're three steps behind everyone else. And he was *our* dad, you know?' CeCe said.

'I understand, Cee. Maybe we can discuss this later?' Ally replied.

'Yes, of course. I apologise, everyone. All I meant was that it's wonderful to have you here, Merry. In a way we've grown up with you our entire lives. You were a story. A fairy tale. And yet here you are.'

'Yes. And this entire time, I didn't know I was even missing!' I desperately tried to lighten the heavy atmosphere.

'I suppose I just wanted to know how you went *missing* in the first place,' CeCe continued. Clearly she was a dog with a bone. 'That's what I was referring to when I said Georg was keeping something from us. I think he knows exactly how you went missing. And maybe, Merry, he told you last night. Which is why you've decided to come. I'm just upset that he wouldn't tell us, too.' CeCe looked genuinely deflated.

'CeCe! What are you doing? Please,' Star said to her sister. 'I'm so sorry, Merry.'

'Gosh,' I said calmly. 'Well, I can quite understand why you might be upset, CeCe. But I can promise you that Georg most certainly didn't tell me how I came to be "the missing sister". I also, most assuredly, do not know the answer to that myself.' I looked to Georg for help.

'Girls,' he began, 'your father was my client. Please know that I have never, and would never, *personally* keep information from you.' He sighed again, deeply. 'It is true, however, that I have, at times, been responsible for following strict instructions outlined by your pa before his death. For example, it was very important to him that you should all have the choice about whether or not you wished to discover the truth about your birth families. So, whilst it is correct that I knew of your heritage, for example, the information was not for me to divulge. As Ma says, I love each of you very much.'

I glanced over at poor Charlie Kinnaird. He looked as if he wanted the ground to swallow him up. I felt for him. He wasn't amongst the British now, who would rather throw themselves overboard than suffer any confrontation as a result of stating their true feelings about anything. The awkwardness didn't seem to be shared by Floriano or Miles, who were both absorbed by the exchange, as if they were watching a play.

Georg continued. 'You must believe me when I tell you this: whatever secrets your father kept in his life were kept in service of protecting you.'

'Protection? What do we need protecting from?' Star asked.

'It's all right, Star,' soothed Maia. 'I think what Georg is trying to say is that Pa wanted to make sure we were all looked after once he had gone.

'Yes,' continued Georg. 'But also during his time on earth. There are reasons why you knew him so well as a father, but little about his life outside of Atlantis.' I noticed Ma shooting Georg a look, her eyes wide with angst.

'What are you saying, Georg?' asked Maia.

Georg shook his head, accepting that whatever freight train was currently running down the tracks, it was too late to slam the brakes. 'I am saying that nobody was closer to Pa Salt than you, his six daughters. You saw his kindness, his warmth, his passion for humanity…and his love of life. You yourselves are products of it.'

'Carry on,' CeCe urged.

'Nonetheless, your childhoods were unusual. I know that most of you have noted that it is, quite frankly, odd that your pa sought to adopt six girls from different corners of the globe. Similarly, perhaps you wonder why he took no wife, despite being a superb prospect—kind, handsome and financially secure. The reasons for these things, they have never been fully explained to you. For your safety.'

'Georg, we don't understand. Please stop speaking in riddles,' Ally stated firmly.

'There is cause behind everything in life, girls. I am merely trying to explain that if you feel your upbringing, or any of my behaviour following your father's death has been unusual, there is logic behind it.'

The feeling around the table had shifted from tense to uneasy. I didn't know what path Georg was heading down, but I suspected that soon enough I'd have a part to play.

'Your father created a haven for his family, a refuge where he could ensure your protection and well-being. This is why he built Atlantis—an idyllic corner of the universe where you were all cut off from the cruel realities of life. There, he was able to care for you, nurture you, and provide you with all the love any child could ever wish for. It is why he hired myself, and Marina, and Claudia too. The world of Pa Salt was created for you, his children.'

'Georg, whatever you're trying to say here, spit it out,' Maia said.

'I apologise. You would like some answers. Well, perhaps we should start with your father's name. Pa Salt. This is what you have all called him, for as long as you were in his care. Indeed, it is how practically all visitors to Atlantis referred to him. The same went for your teachers, your friends…he was Pa Salt to everyone around him.'

'Yes. He was just…Pa,' Tiggy muttered.

'He was,' Georg continued. 'This is how he wanted it to be.'

'We all asked him about it loads of times. I remember.' CeCe frowned. 'He'd just laugh and say, "You know my name! It's Pa Salt."'

'Whenever we had to write it on an official form, he just told us to write "Mr D'Aplièse",' Star recalled.

'Yes, that's right. It is why I do not want you to experience any…difficult feelings about the fact that you never questioned that it was somewhat odd.'

'Oh God,' Electra moaned. 'We didn't even know his name. The most important person in our goddamn lives, and we didn't even know his name.'

'Once more, you must not berate yourself for this, Electra. It was of his design. Your father fully intended for this to be the case,' Georg attempted to reassure her. 'It is a credit to him, and the world he built, that you never felt a burning desire to debate it fully.'

'Georg, you're scaring us. What was Pa's name?'

Georg looked at me, and gave me a sympathetic nod. It seemed that my moment had come. I inhaled deeply, and steeled myself.

'Atlas,' I muttered meekly. 'I think that his name was Atlas.' The table turned to me now. I looked into the eyes of the sisters, who were clearly desperate for more information.

'Floriano, Charlie, Miles, Chrissie…would you mind awfully giving us some time together?' Maia asked, after a moment.

'Oh gosh, of course. Absolutely. We'll leave you to it. Tiggy, give me a shout if you need anything,' Charlie stood up at lightning speed, and was through the salon doors quicker than a whippet.

'You all right, Mum?' Jack leant in to ask me.

'I am, thank you, darling. You and your sister can make tracks. I'll be okay.'

'Are you sure? We'll just hang around on the aft deck for whenever you need us.'

Jack and Mary-Kate both stood and left. Only Ma, Georg and the sisters remained.

'Sorry, Merry. You were saying?' Maia prompted.

'Yes. Your father. Atlas was his name.'

The girls looked at me with a mixture of confusion and suspicion. Apart, that is, from Tiggy, who was sat there with the most enormous smile on her face. I held eye contact with her, and she nodded at me supportively.

'No big prizes for working out the anagram,' Ally said. 'Pa Salt…' she mused as she doodled on a napkin. 'It contains the letters within Atlas. Plus a spare P.'

'What does the P stand for? As we're continuing to learn, it would be unusual of Pa to have done anything by chance,' Star said.

'I think I can answer this question…' said Ma. 'The P simply represents Pleiades.'

'Marina is right,' Georg confirmed.

'Well, I suppose it resolves one fairly large mystery—our names,' Maia said. 'The daughters of Atlas.'

'I remember something about him being called Pa Salt because Maia said he always smelt of the sea. Did he make that up?' Electra asked.

'I honestly don't know,' Maia replied. 'I just accepted it was true.'

'We all did,' nodded Ally. 'But Merry, tell us more. How do you know our father's name?'

'He wrote me a letter.'

'A letter?'

'Yes, that's right. After Georg arrived in Dublin last night and convinced me to fly out and join you all, he presented me with a package when we were on the jet. In that package was a letter, and a diary.' I spoke slowly and cautiously, not wanting to leave out any detail or get something wrong.

'The letter was from Pa?' Star asked.

'Yes. I believe I'm right in saying that all of you received a letter from him?' There was general nodding. 'Well, I received one too. As you can imagine, this is all very nerve-racking for me, particularly after you spoke so…passionately earlier, CeCe.' I noted some of the women shooting a look to their sister, who stared down at the floor.

I reached into my bag to retrieve the letter, along with the copy of the charcoal drawing of my mother. As I returned them to the table, I noted how badly my hands were shaking.

'Please, Merry, there's no need to be nervous. We just want to know what's going on,' said Ally comfortingly.

'Firstly, I'd like to show you a drawing,' I held it up for the table to examine.

'Oh my goodness. Merry…I knew I recognised your face from somewhere,' Star said. 'Does everyone know what this picture is?'

'Excuse my French but *holy shit*!' added Electra. 'That thing's been in Pa's office for as long as I can remember.'

'And it's you! The charcoal drawing was always you!' exclaimed CeCe.

'Actually, no, this drawing is not of me. But I do agree with you, the likeness is uncanny. Georg confirmed to me last night that this is a picture of my mother. When I saw it, it stirred some emotional, primal reaction in me,' I confessed.

'The drawing that Pa's had in his study for all these years is your mother…' Maia said, slowly looking round at her sisters. I sensed that they were beginning to connect the dots.

'I noticed that it vanished from Pa's office at some stage during the last year. That explains that mystery.' Ally turned to Georg. 'I imagine you removed it and made that copy to help in the search for Merry?'

Georg nodded.

'I'm assuming you still have the original somewhere?' asked CeCe.

Georg paused. 'I know where the original is, yes.'

I picked up the baton again. 'In truth, girls, I'm here for myself, as much as I'm here to share this journey with you. I want to discover my true heritage, and it's a riddle that starts with your father.' I shook my head. 'The thing is, Georg has made it clear to me that in terms of your Pa Salt's life, you seem to have as little knowledge as I do.'

'That's certainly turning out to be true,' Electra mumbled.

'He was *your* father. He raised you, and you loved him. And that is why I hope that we can learn about him together.' I picked up the letter, and removed it from the envelope. 'Will I go ahead and read it?'

There was a keen nod of agreement.

'"My darling daughter…"'

I put the letter down and returned my gaze to the table. Tiggy walked over to me and enveloped me in an enormous hug.

'I thought I felt him close by,' she said. 'But it was you.'

'Nothing went wrong with your adoption process. You were *his*…' Maia whispered.

'You're Pa's flesh and blood, Merry. That's amazing,' added Ally.

'All this time, he had a *real* daughter,' CeCe said.

'No. That is not the appropriate word, CeCe.' Georg spoke forcefully, the lawyer in him seeping out. 'You were, each of you, his *real* daughters, and he loved you as if you were of his own lineage. I sincerely hope none of you would disagree with that.'

'No, of course not,' replied Star.

There was a pause as the sisters tried to absorb what this all meant.

Electra spoke next. 'So, Pa Salt's bloodline continues. That's crazy.'

'I think it's beautiful,' Tiggy said soothingly. 'And your eyes, Merry. I can see it now…they're Pa's.'

'My goodness, you are correct, *chérie*,' Ma said in wonder, her jaw dropping.

'I suppose you became the missing sister because something happened to your mother,' Star surmised. 'He must have lost both of you simultaneously. That's so sad.' She put her hand to her mouth.

'But he never gave up,' Georg stated. 'He dedicated his entire life to the search. In truth, it was why he was so often away.'

'I thought Pa was away so often for work?' said CeCe.

'Your father retired many years ago. He made all of his money very young. As the years passed, his shares and interests grew, and he amassed a fortune.'

'What exactly did he do for work, Georg? Whenever we asked him about it he'd tell us something vague about investments and finances until we became bored and left the subject alone.'

Georg looked back to me, and I took my cue.

'So, Atlas has entrusted me with his diary, and the letter asks me to share its contents with you after I have completed my study of it. However, despite the instructions, I do not believe it is my right to know Pa Salt's story before the daughters he knew.' I gestured to Georg. 'Which is why I have asked for six copies. If it is your wish, we can all learn his story simultaneously.'

After a pause, Ally spoke. 'Thank you, Merry. That's incredibly generous of you.'

'I just wish he felt he could tell us all of this himself,' Electra added sadly.

'As I mentioned previously, nothing was done without cause. Atlas was the most intelligent man I've ever known. He kept Merry's origins secret to ensure your protection,' Georg asserted.

'Georg, you keep going on about "protection" and "safety", but I don't have a clue what you mean. Not once growing up did I ever feel under threat,' Maia said.

'Then his plan worked.'

'What plan? Seriously, I want some answers now!' I hadn't predicted that Maia would be the first sister to raise her voice.

'Georg,' I jumped in quickly, 'have you been able to make copies of the diary yet?'

'I have, Merry, they're safely stowed downstairs.'

'Would you be so kind as to bring them up and hand them out? I think we'll all feel a lot better when we have something physical in our hands,' I added decisively.

The lawyer nodded, and as he passed Ma, I noticed that she grabbed his hand and squeezed it. Both had clearly been anticipating this moment.

'This trip was supposed to be about honouring Pa's memory. Instead, I feel like we didn't even know him at all,' Electra muttered, her eyes cast down.

'This *world* he created for us,' CeCe said. 'Why didn't we question it further? It's not like any of us are stupid, is it?' Her voice cracked, and she inhaled sharply as the sobs began. Star stood and went to put an arm around her sister. 'Sorry, guys. I'm just tired. We've all had to grow up so quickly in the last year. Learning to live without Pa, travelling the world, finding our birth families—it's been a whirlwind. I thought that this trip would be a chance for all of us to say a goodbye and begin a new chapter. But guess what? There's more! I'm just exhausted.'

CeCe's speech had a cumulative effect on the others. They all clearly empathised with their sister's opinion. I shifted uncomfortably in my chair.

'My girls,' Ma began. 'My beautiful, talented, kind girls. I am sorry that your lives have been so full of drama lately. You have all experienced such prolific grief in the last year. But remember, alongside it, many highs too.'

I noted how the sisters looked at her. Suddenly, the grown women in front of me were children again, unnerved and seeking parental comfort.

'Do you know what I think?' she continued. 'I think that our lives are like heartbeats, displayed on a monitor. They go up and down. And what does that tell you? That you are *alive*, my dears.' I noted one or two smiles from the sisters. 'If each of you had a dull and boring existence, then the monitor would not go up and down. It would be flat! And what would that mean? That you are not alive at all!' Some of the smiles turned into giggles. 'So you see, it is better to have this…excitement in your life, than for the days to pass like buses, one after the other, forever and ever…'

'Pa used to say that to experience the best moments in life, you have to know the worst,' Tiggy said.

'That's right, *chérie*. You will soon learn that your father did experience the worst moments that life can deliver. But he also experienced the best, which were all tied to you, his children.'

'So you *and* Georg know about Pa's past then, Ma? Why would you keep it from us?' asked Maia.

'*Non!* Enough now. This is not about myself and Monsieur Hoffman. It is about your beloved pa, and the path he wished for you to follow.'

'Sorry, Ma.' Maia was cowed.

'I wish to tell you how proud I am of each of you. You have all handled the events of the last twelve months with a bravery, determination and wisdom which would have made your father so happy. I know that you will now continue to be the tolerant, generous and intelligent women that your father, and, if I may take a small amount of credit, I raised you to be.'

The effect she had on the sisters was significant. From what I had observed so far, I would wager that she was a woman who chose the moments to assert her authority carefully.

Ally broke the silence. 'Merry, I know I speak for all of us when I say that we really are so happy and proud that you are here. You must forgive us if we let our emotions get the better of us at any point.'

'It's quite all right,' I assured her. 'If there's anyone who understands the feeling of having your world turned upside down, it's me.'

Georg returned from the salon carrying pages piled high, and on top, the original beaten leather-bound diary. 'Six copies and the original.' He proceeded to place the individual facsimiles in front of the sisters, and handed me the diary.

'Gosh, it's enormous,' said Star. 'It must be hundreds of pages long.' She lifted her copy from the table and examined it.

'You're not wrong there. I should tell you that I have read some of it,' I told them. 'But not a great deal. He's still a little boy. It's quite a story so far, I have to say.'

'Well, that sounds like Pa.' Tiggy smiled.

'It's a bit of an education, too. Come to think of it, I must put Rio on my "to visit" list.'

'I'm sorry?' Maia said, leaning in towards me.

'Oh, apologies, I'm just thinking out loud. The diary starts with your Pa meeting the chap who sculpted *Christ the Redeemer*. As one does.' Maia's jaw began to drop. 'Sorry, is that significant?' I asked earnestly.

'You might say that, yes,' said Ally. 'His assistant was Maia's great-grandfather.'

I began to mirror Maia's expression. 'You're joking? Laurent…what was it?'

'Brouilly,' Maia managed to stumble.

'My word… That's incredible. I'm so sorry, Maia, I didn't mean to give a spoiler.'

'No, not at all. It's…wow.' She slowly shook her head. Around the table, I noticed the sisters glancing excitedly at one another.

'Is that what this diary is going to be like?' Electra asked. 'We'll all find out exactly why Pa chose to adopt us? Georg?'

'You must read and find out,' he replied stoically.

Tiggy clapped her hands together. 'Right, how shall we do this? Does everyone want to read it together?' she asked.

Maia was the first to reply. 'Oh, no. I think I'd like to have some space to process things as I'm learning them. How does everyone else feel?'

'I think that's a good idea, Maia,' Ally replied. 'It looks like there won't be much time spent in the hot tub on this particular cruise. We'll all have our heads buried in Pa's life story.' There was a burble of agreement amongst the table.

'I'm not as fast at getting through books as you guys are,' CeCe added meekly. 'Particularly if I'm under pressure to try and read something quickly. My dyslexia just causes letters to become a great big jumble.' She looked to the floor.

'Oh, sorry, CeCe, of course. Would you like to read it together? I certainly wouldn't mind speaking it out loud,' Star said.

CeCe gave her a grateful smile. 'Thanks, Star. That'd be great. As long as you're sure you don't mind?'

'Don't be silly, of course I don't.'

Ally stood up. 'That's settled then. We've got three days. That should give us enough time to get through everything,' she confirmed.

'It's sort of fitting in a way, isn't it?' Electra said. 'By the time we come to say goodbye to him, we'll know who Pa really was.'

11

Maia began to make her way to the second deck. Ever since Merry had mentioned that Brouilly featured in the diary, her mind had been racing. What was Pa's connection? She thought back to her own personal journey of self-discovery one year ago. The pieces of her biological jigsaw had been firmly assembled, and she was fully aware of the genetic inheritance that had gifted her the shiny dark brown hair and unblemished honey-brown skin. But now, Maia was beginning to realise that the picture was incomplete. Why had Pa chosen her to rescue? And how did he himself know so much about her family history?

Maia found Floriano luxuriating in a deep leather chair in the corner of the reading room, book in hand. The image sent butterflies fluttering in Maia's stomach. It reminded her of Pa, who used to spend so much of his time on the *Titan* in that particular spot. The room was undeniably one of her favourite places on board—a grand floating library with bespoke bookshelves lining every wall, each packed to the brim with Pa's favourite tomes. Maia recalled endless, sumptuous summers picking out novels and retreating up to the sun deck to spend a day reading under golden rays. She closed her eyes and inhaled the sweet, musky smell of the books. It hadn't changed a bit since she was ten, and first took an interest in the contents of the reading room. She cast her mind back...

'Pa?' Maia enquired, not wishing to interrupt her father's deep contemplation of Victor Hugo's *Les Misérables*. He raised his eyes to his daughter.

'Maia, my dearest. Are you enjoying the cruise?'

'Yes, Pa, thank you. But I've finished my book. May I take one from one of your shelves?'

His eyes lit up. 'Of course, my *petite princesse*! Nothing would make me happier.' He stood up and took Maia's hand, leading her towards the largest of the shelves. 'Here is where I keep the fiction.'

'The made-up stories?'

'Ah, my dear, there are no made-up stories. They all happened once upon a time.'

'Really?'

'Oh, I expect so.' He glanced at his beaten copy of *Les Misérables*. It looked to Maia as though it had been read many times before. 'Eventually someone writes them down. Now, what do you wish for?'

Maia pondered the question. 'I think a love story. But not a boring one.'

'Hmm, a wise choice indeed. But you test my ability as a librarian. Let me see…' He scanned the shelves, running his finger over the rows of books that he had accumulated over the years. Eventually he came to rest on one. 'Ah! Of course.' He removed it from the shelf and smiled as he examined the cover. '*The Phantom of the Opera*, by Monsieur Gaston Leroux.'

'Phantom? It sounds frightening, Pa.'

'I promise it is a tale of romance. You will love it, I am sure. In fact, if you do not, then I give you permission to throw me into the swimming pool.' Maia laughed, and Atlas went to hand the book to her. 'Ah, no! I am sorry, my darling, but this copy is in English. Allow me to see if I have a French edition.'

'It's okay, Pa, I'd like to try it in English.'

'My goodness. You are brave indeed. Are you sure you don't wish me to find a French version? You are on holiday after all, there is no need to force study upon yourself.'

'It doesn't feel like studying. I like it.'

'Very well, my *petite princesse*.'

Floriano's voice intruded on Maia's memory. 'Maia? Are you all right?' he asked, looking at her from the chair.

'Sorry, yes. I was in my own world there. Where's Valentina?'

'Ma has taken her and young Rory for a swim. Come and sit with me. Tell me about what happened upstairs. What's this big pile of paper you have?' he said, taking the pages from her and placing them on the old oak coffee table.

She filled him in on the morning's events.

'*Meu Deus*, Maia. That is a great deal to take in. How are you feeling?'

'All right, I think. Merry is totally wonderful, and how she's coping so well in the middle of this chaos I really can't fathom. She *must* be Pa's daughter.'

'And the diary…you said she mentioned Laurent Brouilly? Is it possible your Pa Salt knew him?'

'That's certainly what it seems to suggest, yes.'

'Well then, what are you doing speaking to me? Why aren't you reading?' Floriano gestured to one of the rich blue velvet sofas in the middle of the room.

'It might sound odd, but I'm a little nervous. What if I discover something upsetting? I don't know, Floriano, what if it turns out Pa was some sort of international drug kingpin?'

Floriano put a hand on her lap. 'I do understand. Although I am unsure how many international drug kingpins are admirers of the works of Shakespeare and Proust.' He glanced around the room.

Maia sighed. 'No, but you understand what I mean.'

'Of course. All I can tell you is that you have walked into the darkness without a candle before, and at the end of your journey, found a light. Truly, there is never a dull moment in the D'Aplièse family.'

'You're right there. Do you wish you'd found someone who lived on a quiet *fazenda*, with four chickens, a dog and an ailing grandmother?'

Floriano laughed. 'My dearest Maia, I would not have it any other way. Remember that it was I who encouraged you to return to the *casa* of the Aires-Cabrals. And it is I who now tells you that, whatever you discover in that diary, you will find peace in knowing the full circumstances of your father's connection to Brazil. What would my readers think if I presented them with a story only half told?' Floriano moved his hand onto Maia's stomach, and leant in to whisper. 'Remember, in order to have hope for the future, one must look to the past.' Maia felt immediately reassured, her partner's easy nature providing the tether she needed to dive back into the past once more. 'When will we tell the others, by the way? I know you've discussed it with Ally, but surely your sisters will start to question why you have swapped wine for water?'

'Gosh. I'd thought about announcing it on the trip, but now there's so much more happening... Would you mind if we waited a little longer?'

'Of course not, my dearest. I will follow your lead.' He leant in and kissed her. 'I am glad that our little *bebê* is going to know exactly who his grandfather is.'

'*His?* What makes you so sure it's going to be a boy?'

He chuckled and shrugged. 'Sorry, I misspoke. Although, what can I say, it would be nice to have a little *garoto* to share the pain of supporting the Botafogo football team.'

'Agreed. It would certainly take some of the pressure off me.'

'Quite. Now, I imagine you wish to have the room to yourself as you begin the diary?'

'Thank you, Floriano.'

'Not at all. Remember that I am close by if you need me.'

He made his way through the open double doors, and closed them behind him. Maia surveyed the empty room before heading over to the sofa, pages in hand. The silence, save for the low hum of the *Titan*'s engines, was just what she needed to focus on the task at hand.

The Diary of Atlas

1929

12

Monsieur Landowski made a point of coming out from the atelier to meet me and Evelyn upon our return from the *conservatoire*.

'Well?' he enquired, with what seemed like genuine anticipation.

'Monsieur Ivan declared him a triumph, and would like to tutor Bo twice a week,' Evelyn replied.

The look on Monsieur Landowski's face had caught me off guard. His eyes lit up and he broke into an enormous smile.

'Ah! Excellent! Congratulations, boy. Very well deserved.' He clasped my hand and shook it vigorously. A smile appeared on my lips too. It had been so long since another human had shown an interest in my own happiness that I wasn't quite sure how to react. 'This is good news,' Landowski continued. 'With your permission, I shall raise a toast to you tonight at dinner and tell the family.'

I removed my scrap paper from my pocket, scribbled something, and held it up to Monsieur Landowski.

Money?

'Young sir. It is the privilege of one *artiste* to help another. I have been immensely lucky in that I have been generously compensated for my commissions. I will not hesitate to help you.'

Thank you, monsieur, I scribbled, fighting the tears that were forming.

'Are you aware of the *Prix Blumenthal*, boy?' I shook my head. 'It is a large financial prize awarded by the American philanthropist Florence Blumenthal—and her husband George— to a young artist, sculptor, writer or musician. I am one of the jurors here in France. I have always felt a little…odd about giving someone else's money away, so I am happy to personally provide assistance on this occasion. Plus, I am sure that one day, you will find yourself in a position to help others. Be sure to accept the privilege.'

I nodded emphatically.

That evening, the Landowskis were all sincere in their congratulations—apart from Marcel, who spent the entire evening looking as if he had consumed a sour gooseberry.

As I lay in bed, I considered how fortunate I had been to collapse in the garden of this particular household. I had been so exhausted, malnourished and dazed that I merely fell where I stood, and crawled under the nearest hedge for shelter. It might have belonged to anyone, and my fate could have been determined by the local gendarmerie. I might have been sentenced to an orphanage, a workhouse or psychiatric care, given my refusal to speak. More likely, of course, I would have died that night under the French stars. But my Angel, Bel, had been my saviour. Had it been mere coincidence that she had found me? I thought of my starry guardians, the Seven Sisters. Perhaps they had sent her to me, just as I believed they had kept me safe on my impossible journey…

I do not doubt that the Landowski family find some romance in the mute boy from under the hedge, who possesses a talent for the violin. It is probable that they are concocting stories about just who I am. The fact is, of course, that whatever fiction they are theorising about, the truth is more devastating than they could possibly imagine.

I must continue to remind myself that the Landowski atelier is not the end point of my journey. I have set out into the world with a purpose, and it is not yet complete.

I shut my eyes and thought of what my father had said to me on the last day I saw him: *My son…I fear the moment has come when I do not have a choice about whether to stay or go. Our situation is not sustainable. I must try and find help.*

My heart sank and I was consumed by an urgent anxiety. 'Please, Papa. You can't go. What will we do without you?'

'You are strong, my child. Perhaps not in your body, but in your mind. It is that which will keep you safe whilst I am gone.' I threw myself into his arms, the warmth of his being enveloping me.

'How long will it take?' I managed, through ever-increasing sobs.

'I do not know. Many months.'

'We will not survive without you.'

'That is where you are wrong. If I do not leave, I do not think any of us have a future. I promise on your beloved mother's life that I shall return for you... Pray for me, wait for me.'

I nodded meekly.

'Remember the words of Laozi. "If you do not change direction, you may end up where you are going."'

I rolled onto my front, hoping a positional shift might rid my brain of that particular memory. I felt a stabbing sensation in my chest, and realised that I had not yet removed the pouch from around my neck. Was it possible that, for the first time in months, I had forgotten about its presence?

As I passed the drawstring over my neck, I permitted myself a look within. The room was dark, but bright moonbeams shone through my window. The light caught the sharp points of the item inside, and I marvelled at the shards of yellowy-white that danced about the walls. It pained me to think that something so incredibly beautiful could cause so much pain and suffering. Jealousy can make human beings do terrible things.

I contemplated what my next move would be. I had traversed arctic deserts and mountain ranges in the hope that I would see my father once more. Did I believe he could still be alive? Even if I confessed that I felt the odds were slim, how could I put my search on hold having come so far?

The truth of the matter was that in the Landowski household, I had found shelter, safety and now, with the promise of tuition from Monsieur Ivan, so much more. I threw back my bed covers, slid my feet onto the wooden floor, and walked across to the window. The milky light of the moon illuminated the courtyard below, and I stared up at the gleaming celestial sphere which hangs above our planet.

'Are you out there, Papa?'

I carefully unlatched the window and let the cool night air envelop me. I came from the cold, and still liked to feel its crisp freshness on my skin. All was still outside, and I drank in the night. As I looked up at the clear sky, I searched for my guardians. Sure enough, there they were, the Seven Sisters of the Pleiades. Their presence was a certainty, which is perhaps why I found so much comfort in them. Whatever may change in my life, whatever losses I may still have to endure, the stars would always be there, looking down on creation for eternity. I noted that, tonight, it was Maia who was shining the brightest, as she always did in the winter.

'Maia,' I whispered, 'what should I do?'

I was always childishly hopeful when I spoke to the stars that one day, they may actually reply. After I'd shut the window and turned around to get back into bed, my foot brushed against something and I nearly tripped. I looked down to see my violin case, which I'd failed to slide all the way under the bed. The thought of playing for Monsieur Ivan at the *conservatoire* produced such a sense of excitement and glee in me that it had a dizzying effect, and I climbed back under my blankets.

After placing the leather pouch between my legs, I pulled the bedding tight around me. In my short life, I had already endured more trauma than any human being should ever have to. For the first time in years, I found myself in a place of safety, surrounded by people who seemed to care for my well-being. Would it be so wrong to spend a while at the Landowski atelier? If indeed Papa was alive, would he chastise me if I were to postpone my search for him? More likely, he would be a little proud of what his son had achieved. I had crossed dangerous borders to escape the horror of my former life, befriended a famous sculptor and, most impossibly, become a student of the esteemed Conservatoire de Paris. My father's voice crept into my head: *If you do not change direction, you may end up where you are going.*

Yes…yes. If I were to continue my journey now, with only the vaguest of information to guide me, the fate I feared most could well become my reality. I would have to return to stealing food and drinking rainwater, not to mention trying to find shelter along the way. I doubted it was the life my father would want for his son.

It was decided. I would stay with the Landowski family for as long as they would allow me to. Then I would complete the task that had brought me here in the first place: the search for my father.

'When is your birthday, boy?' Monsieur Landowski asked, as Evelyn presented him with a pile of forms from the *conservatoire*. 'These papers require a lot of information which I do not know. Your date of birth, an account of your experience on the violin…and, some might argue, principally your name.' He chuckled and shook his head. 'Young Bo. You're going to need a surname, you know. Do you already have one?'

I hesitated.

'One that you would be willing to share with me, for the purposes of your enrolment at the conservatory?'

I thought for a moment, and took out my paper. I began scribbling some of my favourite words: stars, aurora, serendipity, Pleiades… Ah, yes…that had about the right number of consonants and vowels to create something interesting. I scribbled further, rearranging letters as Monsieur Landowski examined the forms. I handed the scrap paper to him.

My name is Bo D'Aplièse.

He raised an eyebrow. 'Bravo, young man. You have successfully invented a name that will serve you well at the conservatory. As for your previous experience…well, who better to write it down than yourself. He handed me the papers. Under *l'expérience antérieure de l'élève*, I wrote:

No technical training or professional experience.

Monsieur Landowski looked at my effort and said, 'Goodness, you *are* young, dear boy! One of the most important things an *artiste* can learn is to sell himself!' He noted the surprise on my face. 'Do not confuse this with arrogance. One may remain modest, but also know one's self-worth. Perhaps you might talk about when you first began to play.' He returned the forms to me. I thought for a moment, and put pen to paper:

I have played the violin for as long as my hands were large enough to grasp the neck. I watched my father play and marvelled at the way his bow danced over the strings. He was kind enough to share his passion with me. At first, I learnt to play by ear, copying my father note for note. This is still my favourite method, for others find it magical. However, my father dedicated a generous amount of time to teaching me sight reading, and I have come to understand 'natural harmonics' as if they were themselves a spoken language. My father would often tell me that playing can improve memory and attention span, as well as mental function and overall health. I am unsure if I have benefitted from these things, but I know that when I play, time stops, and I travel to a place that is not on this planet; I dance on the wings of the universe.

I returned the papers to Landowski. 'Perhaps you should be a poet, too,' he said. 'Tell me, who was your father? Where is he now?'

I shook my head.

'Well, young man, wherever he is now, in this universe or the next, I am confident that he would be proud of your achievement. As am I, if you don't mind me saying so.'

I met Monsieur Landowski's eye.

'Young Bo, I am a sculptor. It is my job to immortalise another individual's essence, forever, in stone. The client must sense the *emotion* in the piece, they must *feel* something. In this respect, I am adept at knowing what lies beneath the surface of an individual. And you, young monsieur, have known great pain.'

I cast my eyes down, sighed and nodded.

'It is, of course, why I am happy to home you here with my family. I hope that this goes some way to restoring your faith in humanity.' He looked out of the atelier window. 'It is hard to remember sometimes, particularly when you have experienced the sadness which I can sense in you…but in this life, there are far more good people than there are bad.'

I put pen to paper. *You are a good person.*

'Ah! I try. Although I may be forced to go into a murderous rage if Brouilly fails to deliver my *Cristo* to Rio in perfect condition.'

I let out a small chuckle.

'Was that a laugh, dear boy?! Goodness, I *am* privileged today.' Landowski went back to filling out the forms required by Monsieur Ivan for my enrolment.

I suddenly felt compelled to give Monsieur Landowski something to demonstrate how grateful I was. His selflessness was not something to which I was accustomed, and the sight of him dedicating precious moments of his day to doing something for me compelled me to act. Despite the ball of nervous energy building in my stomach, I steeled myself, and opened my mouth.

'Thank you, monsieur,' I uttered meekly.

Landowski's eyes widened, and an enormous smile appeared on his face. 'Well. Good. It is my pleasure.'

I put a finger to my lips, and used my eyes to plead with him.

'Do not worry, boy. Your spoken gratitude will remain between you and me. Now, I shall have Evelyn post these papers back to the *conservatoire*. Monsieur Ivan has suggested that you begin next week. With that in mind, I think perhaps we should refresh your wardrobe.'

14th January 1929

Today, Evelyn took me to Paris. We travelled to an enormous building on the Left Bank in the 7th arrondissement, called Le Bon Marché. It was a shop like no other I had seen before. Under one roof, one is able to purchase food, furniture and clothing. Evelyn told me that this was called a 'department store'. I am indebted to Monsieur Landowski and his family for purchasing me a pair of new brown shoes and a blazer of my own, in addition to a number of shorts, shirts and undergarments. I had never before experienced the services of a tailor, who is a gentleman who measures clothing to ensure it fits the body perfectly. Evelyn instructed him to leave some room in the jacket, for she predicts that I will grow quite quickly. Whilst we waited for the good monsieur to finish his work, Evelyn kindly bought me an éclair au chocolat from the Grande Épicerie on the bottom floor, which is a sprawling food hall that stretches on for miles. Then we walked down by the River Seine. I felt as though I was in the famous painting by Monsieur Seurat. After we had collected the clothing and returned home, I rushed up to my room to practise my scales for Monsieur Ivan, as my tuition begins tomorrow.

13

'Bo D'Aplièse! *Entre, s'il te plaît.*' Monsieur Ivan's thin frame beckoned me into his small classroom. Although the exterior of the *conservatoire* was very grand, the tuition spaces were not. Red felt had been attached to the peeling wallpaper to absorb the sound, and there was a distinctly stale smell which hung in the air. Not that I was going to be put off by that. 'May I compliment you on your fine surname, which I have learnt since our last meeting. Quite unique.' Monsieur Ivan stroked his scrawny chin.

I bowed my head.

'Ah, yes! The boy who does not speak. Well, I shall not waste time with chit-chat, *petit monsieur.* Let us begin.'

I went to open my violin case.

'*Non!* We must allow the instrument to acclimatise to the room. It is fresh in from the Parisian streets in January, and must warm up. Speaking of which, please follow my lead.' Monsieur Ivan raised his left hand and stretched out his fingers.

'*Un, deux,* squeeze!' He promptly formed a fist, and I followed his lead. 'We must do this five times, both hands.'

After, Monsieur Ivan made me lay my hands on his desk. Then he asked that I lift each finger as far as possible, and hold it in place for a one-two count. Clearly, Monsieur Ivan sensed my confusion, as this had certainly never featured in my sessions with Papa.

'*Petit monsieur*, do you not think that a runner would stretch before taking to the track? We owe it to the instrument to be ready to play.'

I nodded, and only after several minutes of finger and wrist preparation was I permitted to remove my violin from its case.

'Now, follow me, please,' Monsieur Ivan instructed. I copied his trills and études, before we moved on to scales and arpeggios. 'Very good, little Bo. I notice you have improved since our first meeting. Have you been practising?'

I nodded once more.

'Very promising. It is this characteristic which can allow an average player to ascend to greatness. So, as your tutor, I will teach you higher-level string techniques such as control of *vibrato*, different bowing attacks and the harmonic series. I will attempt to correct problems in your technique, and encourage you to push the boundaries of musical interpretation. Does this sound acceptable to you?'

It sounded more than acceptable. Indeed, it seemed that God himself had offered to show me the gateway to heaven.

The rest of the lesson was exhausting. I never managed to play more than a few notes as Monsieur Ivan would stop me to comment on my finger placement, my posture or my musicality. It was a whirlwind of admonishment, and I started to question why I had ever picked up a violin in the first place. Just as I was about to begin crying, Monsieur Ivan declared that our first session was over.

'I do believe that our time is up, Monsieur Bo.'

I removed my chin from the saddle, and allowed the violin and bow to swing down by my knees.

'Tiring, no? Do not worry, this is normal. You have never had a proper lesson before. Many of our sessions will be similarly tough, for your body and for your mind. But it will get easier each time, I promise you that. I shall see you on Friday. In the meantime, please practise relaxing your shoulders. I noticed that each time I stopped you from playing, they became tighter and tighter. This is no good for us.'

How? I wrote.

'A good question. You must try to go to a "sacred space" in

your mind. Perhaps picture a moment in your life when you felt at peace. This is your task over the next few days. I will see you on Friday. Thank you, *petit monsieur.*'

I finished clipping my violin into my case and left Monsieur Ivan's room. Most people would not be able to tell if a silent boy were upset or elated, but Evelyn was aware that something wasn't right.

'Was it a difficult lesson, my dear?'

I looked down at my shoes.

'You must remember that Monsieur Ivan is not used to tutoring such young pupils. The *conservatoire* is a place for undergraduates, who spend every hour of the day studying. As I waited for you in the reception area, I watched students twice your age filter in and out. I doubt that he treats you any differently to them.' I looked up at Evelyn and smiled. 'You must be the youngest pupil at the *conservatoire* by ten years, *chéri*. Your achievement is beyond outstanding.'

Over the following weeks, I worked furiously. My evenings were consumed with visits to Evelyn in her cottage, and I would practise my scales, show her my posture, and play 'Venus' from Holst's *The Planets*. Poor woman, she must have heard the piece one hundred times, but each night she would applaud and say she enjoyed it even more than the last time. During the days when I was not at the *conservatoire*, I would spend time in the atelier with Monsieur Landowski. Monsieur Brouilly was well on his way to Rio de Janeiro, and in his absence, I had become the de facto assistant—passing tools, brewing coffee and listening to Monsieur Landowski exclaim in delight or cry out in anguish as he worked on his commissions. As a reward, I was permitted to borrow books from his personal library. He had bestowed that honour upon me when he had caught me looking longingly at one of the bookshelves after dinner one evening. As a result, I devoured the likes of Flaubert, Proust and Maupassant. After I'd returned my third book within a week, Monsieur Landowski had widened his eyes.

'Goodness me, boy, at the rate at which you're going through my collection, I shall have to purchase the entire *Bibliothèque de la Sorbonne*.' I gave him a wide smile. 'You know, I must confess that

I do not know many young men who have such a passion for literature. You are wise beyond your years. Are you positive that you are not a forty-year-old who has discovered the fountain of youth?'

At the *conservatoire*, my lessons with Monsieur Ivan continued apace, and with each session I became more accustomed to his manner.

'Relax your shoulders, *petit monsieur*! Go to your sacred space!' This was, admittedly, something I found myself struggling with. 'Each time I give you a note, you become more and more tense. These are lessons, little Bo, and you are a student, here to learn!'

There was an irony in what Monsieur Ivan was asking of me whilst simultaneously raising his voice and thrashing his arms about. If I had the option to speak, I think I would have shouted in frustration. But instead, I gritted my teeth and played on. Although I was exasperated, I certainly did not begrudge my teacher. He was not aggressive, nor mean-spirited. He was simply passionate about his craft, and keen that I should improve. If anything, my irritation was born from a desire to achieve perfection. Each night I would break into a sweat as I practised all that Monsieur Ivan had taught me. With my hard work, I simply assumed that his critiques would slowly cease.

A few weeks in, Monsieur Ivan allowed me to play an entire solo without interrupting.

'Good, Bo. Your *legato* is improving. This is progress.'

I bowed my head.

'Now, because I do not believe you are able to do this on your own, we will make a list of things which make you happy. Then, as you become angry when I give you notes, you will be able to think of these things, and the tension will disappear. Please, sit.' He gestured to the stool beside his own chair at the desk. 'It seems, young man, that you have the weight of the world on your shoulders.' I froze, wondering if Monsieur Ivan had somehow discovered my true name. He had already detected that we were from the same part of the globe. Who did he know? My stomach lurched as I thought of the consequences. 'It is no good, Bo. A great violinist simply cannot perform with such heaviness anchoring him down. Your shoulders must be free to move with the instrument. So, together, we will try and lift this weight.'

I realised that his choice of analogy was merely a coincidence. My heart began to beat a little slower. I sat beside him, and took out my paper.

'So, we will begin our happy list.' My pen hovered, and Monsieur Ivan chuckled. 'Okay, I will start,' he said. 'What makes me happy?... Ah, yes...' *Good vodka*, he wrote. 'All right. It is your turn.' My pen continued to hover. 'Do you have friends, *petit monsieur*?'

Landowskis, I wrote.

'Yes, yes, outside of the Landowski family.'

I do not attend school, so I do not see other children.

'Hmm. You raise a good point. When I cast my mind back to what made me happy as a young boy, I think of my schoolfriends. We would wreak havoc on the streets of Moscow for hours upon end.' Monsieur Ivan folded his arms over his sleeveless jumper and leant back in his chair. 'I remember throwing snowballs and building igloos. But you do not currently have such an opportunity.'

Violin, books, I wrote.

'Oh yes, these things are wonderful indeed. But they are isolating. When I ask you to go to a "sacred space", neither can provide that. You need *experiences*, young man. I am going to see if we can arrange for you to spend some time with others who are of a similar age. A former pupil of mine attends the *Apprentis d'Auteuil* orphanage several times a week to play for the children. I shall contact him and ask if you could attend their recreational activities at lunchtime, or perhaps in the evening, when you come to Paris.' He noted the look of horror in my eyes. 'Do not look so afraid, *petit monsieur*! What do you fear? That you will be committed to the orphanage yourself?' I nodded vigorously, and Monsieur Ivan laughed. 'No need to worry about that, young man. Monsieur Landowski and I speak often, and I happen to know just how much he values your presence in his household. Do we have an agreement?' I held firm, and shook my head. 'Bah. Take it from one who knows. Life is about people, and there is no worse punishment than loneliness. I am only acting in your best interests.' I looked down at the floor, but Monsieur Ivan continued. 'In addition, these young people are without parents themselves, and have come to know the hardships of life well before they should, much like yourself. I believe it would do you good to spend time with them.' I did not respond. Monsieur Ivan let out a sigh. 'All right. If you say yes, I promise that I will refrain from critiquing you for a whole session, and you can play whatever you wish. This is a rare opportunity. You would not catch me making such an arrangement with my undergraduates, you know. May we make a deal?' Sensing that it wasn't truly an option to deny his request, I raised my hand and shook his. 'Excellent. I shall telephone Monsieur Landowski and ensure we have his permission, then seek out my old pupil. Merci, *petit monsieur*. I shall see you on Tuesday.'

14

'Goodness me, my little *chéri*. If nothing else, these sojourns will only serve to increase your gratitude to Monsieur and Madame Landowski.'

Evelyn was not wrong in her summation of the *Apprentis d'Auteuil* orphanage. It was truly gothic in its appearance, with rotting windows and dilapidated brickwork. We were met at the large iron gates by a tall, spindly woman called Madame Gagnon, who let us in and led us across the concrete forecourt.

'This is only a favour because of the contribution young Monsieur Baudin makes with his violin. Really, we do not have the time to supervise an extra child. Madame, are you aware of how full we are after the Great War? I hardly have an inch to spare.'

'Madame Gagnon, I know that Monsieur Landowski and Monsieur Ivan are incredibly grateful to you for allowing Bo to spend some time with other children.'

'Well, I do not know what good it will do the boy. He cannot speak, so I am unable to see what he will gain from cluttering up my playground.'

'Madame Gagnon, Monsieur Landowski has indicated to me that he would like to contribute towards the upkeep of the orphanage.'

'If that cleanses his soul, so be it, madame. We have many Parisians with guilty consciences whose donations just about allow us to keep the doors open and feed the children. If Monsieur Landowski really wished to make a difference, he might see fit to provide some of these children with a loving home.' I saw Evelyn bristle, and gesture down towards me. Madame Gagnon raised her eyebrows. 'Well, it is time for the children to come out into the fresh air. They will be here for one hour only, and I expect you to be prompt in your return, Madame Evelyn. After recreation, I will let the boy out of the gates, and he will no longer be my responsibility.'

'I understand, Madame Gagnon,' Evelyn replied.

The spindly woman turned on her heels and entered the orphanage. When the great wooden doors closed behind her, the thud echoed across the forecourt.

'Goodness me! I shall not be too swift to judge, little Bo, for she has a difficult job, but I sense lava runs through that woman's veins. Still, I'm sure the children she cares for will prove a different story. Remember, I shall only be gone one hour. Try and have fun, *chéri*. Would you like me to take this?' Evelyn grabbed my violin case, which I was still holding after my earlier lesson with Monsieur Ivan. Instinctively, I clutched on to it. It was my most prized possession, and I struggled with the concept of even Evelyn taking it from me. 'Very well, Bo. You may keep it with you if you wish.'

The doors of the *Apprentis d'Auteuil* opened once again, and children began to flood out into the forecourt.

'Goodness. Some of those winter coats have more holes in than Swiss cheese,' Evelyn said under her breath. 'Good luck, little Bo. I will see you shortly.' With that, she left through the iron gates. I had often wondered what the ancient slaves might have felt as they waited to walk out into a seething Colosseum of Romans to face the lions. Suddenly, I felt I knew.

The variety of ages shocked me. It appeared to me that some of the residents could hardly be described as children at all, whilst others weren't older than two or three years old, their little hands clasped by older inhabitants. The forecourt filled quickly, and I was eyed suspiciously by those who passed me. Some children took out chalk from their pockets and began to draw squares on the ground. Others had old rubber balls which they threw to one another. As this frenzy of activity ensued, I simply remained still and looked around, unsure of what to do.

In truth, having never attended school, I was not used to socialising with other children. Apart from one individual, of course: the boy who had been my best friend, the boy who I had loved as a brother and…the boy from whom I had run. *He* was the reason I had fled into the snow on the worst day of my life. A shiver travelled down my spine as I contemplated the consequences of ever seeing him again. He had vowed to kill me, and from the murderous look in his eye on that terrible morning, I had no reason to doubt him.

'Who are you?' A boy with an angular face and worn woollen hat stood before me.

I reached for the paper in my pocket and began writing.

'What are you doing? He asked you a question,' said another boy, who had thick, dark eyebrows.

My name is Bo, I cannot speak. Hello. I held the paper in front of me.

Both boys squinted at it. It suddenly occurred to me that I was arrogant in my assumption that everyone I met here would have the ability to read.

'What does it say, Maurice?' the boy with the hat asked.

'It says he can't talk.'

'Well, what's the point of him then? What's the point of you?' I somehow sensed that the young man's question wasn't related to the philosophy of my compatriot Dostoyevsky. 'What did your parents die of?'

I am only a visitor here, I scribbled.

'I don't get it. Why do you want to visit this dump?'

I would like to make friends, I penned hopefully.

Both boys broke out into laughter.

'Friends? You belong in the circus. And what is this, circus boy?'

The one known as Maurice grabbed my violin case. A surge of panic rushed through me. I shook my head with as much energy as I could muster, and brought my hands together in prayer, silently pleading with him to return it to me.

'A fiddle, is it? Why would you bring this here? Who do you

think you are, that ponce Baudin?'

'Yeah, he does, Jondrette. Just look at his clothes. He reckons he's a fancy little *monsieur*, doesn't he?'

'You think it's funny, do you? Coming in here to have a laugh at us, who've got nothing?' I continued to shake my head, and dropped to my knees, in the hope that they'd see my desperation. 'Praying won't help you in here. Let's have a little look at what we've got inside here then.'

Jondrette began unclipping the case. Every fibre of my being wished to cry out, to verbally attack him, or to use my reason to win my violin back. But I knew I could not draw attention to myself.

'Give it here, you weakling.' Maurice ripped it from Jondrette, and began pulling at the clips, attempting to force them from the casing. The brute was successful, and he threw the metal buckles to the floor. Then Jondrette hungrily flipped the lid up and, with his grubby hands, lifted my precious cargo from within.

'Well, would you look at that. I'd say it's even nicer than Baudin's. What do you reckon, Jondrette? Shall we try and sell it?'

'Who do you know that'll pay us for something like this, and not immediately report us to the gendarmerie for trying to flog stolen goods?'

'Yeah. You're right. Seems to me that this would be a good opportunity to teach *Monsieur Fancy* a bit of a lesson.' Jondrette raised my violin above his head. I closed my eyes, and prepared myself for the crash of wood on concrete. To my surprise, the sound didn't materialise.

'What on earth do you think you're doing, you horrible little toad?' I opened my eyes to see a girl with blonde hair grabbing Jondrette's arm.

'Oi! Get off me!' he cried. The girl appeared to tighten her grip. 'Ow!'

'You will give this instrument back, Jondrette, or I will tell Madame Gagnon that it is the pair of you who broke into the storeroom and stole the biscuits.'

'You have no proof of that, you tell-tale!'

'I have a feeling that the crumbs under your bed might suffice, Maurice.' The girl pointed to the door, where Madame

Gagnon was smoking a cigarette and observing the youngest of the children. 'If I run over to her now and tell her, she'll be up to check quicker than a flash, and you know it.'

Maurice and Jondrette looked at each other.

'Why are you sticking up for this little worm? Have you not seen the clothes he's wearing? He's got money. He's come here to mock us.'

'Not everyone in this world is out to get you, Maurice. Now, Jondrette, hand back the violin.'

Jondrette hesitated, and the girl rolled her eyes. 'Fine, have it your way. She turned her head towards the building, and raised her voice. 'Madame…'

'All right, all right.' Jondrette shushed her. 'Here.' He ripped his arm from the girl's grip, and handed me the violin. 'Do you always need girls to stand up for you?' he hissed.

'That's enough. Run along, you silly little boys,' said my saviour.

Maurice and Jondrette reluctantly began to shuffle off, but not before the latter had given my broken case a good kick, and it skidded across the forecourt. The girl walked over to retrieve it, and brought it back to me. I was sitting on the ground, cradling my violin like a sick puppy.

'Sorry about them. I wouldn't take it personally, they're horrible to everyone. Here, let me help.' She began to gather the pieces of paper that had fallen to the ground as I had pleaded with the boys. She glanced at the top sheet. 'You can't speak?' I shook my head. 'Goodness. I was wondering why you didn't cry out. What's your name?' I quickly shuffled through the papers and found the appropriate page. '*Bo?*' I nodded. The girl giggled. The sound was so pleasing to me that I thought my heart might simply stop there and then. 'I like your name, Bo. Is that why you carry a violin?' I shrugged, and without realising it, a smile had made its way onto my lips. I removed my pen from my pocket and began to write.

What is your name?

'Oh, yes, sorry. My name is Elle. It's good to meet you, Bo.'

20th March 1929

Monsieur Ivan has insisted I attend recreational activities at the Apprentis d'Auteuil orphanage so that I might enjoy some positive experiences with other children. He believes that if I can make friends, then the weight of the world will be lifted from my shoulders and I will become a better violinist. I respect Monsieur Ivan's wishes, and for the past few weeks I have attended lunchtime breaks on Tuesdays, and evening recreation on Fridays. I am grateful for the experience, and have learnt how lucky I am to have been taken in by the generous Landowski family. Many of the children in the orphanage lost their parents in the Great War. In truth, it is somewhat difficult for me to acquaint myself with others, due to my condition. I am unable to call for balls, or sing during the game which is called 'hopscotch'. Nonetheless, I am determined in my quest to become a virtuoso violinist, and I will persist. There is one person I have met at the Apprentis d'Auteuil who I do enjoy spending time with. Her name is Elle, and she does not mind that I do not speak. She is a great deal more interested in my music, and has asked me on several occasions if I will play my violin for her. I confess that I have not yet gathered enough courage to do so, not out of fear of what the other children might do (although based on experience, that is a legitimate concern). In truth, I would be so afraid of disappointing her in any way that I am crippled by anxiety. Her golden hair and blue eyes make me think of an angel, and the thought of dispiriting an angel is too upsetting to imagine.

I pulled my pen from the page. I didn't think recording my feelings in my *official* diary would be appropriate, just in case the Landowski family ever did try to read its contents. I will switch over to my secret pages, of which these are a part. If it is not already obvious, the horrors of the *Apprentis d'Auteuil* orphanage are worth enduring to spend two hours per week with Elle Leopine.

In the brief time that I have known her, I have discovered that she plays both the viola and the flute, and is self-taught. The instruments belonged to Elle's parents, and serve as the only connection she has to them. Both were lost in the war. Elle's father died in the trenches, and her mother perished during the influenza outbreak of 1918. She is thirteen years old, and as such, has no memory of either. Perhaps the saddest thing that I have come to learn about Elle is that she had a baby brother, only a few weeks old when her mother died. The orphanage had been able to arrange for his immediate adoption, as there was a high demand for newborns from families who had lost so much in the conflict. But Elle was not so fortunate. She had been a resident of *Apprentis d'Auteuil* for eleven years.

When I am with her, I find that I do not think of anything else. In those moments, I am not contemplating my past, or the pain and tragedy which I have experienced. She is like music in that way, able to transport me to a place beyond the physical ground beneath my feet. Goodness! Who do I think I am, Lord Byron?

In truth, I have always found his poetry a little difficult to stomach. But now, I find his verses resonate with me wholeheartedly. Since meeting Elle, I am ashamed to say that I now care about little else. My nightly visits to Evelyn are secondary, as are the books I borrow from Monsieur Landowski. Even my violin lessons with Monsieur Ivan now take an incidental position in my mind. My bi-weekly trips to Paris are no longer fuelled by the excitement of playing at the *conservatoire*, but the thought of spending time with my new friend.

I am aware of the effects of 'love' and what it can do to a mind. From literature I have read, I understand that even the sturdiest of brains can lose all sense of reason and logic. And yet, even though I know this, I do not find myself caring.

Elle has told me that she has read every book in the library at the orphanage twice over, and so I have taken it upon myself to bring her novels from Monsieur Landowski's collection. If this is not proof that I am taking leave of my senses, I am unsure what is. The books are not mine to lend out, and I hate to think of how Monsieur Landowski might feel if he discovers what I am up to. But I cannot stop myself; my urge to please Elle supersedes any repercussions my actions might have. When she has finished with a book, we discuss it together (I use the term 'discuss' liberally—

she talks, and I write). Although, remarkably, she often knows what I wish to say without my pen ever having to touch the paper.

Tomorrow is a Tuesday, and I am hoping that Elle will have finished *The Phantom of the Opera*. I am blushing as I think about it, for it is the tale of a gifted musician who tries to win over an unattainably beautiful woman with his talent. I would like to think that I have a significant advantage, too, for my face is not disfigured, like the phantom. Although, I must concede, if I am to impress Elle with my musical skill, it would necessitate actually playing for her first.

I packed away my diary and climbed into bed. I'd played a particularly challenging set of arpeggios for Evelyn that evening, and soon enough I found my eyes closing, aided by thoughts of Elle's sweet face. I turned onto my front, and once again I felt a stabbing in my chest. Forgetting to remove the pouch from around my neck was becoming a more frequent occurrence. As the days passed, it was simply getting easier and easier to forget who I was and why I was here.

On Friday evenings, I was permitted to enter the *Apprentis d'Auteuil* and go to the common room on the first floor with the other children. Elle and I would perch ourselves in the window seat, and look down on to the Rue Jean-de-La-Fontaine.

'I just can't believe that Christine would ever be truly happy with Raoul!' Elle said of Gaston Leroux's novel. 'Music is her passion, and only the Phantom truly understands that. Raoul is boring. He's just…good-looking and rich…'

The Phantom is a murderer! I wrote in response.

Elle laughed. 'True enough, Bo!'

Who would you choose?

She looked at me, her blue eyes somehow gazing beyond my own and into my soul.

'Hmm. The rich, boring man, or the interesting murderer,' she pondered. 'Maybe it sounds insane, but I think I'd have to take my chance with the Phantom. I suppose, if he did turn on me, that it's better to lead a short, passionate life than a long, boring one.'

You are very wise.

'No, I think you have us confused, Bo. You are the wise one. You don't speak, but you are able to convey in one written sentence what it would take me hours to say.'

It is a necessity.

'Is it?' She smiled and looked out of the window. 'Sometimes it looks like you wish to talk.' My stomach tightened. So many words hung on my lips. 'Anyway, why won't you play for me, Bo? I promise, Maurice and Jondrette won't dare bother you now.'

You have not yet played for me…

'I am merely an amateur who has taught herself to play through books and practice. In truth, I do not even know if I possess any ability whatsoever! I would be embarrassed to play for you. You, on the other hand, are a student of Monsieur Ivan!'

I am not yet perfect, I wrote.

'Well, no one can ever be perfect. But you're receiving lessons at the Conservatoire de Paris. I don't know anyone else our age who has ever been admitted. It's my dream to go there one day, but…'—she gestured around her—'how could I ever afford the fees?' Elle cast her eyes downward, and in that moment, I thought my heart would break in two.

You will go, one day.

'Thank you. But I doubt that's true. I can't imagine the day when I'll ever be allowed out of here, let alone through the doors of the conservatory.' Elle's eyes were beginning to fill with tears.

Every fibre of my being wanted to open my mouth and give her platitudes, to assure her that I was living proof that *anything* is possible. I knew, however, that it was imperative I resist.

I had a thought.

I quickly untied the strings which secured my violin in its broken case and lifted the instrument to my chin. I grabbed my bow, closed my eyes, and began Beethoven's Sonata No. 9. As I played for Elle, I felt my performance elevate, the importance of each note heightened. I flicked the bow away from the violin to conclude the piece and dared to open my eyes to gauge her reaction.

She was staring at me, her own eyes wide and no longer weepy.

'Bo… That was incredible. I knew you must have been talented for Monsieur Ivan to take you on, but even so…'

I bowed my head. Adrenaline was coursing through my veins, and knowing that my performance had the desired effect made my heart soar. Suddenly, it dawned on me that my audience had been considerably bigger than just Elle. I slowly turned inwards to face the common room, and saw a sea of stunned faces looking my way. At the back of the room, Madame Gagnon's eyebrows were raised so high that I thought they might lift her off the ground. To my total surprise, she slowly raised her hands and began to clap. The rest of the room began to follow suit, and shortly, I was the recipient of rapturous applause. Even Maurice and Jondrette, though not clapping, had a look of surprise on their faces. Elle must have sensed I was becoming overwhelmed, so she grabbed my hand, and it was about the most perfect moment of my life.

The applause died down, and Madame Gagnon decided to pay me a compliment. 'Bravo. Despite your age, I sense that you could give Monsieur Baudin a run for his money.'

'See,' Elle whispered, 'you must have been good.' She kissed me on the cheek. 'Thank you, Bo.'

Blood rushed immediately to my face and I tried to limit the embarrassment by packing away my violin. *When can I hear you play?* I wrote, once I had secured the string on my case.

'You think I wish to play for you *now*, after that?! It would be like a newborn infant attempting to recite verse to Shakespeare.'

It would make me happy.

Elle put her smiling face in her hands. 'Ah! All right. I will practise over the weekend and be ready for when you come next Tuesday. At the very least you might be able to give me some tips on how I might improve.'

When Evelyn arrived to take me back to Boulogne-Billancourt, Madame Gagnon deposited me at the gates, and relayed what had happened.

'He is a great talent, and welcome here.'

On the bus home, Evelyn picked up on my joyous mood.

'I cannot believe you played for the children! This is fantastic news, Bo. I know how happy Monsieur Landowski will be to hear that you are growing in confidence.'

What Evelyn did not know, of course, was that I had not played for the children. Just one single girl, who seemed to be rapidly changing the direction of my life.

When I returned to the *Apprentis d'Auteuil* on Tuesday, Elle grabbed me and told me to follow her. We crossed the forecourt, and to my surprise, Madame Gagnon opened the door and permitted us to pass.

'She has given permission for me to perform alone in the common room. I am too shy to deliver a show for the masses as you did the other day.'

We sped through the corridors, Elle dragging me with such force that I had to jog to keep up with her. When we arrived, I sat on one of the old chairs where the leather seat pad had worn down to the metal beneath. Elle unpacked and rapidly assembled her flute.

'I have decided I will play Debussy—*'Prélude à l'après-midi d'un faune'*. Please do not criticise my ability too harshly. Remember, I have never had any professional tuition.' I could hardly believe that the most beautiful human in the world was about to treat me to a private concert. 'Now I will begin.' She lifted the flute to her mouth, and inhaled deeply.

It was clear how musically proficient she was. What was magical, though, was that Elle had taught herself to play from books alone. I do not believe that I would have had the capacity to do such a thing. Her reason for picking up an instrument in the first place was far more noble than my own. She played because it was a tribute to her lost parents, a way to connect with them even though they were no longer here.

I closed my eyes. The resonance of this once-grand old building ensured that the notes hummed pleasantly in the air. Nonetheless, I forced the musician in me to assess the technicalities of Elle's playing, as requested. I noted her breathing was erratic, and she was rushing through Debussy's work. I took out my pen.

Relax. I held up my note.

She lifted her eyes and read my message, then removed the flute from her mouth.

I scribbled once more. *Remember, I am only an eleven-year-old boy!*

To my delight, she laughed, and nodded at me. She inhaled again, and started the piece from the beginning. This time, the notes were without their staccato edge, and suddenly I understood the benefit of travelling to the 'sacred space' which Monsieur Ivan describes. When she finished, I stood up to applaud.

'Stop it. That was better, but you're right, the first time was terrible.' I shook my head. 'You don't need to be kind. I was just so nervous to play for you, Bo. All I've been able to think about since you left last time is how much I wanted to impress you.'

You did! I was secretly thrilled that my opinion meant so much to Elle.

'Now, I'll play my viola. I feel as if I'm less established on it than I am on the flute.'

Elle raised the instrument to her chin and began to play Strauss's *Don Quixote*. She was correct in her assessment—she was stronger on the flute, but showed clear promise on the viola, too. When she finished, I made sure my applause was as rapturous as before.

I cannot believe you are self-taught.

'Thank you. Neither can I, sometimes. I suppose it is the result of hours of loneliness. But anyway, please, tell me what you think, Bo. How can I improve?'

Neither are my instrument, but I shall try to provide general tips! I proceeded to write a list of basic tricks that I had learnt during my study with Monsieur Ivan.

'Gosh, thank you, Bo. I'll make sure to put everything into practice.' She examined the list. 'You've written *practise bow placement* here. Can you show me what you mean?' I walked towards Elle and picked up her bow. Then I stood behind her and took her right hand. I gently stretched it in front of her, turning her palm so that it faced us both. Next, I brought the bow in, and lined it up with the base of her fingers. 'Like that?' Elle asked. I nodded.

I took her thumb, and ensured it was pushing into the wood with a slight firmness. Then I placed her middle finger directly opposite, the joint just touching the bow. Of course, the viola itself was much larger than it should be for a child musician, on account of it belonging to Elle's mother, so my adjustments would have felt doubly alien to her.

'Gosh, I didn't realise I'd been getting it so wrong.' I returned to face Elle, and continued to manipulate her fingers into the position now drilled into me by Monsieur Ivan. As I was doing so, I caught Elle's eye. She was looking at me in a funny sort of way, like she wanted me to do something, but wasn't saying what it was. I must have returned her gaze in a quizzical way, because she giggled. Then she leant in, and kissed me. Her soft lips pressed against mine, and my world changed forever.

'I see we are done with our music lesson.'

A chill passed down my spine as I spun around to see the figure of Madame Gagnon lurking in the open doorway. Elle immediately went to clip her viola into her case, and picked up her flute. She rushed towards the door.

'I will put these away in the dormitory, Madame Gagnon.'

Madame Gagnon raised a single eyebrow in response, but allowed Elle to pass and scurry away. The two of us were left in the common room, and Madame Gagnon was giving me a stare that could fell a carthorse mid-gallop. I was suddenly overcome with immense shame. Special permission had been granted for Elle to play for me away from the eyes of the other children, and it must have seemed that I was abusing Madame Gagnon's leniency. I hurriedly picked up my pen and began scribbling an apology.

'Don't write, just sit,' Madame Gagnon said, pointing at a chair.

I was convinced that she was about to tell me I was no longer welcome at the orphanage, which would, of course, mean that I would no longer be able to see Elle. In seconds, I felt my world would unravel around me, and my hope turn to despair. I took a seat and, to my surprise, Madame Gagnon closed the door to the common room and sat opposite me. She must have seen the look of terror in my eyes, because, quite incredibly, she said something comforting.

'She is quite taken with you, young monsieur. I hope you know how fragile young women's hearts are. You are to be very delicate with it.' I nodded. 'Needless to say, if I ever see any of that…business again, I will not hesitate to whack you with my stick. Do you understand me clearly?'

Yes, Madame Gagnon.

'Good. Now, I have something to discuss with you. I have worked here at the *Apprentis d'Auteuil* for the past twenty years, and seen hundreds of children pass through its doors. It has always been my priority to try and find my wards new homes as quickly as possible, but never at the expense of their own well-being.' Madame Gagnon paused and took in a deep breath. 'After the war, we faced a very difficult period, with no resources and many children. I was not sure that it would be possible to feed so many mouths, let alone provide everyone with medicines, bedding, clothing and all the other necessities for rearing a child. It was a very difficult situation. This meant that I was forced into making some hard decisions. Elle and her brother arrived shortly after their mother had succumbed to influenza. A month previously, a wealthy couple from abroad asked me to inform them if the orphanage received any newborns, for they could not conceive a child. I assured them that I would, and normally I would have been all too happy to arrange for a child to move straight into a loving home. But…this baby had an older sibling. Under normal circumstances I would not have permitted adoption unless the family agreed to take them both. As far as I am concerned, when children have already lost their parents, it is imperative that they stay together. However, as I mentioned, I feared for the future of the orphanage, and I am ashamed to say that I allowed practicality to overrule morality. In short, I should not have permitted Elle's younger brother to be separated from her. Each year that she has been here at the orphanage, overlooked by families, my guilt has increased. As she has no doubt told you, she plays her instruments so that she feels a connection to her parents?' I nodded. 'Perhaps you can imagine just how upsetting that sound is to me, when I am solely responsible for taking away the true link to her past— her younger brother.'

Who took Elle's brother?

Madame Gagnon cast her eyes down to the floor. 'I'm sure you would not doubt that someone as officious as myself keeps impeccable records of every young person that passes through our doors. But on this occasion, the couple who took the baby wished to remain completely anonymous, so it could never be discovered that the son was not their own. As I said previously, I was under incredible pressure. In addition, the family agreed to make a substantial donation to the orphanage. As they say, one should not look a gift horse in the mouth. But, as a consequence, not only is Elle separated from her brother, she has no hope of ever finding him.'

What nationality were the wealthy couple? I wrote, in the hope that at least I'd have something to tell Elle if this conversation were ever to be mentioned.

'I genuinely cannot recall. Anyway, now I have given you some context, I have a request. I have not known a gentler, wiser soul than young Elle Leopine in the many years I have been here.'

Why does nobody wish to adopt Elle?

'Many have come close, but always decided against it. If I were to guess at why...'—Madame Gagnon shook her head—'Elle's family, the Leopines, fled the horrific pogroms of Eastern Europe and emigrated to Paris. Do you know what a pogrom is?' I nodded sadly. My father had often talked of the insanity and depravity of racial injustice. 'Hmm. I do not know if you are aware, young man, but there are whispers of a growing movement in Germany, which may well threaten the safety of the Jewish population. The French are aware of the power of the German state, after the horrors of the last decade. It is, I think, possible that potential parents do not wish to bring any trouble into their homes should there be any further conflict.'

Elle has not been adopted because she is Jewish?

'It is speculation, but I think it is possible, yes.'

Brother?

'As I said, the baby was taken to a new country and registered under a new name. Anyway, at that time the world's mind was elsewhere. It was not a significant factor. In any case, whatever the reason, Elle is still here, and I feel an immense guilt. You have known her for a few short weeks, but clearly you have a kinship with one another. Anything that enlivens the young girl's life eases the burden on mine, so I am grateful to you.' I tried to give her a smile, but I think it came out slightly manic, as I was unnerved by the steely Madame Gagnon opening up to me in such a way. 'So, to my request. From my conversations with Madame Evelyn, you are tutored at the Conservatoire de Paris by Monsieur Ivan. Elle's dream is to attend the conservatory. Ever since she was able to physically lift her instruments, she has played them, teaching herself through books I was able to procure via library donations. I have no musical ability whatsoever, you understand, but across the years I have noted that Elle's talent has begun to soar. I have often asked her to play for Monsieur Baudin his visits, but she has always refused, citing fear of criticism. It is quite the achievement that you have managed to convince her to play for you.'

It was a pleasure to hear her.

'Tell me, from one who understands, does she have promise?'

Infinite promise.

A faint hint of relief passed across Madame Gagnon's face.

'I am glad that my musical ear is not so out of tune that I am unable to detect good musicianship when I hear it. Do you believe that she is good enough for conservatory tuition?'

Without a doubt.

'As I am sure you can surmise, Elle's chances of attending the *conservatoire* as an undergraduate are slim, for no other reason than the high fees. She would require a full scholarship, and I understand those are harder to come by than blue diamonds.' My stomach turned at Madame Gagnon's choice of analogy. 'Perhaps you know what I am about to ask of you, Bo. I wonder whether you might be able to convince Monsieur Ivan to take on Elle for lessons.'

I tensed up. How on earth was I supposed to do that? Who would pay? What if Elle knew that I had failed? *Monsieur Ivan teaches only violin*, I wrote.

'I am sure that he would be familiar with the appropriate individuals to nurture Elle's talents.'

Money?

'Of course. I have a savings account with which I have been very frugal over the years. I have accrued a not insignificant amount for my retirement, but I can think of no better use of my savings than to help right a wrong for which I am responsible.'

Madame Gagnon was still, and continued to look me straight in the eye. Behind her upright posture and steely frame, I sensed that she was a little nervous about my reply. Clearly her remorse at what she had told me was genuine, and after many years, she believed I was some sort of answer to her guilt.

I can try, Madame Gagnon.

'Good! I am very pleased. Needless to say, I will not be informing Elle of the secret task I have given you. It shall remain between you and me, until we have a positive outcome.'

Thank you.

Her relief was palpable. 'I will ensure you are recompensed for your efforts, young monsieur. Perhaps when you visit from now on, you may be given permission to be alone with Elle in here, or in one of the studies, rather than be surrounded by the noisy masses.' My eyes lit up. 'For the purposes of improving her musicianship only, you understand. I will continue to watch you like a hawk.' To my surprise, Madame Gagnon smiled. 'Thank you, Bo. You are a good person.'

15

'What ails you today, *petit monsieur*?' Monsieur Ivan threw his gaunt arms in the air. 'Over the last few weeks, you have improved significantly. Your shoulders, they are much looser. This is very good! I knew that spending some time with your peers would be beneficial.' I didn't stop to tell Monsieur Ivan that it was *peer* rather than *peers* that had yielded the improvement. 'But today, you are like an ice statue! So tense and full of angst. Tell me, what ails you?'

Monsieur Ivan was not wrong in his assessment of my mental state. After a few sessions where I had made sure to adhere meticulously to all of his instructions, smiled at his witticisms and nodded along as he ranted about the pay some orchestras offered, today was the day I had steeled myself to ask him about Elle. I put pen to paper.

Thank you for your suggestion of attending recreation at the Apprentis d'Auteuil. It has changed my life for the better.

Monsieur Ivan shrugged smugly. 'No need to thank me, young Bo.' He tapped his temple with his index finger. 'Never let it be said that I do not know how to get the best from my pupils, whatever age they may be. It does not answer my question, though. Why are you so tense today? Is all well in the Landowski household?'

Yes, thank you. Monsieur Landowski and family are in good spirits.

I have a question to ask you that is personal in nature.

'Oh. I shall steel myself. Do not be embarrassed, young man. We are émigrés, remember. Here for one another.' Monsieur Ivan sat back in his chair and folded his arms. 'This question, is it perhaps…anatomical in nature? You are embarrassed to ask Monsieur Landowski or Madame Evelyn? Fear not, I remember when I was a young man, and was surprised to learn that the male body experiences certain changes that—'

I frantically waved my arms and shook my head. That was *not* a conversation I wished to have with Monsieur Ivan, or, for that matter, anyone. I hurriedly scribbled.

It is about a child at the orphanage, and their musical talent.

'Oh… I see. I will contact Baudin and have him listen to the boy. Then he will be able to give him a direct critique about how he might improve his chances of admission to the *conservatoire*. Okay? See! Sometimes problems can be easily solved. There was no need to be so nervous. Now, we will run through the Tchaikovsky again.'

I was already writing *Her.*

'Apologies, I should not have assumed gender. I merely thought you would be spending the majority of your time playing marbles and scheming with other little boys. Either way, I will have Baudin listen to her and give her an assessment.'

I had sensed this task was not going to be simple. *I wished to enquire about the possibility of her having lessons at the conservatory, like me.*

There was a lengthy pause as Monsieur Ivan absorbed the information. Then he looked at me quizzically, and began to laugh.

'Oh, no! Clearly, I have made a mistake in sending you to the *Apprentis d'Auteuil.* Now you are going to try and send every child through our doors here.' Monsieur Ivan continued to chuckle, then slapped his hands on his knees. 'As I sense you already know, that would not be possible. The conservatory is for undergraduate study and beyond. We are not a music school for infants. There are many private tutors who devote their time to listening to the screeching and honking produced by children.

I'm sure I can find the details of someone willing to tutor your little friend. All right? Now, the Tchaikovsky.'

She is self-taught over many years. I have heard her play and she is supremely talented. I believe she would benefit from conservatory training only.

'Oh, now I see. That changes everything.' Monsieur Ivan cupped his hand by his mouth and pretended to shout. 'The young prophet has decreed that only conservatory training will help his friend! Clear the schedules and ready the tutors! Our *petit* scout has found us the next great genius!' I cast my eyes downward. 'Young Bo, I do not doubt that your intentions are good and you are just trying to help your friend, but you are a mere boy, here by special arrangement because Monsieur Landowski has connections to Monsieur Rachmaninoff. Without that connection, regrettably, I never would have agreed to see you. In truth, I was expecting to listen to you play as a courtesy and nothing more. It is only because of your unique ability that we are here. You have a…maturity which is highly unusual in a boy of your age. The *conservatoire* does not teach children, and that is the end of the story. Now, please, the Tchaikovsky.'

She is also unique in that she is self-taught. I cannot imagine the mental strength that… Monsieur Ivan ripped the paper from my hands and threw it to the floor.

'Enough! The Tchaikovsky, boy!'

I shakily reached for my violin, and placed my chin in the saddle. I picked up the bow and began to play. Before I knew it, tears were streaming down my face, and my breathing was erratic, leading to a plethora of errors. Monsieur Ivan put his head in his hands.

'Stop, Bo, stop. I apologise. There was no need for my reaction. I am sorry.'

His platitudes were no use; the floodgates had opened, and I was unable to shut them. I realised that it had been so long since I had sobbed like this. There had been dark nights on my journey when my body had gone through the motions of crying, but I was simply too dehydrated to actually produce the tears. Monsieur Ivan rifled through his desk drawers and produced a handkerchief.

'It's clean,' he said, handing it to me. 'Once again, young man, I should not have shouted at you. You were just trying to help someone. And that is something that should never be discouraged.' He put a comforting hand on my shoulder.

It didn't work. I cried and cried. The fact that I had been shouted at merely acted as the catalyst for a release which had been due for many months. I cried for my father, my mother, and the boy who I thought of as my brother, but who now wanted me dead. I cried for the many lives I might have led, had I not been forced to run. I cried as I thought of Monsieur Landowski's generosity, and Monsieur Ivan's willingness to tutor me. I cried out of exhaustion, grief, despair, gratitude, but perhaps most significantly of all, I cried for love. I cried because I was not going to be able to give Elle the opportunity which she deserved. My bawling must have lasted for a good fifteen minutes, during which time Monsieur Ivan stoically kept his hand on my shoulder and said, 'There, there,' over and over. Poor man. I doubted he would have bargained on such a dramatic reaction when raising his voice to me. It was unlikely he faced such a problem with his undergraduates.

Eventually, the well inside my body dried up, and I was left taking deep, long breaths.

'Goodness. I must say that although I am in the wrong, that was a more extreme response than I was anticipating. Are you all right now?' I nodded, wiping my nose on my sleeve. 'I am pleased. Needless to say, I think it is for the best that we leave the rest of the lesson for today.'

I am sorry, Monsieur Ivan, I wrote.

'No need to apologise, *petit monsieur*. It is clear to me that there is a great deal else at play. Would a friendly ear help? Or should I say, a friendly pair of eyes? Remember, we are émigrés, and even if we shout at one another, there is an eternal bond between us.'

I began to write, but then stopped again. Perhaps it was the internal chemicals released by my tears, but I suddenly felt a sea of calm wash over me. If I spoke, what was the worst that could happen? Perhaps it would lead to my death. Then, at least, I would be in the world beyond, to join my mother, and perhaps my father too. Everything seemed so utterly, beautifully pointless. The desire to unburden myself made me take leave of my senses. So I did the unthinkable. I opened my mouth.

'If you will listen, then I will tell you my story, monsieur,' I said, in my mother tongue.

Monsieur Ivan did a double take. 'My word…'

'I have lived a short life, but the tale is long. I do not think I will be able to recount everything in the ten minutes we have left.'

'No, no, of course not. Well, let me clear my schedule. This is important. What about your Madame Evelyn? I will leave a message at reception that we are extending today's lesson to prepare for a recital.' He shot up, almost tripping over his wooden chair as he did so.

'Thank you, Monsieur Ivan.' I would be lying if I said it wasn't somewhat enjoyable to have him on the back foot for once.

Using my voice was a little like flexing a muscle that had been resting for months during rehabilitation. It felt fresh, and strange, almost as if it did not belong to me. Of course, I'd used it here and there, to remind myself that I still possessed the ability to speak, and to thank Monsieur Landowski a few weeks ago. But the sentence I had just uttered to Monsieur Ivan was the most I had spoken in the best part of a year. 'My name…is Bo,' I said. 'My name is Bo. I. Am. Bo.' My voice was noticeably deeper than I remembered it, although nowhere near breaking. What a strange sensation.

Monsieur Ivan stumbled back into the room. 'All right, we are ready.' He sat back in his chair and gestured to me.

I closed my eyes, took a deep breath, and told him the truth.

The tale took me the best part of an hour, during which time Monsieur Ivan sat quietly, eyes wide, completely absorbed by the shocking nature of the information I was revealing. When I eventually concluded, with my discovery by Bel under Monsieur Landowski's hedge, a period of stunned silence followed.

'My Lord…my Lord…my Lord…' Monsieur Ivan continued to repeat this refrain, shaking his head and biting his nails as he worked out his response. 'Young Bo... Or *not* Bo, as we are both aware, I am simply lost for words.' He stood up and grabbed me, giving me an embrace so firm that the air was crushed out of my lungs. 'But I knew it! *Émigrés*. We are strong, Bo. Stronger than anyone can ever know.'

'Monsieur Ivan, if anyone were to ever find out...'

'Please, *petit monsieur*. We are bonded by our place of birth. Remember, I understand the land from which you have come, and the trauma you have lived through. I swear, on the graves of my family, that I will never utter a word of what you have just spoken to me.'

'Thank you, monsieur.'

'I feel moved to tell you that I believe your parents would be very proud of you, Bo. Your father...do you truly believe that he still lives?'

'I do not know.'

'And the...item you mentioned, is it still in your possession?' Perhaps this is the one part of my tale that I should have kept from Monsieur Ivan. As I had learnt, greed can infect minds and drive the rational insane. He sensed my hesitation. 'Please, I have no interest in it, you may be assured of that. I merely mean to tell you that you must protect it at all costs. Not because of its material value, you understand, but because it may well be used as a bargaining chip to one day save your life.'

'I will. I do.'

'I am glad to hear it. Now, please, tell me more about Elle. After what you have faced, I understand the significance of having such a friend in your life.'

I related her story to him. 'She is a very special person, Monsieur Ivan, to remain so positive and brave despite her circumstances. I think she is a little like gravity, pulling all towards her.'

Monsieur Ivan chuckled. 'Ah, Bo. Now I see. I think that perhaps she does not pull *everyone* towards her, but only yourself. God help you, young man, as if you didn't already have enough problems, you are in love!'

'I do not know if it is possible for an eleven-year-old to be in love.'

'Don't be silly, *petit monsieur*! Of course it is! *Love* doesn't care that you are so young. She has you in her grasp, and now you are a slave to her.'

'I'm sorry.'

'Sorry? Please, there is no need to be sorry! It is something to celebrate. Indeed, if you were older, I would pour you a vodka and we could talk long into the night about your passion.'

'Will you see her, Monsieur Ivan?'

'If I discover what you have shared with me is an elaborate ruse to get your girlfriend through the doors of the conservatory, I shall rain down hellfire on you…' He held my gaze, before breaking into an enormous grin. 'I am joking, *petit monsieur*. Of course we will see her. Monsieur Toussaint teaches the flute, and Monsieur Moulin the viola. She will have her audition. Needless to say, though, *if* we arrange to provide tuition, the *professeurs* will not work for free.'

'That is catered for by a charitable individual at the orphanage.'

'Very well. I will arrange details and let you know upon your next visit. Am I to assume that when you return through that door, you will go back to being mute in our lessons?'

I paused to think. 'No, Monsieur Ivan. We are bonded by our place of birth.'

'Thank you for your trust, *petit monsieur*. I assure you that you will not regret placing it in me.' I nodded, and reached for the door handle. 'One more thing. You have told me all but your true name. Will you share it with me?'

I did.

'Well. Now it makes sense.'

'What does?'

'Why, when you play, you have the weight of the world on your shoulders.'

In the end, Elle's audition had been a formality. Monsieur Ivan had certainly intimated as such when arranging it.

'Little Bo, I have had to tell a small white lie to ensure that your girlfriend is guaranteed acceptance.'

'She is not my girlfriend, Monsieur Ivan.'

'Of course she is. Anyway, needless to say, the other *professeurs* would be none too happy about the *conservatoire* turning into a crèche.'

'What was the lie?' I asked nervously.

'Merely that your young friend is connected to Monsieur Rachmaninoff, and he himself is keen that her blossoming musical talents be nurtured.'

'Monsieur Sergei Rachmaninoff?'

'Indeed. Quite genius, is it not?'

'But Monsieur Ivan, I don't understand. Elle lives at the orphanage!'

'Young Bo, how do I say this with tact… Monsieur Rachmaninoff, though a truly kind and talented man, is renowned for his female protégés, many of whom have resided in Paris. It is, therefore, perfectly conceivable that young Elle is the product of one of his dalliances with a female, and guilt is compelling him to act in this instance.'

'Monsieur Ivan, I'm not sure that Elle will be able to maintain such a ridiculous facade,' I countered.

'No facade is required, *petit monsieur*. I have informed Toussaint and Moulin that the young girl does not know of her lineage, and Monsieur Rachmaninoff would be enraged if she were to find out. I can guarantee their silence; they would not wish to upset the *Great Russian*.'

'Monsieur Ivan…'

'Bo, I assume it is your wish that you should both take tuition at the same time? Schedules will no doubt have to be rearranged, and the detail about Monsieur Rachmaninoff will ensure that happens without fuss.'

I had reluctantly agreed to support Monsieur Ivan's plan, on the proviso that it would, in a roundabout way, provide Elle with an extra layer of protection. Toussaint and Moulin would not dare be so scathing in their criticism of Rachmaninoff's daughter. Although I must admit, I did feel quite terrible about blemishing the good composer's reputation.

And so it was that Elle and I, together, became the youngest students at the Conservatoire de Paris. In recent weeks, Evelyn has allowed me to take the bus to and from Paris unaccompanied, provided I check in with her whenever I return home. This concern was somewhat unnecessary considering my experiences during the last eighteen months, but it felt wonderful to have someone so worried about my well-being.

After our bi-weekly lessons, before returning to the *Apprentis d'Auteuil*, Elle and I have taken to buying ice creams from a small parlour on the Avenue Jean-Jaurès, followed by strolls down by the Seine. This is a privilege afforded to us by Madame Gagnon, who remains thrilled beyond all recognition that I have somehow managed to secure conservatory tuition for her ward. In fact, as the weeks have passed, we have begun to push the boundaries a little more, daring to stay out later and later. Sometimes we take books and pencils down to the water. Elle reads aloud, and I draw. I do not profess to be particularly good, but my landscapes are slowly improving.

A few days ago, Elle rested her head on my shoulder and narrated *The Hunchback of Notre-Dame*. I halted my attempt to capture the green horse chestnut tree, and looked down at her blonde hair, then at the rolling river. The May sunlight danced on the ripples of the water.

'Love is like a tree: it grows by itself, roots itself deeply in our being and continues to flourish over a heart in ruin. The inexplicable fact is that the blinder it is, the more tenacious it is. It is never stronger than when it is completely unreasonable...' Elle recited. 'Do you think that's true, Bo? Can people be blinded by love?'

She looked up at me. I shook my head and grabbed my pen.

On the contrary, I think that love finally allows a person's eyes to truly open.

I held her gaze. Elle lifted her head to give me a kiss. It was longer than before, and her warm lips moved delicately against mine. When she drew away, I felt light and floaty, and my stomach filled with a pleasant tingling sensation. I couldn't help but let out a laugh. That made Elle laugh, too. Feeling emboldened, I took her hand and held it in mine. Whenever we have seen each other since, I have not let it go.

She makes me feel safe. Previously, I had believed that was the domain of warm buildings, food on the table and money in the bank. But Elle has taught me that you may live happily without those things, as long as you are with someone you...

After much internal debate and self-reflection, I have concluded that, yes: I am totally, hopelessly and unconditionally in love with Elle Leopine.

16

I hope that my ability to craft written prose has not diminished over these last few months. In truth, since taking the step of speaking to Monsieur Landowski all those months ago, I have not felt the need to pen a diary for the sake of my kind host, and if somehow you are reading this, you will note that I have done away with the bland inserts designed to placate any prying eyes. It is because I have grown to trust the Landowski family entirely. These kind people continue to feed me and provide a roof over my head.

I suppose that I found it therapeutic to write my innermost thoughts down on paper. Of course, most people are able to verbally express them to a friend or family member, but when I began this process, I did not have that luxury. Now, I have Monsieur Ivan to talk to, and in terms of keeping my secrets, he has been as good as his word. At the start of the autumn term, he had some thoughts to share with me.

'Bo, I have taken some time to reflect on your progress during the summer break. Many would be envious of the life you are living: tuition at the Conservatoire de Paris, the opportunity to work alongside a world-renowned sculptor…not to mention the attention you are receiving from a certain blue-eyed blonde girl down the hallway.'

I blushed. 'Yes. I feel very grateful, Monsieur Ivan.'

'And yet…we have so far been unsuccessful in unlocking the ability to *truly* relax those shoulders of yours.'

'What do you mean?'

'I am convinced that you possess the ability to be a virtuoso musician. Indeed, your ability on the violin far exceeds many who earn a living from playing.'

'Thank you, monsieur.'

'But the shoulders are just not right. I do not think it is a problem we can so easily fix.'

'Oh.' Monsieur Ivan's honest assessment cut through me like a knife.

'Do not look dispirited, young Bo. I will continue to tutor you on your preferred instrument, of course. But I insist we add another to your repertoire.' He stood up and walked over to a large case which was resting against his desk. 'You have grown a lot taller over the summer, which will help us enormously.' I eyed the case. 'What do you think of the cello, Bo?'

In all honesty, I had no opinion on the subject, and said as much.

'It is a beautiful instrument. Mellow, sonorous, transcendental…it possesses a wide variety of tone, from the calm and solemn lower register to bursts of passion in the uppermost register. It reminds me a little of you. In your life, you have known immense pain and suffering. And yet, there is something of the hero about you. I cannot help but sense that, despite it all, you are destined for greatness.'

'On the cello?' I asked sincerely.

Monsieur Ivan chuckled. 'Perhaps on the cello, yes. Perhaps elsewhere. What I mean to say is that the cello is something of a split personality. On the one hand, it plays the part of the solid, if melancholic bass instrument, but on the other, it aspires to the passion of a heroic tenor. I think it will suit you.'

'I have never played such a large instrument. But of course, I am willing to try anything you suggest, Monsieur Ivan.'

'Good. The best part of my plan, of course, is that the cello rests comfortably between the legs. There will be no need to employ those heavy shoulders of yours in the same way the violin requires. It is my own second instrument, so I will instruct you myself.'

And so I began to play violin on Tuesdays and cello on Fridays. Initially it had felt alien to have such a large object placed between my legs, and to hold my bow at stomach level. But I had thrown myself into it wholeheartedly, and was pleased with my progress. Of course, I am not in possession of a cello, so am unable to practise at home. If anything, it has sharpened my mind and fuelled my desire to make the most of my tuition at the conservatory.

I suppose I felt the need to take up my pen once more because tonight is Christmas Eve, and my father used to impress upon me that it was a time to reflect on the previous year, and to mark the passing of time in one's mind. Therefore, I have been thinking a great deal about Bel…but perhaps not as much as Monsieur Brouilly, who has been a wreck since his return from Brazil. Needless to say, I continue to assist in the workshop, as Laurent, though physically present, is elsewhere in his mind. A few days ago, he heard me practising 'Morning Mood' on the bench outside the atelier, and approached me with tears in his eyes.

'Where did you learn to play like that?' I returned his stare. 'Who gave you the fiddle? Landowski?' I nodded. 'I see,' he said quietly, 'that like any artist, you speak through your craft. Truly, you have a gift. Treasure it, won't you?' I smiled and nodded once more, and Monsieur Brouilly placed a hand on my shoulder. He gave me a small wave goodbye, then wandered off to further contemplate his own misery in the bars of Montparnasse, which is where he seemed to spend all of his time outside of work.

Last night, I was woken by a strange wailing noise coming from outside my window. I checked my clock. It was just after two. Unless Père Noël was making a particularly early stop at the Landowski atelier, the noise belonged to someone altogether more real. I removed the leather pouch from between my thighs and hung it around my neck. Then I cracked the window and looked down into the courtyard below. I spied the figure of Monsieur Brouilly, and next to him, several bottles. I quickly concluded that attempting to get any sleep was going to be a futile effort, and my father had taught me that at Christmas, you should seek opportunities to help your fellow man. I took my cue, and reached for my warmest coat. Then I gently opened my bedroom door, padded downstairs and left the house. I followed the sound of sobs to the courtyard, where I found Monsieur Brouilly with his head in his hands. I thought what a good job it was that he had chosen to cry below my window at the back of the house, rather than any of the family's at the front.

As I approached, I deliberately made my footsteps louder so that he would notice me, and in his stupor, not mistake me for the Ghost of Christmas Past. This had the desired effect, and Brouilly spun around, knocking over a bottle in the process. I instinctively put my finger to my lips, and laid my cheek on my hands to mime 'sleep'.

'Bo. I am sorry,' he sniffed. 'Did I wake you?' I nodded. 'Oh dear. I am ashamed. You are the child here, not I.' I went to sit down next to him. He looked at me, slightly perplexed. 'I assure you, I will be quiet now. Please, return to your bed.' I pointed up at the moon, and then to Monsieur Brouilly's heart. 'Monsieur Landowski is very kind to keep me on here, when clearly at the moment I am about as useful as melted chocolate.' Brouilly chuckled suddenly. 'He even agreed to send me to Brazil, when he knew full well that my purpose went beyond the safe delivery of the *Cristo*. He is a great man.' I pointed to myself. 'Quite right. He has shown both of us immense humanity.' He looked down at me. 'You have grown a great deal whilst I have been away. Filled out, too. And I do not just mean physically. It is pleasing to see you beginning to flourish. Bel would be so happy. If only I could tell her.' I raised my eyebrows and shrugged. 'You wish to know what happened? In truth, I am still trying to work it out myself. We were together in Rio. But we both knew I had to return to Paris. I could not let my opportunity with Monsieur Landowski fade away. I begged her to come with me, and to leave that pathetic little slug Gustavo. I thought she would choose me, Bo. But she did not. And that is that. I may never understand why.' Brouilly sobbed, and I placed a hand on his shoulder. 'I understand that since I have been away you have gained a special friend in your life, is that correct?' I nodded sympathetically. 'Can you imagine your life without her now?' I shook my head this time. 'Perhaps then, young man, you can understand a little of the fate that has befallen me.' Brouilly sobbed again. 'You know Bel's gentleness better than most. After all, you would not be here without her.'

This was certainly true. In all honesty, I was a little surprised that Monsieur Brouilly had returned to Paris at all. From what I had seen of Bel and Laurent in the atelier, there was no doubt in my mind that they loved one another. If I were to place a bet, I would have staked everything on the two of them running away to some far-off corner of the world, where they would have been happy with only each other. Of course, as I had already learnt in life, sometimes love is not enough to keep two people together.

'You know, she didn't even come to say goodbye to me. Perhaps she would have found the prospect too traumatising. In the end, she sent her maid with this.' Brouilly reached into his pocket and produced something white and smooth. 'Do you know what this is, Bo?' I squinted, but in the moonlight I recognised what Laurent was holding out. 'A tile from the *Cristo* himself. It became a tradition amongst the workers to write messages of undying love on the reverse, and have them sealed on the statue for eternity. Here.'

He handed me the tile, and I held it up to my eyes. I could just make out the inscription:

> *30th October 1929*
> *Izabela Aires-Cabral*
> *Laurent Brouilly*

'I have thought a great deal about her decision to give me this tile. In doing so, she has chosen not to bind our love forever, but to return it to me, unreciprocated. As a consequence, I do not wish to keep it in my possession. Please. Have it.' I tried to force it back into his hand, but Laurent would not accept it. 'Perhaps you do not understand, Bo. If the reception to the *Cristo* is as welcome as I predict it will be, this little tile will one day have quite a value, I imagine. It is a gift. Maybe you will sell it.' Laurent stood up, stumbling slightly against the wall as he did so. 'Or perhaps you will keep it forever. As a reminder that you must never lose the one you love. Or you will become like me!' I stood up too. 'Lost love is a curse, Bo. It hurts. Not just in the mind. It has the ability to make your very core ache. I hope for you that you never have to experience what I am feeling.' He reached down and grabbed the one bottle with a remnant of liquid within it, and took a dramatic glug, then looked up at the moon. 'Odd, don't you think?' I glanced at him quizzically. 'She is on the other side of the world, but now, she will be looking up at the same thing.' He closed his eyes, and stood for a moment. 'Well then, goodnight, little Bo. I look forward to working alongside you in the workshop. And a Merry Christmas to you.'

With that, Laurent Brouilly staggered away into the night.

I returned to my bedroom, and placed the soapstone tile in the pouch alongside the item I continued to protect, climbed into bed, and placed it once more between my thighs. The pain Brouilly was suffering was deep and visceral. I sent a silent prayer up to my Seven Sisters to look after him and, of course, Bel too.

Christmas Day was magical. Under the grand fir tree, which was decorated beautifully with candles and paper ornaments, I was amazed to find there was a gift for me.

'Père Noël was very impressed that you have been so helpful to Monsieur Landowski in the absence of Monsieur Brouilly, so was keen to reward you,' smiled Madame Landowski.

The package was a recognisable shape. I delicately removed the brown wrapping paper, and then unclasped the large leather case beneath. Inside was one of the most magnificent instruments I have ever seen. The cello had a slick, spruce top, and a glistening maple on the back and sides. It was so well polished that I could see my own face in it, and as I removed it fully from the case, a pleasing smell of vanilla and almond wafted into my nostrils.

Monsieur Landowski put a hand on my shoulder. 'It is made by the German craftsman G. A. Pfretzschner, so barring any accidents, it should last you a lifetime. Monsieur Ivan predicts you will grow quickly, so I thought an adult size would be appropriate. I enquired about it myself.' Madame Landowski shot him a look. 'I mean to say that Père Noël asked me to enquire about it on his behalf.'

Instinctively, I threw my arms around him.

The generous gift was far from the best part of the day, however. The family knew all about Elle from Monsieur Landowski's regular conversations with Monsieur Ivan. As a result, they had been kind enough to suggest I invite her for Christmas dinner. Although I had initially been nervous, it turned out to be a joyous affair, and my soul soared as I looked around at the table full of people who meant so much to me. Elle, of course, acquitted herself magnificently, captivating the Landowskis with her charm and easy nature.

After the food, an air of melancholic malaise descended on the room. One by one, the Landowski family slipped away from the dining table onto one of the living room sofas, accompanied by a book, a puzzle, or to catch forty winks. Elle and I helped to clear the plates, and after, we put on our coats and I took her to the bench outside the atelier.

I put her hand in mine and steeled myself. I had been planning this moment for the last few weeks. It was Christmas Day, Elle was here, and I knew what I wanted to do. The time was right. I looked up to my shining guardians for strength, and, finally, the words I had longed to say for so long left my mouth.

'I love you, Elle.'

Her grip on my hand tightened, and her eyes grew wide. 'Tell me I didn't just dream that, Bo?'

'No, you didn't,' I replied.

Her face lit up. 'I didn't think I did!' She broke out into a laugh, then threw her arms around me. 'Hello, Bo!'

'Hello, Elle.' I felt euphoric. 'I love you.'

'I love you too!' She practically squealed with excitement. 'Oh Bo, I've been waiting so long for you to speak to me. I knew you could! But tell me, why has it taken you all this time?'

I looked up into the clear Parisian sky, where the Seven Sisters twinkled. 'Before I explain to you why I took a vow of silence, tell me…do you know about the Pleiades star cluster, Elle?'

She shook her head, still somewhat in disbelief that we were actually conversing. 'No… I must confess that I do not.'

'Well, I can think of no better topic for our first conversation. I have not been able to share their story with another for so long.'

She leant her head on my shoulder. 'Then tell me, Bo.'

'Do you see the brightest star in the sky? Just above the church spire?'

'Yes! How beautiful.'

'Her name is Maia. Now, if you look closely, you'll see some other bright stars surrounding her, in the shape of a waxing crescent moon.'

'I can see…'

'These are the other six of the Seven Sisters—from the top, Alcyone, Asterope, Taygete, Celaeno, Electra…and Merope, the missing sister.'

'The missing sister? Why do they call her that? I can see her.'

'I know, I've always thought that was interesting. I can only assume that she was missing once, and was found. I like to think of her star as hopeful. Now, to Merope's left, can you make out one bright star on top of the other? The smaller is Pleione, and the larger…is Atlas.' I took a deep breath. 'They are the parents of the Seven Sisters.'

'You talk about them as if they are real people, Bo.'

'Who are we to say that they were not? The legend says that whilst their father was condemned to carry the weight of the world on his shoulders, the sisters were pursued by the relentless Orion. So, the all-powerful Zeus turned the girls into stars to comfort Atlas.'

Elle's eyes sparkled as she stared up at the heavens. 'How beautiful.'

'I think so. There are other interpretations, of course, which are not quite as romantic. But this is the story I choose to believe.' I looked back at Elle. 'I have spent a large part of my life alone, but never without the stars above me. To me, they are my protectors.' I looked down at my feet. 'My father used to tell me that.'

'Your father? Where is he, Bo?'

I shook my head. 'I do not know. I have not seen him for

years now. I set out to find him, but…although it is hard to admit, I do not believe he is alive.'

'And your mother?'

'Dead.'

'I am so sorry, Bo.'

I dared to put my arm around her. 'It is a situation you have endured for your entire life.'

'Which is why I sympathise so much, Bo.' She put a hand on my cheek. 'Sincerely, I am so very sorry.'

A lump unexpectedly arrived in my throat. 'Thank you, Elle.'

'So tell me…why have you chosen to speak to me today? You could have opened your mouth at any time, my darling!'

I paused to consider her question. 'Well, it is Christmas Day after all—a time which reminds us that we are only alive once, and must not waste a moment.'

'That is exceedingly sweet, but absolute nonsense. Please, you are here with me, and we are alone. Tell me the truth.'

I looked to the stars once again. Their silent, stoic majesty gave me the confidence I needed to reveal the truth to Elle. 'I do not speak because I am afraid that if I say the wrong thing, it could get me into trouble.'

'Trouble?' she repeated, worry appearing on her face.

'Yes. But when I'm with you, I don't feel afraid, Elle. I feel brave. Therefore, there is no reason to remain silent.'

'Oh Bo. What is it that silence protects you from?'

'I am running from someone, Elle. Someone who has sworn to kill me. The only thing that is currently protecting me is my location, which is unknown to my pursuer. If I talk, then there is a higher chance of information of my whereabouts spreading, and it is not a risk I feel confident taking.'

'*Mon Dieu*, Bo. Who is it that wishes you harm?'

I paused. 'Another boy.'

'A boy? Bo, you should have said. I'd very much like to meet him. The one thing that little boys are afraid of, more than anything else, is an older, wiser girl. You've seen how I control Maurice and Jondrette.'

Elle's kindness made my heart swell in my chest. 'Thank you for your offer of protection, Elle. But with respect, little boys like

Maurice and Jondrette are of no real consequence. The boy I run from believes that I did something terrible, and that makes him very dangerous.'

'How dangerous can one boy be?'

'He holds me responsible for…a death that occurred.'

'A death?' Elle said, trying to suppress a gasp.

'Yes.' Elle and I locked eyes, and there was an uncomfortable pause in the conversation.

'Were you…responsible for the death?'

'No, I was not. But he will never believe the truth. So, I have been forced to run from him. I fear that I am cursed to do so forever.'

'Where is the boy now? Is he in France?'

'I do not believe he can be, no. I am hoping he is still several countries away.'

'*Countries*, Bo? You've crossed countries?'

I nodded solemnly. 'Running *from* him, and *towards* my father. He was on his way to Switzerland—the country of his birth—in an attempt to try and save me…and the boy's family too. That is where I was trying to get to when I was found collapsed under the Landowskis' hedge over one year ago.'

'Bo…there's so much I don't yet understand, but how on earth could this boy, whoever he is, ever know your whereabouts?'

'There is something which complicates matters.' I took a deep breath, and removed the leather pouch from around my neck. 'This…item…this is the cause of all the misery.' I looked around to ensure that there were no prying eyes lurking in the shadows, and removed the object from within. Even in the dark of the night, and despite the fact it had been covered in boot polish and glue, it somehow had the ability to attract the nearest source of light, and shimmered before our eyes.

'Bo…' Elle said in shock.

I held it up so she could see clearly. 'It's a diamond.'

'It can't be, it's enormous. The biggest I've ever seen.'

'I assure you, this diamond is real. The other boy believes that I stole it from his mother and murdered her.' Elle put her hand to her mouth. 'Please trust me when I say that this could not be further from the truth. But I believe that as long as he knows I possess the stone, he will stop at nothing to reclaim it from me, and end my life. He is clever…'

'As clever as you?'

I managed another smile at Elle's kind words. 'Perhaps. Do you now understand why I do not speak, Elle? And why you must not reveal to others that I can, nor any of what I have told you this evening?' I put the diamond back in its leather pouch, and secured it around my neck.

'You have to tell me your story, Bo—every bit of it.'

I shook my head. 'The tale is long and upsetting.'

Elle sat up straight and adopted a forthright tone. 'Look at me. I am your Elle and I love you more than I have ever loved anyone or anything. I promise that whatever you tell me tonight, I will keep secret until the day I die. This I swear to you, beneath the Seven Sisters of the Pleiades.'

In truth, I longed to share every detail with her. But it was my duty to make her aware of the consequences. 'Elle,' I began, 'since you have arrived in my life, I feel *alive* again. I can take pleasure from the smell of Monsieur Landowski's strong coffee, the warmth of blankets, and the sound of the flowing Seine. All because I have met you.'

'I feel the same way,' she replied tenderly.

'You must understand that by telling you my story, I may put your life in danger, too. If anything happened to you, I would never forgive myself.' I looked away from her. 'Indeed, I could see no more point in existence.'

Elle turned my face towards her again. 'Well,' she said, 'I should not like to live without you either. But perhaps *you* can understand, Bo, that I accept *all* of you.'

How could I ever deny those blue eyes? 'Very well. I will tell you the story of my life,' I replied.

I told her everything, from the moment of my birth in a rail carriage in 1918 to the present day. I told her of my father, of brutal winters, of stargazing and violins, of divided families and hungry bellies. I told her of the invention of 'Bo', and of my real name, and that she was never to use it.

Elle sat in stunned silence as I recounted my tale to her. When I had finished, I noticed she was crying. 'Why the tears, Elle?'

'Because you are such a kind person, and the universe has treated you so poorly.'

'I feel the same way about you. But now we have each other. Always…'

'And forever,' Elle replied.

We held each other under the gaze of the Seven Sisters. In that moment, we were not children, but two old souls, world-wearied before their time.

'Does anything change now?' I asked.

'Oh, yes,' said Elle. My heart sank. 'My love for you has only grown, and my desire to keep you safe become stronger.'

'That is good news,' I replied. 'In all honesty, I thought you might be put off by my voice, which now seems to squeak at inopportune moments.'

She giggled. 'I think it's sweet. And don't worry, I have seen other boys at the orphanage go through this phase before their vocal cords settle. It will pass.'

'Well, that *is* a relief.'

'Bo…'

'Yes, Elle?'

'There is one detail you have omitted. The boy who has sworn to kill you—what is his name?'

I stared up at the stars, knowing that on the other side of the world, he was inevitably doing the same.

'Kreeg Eszu.'

The Titan

June 2008

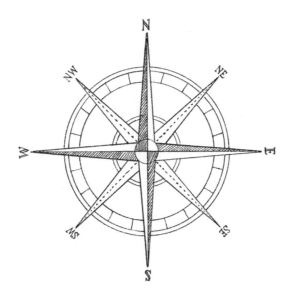

17

Bear's cries dragged Ally back into the present, and she shakily placed the heavy pages of the diary on the dresser in her cabin.

'There, there, sweetheart.' Ally lifted Bear out of his cot, where he had been happily slumbering until moments ago. The enormous roar of the *Titan*'s engines had just quietened, and ironically it seemed to be the change in tone which had woken him. 'Captain Hans must have found a place to anchor for the night, Bear, that's all.'

She sat back down on the bed and, operating on autopilot, bounced her child on her knee. Ally blinked heavily, realizing that she had been so absorbed in the diary for the last few hours that afternoon had turned into evening. She switched on her bedside light, and then put Bear to her breast as her mind whirled. She imagined that the others were similarly reeling from the concrete revelation that Pa *had* known Kreeg Eszu, and moreover, that he seemed to be running from him. Ally thought especially of Maia, for whom the truth must be particularly difficult to accept. She was grateful that Floriano was close by.

But for Ally, there was more to take in. Pa's alias—Bo, and his love, Elle… Ally knew the names. They had been close friends of her grandparents, Pip and Karine Halvorsen, and were mentioned frequently in the manuscript of *Grieg, Solveig og Jeg*, the primary document through which Ally had learnt of her heritage. Bo was Pa all along. Tears formed in Ally's eyes as she recalled that he didn't say much, but was the most talented musician at the

Leipzig Conservatory. She desperately tried to remember any more information about her grandparents' friends, but beyond the fact they fled to Norway—because Elle and Karine were Jewish—there was little she could recall. What had become of the pair? Did she remember something about them travelling to Scotland? Her thoughts were broken by a knock on her door.

'Come in,' she said automatically.

The door opened, and the tall, handsome figure of Jack entered the room. 'Hiya, Ally, I…' He spotted her feeding Bear. 'Oops, so sorry, I can come back later. I didn't mean to…'

Ally's cheeks reddened. 'No, sorry, Jack, I was in my own world… It's fine, please come in. He'll be finished in a moment.'

'Righto.' Jack took a seat on the leather chair next to the dresser. 'I just wanted to come and check on you. Are you doing all right?'

'Yes, thank you, Jack.' Ally gave him a weak smile.

'Have you eaten? Or at least managed some water, or a cup of tea?'

Ally thought for a moment. 'You know, actually, I haven't.'

'That might explain why you're white as a sheet.' She didn't have the energy to explain the full implications of what she had learnt from the diary that afternoon. 'Here, let me get the kettle on. You can make a start on this in the meantime.' He tried to hand her an unopened bottle of Evian from the room's fridge.

'Thanks. Would you mind…?' Ally nodded at the bottle.

'Oh, sorry, of course.' Jack unscrewed the top and Ally held the water in her spare hand. She took a deep glug.

'That's better. What's everyone doing up there, by the way?' she asked, looking to the ceiling.

'To be honest, it's a total ghost town. Everyone's hunkered down reading. I haven't even seen Mum this afternoon. She must be as engrossed as you are. All of us "spare parts" are just sort of milling around making awkward chit-chat, too embarrassed to ask any of the staff for anything!'

'Jack, don't be silly. You're not spare parts at all. In fact, based on what I've just read, you're all going to have very important roles to play in supporting my sisters.'

'And you, of course.' Jack smiled at her as he prepared the

tea, and Ally's heart fluttered like a teenage girl's.

'That's very sweet of you, Jack, thank you. But honestly, I'm fine. I have this one.' She glanced down at Bear.

'Now, I'm no expert, but from what I remember about babies, they're not traditionally the best conversationalists.' Ally laughed. 'You see, I reckon that you're some sort of leader up there. The other girls look to you for guidance. But they've all got partners who they can moan and whine to when they close their cabin doors. You don't have that luxury, just this little tyke to give you the runaround. So, basically, I wanted to say that…'—he opened his arms out—'I'm here for ya.'

'That's really very sweet of you, Jack, thank you,' Ally replied sincerely. He placed the tea on the dresser and returned the milk to the fridge. 'Jack…'

'Yes, Ally?'

'I just wanted to say that…' Bear spluttered and looked up at Ally. 'Sorry, just give me one moment.'

'Oh, sure, take your time.' Ally removed Bear from her breast. She noted that Jack averted his eyes, which she thought was sweet. She placed her son on the bed, and he gurgled contentedly. 'You were saying?'

Ally blushed. 'Oh, nothing.' Jack nodded and looked down at the floor. Ally chastised herself, and attempted to quickly change the subject. 'I haven't even told you the biggest revelation from the diary.' She went to pick up the pages from the dresser. 'What was the name of the house in Ireland? The one in West Cork, where your Mum's coordinates led…'

'Argideen House?' Jack replied.

'Yes. You remember that you traced it back to the name of Eszu?'

'I do.'

'Well, my father knew him. Quite well it seems.'

'Interesting. What are the implications of that?'

'I don't have all the answers yet, but I'm getting there. Come to think of it, I really should go to Maia. That information will have affected her the most.'

'May I ask why?'

'Sorry, Jack. It's not my story to tell.'

'Of course. Tell you what, shall I look after the little nipper while you go and see your sister?'

'Would you do that for me?'

'Sure, no problem.'

'Thank you, Jack. Feel free to take him somewhere else if you don't want to stay in here. And if you get bored, then Ma should be about too.' She grabbed her tea and made for the door.

'Righto. Come on, Grizzly Bear, why don't we take you upstairs? You go on ahead, Ally. We'll see you later.'

Maia felt physically sick. Awful memories of the smarmy, oily Zed Eszu's—Kreeg's son—filled her mind, and the thought that a generation before, Pa had been forced to flee from his father made her want to cry. Did Zed know their family history? He must have done. Perhaps that explained why he seemed to target the D'Aplièse sisters. She was well aware that he and Electra had been together, and Tiggy had told her all about his arrival in the Scottish Highlands. Zed's presence in the girls' lives must have caused Pa a lot of pain, and it was all too much to bear.

'Bastard!' Maia cried, throwing the pages of the diary to the floor.

'Maia?' Star said. She and CeCe had appeared at the door of the reading room just as Maia put her head in her hands and began to sob. Her two sisters ran and wrapped their arms around her. 'I'm so sorry, Maia. How awful for you.'

'For what it's worth, I agree with you, Maia. What a vile piece of shit,' added CeCe.

'He knew, didn't he? He knew about Kreeg and Pa. That's why he's buzzed around our lives, like a wasp that can't be gotten rid of. I feel so used. I had his *baby*!' Maia shrieked.

'I know, sweetie, I know. It wasn't your fault.' Even though Maia had only ever told Ally, her other sisters had always suspected, given her move to the Pavilion at Atlantis under the pretence of 'glandular fever' for nine months. 'We came up as soon as we'd read it.'

'Thank you, Star.' Maia sniffed. 'Oh dear. It's all so *emotional*, isn't it? I hate to think of Pa so desperate and alone.'

'At least he's found Elle now. She's changed his life. Even his handwriting seems to be more…twirly. Do you know what I mean?' CeCe said.

Maia gave a half sob, half chuckle. 'Weirdly I do, yes. And it makes me happy to read about how kind the Landowski family were to him.'

'Gosh, of course. I hadn't properly considered that. It must have been odd enough for you reading about Pa's time at the atelier, and his interactions with Laurent Brouilly,' Star said softly.

'Yes. He was the silent little boy I'd read about in Bel's letters. I couldn't believe it.'

'It explains how he got the soapstone tile that Pa left you in your letter, too,' Star continued.

'It does, yes.'

Ally entered the room and approached her sisters. She took Maia's hand and squeezed it. 'Oh darling. We're all here for you. Whatever you need.'

'I know. Sorry, I'll pull myself together.' Maia wiped her tears on the back of her sleeve. 'Zed's a piece of work, what's new?' Ally handed her a tissue from her pocket. Maia took it gratefully and dabbed her eyes. 'So, Pa knew Kreeg.'

'I think that "knew" is a bit of an understatement,' CeCe added sharply.

'Why didn't he ever *say* anything about it? He must have had a heart attack when I first mentioned that I'd met a boy called Zed Eszu,' Maia snivelled.

'I don't know, sweetie. Maybe they resolved their grievances? We only know part of the story after all,' Star added, stroking her sister's hair.

'Something tells me that didn't happen, Star,' Maia replied. 'We all know that on the day Pa died, Kreeg committed suicide. And Ally, you said that you saw the *Olympus* next to the *Titan* that day too?'

'I didn't see it myself, but Theo's friend mentioned it over the radio,' Ally confirmed. She sighed and ran her hands through her hair. 'Actually, I think it's time that I brought everyone up to speed on something.'

'What do you mean, Ally?' CeCe asked sharply.

'Do you remember that Merry's coordinates led to Argideen House in West Cork?' Her sisters thought for a moment, then nodded. 'Well, even though the house is long abandoned, it belongs to the Eszu family. Jack found out when he was looking into it on our behalf.'

There was a silence as the women tried to process the significance of the connection. 'What does that mean?' asked Star eventually.

'I honestly don't know yet. But one thing is clear—with Zed, Argideen House and the presence of the *Olympus* on the day of Pa's death...the relationship between Pa and Kreeg is the key to understanding everything.'

'Agreed,' sniffed Maia.

'I'll round up the others and check where they've read up to in the diary. Then we can discuss the connection over a couple of bottles of rosé.'

'Good idea, Ally,' nodded Star. 'There's so much of the story we still don't know. Where Pa came from, why Kreeg believes he murdered his mother...the diamond...'

'We can only hope that things become clearer as we all read on,' Ally said, putting a hand on Star's shoulder.

18

Georg Hoffman swirled the whisky in his hand and focused on the clink of the ice in his glass. From the upper sky lounge, he looked across the Mediterranean Sea at the Italian coastline, which burnt a bright gold in the setting sun. He could just make out Naples, and beyond that, the ancient city of Pompeii, its citizens frozen in time for thousands of years. He thought it an apt metaphor for this trip—as the events of the past were still somehow shaping the present.

Georg considered the last twelve months. What a whirlwind they had been for the D'Aplièse sisters. Each one had, without exception, handled the truth of their past with such maturity and wisdom.

'You would be so proud,' he said to the empty room.

The last few weeks in particular had been sleepless. The phone calls he had received with constant updates of 'the situation' were enormously distressing. Although he was attempting to deal with it as best he could, once more, Georg was torn between the lawyer in him, duty-bound to fulfil the wishes of his client, and the human being, who loved this family as his own. There was a tap on the sky lounge door. Georg turned to see Ma poking her head around the frame.

'I just wanted to check on you, *chéri*. Are you coping?' she asked.

'Yes—thank you. Please come in, Marina. Will you join me in a drink?'

She closed the door softly behind her. 'You know, Georg, on this occasion, I think I will.' He reached for the decanter, and duly poured his old friend a glass.

'This was his. A Macallan 1926. In fact, I do not doubt that the last hand to touch this decanter was his.' He handed the drink to her.

'Thank you. Yes, I remember him saying that he developed quite a taste for the local drams after spending that time in Scotland.' Marina took a delicate sip, and felt the warm, mellow liquid travel down her throat and into her stomach. 'Do you think the girls have reached that point in the diary yet?'

'I am unsure. How do you think they will receive it all, Marina?'

'It is difficult to predict. Some may find certain elements of his story easier to digest than others. But I am simply glad that, for once, we will all be in complete accord.'

'Yes.'

'May I ask for the latest news?' Marina looked at Georg searchingly.

'There is nothing beyond what I told you this morning. Things are deteriorating quickly. There is not long left.'

Marina crossed herself. 'Whatever happens, you must not blame yourself, Georg. You have acted honourably.' She placed a hand on his.

'Thank you, Marina. That means a great deal coming from you. We have been through so much together over the years. I just feel I owe it to him to get this *right*.'

'I know you will, Georg, whatever you choose. I fear it is not often said, but Atlas would be enormously proud of you, too. And your sister, of course. I am sorry not to have asked…how is she coping with it all?'

'She is finding it difficult, as anyone would in such circumstances.'

'I can only imagine.' Marina looked out to the ocean. 'He always loved this coastline.' Georg did not respond, and Marina looked up at her friend to see tears in his eyes.

'Oh *chéri*, please do not cry. It breaks my heart.'

'I owe him everything, Marina. Everything.'

'As do I. I've always meant to ask…when Atlas found you two on the shores of Lake Geneva, did you ever wonder if he'd turn you in to the authorities?'

Georg lifted the decanter and replenished his glass. 'Of course. We were just a pair of terrified children. But he himself had fled persecution.' He sipped his whisky slowly. 'Atlas was so kind to us.'

'You have repaid him well, Georg. You have given your life to his service.'

'It was the least I could do, Marina. Without him, I would not have a life.'

Marina had emptied her glass too, and Georg refilled it. 'Thank you. How long does your sister anticipate is left?'

Georg shrugged. 'Only days.'

'Will that influence your decision, Georg? About—'

'Perhaps.' He cut her off. 'I confess, finding Merry and bringing her aboard the *Titan* just in time for it to set sail might determine my course of action.'

'It seems only fitting. Perhaps it is a sign from above.'

'As so much of his world has always been.'

There was another knock on the door, and Merry appeared. 'Hello, you two. How are you getting on?'

'Merry! Yes, well, thank you,' Ma replied. 'More importantly, how are you, *chérie*?'

'Oh, grand, thanks. The diary is a fascinating read. Atlas had quite the way with words, didn't he? For a boy so young, he's incredibly eloquent.'

'He was always linguistically gifted.' Ma smiled.

'I just wanted to ask about this Kreeg Eszu chap. He's only really got a brief mention so far, but Jack has told me that Argideen House was owned by his family. Could you tell me a bit more about how that came to be?'

Ma looked up to Georg, who polished off his whisky in a single gulp. 'Ah, yes. I imagine you must be very curious about that connection.' Merry noted the steely way Ma was staring at Georg. 'But to tell you the truth, Merry, we do not know.'

'Oh. Really?'

'Yes. I suppose it is better to tell you that now than for you to read the entire contents of the diary and be disappointed.'

'Right. Well, that's more than a little annoying.'

'Perhaps we will find out one day. Or perhaps it is mere coincidence, Merry,' Georg lied.

Merry wrinkled her nose and tutted sharply. 'Ah, yes, you're absolutely right. I'm sure I'm overthinking it. After all, it's a very popular Irish name. Sure, there's thousands of Murphys, O'Briens and Eszus,' she retorted. Merry placed her hands on her hips and raised her eyebrows at Georg, causing him to take out his pocket square to dab his brow. 'Now, I'd like to make a call to Dublin, if that's possible, to update Ambrose on everything. I can hardly believe it's been less than twenty-four hours since I last saw him. It feels like a lifetime since then.'

'I am inclined to agree, yes,' replied Georg. 'There is a satellite phone in the office. Most of the staff are familiar with its operation. Marina, would you mind accompanying Merry?'

'Of course not. Come along, *chérie*. Afterwards, shall we perhaps enjoy a glass of wine on the aft deck before dinner?'

The ladies left the sky lounge and Georg was alone once again. He sighed heavily. It was regrettable that he had just lied to Atlas's daughter. Perhaps he should have come out with the whole truth then and there, which would certainly have eased the enormous burden he felt he was carrying. But, of course, it was not what his employer would want. Georg's pocket vibrated, and he hurriedly fumbled to retrieve his phone. Although it displayed *Unknown Number*, he knew exactly who was on the other end of the line. Inhaling deeply, he accepted the call.

'Pleione,' said Georg.

'Orion,' came the reply.

These were the words required by both parties so that each knew it was safe to talk.

Georg steeled himself for the evening update.

19

Ally tossed and turned in her hot cabin. Dinner had been uneasy, with each of the sisters independently struggling to understand the gravity of what they had read earlier. Floriano and Chrissie had done a good job of filling any silences, and Rory and Valentina had entertained the table with their charming developing friendship. Nonetheless, the atmosphere was noticeably tense, which was hardly a surprise given the circumstances. Ally had caught Jack's eye a few times as they ate, but he had looked away to avoid any awkwardness. She wished she'd addressed the 'Bear situation' in the cabin earlier, but had been too nervous. She felt stupid. The longer it went unspoken, the stranger it surely seemed to Jack.

Ally's phone buzzed, and she saw that she had a new voicemail. Reception was patchy out at sea, but clearly Hans had anchored them within reach of a local mast. She dialled her message service.

'Hello, Ally. It's Celia here…' Theo's mother's voice crackled on the recording. 'I hope you're well, my darling, and little Bear! I'm so looking forward to seeing the pair of you again in London. Do let me know if you have any plans to come over. If not, I shall pack my thermals and make my way to Norway! Listen, I know that you're on your cruise in honour of your wonderful pa… So I just wanted to give you a call to let you know I'm thinking of you, dear. And I'm sure that wherever he is, Theo is smiling down on you, too. Sending lots of love to you, darling. Bye.'

Ally put the phone down, and a fresh wave of guilt washed over her. Celia Falys-Kings's voice was so full of genuine affecttion. Yes, she had feelings for Jack, but shuddered at the thought of disrespecting Bear's father's memory.

'I'm sorry, Theo,' she whispered.

Even though her sisters were cheering her on, Ally reflected on what others might think—what would her brother Thom's opinion be if she and Jack ever…? It wasn't exactly a great look to snag a new boyfriend less than one year after your partner had died. In addition to that, the last thing she wished to do was to upset Merry, who must have been finding this whole experience surreal enough, without her new adopted sister being inappropriately affectionate towards her own son.

'Oh God.' Ally sighed.

'Ally? Are you awake?' whispered a voice from outside her cabin door. She tiptoed over and gently opened it. Tiggy stood there, in her *Titan* robe. 'Hi! Sorry, I didn't want to knock and risk waking Bear.'

'Oh, don't worry about it. He's out for the count. Would you like to come in?'

'Thank you.' Tiggy had an uncanny ability to glide into rooms, like a graceful, elegant spirit. It was a light, ethereal quality which Ally had always admired. 'I just wanted to check something, as I zoned out a little at dinner. Did we agree to read another one hundred pages of the diary by tomorrow lunchtime?'

'Yes, that's right. Then we're going to regroup and discuss.'

'Lovely, sounds like a plan. Thanks, Ally.' Tiggy turned towards the door, but paused by Bear's cot. She looked down at her sleeping nephew. 'Little Bear. Hard to believe that it was only a few months ago in a cave in Granada when you decided to surprise us all…particularly your mummy!' she whispered.

Ally smiled at the memory. 'You know, I don't think Charlie will ever be quite the same after watching Angelina that night. Five years of medical school were no substitute for a *bruja* and her knowledge when Bear decided to appear so suddenly.'

'Well, he shouldn't be too downhearted. There's only so

much a *bruja* can do at the end of the day… I'm sure you were grateful for the painkillers he prescribed you afterwards!' Tiggy gave her sister a wink. Then she looked back down at Bear. 'He says to look at the letter, by the way.'

'I'm sorry?'

'He wants you to look at the letter.' Tiggy gave Ally a wide smile.

'Who? Bear? What do you mean? I…'

'I'm not sure. I hope that's helpful. I'm off to bed. Night, Ally.' Tiggy embraced her sister and headed for the door.

Once it was shut, Ally's heart skipped a beat. Tiggy could only have been referring to one thing. She walked over to her suitcase and opened a zip pocket in the lining. From within, she retrieved the only letter in her possession. It was Theo's, of course, which she carried with her everywhere. This was not information Ally shared around, and nobody else had ever laid eyes on it. Trembling a little, she slowly opened the envelope, and her eyes skipped down to Theo's penultimate paragraph, like they always did.

And if by any chance you get to read this, look up at the stars, and know I am looking down on you. And probably having a beer with your pa, as I hear all about your childhood habits.

My Ally—Alcyone—you have no idea what joy you've brought me.

Be HAPPY! That is your gift.

Theo xxx

The image of Theo and Pa sharing a drink and a smile brought Ally an enormous amount of happiness. She knew how much her father would have approved of him, and hoped very much that they had been able to meet in another life. Now, what was it that Tiggy had said?

He wants you to read the letter.

Ally stared down at the only capitalised word on the page, which her eye was drawn to like a magnet.

Be HAPPY!

A lump arrived in Ally's throat. She walked over to the cabin window and bent her knees so that she could look up to the stars.

'Thank you, Theo. Give Pa a hug from me.' She placed the letter safely back in the zip lining of her suitcase, and climbed into bed. Ally knew immediately that trying to sleep would prove futile, since her mind was more crowded than the Grand Plaza in Oslo. She grabbed her phone once more and sent Jack a text.

Thanks for looking after Bear earlier. Sleep well! x

She received a response almost immediately:

Pleasure Al! You too x

She eyed the pages of the diary on the dresser. Inside were answers. The agreement had been that the sisters would read another hundred pages in the morning, but knowing there were revelations just inches away, she decided she would read on.

The Diary of Atlas

1936–40

20

Leipzig, Germany

The casual reader, should they find themselves engrossed in these pages, may wonder why there is no diary entry recorded for over six years, and how it has come to be that the little boy who was a *citoyen de Paris* is now on the cusp of adulthood in a new European city. The tale is a turbulent one. In truth, during the past six years, I wrote pages for my diary often. The contents were probably too sentimental for some literary tastes, but stood as a record of the happiness I experienced over the course of my time in France. It is my unfortunate duty to report that the majority of the pages were left in the Landowski household, when I was forced to make an unplanned, untimely exit, due to circumstances that arose as a result of my grave mistake: opening my mouth and talking.

Although, as I write, it is 1936 and I am eighteen years old, I appreciate that it would be lax of me to offer an incomplete story. Allow me to explain. From 1930 to 1933, life in Paris continued for me in much the same pattern as it had for the previous two years: I assisted Monsieur Landowski and Monsieur Brouilly in the atelier, and attended my lessons with Monsieur Ivan at the *conservatoire*, as did Elle. As we both grew older, we were awarded more and more freedom by our respective keepers—Madame Gagnon in Elle's case, and Evelyn in my own. We spent halcyon mornings discovering coffee in Parisian cafes, and in the evenings, we would wander the streets, each time finding some new architectural detail which would provide enchantment and wonder. My decision to speak that Christmas Day had truly allowed my relationship with Elle to flourish…who could have predicted? It was my great privilege to read to *her* on our picnic luncheons, and to seek her opinions on every facet of my fast-improving life. Ironically, it would be the same decision that would lead to my undoing.

One morning in early 1933, whilst we were in the workshop, Monsieur Landowski made an announcement: 'Gentlemen! I have some news to impart. It is not of an insignificant nature, so listen carefully. Our journey together is coming to an end.'

'Monsieur Landowski?' Brouilly said, the colour draining from his face. After all, he had made the decision to leave Rio to pursue his career in Paris.

'As of this morning, I have been offered the position of Director at the French Academy in Rome.' Brouilly did not respond. I found myself feeling similarly anxious, for Monsieur Landowski provided me with shelter, food and, of course, generously paid for my tuition at the conservatory. 'Monsieur Brouilly, have you nothing to say?'

'Apologies, monsieur. Congratulations. They have made a fine choice.' I joined Brouilly's praise by offering a wide (if artificial) grin, and a solo round of applause.

'Thank you, gentlemen. Imagine. Me! With an office! And a salary!'

'The world will miss your talent, monsieur,' Brouilly said, with genuine sadness.

'Oh, don't be ridiculous, Brouilly. I shall still sculpt. I will always sculpt! The main motivation for taking the position is…well, I suppose you could say that it is the fault of our young friend here.' Landowski gestured to me, and registered my shock. 'What I mean to say is that I have derived a great deal of pleasure, both artistic and personal, from seeing Bo progress during these last few years. Monsieur Ivan says that he is well on his way to becoming a virtuoso cellist. All this, from a child who could hardly stand when we first met. In truth, I am a little jealous of your teacher, Bo! Although I have contributed financially, I wish I could have been the one to nurture your artistic gifts. As such, it is my hope that at the French Academy, I will be able to develop the talent of other young people in my own field.'

My artificial smile had turned into something genuine.

'That's a very beautiful sentiment, monsieur,' Brouilly said glumly.

'Oh Brouilly! Don't look so downcast, man!' Landowski walked over to his assistant and placed a hand on his shoulder. 'Do you really think that I would leave you directionless? Before accepting the position, I made some arrangements with our colleague Monsieur Blanchet at the École des Beaux-Arts. You will take up a position as a junior teacher there when I leave for Rome in one week.'

'Really, Monsieur?' Brouilly's eyes widened.

'Yes. Blanchet was more than happy to accept my letter of recommendation. It is a fine institution, and you will be a valuable asset. They'll certainly pay you a great deal more than I do, at the very least. Enjoy the regular income whilst you work on your own career.'

'Thank you, Monsieur Landowski, thank you. I will never forget what you have done for me.' Brouilly shook his teacher's hand vigorously.

'It is deserved. After all, I could not have completed the *Cristo* without you...' After shaking Brouilly's hand, Landowski held it steady and examined it, then gave him a wink. 'Your work will live on forever.' Next he turned to me. 'Young Bo! Your life will continue largely unchanged. I have no plans to sell the house here, and of course we will be back for summer breaks, and Christmas too. Most of the staff will be forced to take up new positions...but Evelyn will remain. Is this agreeable to you?' I nodded. 'Good! Then I do believe that it is tradition to celebrate change with a bottle of champagne...'

Within seven days, the Landowski family was packed and ready to leave for their new life in Rome. I believe I would have been a great deal more emotional about their imminent departure had it not been for Elle. As long as she remained, I felt invincible.

As Monsieur Landowski had promised, my life was hardly

altered, save for me spending more time with Evelyn, who was now solely responsible for the upkeep of the household. I would correspond via letter with Monsieur Landowski often. He would tell me the stories of the young *artistes* who passed through his doors at the French Academy, and give me updates on the family:

Marcel is working furiously on his piano playing. As you know, he hopes to attend the conservatoire in the next two years… I think that he has a good chance. I do not doubt that your presence has provided the motivation required for him to achieve his dreams!

I must say, it was not altogether unpleasant to have the entire household to myself, with completely free access to the library…and to the kitchen. I was even bold enough to hold brief conversations with Evelyn. When I had eventually opened my mouth to her, she cried. Looking back now, I lived in a dream-like state, entranced by the intoxicating potion of Elle, music, and what had begun to feel like total security.

How naive I was.

The beginning of the end started in the autumn of 1935.

Elle and I sat in a cafe on the Rue Jean-de-la-Fontaine. As Elle was now older than eighteen, she had left the *Apprentis d'Auteuil*, and inhabited a dark, dingy room in the attic of a friend of Madame Gagnon's. She made a meagre wage from cleaning for the owner—Madame Dupont—but accepted it, as the arrangement meant she could still attend her bi-weekly tuition at the *conservatoire*. I leant back in my metal chair and I looked at Elle, who was sat staring blankly into her coffee. Clearly something was bothering her.

'Is everything all right, my love?' I asked.

'Yes, fine…it's just that Monsieur Toussaint shouted at me during our last lesson.'

I gave her a warm smile. 'As you know, that's not unusual at the *conservatoire*.'

Elle shrugged. 'I know. But to be quite honest, I don't think Toussaint has ever really liked me. He believes himself to be above tutoring a novice teenage girl. He is right, of course. But these last few weeks, as he has been attempting to improve my sight reading, his venom has been particularly poisonous.'

'Don't worry about that. I'm sure he is just frustrated that you haven't learnt *the proper way*. I had a similar experience with Monsieur Ivan,' I placated her.

'You're right. He did say something odd during the outburst, though.'

'What was it?' I asked.

'He said that if I wasn't the spawn of "the Great Russian", he'd force me to stay up all night and study.' My blood ran a little cold. 'I asked him what he meant by the "Great Russian" comment, and he laughed, saying that *surely* I didn't think that I was in his classroom on merit alone. I continued to press him, and he became enraged, saying that he didn't have time to teach children, and that Rachmaninoff should climb down from his throne and do it himself.'

'Ah,' I stuttered.

Elle frowned. 'I said that I didn't understand, and he laughed and told me that he was going to write to the Great Russian to tell him his daughter was useless. Then Monsieur Ivan appeared, and asked to speak to Toussaint in the corridor. They stepped outside, talked for a while, then he returned and dismissed me.' Elle looked at me quizzically. 'What do you think he meant by that reference to Rachmaninoff?'

I slowly took a sip of my English Breakfast Tea. 'I may be able to shed a little light on the situation.'

She looked confused. 'What do you mean, Bo?' I sighed and explained the fiction which Monsieur Ivan had invented. When I had done so, Elle looked understandably crestfallen. 'So...I would not have gained a place at the conservatory had it been based on talent alone?'

'That's not it at all. Monsieur Ivan said that you were Rachmaninoff's daughter so you would be granted an audition. The rest, I assure you, was achieved through your musical prowess.'

'They all think I am Rachmaninoff's abandoned daughter?'

'Well, Toussaint and Moulin do. Please, try not to worry. I will speak to Monsieur Ivan at our next lesson and get his account of the situation.'

I never had the chance to speak to Monsieur Ivan. A few nights later, I was woken by a crash as I slept in the Landowski home. My eyes shot open, and I threw the covers from my body. Despite my new life of safety, I was glad to learn that, at least on a subconscious level, my senses remained on high alert. My former existence in the frozen wastelands ensured that I always 'slept with one eye open', as my father used to term it.

The clock on my desk showed that it was just past two a.m. Now fully awake, I heard a second distinct sound from the bowels of the house—a door opening.

I was not alone. Looking out of the window and seeing no light in Evelyn's cottage, there was no use comforting myself with the idea that she had decided to enter the main household at this time of night. I padded over to my bedroom door as softly as I possibly could, and turned the handle with precision. Thankfully, it opened silently. Listening closely, I heard the sound of footsteps creaking on the wooden floorboards below. Instinctively, I felt for the pouch around my neck.

Was it him? Had he somehow found me?

This was the moment I had feared.

Despite the terror now coursing through my body, I knew that I had one tactical advantage over the intruder. I knew the Landowski house well, and based on the crashes and creaks, I had to assume the intruder did not. I contemplated hiding, but knew that would be of little use—it was the middle of the night, and they might simply keep searching until I was found. I thought of running, too—simply racing down to the doorway and sprinting into the night. If it *was* him, I doubted that the few miles of distance I would be able to put between us tonight would be enough to protect me. Regrettably, I concluded that offensive action was necessary.

I slowly walked over to the top of the stairs, and listened for the footsteps below. It seemed that the intruder was methodically searching the house, as if looking for something. Or, more likely, someone—me. Eventually, the footsteps progressed towards the east wing of the house—the drawing room and the library—and I took my chance. Maintaining my light-footedness, I crept down the stairs to the ground floor, and headed in the opposite direction. I made straight for the atelier, and Monsieur Landowski's chisels. Picking up the sharpest of the tools, I walked back into the hallway, staying close to the walls to avoid being caught in the moonlight. Once I had reached the staircase again, I stopped to listen. There was silence. Where were they? I took another step forward into the corridor, and a great force whipped me off my feet and into the air. The intruder had grabbed me from behind in an attempt to lock my arms together. I kicked back at my assailant as hard as I could, aiming for the knees. The subsequent yelp told me I had hit my target. The intruder buckled and released their grip as we both tumbled to the floor. I dropped the chisel in the struggle, and scrambled around in a desperate attempt to find it. During those few seconds, the assailant leapt to their feet and hurtled down the corridor towards the living room. Thankfully, my hand brushed the chisel and, grasping it, I stumbled down the corridor after them.

'Show yourself!' I shouted, not able to control the rage in my voice. The drawing room was still, and I could only make out shapes of furniture in the moonlight.

'You were never a coward, Kreeg. Let us see each other.' The room remained eerily silent. 'You know, I do not wish to fight you. I never have. I carry this chisel only so that I might defend myself from you. There are things you do not understand...things that I long to tell you. Please, come out and I'll explain everything.' Still nothing. 'I didn't kill her, Kreeg. You must believe me.' Tears began to form in my eyes. 'How could you ever think that I would be capable of such an act? We were friends. We were brothers.' I wiped the tears from my eyes, and tried to remain focused. 'I only ran that day because I knew you would kill me. I was just a little boy, Kreeg, as were you. Now we are young men and should settle this as such.' I offered one final statement which I hoped would tempt him out of hiding. 'I have the diamond. I would never sell it, as you assumed. I can give it to you now. It hangs from a leather pouch that I keep around my neck. Simply show yourself and we will make the transaction. Then you can leave and we need never see one another again, if that is your choice.'

There was a creak from behind the armoire in the corner of the room. I knew that the mention of the precious stone would be enough to lure him out of hiding.

'A diamond, you say? So that's what you keep in that pouch.'

I knew the voice. But it was not Kreeg's. A figure emerged, and in the gloom, I saw a face.

'Monsieur Toussaint?'

'You know, for a boy who is apparently unable to speak, you are most eloquent.'

'What are you doing here? What do you want?'

'I don't like being scammed, boy. The Conservatoire de Paris is the greatest musical institution in the world, not a nursery. As you very well know, that little Russian rat Ivan led us to believe that your girlfriend was the lovechild of Rachmaninoff. When I threatened to write to him, Ivan came clean and said he had lied.' He took a step towards me. 'I asked him about you. He said that you were the ward of Paul Landowski...who I know has taken a position in Rome. So, as penance for swindling me, I thought I'd come and help myself to a couple of Landowski's vases. But now, I know there's something much more valuable.' He took another step.

'You don't understand.'

'In fact, there are two things of value in this room, boy. The diamond, which I now know hangs around your neck...and you.'

I hesitated. 'Me?'

'It stands to reason that this "Kreeg" you mention would be quite eager to know your whereabouts, given the situation you have just readily revealed to me. I'm sure that he'd pay handsomely for information about you.'

'He's little older than me, Toussaint. He has no money. And if he finds out you stole the diamond from me, he'll kill you too.'

Toussaint snorted. 'There are deals that can be done, boy. Perhaps if I simply end your life now and return the diamond to young Mister Kreeg, we can find a way to split the rewards...' Toussaint slurred his words. He was clearly drunk.

'Monsieur, please. You are a flautist. Not a murderer!' I

pleaded.

'Boy, with that diamond in my possession, I can be anything I want to be. Now, come here!'

Toussaint leapt at me, but I had anticipated his manoeuvre and jumped onto the sofa. With my height advantage, I leapt onto his back. But the tutor was surprisingly strong, and was able to swing around so both of us crashed to the floor. I absorbed his full weight and was badly winded as a result. Seizing his opportunity, Toussaint spun around and ripped the pouch from my neck. He threw it to the side before placing his hands around my neck.

I remember feeling oddly peaceful as the life force slowly began to leave my body. There was no immediate panic…until an image of Elle entered my head, and I was immediately filled with the urge to fight. Summoning every ounce of strength in me, I took the chisel in my hand and forced it into Toussaint's arm.

'Argh!' he cried, removing his hands from my neck. I seized my opportunity and reclaimed the pouch, shoving it into my pocket.

Suddenly, the room was flooded with light, and a loud scream came from the doorway. I wheeled round to see Evelyn at the door, with one hand on the light switch and the other over her mouth. Toussaint, still cradling his arm, stood up and tried to conceal his face by hunching himself over. Then he barrelled past Evelyn and sprinted out of the front door.

'Bo! What's going on? Oh, my dear Lord, is that blood on the floor?' I nodded. 'Are you all right?' I nodded once more through heavy breaths. Evelyn knelt by my side and was frantically searching for any wounds. 'You will speak to me. Who was that man? Why was he here?' I looked back at her, stunned. 'Bo, please. Tell me everything.'

I explained the situation with as much urgency as I could muster.

'*Mon Dieu*, Bo. Do you have this diamond?' I patted my pocket. 'Good. But you are not safe here now. He may return, and I do not know who with. It is time to leave.'

'Leave? Where?'

'Monsieur Brouilly's apartment in Montparnasse. He will take you in and you will be safe there until I can think of a solution.'

'I'm worried that Toussaint will go to Elle. He's her tutor. It is possible he knows where she lives.'

Evelyn closed her eyes and nodded. 'I think you are right to be concerned. You must go to her first.'

'But Evelyn, what about you? What if Toussaint does come back here?'

'Let him come. I don't think he wants anything to do with me. I will send for Louis tomorrow, and he will come to stay here. Now hurry up. You can make it to Elle on the Rue Riquet in under an hour if you jog. Go upstairs and pack some clothes—only the essentials. I will write down the address of Monsieur Brouilly.' I scarpered upstairs and shoved some shirts and underwear into my leather satchel.

I took Brouilly's address from Evelyn, and after a long hug, ran out into the night.

I arrived at Elle's lodgings on the Rue Riquet drenched in sweat and panting after my seven-mile journey. Her window was at the very top of the house, and I cursed myself for failing to plan this far ahead. I had to resort to gathering some small pebbles from the roadside and launching them at the attic pane. It was a risky strategy, but I had little choice. After a minute or two, it yielded a result, and Elle's sleepy face appeared.

'Bo?' she mouthed to me. I gestured for her to come downstairs. She nodded.

After a few moments, the front door opened quietly, and Elle stood before me in her white nightdress. She embraced me. 'What's happening, Bo?'

'I will explain everything once we're safe…but now I need you to come with me.'

Her face dropped. 'Is it *him*?' she asked, fear in her eyes.

'Not exactly. But I need you to pack a few clothes and come back down. We're going to Monsieur Brouilly's apartment.'

No further explanation was needed. Within minutes Elle had returned and we quietly navigated through the back streets to Montparnasse. Thankfully, finding Laurent's address proved a relatively easy task, because his window was adorned with pink orchids…which I knew to be the national flower of Brazil. Several rings on the doorbell produced a bleary-eyed Brouilly, who, once he had registered that it was I on his doorstep, welcomed us in. He graciously brewed a strong pot of coffee, and I relayed the night's events to both him and Elle.

'My God! My God!' Brouilly kept saying. 'You are an enigma, Bo. The silent boy. Look how he talks now. My God!'

Elle held my hand, and her presence provided more comfort than I could truly express. 'Thank you for coming for me,' she said.

'If only I hadn't talked, Elle. I assumed it was Kreeg. I was trying to reason with someone who wasn't even in the room…'

'Of course you assumed that. I would have done exactly the same.'

I paused to look around Brouilly's cramped apartment. A dim lamp served to illuminate his collection of semi-finished projects and half-baked ideas. Sculptures, canvases and tools literally littered the place. The chaos didn't help my mental state, and I put my head in my hands. 'If only I hadn't woken up! Toussaint would have taken his vases and been on his way. I probably would have been none the wiser.'

'I wish that Bel could hear you speak,' Brouilly said melancholically.

I looked at him. Even after what I had just described, his mind was elsewhere. 'Have you had any further contact, Monsieur Brouilly?' I asked.

My former atelier partner had a haunted look on his face. 'No.'

Eventually, Brouilly brought through some blankets. I insisted that Elle slept on the small sofa, and I placed a pillow on the floor. Elle dropped her hand down and I held it before exhaustion took a hold of me and I drifted off to sleep.

The doorbell rang early the next morning, and Brouilly opened the door to Evelyn.

'My dears, it is good to see you.' I raced over and hugged her tightly. 'Hello, Elle. I am glad you are safe. I have contacted the gendarmerie.'

'The gendarmerie?' I said, horrified.

'Yes, Bo. Do not forget that my employer's house was broken in to last night, not to mention the small matter of Elle's drunken tutor trying to kill you. Toussaint needs to be apprehended and dealt with. After all, we cannot have a raving lunatic return to the Conservatoire de Paris to tutor vulnerable young people.'

'But Evelyn, the gendarmerie will want to speak to me! They'll have questions about the diamond. You don't understand, I can't—'

'I do understand, Bo, perfectly well.' She took my hand. 'I have always understood, ever since that little boy knocked on my door for the very first time. You have known more terror in your life than any one human should experience, from forces far beyond the comprehension of a simple woman such as I. So yes, whilst the gendarmerie will wish to speak with you as a matter of urgency, luckily I do not have the faintest idea of where you are.' She gave me a wink.

Elle spoke next. 'When the police pick up Toussaint, he'll twist the story and tell them about Bo's outburst.' She looked at me with sorrow. 'Remember, last night you mentioned…killing a woman.'

I clenched my fists in frustration. 'No! I said that I could *never* have killed a woman!'

Elle put a comforting hand on my back. 'I sincerely doubt that's what Toussaint will say. And remember, Bo, you did stab him with a chisel.' I saw Brouilly's eyes widen.

'Only in self-defence,' I replied honestly.

'I know that. But you have no paperwork, and therefore Toussaint will have the advantage.'

I could feel tears stinging my eyes. 'I will have to run again. As you all know, I am well practised in it. After all, I need to finish the search for my father. If he is anywhere, it will be in Switzerland. I will make for the border. Elle, I—'

'Will be accompanied by me,' she interrupted me.

I shook my head vigorously. 'No, you don't understand. You have witnessed what an attachment to me entails. I cannot allow you to come with me.'

Elle took my hand. 'Bo, until I met you, my existence was sad and monotonous. You changed everything. If you are leaving, then I am too.' She hugged me. Evelyn clasped her hand to her chest, and I saw Brouilly throw his head back in an attempt to assuage any tears.

'Please,' I begged. 'I need you safe.'

Laurent snapped. 'For God's sake, Bo, will you listen to her?' He threw his hands up in frustration. 'Do you not realise that love is all there is? Take it from one who knows. This young woman worships the ground you walk on, and clearly you reciprocate. Do not make the same mistakes that I have, Bo. Life is short. Live for love, and nothing else.'

I looked into Elle's eyes, and knew that the matter required no further contemplation. 'Very well. We will make our way to the border when night falls this evening.'

'Borders this and borders that!' Evelyn exclaimed. 'For goodness' sake, Bo, do you really think that your Evelyn would allow you to be resigned to such a fate?'

I looked at her, confused. 'I do not understand.'

She sighed. 'Ever since the day you arrived in Paris, Monsieur Landowski has known that you were running from something, and that you chose not to speak because you were scared. As a consequence, he was shrewd enough to know that at some stage, you might need to leave Paris. He resolved to help you, and has made plans accordingly.' Evelyn presented me with a cream envelope. 'I am pleased to tell you that as of this morning, Bo, you are the winner of the esteemed *Prix Blumenthal.*'

My jaw dropped.

'What's that, Evelyn?' Elle asked.

'Do you remember, Bo?' She looked at me, and I took my cue.

'It is a prize awarded by the American philanthropist Florence Blumenthal to a young artist or musician. Monsieur Landowski is a judge. But Evelyn, I don't understand… How is it that I have come to win the prize?'

'Monsieur Landowski made arrangements with Florence in 1930, shortly before her death. Apparently, Miss Florence was very moved by your story, and it was agreed that if you were to face jeopardy here in Paris, you would be awarded the prize, and the subsequent funds used to ensure your safety.'

I was in a state of disbelief.

'Congratulations, Bo,' Elle said warmly.

'Apologies,' Evelyn smiled. 'I should have mentioned that the prize will be shared.'

'I'm sorry?' Elle queried.

'You are also a recipient of the *Prix Blumenthal*. Monsieur Landowski ensured that both of you would be looked after in the event of a disaster.'

'Oh my goodness,' Elle said, in a state of shock. I took her hand, a grin creeping onto my face despite everything.

'Of course, you'll both be glad to know that a condition of the prize is that you must continue your instrumental studies. You have been awarded it for your musicianship after all.'

'How will that work, Evelyn?' I asked.

'Arrangements will be made for you to transfer from the Conservatoire de Paris to another European conservatory. Luckily Monsieur Landowski is not short of contacts, and I am waiting to hear back from him regarding instructions for your onward journey.'

'That man with the ridiculous moustache is quite brilliant,' stammered Brouilly.

'He is, Laurent. I telegrammed him this morning. He is working out a plan and will inform me of his decision later.'

I was simply lost for words. 'Evelyn, I don't know what to say…'

She chuckled. 'Wasn't that always your problem, young master Bo?' I hugged her again.

'Thank you, Evelyn. Thank you for everything.'

She whispered in my ear. 'Keep her close, Bo. She is a gift from the stars.' When I pulled away, I saw her brown eyes were glistening. 'Now!' Evelyn clapped her hands together, recovering herself. I must return home and await my telegram from Monsieur Landowski. When I come back, I will bring your instruments. Elle, I wonder whether you might pen a note for Madame Dupont confirming that I am your aunt and have permission to pick up some of your possessions.'

'Good idea.' Elle went to grab a piece of paper from Brouilly's desk and began to scribble.

'Speaking of which, if there are any final arrangements that either of you wish to make before leaving Paris, now is the time. Goodbye, *mes chéris*.' With that, Evelyn turned and left the apartment.

The three of us who remained stood in silence for a moment, as the whirlwind began to calm. Eventually, I turned to Elle. 'We must write letters. There are few things more hurtful than when someone disappears from your life without explanation. I will write to Monsieur Ivan.'

Elle nodded. 'And I to Madame Gagnon, I suppose.'

I wished to keep my letter to Monsieur Ivan brief, but heartfelt.

Dear Monsieur Ivan,

I hope that Evelyn has been in touch with you, and that this letter finds you safely. I regret that I will not be able to attend Tuesday's lesson. I wished to write to you to thank you for everything. Not only have you been a finer tutor than any young musician could ever wish for, you have been something far greater—the first true friend I believe I have ever had.

I hope that we may one day meet again. Failing that, I shall listen closely to all future recordings of Parisian symphony orchestras, and see if I can detect the distinct glide of your bow across the strings. Perhaps you might do the same, and this way, we shall always keep one another in our hearts.

I wish you to know that I hold you in no way responsible for the events that have unfortunately transpired. Without your ingenuity, and the...help of Monsieur Rachmaninoff, I know that it would not have been possible to grant Elle tuition. I am eternally grateful to you for giving us both a chance.

Finally, please remain vigilant of a certain flute teacher. He cannot be trusted. I wanted to give you this information, because, well...we émigrés must help one another, mustn't we?

Bo D'Aplièse

Evelyn returned in a taxi cab with our instruments later that evening. I went to help her unload them, but she put a hand out to stop me.

'Stay inside, Bo. You never know who might be watching.' She and Brouilly swiftly emptied the car, and Evelyn waved it off. 'I won't be staying long. I have the instructions from Monsieur Landowski. He has a colleague at the French Academy who is also a sculptor from Paris. His name is Pavel Rosenblum. The timing is fortuitous. His daughter, Karine, is about to start her first term at the Leipzig Conservatory. He was able to make some telephone calls, and you have both been accepted as undergraduates.'

'Leipzig? In Germany?' Elle asked nervously. I put an arm around her.

'You are correct, yes. Obviously, as undergraduates, it will probably be necessary for you to adjust your ages a little. I do not anticipate that this will be a problem—you both look older than you are.'

'When will we leave, Evelyn? And how will we travel to Germany?' I enquired.

'Do you remember that my son Louis works at the Peugeot factory?' I nodded. 'As luck would have it, he is delivering a new motor car to a client in Luxembourg tomorrow morning. He will drive you across the border, and from there on in it will be safe to make your way to Leipzig on trains. As for documentation, Bo, you will borrow some of Marcel's papers, and Elle, you will use Nadine's. As you are both young, I do not anticipate any close scrutiny. You must return them by post when you arrive in Germany.'

The thought of such kindness choked me. 'Do you know where we will live, Evelyn?'

'I am informed that you have lodgings in a district called Johannisgasse, organised through Monsieur Rosenblum. It is where Karine is staying. I don't have many details—all this has been organised in just one day—but apparently it is nice enough.'

I cycled through the remaining practical questions in my head. 'What about money?'

'My dears, you are the recipients of the *Prix Blumenthal*. I assure you, the financial remuneration will be adequate to sustain you during your three years of undergraduate study. Tuition will be paid, and bank accounts established…the *Prix* will see to it all. In the meantime, here is some money for train tickets and food.' She handed me a brown envelope. 'You will also find the address of your lodgings in there.'

I looked into Evelyn's gentle eyes. 'Evelyn, I will never be able to…' My voice cracked slightly. I had realised that this could be the last time I ever saw her, and my heart was breaking. Without saying a word, she gripped me tightly, and I buried my face in her coat.

'Thank you for being my *petit* companion, Bo. Remember, despite everything, there are more good people in the world than there are bad. I love you very much.' She pulled away and reached into her pocket. 'I have a telegram for you, from Monsieur Landowski.' I took it from her and placed it in my own pocket, doing my utmost to hold back the sobs. Evelyn inhaled and gathered herself. 'Elle! I am so sorry that your exit from Paris is filled with so much drama.' She embraced her. 'Look after him, won't you?'

'Always,' replied Elle.

'Good. Now, Louis will be here at six a.m. sharp. Do you have any letters?'

'Yes.' I sniffed, and handed her my note for Monsieur Ivan, and Elle her letter to Madame Gagnon.

'Rest assured, I shall deliver them safely. When everything settles down, I hope that we will meet again. I will try to write to you in Leipzig, depending on how intensely the gendarmerie intend to follow the events of last night. Be good, the pair of you. And travel safely.' This time, it was Evelyn's voice that faltered, and she hurried out of Brouilly's front door.

'Do you know, I don't think I have ever said more than a few words to Madame Evelyn,' Brouilly said. 'You are lucky to have had her in your life,' he said to me.

'I know,' I replied.

A sleepless night followed, and on the stroke of six, we heard the rumbling of an engine outside. Brouilly, though bleary-eyed, helped us to load our instruments into the shiny new Peugeot motor car.

'Good morning, Bo! What a pleasure to have such fine

company on this long drive.' My old acquaintance Louis gave me a grin, and my nerves were calmed.

Before stepping back inside, Brouilly put a hand on my shoulder. 'Bel knew you were worth saving. Please, keep her in your thoughts. You will be in mine.'

I shook his hand and climbed into the car. Soon, we were driving out of Paris and into the future. As I tried to get comfortable and catch some sleep, I felt a sharp sensation on my outer thigh. I remembered that I still had the telegram from Monsieur Landowski, which I had forgotten to open the previous evening:

'If you do not change direction, you may end up where you are going'—Laozi.

Bonne chance, boy.

21

I hope that I was able to give a decent overview of the circumstances that led to our flight from Paris last year. The journey to Leipzig was simple enough, and Evelyn and Monsieur Landowski have been as good as their word. The *Prix* pays for our tuition and accommodation, and provides an allowance for us to live whilst studying too. Sadly, I have had no direct contact with either of my friends since leaving Paris. However, on the night of my first solo performance at the Leipzig Conservatory, a large bunch of roses was sent anonymously to my dressing room, with a card reading *Regards from Rome*.

Our new life in Germany has proved to be a varied experience. Elle and I live in separate lodgings in Johannisgasse, with a coffee shop halfway between that has become a favourite haunt of ours over the past year. Unlike me, Elle has a roommate, which is standard practice for all the women here. Whether by chance, or by design, it is none other than Karine Rosenblum, and the pair have developed into the firmest of friends. Miss Rosenblum is the polar opposite to Elle in every conceivable way—so naturally they get along famously.

Karine is a true bohemian, opting to wear trousers and a French painter's jacket most days, in total opposition to Elle's conventional skirt, shirt and jumper. She has a mane of black, velvety hair that reminds me of a panther's coat, and her glittering dark eyes are offset by the palest of skin. We have spent many evenings being entertained by tales of her parents—especially her mother, who is apparently a Russian opera singer! Speaking of families, I haven't made mention of Monsieur Landowski, or anything else for that matter. It would only lead to questions I could not answer. I try to keep myself as quiet as I possibly can, and allow Elle to do the talking for both of us.

As far as Elle is concerned, there is little need to deviate from the truth. She has told Karine that she is an orphan, but had a music teacher in Paris who spotted her talent and put her forward for a scholarship. In terms of my own history, if anyone has asked, I simply say that I come from a small artistic family in Paris. I have found that generally suffices. Ironically, I have learnt with age that staying mute actually invites far more questions than talking does.

The tuition at the conservatory is outstanding. The sheer joy of dedicating full days to musical study, rather than my customary two afternoons per week, is unbounded. There was a swift decision made by the conservatory that I should focus only on the cello, for the staff feel that I am more gifted on the larger of my instruments. Nonetheless, I keep my violin safely stored under my bed, just as I did in Paris, and play it frequently to relax my mind. In truth, it has allowed me to rediscover my childlike joy for the instrument. As Elle says, I now have 'one for business, and one for pleasure'.

Here in Leipzig, we are treated to the whole spectrum of conservatory life—playing in orchestras, giving concerts, writing compositions… I exist largely in a dreamlike state. This is essential, as the reality around us is far more frightening than I ever considered.

In March of 1933, Adolf Hitler's Nazi Party gained power in Germany. To my shame, I knew little of the disgraceful ideologies of the man with the little moustache. Elle had naturally been paying closer attention to the growing movement, but only through articles in French newspapers, which were few and far between. It was Karine—herself Jewish—who informed us of the true political evil of Nazism. We were told that one of the first things Hitler had done in power was to pass a ruling that enabled the cabinet to enact laws without the consent of parliament. In effect, this gave Hitler dictatorial control of the nation, and totalitarianism had begun to take hold in Germany. The Nazis have dissolved all other political parties, abolished labour unions and are attempting to imprison anyone who opposes the regime. There are even dark rumours of camps where they place their enemies and subject them to torture beyond any capacity which could be defined as human.

Hitler has made no secret of his hatred for Elle's people. Apparently, he blames them for Germany's defeat during the Great War—a despicable sentiment which turns my stomach. As a result of one man's bigoted insanity, anti-Semitism is now official government policy. It seems that the majority of the country are willing to accept it, believing that Hitler will restore Germany's status as a global superpower.

As such, the conditions we live under here in Leipzig are tense, mainly due to the fact that the city's mayor, Carl Friedrich Goerdeler, is a staunch opponent of Hitler's ethos. None of us are quite sure how he is surviving at present—perhaps because his deputy, a diminutive little man called Haake, is an officious and obedient party member. As I write, Goerdeler is in Munich, meeting with Hitler's minions, where I do not doubt that he is being pressured to employ their anti-Semitic rhetoric here in Leipzig. Whilst Goerdeler is in power to protect us, the citizens of Leipzig feel relatively safe. But in truth, I do not know how long it can last.

My heart breaks each day to see the worry that is etched on Elle's face. It is not unusual to see SS officers roaming the streets here, and the Hitler Youth—the Nazi party's way of shoring up its future via indoctrination—are frequently paraded through the streets. Soon we will have a generation of citizens who accept racial hatred as normal.

It is growing increasingly likely that Elle and I will not be able to see out our undergraduate years at the Leipzig Conservatory. We have discussed returning to Paris—or perhaps somewhere else in France—but I worry that if Germany wishes to make war, it will reach Elle's home country too.

This evening, Elle and I are due to meet Karine for coffee

to discuss the situation, alongside her boyfriend—a Norwegian called Jens Halvorsen (although he is known as 'Pip' to his friends). As far as I am concerned, he is far too relaxed about the situation in this city. He has a belief that the Nazis won't touch students at the conservatory, claiming that, despite everything, Hitler is a supporter of music and culture. Karine is growing increasingly frustrated with his calls for calm.

22

It was him.

Kreeg Eszu.

I would know those penetrating green eyes anywhere.

How did he find me? Did he manage to track me to Paris, and did someone there talk? Toussaint, maybe? My mind is racing, and I am turning to my diary so that I can order my thoughts.

We met Pip and Karine in the cafe as planned, and conversation quickly turned to the political situation in Leipzig.

'Elle and Bo are worried too,' Karine had repeated to Pip. 'Elle is also Jewish, even if she doesn't look it. Lucky her,' she murmured.

'We think it must only be a matter of time before what is happening in Bavaria starts to happen here,' Elle said quietly.

Pip bristled. 'We must wait and see what the mayor can do whilst he is in Munich. But even if the worst happens, I'm sure they won't touch students at our school.' Karine shook her head and sighed. Pip turned his attention to me. 'How are you, Bo?' he asked.

'I am well enough,' I said.

'Where will you spend Christmas?'

I paused to consider. 'I...'

Before I could reply to Pip, I watched two SS officers enter the cafe, sauntering through in their distinctive grey uniforms, pistols sheathed in leather holsters around their waists. When I saw the face of the younger of the two men, I physically felt the blood drain from my face.

Although a decade older, Kreeg still possessed his strong jawline and laser-like eyes which sat above sharp cheekbones in olive-toned skin. He returned my gaze. As calmly as possible, I lowered my eyes and turned my face away. Eszu and his colleague sat at a table only a few feet from my own. The man who had vowed to kill me was within touching distance.

'We are not sure of our plans yet,' I stuttered to Pip, who had been waiting for a response. I subtly turned to Elle and whispered to her. 'He is here. Kreeg.'

Her eyes widened.

'Do not move. We will wait a few minutes and then calmly exit the cafe.'

She gripped my hand tightly.

Seeing Kreeg was shocking enough, but the sight of him in the grey uniform of the SS turned my stomach. As children, we had built igloos in the snow, climbed frozen trees, and told each other stories to pass the long, dark Siberian evenings. And now he served the Nazi Party. I looked down at my feet. Even though I longed to jump up and run, I knew it would be futile. I wouldn't last a minute.

'It's been lovely catching up, but Bo and I really have to be getting home—we have some essays to finish, don't we, Bo?' Elle announced. I nodded. 'I'll see you later, Karine. Bye, Pip.'

'Oh. Goodbye then,' he replied. Karine had a sympathetic look on her face, assuming that we had merely been unsettled by the presence of the officers.

Still gripping my hand, Elle calmly stood up and began to make her way purposefully towards the door. Although I had broken eye contact with Kreeg a while ago, I felt his gaze follow me across the room. With each step, my expectation of receiving a bullet in the back increased, but there was no shot. When we reached the exit, I found myself unable to resist the temptation to turn and look at him once more. To my surprise, he had his back to me, and was sipping the coffee which had just arrived at his table.

We returned to my lodgings as quickly as we could, but maintained a steady pace so as not to attract attention.

'You're sure it was him, Bo?' Elle gasped.

'I am nearly positive. It's been so many years…but his eyes are the same. My Lord, my Lord!' My exasperation was increasing with every second.

'Please, try to keep composure, my love. Do you think that he has tracked you here?'

I shrugged. 'He must have… I cannot think of another explanation. But when we left the cafe, he did not watch us go. He had his back to us.'

Elle nodded, relieved. 'Good. Perhaps he did not recognise you. But Bo, you're both Russian. How is it that Kreeg can be a member of the SS?'

'His father was Prussian. Do you recall? I told you all about Cronus Eszu.'

'Of course,' she replied, remembering the history.

We arrived back at the battered limestone terrace I call home and hurriedly climbed the narrow stairs to the third floor. When we reached my room, I locked the door and made sure to close the thin curtains. Luckily, the woman who runs the lodgings, Frau Schneider, is an old Bohemian, and hardly raises an eyebrow at a female entering the building, as long as 'I don't hear anything and they're out by nine'.

I sat on the creaking bed and put my head in my hands. 'If we were looking for signs that we must leave Leipzig, I think we just had a big one. We have to make arrangements to flee as soon as possible.' I ran my hands through my hair. My breath was short and sharp, and felt simultaneously hot and cold. 'I don't…I don't feel…' The world turned blurry, and my field of vision began to narrow.

Elle joined me on the bed. 'It's fine, my love. You're all right.' She put a comforting arm around me. 'Be calm. You are safe, and I am here. You have had a shock, but you will recover.'

'We have to leave, Elle. He'll come for me… He'll come for us…'

'I agree, my love. But will you listen to me a moment?' I

gathered myself together and nodded. 'Thank you. Now, from what you have told me, Kreeg Eszu has one mission in life—to end yours. Yes?'

'You know the answer to that question.'

'Well then, if he had recognised you in the cafe, he would not have failed to act, no matter the consequences. Do you concur?'

I paused for a moment, before agreeing. 'I suppose, yes.'

'It stands to reason, therefore, that he did not realise who you were. On that basis, we can assume that there is no immediate danger to you. Do you follow my logic?' she asked. I hesitated. 'Just in the way that there is no immediate danger to me from Leipzig's political situation. No one is breaking into our homes and segregating us—yet. That is not to say that things cannot change quickly, but for now, in this moment, we are safe, and we are together. So please, my dearest, stay calm. For me, if nothing else.'

I slowed my breathing, and looked into Elle's eyes. 'I am sorry.'

'Please, my love, there is no need to apologise. I just want you to know that you are all right, and I am here.' She ran her fingers through my hair, which always had a soothing effect.

After a few moments, I stood up from the bed. 'Time for action. I will begin to formulate plans for our exit.' I pulled my suitcase from the wardrobe in the corner of the room. 'You must make a trip to the Deutsche Bank tomorrow and withdraw all the funds you can. Then we will simply take the latest train out of the city.'

'Where do you propose we run to, Bo? Back to France? Back to a gendarmerie who are still, in all probability, wanting to arrest you? We wouldn't be able to talk to Evelyn or the Landowskis. Word would get around Boulogne-Billancourt that you had returned after your mysterious disappearance, and the police would find you.'

'You're right. We won't travel to France, it poses too great a risk. We will go to Switzerland. It's time. I have to find out what happened to my father.'

Elle sighed. 'How many years have you talked of reaching

Switzerland, Bo? Is there any part of you that believes he is alive?'

I was taken aback. 'No, of course there isn't. But what do you propose? Shall we stay here in Germany? Do I just accept that Kreeg may murder me? Or that Hitler might do the same to you?' I kicked my suitcase in frustration and immediately felt guilty. Elle was trying to help, but I was consumed by a whirlwind of panic.

'Listen to me,' she implored. 'There is nothing we can do about Hitler. But perhaps there is something we can do about Kreeg.'

I put my hands on my hips. 'And what is that, Elle?'

'I have thought about this across the years. Why don't you simply return the diamond?' she asked.

I couldn't help but emit a laugh. 'Oh Elle. You know I tried to hand it to him in Siberia. But he would not listen. He simply attacked me.'

Elle nodded. 'I know, but much has changed since then. You were children. And given the situation you have described to me, I do not know what else Kreeg was supposed to think.' She paused, clearly contemplating whether her next words were wise. 'You were stood over his mother's body, after all.'

I shuddered at the memory. I had tried, for many years, to erase it from my mind. 'Why must you remind me?'

'Because, my love, you have to remember that you are not a murderer. I worry that sometimes you forget. You are innocent, and have nothing to fear from your maker.'

'My maker, no. My brother…Kreeg…that's a different story.'

'Kreeg believes that you killed his mother to take possession of the diamond. We both know that is simply not the case. He needs to accept the truth of the situation.'

'And how do you propose I do that, Elle? Shall I walk up to him in the street, tap him on the shoulder and embrace him? Would you have me throw him the diamond and say, "No hard feelings, brother"?'

'I understand how you must be feeling, Bo, but there is no need to be aggressive towards me.' She looked crestfallen.

'I am sorry, my love, but I worry you forget why we are here in the first place. Kreeg swore to hunt me down and avenge his mother, or die in the process. I know him, Elle. Perhaps better than anyone on our planet. He will keep his word.'

'I know. But there are several things we must remember. Number one, he does not know your alias. You are Bo D'Aplièse here. Number two, you have aged. I know that you recognised Kreeg immediately, but it will not necessarily be so easy for him. Thirdly, what instrument is it that Kreeg knows you to play?'

'The violin.' The realisation dawned on me. 'Ah...'

'Exactly. He certainly won't be making enquiries about a student named Bo D'Aplièse who plays the cello. If he's been sniffing around, perhaps he's beginning to lose hope that you are here in the first place.'

'I suppose it is possible, yes,' I conceded.

'Well then, perhaps the stars have given you an opportunity. Kreeg does not have the element of surprise which you fear. If we can formulate a plan to return the diamond to him, perhaps with a letter explaining the full and true circumstances surrounding his mother's death, then perhaps he will give up his pursuit.'

I shook my head sadly. 'It will never be enough, Elle, despite the truth. He wants my life.'

She put her cupped hand to my cheek. 'Is it not worth a try, my love? You and I could live in true peace.'

'I am scared, Elle. I am scared of him.'

'I know. But you have your Elle here with you.' She stood and began to pace around the room, thinking out loud as she did so. 'Firstly, it is imperative that you stay inside for the time being, so that I might work out where Kreeg is stationed, and what his daily routine is. Does that sound like a reasonable start?'

I let out a sigh. 'Yes,' I agreed.

'Good! Then we will commence.'

'Elle...'

'Yes, my love?'

'I implore you to be careful. We are only assuming that Kreeg did not recognise me tonight. He is a shrewd operator, and very dangerous. If anything happened to you, I would surrender myself to Eszu willingly.'

'I know. That is why we are going to try and bring this to an end, one way or another.' Elle kissed me. 'Goodbye, my love. I will return with information when I am able to.'

With that, she unlocked my bedroom door and left my lodgings.

And now, here I sit, frozen with fear that something will happen to Elle, or that Kreeg knew it was me in the cafe. Every so often I draw my curtain slightly and peer out onto the street below, half expecting to see a man in an SS uniform staring back up at me. I predict I have a long night ahead.

23

Elle returned at ten a.m. the next morning, looking pale and shaken. She could hardly get any words out, so I sat her down and fetched her a cup of sweet tea from the small kitchen on the ground floor. As she sipped, I held her in my arms until some colour had returned to her face.

'It was awful, Bo. So awful.'

When she finally felt able, Elle described the horrific scene she had just witnessed at the Gewandhaus—the city's largest concert hall. The square outside boasted a statue of the great Felix Mendelssohn—the Jewish founder of the original Leipzig Conservatory. This morning, members of the Hitler Youth had torn down the statue and hammered it into a pile of rubble.

'Their faces were furious and their teeth gnashing, Bo. They were like rabid animals, blinded by rage and hatred. I simply had to hold my nerve and walk past, showing as little emotion as possible.' Elle shut her eyes in an attempt to block the memory.

'Goerdeler will be enraged,' I said. 'How could anyone hate a man who gave so much to the world?'

'I'll bet you anything that it was his poisonous deputy, Haake, who organised it. It would make sense for him to make an intimidating move whilst Goerdeler is in Munich. Now, surely, he will be forced out. Then Leipzig will be lost.'

'Elle, I'm so sorry.'

She took out a handkerchief and dabbed her eyes. 'There's more. I saw Kreeg, stood near the rubble, shouting instructions at the children. I think he oversees the Hitler Youth brigade.' I shuddered to think of his influence on innocent children. 'I should be able to learn his movements relatively easily as a result. I just need to find out the brigade's schedule. Then I will know where Kreeg will be at all times.'

'Well, I suppose that if there was a silver lining to this morning, it is that.'

Elle cast her eyes to the floor. 'I would not say so, Bo.'

I chastised myself. 'That was a stupid thing to say. I won't let them hurt you, my love, I swear.' She gave me a sad smile. 'Do you not have tuition to attend, by the way?'

'No. Principal Davisson has shut the conservatory. He has deemed it too dangerous for the students, so I'm going to meet Karine in Wasserstraße.' She stood up.

'Elle, I don't think that's wise. Karine is visibly Jewish. If there is high anti-Semitic sentiment on the streets today, then I worry for your safety.'

'Bo, we must remember that we have a duty to our friend. We both know that Pip doesn't see the severity of the situation. He's far more concerned about finishing his assessed piece.'

I nodded. 'I'm supposed to be playing cello in the orchestra…' I waved the thought away. 'Anyway, I can't let you go out by yourself today. I want to accompany you.'

Elle considered it. 'I admit, I would feel better if you did. Kreeg and his Hitler Youth brigade are hosting a book burning by the rubble of Mendelssohn's statue. They are demanding that students throw scores written by Jewish composers onto the inferno…' Elle became understandably choked. I stood up and took her in my arms. 'Put on your large coat,' she eventually instructed. 'Your hat, too. Let's not take any chances.'

We sat in a secluded alcove in the Wasserstraße coffee shop, and waited for Pip and Karine to arrive. When they joined us, Karine was shell-shocked and had clearly been crying. Nonetheless, Elle's best friend was predictably resilient when addressing the table.

'Now that this has happened, we have no one to protect us.

We all know that Haake is an anti-Semite. Look at how he tried to enforce these horrible laws from the rest of Germany. How long before they stop Jewish doctors from practising and Aryans from consulting them here in Leipzig?' she asked.

Pip put his hands up to call for calm. 'We shouldn't panic, but wait until Goerdeler returns. The newspapers say it will be in a few days. He went from Munich to Finland on an errand for the Chamber of Commerce. I'm sure that when he hears of this he will head back to Leipzig immediately,' he said.

'But the mood in the city is so hateful!' Elle blurted out. 'Everyone knows how many Jews are studying at the conservatory. What if they decide to go further and raze the whole place to the ground, like they have done with synagogues in other cities?'

'The conservatory is a temple to music, not to political or religious power. Please, we must all try to keep calm,' Pip reiterated.

'That is all very easy for you to say,' Karine remarked to him in an undertone. 'You are not Jewish, and will pass for one of their own.' She studied Pip's wavy red-blonde hair and light blue eyes. 'It's different for me. Just after the statue was taken down, I passed a group of youths on my way to the conservatory and they screamed out "Jüdische Hündin!"' She dipped her eyes at the memory. All of us knew that it meant 'Jewish bitch'. 'And what's more,' Karine continued, 'I cannot even speak to my parents. They are in America to prepare for my father's new sculpture exhibition.'

Pip suddenly looked as if his blood was boiling beneath the surface of his skin. He took Karine's hand. 'My love, I will keep you safe, even if I have to take you back to Norway to do it. No harm will come to you.' He grasped her hand in his and smoothed a strand of glossy black hair from her anxious face.

'Do you promise?' Karine asked, with heart-wrenching sincerity.

Pip kissed her forehead tenderly. 'I promise.'

Elle and I were satisfied that, for the first time, Pip seemed to have accepted the gravity of the situation.

During the next few days, I remained in my lodgings and sent a note with Elle to tell my professors that I had come down with the winter flu. She came to visit me each evening, and update me on Eszu's movements. On the third night, she returned with some new information.

'I followed some of the SS officers into the centre of the city today. I've learnt that they stay in a hotel near to the NSDAP building,' she said, with a hint of excitement in her voice.

'What's the NSDAP building?'

'A sort of administrative headquarters. The state police are based there.'

I leant on my flimsy wooden desk. 'Do you think that's where Kreeg is located?'

'Almost certainly, yes. Although…' She looked away.

'What is it, Elle?'

'I've discovered that there is a rotation system in place. Kreeg travels around the country, visiting different Hitler Youth brigades, ensuring that the local indoctrination techniques are up to scratch. He will be leaving Leipzig imminently.'

I gave a chuckle in disbelief. 'How did you learn this?'

'I talked to one of them.'

My mood swiftly changed. 'WHAT?! Elle, what on earth were you thinking? I only agreed to this plan on the proviso that you would not put yourself in harm's way!'

She took my hands. 'What better way to protect myself than to show support for their cause? I sidled up to one of the fresh-faced boys, who was smoking in the conservatory colonnade. I told him how handsome he looked in his uniform, and what a wonderful job he had done in taking down the statue the other day.'

I let go of Elle's hands and began massaging my temples. 'Oh Elle. Go on.'

'I asked the soldier what his job was, and he told me that he was responsible for training the youth brigade under supervision from First Lieutenant Eszu…who is leaving tomorrow.'

My anger spilt out. 'You are playing with fire, Elle. What if he knew that you were Jewish?!'

Elle rolled her eyes. 'For goodness' sake, will you look at me? My blonde hair and blue eyes could hardly be more fitting for their Aryan vision for Germany, could it? And it's amazing what a little batting of eyelids can do…'

I sighed. 'I don't know how to feel. I suppose I should be happy that if I lie low for the next twenty-four hours, then Kreeg will leave Leipzig and I will be protected again. On the other hand, we won't be able to enact your plan.'

'No. Although the young officer told me that Lieutenant Eszu will be returning in six months to ensure that standards had not slipped. It will give us time to come up with a more concrete idea of how to return the diamond to him and ensure your safety.'

I began to pace around my small bedroom. 'Yes. But it doesn't change the position in which we find ourselves here, Elle. The Nazis aren't just packing up and leaving like Kreeg. It's still not safe for you.'

Elle took a moment to formulate her response. 'As Pip predicted, Goerdeler is back. Just this afternoon, he promised to rebuild the Mendelssohn statue. Haake's plan to oust him has failed. I think…things feel more stable out there. Whilst Goerdeler holds office, there is no imminent threat.'

I stopped pacing and looked into her eyes. 'Are you really proposing we stay, Elle?'

She slowly nodded her head. 'I have a duty to Karine. Pip isn't going anywhere for the time being, and she needs our support. Don't forget, Bo, without her father, we wouldn't be here in the first place. We must stay to protect her.'

I couldn't argue with Elle's point. If Karine was staying, then evidently so were we. 'I understand,' I replied.

'Thank you, Bo.' I was rewarded with a kiss on my cheek. 'You realise that it's only a few days until the Christmas break? Pip and Karine plan to spend a week in a small hotel, checking in as man and wife. Frau Fischer, who runs my lodgings, is visiting family in Berlin at the same time.' Elle blushed a little. 'I thought, that…if you wanted to, you could perhaps come and stay with me for the week.'

My heart fluttered slightly. Even though Elle and I had been 'together' for seven years, we had never…consummated the relationship. Forgive me, I feel a little embarrassed writing about it. Our formative years have been predicated on innocence. However, now twenty and eighteen, there are clearly certain urges that had not been present when we were children. We had come close to indulging them on a few occasions, but had always found ourselves interrupted by something—normally another lodger. We had discussed perhaps booking a hotel, but always felt that it would somehow be disrespectful to Monsieur Landowski and the *Prix Blumenthal*.

'Life is short, Bo,' Elle said, giving me a wink and making for my door.

The Christmas break arrived, and the conservatory cleared out, with pupils and staff alike returning home for the festivities. The lodgings were basically empty, and I packed a small suitcase of belongings to take over to Elle's bedroom.

That night, we made love for the first time. We were both incredibly shy, and the experience was short and fumbling. Afterwards, as I held her in my arms, we looked at one another, in a bizarre attempt to force a romantic moment—for I think it was what we have both read about in novels. In truth, the...act...had been slightly underwhelming, and the subsequent eye contact simply caused us to burst into peals of laughter. Then, the laughter became kissing, which in turn became something more, and...well, I am glad to report that the second attempt was far more successful. I am hesitant to write any details here, to preserve Elle's modesty and my own embarrassment, but it was quite remarkable.

We spent the week schooling one another in the art of physical intimacy, and happily drowning in the sins of the flesh. We discovered that, after a false start, it is the most natural process for two people in love. Our bodies are designed to give us pleasure, so why should we deny them?

The new term arrived, and with Goerdeler back in the city, the political temperature was lowered, just as Elle had predicted. I returned to my studies, and life largely continued as it had before the arrival (and departure) of Kreeg Eszu. Pip was working furiously on his composition, in the desperate hope that it could be performed before Karine had no choice but to leave Leipzig. He held occasional rehearsals for new elements of the score and, from behind my cello, I would genuinely marvel at the work. Even if he is lacking in other areas, Pip Halvorsen is a supremely talented composer.

'Is it any good, Bo? I trust your opinion.'

'I think it will be a triumph,' I answered honestly.

'That is very gracious of you to say.' He closed the piano lid and leant over to me. 'You know, there is a rumour around the school that you are called "Bo" because you are never seen without your cello bow. Is there any truth in it?'

I chuckled confidently, masking my pang of anxiety. 'Nonsense, I'm afraid. Although, of course, that is why I picked up a bow in the first place!' I internally congratulated myself on the smoothness of the lie.

'Ah, of course. Bo by name...'

'Bow by nature,' I replied.

Pip looked around the wood-panelled rehearsal room. 'You know, Goerdeler is standing for re-election in March. He announced it today.'

I stood up and began to pack my cello away. 'Well, that is undoubtedly good news.' I was aware that Pip was watching me closely to see my response.

'Yes,' he continued. 'I'm rather hoping that, as the whole conservatory and the majority of Leipzig are behind him, his re-election will rid this place of its unwelcome visitors. For the sake of our significant others.'

I clipped my case shut, then turned to face him. 'I believe that might be an ambitious prediction, Pip. Goerdeler hasn't even managed to get Mendelssohn's statue rebuilt.'

He shrugged. 'Granted. But surely once the people have spoken, and he is returned to office, the Reich will have no choice but to support him?'

'I'm not so sure. We all know that Haake is openly canvassing against his re-election. The destruction of the statue has fully revealed his stance on the Jews.'

Pip sighed deeply. Clearly I was not providing him with the

responses he was hoping for. 'I know. I'm constantly trying to convince myself that this isn't real. I'm in my third year, of course. There is a high probability that I will get to finish my time here in Leipzig. But for Karine, Elle and yourself, of course...you might have to leave before your final year even begins.'

'It is a small price to pay for guaranteed safety, Pip.'

He paused, and then nodded. 'Quite right, yes.'

Over the next few weeks in the run-up to Goerdeler's re-election, Elle, Karine and many other conservatory students canvassed for him. On the night the votes were counted, we joined the crowds outside City Hall and cheered euphorically when we heard our candidate had been re-elected. For the first time in a while, it felt like we had experienced a true victory.

24

Despite Goerdeler's best efforts, the statue was not rebuilt. Given this failure, he resigned from office on 31st March 1937, declining to formally accept his re-election.

I must apologise for the quality of my handwriting, which the reader will no doubt observe has deteriorated significantly since my last entry. Unfortunately, I have endured an injury to my right arm, and it is painful to lift it up onto the desk. Each time I start a new line, a jolt of pain passes through my elbow, up into my shoulder, and crescendos in my neck. It serves as a reminder that the human body is an intricate mass of connected nerves, and I seem to have done enough damage to ensure that my pain is felt in a number of places. I am currently wearing a makeshift sling which Elle formed out of her scarf, and she helps me in and out of it several times per day. In addition, my face is currently the colour of the *glühwein* we drank to warm ourselves on winter's nights.

I should explain that I am currently in a cabin aboard a rickety old ferry, transporting me and Elle to a new land which neither of us have ever seen. Despite all that has happened, I am excited by the promise of a fresh, green country. Alongside us on the ferry are Pip and Karine, to whom I think Elle and I probably owe our lives. Pip has selflessly agreed to allow Elle and me to join him and Karine at his family home in Norway. The two-day voyage is providing a welcome opportunity to write in my diary, and I will chronicle the events which led to our departure from Leipzig.

Over the past few months, we had remained vigilant—particularly Elle, who had kept a keen eye out for Kreeg's reappearance in the Hitler Youth brigade. Despite the fact there was no sign of Eszu, both Elle and I had felt that, come May, it was time to go. We had both agreed to wait until the end of term, so that we might take our second-year exams, and then pack up for good. Now Goerdeler had gone, the National Socialists were free to decree any sanctions they liked against the Jewish population. It was simply too dangerous to remain. Elle had eventually convinced Karine to leave Germany with or without Pip, but he had accepted the severity of the situation, and invited Karine to return with him to Norway at the end of term.

Elle and I thought that the United States would be a sensible location for us to explore. We had just enough funds to make the crossing, and I had formulated a vague strategy to seek out the Blumenthal family to thank them for saving my life and to find work.

With plans made for all of us, it felt fitting that the concluding act of my time in Leipzig was to perform in the orchestra for Pip's assessed piece. It was a light summer's evening, and hundreds of students gathered outside the Gewandhaus in anticipation of hearing the orchestrations of the third-year composers. The square outside the conservatory really did look idyllic, despite the obvious absence of Herr Mendelssohn. Students milled about (many dressed in tails for the performance), sipping wine, discussing music and laughing with one another. Festooned lights provided a serene yellow glow, and if someone had parachuted down with no knowledge of the tension that plagued the city, they would surely have found this to be one of the most delightful atmospheres on earth.

I think it is how I will choose to remember the conservatory until the end of my days: a halcyon beacon of creative expression, which encouraged immense growth in me, both musical and personal.

'You look very handsome, Bo. Tails really do suit you,' Elle said, slinking her arm into mine.

'Thank you, my love. But tails suit any man. We have it very easy. You and your female peers on the other hand are analysed and judged for whatever fashion choices you make. It's silly, really…'

'Is there a compliment forthcoming, or should I be worried?' Elle joked.

'Sorry, of course. You know that you always look radiant. But tonight, exceptionally so.' It was no exaggeration. Elle wore a strapless navy-blue ballgown, which wrapped her torso snugly before splaying out into a ruffle below her hips.

'Thank you, Bo. You're right about women's fashion. I imagine Poor Karine will be receiving sly comments all night!' Our friend had, naturally, decided against wearing a dress, and had opted instead for a black suit with an oversized white bow tie completing the ensemble.

'I think she looks perfect,' I said.

'So do I. She is so…herself. Something that you and I might never master.'

I chuckled. 'You might be right there. Listen, you should take your seats. It's not ticketed tonight, and you don't want to miss out.'

She gave me a peck on the cheek. 'Good luck. Try not to ruin Pip's career…' Elle walked off to grab Karine before making her way inside the Gewandhaus.

Pip was clearly nervous, and not without cause. There was a great deal of buzz around his piece, and this event was better attended than usual. As his audience moved in to take their seats, he paced anxiously around the foyer.

'Do not worry, my friend,' I reassured him. 'We will ensure to do your fine piece justice this evening.'

'Thank you, Bo. You make a valuable contribution on your cello.'

I put a hand on his shoulder. 'I must take my seat. Good luck, Pip.'

After taking my place on stage, I watched as Pip was led in by Principal Walther Davisson, along with the other five composers who were sharing the showcase. They took a seat in the front row of the Großer Saal, each one looking paler than the last with nerves. Then Principal Davisson took to the stage, and received a warm round of applause. He, like Goerdeler, had become a stalwart figure of calm and reason in these turbulent times. All of us at the conservatory felt that he was our champion and protector.

'Thank you, all, thank you.' He raised his hand, and the applause died down. 'Welcome to the Gewandhaus, and to the end-of-term performances. I am sure you are all excited to hear the results of your contemporaries' hard work and dedication, so I shall keep my wittering short. I wish to commend everyone gathered here tonight on an incredible year of resilience and determination. Most of you will be familiar with my advice to put on your imaginary horse blinkers, so that you might not be distracted by all that is going on in the world around you. Tonight is not just a celebration of the six young composers you will hear from, but all of your achievements throughout the last year. I am extraordinarily proud to be your principal. Please, give yourselves a round of applause.' The Gewandhaus obliged, and the room was filled with whoops and cheers. 'In the coming years, people are going to look to you for comfort, for happiness, and for escape. You are all well equipped to deliver. See that you do.' There was a stillness in the hall as the congregation reflected on his words. 'Now, I shall introduce our first composer of the evening—Petra Weber. Petra's piece, "The Ascension of Hope…"'

As Davisson continued his speech, I looked at Pip. His eyes were darting around the Gewandhaus. Unfortunately, he was last on the bill, and would have to wait approximately ninety minutes before his piece was performed. The prospect must have been agonising for him.

Eventually, after five successful performances, it was his turn to take to the stage. When his moment came, I noted that his legs were trembling a little. He took a brief bow, then sat down at the piano. The conductor raised his baton, and we began.

Pip needn't have worried. The lights dimmed and the audience were transported to a euphoric place. The delicate harmonies and swelling crescendos of Pip's score didn't fail to land. Somehow, the piece felt charged, pulsating with emotion and capturing the resilience of the entire conservatory. It was a pleasure to be a part of. As the final notes played—a lingering trickle on the harp—there was a brief silence, followed by rapturous applause. The audience stood for Pip, and this time his bow was full of confidence.

There were joyous celebrations in the Gewandhaus foyer afterwards. I felt a little emotional watching Pip being slapped on the back and congratulated by peers and professors alike. There was even a newspaper journalist who asked him for an interview. It was undeniable that he had worked furiously over the last few months, and deserved to reap the rewards. I saw Karine fighting through the crowds to embrace him. 'My very own Grieg,' she said. '*Chéri*, your glittering career has just begun.' It was hard to disagree with her assessment.

Champagne was provided by the conservatory, and it seemed that this year, the boat had been well and truly pushed out. The fizz flowed like water, and the majority were indulging heavily. One couldn't blame them—they were merely seizing the day and celebrating the moment. I was offered flute after flute, but at each opportunity turned them down.

I have slowly let my guard down over many years, opening my mouth to speak and even tell others my story—something I never anticipated sharing. But alcohol loosens the lips and dulls the senses, so I have found it best to avoid what many consider to be the sweetest nectar. It became apparent early on in the evening that I was in a fierce minority, and as such, made the decision to return to my lodgings—happy, but sober.

I went to inform Elle of my decision. 'I think I'll stay out a little longer with Karine,' she said.

'As you wish, my love. Shall we meet for coffee in the morning?'

'Perfect,' she replied, and gave me a kiss on the cheek.

I turned to Elle's roommate. 'Goodnight, Karine. Please tell Pip once again what a pleasure it was to play his music tonight.'

'I will, Bo, thank you! Goodnight.'

When I left the Gewandhaus it was nearing midnight and there were no trams running, so I began the twenty-minute stroll home. In the daytime, it was a very pleasant walk, but now the sun had gone down, the night air was chilly. I pulled my coat collar up around my neck. The road from the Gewandhaus back to Johannisgasse was long and empty, lined by enormous fir trees, and dimly lit by gas lamps at intervals of fifty feet or so. To either side of the road lay enormous open fields, used primarily by the citizens of Leipzig for exercise or walking dogs. At night, it produced an eerie effect, making me feel as though I was walking on a floating bridge over a deep abyss. Owing to the lateness of the hour, there wasn't another soul in sight.

I'd been walking for ten minutes when I heard the snap of a twig behind me. I turned around, expecting to see a fox, or perhaps a deer making its way across the road, passing from one field to another. But to my surprise, there was nothing in sight. I paused, silently scanning the area for signs of movement. Seeing none, I continued on my way. After walking for another twenty feet, I could have sworn I heard footsteps coming from the other side of the trees. I spun around once again.

'Hello?' I cried. 'Is someone there?' Silence greeted me once more.

Feeling uneasy now, I quickened my pace. Sure enough, the footsteps I'd heard before became louder, the individual now unable to move with any subtlety. Formulating a plan, and knowing that attack is the best form of defence, I wheeled around on my heels, and sprinted towards the trees, and the footsteps.

'Why are you following me? Why won't you show yourself? Don't be a coward, if you have something to say to me, I want to hear it!' I ran in and out of the trees, expecting to catch someone lurking. Finding nothing, I continued onto the field, where I was surrounded by darkness. I stood deathly still, and listened for the footsteps again. After a moment, I heard them again, the squelchy earth of the field betraying the mysterious individual. The footsteps were receding deeper into the darkness, and away from me. Satisfied that whoever had been following me was warded off by the confrontation, I returned to the road and broke into a jog for the remainder of my journey.

I was out of breath when I approached my front door, and a little shaken, too. I put my hand in my pocket and fumbled with my keys, eventually dropping them on the floor behind me. As I turned to pick them up, I saw a shadowy figure dart behind a building on the corner of the street.

Had he returned to Leipzig? Did he know who I was?

I assessed my options, which were limited. If the mysterious figure was Kreeg, then running up to confront him again would be foolish. In all probability he was carrying his gun, and would just shoot me dead. My immediate thought was to protect Elle, but if I were to travel back down the long road to the Gewandhaus, I would lead Eszu right to her, putting my love, and our friends, in danger. It was clear to me that I had to take the only option available, and continue into my lodgings. I put the key in the door and made my way swiftly up to my room. I locked the bedroom door behind me, and didn't turn the light on. Then I made my way to the window to observe the street below, looking for signs of the shadowy figure. All seemed quiet.

Nonetheless, I thought it sensible to take precautions. From my bedside drawer, I grabbed my pocket knife. Then I returned to my vantage point at the window and closed the curtains this time, save for a single sliver of glass for me to look through. From my position I could just about make out the corner of Elle's lodgings. At least I would be able to see that she and Karine returned home safely.

This would be a long night.

I pulled up a chair, and placed a pillow behind my head. At least the next few hours would give me an opportunity to come up with a plan to escape Kreeg, if indeed it was him. I sat vigilantly watching the empty street below. Time passed, and there was no sign of the figure that I was sure had been following me. Or…was I so sure? Perhaps my mind had been playing tricks. I had been under a great deal of stress lately, and it was possible my imagination was running away with me.

The room, by virtue of being at the top of the lodgings, was warm, and the hiss and click of the iron radiators was soothing. I felt my eyes becoming heavy. In an attempt to revive myself, I opened the bedroom window a crack, and the cold night air rushed in. My plan worked for a brief period, but eventually my body conceded to the inevitability of slumber.

I woke up choking. My eyes opened, but I couldn't see anything in front of me. Instinctively I stood up and blindly took several steps forwards. My foot made contact with a table leg, and I was sent tumbling to the floor. Despite the pain of the fall, my vision was instantly clearer. As I rolled onto my back, I realised with horror that my room was filled with black, acrid smoke.

Panic surged through me. I scrambled to my feet, but took a lungful of the smoke and began to choke again. I dropped back to the floor, my heart thumping. I crawled along the floor, using the corners of the room to guide me to the bedroom door. When I reached it, to my horror, I realised that the smoke was pouring in from the corridor. Clearly I would have a battle on my hands to get downstairs. But what choice did I have? Grabbing the door's handle, I pulled myself up, holding my breath as I did so. My hand searched for the bolt lock, and when I found it, it was scorching to the touch. I gritted my teeth and ripped the bolt with as much force as I could muster, and to my relief, it came free.

I positioned myself behind the door to shield myself and wrenched it open. Large orange flames flicked into the room like the giant tongue of an angry serpent. With a sinking heart, I realised that escape was an impossibility.

I closed the door again. It was only a matter of time before the fire incinerated it, and I wondered whether I would be a victim of the flames or the smoke. I slumped back down to the floor, and placed myself on my belly.

'I'm sorry,' I cried, although I wasn't entirely sure who I was speaking to. Perhaps Elle, for leaving her alone in Leipzig in the face of enormous danger. Perhaps my father, whom I had failed to find, despite promising myself that I would. Perhaps to the Landowskis, Evelyn, Monsieur Ivan, and all those who had believed in me when I had nothing. Maybe even to Kreeg Eszu, for the simple misunderstanding that had led to so much suffering and heartbreak.

He was making me pay for it now.

I had crossed continents, surviving cold and starvation. Despite everything, I had found someone who had made my life worth living…and this was how it was all going to end. Unceremoniously, in a plume of smoke.

I turned onto my back, and closed my eyes. When I was a young boy, my father used to use a relaxation technique invented by the theatre practitioner, Konstantin Stanislavski, to send me to sleep. I recalled his voice: *The muscle controller is in your little toe at the moment. He has to start at the smallest point in the body, you see…and he switches it off. Then he travels to the next toe, and the next…and now he is in the sole of your foot. Gosh, how tense it is there, carrying the weight of your body all day long. But it is not a problem for the muscle controller. He switches it off as easily as turning out a light. Now he moves up to your ankle…*

My father, imaginary or not in that moment, talked me to sleep. More likely, it was the smoke I had inhaled. As for what happened next, my assumption is that I dreamt it.

I saw the stars above me.

I remember being happy that they were here for me at the end. The constellation of the Seven Sisters glistened and twinkled before my eyes—my guiding lights, my constants. Then, the stars began to rearrange themselves into seven female faces that I did not recognise. Each seemed to radiate so much warmth and love. In that moment, I felt peaceful… I was ready.

Then, I heard a voice.

'Not now, Atlas. There is more to do.'

The seven faces disappeared from view, and the stars once more rearranged themselves into a single figure. She had long hair, and a flowing dress which seemed to spread out behind her into eternity. Then the stars themselves faded, and the figure was revealed to me in technicolour. Her dress was a rich red, and she was adorned in garlands of white and blue flowers. Her hair—a shimmering blonde mane—was arranged elegantly around her heart-shaped face. Her huge, blue opalescent eyes appeared to glimmer and sparkle, and I found myself transfixed. She spoke to me again.

'The boy with the world on his shoulders. You must carry it for a little longer. Others depend on you.' I noted a European accent, though she spoke to me in my own mother tongue.

'What do you mean?' I replied breathlessly. 'Who are you?'

'Your destiny is not yet fulfilled. You need not pass through this door yet.'

'What door? What are you talking about?'

The woman smiled. 'You are looking at me through a window, Atlas. I find that they are much preferable to doors, for one may see the path ahead before leaving.'

I understood her message. 'The window... But I'm three stories up, I will never survive the fall!'

'You will not survive in here either. Take a leap of faith.'

The woman began to disappear from view, consumed by the black smoke that billowed and pulsated above me.

Now fully awake, I rolled over onto my stomach and crawled towards the window. As I made my way across the floor, my hand brushed a long, thin item. I looked down to see my cello bow. I grabbed it. I could just make out the light behind the window through the smoke, which was being drawn out through the open crack. That was what was encouraging the smoke to flow so forcefully.

Using the curtain, I managed to stand, and heaved up the heavy window sash. There was brief respite from the blanket of smoke that surrounded me, before it enveloped me once more, more furiously than ever. I looked down at the ground, where I could just make out Frau Schneider along with the others who had escaped the blaze. They spotted me at the window.

'He's alive! My God!' Frau Schneider wailed. 'Wait there, young man! The fire service has been contacted, we will save you!'

There was a terrifying bang from behind me. I turned around to see that the door, and along with it the frame, had given way to the flames. My decision to open the window so widely had served to anger the blaze, and the scorching orange flames encroached into the room like an octopus entering a cave. The fire was hungry. It wanted me. Now, there really was no choice. The last thing I grabbed from the room was my diary, which I could just make out on the desk nearby. Then I climbed out onto the windowsill.

'Don't you dare! You stay there!' Frau Schneider screamed up at me.

I estimated the drop was more than fifty feet. I placed my bow, and the diary, in the waistband of my trousers. Then, tentatively, I grabbed the sill and slowly lowered myself down, so that my legs dangled from the window. Each inch that I could reduce my fall by was crucial. I mentally prepared myself for what was to come.

'The flower bed, the flower bed!' Frau Schneider cried. 'I watered it only this evening!' I let go of the sill with my left arm and swung freely, so that I could look below. Even though it was dark, the white and blue flowers acted like landing lights. If I could just propel myself slightly and land in the soft mud, I predicted I had a chance. There was a loud creak from within my bedroom, and I accepted that it was now or never. Gripping back onto the sill with my arm, I used the momentum to swing my body to the right, then the left, and let go.

My landing, although imperfect, was pretty good, all things considered. My feet hit the flower bed as I hoped they would, and on impact I bent my knees and rolled. I only felt the true force of the fall as my right arm hit the stone pavement by the flowers, followed promptly by my face.

'Argh!' I cried out in pain.

'My boy, my boy!' Frau Schneider cried, appearing over me. 'Where are you injured? Can you feel your legs? Can you wiggle your toes?'

'Yes,' I replied. 'It's my arm that's hurt.' I rolled up my sleeve with my good arm, and was met by a pretty ugly sight. Clearly my elbow had been dislocated, and the effect was eye-watering.

'We must move him away from the building. Help me!' Frau Schneider was immediately joined by a couple of the other boys from the lodgings, who, in an attempt to pull me away from the house, grabbed my arms.

'No!' I cried, but it was too late. The boys heaved me, and my right arm produced a sickening crunch. This was followed by a wave of hot pain that started at my elbow but somehow managed to travel around my entire body. I screamed, but the boys were resolute in moving me away from the flames. When they let go, I huddled myself into a ball as the shockwaves of pain continued.

'Breathe, young man. Courage,' said Frau Schneider, who was by my side once again and stroking my hair. 'You have survived.'

'Did…everyone…get out?' I eventually managed to ask.

'All are accounted for. Thankfully there weren't many in the lodgings, most are still out in the town centre after the performance tonight…though I cannot speak for the other houses.'

'Other houses?' I uttered.

'I'm afraid so, young man. It really has begun. I'm so sorry. None of this would have happened without me. It was I who they were after.'

I furrowed my brow in confusion. 'I don't understand, Frau Schneider.'

'I am Jewish. They torched the building to take my business from me and show that I am not welcome here. Regrettably, tonight, they have succeeded.'

Cogs began to whir in my head. 'I'm sorry, Frau Schneider.'

'There is certainly no need for an apology. You could have been killed tonight, and I would have been responsible.' She bowed her head.

'No, Frau Schneider,' I replied. 'You most certainly would not have been.' A rock formed in the pit of my stomach. 'You said "other houses". So the SS have visited other premises housing Jews?'

'I'm afraid so, yes.' I staggered to my feet, renewed bolts of pain shooting down my arm. I winced and inhaled sharply. 'Be careful! I will send for a doctor,' Frau Schneider insisted.

I ran towards the coffee shop, and Elle's intact lodgings came into view. The relief that washed over me was a more effective antidote to pain than morphine. 'There is no need for a doctor, Frau Schneider. I will be fine, thank you. I just have to find Elle.'

Frau Schneider nodded. 'I have not seen her. Perhaps if you ask around, then…' She put her hand to her mouth and began to cry, suddenly overcome by the night's events.

I raised my good arm, and placed it on her shoulder. 'It is so very unfair, Frau Schneider. I am truly sorry for your loss.'

'Thank you,' she sniffed. 'But I wonder why they decided to target me? My religion is hardly well advertised, unlike many others in the city.'

A pang of guilt ran through me. I knew that tonight, Frau Schneider was not the target. It had been me.

'Bo!' Over Frau Schneider's shoulder, I saw Elle running towards me, accompanied by Karine. As I went to embrace her, another surge of pain rushed through my arm, and I couldn't hold in my grimace. 'My love…what on earth happened? Are you all right?'

'Oh Bo,' Karine added.

I gestured to the smouldering building. 'I had to jump. They're torching Jewish residences. But, Elle…it was him. He knows. We have to go, tonight if possible.'

'What do you mean *him*?' Karine asked.

Elle turned to her friend. 'He means this…particularly nasty SS officer we've seen around the city. Isn't that right, Bo?'

'Yes,' I replied, grateful that Elle's brain was functioning better than my own. 'He just has a very aggressive aura. Frau Schneider, who runs my lodgings, is Jewish, so we were on the list for tonight's torchings. Where is Pip?'

'Still out on the town, enjoying his success,' Karine said. 'Was everyone able to make it out?'

'Apparently so. But none of us are safe here now. We must make plans to leave immediately.' I put my left arm around Elle and she buried her head in my chest. I looked back up at the building as the sound of sirens began to encroach, my cello bow against my leg. The pattern of my life had repeated itself, and I had lost everything. But this time, I had Elle by my side.

'Where will you go?' asked Karine.

'As far away as possible. America, we hope.'

'We will miss you, Karine,' Elle sobbed. 'You have been like a sister to me.'

'And you to me, Elle.' Karine bit her lip. 'What if there was a way that we could all stay together? Would you be interested?'

Elle and I looked at one another. 'Of course, Karine,' she replied. 'You are more than welcome to come with us. Perhaps you could join us on our voyage to America?'

'Actually, I was thinking that you could accompany me. As you know, Pip has offered to take me to Norway. I'm sure, given what has happened tonight, that he would be more than willing to extend the offer to you. What do you think?'

'Yes. Oh, yes!' Elle replied, before I'd even had a chance to absorb the information. She turned to me. 'Bo, it's a perfect plan.'

Still in a daze, I nodded. 'If Pip agrees, of course we would come. Thank you, Karine. You have no idea how much that offer means to us.'

'It is settled. The end of term is only a few days away, and then we can take the passage to Bergen.'

'No,' I said firmly. 'When I said that Elle and I would be gone by tomorrow night, I meant it. It is of the utmost importance for our...for *Elle*'s safety that we leave Leipzig immediately.' I glanced pointedly at my lodgings.

'I understand,' Karine accepted. 'I will talk to Pip first thing. All he cared about was having his work performed, and he achieved his objective tonight. Hopefully we can all be out of Leipzig by the evening.'

'In the meantime, Bo, you need somewhere to stay,' Elle said. 'I'm sure Frau Fischer wouldn't object to you spending the night on our floor, given the circumstances. Is that all right with you, Karine?'

'Of course.'

Thankfully, my presence was permitted. I took the wooden chair in Elle and Karine's room and placed it by the window, determined to make amends for what had happened earlier. If only I had been more vigilant, this could all have been avoided. With the protection of Elle my responsibility, I was confident that I would not falter at this second opportunity. I waited until the sun rose at just before five a.m., before finally retreating to the floor to get some rest, certain that Kreeg wouldn't try anything during daylight hours. At seven, I heard Karine leave to speak with Pip.

She returned a few hours later and assured us that the family would welcome us into their home, and that Pip was currently in the process of making a hurried phone call from Principal Davisson's office to at least provide some warning to his kin in Bergen.

The rest of the day was a flurry of packing. I helped Elle to sort her possessions, oddly relieved that I didn't have to do the same, given that mine were now a pile of ash. Only my cello had survived, left at the Gewandhaus last night—not that I would be able to collect it; the operation was simply too much of a risk. A lump formed in my throat as I bid a silent farewell to my instruments. At least the diamond was safe, secured as always around my neck. As I bent my arm to feel its familiar shape in the pouch, a bolt of pain surged through my elbow. I yelped.

'Oh Bo. You must see a doctor,' Elle said. 'Here.' She took one of her scarves and tied it around my neck as a makeshift sling. She gave me a gentle kiss on the cheek and stroked my bruised face. 'My poor love. You're going to be the colour of beetroot before too long.'

'And then mustard after a week or so,' I added.

'I forgot to mention,' Karine interjected. 'Pip's mother, Astrid, is a nurse. She'll be able to see to your arm.'

'There you go, Bo.' Elle managed a smile. 'Things are looking up already.'

Regardless of all that had occurred during the last six months, I was still a little heartbroken to be forced out of Leipzig. When Elle and I had arrived, I dared to dream that we might finally be free to live out our lives together—as musicians, no less— unburdened by the past. However, as I suppose it was always going to, it had caught up with me, conspiring with the present to not only harm me, but Elle too.

Selfishly, I pray that Norway is far enough from Kreeg.

25

Bergen Harbour, Norway
New Year's Eve 1938

Please, dear reader, forgive my long absence. As I write now, I can scarcely believe that over eighteen months have passed since my last entry. One factor alone accounts for my lack of chronicling—my arm. It transpired that my 'fall' in Leipzig resulted in both a dislocated elbow and a compound fracture. Apparently, the situation was not helped by the fact I stoically penned a number of pages on the two-day voyage from Leipzig to Bergen.

Upon our arrival in Norway, the kind and wondrous Astrid Halvorsen ensured that I received immediate care from the Haukeland Hospital. My arm was sealed in a cast for six weeks, and I was told that healing could take a year or more. Although I do seem to improve marginally each day, writing has continued to prove difficult. Many times, I have attempted to lift my elbow and put pen to paper, and subsequently given up due to the pain. However, I am glad to report that what was once a searing heat in my arm is now merely a dull ache, and therefore…I am able to continue my diary. What a luxury!

I will endeavour to recall events in detail, for I believe that if you are still reading this, you have a vested interest in my tale.

After walking down the steamer gangplank, Astrid had taken one look at my elbow and decreed that I would almost definitely need an operation. She was proved right, and despite resistance from the kind Halvorsen family, I had insisted that all hospital costs were paid for by myself. This, in effect, saw the end to the funds provided by Monsieur Landowski's *Prix Blumenthal*.

Mercifully, the Halvorsens were beyond generous to us. In those early days, they provided us with a roof, sustenance, and countless happy evenings filled with music and laughter. Pip and his parents treated me and Elle like family (and Karine too, of course).

Pip's father, Horst, is a fellow cellist, and plays in the Bergen Philharmonic. I have therefore received inordinate amounts of sympathy from him during my time in Norway, as I can no longer properly lift my bow arm. It is simply too stiff. I was therefore never able to engage in what became traditional post-dinner performances, featuring Pip at the piano, Karine on the oboe, Elle on the flute or viola (depending on the piece) and Horst on the aforementioned cello. Pangs of sadness would crash inside my chest like waves as I stared longingly at my former instrument.

Those first few months in Norway were just what was required after our turbulent exit from Germany. Here, Elle and I felt safe. Norway is perhaps the most beautiful country on the planet. In my short time here, I have marvelled at misty mountains and stared in wonder at waterways that drift off into eternity. One of my favourite pastimes is to hike up into the local park, the Bergens Fjellstrekninger, with a sketchbook and a set of pens to try and capture some of the natural beauty the country boasts. Even the air here has a certain purity. One can almost become drunk on it, intoxicated by the sharp, fresh chill.

I was fully aware that we could not rely on the Halvorsens forever, no matter how comfortable they made me and Elle feel. The fact of the matter was that we were not family, we were refugees. In Paris, I had allowed Monsieur Landowski to finance me, and in Leipzig, the *Prix Blumenthal* ensured that we wanted for nothing. I was determined that I should begin to pay the way for myself and Elle.

During my strolls in Bergen Harbour, I had earmarked a chart maker's shop—Scholz and Scholz. From conversations I'd had with Horst, I knew that the elderly proprietor was German, and his son had recently left Norway for the Fatherland to join the ever-growing Nazi movement, which was a source of great upset to the old man. I wagered that, under the circumstances, he might be willing to take me on as an assistant, even with my bad arm. After all, my knowledge of the stars is unparalleled, if I do say so myself.

I am glad to say that my wager was proved right, and I have been working for Mr Scholz ever since. He is a kindly old man, and his wife is an expert in the dark arts of pumpernickel baking. In truth, I do very little here. I certainly don't bear the responsibility of making any charts myself, but merely corroborate Mr Scholz's work. The wage is deservedly meagre, but I proved to be such an amiable presence that upon discovering my living situation, he and his wife offered me the small apartment above the shop, previously occupied by their son. I jumped at the chance, and asked if my 'wife' might be able to join me. They readily agreed with the promise that Elle would help Mrs Scholz to clean.

Elle was initially concerned that Karine might be jealous. She and Pip had announced their intention to marry a few months after arriving in Bergen, and Karine was desperate to move out of the Halvorsen household.

'They need their own space,' Elle had sighed.

'I am sure they will have it soon enough,' I replied. 'If Pip passes his audition, he'll join Horst in the Bergen Philharmonic. They'll soon have enough money for a house of their own.'

'I'm sure you're right.' She took my hand. 'Do you think that, one day, we might...?' Elle hesitated. Since the announcement of our friends' engagement, there was an unspoken sense of sadness that we were not yet joining them on the journey of matrimony.

I grabbed her hands. 'My love, the only thing that is certain in our lives is that we will be together forever. We will marry as soon as we have the funds together, and a place of permanent safety. I promise.'

So, just like that, Elle and I have been living as 'man and wife' for eighteen months. It has been, in a word, blissful. We spend the evenings in our tiny apartment huddled around a wood-burning stove, staring out across the water at the little houses which climb the hill. At night, the windows glow a warm yellow, the colour of melting butter. With just the two of us cocooned away from the rest of the world, it is all too easy to forget what we have run from.

I do my best to live in the present, as do our friends. Pip and Karine were married a year ago, on Christmas Eve 1937, with Karine 'converting' to Pip's Lutheran faith. She had discussed the formality with Elle, stating that, 'A few drops of water and a cross on my forehead does not make me a Christian in my heart.' Nonetheless, her new surname and documentation provide a buffer of protection should the Nazi threat one day arrive on Norway's shores, which remains a possibility.

Pip was successful in his audition, and now sits alongside his father in the Bergen Philharmonic. Any hint of jealousy I may have harboured at his success is overridden by the fact that he is my saviour—not to mention that he is deserving of his position. Alongside his commitments to the philharmonic, Pip continues to work furiously on his debut concerto, refusing to share the results with anyone until it is complete. He says that when it is finished, he will dedicate it to his wife. I do not doubt that my friend will produce a masterpiece.

In the spring of 1938, Pip and Karine were able to scrape enough funds together to rent a house on Teatergaten, just a stone's throw away from the Bergen concert hall. Karine had asked if I would choose a piano for the living room, and I went to great lengths to ensure that the finest instrument within her budget was procured. The housewarming gift from me and Elle was humbler—we presented the couple with a handmade stool for the new piano, which I carved and Elle upholstered. Although it was not the world's most expensive piece, it was made with a great deal of love.

Not long after that, Karine announced that she was expecting a baby, and in November, little Felix Halvorsen was born. When we met Pip and Karine's baby, I noticed the wistful, longing look Elle had in her eye. I took her hand.

'One day,' I assured her, kissing her lightly on the forehead.

Neither of us are naive enough to believe that safety from Kreeg and the Nazis will last forever. How could it, given all we have been through? We are merely waiting for disaster to arrive on Norway's shores, in the form of war, or a man who wishes me dead. Perhaps both.

The newspapers make for particularly grim reading. Tensions in Europe are escalating by the day. Back in March, Germany annexed Austria. There had been a brief glimmer of hope in September that conflict could be averted. Britain, France, Germany and Italy all signed the Munich Agreement, which conceded the Sudetenland area of Czechoslovakia to Germany, in return for a pledge from Hitler that he would make no further territorial demands. But now, just three months later, there are few who truly believe the agreement will hold.

With our philosophy of living in the present, Pip, Karine, Elle and I are booked aboard the *Hurtigruten* ship which will take us up the magnificent western coast of Norway to celebrate the arrival of 1939. It was my own suggestion, for the journey will take us past many breathtaking landmarks, including, most tantalisingly of all, suspended on the edge of the Geirangerfjord, the Seven Sisters waterfall.

26

It is impossible to translate the beauty of what I witnessed whilst aboard the *Hurtigruten* through the written word. No man possesses the capacity to truly capture the serene, still magnificence of the waterfall, nor the overwhelming gracefulness of the light show which followed. Nonetheless, I feel compelled to turn to my diary to give the reader some sense of the wonder I am currently experiencing.

At about eleven a.m., the *Hurtigruten* rounded the riverbend of the Geirangerfjord, and the Seven Sisters waterfall appeared. I am not ashamed to say that my stomach fluttered with infant-like anticipation as the ship edged closer and closer, until I was face to face with one of the most remarkable sights I have ever seen. Climbing up the rocky outcrop from the fjord were seven opaque paths of white ice, adorned with spindly branches that splintered and diverged infinitely. I have never seen anything of the sort. The frozen streams appeared to me as the ethereal locks of the sisters themselves, blowing in the cosmic winds. Elle grabbed my hand, sensing I was overwhelmed.

'It is truly breathtaking, *chéri*,' Karine said to Pip, embracing him, before turning to the group. 'Why do they call the waterfall the Seven Sisters?'

'Bo can answer that one,' Elle replied, smiling up at me.

'Oh, of course,' I said. 'In this particular case, the legend states that the seven streams—or '"Sisters"—dance playfully down the mountain, as they tease and "flirt" with that waterfall over there.' I pointed to the single stream of water on the opposite side of the fjord. 'He is known as "the Suitor". I must say, it's not my favourite legend that concerns the Seven Sisters, but I am fascinated by their appearances in almost every culture and time period.'

'Please, Bo, continue,' Pip asked, with what seemed like a genuine interest.

'Different cultures believe different things. But for millennia, they have been immortalised in the famous star cluster, and are objects of fascination and wonder across the globe. Tales of the Sisters have been passed on by word of mouth, poetry, art, music, architecture…they are embedded in every facet of our world.'

'Do you know, Bo D'Aplièse,' Pip said, 'in the three years that I have known you, that is the most I've ever heard you talk!' He wasn't wrong, and his comment caused us all to break into laughter.

The passage up from Tromsø eventually became so choppy that Karine decided to go to her cabin, and Elle volunteered to take her down. The steward had announced that this was our best vantage point to see the Northern Lights from, so Pip stayed for a while.

'You spoke so passionately about the Seven Sisters earlier. Tell me, how do you know so much about the stars?' he asked.

'My father was a teacher.'

'Oh really? Of what?'

I felt safe enough in giving Pip the information he was after. 'Music and Classics. The latter encompasses philosophy, anthropology, art, history…plus astrology and mythology. He was particularly fascinated by the relationship between the final two.' I smiled at the memory. 'Naturally, he passed that fascination on to me.'

'This was back in Paris?' Pip asked.

'Er, yes, that's right. In Paris. He served as a private tutor for…wealthy clients.' The latter sentence was not a lie.

Pip gave a chuckle. 'It explains your intelligence, Bo. I am not ashamed to admit that it is far greater than my own.'

I shook my head. 'My friend, I am the one who is jealous of you! Step back and look at your life. You are a member of the Bergen Philharmonic orchestra! The *Hero Concerto* is going to have success beyond your imagination, and you have a beautiful family,' I replied honestly. 'No doubt baby Felix will be missing you today.'

Pip leant on the railings of the *Hurtigruten*. 'I'm sure he's happy enough with his *bestemor* and *bestefar*. Thank you for your kind words, Bo. Though we both know that if it wasn't for your blasted arm, we'd be looking across at one another in the orchestra pit.'

I smiled. 'Perhaps, in another life.'

Pip looked wistfully out to the black water. 'I love Karine so very much, Bo. I feel like the luckiest man that has ever lived.' He reached into his pocket and produced what appeared to be a small ornament. 'Before I moved to Leipzig to attend the conservatory, my father gave me this.'

'What is it?' I asked.

'This, my friend, is a lucky frog...or so my father tells me. They say that Edvard Grieg used to keep them dotted around his home to bring him good fortune. Apparently this one belonged to my grandmother, Anna. Here.' He handed it to me. 'It's yours.'

'Goodness, Pip, I could never take this. It's a family heirloom.'

'Bo, it has brought me all the luck in the universe, so it only seems fair that I should pass it on so another may benefit.' He thought for a moment. 'I wish that you and Elle may live without fear.'

I was deeply moved. 'Pip, I don't know what to say. Thank you.'

'My pleasure. You know, I really should go to Karine. She's awfully seasick. Are you going to stay out here?' he asked.

'All night, if that's what it takes to see the Lights.' Pip put a friendly hand on my shoulder and walked inside.

My eyes were glued to the night sky, which remained crystal clear above me. I am not sure how long I stood there for. Hours, perhaps, bathing in the starlight and communing with my sparkling guardians.

At some stage the Pleiades disappeared from view. I blinked hard, and when I reopened my eyes, the sky above me was covered by a shimmering, iridescent cloak that danced and pulsed across the heavens. I stood in awe beneath the sheer brilliance, the gleam…the lustrous luminosity of the lights…What a privilege it was to witness the vast cosmic beauty of our universe, greater than any manmade work of art or architecture.

After a few minutes, the Aurora Borealis disappeared as mysteriously and abruptly as it had arrived. I couldn't help but break out into ecstatic laughter. I even threw my hands up and cried out, 'THANK YOU!' which shocked a few of my fellow stargazers on the deck.

Soon after, dawn broke over the tranquil waters of the North Cape. In no time at all, we would be turning back towards Bergen. Eventually, I walked back inside the boat to wake Elle and tell her about what I had seen. On the way to our cabin, I passed through the dining room, and saw Pip and Karine sitting down for breakfast. I jogged over to them.

'My friend, I saw them! I saw the miracle! And its majesty was enough to convince even the most fervent non-believer in a higher power. The colours…green, yellow, blue…the entire sky was lit with radiance! I…' I found myself choking on my words, before recovering. I reached my arms out to Pip and clasped him in a hug, which I'm relatively certain took him by surprise. 'Thank you,' I said. 'Thank you.'

Feeling like I was floating on air, I waltzed downstairs and into my cabin, where Elle was peacefully slumbering.

I will never forget the night the sky danced for me.

27

As I reread those pages from the *Hurtigruten*, the lights of the Aurora Borealis and the waterfall feel like a lifetime ago. I find tears coming to my eyes as I read about our dear, dear friends, who no longer... Apologies, faithful reader, I am getting ahead of myself.

I need this time to make no apology for the fact that I have not written in this diary for well over a year. Following our trip on the *Hurtigruten* in 1939, and with a steadily improving elbow, I felt reinvigorated, and penned pages full to the brim with memories. But I regret to inform you that history repeated itself, and those pages remain above the chart-maker's shop in Bergen, as Elle and I were forced to flee once more.

The German war machine attacked Norway on 9th April 1940. The country was taken completely unawares, with its navy busy helping Britain to provide a blockade in the English Channel. In the end, the battle for Bergen was short and brutal, and the city was soon fully occupied. Soldiers patrolled the streets and enormous swastikas hung from City Hall. The new regime, of course, cancelled all Norwegian cultural events, including the premiere of Pip's *Hero Concerto*.

In the weeks preceding the invasion, Karine had been out of her mind with worry. She begged Pip to leave Europe with her, but her husband was resolute in his desire to remain. On several occasions she arrived at our apartment in tears.

'He thinks my new surname and the Lutheran baptism will protect me. I love him, but he is so very naive. The soldiers will take one look at me and see the truth. All it would take is a little investigation, and then…' Karine put her head in her hands, before pointing at Elle. 'You should be fearful too. Your blonde hair and blue eyes can only go so far in protecting you. None of our people are safe in Europe.'

'I know, Karine,' Elle had replied. 'We are making plans.'

'You are right to do so, despite what my husband says. It is impossible to underestimate *their* thoroughness. They will stop at nothing to root us out. And little Felix has Jewish blood, of course. What if they take him too?'

Elle embraced her friend. 'My dearest Karine. I cannot imagine the worry you are experiencing. But your husband would lay down his life to protect your son. I am positive that Pip will do anything to keep him safe.'

Karine began to sob. 'I want to believe it, Elle, I really do.' She shook her head. 'But the *Hero Concerto* is all he thinks about. My parents have begged us to join them in America. They've even sent money. But Pip simply refuses. He says that in a new land he would be just another would-be composer. But here he is *the great Jens Halvorsen*!'

'Do you really believe that he would put his own ego before your personal safety?' Elle asked.

'I do not want to. He insists that Norway is safe because she remained neutral in the Great War. But we know these people, Elle. They will never stop. I am convinced that they will arrive on these shores. And when they do, we must be ready.'

We were. On the night the Nazis came, Elle and I took refuge high up in the hills of Froskehuset alongside the entire Halvorsen clan. As part of my preparations for this very moment, I had engaged the services of a local fisherman, Karl Olsen, who worked out of Bergen Harbour. Karl had agreed to take us to the safety of Great Britain. He was a good man—friendly and reliable—and I talked with him each day as I entered Scholz and Scholz. However, I should state that Karl was not acting out of pure altruism—I had been supplying him with free charts for eighteen months.

On the first morning of the occupation, I rose early and met Karl in the harbour as he began his day. He swore that in twenty-four hours, he would be ready and waiting to ferry us to Scotland.

I reported back to Elle. 'We have to tell Pip and Karine,' she pleaded.

I hesitated. 'Karine, yes. But Pip, and his parents…the more people that know of our plan, the more likely it is we will be discovered.'

She held her ground. 'Bo, we *must* offer them the chance to accompany us.'

'Absolutely we must. But you know how stubborn Pip is. The last thing we want to do is create a scene. Promise me you'll speak to Karine and gauge her reaction first?'

That evening, our last in Norway, we met with the Halvorsens. I made conversation with Astrid and Horst whilst Elle talked to Karine. I studied their faces as Elle imparted the news of our imminent departure. It broke my heart to watch two best friends saying their heart-wrenching farewells.

'What did Karine say?' I asked, as we walked out of the front door towards the tiny hunting cabin we were temporarily occupying.

'She told me that she would always be waiting here for me, and that I must write to her when we reach Scotland.'

'She didn't even contemplate coming with us?'

Elle shook her head. 'She said that Pip would not consider it, and she would rather die than leave his side.' I took Elle's hand, as we both silently contemplated the fate that Pip was condemning her to.

The next morning, at five a.m. sharp, Elle and I met Karl in the harbour. We climbed aboard his trawler, and endured a choppy but uneventful crossing to Inverness, Scotland. It took the best part of the day, during which time I prayed that we would not encounter any military vessels. However, the Pleiades smiled upon us, and our passage to Britain was mercifully clear. I held Elle tight against me as we both mentally bade farewell to our former life. It was something that we were tragically accustomed to, but it didn't get any easier. I knew in particular how heavy Elle's heart was. Karine meant so much to her, and there was no doubt that we were leaving our friend in danger. But, aside from physically kidnapping her and little Felix, there was very little we could do.

'Remember, Karl, you need to drop us somewhere secluded. We don't have any paperwork.'

He waved my concern away. 'No problem, Bo. We'll find an empty beach. From memory, there's no shortage of those here. You'll have to walk ashore, mind.' Elle and I looked to one another and raised our eyebrows.

After some scouting, Karl found somewhere suitable, and took the trawler as close to the shore as he dared.

'That's as good as I can manage.' He shrugged. 'You'll have to go in.' I nodded, then reluctantly hopped over the side of the boat into the freezing water, which came up to my thighs.

'Goodness,' I said, exasperated. 'It's best that I carry you, Elle. Grab our bag.' She took a hold of the singular leather satchel that contained the belongings we'd managed to grab, and Karl helped to lower her into my arms.

'If you have a chance, please tell Karine that we made it safely!' Elle called up to him. 'I'll write to her!'

Karl gave a thumbs up. 'Good luck, you two. I appreciate the charts, Bo.'

'Thank you for everything, Karl. Are you sure you're not getting off, too?'

He laughed. 'Bergen is my home. I want to return and help rid it of its unwelcome visitors. I assure you, the Norwegian people will succeed.' With that, he revved the engine, and began his return journey.

I slowly trudged out of the ocean and onto the beach of pure white sand, where I gently put Elle back on her feet.

'Thank you, my love,' she said gratefully.

The day was grey and windy, which suited this rugged coastline. I took in our surroundings. If Norway had been picturesque and serene, my first impression of Scotland was that it was jagged and raw, but both were equally beautiful. Rocky outcrops, grassy knolls and the ominous sky above us made for quite the first impression. We made our way up a dune, and onto a deserted road.

'I don't think it will take us too long to walk to Inverness,' I wagered. 'From what I could see from the ocean, it's a couple of miles from here at most.'

In under an hour, we'd reached the large coastal town, which described itself as 'the centre of the Highlands'. I don't know what I expected from such a place, but it felt practically deserted. Part of me suspected it was due to British military conscription, which had come into force on the day Neville Chamberlain had declared war on Germany. I shuddered to think of the families in small towns such as this who had been devastated by that decision. Populations must have practically halved.

As we approached the town centre, we came across the red sandstone castle which cut an imposing figure on the banks of the River Ness. I recalled it was where Macbeth had murdered King Duncan in Shakespeare's play, and I couldn't fend off the shiver which travelled down my spine.

Thankfully, by the time we'd arrived on the cobbled high street, my trousers had dried off, although I couldn't quite say the same for my shoes. My feet were positively frozen, and I was desperate to get inside as quickly as possible. Thankfully, it wasn't long until we spotted a battered old sign that swung above us in the strong breeze. It read:

The Sheep Heid Inn, bed and board

'What do you think?' I asked Elle.

She nodded emphatically. 'Let's go in.'

We opened the door to the decrepit terraced building, and walked inside. It was dark and cramped, with only a dim electric light illuminating the reception desk. I tentatively rang the bell, and an elderly gentleman with glasses and a hunch appeared from the bar in the next room.

'Yes?' he asked.

'Hello, sir, do you have a room spare for me and my wife?'

He eyed me suspiciously. 'How long for?' he muttered in his thick accent.

'The next few nights at least. Perhaps longer.'

The man raised an eyebrow. 'What's yer business in Inversneckie?'

'I'm sorry, where?'

He rolled his eyes at me. 'Inverness. What are you doing here in the city? You don't sound local.'

'You have an impressive ear. We are French by birth, but here to visit our ailing Scottish grandmother.'

'Oh, aye, and where does she live then?' he pressed.

'Munlochy,' I replied, as quick as a flash. I had seen a sign for the town on our walk in, and made a mental note of the name as it was pleasing to the ear. This seemed to satisfy the proprietor.

'A room for two it is. You cannae be too careful. Mr Chamberlain's got all of us looking out for anyone strange, you see.'

'Quite right too, sir.'

We were shown up to our room, which was dingy and damp, very much like the weather outside. The mattress was hideously thin, and when I dared to lie down for a moment's rest, my back was assaulted by a barrage of springs. Mercifully, the low quality was reflected in the meagre price of the room, which nonetheless had made a dent in our tiny savings.

'We must discuss our dialect, my love,' I said, as Elle joined me on the bed. 'As we have just learnt, to the British ear we are both softly accented. The last thing we want is attention. Imagine if someone accuses us of being spies!'

She rolled onto her side to face me. 'You're right. But what can we do?'

'Well, I suggest the first thing we do if we're going to be here long-term is adapt our names. If I am Bo, perhaps I could now be...' I searched my brain for an English equivalent. 'Bob!'

Elle frowned. 'I can't call you Bob with a straight face. What about Robert?'

I considered it. 'All right. Robert it is. And perhaps you will become Elle...anor? Like Elinor Dashwood from *Sense and Sensibility*.'

Her frown turned into a small smile. I thought the reference to Jane Austen would please her. 'Okay, so we're Robert and Eleanor. And what about our surname? D'Aplièse is unusual to say the least.'

'I agree. We can't risk any unwanted attention, particularly with conscription in full force. I am young, and locals might start to ask why I am not on the front line.' I sighed in frustration, the weight of the unknown beginning to crush my spirit.

'Bo, even if you wanted to fight, you would not be permitted to. You still struggle to lift a cello bow. Lifting a rifle is out of the question,' Elle reminded me. 'Any doctor would quickly verify that.'

I let out an ironic chuckle. 'Ah, yes. How convenient.'

Elle rolled onto her back and stared at the ceiling. 'If people ask questions about our past, and want to know what we are doing in Britain, I think it makes sense to tell them that we are Jewish refugees, who fled France due to the threat of Nazi invasion. It will at least explain our accents. For half of us, it's simply the truth.'

'You're right.' I rubbed my temples in thought. 'We just need some quiet corner of the country where we can remain hidden away.'

'And finance our existence too, of course,' Elle added.

'What about the Highlands? We could go even further north. I see no reason to change the situation we had in Bergen, where we worked as a pair. Perhaps we could take up work on an estate? They're bound to be short-staffed because of the war.'

Elle sat up and looked out of the grubby window at the dreary street. 'I miss our little apartment with a view of Bergen Harbour. I could have stayed there forever with you.'

'Me too. But we must remember that we are here out of necessity. In this country, I believe we are safe from German invasion. Britain's military is strong and its people resilient.' I took her hand and squeezed it hard. 'I promise, my love, we will have our happy ending.'

Elle spent the afternoon writing a letter to Karine, and I took the opportunity to go exploring. Despite the weather, Inverness had a quaint charm to it. I tried to imagine the place in the height of a peacetime summer, bustling with Highland tourists, which helped my appreciation. I strolled down by the River Ness, which bisects the town and acts as a link between the North Sea and the famous monster-inhabited loch. On my route back to the inn I passed a myriad of little cafes, each claiming to serve *the best Scottish breakfast in town*. I dared look at a few of the menus, and saw that most came with a healthy offering of black pudding, which I understand is made of dried blood. The British do have strange tastes.

After Elle and I had posted her letter to Norway, we settled down in the bar of the Sheep Heid Inn for the evening. In contrast to our bedroom, the bar actually felt relatively cosy now the sun was setting. We were perched on an old wooden bench and stared at the hearty fire which was burning brightly in the grate. When it became dark outside, the barman began to hang up blackout blinds in case of an enemy air raid. I got up to assist him.

'Thanks, pal,' he said with a smile. 'Can I get ye a whisky?'

I hesitated. The reader will be familiar with my reticence to drink alcohol. However, earlier that day I had been up to my thighs in the North Sea and had still not quite recovered from the cold. I decided that on this occasion, I would make an exception, due to the spirit's famed warming properties.

The amber liquid was strong, but undeniably delicious. It had a pleasant mellowing effect on the constitution, and Elle and I enjoyed several glasses of different single malts that evening. The friendly barman, Hamish, clearly enjoyed educating two 'French' refugees on the intricacies of distillation, and why it was so superior to wine. I was worried just how much I'd enjoyed the whisky. I made a mental note not to indulge myself again for a while.

The next few days were spent adapting to life in this new country. My observations were that its people, once their guard was let down, were friendly, welcoming and buoyant. The food, however, was proving a difficult hurdle to jump. The British diet seemed to consist almost entirely of meat, gravy and potatoes. Quite how they had so many famous athletes, I wasn't entirely sure.

On our fifth night in Inverness, we went to dinner at a local tavern—or 'pub' as the British call them—called The Drovers Inn. There were many such pubs in Inverness, and to my untrained eye, they all appeared hugely similar. However, locals would beg to differ and staunchly defend their favourite. 'The Drovers' had been recommended by Hamish. Although not particularly big, it was full of character, with horse brasses and tartan hanging from nearly every wall. Behind the bar were a collection of pewter tankards with names etched on that belonged to the regulars. Naturally, I was able to spot a 'Hamish' amongst them.

Browsing the menu, I was excited to finally see haggis advertised. Hamish had told me it was the national dish, but when I asked him what it *was* exactly, he had laughed and encouraged me to taste it before daring to ask. The tall, burly landlord came over to take our order.

'I'd like to try the haggis, please,' I said confidently, before deciding I wasn't brave enough to go in blind. 'But may I ask what it actually is?'

'"Tis the liver, heart and lungs of a wee sheep,' the landlord replied.

I recoiled slightly. 'Oh, goodness... How is it presented?' I enquired, genuinely wondering if I'd be able to stomach the sight of all that on a plate.

'Dunnae worry yourself, it's all wrapped up in the wee fella's stomach!' he said jovially.

That didn't fill me with much confidence. 'Does it come with anything else?' I enquired.

'Neeps and tatties,' came the reply.

'Neeps and tatties? I'm not quite sure I understand...'

'Turnips and potatoes,' said a deep, rich voice from the bar. A man, approximately fifty years of age, turned around and smiled at Elle and me at our corner table. Even though his hair was greying, his dark eyes and chiselled jawline made him handsome.

'Oh, thank you very much, sir.' I nodded at the man at the bar. 'I'd like to order that, please.'

'And for your filly there?' the landlord asked.

'My what?'

'Your lady friend,' said the man from the bar, now openly laughing. His accent was a clipped English, and he wore a bottle-green tweed suit.

'I'll have the soup, please,' Elle said to the landlord.

'As ye wish.' He nodded, and slunk off to the kitchen with

our order.

The Englishman from the bar made his way over to our table, and I noted that he had a pronounced limp. Setting his frothy beer glass down, he pulled up a stool. 'The Scots only live next door to us English folk, but even I struggle to understand those thick accents sometimes!' He stuck his hand out. 'Archie Vaughan. Nice to make your acquaintance.'

'Oh, hello,' I said. 'My name is Robert, and this is Eleanor.'

'Lovely to meet you,' she added.

Archie gave us a wide smile. 'Charmed, I'm sure. Sorry, I'm probably being terribly rude. Do you mind if I join you for a drink?'

I glanced at Elle, who remained calm and returned his grin. 'Of course not,' she replied, raising her glass of port and lemon.

'Smashing!' Archie cried. 'Now tell me, with those most English of names, where did you pick up those unusual accents?' He took a swig of his beer.

'We're French. We recently fled here to avoid the imminent invasion.' Elle paused, sticking to the script. 'Our people are under threat everywhere,' she added.

'Who, the French?' He snorted, looking comically perplexed. Elle shook her head, and Archie briefly shut his eyes as comprehension dawned. 'Oh, gosh. I see. Well, you're most welcome here. And don't worry, I'm confident we've got the Hun on the run.' He rearranged his legs under the table, wincing as he did so. 'What brings you to Inverness specifically?'

'We're trying to find work,' I replied honestly.

He chuckled. 'Well, sorry to be the bearer of bad news, but you're in the wrong area. Whoever advised you to come up to northern Scotland deserves a slap on the wrist. As you've probably realised, it's mountains and lochs as far as the eye can see.'

'Are you from the area?' Elle asked.

'No, most definitely not. I'm very familiar with it, though. I've been coming up here for shooting weekends ever since I was a lad. It's why I'm here at the moment. I have a week of leave from the Royal Air Force, so I've come to get some Highland air.'

'Where are you based?' I enquired.

He paused for a moment, choosing his reply carefully. 'The

south of England. Kent, as it happens. Not that it will mean much to you!'

'The home of Charles Dickens,' I remarked.

Archie looked genuinely surprised. 'Good Lord, are you sure you're French?! I commend you on your British literary knowledge.' He leant back and folded his arms. 'Don't forget that Miss Vita Sackville-West is from our neck of the woods, too!' Elle and I stared blankly back at him. 'Yes, all right. That one might have been a bit of a stretch.' He took another sip of beer, before training his eyes on me. 'May I ask how you've managed to avoid the battlefield, Robert?'

I felt a little nervous at his line of questioning, but was assured in my reply. 'I'm unable to fight because of an injury to my arm. We're really looking for anything to pay our way.'

Archie raised his eyebrows. 'Ah, a fellow invalid. Sorry to hear that, old chap. You might have noticed I have a dodgy leg, so I can't fight either.' He gave it a slap. 'The Boche are to blame, but it's not a recent injury. I copped this one in the Great War. Now I'm stationed behind a desk.'

'And I'm sorry to hear that too,' I replied.

He looked at me with sympathy. 'I know what it's like for a young man unable to fight. I've got a son, perhaps only a little younger than you, Robert. His name's Teddy. He's got flat feet.' I shook my head. 'Very unfortunate business. Not that he's particularly cut up about the whole thing.' Archie rolled his eyes.

'How does he spend his time?' Elle asked. 'Is he behind a desk like you?'

Archie gave a beleaguered smile. 'No. Teddy is twenty-one and the heir to my enormous country estate.' My ears pricked up. 'Despite my best efforts, I can't seem to motivate him. As a result, he dandies around, getting into scrapes, most of which have to be cleared up by my long-suffering wife Flora.'

I seized my opportunity. 'A country estate? You must have a lot of staff to run things for you.'

Archie chuckled. 'I'm rather afraid those days might be gone for High Weald. Things have been a little…tight since the Great War. And the staff we did have are now either on the front lines or working in munitions factories.' He sighed. 'Flora does almost everything. It's very unfair. But unfortunately, there's little choice at the moment.' Archie looked into his near-empty beer glass. Elle put a hand on my leg, urging me to continue.

'That sounds very difficult for her. Perhaps we might be able to fill the void?' I offered.

Archie looked up, suddenly embarrassed. 'Right, of course. Sorry, I can be a little slow on the uptake. You said you were looking for work.' His eyes darted around the pub as he attempted to formulate his rejection. 'You seem like awfully decent chaps, but as I mentioned, finances are a little difficult in the Vaughan family at the moment. My home, High Weald, is slowly crumbling, and virtually every penny I earn goes back into keeping it from falling down.' He rubbed his eyes. 'It's been in my family for generations and I don't want to be the Vaughan that let the side down. In short, I could hardly offer you anything in terms of payment.'

I had resigned myself to Archie's rebuff, but Elle wasn't going to give up. 'Oh, we're quite used to a petty income, Mister Vaughan. In Paris, we only had a tiny apartment.'

'Actually, it's *Lord* Vaughan, if we're being strict about it,' he said with a wink. 'All right then. Tell me, what was it you did for work in Paris?'

'Apologies, Lord Vaughan.' Archie waved it away with a laugh. Elle looked at me. 'Robert and I worked together at an orphanage,' she lied. 'Robert was the caretaker and gardener, and I cooked for the children, and did some cleaning too. Naturally, orphanage funds were limited, and so we weren't paid much at all.' The smoothness of Elle's fiction was astounding.

'Was it a big place?' Lord Vaughan asked, eyebrows raised.

Elle nodded vigorously. 'Oh yes, enormous. It's called the *Apprentis d'Auteuil* if you'd like to look it up. And we guarantee you, whatever mess young Master Teddy may create, it will be nothing compared to the chaos which one hundred children caused!'

Archie raised his eyebrows and swilled his remaining beer around his pint glass. 'No, I don't imagine much *would* be a challenge after that. Well, I can't deny that Flora would be very grateful, particularly with me tied up at the airbase.' He thought for a moment. 'Listen, although I couldn't pay you much, High Weald does have a number of cottages on the estate, all of which are currently unoccupied. Would a roof over your head and all the game you can shoot be adequate?'

Elle beamed. 'Oh sir, we would be forever grateful to you!'

I joined in her enthusiasm. 'Honestly, Lord Vaughan, we would be indebted to you.'

'Well then'—he slapped his thighs and stood up—'welcome aboard!' He shook both of our hands warmly. 'What a fortunate meeting this has proved to be.' He didn't know the half of the matter. 'But I must be getting back to my lodgings. I'm on the sleeper in a few hours.' I looked at him quizzically. 'Oh, sorry. The overnight train. It runs from Glasgow to London. Speaking of which, where are you staying at the moment? I'll have some tickets arranged. Could you start next week?'

Elle and I looked at each other. 'Of course, we'd be grateful to,' I replied. 'We're at the Sheep Heid Inn.'

'Excellent.' He clapped his hand together. 'I'll have the tickets sent there.'

'Oh, we're more than happy to pay for—' Elle began.

Archie held his hand up. 'Nonsense, you're under my employ now, and things haven't grown so bad that I'm unable to fund a night on the Caledonian Railway.' He downed the remnants of his pint of beer. 'Forgive me, do you know, I don't think I caught your surname?' He looked at us quizzically. 'It's Robert and Eleanor...'

'Tanit,' I replied, as quickly and smoothly as possible.

'Perfect. I'll have the tickets sent to Mr and Mrs Tanit.' With a nod and a smile, Archie Vaughan took his long, blue great coat from the hook by the door and walked out of the tavern.

Elle and I turned to one another, and started to laugh. 'You see, my darling,' I said. 'Do you understand why, despite everything, I put my trust in the universe?!'

She took my hands. 'I'm certainly beginning to. What a stroke of luck!'

'Indeed.' I looked skywards and gave a small shrug. 'Or, perhaps, something more powerful than luck. Who are we to say?' We stared into each other's eyes for a while, both probably a little baffled that we had been granted a new opportunity so quickly. Eventually Elle frowned.

'What about the surname you gave him? What were you thinking?'

Reader, in a moment of sheer panic, I had provided Archie Vaughan with my true name—the one that, somewhere in the wastelands of Siberia, is written on my birth certificate: Tanit.

I ran my hands through my hair. 'I know, it was foolish of me. But I didn't wish to hesitate for a second, particularly after all those questions about our accents. It was merely what was in my brain.'

Elle rolled her eyes, but the smile returned to her face. 'So, we are to be Mr and Mrs Tanit.'

'I suppose that if Kreeg ever does make it to Britain,' I reasoned, 'the last thing he'd expect is for me to be using my real surname...'

Over dinner, we discussed all the possibilities that our new life on the country estate might afford us. We fantasised about the little cottage we had been promised, and the lush green surroundings of the English countryside. In that moment, the peril of Kreeg and German invasion felt very far away.

We strolled back down the high street to our lodgings, whereupon the proprietor presented us with a letter addressed to 'Bo and Elle'—which, thankfully, were the names we had used to check in. Elle's face lit up, and she rushed upstairs to our room.

'It must be Karine!' she said excitedly. 'I can't wait to tell her about what happened this evening. She'll think it's so funny.' She examined the front of the envelope and frowned. 'It's strange, this doesn't look like Karine's handwriting.'

'Open it and find out,' I encouraged her.

Once she had torn into the envelope, Elle pulled out two pieces of paper. 'There's something from Horst in here,' she said quizzically.

'Horst? Is everything all right?'

I studied Elle's face as she read the contents. 'I don't understand.'

'Read it aloud,' I suggested.

'"Dear Bo, Dear Elle..."' she began.

I hope this envelope reaches you. I discovered your address from the recent letter you sent to Karine. I apologise for opening it, but you will soon learn why I had no choice. I am glad that you are safely in Scotland, and hope that the horror of this senseless conflict does not follow you there. I wish that I was not writing to you in such sorry circumstances. But it is my duty to send this letter to you, as per my dear son's wishes.

I beg of you, do not think badly of him. He was not a rotten person. He merely made a mistake, and has paid the highest price imaginable. Thank you for being such dear friends to my son, and to Karine. Know that they both loved you deeply.

Please, treasure each other, love each other, and listen to each other.

Your friend,

Horst Halvorsen

Elle put the letter down and looked at me with concern.

There was a sinking feeling in the pit of my stomach. 'Let me read the other letter.' I walked over to Elle and gently took it from her hands.

Dear Bo, Dear Elle,

By the time this letter reaches you (if it ever does), I will be gone. It is my sad duty to inform you that, this morning, the love of my life, Karine Eliana Rosenblum, was shot and killed by our invaders.

Her crime was that she had dared to walk into town to buy bread and milk.

As you both know, it was Karine's wish to leave Norway. I selfishly failed to heed her warning, and for that, I can offer no excuses. My wife was kinder, cleverer and BETTER than I, and I should have listened to her.

My heart is broken, and can never be fixed.

Elle, I must apologise to you in particular. You were Karine's best friend, and shared a bond with her perhaps even deeper than my own. It is my fault, and no one else's, that you will never meet again.

My friends, I throw myself at the mercy of our Lord, but do not expect forgiveness. Writing this letter will be my penultimate earthly act. Then I will take my father's hunting gun from the shed, and end my life in the woods above the house. Rest assured, Felix is safe with my loving parents, who I know will be as adoring to my son as they were to their own.

All I ever wanted was to be lauded for my musical prowess. So please, my friends, do not remember me—let that be my eternal punishment. Allow me to be consigned to ash and dirt.

But remember our dear Karine. In a world shrouded by darkness, she was a light, and must shine forever.

Yours,

Jens 'Pip' Halvorsen

Neither Elle nor I were able to speak. We simply sat in silence, until Elle's body began to shake and shudder as her tears arrived. I held her for hours, until she finally relaxed and fell asleep in my arms, exhausted by the emotional toll of what we had learnt.

The morning light eventually arrived, and so did the Caledonian sleeper tickets for 'Mr and Mrs Tanit', which caused a fair amount of confusion at the reception desk, for we had signed in under 'D'Aplièse'. Thankfully, the proprietor accepted my excuse that 'Tanit' was my ailing grandmother's name, and there had clearly been a mistake.

That evening, we took a train from Aberdeen to Glasgow, and boarded the sleeper just before eleven p.m. Having settled into our small cabin—which comprised of a metal bunk bed, a small sink and a foldaway table—I joined Elle on the bottom mattress and squeezed her hand.

'We will live our lives in her honour. In *their* honour,' I assured her. 'Our happiness will be in remembrance of them,' I said as the wheels began to roll on the track.

I was distressed to see just how broken Elle looked. 'I can't stop thinking about little Felix,' she sniffed. 'What will become of him? To lose both of one's parents at the same time is…well, I know just how painful it is.' She looked at me dead in the eye. 'Do we not have a duty to go back for him?'

I pondered Elle's question. Searching my heart, I felt that the truth was…yes, we did have a duty. But we could not return to Bergen at this moment in time. It would be suicide. 'Felix will be safe with Horst and Astrid. We know what good people they are. And Karine can rest peacefully knowing that no connection to his religious heritage can now be made. He is well protected where he is.'

Elle put a hand to her mouth. 'I just feel so very indebted to both of them. Without them, who knows where we would be? And now…it's too late to repay them for their kindness.'

Elle's words circled around my head as the train chugged on into the night. Eventually, the gentle rhythm of the train and the clacking of the track lulled me to sleep, and we left Scotland for a new life.

The Titan

June 2008

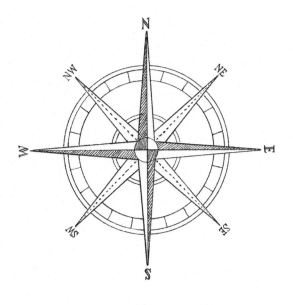

28

Merry

All things considered, I'd managed a decent amount of sleep last night. Perhaps I owed it to my brief conversation with Ambrose. He had been on his way to dinner, but hearing his clipped, jovial tones relaxed me. I had promised to call back early this morning with updates. I yawned and looked around my cabin, which was bathed in a pleasant orange glow as dawn crept in through the porthole.

There was a familiar rumble in the belly of the ship as Captain Hans throttled up the engines for another day of cruising. I was certainly glad of the opulent luxury of the *Titan*, and that I wasn't crossing the choppy North Sea in a trawler as my parents had done. I rubbed my eyes at the thought of all they had been through. There was no question that I was now deeply emotionally invested in their story, and when we came to lay the wreath for Atlas, I predicted I would be as teary as his other daughters.

They all spoke of their pa with such sincere love. Rather unexpectedly, I found myself a little jealous that I had never been able to receive his affection, despite my biological connection.

My alarm went off—not that I needed it—and I sat up in bed. Then I reached for the satellite phone which had been stationed next to my bed by a friendly young crew member, and punched in Ambrose's number, and after a few rings, he picked up.

'Might I presume I am connected to the Mermaid of the

Mediterranean?'

'Good morning, Ambrose,' I chuckled. 'Did you have a good time last night?'

'Sublime, thank you, my dear. I was treated to dinner at the Drury Buildings by a former student of mine. It was "good craic", as they say...' He stopped himself, which was generous for Ambrose, as he could have gone on for hours. 'But enough of me! I insist you tell me everything!'

I leant back on my pillow. 'I really must thank you for convincing me to fly out here, Ambrose. I have a feeling that it's going to change my life.'

'You know, my dear, so do I. Now come along, give me the juicy bits, if you don't mind.'

'All right, brace yourself...' I filled him in on what I'd learnt so far.

Ambrose was flabbergasted. 'Golly, Merry. Pardon the cliché, but what a roller-coaster.'

'That's not even the half of it,' I continued. 'In the diary, Atlas is being pursued across the world by a childhood friend turned enemy. Maybe you've heard of him. He's that communications tycoon Kreeg Eszu—the one who committed suicide a year ago.'

There was a pause on the line as Ambrose pondered the name. 'Oh yes... How odd! Come to mention it, I think his company *does* my internet. It's rubbish.'

I couldn't help but laugh. 'I'm sure everyone on board the *Titan* would be glad to hear it. Kreeg and his son Zed are absolute *personae non gratae*.'

'No wonder,' Ambrose replied. 'From memory, that man had fingers in all sorts of pies, didn't he? Broadband, mobile phone networks... I think he even had a controlling stake in a couple of television channels.'

I swung my feet out of bed and stood up. 'Apparently so, yes. Zed took over things following Kreeg's death.'

Ambrose tutted. 'Well, if you do happen to bump into him at any stage, please send him over to Dublin to boost my signal.'

I shook my head. 'I'll be sure to, Ambrose.'

'Thank you.' He sniffed. 'Now, are you any closer to finding out how you ended up on Father O'Brien's doorstep in West Cork?'

I sighed as I looked out of the porthole at the rising sun. 'Not yet. Although there is something mysterious that I haven't mentioned.'

'Excellent,' Ambrose cooed. 'I love mysterious. Do tell.'

'You'll recall that Jack did a bit of digging into Argideen House. It turns out that the last registered owner was none other than this Kreeg Eszu fella.'

'Hmm…' Ambrose mused. 'What an intriguing coincidence. If, indeed, it *is* a coincidence…' His voice trailed off.

'Quite. You don't happen to know anything about what happened with the house from the fifties onwards, do you, Ambrose?'

He sighed, clearly annoyed with himself. 'I must confess that I don't. I had little to do with Argideen House on my visits to West Cork. Surely the diary will provide you with answers?'

'Apparently not, according to Mr Hoffman. Although I'm not sure I completely believe him. I could swear he's not telling us the whole truth.'

Ambrose chuckled. 'Lawyers do not, generally speaking. I'm very happy to do a little bit of digging at this end, if that would be helpful? I've still got plenty of contacts in West Cork. You know how small the place is. There's bound to be someone who remembers *something* about that time.'

'Thank you, Ambrose, I'd be incredibly grateful if you would.' I smiled at his kindness.

'Don't mention it, Merry. As you know, I've always rather liked the idea of being a detective.'

'Poirot would be quaking in his boots,' I quipped.

'Indeed. Rest assured, I shall do my bit this end and see what I can learn about the former inhabitants of Argideen House.'

'Thank you, Ambrose. I'll ring you tomorrow morning ahead of the wreath laying.'

'Jolly good! Enjoy the high seas and the continued adventure of your true heritage. Goodbye, Merry.'

'Goodbye, Ambrose.' I put the satellite phone down, stretched and headed for the shower.

29

Ally sipped her latte and looked out onto the Mediterranean from the port viewing deck. The sea was like a millpond this morning, and she envied the perfect sailing conditions. How she wished she could get off the *Titan* for a few hours and take her Laser for a spin. It was just what she needed to clear her head. Reliving the awful fate her grandparents had suffered had been difficult. She still found Pip's decision to stay in Norway difficult to reconcile. If only her grandmother had listened to Pa and Elle, how different things might have been. She could have travelled with them to Scotland, started a whole new life…

Ally shook her head. It was amazing what the bond of love could force a person to do against their better judgement.

Reading the story from a new perspective had given her an even greater sense of sympathy for her biological father, Felix Halvorsen. He had been the real victim of that whole horrific episode. Was it any wonder that he had turned out the way he had? Ally felt a sudden urge to text her brother Thom, and took her phone from her pocket. She checked for any bars of signal, but the *Titan* was moving and now out of the range of a mast.

'Ally?' She jumped, and managed to spill half of her coffee down her white linen shirt. 'Shit, I'm so sorry.' Jack jogged down the deck towards her.

'Jack…it's not your fault. I was lost in my thoughts, that's all.'

'Yeah?' He put a gentle arm on her back, and Ally's spine tingled. 'Are you doing all right?'

Ally nodded. 'I am. Thank you, Jack.'

He raised his eyebrows at her. 'Now, are you going to give me the real answer?'

She gave him a resigned smile. 'All right. That last section of the diary was particularly difficult for me.'

Jack sighed and leant on the *Titan*'s railing. 'I'm sorry, Al. This must be so rough on you in particular.'

'It's hard for all of us,' Ally replied. 'I can't even guess at what your mum's going through.'

'Ah, she's a tough old bird.'

'Jack!' Ally couldn't help but snigger at his outrageous comment.

He chuckled, too. 'Hey, she'd freely admit it!' Jack carried on with the point he was determined to make. 'But I really feel for you, Ally, with Bear and everything. Speaking of which, where is the little man this morning?'

'He's currently with Ma.'

'Lucky him. She's pretty great with the kids, eh?'

'Absolutely.' Ally folded her arms and looked to the floor, unsure how to phrase the compliment she wanted to give. 'You weren't so bad yourself with him yesterday. You're a natural.' She nodded.

'Oh, thanks. I've always fancied being a dad.' He cursed himself. 'Not that…I am his dad. Or…ever would be his dad.' He shook his head and gripped on to the railing.

'It's all right.' Ally let out a tender giggle.

Jack took a deep breath. 'I'm crap at this, Ally. But I really wanted to say that…I imagine you'll be thinking about Theo a lot, in addition to everything else. You must miss him hugely. And that's on top of everything you're already going through.'

Jack's heartfelt words and thoughtfulness touched Ally deeply.

'I really appreciate you saying that, Jack. Thank you.'

'I mean it,' Jack continued. 'He'd be really proud of you. And Bear too, of course.'

Ally tried to suppress the lump in her throat. 'Thank you.'

They stood together in silence for a moment, both staring out at the sea. Then Ally slowly reached out a hand. 'Whilst we're having awkward conversations, I owe you an apology.'

Jack took her hand, but looked genuinely puzzled. 'What on earth for, Ally?'

'For not telling you about Bear when we met in France. It must have been very strange to see him when you arrived.'

'Oh.' He shrugged and tried to play it off. 'Don't mention it. It's absolutely none of my business.'

Ally pushed on. 'Thank you. But Jack...it really sort of *is* your business, and I feel stupid for not telling you. I really am sorry.'

He shook his head. 'Don't be silly. How d'you reckon it's "my business" anyhow?'

Ally steeled herself. 'Oh boy. Jack...I didn't tell you because I didn't want to...'

He gripped her hand tighter. 'Didn't want to what, Ally?'

'I didn't want to drive you away from me,' Ally admitted.

There was a brief silence. 'Oh,' was all Jack could manage in response.

Ally continued. 'I just assumed, rightly or wrongly, that you might be put off by the fact that I had a new baby. Not to mention that he's the child of my dead lover.' Ally put her head in her hands. 'Honestly, Jack, you couldn't write it.'

Jack let out a nervous laugh. 'No. To be honest, I thought you didn't mention him to me because you didn't see me as a "serious thing".'

'A "serious thing"?'

'Yeah, you know.' Jack's eyes skirted about the deck. 'Potential boyfriend material, I guess.'

'That's not the reason, no.' Ally grinned. 'Did you really just use the phrase "potential boyfriend material"?'

This time it was Jack who put his head in his hands. 'God. Sorry.'

Ally rubbed his back. 'It's okay! But whilst we're having this conversation, can I ask what you really think of the whole situation? Feel free to be honest.'

Jack's eyes were wide. 'You mean Bear?' he asked. Ally nodded. 'Well...' He struggled to find the right words. 'I think it's great! I mean, he's great! It's all…great.'

Ally couldn't help but laugh at his outburst. Jack joined her. 'Sorry about that. I've never been very articulate. But I mean it, Ally. I think it's very special what's happened with your boy. I think it's kind of beautiful that Theo lives on. Anyway. That's all I'll say on the matter before I tie myself into any more knots.' They stared at each other for a moment, until Ally leant in to gently kiss him.

'Blimey,' Jack said. 'We should have had this awkward conversation weeks ago!' He pulled Ally into his arms. He kissed her passionately this time, and felt her soften in his arms.

'Thank you, Jack,' Ally said.

'What for?'

'For being here.'

30

By eleven o'clock, five of the six D'Aplièse sisters had gathered on the large, comfortable sofas in the main salon. Most had brought juices and freshly baked croissants down from the breakfast table, having only just surfaced after a long night of reading.

'I couldn't put the diary down,' Tiggy said.

'Nor could I,' agreed Maia. 'You know the bit I found really interesting? When Pa's in the fire. That woman in the red dress appeared to him…'

'Yeah, amazing what a little smoke inhalation can do to the brain, huh?' Electra scoffed, and shoved a pastry into her mouth.

'Oh, I wouldn't be so sure, Electra.' Tiggy gave her a wistful smile, and tried not to be offended when her younger sister rolled her eyes.

'I think everyone's missing the main point.' CeCe frowned. 'That bastard Kreeg literally tried to burn Pa alive. I don't know about you, but I feel such…rage.'

'I know, CeCe,' Star comforted. 'The weird thing is that he failed. Kreeg never managed to kill Pa. They both died as old men. So did Kreeg give up the chase, or did they reconcile?' The room fell silent as each sister wondered what the truth might turn out to be.

The quiet was broken as Ally walked into the salon, followed by Jack.

'Morning, everyone,' she said.

'Yeah, morning, ladies.' Jack awkwardly manoeuvred himself away from Ally, clearly unsure of whether he should be standing next to her or not.

Ally clasped her hands together. 'From all the chatter, I assume everyone's up to speed on Pa's diary?' There was a general nod of agreement. 'Where's Merry?'

'She's been up,' Star replied. 'I think she's snuck off to the hot tub to mull things over. Are you okay, Ally?' she asked tentatively. 'It was horrid to read about your grandparents.'

Ally forced a smile and nodded. 'I'm fine. It's nothing I wasn't fully aware of.'

Suddenly, Maia shrieked, 'Oh my God!'

The eldest D'Aplièse sister was pointing at a television in the corner of the room, which was broadcasting the BBC News Channel. Although it was on mute, the entire room was now all virtually face to face with Zed Eszu.

'Oh shit, what's that animal doing on the screen? Sorry, Maia. Someone turn it off!' Electra hurriedly said.

'No!' Maia replied firmly. 'I want to hear it. Let's turn it up.' CeCe grabbed the remote and hammered the volume button.

'...and as part of our *futures* week, we're joined by the CEO of Lightning Communications, Zed Eszu, to talk about his plans for the growth of fibre-based internet. You're very welcome to the programme, Mr Eszu.'

'Thank you so much,' he replied, with his trademark mawkish smile. Zed was dressed in one of his awful shiny suits, though had elected not to wear a tie. In fact, his shirt was unbuttoned so far that the viewer might catch a glimpse of his large pectoral muscles. His black hair was slicked back, and he exuded oiliness, in every sense of the word.

'Oh God, just look at him,' cried Electra. 'He'll be loving every second of this.'

'Shh,' said Maia, who was staring intently at the screen.

'Firstly,' the presenter continued, 'our sincere condolences on the death of your father, Kreeg, who ran Lightning for decades.'

'Yes, nearly thirty years,' Zed replied.

The presenter gave him a heartfelt nod. 'In that time, he

achieved a great deal, helping to update internet infrastructure in homes across the globe. Which naturally made him a very wealthy man.'

Zed gave an artificial chuckle that made Maia's skin crawl. 'The money wasn't important to my father.' He spread his hands expansively. 'He just cared about helping people. That was his true passion.'

'What is this bullshit?' Electra hissed.

'Shh, please,' Maia pleaded.

'My father loved humanity. He wanted us all to live better lives, to be better connected, and…'—Zed looked straight down the barrel of the camera—'…to never lose touch with the people that really matter.'

The interviewer folded his arms and reflected on Zed's comments. 'Do you think that's what drove him?'

Zed leant back in his chair and gave another sickly sweet grin. 'You know, he didn't like the idea that someone could just disappear off the face of the earth. Everyone deserves to stay connected. I think that's what fascinated him about communications and the internet.'

'It's an inspiring story. You yourself have been running the company for a year now, appointed director upon your father's death. Was it always the plan for you to take over one day?'

'Oh, absolutely. My father was a meticulous planner. Everything was always…incredibly well thought through.' He nodded soberly, his face all concern.

Tiggy interjected. 'He makes me shudder. Why do I feel like he's speaking directly to us?'

'I know what you mean,' Ally replied under her breath.

The presenter continued. 'Well, as part of our *futures* week, you're here to talk about the expansion plans you have for Lightning, and how we might see our internet speeds increase!'

'That's exactly right, thank you.' He tapped his fingers together, playing the part of the intelligent businessman. It was all for show, of course. It was one big performance, and the D'Aplièse sisters knew it. 'I can today announce that Lightning Communications intends to replace our outdated satellite network with state-of-the-art fibre optic cables, which will connect our continents more reliably than anything in space ever could.'

The presenter appeared confused. 'Cables? Isn't that a step backwards from satellites?'

'Great question. Thank you for asking it.' He grinned.

'Bleurgh,' CeCe muttered.

'My cables will offer significantly improved performance in terms of bandwidth and data carrying. I know it might be a little difficult for some of your viewers to understand.' He smiled patronisingly. 'These cables work by transferring information via pulses of light which pass along transparent glass pipes. Like magic,' he chortled. 'Think of me as a magician.'

'A magician with a very punchable face,' Jack chipped in.

The presenter continued his line of questioning. 'Will these cables hang above our heads like telephone lines?'

'My goodness, you really are full of excellent questions today.' Zed's attempts to sound sincere were growing increasingly frustrating. 'In fact, these cables will be placed under our oceans. Just imagine it…the seabed itself will teem with technology!'

'It sounds very ambitious, Mr Eszu. Naturally, I should address the environmental concerns. Will you be able to do the job without disturbing marine life?'

Zed frowned, and his guard momentarily slipped. 'This new network will form the basis of global telecommunications for the human race. If a few fish get in the way, then I'm sure it is a sacrifice that people will be willing to accept.'

'Well, not everyone would agree with—'

Zed cut the presenter off. 'It's all a matter of risk and reward. In order to win, we must accept that there will be casualties along the way.' He checked himself and delivered a further nauseating smirk. 'Of course, to be absolutely clear, we at Lightning will do our utmost to ensure that Nemo and his little fishy friends go unharmed.'

'I'm sure many viewers will be relieved to hear that,' said the presenter, now a little flustered. 'I was going to ask—'

Zed interjected once more. 'You see, my father isn't dead, not really. He lives on through this project. And if all goes to plan, he'll live on forever. Everyone will remember the Eszu name.'

'That's a…uh…nice sentiment. But to get back on track, this

is an absolutely enormous task, isn't it?'

'That's true.' Zed gave a modest shrug. 'But I am thrilled to announce that Lightning Communications will be partnering with Berners Bank to ensure the project's completion.' The younger Eszu looked very satisfied with himself.

'You're going to be bankrolled by Berners?' the presenter asked.

'You've chosen a crass term, but yes. David Rutter, the CEO, is a personal friend of mine. He's a great man. He shares my vision for the future.'

'David Rutter...' CeCe whispered. 'Where have I heard that name before?'

'Mr Rutter's telephone number is certainly a handy one to have in the phonebook,' the presenter quipped.

Zed raised his immaculately plucked eyebrows. 'I would tend to agree, yes.'

'Where will you start this enormous project?'

'We'll begin by connecting Australia to New Zealand. It's our little Antipodean test run,' he laughed. 'We're about to send out a small army of "trenchers" to start digging under the Tasman Sea.'

The presenter gave Zed a nod. 'Well, we shall follow your progress with interest, Mr Eszu. You must promise to return to the programme and update us on the progress of the project.'

'Oh, it would be my pleasure to, thank you.' He flashed his whitened teeth. 'But just before I go, I should say that we like to brand everything to the hilt at Lightning. Perhaps you'd like to know the name of this project?'

The presenter was taken aback once more. 'Of course,' he said, through gritted teeth.

'Well, seeing as this project will do the heavy lifting for humanity, it makes sense that we should term the project... "Atlas".'

Electra took the remote control and switched the television off. The salon was silent. 'All right, ladies. I'm sure he knows we're on this trip. And I'm sure he knows all about Pa and Kreeg's past.' She pointed to the television. 'That creep wants a reaction. But we're not going to give it to him. Okay?'

CeCe stood up. 'It's like a final piece of revenge. The whole world is going to know about this cable thing. And he's using Pa's name to do it.'

'Sorry, exactly who was that guy?' Jack whispered to Ally.

'Kreeg Eszu's son,' she replied.

'God. I can smell the hair oil on him from here.' He paused, sensing the change of atmosphere. 'Listen, I'm going to do a coffee run, I think you girls could do with a top-up.'

'Make it a rosé run, Jack, if you don't mind,' Star said.

'Coming right up,' he replied, and made for the salon door.

'Jesus. I feel sick. He just…' Maia's voice tailed off as a lump arrived in her throat.

'I know, sweetie,' Electra replied, taking her sister's hand. 'But let's stay calm, and stay together. Think about what Pa would do. He'd pause and think things through. What was that thing he always said? About chess?'

'Lose pieces wisely,' Star whispered.

'That's it. I think he meant that you have to pick your battles. And this is one that we can't do much about at the moment,' Electra continued. 'We know that the timing isn't a coincidence. He's trying to ruin our trip to honour Pa. So we're not going to let him.'

Ally stepped outside onto the aft deck, her head spinning. It had been quite the morning, from having to relive her grandparents' horrific deaths, to Zed Eszu appearing like an omnipotent and evil god on the *Titan*'s televisions. Not forgetting, of course, Jack… Her heart skipped a beat as she thought of their earlier kiss. She desperately hoped that the awkward tension was now behind them, and that they might have a chance… She carried on towards the rear of the yacht, thinking that she might track down Ma and relieve her of 'Bear duty'.

As Ally approached the stern, she spied Georg Hoffman. He was running one hand through his hair, whilst the other grasped a satellite phone. The lawyer was pacing up and down, shaking his head vigorously. Then Ally stared in disbelief as Georg put the phone down, dropped to his knees and began to thump the teak decking. She rushed over to him. 'Georg! Are you all right?'

He jumped out of his skin, and rushed to his feet. 'Ally, forgive me. I thought I was alone.'

'What's wrong? Who were you talking to?'

'Oh,' he stumbled. 'It was only my sister. She was giving me some…difficult news.'

'Georg, I'm so sorry. If there's anyone who understands difficult, it's me. Would you like to talk about it?'

He went red in the face. 'Oh, no. Thank you, though. I really cannot apologise enough. I very rarely lose my cool, so to speak.'

'Don't worry about it, Georg,' Ally comforted him. 'It's a stressful time for us all. Are you positive that sharing won't help?'

He let out a large sigh. 'It's nothing, really. Claudia was just updating me on some personal matters that I'm currently unable to resolve. That's my job, Ally, I solve things. And it frustrates me that I'm powerless to help someone very important to me.'

Ally frowned. 'Sorry, Georg, did you say Claudia? *Our* Claudia, from Atlantis? I thought you were on the phone to your sister.'

Georg's mouth opened wide. 'Uh, I'm sorry. Yes, I made a mistake. Well, no,' he corrected himself, 'I didn't. My sister is also called Claudia. The two Claudias, aha!'

'Did you make a mistake, Georg? Or, for once, did you actually speak the unfiltered truth?'

Georg Hoffman put his head in his hands. 'Where are you up to in the diary?'

'Pa's living at High Weald.'

He took a moment to mentally check something. 'Yes, Ally. Claudia is my younger sister. The circumstances of our meeting with your father are detailed in the pages of his journal. I will let him tell you in his own words.'

Ally was lost for words. 'Georg… I…why on earth would that be kept a secret?'

Georg shrugged, his thread well and truly unravelled. 'Your father was doing what he did best—protecting us, that's all. Read on, you will see.'

Ally thought this day couldn't get any more chaotic. The sight of a manic Georg was deeply unsettling. It was a bit like seeing the little man behind the curtain in *The Wizard of Oz*, frantically operating the complex machinery to maintain the illusion. Suddenly, Ally felt a strong urge to gain control of the situation. 'Now tell me, Georg, what was the news that Claudia was giving you? The news that literally caused you to pound the floor with rage?'

Georg threw his hands out. 'Really, Ally, it's nothing related to—'

Ally snapped, and grabbed Georg by the lapels of his linen jacket. 'Georg Hoffman, for the first time in your life, you are going to tell me *exactly* what is going on. I want to know what Claudia was telling you, and I want to know why it made you so very angry. Then I want to know why you've had so many secretive phone calls during the past month, and why they started as soon as Claudia went on leave from Atlantis. Remember, Georg, you work for me and my sisters. And we want answers. This isn't negotiable.'

Georg's shoulders slumped down, and Ally looked deep into his reddening eyes.

'Okay, Ally. I will do as you have asked. But please, do not blame me. Believe me when I tell you that I have done my best.' Georg began to quietly sob.

'I don't doubt it, Georg. But we are ready for the truth.' She released him and looked into his tear-stained eyes once more.

'Yes. You are,' he said emphatically.

The Diary of Atlas

1944–51

31

High Weald, Kent, England

Personally, I have no idea why the Vaughans wish to live in their old, crumbling mansion, when this picture-perfect estate cottage, which Elle and I inhabit, exists. It has a wood-burning stove, large exposed beams and views over the rolling green expanses of the 'Garden of England'. I love it.

In terms of work, Elle and I have found fulfilment in our everyday activities. Elle cooks for grateful mouths, and I tend the beautiful grounds that High Weald boasts. On occasion, we even manage to collaborate, with Elle utilising the produce that I grow in the vegetable patch. In all honesty, I thought that our minds would be restless and unsettled, as neither of us are able to express our passions in symphony orchestras—but the quiet, wholesome life we now live is, dare I say…preferable? Never in my life have I felt safer, or more tranquil. My landscape sketches have certainly improved, with Elle even permitting me to hang one or two on the walls of the living room.

In the evenings, we huddle together in front of the fire and read books. Occasionally we'll switch on the wireless, to be reassured that the Allies are holding the Axis powers at bay, but in all honesty, the war seems a million miles away from the pastoral idyll in which we exist. As the conflict has progressed, Archie Vaughan has had to spend more time at Ashford airbase, but is endlessly chipper. His wife, Flora, is a true delight, too. She spends hours working alongside me in the gardens. Her passion for flowers clearly has the ability to soothe her soul and transport her to another world. I recognise this in her, because music does the same for me.

Flora is particularly patient with me, as she realised very quickly that I am not a gardener by trade. Each day I have learnt something new from her, and have grown to appreciate the true beauty of the natural world. It is delicate, intricate and harmonious in its majesty. During our long afternoons tending perennials and pruning shrubs, Flora has told me her story, which I must say nearly rivals my own in terms of drama. I am very happy that she and Archie have eventually found one another.

'I spent many years trying to deny love, Mr Tanit,' she confessed to me. 'But I have come to realise that it is a force stronger than any human being has the capacity to control.'

I smiled. 'You're correct there, Lady Vaughan.'

'I know I am.' Flora snipped a browning bud from her white rose bush. 'Now tell me, Mr Tanit, how did you meet Eleanor?'

I pondered my response for a while as I dug out a tenacious weed. 'We met as orphans in Paris, Lady Vaughan.'

She put her hands on her hips. 'Goodness me! I didn't realise that you were both parentless.' She paused. 'You know, Teddy…' Flora stopped herself, and shook her head. 'Anyway, you are both very well suited, I have to say.' She examined a delicate white petal. 'The older I grow, the more I begin to think that love is simply written in the stars.'

I looked up to meet her eye. 'Oh yes, Lady Vaughan. That I know for certain.'

She tutted. 'Please, Mr Tanit, I don't know how many times I have to tell you. You can call me Flora.'

'Sorry, Flora. Please, call me Bo…Bob. Robert.'

She giggled. 'All right, Bo-Bob-Robert, will do.'

I shook my head and moved on to the next weed. 'Apologies. Thinking in English rather than French occasionally leads to confusion,' I explained.

'It's quite all right. I can't imagine what the both of you have been through. But I'm so glad you have each other. The way you look at each other is really quite magical. When did you marry?'

I was glad that I was able to focus on the mud in front of me. 'Oh, that would be a few years ago now, just before we crossed from France. It wasn't an expensive affair.'

Flora sighed melancholically. 'I think that's better. It's about two people at the end of the day, and no one else.'

Archie and Flora have a daughter, the charming and intelligent Louise. She is sweet and caring, and manages a team of 'Land Girls' who are at High Weald to help with the war effort, growing crops on the estate. Her leadership is inspiring, and her wards simply adore her.

Just recently, we celebrated Louise's engagement to Rupert Forbes—a gentle, bookish man who had been prevented from joining the front lines by his myopia. Nonetheless, Rupert's immense intelligence and assured demeanour led him to be snapped up by the British Security Service—something of which Archie in particular was immensely proud.

The couple have moved into Home Farm across the lane from High Weald, which has been empty since the farm manager left following his conscription. It is always a pleasure when the couple stop to chat to me in the gardens, and a privilege when they join us for an evening meal, which they have done on several occasions.

The only member of the family who we have failed to warm to is the Vaughans' son, Teddy. He was recently asked to leave Oxford University for reasons I'm not entirely sure of, and since then has tried his hand at the Home Guard (which he was doomed to fail in, for Teddy cannot take orders). He was also briefly allowed to manage the farm at High Weald, but under his short stewardship the annual yield dropped by nearly forty per cent due to his inattention. Out of desperation, Archie found him an administrative job at the Air Ministry, which lasted only a few weeks.

Elle and I will often hear the roar of his sports car passing our cottage at an early hour of the morning, following one of his evenings out on the town, no doubt in the company of various different women who all seem to inexplicably swoon at his presence. Goodness knows what they see in him. Personally, he treats me like a piece of dirt on his expensive shoe. But the young man's ego hardly bothers me. Teddy Vaughan is a pathetic runt compared to the ferocious Rottweiler of Kreeg Eszu.

However, not so long ago, the runt nipped at my heels a little too aggressively. The nature of his crime was making some suggestive comments to Elle, which caused her great upset. Teddy may call me what he likes and face no consequences, but any threatening behaviour towards *her* is unforgivable.

'I want to talk to him now!' I had seethed after Elle had told me about his lewd mouth. I stood up, grabbed my coat, and made for the cottage door.

'Bo, no!' (We are still 'Bo and Elle' in private.) She grabbed my arm and looked at me pleadingly. 'We can't risk what we have here. It's simply too perfect. He didn't actually *do* anything.'

'I don't care. What he said made you feel uncomfortable, and I won't stand for it.'

Elle took me by the hand and led me back to the ageing pink sofa in the centre of the living room. 'You can't forget our place here. We're just staff. It is not our place to speak to any of the Vaughans with anything other than deference.'

I was furious, but reluctantly agreed. 'If he ever tries anything with you, then…' I didn't wish to continue the sentence.

'Yes.' Elle nodded.

'There are rumours about his promiscuity, you know. I heard a couple of the Land Girls talking about it. Apparently one of them is pregnant with his child!'

Elle sighed and leant back into the sofa. 'Tessie Smith, yes. The rumours are true. She's beginning to show. What's worse is that she has a fiancé fighting in France.'

I shook my head. 'Good Lord. What the gentry think they are entitled to will never fail to shock me.'

'I've been sneaking her meals,' Elle continued. 'She's eating for two now, and the rations they receive are absolutely pathetic.'

Elle's kindness diffused my anger, and I took her in my arms.

Over the last few months, Teddy Vaughan's advances have

become less and less ambiguous. Elle has described to me his grotesque words and wandering hands. Just the other day, he had been so bold as to put his arm on Elle's back whilst Flora was in the kitchen. He is a man that knows no boundaries.

Two nights ago, I was working late in the vegetable patch, securing cages around the produce, as we had been subject to nightly raids from peckish rabbits. I was in the process of cutting some chicken wire when I heard the familiar rumble of a car coming down High Weald's long gravel drive. It was Teddy, no doubt rolling in from a day at the pub. On this occasion, instead of continuing his journey towards the main house, Teddy stopped the car outside our cottage. I saw him stumble out of the door and disappear behind the vehicle. Aware that something was amiss, I dropped my torch and began to run back to our cottage. When I arrived, the door was open, and Teddy Vaughan was on top of Elle on our sofa.

'Come on, that husband of yours doesn't have to know,' he slurred.

'Please, get off me!' Elle cried.

Blinded by rage, I grabbed Teddy and threw him off. Elle cowered behind me.

'He just walked in and jumped on me!' she sobbed.

Teddy stumbled up off the floor and lurched towards me, attempting to throw a punch, but missing by a country mile when I swerved out of the way.

'Leave our house!' I yelled. 'Now!'

'Whatda yamean, YOUR house? Thisus my house. It's all my house,' came his garbled reply.

'It most certainly is not, you vile little man. This house belongs to your parents.'

'Yeah, but they'll be dead one a these days and then you'll work for me.' He leered at Elle. 'And then I'll have wherever I want.'

'We will never work for you. Now get out. You're drunk.'

'Yeah, I am.' He stumbled closer to me. 'Now I might be drunk, but at least I'm honest.' He jabbed a finger into my chest.

My stomach sank and my heart filled with dread. 'What on earth do you mean?'

'You're not French. I had a French roommate at Oxford. He didn't sound anything like you. You're a little liar, Tanit.' He stumbled backwards and threw his arms up in the air. 'Maybe you're a spy! I should report you to the War Office.'

I held my ground. 'And what exactly is it that you think I'm spying on at High Weald? Potatoes?'

'My father issa very important man. Maybe you wanta know what he gets up to at the airbase? Hmm?' He held his index finger up to my face. 'One call is all it would take to get the police round here. You wouldn't like that, would you, Tanit? Digging around, asking all kinds of uncomfortable questions. Maybe they'll lock you up. But don't worry. I'll take very good care of your wife...' He gave Elle a lecherous grin. I grabbed Teddy by his collar, knocking him off his feet, and dragged him to the door. 'Hey! Gerroff me! You're just a good for nothing servant. That's all you'll ever be...' I slammed the door in his face, before turning back to Elle.

'Are you all right?'

'Yes... I was reading. He just burst in and... I didn't know if you were going to come...' she sobbed.

'I will always be here to protect you, Elle.' I squeezed her tightly. 'I know he's often down the local pub, but I've never seen him that drunk before. The man was completely out of control.' Elle began to shake. 'Come and sit down, my love. I'll make you a sweet tea.' I led her to the sofa and crossed into our cosy kitchen. I filled the small copper kettle and placed it on the stove. As I looked around the blissful cottage, my heart became heavy. I knew that there was only one outcome.

'I think I know why Teddy was so drunk.' Elle sniffed. 'Apparently Lady Vaughan sat him down to talk about Tessie Smith earlier. That's the gossip from the Land Girls.'

I sighed. 'I suppose that would explain it, yes.' I joined her on the sofa. 'We'll have to hand in our notice to Flora first thing tomorrow morning.'

Elle dropped her head. 'No...'

I put my arm around her. 'I know, my love. But there's no debate to be had. We're not safe here any longer. We can't have Teddy anywhere near you, and I can't risk him phoning the War

Office. There's no choice,' I said solemnly.

Elle looked up at me. 'Do you honestly think Teddy would call?'

I gave a sad shrug. 'Who's to say? I know he was drunk. But I don't think it's worth the risk.'

'But Bo, we've been so happy here!' Elle mourned. 'I'm not sure I can face uprooting our lives again. It's too much.'

I stood and crossed back over to the whistling kettle. 'I wish we could have remained forever. But if we want to stay together, we have to move, Elle.' I poured the boiling water into a cup and steeped the tea leaves with the strainer.

'Can you do it all again, Bo? Start afresh? Throw away everything we've built here?'

I handed her the hot drink and sat down. 'Elle, when I was a boy, I thought that "home" meant shelter, safety and food on the table.' I took her spare hand. 'You have shown me that it is not a physical place, but a feeling engendered by those we love. As long as I am with you, I *am* home.'

We sat hand in hand for a while, contemplating the loss we were, once again, being forced to suffer.

Eventually, Elle spoke. 'Where will we go this time?'

I rested my head in my hands. The adrenaline of Teddy's attack had worn off, and I found myself totally exhausted. 'What about London?' I asked. 'There'll be no shortage of work there.'

'What, in a munitions factory?' Elle baulked.

I shook my head. 'No, my love. Archie says that an operation to liberate France will begin any day now. He's talked about an enormous beach landing in Normandy. I believe London will be safe.'

Elle sipped her tea, some colour finally returning to her face. 'You know what the end of the war means, though. I may be safe from persecution, but Kreeg Eszu will be free to travel wherever he likes. If he finds out where we are—'

'I know,' I interrupted. 'All the more reason to move again.'

The next morning, I waited for Flora Vaughan in High Weald's impressive kitchen whilst Elle packed up our belongings in the cottage. The grandiosity of the house only increased the pain of our imminent departure.

'Good morning, Mr Tanit!' Flora beamed, apparently genuinely cheered by my presence. 'I rarely see you here in the kitchen.' She looked concerned. 'Is Mrs Tanit unwell?'

'Oh, no, she's fine. Thank you, Lady Vaughan.'

She rolled her eyes playfully. 'I don't know how many times I have to tell you, it's Flora to you, Mr T.'

'Thank you, Lady Vaughan,' I replied purposefully, which caused her face to drop. 'I'm here today with the unfortunate news that Mrs Tanit and I have decided to leave High Weald immediately. We will both be gone by this evening.'

Flora looked confused. 'Please, Mr Tanit, I don't understand. May I ask the reason?'

I hesitated. She deserved to know about Teddy's behaviour, but I was wary that, after the Tessie situation, she probably couldn't endure much more. 'I won't be drawn on the reason, Lady Vaughan,' I responded. 'But truly, from the bottom of our hearts, we want to thank you for everything you've done for us. It would not be an overstatement to say that some of the happiest years of our life have been spent here at High Weald.'

Flora simply shook her head. 'I won't accept your resignation without a reason, Mr Tanit. I think I am owed that, at least.'

I accepted her argument. 'It's best, ma'am.' I paused. 'Mrs Tanit no longer feels comfortable at High Weald.'

Flora slowly shut her eyes and inhaled deeply. 'Teddy,' she replied.

'As I said, Lady Vaughan, I won't be drawn on the reason.'

Flora massaged her temples. 'I'm truly sorry, Mr Tanit. The boy is out of control.' She stared out of the kitchen window at the vegetable patch we'd spent hours cultivating together. 'I will miss our conversations putting the world to rights.' She turned back to face me. 'Not to mention your horticultural prowess.'

'All of which has been learnt from you, Lady…Flora.'

She gave me a sad smile. 'I don't expect Eleanor to come up here, but please send her my warmest thanks, and tell her that she will also be greatly missed.' Flora looked contemplative. 'You know, I struggle to remember what High Weald was like without you.'

'That's very kind of you to say,' I replied honestly.

'Where will you go now?' she enquired.

I gave a small shrug. 'We plan to go to London. It's our best chance at finding work.'

'Will you be all right for money? I want to make sure you're looked after, seeing as that vile son of mine has made you feel uncomfortable.'

'I never said that your son—'

'You don't need to, Mr Tanit.' Suddenly, Flora's eyes lit up. 'Will you wait here a moment? There's something I wish to give you.' Before I had a chance to agree, Flora was already out of the door and running up the main staircase. When she returned, she had a small blue box in her hand. 'This is a gift from me to you. Without wishing to be crass, its value is enormous. Were you to sell it, then it would provide all the funds you need for a new start.'

I was shocked. 'Oh, Flora, I could never—'

'You haven't even seen what it is yet!' She delicately opened the box. A small onyx panther lay within. 'Now, it might not look much, but this panther is manufactured by a company called Fabergé. They're incredibly prestigious.'

Little did Flora know how familiar I was with the House of Fabergé. My father had often told me about its exquisite pieces. 'Please, Flora, I know what the value of that item must be, and there is absolutely no question of me taking it. Thank you…but no.'

Flora held firm. 'Mr Tanit. The man who gave me this panther—my father—no longer walks this earth. I think that part of the reason he left it to me was so that I might use it to better my circumstances, should I ever need to.' Her eyes momentarily glazed over. 'Since my father's death, Archie has reappeared in my life, and now I live here at High Weald in comfort and in happiness. I do not need this piece, which I keep in a drawer, and never so much as look at. I strongly believe that my father would want you to have it.' She squeezed it into my hand. 'From one good man to another.'

'Flora, this is a family heirloom.'

She smiled slyly. 'Well, it *is* a family heirloom…but probably not in the most conventional of ways, Mr Tanit. I assure you, I am most happy to part with it. If nothing else, please keep it as a reminder of your time here at High Weald.'

There was no arguing. Flora wished me to take the panther. 'Very well. I will keep it with me. Thank you for everything.' Rather unexpectedly, she enveloped me in an enormous embrace, which I reciprocated.

'Thank *you*, Mr Tanit.' I turned to leave the kitchen. 'You're absolutely insisting that you leave High Weald tonight?'

'Yes.' The idea of seeing Teddy again was not one I could consider. 'It has to be tonight.'

'What will you do about accommodation? London is an expensive city.'

I gave a long exhale. 'I'm not entirely sure, but we'll find something,' I assured her.

Flora pondered for a moment. 'Perhaps you don't have to... I've mentioned my friend Beatrix Potter to you, haven't I, Mr T?'

'Of course,' I replied. I had loved hearing tales of the children's author, and recalled how devasted Flora had been when she had died last Christmas.

'Did I mention that she bequeathed me her bookshop?'

I racked my brains. 'I don't think you did, no.'

'It's in a lovely location in Kensington,' she said excitedly. 'I intend to hand it over to Louise and Rupert as a wedding gift, but until then, it is mine to do with as I wish. I mention it because there is a small flat above the shop. Please feel free to make use of it for the time being, until you become settled.'

I was lost for words. 'Flora, are you sure?'

She grinned broadly. 'Positively certain. Here, let me write down the address for you.' She opened a kitchen drawer and pulled out a pencil and paper. 'I don't imagine that the flat is in particularly good condition, but hopefully it's habitable.' She handed me the address:

Arthur Morston Books
190 Kensington Church Street
London W8 4DS

'Flora…thank you,' I replied, trying to keep a check on my emotions.

'It's the least I can do, Mr T. Let me get you the keys.'

I left the kitchen and began the walk back down the drive to our cottage. When I was halfway, I turned to look back at the main house. Even though some of the stonework was crumbling, and a couple of the windows rotting, it still looked resplendent. It had *endured* for so many years, through change, wars and different generations of Vaughans. Yet still it stood, unmoving and awe-inspiring in its aspect.

Then I turned my head away and walked off into another new future.

32

Elle and I arrived at Arthur Morston Books on Kensington Church Street with our two suitcases, and I put the key in the lock. When I pushed the door open, a bell tinkled, and I searched for a light switch. When I'd located one and flicked it on, Elle and I were greeted by a rather magnificent sight. Enormous oak shelves lined the walls, full to the brim with publications of every genre. That's not to mention the several shop tables, which were covered in mountains of unorganised books, arranged chaotically, as if someone had been searching for a particular passage in amongst the thousands of pages.

'It's amazing!' said Elle.

We wandered through the shop, breathing in the faint smell of vanilla which seemed to mysteriously permeate from ancient tomes. Eventually, we located a door behind the till which led up to the slightly drab flat. In contrast to the antiquarian grandeur of the shop below, it had peeling green wallpaper and a desperately thin carpet. Nonetheless, it would most certainly do for the time being. After unpacking our bags, we walked back downstairs and, like children in a sweetshop, hungrily investigated the works on Arthur Morston's shelves.

The books were certainly helping to take our minds off the idyllic life we had been forced to leave behind. 'There's enough to keep us entertained for years here, Elle!' I laughed.

'I know. I think it's quite magical to live above a bookshop.'

I crossed the shop floor to her. 'You know, I think London will be good for us. We'll be able to watch concerts again, go to the theatre…we can take strolls by the River Thames, just as we did along the Seine in Paris when we were children.'

She returned the book of poetry she'd been reading to the shelf and gave a sigh. 'You're right. I'll try and see this as a positive move, but…'—she hesitated—'I really saw us staying at High Weald forever. I thought we would eventually marry, have children together…and now I wonder if either of those things can ever happen.'

I gave her a gentle kiss on the forehead. 'I understand. Please know that I long for nothing else. One day, when we are safe, we will marry.'

Elle sniffed. 'I know it's only a piece of paper.'

'But an important one,' I said, stroking her hair. 'And then, when that's done, I promise we will have a thousand children.'

'A thousand?!' She managed a giggle.

'Oh, at least,' I continued. 'We will need something to keep us busy after we settle down.'

'Why don't we start with one, and see how we go?'

'As you wish, Elle. But if we're only going to start with one, do you wish for a boy or girl?' I asked.

She thought for a moment. 'As long as the baby is fifty per cent of you, I will love it unconditionally.' She leant her head into my shoulder.

Elle and I spent the next few days sorting and categorising the thousands of books which filled the shop. It certainly occupied our minds, and once again, we fell into a routine.

'I wonder whether Flora would consider allowing us to sell any of these books for her? It's senseless that all this wonderful stock sits gathering dust on the shelves,' Elle said. 'The money we take can go straight back to High Weald.' She looked suddenly enthusiastic. 'We could even order in new books, if Flora would let us…before Louise and Rupert arrive, of course.'

I considered it for a moment. 'I think it's certainly worth enquiring,' I replied.

We wrote to Flora, but did not receive a reply for over ten days. By the time a letter did drop through the door, Arthur

Morston Books was in pristine condition and ready for trading. Unfortunately, the letter's sad contents explained the reason behind Flora's delay.

> *Dear Mr and Mrs Tanit,*
>
> *It is with regret that I must inform you that my husband died the night after you left, alongside fourteen others at RAF Ashford, when a bomb directly hit the tent he was sleeping in. As such, Teddy has immediately inherited High Weald and all of his father's associated assets, as is his birthright.*
>
> *Please rest assured that Arthur Morston Books remains my property, and Teddy is unable to take it from me. I still intend to give the shop to my daughter and her husband after their wedding in the summer, but in the meantime, I am more than happy to allow you to sell the books and restock the premises. Perhaps, if you are able to make a success of it, then Rupert and Louise might feel inclined to keep you in situ as managers...though that is, of course, their decision.*
>
> *Regrettably, I will no longer be contactable via High Weald itself, as Teddy intends to take a wife, and as such I will move to the Dower House. I will send exact details once I am sure of them. It is a kind thought that you should wish to send the profits back to High Weald, but I would request that any surplus funds are kept by yourselves.*
>
> *Kind regards,*
> *Flora V.*

'He's kicked his own mother out of the house! How dare he!' Elle raged.

The news had shaken us both. 'Poor Flora. The love of her life perishes and her scallywag son gets everything. How horrendously unfair.'

'Do you think it's us, Bo?' Elle asked. 'Are we cursed? It seems that everywhere we go, we leave a trail of human despair.'

We spent that evening sharing stories of Archie Vaughan and all the ways he had influenced our lives for the good.

Within three days, we had opened up Arthur Morston Books for trading. We soon discovered it to be an incredibly fruitful business, with locals desperate for stories and escapism after the dark days of the London Blitz.

33

After a successful year of trading, on 8th May 1945 the BBC announced victory in Europe, and the country celebrated the formal acceptance of Germany's unconditional surrender. The war on the continent was over. Elle and I danced in the street with the British people. Then, at the start of June, a cream vellum envelope arrived through the letter box of Arthur Morston Books, addressed to 'Mr Tanit'. I took it back to my small desk at the rear of the shop, and opened it.

Dear Mr Tanit,

It is my sincere hope that this letter reaches the individual for which it is intended.

My name is Eric Kohler, and I am a lawyer at a firm in Geneva, Switzerland. It is my sad duty to inform you that your grandmother, Agatha Tanit, passed away some years ago now—in 1929—at the age of ninety-one. I am in the rather difficult position of being unaware of how well connected you are to your family, so if what I write shocks you, I apologise.

The heir to Agatha's estate—your father, Lapetus Tanit—is also sadly deceased. He was found in South Ossetia, Georgia, in the winter of 1923. The cause of death was deemed to be exposure to the bitter elements.

His body was recognised by the soldiers who discovered him, given his position in the Russian royal family, and very slowly the news made its way across Europe to your grandmother.

When Agatha learnt of her son's death, she endeavoured to find you, her only grandchild, exhausting large amounts of money and time during the search. She eventually managed to establish that you were in Siberia, but by the time her representatives arrived, you had gone.

For over a decade now, I have scoured the continent for the name 'Tanit', and a man that would be your approximate age. In fact, I must confess that I have written versions of this letter several times, but had no success with previous recipients. Recently, during my monthly enquiries on behalf of your late grandmother, I saw your name appear, registered as the manager of this bookshop in London.

Mr Tanit, it is my very sincere hope that you are indeed Agatha's grandson, and the beneficiary of her estate. However, to ensure this, I must ask that you make the journey to Geneva to meet me in person, where I will be able to ask you some questions which will determine the outcome. Your travel costs will, of course, be covered, so if you might be so kind as to write to me concerning your availability, it would be my pleasure to arrange your trip.

Kind regards,

E. Kohler

I placed the letter down on the desk, and without warning, tears filled my eyes. It was as though, somehow, my father's hand was reaching out from the page.

'Bo? What's wrong?' Elle asked, seeing my distress. I handed her the letter.

She absorbed the contents. 'Oh Bo… I'm lost for words myself. I can't imagine how you must be feeling.' She hugged me hard. 'I'm so sorry about your father.'

I shook my head. 'I'm being silly. Obviously I knew, Elle. But seeing it written down on paper has brought everything to the surface.' I sighed deeply. 'After all these years of wondering, now I know that he only made it as far as Georgia.'

Elle gently rubbed my back. 'It makes your achievement of reaching Paris all the more remarkable. But what about your grandmother, Agatha…did you know about her?'

I shook my head. 'No. When my father left me on that awful day in nineteen twenty-three, he told me he was going to Switzerland for help.' I stood up, crossed to the shop entrance, and turned the *open* sign round to *closed*. 'I never knew where he intended to find help. Clearly he was trying to reach his mother.' I sniffed.

Elle furrowed her brow. 'Now there's one thing I don't understand. If Lapetus had such a wealthy mother, how was it that he found himself in such strife in Siberia?'

I shrugged. 'I've told you who he was. As you've read in the letter, he was often seen with the Romanovs. After the revolution, keeping a low profile was a necessity to ensure our safety.'

Elle sat in one of the large wing-backed chairs we'd installed in the shop for customers. 'I just can't believe that this lawyer has tracked you down.'

I agreed. 'Flora must have sent off some official documents to someone or other with our names on.' I stroked my chin as I processed the chain of events which had led to my discovery. 'It appears to have been an ironic stroke of fortune that I gave Archie Vaughan my real surname all those years ago. Although, it does worry me that we were found so easily by Mr Kohler. As you have pointed out, now the war is over, Kreeg is free to roam wherever he likes.'

'If he survived,' Elle reminded me. 'So many have not.'

I shook my head. 'I doubt that I would be that fortunate.'

Elle gave me a sympathetic smile. 'Will you meet with Mr Kohler?' she asked.

'Yes,' I replied confidently. 'When I set off into the snow as a boy, Switzerland was my destination. It's finally time to end that journey.'

'When will you go?'

'As soon as Mr Kohler can manage.' I cast my eyes over the shelves of Arthur Morston Books. 'I have no idea how much money Agatha has in her estate, but imagine what we might be able to do with a significant sum? It could finally buy us safety.' I dared to dream for a moment. 'We could get a little house in the middle of nowhere. Elle, with enough money, and a little cleverness…'

'We could protect ourselves from Kreeg forever.'

After making enquiries, I found the law firm Kohler & Schweikart to be legitimate, and boarded the ferry to France one week later. After three days of trains, I arrived to meet Eric

Kohler in his grand building on Geneva's Rue du Rhône. The imposing reception boasted, of all things, a water feature, and I watched it babble elegantly for twenty minutes whilst I waited for the lawyer. Eventually, a large walnut door opened, and an immaculately dressed man with coiffed blond hair appeared.

'Mr Robert Tanit?' I nodded, and he shook my hand. 'Eric Kohler. Please, follow me.' He led me through the walnut door to an office with an impressively high ceiling. His desk was set against enormous Palladian windows, which provided panoramic views of the stunning, still Lake Geneva. 'Take a seat.' He gestured to the green leather chair on the other side of his desk.

'Thank you.'

Eric looked at me, I assume in an attempt to decide if I had a likeness to Agatha. 'I trust your journey was pleasant?' he asked.

'Yes, thank you. I don't think I've ever taken such an agreeable train journey. You really do have a beautiful country.'

Eric smiled. 'I like to think so. Small, but perfectly formed.' He turned to gesture out of the window. 'With a big lake.' I was put at ease by his amiable manner. 'Although, I must confess, Mr Tanit, I am perplexed as to why you call it *my* country. It is yours, too, is it not?'

'Oh.' I thought for a moment. 'I suppose it is, in the sense that it's the land of my father. But I was not born here, and I have never visited.'

Eric nodded. 'You were born in Russia, correct?'

I hesitated, unsure of what exactly the lawyer knew. 'Yes.'

'Hmm.' Eric leant back in his chair. 'We have much to discuss. But before we proceed, I do need to confirm your identity. Do you have your papers?'

I hesitated. 'I have my British identity card, and a passport.'

'Perfect!' Mr Kohler clapped his hands together.

'But, Mr Kohler, in the spirit of honesty, both were procured for me by my former employer, Archie Vaughan. He had connections high up in the British military, and so was generously able to source these documents for me and my partner.' Mr Kohler narrowed his eyes. 'What I am attempting to say is that the information, such as my birthplace and age, may not match your own records.'

Eric clasped his hands together and leant forward onto his desk. 'May I ask why you possess no original documents, Mr Tanit?'

'If my birth certificate does exist, it is buried under Siberian snow. I fled Russia as a young boy. I had no choice, Mr Kohler. I feared for my life. My father had left a long time before, and I thought—'

'You had to run.' Eric cut me off with a nod of acknow-ledgement. I watched a knowing smile appear on the lawyer's face. Was he somehow aware of Kreeg Eszu's mission to end my life? 'I thought this may be the case, Mr Tanit,' he continued. 'Your grandmother prepared me for it.'

I proceeded carefully, gripped by a mix of nerves and intrigue. 'I'm sorry, Mr Kohler, I'm not sure I understand.'

'There are no secrets here, Mr Tanit. I know everything.' I steeled myself. 'Your father, Lapetus Tanit, was a member of Tsar Nicholas II's royal household, before the revolution. Correct?' I slowly nodded. 'He taught Classics and Music to the tsarevich and his sisters. As a result, he was well known to the Bolsheviks, as were all those associated with the royal family. Following the October Revolution, when the tsar was overthrown and killed, your father feared for his safety and fled. Then, when he failed to return to you, you followed him, fearing for your life too.' Eric looked a little smug. 'Am I close?'

Nothing he had said was untrue. He had merely missed out the key detail of Kreeg and the diamond. I deferred to him. 'Yes, Mr Kohler. You are correct in all you have said.'

He stood up from his chair and began to slowly pace in front of the window, as if he were Poirot explaining a case. 'For the reasons I have mentioned, you have been running your entire life, desperately afraid that a member of the Red Army might appear at any moment and slit your throat, as you were a member of the royal household.' He raised his eyebrows at me. 'In fear, you have travelled across Europe, changing occupations and, I venture, names too.'

His explanation really was close enough. 'You are most astute, Mr Kohler,' I said.

'I've had a long time to piece together the narrative.' He took a seat again and reached into a drawer. 'Now that we've got everything out in the open, I want to start by having you confirm your birth name, for we both know that it is not "Robert". I remained silent. 'I assume you remember it?' he said, somewhat sympathetically.

'Yes,' I stumbled. 'I just…it was a different life.'

'I understand. Well, one thing I wish to assure you of, Mr Tanit, is that you are quite safe from Soviet persecution. Their pursuit of royalists ended over a decade ago, and the child of a teacher would be of no interest to them. You are safe, I promise.'

'That's…reassuring to know. Thank you, Mr Kohler,' I replied.

'There will, therefore, be no need for all this running and name-changing. You are a Swiss citizen by birthright, and should you choose to settle here, you would be very welcome. Now, please, your first name?'

'Atlas,' I muttered.

'A good start!' said Eric cheerfully.

I have gone out of my way to avoid using my unique name throughout the years. The observant reader may, of course, recall my reticence in using it in this very diary. But Kreeg has tracked me down regardless.

'As I mentioned, Mr Tanit,' Eric continued, 'your grandmother prepared me well. She told me that her son had been employed by the tsar after his musical studies led him to Russia. You have her to thank for all this, not me.'

'I…only wish I could,' was my honest reply. 'You mentioned that I am a Swiss citizen and would be welcome to stay here. But I am without a passport or birth certificate. How could that work?'

Eric waved his hand. 'If I can prove that you are Agatha Tanit's grandson, which I intend to do in a moment, then the path to citizenship is relatively simple.' Eric adjusted his tie. 'With the backing of my firm—which is very well thought of—you could have documents processed with ease. Though it will, of course, take time.'

I was bemused by the idea of totally authentic citizenship. 'Goodness.'

Eric reached into another desk drawer and took out a file.

'The other Mr Tanits who have sat in that chair have all been able to provide identification, but this is the part of our conversation where they begin to struggle. Knowing that you might be without formal proof of your ancestry, Agatha devised a series of questions, which she believed only her true grandson would know the answer to.'

'How intriguing,' I said, slightly unnerved at what was to come. 'What if I am unable to answer the questions?'

Eric shrugged. 'In that case, Mr Tanit, I'm afraid we will have to part ways, as per Agatha's wishes.'

I gulped. 'I see.'

'There are only three questions, Mr Tanit. May I proceed?'

I moved to the very edge of my seat. 'Please,' I replied with baited breath.

'Very good.' Eric cleared his throat. 'The first question is, together with the open star cluster of the Hyades, the Pleiades form what celestial entity?'

I replied without hesitancy. 'The Golden Gate of the Ecliptic.'

A broad smile appeared on Eric's face. 'Correct. How exciting, Mr Tanit. I have never got to question two before.' He leant in. 'May I ask how you knew the answer?'

'My father was fascinated by astronomy. He taught me everything I know about the night sky.'

Eric chuckled. 'Just as his mother taught him everything she knew. Anyway, the second question is, who crafted Lapetus Tanit's violin?'

'Giuseppe Guarneri del Gesù, Mr Kohler.'

He grinned broadly. 'Quite right, Mr Tanit. It was a gift from Agatha, given to him before he departed for Russia. Did you know that?' I shook my head. 'Well, you are correct nonetheless. So, on to the third and final question…can you tell me *why* Lapetus Tanit owned a Guarneri violin?'

I furrowed my brow and shook my head. 'Oh dear, Mr Kohler. I fear we may have come unstuck. My father used to say that he preferred the deeper resonance of Guarneri's violins.'

'Hmm,' replied Mr Kohler, unsure of whether to accept my answer. 'Lapetus preferred Guarneri's violins rather than…'

I scoffed. 'Well, rather than Stradivari's. He always used to say that Stradivari was "too big for his boots".' Despite the fact I had almost definitely failed my grandmother's identity quiz, the memory brought a smile to my lips. Mr Kohler stared at me, before turning around the piece of paper he was holding, and pointing to one sentence in particular. In beautiful, ornate handwriting were the words *Stradivari was too big for his boots...*

Noting that my jaw was nearly on the floor, Eric spoke. 'It seems that your grandmother's questions were very well chosen. And there I was, over fifteen years ago, desperately advising against the strategy. "No, Mr Kohler," she said. "It is inconceivable my son wouldn't frequently have mentioned that Stradivari was too big for his boots. It is all he talked about!"'

'But... Agatha never even met me,' I said, still in a state of absolute bewilderment.

'No. But she was an exceptionally clever woman, who knew her son better than anyone else on the planet.'

'I am very sorry not to have met her.'

'Quite. Anyway, Mr Tanit. Congratulations. Good to formally meet you, Atlas.' He put his hand out and we shook once again. 'So, allow me to tell you about your family history. What do you already know?'

'Very little,' I replied honestly. 'My parents were members of the Russian royal household. My mother died during my birth, though my father told me all about her. I also knew that my pa had Swiss heritage, but aside from that... I don't know much.'

'In which case, it is my pleasure to inform you that your bloodline is aristocratic. The Tanit family has its roots in the Holy Roman Empire. Have you heard of the House of Habsburg?' I shook my head. 'The house grew to be one of the most prominent dynasties in European history, but they originated from northern Switzerland. The family produced kings of Spain, Croatia, Hungary... I could go on.'

My eyes grew wide. 'Mr Kohler...are you saying that I am a Habsburg?'

The lawyer laughed. 'No, you are not.' I felt my cheeks reddening. 'However, there are historical accounts of Tanits assisting the house as far back as eleven ninety-eight. Your descendants would advise the family on the position of the stars, and whether they hung to the Habsburgs' astrological advantage. They placed a great deal of trust in your family, and for that reason rewarded them with nobility…and a great deal of money. And you, Atlas, are the end of the bloodline. The very last Tanit. I have a fortune of…'—he flicked through his papers—'approximately five million Swiss francs to give you. Once your papers are in order, of course.'

My expression must have appeared comical. 'Five…million?' I whispered.

Eric nodded. 'Indeed. Perhaps now you can appreciate why I was keen to contact you. Not only are you entitled to a great deal of money, but you are the last remaining member of a Swiss cultural dynasty!'

I was lost for words. The money could provide everything Elle and I had dreamt of. The thought choked me. 'I'm unsure of what to say.'

'No need to say anything, Atlas. I will begin the process of formally registering you as a Swiss citizen. As I mentioned, after the war there is a long queue, and it could take years rather than months.'

'I understand,' I replied. My head was spinning. Elle and I would be able to settle down here and start a family. I couldn't wait to tell her the news. 'Might I ask where I am staying tonight, Mr Kohler? Will I be in Agatha's house?'

'Ah. I have arranged a hotel for you for the next few nights. Here's the address.' He handed me a card. 'Agatha bequeathed her large town house to the couple who used to care for her in her old age. After your father left for Russia, they were really the only family she had left. However…' Eric raised his finger, remembering something. He returned to the file on his desk and began rifling through once more. 'About a year before Agatha died, she bought a large plot of land on a secluded peninsula by the lake.' He found the piece of paper he was searching for and scanned it. 'It now also belongs to you. Here is a map of its location. Please feel free to visit if you so wish.' I took the paper from him. 'It's beautiful out there.' Eric turned to look out of the enormous windows. 'You could go this afternoon.'

'I might just do that,' I replied as I stood up, my legs jelly-like. 'Can I get a taxi from outside?'

Eric snorted. 'You might struggle there. The peninsula is only accessible by boat! However, you can hire aquatic transport at a reasonable rate from the dock nearby. Show the driver your map, and he'll know where to take you.'

'Are the boats available for private hire? I'm actually very handy with a map.'

'Yes, I believe so, if you can convince them of your credentials. Oh, there's also this!' He took a small cream envelope from the file. 'It's a letter to you from your grandmother. You know,' he chuckled, 'I never thought I'd see the day when this was handed over. Look!' He pointed to his temple. 'I have grey hair! When I met your grandmother, I was a young man.' He stood up to hand over the envelope and bade me farewell. 'I'll contact you via the hotel. There will be plenty of documents to sign whilst you're here in Geneva. Goodbye, Atlas. See you tomorrow, I imagine.'

'Thank you, Mr Kohler.'

34

Within forty minutes I was chugging across Lake Geneva on a slightly rickety Shepherd Runabout. Despite my vessel, I was entranced by the vast mountains that surrounded the lake. I closed my eyes and enjoyed the cool breeze on my skin. I loved being out on the water, with nothing but my thoughts and the clean air to accompany me.

The journey from the dock near the Rue du Rhône took the best part of twenty minutes on the Runabout, providing me with the distinct feeling that Agatha's peninsula really was isolated. Eventually, the piece of land shown on the map came into view. I stared ahead at the private promontory, which had a crescent of imposing terrain rising up steeply behind it.

I killed the Runabout's engines, and allowed the vessel to glide slowly towards the shoreline. Perfect silence fell, and I was in awe of the majesty of the fairy-tale landscape, which was reflected in the glass-like water. The hull soon made contact with the soft ground, and I hopped out with the boat's line in hand. I heaved the bow of the Runabout onto the sand, and tied it off on a large rock. Taking in a deep breath, I removed Agatha's letter from my pocket.

Dear Atlas,
My dearest grandchild, if you are reading this, then Mr Kohler has kept

his promise and successfully located you—something that regrettably I was unable to do myself.

As I write, I know that I am close to the end of my allotted time here on earth, but if you find yourself with a tear in your eye, please do not shed it, for soon I will be with my beloved son—your father.

Despite the distance that was put between us by your father's job, he would write to me regularly. In this way, I was able to keep up to date with your growth and development. He spoke of you with such pride, Atlas, often relaying that you were wise beyond your years, achieving more than he believed humanly possible. I do not doubt it from a Tanit.

In this regard, Lapetus informed me of your talent for the violin, and of your fascination with the stars—which would come naturally to you, given our family history. Perhaps Mr Kohler has shared some of it with you. If not, make sure to ask him. The story is fascinating and longer than I have the energy to write here.

How I wish that we could have met, reminisced together, and looked to the silent heavens above my cherished Lake Geneva. Speaking of which, no doubt you have been informed that you are now the owner of a secluded plot of land on the lake herself.

I purchased it for you, grandson of mine. I have chosen its location carefully. You will note that it is accessible by water only and hidden away from the prying eyes of others.

I sensed that you may need your own corner of the world, Atlas—a place of peace and safety. I hope this land can provide that for you, and might act as a home for future generations of Tanits to live.

Perhaps I am wrong, though, and you do not require such a gift. Therefore, should you wish to sell the land, you may do so with my full blessing.

I am growing tired now, so regrettably cannot write for much longer. Spend your inheritance wisely, but remember that life is supremely short. It is my sincere wish that you use the money to enhance the lives of my great-grandchildren, and the future generations which they will produce.

I look forward to one day meeting you in the next life. Until then, should you wish to find me, Atlas, look to the stars.

With love,

Your grandmother, Agatha

The letter was powerful, and my eyes were stinging once

again. I looked up at the sky.

'Thank you,' I whispered.

For one mad moment, it seemed that the universe was replying to me directly, as I heard the snap of a twig behind my back. I wheeled round, but was greeted by the bare peninsula. 'Hello?' I called. Wondering if it was perhaps an animal, I made my way over to the trees. As I approached, I heard the sound of hurried footsteps. 'I say again, hello!'

Entering the woodland, I stumbled across some tarpaulin and the remnants of a fire, which had been quickly extinguished by a bucket of water that lay nearby.

The footsteps rushed off into the undergrowth, and I began to chase after the sound. 'Please, stop. I'm the owner of this land. I mean no harm!' After a short jog, I paused to listen for the footsteps once more. Hearing only birdsong, I put my hands on my hips and looked around the untamed land.

Suddenly, a sharp, searing pain shot through the back of my left leg, which buckled. 'Argh!' I cried, and fell to the floor. I looked up to see a young boy wielding a large wooden stick. He raised it above his head again, this time to deliver a blow to my face, and I put an arm out to shield myself.

'Stop it!' came a voice from the trees behind me. A little girl emerged. She was younger than the boy. 'Don't do it, please.'

'What do you want?!' the boy shouted at me, the stick still raised above his head.

I noticed the pair were speaking German, and I replied in kind. 'This is my land. Well, it will be soon. But please, I don't mean you any harm. I didn't know you were here.'

The boy shot a look to the girl before turning back to me. 'Are you German?' he asked. 'You were speaking French before.'

'It is because I am Swiss,' I replied, for simplicity.

'Why can you speak German?' the boy asked.

'I used to live there. In Leipzig, before the war.'

'Claudia, come here.' The little girl made her way over to the boy and stood behind him. He lowered his stick. 'I'm sorry that we are on your land. We will pack our belongings and leave.'

'I don't understand. Why did you hit me?' I asked, slowly getting to my feet. 'You're very welcome to camp here. But you mustn't do harm to strangers!'

'See, I told you!' the girl hissed at the boy. 'I am sorry about my brother. I told him that you weren't going to hurt us.'

'I apologise,' said the boy. 'We'll be going now.'

For the first time, I noticed that the clothes the children were wearing were ripped and incredibly dirty. They were also monstrously oversized—a combination of the fact that they were made for adults, and that the children themselves were uncomfortably skinny. 'As I said, you're more than welcome to camp here. Is that what you're doing? Camping?' I asked.

'Yes, just camping,' replied the boy.

'It looks like you've been here a very long time,' I said.

'We have been. But we will move now.'

'Into the mountains? I didn't see a boat. Is it safe for you to try to climb? It looks very difficult.'

'We will manage,' the boy replied.

'Please, sir,' said the girl, 'do not tell anyone you have seen us. I don't want them to come for us again.'

'Claudia!' the boy chastised her.

'It's all right,' I soothed. 'Claudia? Is that your name?' The girl nodded meekly. 'It's a very nice name.' I turned to the boy. 'And can I ask what your name is, young man?' He shook his head, and I shrugged. 'Very well. My name is Atlas. Can I ask what you meant when you said that you don't want "them to come for us again"? Who are "they"?'

'The bad men,' Claudia replied.

'The bad men?' I repeated. 'Do you mean the soldiers?' Claudia nodded. I was beginning to understand. 'Have you come from Germany?'

'Yes,' said the boy.

I looked at him with enormous sympathy. 'Did you escape from one of their camps?' The boy nodded. I knelt down to meet the children's eye level. 'I assure you, I am not one of them, I promise. I am a friend.' The boy sighed, and gave me a nod. 'How old are you?'

'I am eleven,' he replied. 'My sister is seven.'

'That's very young to be out here on your own—take it from one who knows. How long have you been alone?'

He shrugged. 'I am not sure. I think nearly fifty nights. And we are not alone.' He put his arm around his sister and looked defiant. 'We have each other.'

'Of course,' I said. 'And that is wonderful. I knew these two innocent souls had probably experienced horrors beyond my comprehension, and I tried to pick my words carefully. 'Might I ask how you came to be here?'

The boy cast his eyes to the ground. Very sweetly, his sister held his hand. 'Our mother distracted one of the guards, and we climbed under a piece of fence. We…' The boy tried to continue, but was too choked. Claudia spoke instead.

'We didn't want to leave, but Mother said we had to,' she mumbled softly. 'After what they did to Daddy.'

My heart broke for the children. In their short time on earth, they had experienced the worst of humanity. If anyone could understand their pain, it was me. 'You won't know this, as you've been here for so long, but I have some news for you. The war is over. The camps, like the one you escaped from, are being liberated. I can help you find your mother,' I told them gently.

The boy shook his head. 'No, sir, you cannot. She gave her life for us. We heard the gunshots as we climbed under the fence. Then we ran. Mother told us to get to Switzerland because it was safe. So I took Claudia and did my best,' he sobbed.

Very slowly, I put a hand on his shoulder. 'I cannot tell you how sorry I am. I lost my parents when I was a child too. But remember'—I tapped my chest—'they are alive in here, always.' The boy looked into my eyes. 'You have kept your sister safe. Your mother, wherever she is, is enormously proud.' I had a thought. 'You must be very hungry.' I reached into my trouser pocket and produced a packet of peanuts I had left over from the train journey. 'Here.' The boy took the bag gratefully, and began to share the contents with his sister. 'How did you end up on this peninsula?' I asked.

'We stole a boat from the other side of the lake and drifted here,' he explained between mouthfuls. 'We climbed out with our belongings, and in the morning the boat had drifted away.'

My eyes widened. 'So you've been stranded? How terrible.'

The boy shrugged. 'Boats have passed often, but we dare not

signal them in case they returned us to the camp.'

I rubbed my eyes at the storm of misfortune which had befallen the children. 'Of course. What have you done for food?'

The boy poured out the last of the peanuts and gave the lion's share to his sister. 'I can fish, but I don't catch too much. We've tried a lot of berries. One plant made us very sick.'

I knew I had to get the pair to civilisation as quickly as I could. They needed the care of doctors and warm beds to sleep in. 'I know that we've only just met,' I began tentatively, 'but would you come with me in my boat? I'm going back to the city. I know people that can help.'

The boy froze. 'How do we know we can trust you?'

I contemplated his question. 'You are quite right to ask…but I am unable to give you a satisfactory answer.' I furrowed my brow in frustration. 'I do not have a newspaper with me, so I am unable to prove that the war in Europe is over. I can show you these, though.' I produced my British passport and identity card, and handed them to the boy.

'British?' He took a step back. 'I thought you said you were Swiss.'

'Ah.' I cursed myself internally. 'Yes. Well observed. You are clearly very clever.' I gave him a nervous grin. 'My father was Swiss. I'm actually here to inherit my grandmother's estate.' A lightbulb went on in my head. 'I have a letter from her. Can you read any French?'

'A little,' replied the boy, his eyes narrowed.

I handed him Agatha's letter. 'Please, read it.' I sat crossed-legged on the ground. If you need help with any of the words, just ask.' I smiled. The boy retreated ten yards or so and sat down opposite me, alongside his sister. He slowly made his way through the letter, and after five minutes or so, he stood up.

'All right,' said the boy. 'We will come with you.'

Claudia's little face lit up. 'Really?' she asked her brother. He nodded at her.

I breathed a sigh of relief. 'That *is* wonderful news!' I jumped to my feet. 'Thank you for trusting me. Shall we put your things into the boat?'

'No,' said the boy. 'We can leave everything behind.' He took his sister's hand.

'I quite understand,' I replied. 'Now we are acquainted, might I have the pleasure of knowing your name?'

The boy looked up at me. 'My name is Georg.'

Mr Kohler was somewhat shocked to see me again that afternoon...particularly as I re-entered his office accompanied by two malnourished and begrimed children.

'What on earth is going on?' he asked, nearly knocking his cup of tea from his desk.

I explained the situation as succinctly as I could. Reader, it is amazing what money can do. That afternoon, Mr Kohler was able to arrange a doctor, a social worker and unlimited access to hearty meals—all paid for by Agatha Tanit (he was happy to release some funds from the estate immediately, given the unique circumstances, and confident that my grandmother would approve).

'What will happen to them, Mr Kohler?' I asked.

The lawyer was in a daze, and I could hardly blame him. 'As soon as we have been able to confirm exactly who they are, we shall see if they might be able to return to any family members they might have in Germany.'

I raised an eyebrow at him. 'Do you believe that is likely?'

Eric put his head in his hands. 'No. Should that prove to be the case, the Swiss government will probably fund their care and place them in a children's home, where they will presumably find adoptive parents. As child refugees, their path to citizenship will hopefully prove simple.'

I sat down in the leather chair opposite Mr Kohler. 'An orphanage, you say?' Eric nodded. I cast my mind back to the *Apprentis d'Auteuil*. To condemn Georg and Claudia to such a life after all they had already endured seemed so very cruel. They had run from persecution, as had I. I remembered Boulogne-Billancourt. What were Landowski's words?

I am sure that one day, you will find yourself in a position to help others. Be sure to accept the privilege.

I knew what I wished to do.

'I should like to pay for the children,' I remarked to Eric.

'I'm sorry?'

'Georg and Claudia sought shelter on Agatha's land—my land—and I want to see that they are well treated. The only reason I am stood before you today is due to the kindness of strangers. I haven't been able to exercise much selflessness during my life, and now it seems that my circumstances have changed.'

Mr Kohler leant back in his chair as he considered my proposal. 'That is a very noble sentiment, Atlas, but I do not believe that it will prevent Georg and Claudia from being placed in a children's home. Unless you plan to take them back to London?'

I gazed up at the high ceiling as I thought about the idea. It simply wasn't safe to take the pair home, given that Kreeg may still be at large. 'That is not possible at the moment,' I replied. 'But Mr Kohler, I would desperately like to avoid those children being placed in a home. They have lost their parents, and their world has been turned upside down. They need comfort and security, not the uncertainty that an orphanage fills a heart with. Can you really think of nothing?'

Eric drummed his fingers on his desk. 'I suppose…well, I can't promise anything. But the couple who used to care for your grandmother might be amenable to housing them, if you were able to provide funds for their living costs.'

'Really?' I asked, taken slightly aback.

Eric nodded. 'They are very grateful to Agatha for bequeathing them her town house.' He chuckled suddenly. 'In fact, I had to make quite the effort to convince them to accept the gift in the first place. I will make a phone call this afternoon.'

I stood up to shake Eric's hand. 'Thank you, Mr Kohler! I should love to meet them, pending the outcome of your telephone call. What was their name?'

'The Hoffmans.'

Timeo and Joelle Hoffman were a sweet and humble couple in their sixties, whom I met with several times during my stay in Geneva. They spoke so fondly of Agatha and her kindness, and were genuinely thrilled that Eric Kohler had finally been able to locate me. The lawyer's prediction was proven right, and the couple were all too pleased to welcome Georg and Claudia into the town house, which was impressive and immaculately appointed.

'It would be our honour, Mr Tanit!' Joelle enthused. 'Truth be told, since we lost your grandmother, we've felt a little directionless.'

Timeo nodded. 'It makes no sense us rattling around this enormous place with four spare bedrooms. There's plenty of room to go around. It's the least we can do for the poor little nippers after what they've been through.'

I was touched by the unquestioning generosity of the pair. 'Do you have any children yourselves?' I asked.

The couple appeared a little crestfallen. 'No,' Joelle replied. 'We were not blessed.' She looked suddenly worried. 'But honestly, Mr Tanit, we're very experienced carers, and we would never—'

I put a hand up to stop her. 'I quite understand, Joelle. I cannot tell you how overjoyed I am that you are willing to take Georg and Claudia into your home. Promise me that any expenses whatsoever—food, clothing, schooling—will be invoiced to Mr Kohler. I will authorise him to reimburse you immediately.' I went to shake their hands, but Joelle embraced me in a hug.

Timeo laughed softly. 'Apologies, Mr Tanit. My wife is merely expressing how happy Agatha would be that you are standing here in the living room of her house.'

Joelle pulled away to look at my face. 'Do you think you will return to Switzerland to live?' she asked. 'It is a lovely place to make a home!'

I gave her a warm smile. 'Perhaps, Joelle. I have several

matters to attend to in England before I consider that option, however.' I made for the door. 'Please do keep Mr Kohler updated on the children's progress. I should be absolutely delighted to hear about how they are getting on.'

The rest of my time in Switzerland was spent signing papers, meeting bank managers and sorting affairs with Eric Kohler, who would officially cease working for Agatha, and begin to work for me.

'I will send your passport and any other documents to Arthur Morston Books, Mr Tanit. Please ensure that if you move, you tell me. I don't want to have to chase you for another fifteen years.' He chuckled and shook his head as I closed the enormous walnut door and left his office.

35

The process of acquiring citizenship transpired to be as slow as Eric had predicted. I became accustomed to his monthly letters, detailing what frustrating stage my application had been halted at, usually sent alongside a plethora of new documents to be signed and dated. In addition to the administrative business, it was a continued comfort to hear about the improving lives of the children from the peninsula. Both had begun to attend a local independent school recommended by Mr Kohler, and Georg in particular was showing significant academic promise.

Happily, I did not have to spend any time convincing Elle that our future was in Switzerland. 'As soon as I have my official papers,' I had promised her, 'we will begin construction on a safe haven just for the two of us. Imagine! Our own secluded paradise.'

She had positively beamed at the thought. 'Oh Bo. It sounds too good to be true! And when you have your citizenship, we can marry…openly, officially. The day cannot come soon enough.'

I knew how desperately she longed to settle down. I willed the process of Swiss citizenship to be speedy, but in the meantime, I wanted to make her a promise. With the permission of Mr Kohler, I withdrew some funds from Agatha's estate and made my way to a jeweller's on Bond Street in London.

Although I browsed a plethora of rings, none impressed me. I had never spent such a significant amount of money before, and

I was reticent to exchange it for some jewellery that, despite the price, was generic. I wanted the ring to carry some meaning. After an hour of staring and squinting through thick glass, I enquired if a custom piece could be made.

'Anything is possible for the right price, sir,' the jeweller replied.

I knew that the central stone had to be a diamond—the ultimate symbol of strength in love. As for the setting, I asked for seven individual points to be included, to give the ring the appearance of a glistening star.

'Very good, sir.' The jeweller grinned. 'As the setting will be quite large, perhaps you would like to select a second stone for the points? Sapphire perhaps?'

I thought for a moment, conscious of the fact that the man was trying to extract more money, but desperate for the piece to be totally unique. 'Is there a gem that represents hope?' I asked.

The jeweller nodded. 'Oh yes, sir. Emeralds. Traditionally they signify romance, rebirth…and fertility,' he added, raising an eyebrow.

I clasped my hands together. 'Perfect!'

It took several months to craft, but was eventually hand-delivered to the bookshop. When I unwrapped the box and looked within, I was lost for words.

That night, I took Elle out for dinner in the city's Albert Buildings. She wore a teal dress which somehow made her blue eyes even more vivid than usual. As we shared a bottle of Côtes du Rhône by candlelight, I told her all about the future I planned for us on the shores of Lake Geneva. The rest of the dining room melted away, and I spent the evening lost in her aura.

'I think our time is coming, Elle. We can finally leave the past behind.'

She gave me the same smile that had floored me as a boy in Paris. 'Do you really believe it, Bo? I'm almost scared to dream.'

I took her hand. 'We will have our happy ending.' I gently manoeuvred myself onto one knee, and slipped my spare hand into my jacket pocket. I took a deep breath and stared into her sparkling eyes. 'Elle Leopine. We are destined to spend our lives together. But until the day I can call you my wife, please accept this ring as a symbol of everything you are to me.' I produced the box and opened it in front of her. She covered her mouth with her hands.

'Oh Bo…'

I carefully slipped the ring onto her left fourth finger.

'I don't know what to say,' she stumbled. 'I've never seen anything like this. It's utterly beautiful.'

'Seven points for my Seven Sisters—my guiding lights that have led me to the diamond in the centre of the universe…you.'

When Rupert and Louise Forbes married, Flora signed over the ownership of Arthur Morston Books as she had promised. Happily, the couple asked me and Elle to remain as shop managers. They were content with the business we had succeeded in building, and were busy with the renovation of Home Farm. To add to that, Rupert's role in the British Security Service had apparently become more demanding. Although he was passionate about literature, his country took precedence.

On a quiet January morning in 1947, I put my feet up on my desk and opened the *Financial Times*. As I was soon to be responsible for large quantities of capital, I did my best to keep up to date with the monetary markets—even if the majority of it was confusing to me. The paper was giving its review of 1946. It heralded the formation of the World Bank Group—a family of five international organisations formed to make leveraged loans to countries in need. In its first month, it had approved $250 million for French post-war reconstruction. My eyes widened as I read the article's penultimate paragraph.

The first president of the organisation, Eugene Meyer, is known by most as the publisher of the Washington Post in the United States of America. Mr Meyer spends millions of dollars of his own money to keep the money-losing paper in business, with the aim of improving its quality, and in the spirit of independent journalism. In this regard, one may surmise why Mr Meyer was the perfect candidate for the role of WBG president. Meyer comes from a charitable family. His sister, Florence Meyer Blumenthal, was noted for the philanthropic organisation she formed, the Franco-American 'Blumenthal Foundation', which still awards the Prix Blumenthal to young creatives.

I jumped to my feet and raced upstairs to show Elle the article.

She gave a startled laugh. 'Goodness me! I haven't heard Florence's name in such a long time.'

'Nor I,' I replied. 'It's odd, isn't it? We owe so much to her. I wish we'd had an opportunity to thank her for all she's done for us.' I sat down on our threadbare sofa, which Elle had tried to cheer up with a hand-knitted throw.

'I know, Bo. But Florence died long before we were given the *Prix Blumenthal.*'

'I think that makes my heart ache all the more,' I replied.

Elle joined me on the sofa. 'What about Eugene Meyer?' she asked. 'We could write to him and tell him about the difference his sister made to our lives.'

I sighed. 'I have a feeling that the president of the World Bank Group is unlikely to receive our correspondence.'

Elle nodded, and thought for a moment. 'Okay then. Let's go and see him.'

'What?'

'Why not? Now the war is well and truly over, what do we have to lose? Plus'—she smiled—'I've always wanted to go to the United States.'

I laughed. The idea of travelling freely to a new country without having to flee was still a novel concept to me. 'It's a nice thought, Elle. But I doubt Eugene Meyer will just agree to meet us.'

Elle gave me a pat on the leg. 'Isn't that what your high-flying Swiss lawyer is for? Can't you have him write to Eugene's office in America?'

'Oh, I...' The shop bell rang downstairs, indicating the presence of a customer.

'Think about it!' Elle giggled, as she stood up and walked out of the door.

It took Mr Kohler less than a week to hear back from Eugene Meyer's personal secretary. She informed Eric that her employer was very fond of his late sister, and would be open to a brief meeting. Needless to say, Mr Meyer was incredibly busy. However, he would be in New York in one week's time. Could we make it then?

I thanked Eric and put the telephone receiver back on its stand.

'It sounds like it's one week or never,' I told Elle, who was waiting in anticipation.

'I told you Mr Kohler would produce a result! I'll pack the bags!' she squealed excitedly.

'Hang on,' I laughed. 'Are you sure that we can just up and leave? Who will look after the shop?'

Elle rolled her eyes. 'Bo, we've hardly had a day off in a decade. I'll telephone Louise. I promise you, there'll be no issue.' She ran up to me, grabbed my shirt and gave me a gentle peck on the nose. 'We're going on a holiday! A real-life holiday!'

Two days later, we found ourselves crossing the Atlantic on the *Queen Mary*. Although our second-class quarters were very comfortable, as were the ship's lounges, I spent hours out on the viewing deck. There was something about the emptiness of the open ocean which soothed me. It had the effect of ordering my thoughts. It was akin to me rearranging the bookshelves after a day of customers browsing, but in my own mind.

Elle was ecstatic to be on board. It made my heart swell to see the joy she took from every aspect of the journey, whether it was the fresh coffee served at breakfast, or the jazz singer who performed in the evenings. After the four-day voyage, we checked in to the Winter Quay Hotel in Manhattan early on a Wednesday morning. Elle and I were taken up to our room in the 'elevator' by a young man in a red cap and jacket. He proudly showed us the skyline view from the twentieth floor, which was staggering. I am not ashamed to say that it had a dizzying effect, and I was forced to sit down on the bed. Once he had brought our bags in, the man in the red cap gave us a wide smile and stood expectantly by the door. Mr Kohler had prepared me for the uniquely American custom of 'tipping', and ensured I had some dollar bills to hand. I took one from my pocket and handed it to the man. He tipped his hat.

'Thank you, sir. Have a great stay.'

'I feel like we're on top of the world!' Elle said as she pressed her face to the glass window and took in the overwhelming view.

'Me too. But I'm not sure my stomach has accepted it yet… Now, I must get to the lobby and call Mr Meyer. Remember, he leaves this evening.'

'All right, my love. I'll unpack our suitcase.'

I made my way back down to the slightly sterile white lobby, and over to one of the wooden telephone booths near reception. I reached into my pocket and removed the number given to me by Mr Kohler. Then I put a quarter coin in the machine and dialled.

'Hello?' a man with a gruff American accent answered tersely.

'Mr Meyer? It's Bo D'Aplièse here.'

My name seemed to soften him. 'Bo! You're the guy that knew my sister, right?'

'Yes,' I replied, before correcting myself. 'Well, no, actually. I don't know if the situation has been explained to you, but I was one of the recipients of your sister's *Prix Blumenthal*.'

He exhaled forcefully and I guessed he was puffing on a cigarette. 'That's great, great. Listen, just to save us both time, there's no more funds from my sister's will for previous winners. I hope my people told your lawyer that.'

I was shocked. 'Goodness, you misunderstand, Mr Meyer… I just wanted to thank you.'

He snorted. 'Thank *me*? I didn't do anything for you, buddy.'

'No, but your sister did, in ways that she never knew about. I had hoped to meet her in person to tell her.'

He sighed. 'Sorry to say that you're over a decade too late, kid.'

'I know. I'm so sorry for your loss. I'm absolutely not here for any money. I just wanted to tell you how much your sister unknowingly changed my life.'

There was a pause before Eugene laughed down the line. 'Well, how about that? Who knew that Brits really were that polite?!'

'I'm not British, actually.'

'Look at that, we're getting to know each other already!' He paused to inhale. 'So, you wanna meet? I'm just about to leave my hotel for a story I'm working on this afternoon.'

'That would be wonderful,' I confirmed.

'Great. I'm headed to 132 West and 138th Street. Meet me there in a half hour.'

The numbers meant nothing to me. 'Where is that near?'

'It's Harlem, kid. Listen, just repeat it to a cab driver. There's a diner close to the church. Have him drop you there.'

'Will do. My wife and I will see you shortly.'

He gave a loud cough. 'Woah, hold up. Wife? You didn't mention a wife.'

I apologised. 'Sorry, I should have been clearer. She was also awarded the *Prix Blumenthal*. She'd love to thank you as much as I would.'

Meyer tutted. 'I mean, it's up to you, buddy, but things could get a little hairy out on those streets today. It'd be safer to leave her behind. Either way, I'll see you at the diner.' Mr Meyer hung up the phone.

I returned to the room in a daze and told Elle about my conversation with Eugene. Although initially deflated, the promise of a trip up the Empire State Building that afternoon cheered her up.

'What do you think he means when he says the streets could get dangerous?' Elle asked.

'I honestly have no idea. But I've got to get going. The last thing I want is to miss him.' I gave Elle a kiss and hurried back downstairs. The doorman hailed me a bright yellow taxi cab, and I asked the driver to take me to 132 West and 138th Street.

He turned around to face me. 'You sure, mister?' he asked.

'That's what I've been told,' I confirmed.

The driver shrugged. 'Whatever you say.'

As we made our way towards Harlem, I noticed the enormous, glittering skyscrapers of Midtown start to recede.

'Can I ask what brings you to this part of town, buddy?' asked the driver.

'I'm meeting someone here,' I replied.

'Huh. I'm guessing you're not from round these parts. First

time in New York?'

'That's right, yes.'

He chuckled. 'I thought so. You don't meet many folks from outta town wanting to come to Harlem.'

'Why is that?'

'All I'm saying is most tourists wanna see the Statue of Liberty, Central Park and the Met. They don't want any of the *real* America.'

The neighbourhood we were entering seemed to be in a state of disrepair to say the least. The gleaming glass and neon lights of Downtown Manhattan were replaced by boarded-up windows, rusting signs and overflowing rubbish bins. The cab made its way up a street called Lenox Avenue, and the faces we were passing were now predominantly black. My heart went out to the children sat on the steps of derelict houses, some of which frankly didn't look fit to accommodate anyone.

Eventually, the car approached an imposing gothic church, labelled *Abyssinian Baptist* on the sign outside. Someone was setting up a small stage with a microphone nearby, and I noticed several policemen buzzing around the area, their arms folded imposingly.

'Here we are. 132 West and 138th Street, buddy,' said the driver.

'Thank you.' I looked around the street. 'I was told that there was a diner nearby?'

'Oh, you must mean the Double R.' He turned around and pointed behind my head. 'It's just over there.'

'Great. How much do I owe you?'

'Three dollars and twenty cents.' I fumbled around in my pocket. 'Just be careful out there today, mister. I've heard it could get a little heated.'

'Oh, er, I will be. Thanks again.' I paid and left the cab, not entirely sure what the driver, or Eugene Meyer, had meant.

As I walked back down Lenox Avenue towards the Double R, the street was getting busier, and some people with what looked like placards were beginning to gather in small groups.

The diner's ancient electric sign buzzed and flickered comically, and the door frame was warped and rotten. With a small shove, I managed to gain entry, and was not altogether shocked to find that the interior was even shabbier than the outside. The air was thick with cigarette smoke, and I was forced to wave my hand in front of my face to clear the fug. A few feet away sat a well-dressed man in a pinstripe suit with red braces and a woollen tie. I marked him out as having the only white face in the establishment.

'Mr Meyer?' I asked, approaching him.

He looked up at me through his circular spectacles. 'Bo D'Aplièse, right?'

'Yes, sir,' I replied.

'Helluva name you got there!' he cried, gripping my hand tightly and shaking it. 'Take a seat. By the looks of things, we don't have long.'

'Sorry, Mr Meyer, I'm not quite sure what you mean.'

He took a swig of his coffee. 'Please, call me Eugene. Mr Meyer was my father. Plus, it kinda sounds like *Mister Mayor*...and he'll be along in a minute.'

'Very well, Eugene.' I was really quite confused. 'You mean, the mayor is coming here? To the diner?'

Eugene looked genuinely perplexed. 'No offence, kid, but did my sister give her money out to dummies? No, Mayor O'Dwyer will be on *that* stage in the next fifteen minutes.' Eugene pointed back towards the church. 'I need to be out there when he speaks. I'm here in New York on *Post* business. I take a personal interest in this story.'

I turned back to face him. 'Forgive my ignorance, Eugene, but what story is that?'

'Black citizens being ghettoised here in Harlem. Have you seen the state of the housing out there? It's goddamn abysmal. There's horrendous overcrowding, and that's not to mention the police brutality these people are up against. The cops treat their fellow human beings like animals.'

I put two and two together. 'So there's a protest happening here today?'

He clicked his fingers and pointed at me. 'You got it. Mayor O'Dwyer is speaking. He's a good guy, I think. The man's made promises to the community and we at the *Post* want to make sure he sticks to them.'

'May I ask why you take a personal interest in the story?' I asked.

Eugene sighed and nodded. 'Yeah. I'm Jewish. I've seen what the Nazis did to my people in Europe. I wanna make sure we don't end up doing the same to African Americans.'

'Of course,' I stumbled, embarrassed that I was clearly ignorant about the situation.

Eugene spoke passionately. 'In flies America the Brave to save the day on another continent, without a moment to consider how we're treating our own damn citizens… It's a travesty.' He rubbed his face. 'Anyway, you've got until O'Dwyer arrives. Tell me your story.' He pulled a cigar from his pocket, clipped the end and lit it.

Feeling exasperated, I did my best to explain to Eugene the value of his sister's contribution to my life, and, of course, to Elle's too. To his credit, Mr Meyer listened intently, puffing away as I told him everything that had happened to me.

'Ya know, kid,' he said after I had concluded my tale, 'I think Flo mentioned you before she died. The little kid that didn't speak.'

'That's right.'

'And look at you now, sat here singing like a canary! It's a miracle!'

'I just wanted to impress upon you that your sister truly did save my life. And my…wife's.'

He gave me a firm slap on the shoulder. 'I got it. Listen, I really appreciate you coming all the way over here to tell me in person. Florence'd be proud, I'm sure.' He took a large puff of his cigar. 'You know, she kept her maiden name after she married George. She was Florence Meyer-Blumenthal. I kinda wish the prize had been named the *Prix Meyer-Blumenthal*.' He shrugged. Suddenly, there was a rapturous cheer from outside, and several individuals in the diner stood up to leave. 'That's my cue, kid. I gotta go. But hey, if you're ever in DC, call my secretary. We can catch up over coffee. You can tell me more of your stories.' Eugene reached into his pocket and placed two quarters on the table. 'Maybe we could do an article on you?'

'Oh, I'm not sure about—'

'Yeah, you're right,' he interrupted. 'No one would believe the story anyway.' He gave me a smile and a wink, before making his way out of the door.

As I sat alone in the red leather booth, I somehow doubted that I would ever meet Eugene Meyer again. My meeting had not brought the emotional catharsis I longed for. Like his sister, he clearly had a significant moral conscience, and the protest was obviously at the forefront of his mind.

There was another roar from the street. I stood up to investigate the commotion. When I left the diner, I was shocked to see that the crowd had increased tenfold in the twenty minutes I had been with Eugene. I found myself amongst a sea of protestors, many now waving their handwritten placards, which bore slogans like *EQUAL RIGHTS!* and *HOUSING FOR ALL!*. From the direction of the stage, I heard a muffled Irish accent projected through the microphone, and I began to squeeze my way through the throng to catch a glimpse of Mayor O'Dwyer.

'Harlem! 'Tis an honour to be here!' the mayor cried, and the crowd cheered in response, galvanised by his presence. As O'Dwyer delivered his speech about housing reforms and better funding for schools, the protestors began to jostle forward as one, and I found myself packed in tighter and tighter. After the mayor had finished, he received a huge cheer, and was replaced at the microphone by a police officer, who began to talk through crowd dispersal. Almost instantly, the atmosphere changed. The air was thick with tension, and I became aware of a large number of uniformed officers who had surrounded the protest. With their blue caps pulled down and their wooden nightsticks brandished, they looked threatening.

I heard a woman near the front shout 'MURDERERS!' up at the officer on the stage. Then she turned to face the crowd. 'Those cops attacked Robert Bandy—shot him when he was unarmed and just trying to save a woman's life. Goddamn pigs!'

A wave of anger swept across the crowd, and the microphone was drowned out by furious cries. The mass of protestors began to undulate more and more violently. As I turned away from the stage to seek a way out, my gaze fell upon a young man shielding himself from a nightstick-wielding policeman. I didn't know what he had done to provoke such a reaction, but the officer seemed incensed, and raised the nightstick above his head to strike a blow. The man's cardboard placard provided almost no protection, and he was struck down in the dirty street, trying to shield his head from the continued beating. Others nearby witnessed the scene and began to panic. They quickly started to disperse, and soon the crowd began to stampede. From a nearby street, officers on horseback came into view.

The horses began advancing on protestors, and it was only seconds before a full-on crush developed. My heart thumped hard as I attempted to extricate myself from the crowd, some of whom were now openly clashing with the officers. The thud of nightsticks on human bodies was sickening.

I put my head down and did my best to fight my way through the assembled hordes. As I did so, the couple in front of me stumbled. After taking a few more steps, I became aware that they had tripped over a person who had fallen to the ground in the chaos. To my shock, that person was a small white woman.

'Can you walk?' I cried.

'My ankle,' she replied, wincing.

The woman was clearly in pain. 'Take my hand,' I said, grabbing her tightly and pulling her up to her feet. I placed my arm around her, and we fought our way through the throng.

'My driver…he's waiting for me on Lenox, over there at the end of the street,' she gasped. I noted she had only a faint American accent.

'Then let's get you out of here fast; it looks like things are about to get even uglier,' I replied.

All around us, violent skirmishes were breaking out as the protestors rallied and began to fight back against the police. As we neared the intersection, the woman pointed to an impressive-looking Chrysler car.

'There's Archer!' she yelled above the melee. With a destination in sight, I swept her up in my arms and ran to the vehicle, wrenching open the rear door.

'Thank the Lord you're safe, Miss Cecily!' shouted the driver, starting the engine. 'Let's get outta here!'

I made sure the woman was sitting securely in the back seat.

'You take care, ma'am,' I said. Before I could shut the door, I noted two policemen with nightsticks heading towards the car. I steeled myself, preparing to run for it.

'Archer, wait!' cried the woman. 'Get in *now!*' she screamed, yanking me firmly into the car beside her. 'Go, Archer! Go, go, go!'

The driver gunned the engine and the car sped off. As we pulled away from the nightmare scene we had left behind, the three of us breathed a collective sigh of relief.

'I can't thank you enough for your help...' the woman ventured.

'It's nothing,' I replied. 'I should thank you for yours just then.' I leant back in the seat, allowing the panic to slowly dissipate from my body.

'Can we take you somewhere?' the woman asked. 'Where do you live?'

I shrugged, not wanting to impose upon a stranger. 'Just take me to the nearest subway stop.'

'We're just coming up to 110th Street station,' the driver interjected.

'That will suit me fine,' I replied. The driver pulled the car over.

'Can I at least take your name?' Cecily said.

I hesitated for a moment, before reaching into my pocket and handing her my card from Arthur Morston Books. I gave her a nod, got out of the car, and slammed the door behind me.

That afternoon's trip to the Empire State Building was postponed as I recovered from the trauma of the morning. 'I'm only glad that you weren't there, Elle. I'm not sure I would have been able to protect you.'

'Oh Bo. I can't believe it. This is supposed to be a holiday, and you managed to walk straight into danger.' She gently stroked my hair. 'But let's try and forget the disappointment of Eugene

Meyer and the drama of the protest, and enjoy our week away. It's so special to be here with you.'

Elle and I spent the next five days exploring 'the Big Apple'. It was an amazing city which pulsated with energy and gave the inhabitants the impression that they were in the centre of the universe. New York had the tallest buildings, the biggest shopping centres and the largest plates of food I had ever witnessed in my life. After years of British rationing, my eyes practically bulged at the size of the beef burgers and mountains of french fries which were presented to diners.

I think the thing I loved most about the city was the positivity exuded by its citizens. They had recently endured the economic downturn of the Great Depression and involvement in the second global conflict. Nonetheless, nearly everyone we met brimmed with a cheerful confidence, and it was a delight to experience.

One day before Elle and I were due to board the *Queen Mary* and return home, the telephone in our hotel bedroom rang.

Elle answered. 'Hello?... Yes, he's just here.' She shrugged and passed me the receiver.

'Mr Tanit?' said a vaguely familiar English voice.

'Speaking,' I replied.

'Oh, wonderful! I'm so thrilled that I've finally managed to track you down. I've telephoned just about every hotel in Manhattan!'

'Apologies, but who's calling?' I asked.

There was a giggle on the other end of the line. 'I'm so sorry, Mr Tanit. It's Cecily Huntley-Morgan here. I'm the silly woman you rescued the other day at the civil rights protest in Harlem.'

'Oh, Hello,' I replied, a little surprised. 'How are you?'

'My ankle's slightly bruised, but I'm feeling much better now I've found you! Your card had the address of your bookshop in London, but I wanted to thank you personally for saving me. So I've been ringing hotels to ask if they have a Mr Tanit staying.'

It was my turn to give a laugh. 'That's a very sweet thought, Cecily, but I did what anyone would. I'm glad you're all right.'

'That's not true, Mr Tanit. People were clambering all over me. You, however, saw a fellow human in need and stopped to help. I am indebted to you, and should like to treat you to lunch.'

Cecily's warm voice put me at ease, but I didn't wish to be any bother to her. 'That really won't be necessary, thank you. I really do appreciate the sentiment, though.'

'Sorry, I won't take no for an answer. How are you fixed for this afternoon at the Waldorf?'

'I…'

'And was that your wife I spoke to a moment ago?'

'It was.'

'Perfect! I shall arrange a table for three, and see you at one p.m.'

Before I'd even had a chance to reply, Cecily had hung up the phone. I confirmed to Elle that I had been speaking to the lady I had scooped up and bundled into a car last week. Elle, in the spirit of embracing our time in the city, was thrilled at the invitation. 'Why wouldn't we go? Lunch with a local at a prestigious hotel? How enchanting!'

It was hard to argue with her reasoning, so Elle and I put on the finest clothes we'd dared pack into our suitcase, and by one p.m., we were outside the slender central tower of the Waldorf hotel. We made our way inside to the dining room—an echoing space with a glittering chandelier that was probably worth more than Arthur Morston Books's entire stock. Cecily's blonde coiffured ripples marked her out amongst the diners, and I identified her immediately. I took Elle by the hand and led her to the table.

'Cecily?' I asked.

'Mr Tanit! Hello!' She stood up and shook my hand firmly, before looking to Elle. 'And you must be Mrs Tanit? I think I owe your husband my life.'

I laughed it off. 'Oh, I don't know if I'd be so dramatic.'

'I don't believe I *am* being dramatic. When people are scared, they take leave of their senses,' Cecily said in a serious tone. 'Look!' She continued, and reached into her purse. She produced my business card and showed it to us. 'I even wrote "kind man" on the back!' She laughed. 'I shall keep it with me forever, as a token of good luck.' She gave me a wink. 'Anyway, please take a seat.' She gestured to the two empty red velvet chairs. 'Now, let's order some champagne! Waiter…'

Our lunch with Cecily Huntley-Morgan was a delightful affair. She told us all about her life: her broken engagement, her voyage to Kenya with her godmother Kiki Preston and her eventual marriage to a cattle farmer named Bill.

'You were at the protest the other day, Mr Tanit. You therefore sympathise with the vile racial prejudice that plagues so much of this country.' I hadn't revealed that my presence on Wednesday was accidental. 'I need not keep this information from you.' She took a sip of the Veuve Clicquot she had insisted on ordering us all. 'When I was living in Kenya, a young Masai princess named Njala gave birth to a daughter on our land. She abandoned her, so I took her in. I named the baby Stella. Knowing I was to return to New York, I was forced to hire a maid—Lankenua. As far as my family know, she is the baby's mother, even though, to all intents and purposes, I am.'

'That must be incredibly hard,' Elle sympathised.

Cecily gave a shrug. 'It is necessary. The bristling disapproval of society would be palpable. I could, of course, handle it with no qualms, but Stella, on the other hand…she already faces so many challenges as a young black girl. It is better for her that things are this way.'

'You've done an amazing thing, Cecily.' I gave her a sincere smile. 'Without you, who knows what would have happened to little Stella. Thank you for showing her kindness.'

'As you said earlier, Mr Tanit, I merely did what anyone would have.'

'And as you replied to me…I don't think that is factually accurate,' I retorted.

Cecily chuckled and raised her champagne flute. 'Well then. Cheers to kindness.'

Elle and I talked to Cecily about our life in Britain, working for the Vaughans firstly at High Weald and then at Arthur Morston Books. Cecily asked about Elle's French accent, and we repeated the line that we both fled Paris due to the threat of Nazi occupation.

'But recently, we've had some good fortune,' Elle told Cecily. 'Robert here has inherited some land in Switzerland on the shores of Lake Geneva. We hope to move there as soon as we can.'

'How wonderful!' Cecily replied. 'Nature is so important, isn't it? I imagine the still peace of the lake will be just the ticket after all you've been through.'

After a delicious pudding of deep-dish apple pie, it was time to part ways.

'Thank you so much for lunch, Cecily. It's tremendously nice of you,' I said, shaking her hand.

'Don't be silly, Mr Tanit. I'm only too glad that I managed to track you down before you return to England. Although, if you don't mind, I will keep that business card of yours. After all, one is never quite sure when one might need one's guardian angel.'

36

England, 1949

My involvement in the New York skirmish was the last piece of bad luck I was to have for a while. At the turn of 1949, Mr Kohler informed me that the process of obtaining my Swiss citizenship was in its final stages. In addition, the bookshop had been reporting record sales. After all these years, I felt my shoulders beginning to drop a few inches.

I found myself breathing easier.

I was sleeping better.

Perhaps my relaxed state was underpinned by something else entirely—the absence of Kreeg Eszu. I had not laid eyes on him since that awful night in Leipzig. Reader, I allowed myself to believe that he was dead—killed in the war like so many of his fellow soldiers.

And then I saw him.

It was a cold day in London. Rupert and Louise Forbes were in town, and had come to the bookshop to visit us. It was, as always, a great pleasure to see them both. I was very happy to hear that Flora was well, despite Teddy and his new American wife driving High Weald into the ground.

The couple had brought their new baby with them, a bouncy and bubbly boy named Laurence, whom Elle duly fussed and cooed over. Once the child was asleep, Elle began proudly showing Rupert and Louise the new stock, and I returned to my desk to look through the accounts. As I mentally questioned a calculation, I found myself staring out of the large shop window and onto Kensington Church Street. At that moment, a tall figure in a great coat and trilby hat came in to view, smoking a cigarette. I continued to watch as a young woman passed by him, then turned to admonish him for a comment he must have made. The figure threw back his head and laughed heartily, which is when I saw his face. The blood froze in my veins.

'Elle!' I cried.

The three other inhabitants of the shop wheeled around, to see me pointing out of the window. Elle followed my finger, and immediately ran to the light switch.

'What on earth is wrong, dear chap?' Rupert asked. There was nothing I could do but drop to the floor, below the level of the window. 'Good Lord, what's happening?'

'Mr Tanit, has something frightened you?' Louise enquired, looking fairly concerned herself. I lifted my head above the window line once more, and saw Kreeg crossing the street towards Arthur Morston Books.

'Elle, come here, now!' She ran across the shop, and the pair of us scuttled through the back door which led up to the flat, closing it behind us as the shop bell rang. Elle went to sprint up the stairs, but I grabbed her, fearing that my assailant would hear her footsteps. Elle's eyes were full of fear, and I squeezed her hand tightly. Then I put my finger to my lips, and gently leant my ear to the door.

'Good morning,' Rupert said. 'Welcome to Arthur Morston Books.'

'Thank you very much,' Eszu replied, in his deep, hoarse voice. 'What a charming shop you have here.'

'That's awfully kind of you to say. I wonder, is there a particular book that I can help you locate?'

'Are you the owner?'

'I'm sorry?'

'I asked if you were the owner of this bookshop,' Kreeg repeated coldly.

'Yes. I'm Rupert Forbes. My wife and I co-own the place.'

'Louise Forbes,' she said. 'Nice to meet you'.

'Gus. Gus Zeeker. It's a pleasure to make your acquaintance, Mrs Forbes.' I looked to Elle, frowning at the use of the anagram.

'Do I detect an accent there, Mr Zeeker?' Rupert asked. 'Whereabouts are you from?'

'Oh, that is a difficult question to answer, Mr Forbes. I like to think of myself as a citizen of the world.'

'Well, that's jolly impressive. But even citizens of the world have to be born *somewhere*, don't they, old chap?' Rupert replied, with a laugh.

Eszu chuckled back at him. 'Now, Mr Forbes, you seem like an intelligent man. Would you really define an individual just by their place of birth?'

'Of course not. I was merely making conversation. You see, I pride myself on being able to identify an accent. Yours is fairly unusual, that's all.'

There was a palpable pause before Eszu's reply. 'As I said, I am a citizen of the world.'

'Yes. But I wonder which side a citizen of the world chose to fight on during the war?' I was impressed with the bravery of Rupert's question.

Kreeg laughed once more. 'Are we not all friends now, Mr Forbes?' There was another stony silence. 'Forgive me, you mentioned if you could help me find a particular book.'

'Yes,' Rupert said curtly. 'Can we?'

'That would be most helpful. In fact, I was in here just the other day. I spoke with someone else, though. He was tall, with dark hair and brown eyes. Who might that have been?'

I gripped Elle's hand tightly.

'Hmm,' I heard Rupert say. 'Are you quite sure that it was Arthur Morston Books you wandered into? It pains me to admit, but there are several similar shops in the area. We don't have anyone of that description working here.' I couldn't believe Rupert was protecting me.

'Oh yes, I'm quite sure it was this shop,' Eszu said slowly. 'There was a young blonde girl in, too. She was *very* fair.'

'Forgive me, Mr Zeeker,' Rupert said. 'When you walked in you complimented us on our shop, as if it was the first time you had entered. We have told you that we do not have staff who match your description, so I must ask again—are you *quite* sure it was Arthur Morston Books you visited?'

I listened as the old wooden floorboards creaked under Eszu's slow, deliberate footsteps.

'What a beautiful little baby,' he said. 'I assume it is yours?'

'*He* is, yes,' Louise replied.

'Family is so important, isn't it, Mrs Forbes?' Eszu continued.

'Of course it is, Mr Zeeker.'

I heard Kreeg give a pronounced sigh. 'Look at this little child. So meek and helpless. I imagine he relies on you for everything, does he not, Mrs Forbes?'

'I would rather think so, yes. His name is Laurence.'

'Laurence? Allow me to compliment you on your choice of name, Mrs Forbes. Its origins are French. It means "bright, shining one". As all babies are born free from sin, I feel you could not have selected anything more appropriate.'

'I...didn't know that,' Louise replied steadily. 'How fascinating.'

'Names are, generally. The things we call ourselves... I've always found it very amusing that something so personal to us is used almost exclusively by others.'

Rupert cut in. 'Sorry to be a nuisance, old man, but the wife and I were just about to shut up shop for lunch. What was the book you were looking for?'

'Of course, Mr Forbes. As it happens, I was in here the other day enquiring about an old atlas.'

I screwed my eyes shut. Of course, the name would mean nothing to Rupert or Louise. In fact, I suspected that Kreeg knew I was within earshot, and this performance was for my benefit.

'Well, as I said, I doubt it was Arthur Morston Books you were in, but our geography section is just over here,' Rupert said. 'Was there a certain type of atlas you were looking for?'

'This one is quite unique, Mr Forbes. But I will know it when I see it.'

'Righto. Sounds like you might need a while to browse, so it really would be best if you returned later, if you don't mind.'

Kreeg replied firmly, 'I am convinced it's here, Mr Forbes.

There is no need to browse.'

'Listen, I'm really not sure what you mean…'

The dialogue was broken by the sound of baby Laurence beginning to mewl.

'Poor child. Take him in your arms, Mrs Forbes. Savour each moment with him. There is nothing more sacred than the bond between a mother and her child.' Elle looked at me, and I cast my eyes to the floor. 'May I ask you, Mrs Forbes, what this little baby would do without you?' Kreeg said.

'What do you mean?' Louise replied, shocked by the question.

'Allow me to be clearer: if some nasty fate were to befall you, and your husband too, what would become of little Laurence here?'

Rupert raised his voice. 'I say, steady on, old man. What a vile thing to say in my shop!'

'Just words, Mr Forbes. Nonetheless, I appreciate that it is a difficult question to answer. Because, in truth, you do not know of what would become of your child.'

Laurence was crying now. 'Listen, I'd like you to leave,' Rupert stated firmly. 'You're upsetting my wife.'

Kreeg continued. 'A mother is everything to a child. She is a carer, a friend, an anchor. Without that anchor, a child can drift away, and there is no telling where they might end up.'

'I really don't understand what you're talking about, Mr Zeeker. Now leave this shop,' Rupert demanded once more.

'Imagine if I stole you away now, Mrs Forbes, dooming your child to a motherless existence. Do you not think that Laurence here would have a right to seek revenge on me?'

'Are you threatening my child?' Rupert asked, now with full-throated aggression in his voice.

'Me? I would never do such a thing, Mr Forbes. It is not within my nature. But the tall, brown-eyed man who is in your employ… I wouldn't be so sure about him.'

'For God's sake, man, I've had about enough of this.' I heard the floorboards creak in rapid succession as Rupert crossed the shop to shove Kreeg out. There was a yelp from Louise.

'Put him down!' she cried. I gripped the door handle, ready

to burst forth and confront Kreeg. There was not a chance I was going to let him hurt Rupert.

'I would be happy to let your husband go, Mrs Forbes, as soon as you tell me where the Tanits are,' growled Eszu.

'Who are the Tanits?!' Louise shouted. My heart was breaking at her continued loyalty, despite the threat to her husband.

There was a thud, and a gasp, as Kreeg had obviously allowed Rupert to drop to the floor. 'I know they worked for your family,' he continued. 'I had a very interesting drink with your brother just the other day. Well, I say drink, the reprobate downed nearly the entire whisky bottle. He told me that they left your estate and now ran this bookshop.'

'We don't know that name,' stumbled Rupert, still gasping for breath. 'As you saw, Teddy is a drunk. You can't rely on a single word he says. We have no reason to lie to you.'

'Don't you?' Kreeg asked. 'Whatever Tanit's told you, it's untrue. You have a killer in your employ, Mrs Forbes. I suppose he didn't mention that, did he? Trust me, I would be very glad to alleviate you of the threat he presents to your family.'

'I'm calling the police,' Rupert said, as I heard him jog to the back of the shop and pick up the telephone receiver. 'You'd better clear out. You don't want to be found within the vicinity of this establishment when they arrive. You probably don't realise who you've just assaulted. Perhaps my drunken brother-in-law neglected to mention that the bookshop is a hobby. I work for the British government.'

'Poor you, Mr Forbes. Very well, I shall bid you good day. Before I go, however…at the start of our conversation you mentioned the war. Tell me, would you hold a distinction between the soldier who had murdered your friend, and those who worked to protect him?'

'Get out! Just get out!' screamed Louise, as Laurence's cries became louder.

'As you wish.' I heard the shop bell ring as the door opened. 'Oh, and by the way, his name is not "Robert".' The door slammed.

'Shh, baby, it's all right,' Louise soothed, as Rupert opened the door we were hidden behind.

'Bloody hell, chaps. What on earth was all that about?!' Elle and I blinked in the light as Louise went to lock the shop and close the blinds.

'Thank you, Rupert. Thank you for not giving us up.' I shook his hand.

'That's quite all right, old man. I might have myopia, but I know trouble when I see it. However, after the bugger nearly wrung my neck, I rather think I'm owed an explanation.'

I gave Rupert and Louise the outline of the situation—that Kreeg believed I was responsible for his mother's death, and had vowed revenge.

'Oh, Mr Tanit,' Louise said. 'How frightful. I'm so very sorry. What a terrible situation.'

'It is, Louise. We can never thank you enough for what you have just done. You put your own lives at risk to save ours...' I was choked by their act of bravery. 'I will never forget it. Please know that I would never have willingly put your family in danger. We thought that perhaps he had perished in the war.'

'But no such luck,' Elle added sadly.

'So, what's the plan?' Rupert asked. 'He knows you're here. You can't stay, it's simply not safe.'

'Should we go to Switzerland?' Elle asked. 'Remember, Mr Kohler expects your citizenship to be approved any day now.'

'And what then?' I asked. 'Yes, I will be a Swiss citizen, but registered and living under my own name. He found us here, and will track us there.' I put my head in my hands. 'I can't help but feel that the net is closing.'

'How wedded are you to European life?' Rupert asked.

'I don't think America will work, I'm afraid. I've thought about it many times, but with such developed communications and officious records, I worry that Kreeg would have no problem locating us.'

Rupert narrowed his eyes and nodded. 'I wasn't talking about America, actually.' I looked quizzically at him. 'I had an old school chum who lost his wife to pneumonia. Poor chap couldn't bear to be here. Everything in his life reminded him of his loss. So he got on a boat to the end of the earth.'

'The end of the earth?' I asked.

'Well, not quite,' Rupert replied. 'But it may as well be. I'm talking about Australia.'

'Australia?' Elle said.

Rupert put his hands behind his back and began to pace around the shop. 'Wonderful country, apparently. Gorgeous weather, glorious wildlife…not to mention mile upon mile of isolated, uninhabited outback. I imagine, if one wanted to, one could completely disappear. Start afresh. That's certainly the opinion I have as a member of His Majesty's Security Service.'

Elle looked at me. 'I know nothing about the country,' she said. 'But we have to do something. Like Rupert says, we can't stay here.'

'And if this fiend does decide to chase you,' Louise added, 'you may as well make him chase you a very long way.' She smiled weakly.

'If he comes back, we could…redirect him too,' Rupert added. 'Pretend to give you up. Maybe say you've fled to America? Really put him off the scent.'

'That would be beyond kind of you,' I confessed. 'But this man…he's not safe. You must be very careful around him.'

'Understood, old boy. You seem to forget that I work for MI5. Despite my bookish appearance, I am rather used to dealing with shady characters. Speaking of which, I'm going to have him looked in to immediately. Perhaps there's something that might allow the government to arrest him, even deport him. I can certainly have him banged up for a few days for trying to strangle me. I'd like to check the spelling of "Zeeker" with you…'

'It's a pseudonym. His real surname is Eszu. Kreeg Eszu. I doubt you'll be able to find out much about him. I imagine, like me, he has trodden very lightly across this earth.'

'Nonetheless, I promise to do my best, old boy. Until such a time, is it decided? A trip to Australia?'

Elle and I looked at each other, recognising the pain in one another's eyes. It felt like we had come so close to a happy ending…only to have the rug cruelly pulled from under us once more. 'It's…so far away,' I said eventually.

'Forgive me, Robert, but isn't that rather the point?' Rupert replied gently.

'We would have nothing,' Elle muttered. 'We'd have to start again.'

'Now hang on,' Rupert reasoned. 'No one is suggesting that this need be a permanent solution. Think of it as a sabbatical. You pop abroad for a while—perhaps a few months, maybe a little longer—and I'll see what I can do this end. Does that sound like a plan?'

I took Elle's hand. 'Yes,' I said quietly.

Rupert put a hand on my shoulder. 'Right. We need to get you to Tilbury. With any luck there'll be a ship that leaves in the next forty-eight hours.'

'You're being so kind, Rupert, you really are,' Elle said.

'Oh, please, it's the least we can do,' he said.

'My mother still talks with such fondness of you both,' Louise added. 'And you've done such a wonderful job managing the bookshop for us.'

'We will miss it terribly,' Elle said honestly.

'By the way, this voyage Down Under, it won't be cheap,' Rupert said. 'How are you for funds?'

'We're okay, thank you.' I gestured to the back of the shop. 'The salary you pay us is generous.'

'Jolly good, old man. In which case I suggest you pick up some things and we get you to Essex. I've got the car down here, I can take you.'

'I'll stay here in the shop with Laurence,' Louise said.

'No, you mustn't!' I said. 'This man has a history of arson. I'd fear for your safety.'

'Arson, you say? Well, we can't let that fate befall Beatrix's bookshop. I'll make a couple of telephone calls and arrange for some subtle supervision. If he comes within ten feet, he'll be apprehended.'

'You are relatively useful sometimes, Rupes,' Louise said with a wink.

'I do my best. Now then, why don't you go upstairs and sort yourselves out whilst I get on the blower?'

Elle and I hurried up to the flat and started to perform the routine which we were sadly used to by now. The suitcases were taken out from under beds, and only the bare essentials thrown in.

We moved silently and robotically, both contemplating the enormity of such a decision, which had been so rapidly made.

'I'm sure that Rupert will be able to help with the transfer of bank accounts and everything like that,' I said. 'He's clearly very well connected.'

'What happens to your affairs in Switzerland?' Elle asked. 'Didn't Mr Kohler specifically ask you not to disappear off the face of the earth?'

'He did. I'll have to think of something on the voyage. I imagine that in itself will take weeks.'

'Yes… I…' Elle was unable to finish her sentence, and her eyes filled with tears.

'Oh, my love.' I dropped the shirts I was in the process of stuffing into the suitcase and took her in my arms. 'I'm so sorry. None of this is fair. Particularly not on you. I've added such a tremendous weight to your life.' Her repressed tears grew into deep, full sobs as she nestled into my chest. 'Forgive me, Elle. I have made your life so difficult.'

'It's not that, Bo. I just thought it was over. You always told me to trust in the universe. I thought Kreeg was dead. I dared to dream that we might be able to truly *begin* our lives together. Marriage, children… So this is my own fault.'

I held her tightly. 'Please, Elle. Never say that. Not an iota of this terrible, awful mess is your fault. It is my cross to bear, and you have been my strength and stay in bearing it with me. I do not know what I would have done without you.' Now it was my eyes which began to fill with tears.

'Stop that, Bo. Never talk in that way. Life is a gift, whatever the circumstances. So,' she eventually said, 'Australia.'

'Australia,' I replied.

She withdrew from my arms and clapped her hands together, attempting to remain positive. 'A new adventure. I certainly shan't be complaining about the weather over there. But I've heard gruesome things about the spiders.'

'Don't worry, Elle, I'll protect you. After all, spiders may bite, but they cannot burn down a building,' I said with a weary grin.

'You're quite right,' she sighed. 'With any luck, Kreeg won't be able to track us to the other side of the planet. Maybe, rather than be sad for the security we're losing in Switzerland, I should be excited for the safety we will gain "Down Under". And it doesn't matter where we are, my dearest Bo. As long as we are together, we are home.' I cast my eyes down to look at Elle's ring, and stared at it for a while. 'What's wrong?' she asked.

'I feel exactly the same way.' I went to take her hand. 'As long as we are together, we are home,' I repeated. 'I've spent too long not married to you, Elle Leopine.'

My statement caught her off guard. 'I quite agree, my love,' she replied.

'I have an idea,' I said, a glint in my eye.

Elle looked at me with a mixture of excitement and confusion. 'An idea?'

'A ship's captain can legally marry two individuals whilst at sea, and provide a certificate to affirm the ceremony's authenticity. Elle, we could marry on the voyage to Australia.' I dropped to my knee. 'Elle Leopine. You are the unquestionable, unparalleled, unassailable love of my life. Will you marry me?'

I had succeeded in surprising her, which, if I understand correctly, is the secret to a good proposal. 'Oh Bo,' she said, covering her mouth with her hands. 'Yes. Of course!'

We both stood in the flat above Arthur Morston Books, laughing together. For a few moments, the rest of the world melted away.

The journey to Tilbury Port in Essex was swift and uneventful. Rupert was better than his word, and had a friend with the same model of car pull up outside Arthur Morston Books and drive north, just in case Kreeg was watching from afar. Then Elle and I were bundled into Rupert's vehicle, and once more, we were off in search of a new life.

'There's a steamship which leaves tomorrow, old boy,' Rupert confirmed. 'It docks at Port Said in Egypt, then goes on to Adelaide. I dare say by the time your feet touch Australian soil, I'll have this Kreeg bugger in cuffs for attempted murder. Don't you worry.' Rupert's jolly, British stiff upper lip cheered me, but I was unable to believe him. Serpents are slippery, after all. 'There's a hotel just around the corner from the port which I've heard is decent enough. I'll drop you there. They'll also be able to arrange your passage tickets. It's the RMS *Orient* you need.'

'Thank you, Rupert.'

'Not to worry, old man. When you feel settled, write to me via the bookshop. I'll be able to update you on the situation. With any luck, you'll be able to return to Europe soon enough, and build your enormous castle in Switzerland!' After we had pulled up outside the Voyager Hotel, I shook Rupert's hand and opened the car door. 'Good luck, Mr and Mrs T. Remember, any sign of the scoundrel and we'll put him right off your scent whilst I work on getting him arrested.'

We waved Rupert on his way and walked into the hotel. The lobby had an air of faded glamour about it, with a dusty piano and several wilting pot plants. It had perhaps once been grand, but was obviously neglected during the war.

'Good evening, sir,' said the bespectacled receptionist.

'Hello. I'd like a room, please.'

'Very good. How long will you both be staying?'

'Just for one night. And I'm informed that you might be able to help us with tickets for the steamship which leaves in the morning?'

'No bother, sir, we can certainly organise that for you. If I might take some details…'

'Sorry, I've just realised I made a mistake. I'd actually like *two* rooms,' I interjected. Elle looked up at me.

'Two rooms?'

'Yes please. You see'—I leant over the desk—'my fiancée and I are marrying tomorrow.'

'Oh, congratulations. Two rooms it is,' he said with a smile. 'I'm jealous of you boarding that ship tomorrow. A new start, is it?'

The receptionist didn't know how right he was. 'It is rather, yes,' I confirmed.

'Wonderful. I feel like we could all do with one of those after the last few years, Mr…'

'Tanit. And this is Miss Leopine.'

'Thank you. I'll arrange the tickets under your name, sir. What class would you like booking?'

'Oh.' I hadn't even thought about it. 'Second,' I said.

'Very good. I'll have them sent up to your room, sir. You can pay upon checkout tomorrow morning. The steamship departs at ten a.m. sharp. You'll want to be on board at least half an hour before.'

We left our luggage at the desk, collected our room keys and made our way upstairs.

'What's going on, Bo?' Elle whispered. 'Why did you book us separate rooms?'

'It's an easy question to answer. The groom is not supposed to see the bride the night before the wedding!'

Elle giggled. 'How romantic. Although we will need every penny we have until we get settled in Australia. You should have saved the money.'

'Oh, nonsense. Are we not able to enjoy at least a few of the traditions? Plus,' I added, 'I have enough funds for a dress. I think we should go shopping this afternoon.'

'Bo, that's very sweet, but totally unnecessary.'

'On the contrary, Elle!' I replied. 'It is absolutely necessary. Cinderella *will* have a dress, and go to the ball!'

As it transpired, the rest of the day was a little magical. Elle and I spent the cold January afternoon hand in hand, blinking in the winter sun and sipping English breakfast tea in paper cups to warm up. We even went to inspect the vessel which would transport us across the ocean. Dangling our legs over the water's edge, we peered up at the mighty RMS *Orient*, which was majestic and imposing. She must have been over five hundred foot long, and at least a hundred tall. The ship had a sleek, black hull and two bright white decks adorned with dozens of circular windows.

'Gosh. Can't we just live on there?' Elle asked. 'We'd always be safe out on the sea.'

I thought about it for a moment. 'You know, you're right. We would be. What a good idea. Maybe I should just spend all of Agatha's money on one of those enormous yachts you read about in the magazines?'

'Well, only if it has three swimming pools, Bo.' She laughed, and the way the midwinter sun caught her face made for one of the most beautiful images I have ever seen in my life. I suddenly felt inspired.

'Wait there!' I said, jumping to my feet.

'Bo, what on earth are you doing?!' Elle cried.

'Just don't move!' I ran across the road and back onto the small high street, where we had passed an art shop. I entered and bought a few small sheets of paper and some charcoal, before jogging back to Elle.

'What was all that about?' she asked.

'I want to draw you.'

'Draw me?' Elle asked, giggling.

'Yes. Monsieur Landowski once said something to me in his atelier about capturing the moment. He only knew what he wanted to sculpt once he *saw* it. I think I know what he means now. I've been inspired to capture your beauty.'

'I'm glad you still have the ability to flatter me after all these years.'

'I've never dared to draw a portrait, only landscapes. I hope I can do justice to what I see before me…'

I got to work with the charcoal, doing my best to encapsulate Elle's enormous eyes, dainty nose and full lips, set within her graceful heart-shaped face. Within fifteen minutes, I had completed my drawing. I looked at what I had produced, and then at Elle, and was quietly pleased with my efforts. It was certainly better than any field, river or tree I had ever attempted to encapsulate.

'Show me,' she said. I handed her the piece of paper, and she examined it, before looking back at me. 'I love it. Thank you.'

'I know it's far from perfect. But it will always remind me of this moment.'

'And why is it that you wish to be reminded of this moment, Bo?'

I closed my eyes. The salty ocean scented the air and invigorated my senses. 'Because, my love, despite everything, I am excited by the prospect of a new future. And tomorrow, I will marry the love of my life.'

She kissed me lightly on the cheek. 'I will keep the drawing forever.'

Eventually we got up, asked a passer-by about the local fashion shops, and were pointed in the direction of a quaint little dressmaker's.

'Go on in, Elle. I certainly shouldn't lay eyes on the dress—that's breaking all the rules. Take as long as you need.' I watched her pass through the door and caught sight of myself in the glass front window. There was no doubting it, these days my looks belied my relatively young age. My hair was rapidly greying, and the wrinkles on my forehead seemed to grow deeper by the day. I could only hope that putting oceans between Kreeg and me might slow down the process somewhat.

I stood dutifully for twenty minutes or so, until the shop bell rang and Elle walked out with a light blue paper bag and a beaming smile upon her face.

'Thank you, Bo. I hope you will like it.'

When we arrived back at the hotel, I escorted my fiancée to her room, which was on the floor above mine.

'This is where I must leave you.' I shrugged. 'I mean, I shouldn't really be seeing you until the moment we are to be wed, but I want to make sure you make it on board. So I'll meet you at the top of the *Orient* gangplank at nine thirty a.m.'

'Nine thirty it is,' Elle confirmed.

I removed a rogue strand of blonde hair from her face. 'Your final night of living in sin…'

'Ha! I accept absolutely no responsibility.' She laughed. 'It's all your fault.'

I held my hands up. 'I freely admit that I have forced you into a sullied life. Will you ever be able to forgive me?' I put my palms together in mock prayer.

'Seeing as you're finally making good tomorrow, I believe that forgiveness is on the cards. But, as this really *is* our last night of living in sin, perhaps we should…indulge ourselves?' she said, playfully loosening the top button of my shirt.

'Oh, I see,' I raised an eyebrow. 'Are you worried that things might be *different* after we're married?'

'Absolutely. It won't feel half as exhilarating.'

'Well then. I suppose we owe it to ourselves.' I kissed her, and she pulled me in through the bedroom door.

That night, we spent hours lost in one another. The whole universe could have ceased to exist outside of the door, and neither of us would have noticed, nor cared a damn. As she lay in my arms, the gentle, rhythmic sound of her breath soothed me to sleep. When I awoke a few hours later, I slowly extricated myself from the embrace, to make my way down to my own bedroom. She stirred, and I kissed her forehead.

'I'm sorry to wake you. I'm just going back to my room to organise a few things for the trip,' I whispered.

'Okay. Am I still meeting you on board the *Orient*?'

'Yes. I'll see you at nine thirty. Sleep well, my darling.' As I grabbed the handle on the door, I turned to look at my wife-to-be, lying peacefully on the bed. Her flowing blonde hair and pale white skin gave her the appearance of a madonna plucked from a canvas of Botticelli.

I have often, in my heart, tried to define love. Now I believe I know what it is. To unthinkingly and gladly put another soul before one's own, regardless of the consequences. Finishing my longing look, I gently opened the door and shut it behind me, my heart so full of love and pride for the amazing woman who had been by my side for twenty years. And whom, tomorrow, I would marry.

37

Atlantic Ocean, 1949

Without you I am
Torn into pieces
Of cosmic dust

The stars are black
The night is endless
The Pleiades weep

The light is now gone
My life is now gone

I am
In bed alone

My world is ended. If you are reading this diary entry, I expect it to be the final one, and the story of Atlas Tanit will be complete. I have managed to survive all these years propelled by the fundamental energy that keeps humans striving forwards against all the odds—hope. But now, even that is extinguished, and I do not have the energy to continue. Later tonight, when the deck is quiet, I will willingly throw myself into the ocean, and let the freezing water consume me. I hope the waves are merciful, and it is a quick death.

I only feel moved to write this last entry out of a sense of duty to you, the reader. It is not the ending I dreamt of as a young boy when I first put pen to paper. Perhaps you have discovered this diary and turned straight to the end, to find out what happened to the man who threw himself off a steamship. Or, maybe, you have completed my entire life story, which I hope has been interesting if nothing else. If that is the case, I am sure that you have already surmised the fate that has befallen me.

Elle is gone.

My worst nightmare has become my reality, and I cannot face existing in it for too much longer.

After leaving Elle's room in the early hours of this morning, I returned to my own quarters. I wrote in this diary, reordered my suitcase and then climbed into bed, with dreams of my wife-to-be lulling me into sacred slumber. I awoke at eight, got up and paid the hotel bill, along with our tickets for the passage. Then I made my way on board the RMS *Orient* and found our cabin. I even excitedly told the young steward who helped me with my bag about my plan to marry on the voyage, and he assured me that the captain would be more than happy to oblige. Then I took coffee and strolled out onto the deck, to watch for Elle.

There was an enormous throng of people by the water's edge, clearly reluctant to let go of their loved ones who were departing for Australia. The pain of human separation was visceral, and I thanked my stars that I was boarding this ship with the only family I would ever need.

As the clock approached nine thirty, I made my way down to the gangplank where we had arranged to meet. As the minutes ticked on, and my watch read nine forty, I began to panic that Elle had overslept. I explained the situation to the steward, who assured me that there was enough time for me to run back to the Voyager Hotel and return to the ship before departure.

I sprinted down the gangplank, nearly sending a family flying into the water as I did so. I burst into the hotel lobby and up to Elle's floor, banging loudly on the door, which garnered no response.

I tried calling out. 'Elle!' I cried. 'Elle, the ship is about to leave! Elle!'

Realising my efforts were clearly fruitless, I ran back down to the lobby, where the bespectacled receptionist from the day before was now on shift.

'Ah, good morning, sir! A big day ahead. Actually, shouldn't you be on board? The gangplank is due to be raised in fifteen minutes.'

'Yes, I know, but my fiancée is still in bed. She was supposed to meet me on the steamer, but she hasn't shown up. Could you please unlock her bedroom door so I can rouse her?'

The receptionist looked puzzled. 'Actually, sir, I saw her leave about half an hour ago. She walked through the lobby with her suitcase.'

I frowned. 'That can't be possible. She hasn't boarded the ship. You must be mistaken. Please, I want you to unlock her bedroom.'

'Really, sir, you have to believe me, I—'

'NOW!' I shrieked, as the eyes of the lobby fell upon me.

'As you wish, sir. Let me just ask my colleague to escort you.'

'Give me the key. I'll go myself.' I yanked it out of the receptionist's hand and ran back up the stairs. I shoved the key into the lock and opened the door. The room was empty. The bed had been made and the floor was clear of possessions. What's more, there was a cup with the remnants of coffee within it, the rim smudged with Elle's pink lipstick. She had been here this morning, and had clearly left, just as the receptionist had confirmed.

Briefly, I was overjoyed at the discovery. It meant that Elle had, in all probability, boarded the ship. I had simply missed her. With my watch now reading ten minutes to the hour, I rushed back downstairs and threw the key at the desk. I returned to the gangplank, scanning for Elle.

'Have you seen a lady with blonde hair and a dark blue coat? She would have been carrying one suitcase. She should be on board.'

The gangplank attendant searched his mind, but shook his head. 'Sorry, sir, I don't think I've boarded anyone who matches that description. But it's a large ship, I could be mistaken. If she's on board, she'll probably have been directed to her cabin. You can always check with the floor steward.'

I hurriedly made my way to our second-class cabin, which was empty save for my suitcase. I accosted the steward in the hallway, and begged him to confirm that Elle was on board.

'Leopine is her surname. Or, perhaps she used Tanit. But she has blonde hair. A blue coat. She's my fiancée…' I was aware that I was beginning to babble as my panic increased. My watch now showed only five minutes to the hour. I raced back up to the gangplank, and found myself describing Elle to anyone I could find, with no luck. My heart was pumping ten to the dozen and my vision began to blur in my overwhelming panic.

I heard the ship's engine's roar into life.

'No, no, please, no!' I grabbed the nearest uniformed employee. 'You have to stop the ship! I don't know if my fiancée is on board!'

'Sorry, sir, the gangplank is raised at ten o'clock sharp. There really can be no exceptions.' I clung to the rail of the deck and desperately scanned the shore for any sign of my love. Still seeing nothing, I ran back to the gangplank and pleaded with the attendant, who saw my pain, but was unable to help, bound by those higher up the chain.

'Sir, I understand the situation.' He tried to calm me. 'I really would very much like to help. But in all honesty, I suggest you disembark.'

'But she might be on board!' I cried.

'In which case, sir, there's another ship which leaves in a few weeks. You could follow her then.' I spun around, and came face to face with an elderly lady. She had high cheekbones, pale skin and piercing blue eyes—not dissimilar to Elle's. Although her curly hair was decidedly grey, there were a few distinct flourishes of auburn within her mane.

'Gangplank up!' came the cry from the steward. He was joined by two other uniformed individuals, who placed their hands on the rope and began to pull. The ship's horn hooted a final warning.

'Where is she? She was meant to meet me here on the ship!' I wheeled around once more to the old lady, who was staring up at me. 'Excuse me, madam, have you by any chance seen a blonde-haired woman boarding the ship in the last few minutes?'

'I couldn't say.' Her accent was Scottish. 'There were so many people coming and going, but I'm sure she's on board somewhere.'

The horn sounded again, and the ship very slowly began to edge away from the dock. I considered jumping over the side. Perhaps the steward was right. If I remained on land, then in the worst-case scenario, Elle might be safely on her way to Australia and out of harm's way. I could avoid Kreeg for another few weeks. But if Elle had not boarded the ship, then I needed to stay in England to protect her. My mind raced. 'Oh God, where *are* you...?' I screamed to the wind, my voice drowned out by the engines and the screeching of seagulls. I staggered back along the deck, clinging to the handrail and gasping for breath. 'Elle! Elle! Elle!' I cried helplessly, feeling as though I was falling through an endless void. As I once more peered over the edge of the ship, trying to suck in as much air as I could, I spied something familiar on the dock. I couldn't quite believe it, but just behind a crowd of people waving handkerchiefs and blowing kisses was a light blue paper bag, from the dressmaker Elle and I had been to the day before.

It couldn't be Elle's, could it?

I had very little to lose.

'Excuse me! Excuse me!' I cried out to the crowd below. 'My bag! I've left my bag!' I continued to shout and flail my arms wildly until I attracted the attention of a young boy. 'The blue bag! Just behind you! Please throw it aboard!' The young man turned around and saw what I was pointing to. He pushed his way through the adults around him and grabbed it. 'Yes! Please, throw it!' The ship was perhaps three metres away from the dock's edge, with the distance increasing by the second. The boy made his way to the water's edge, looking up at me. I realised that I was too high up, and the bag didn't have a chance of making it. I pushed my way back through passengers to the steward at the gangplank. 'Please, my bag, that boy has it!' He had clearly been willing to help a moment before, so nodded, and, quick as a flash, hopped over the ship's edge. For a moment, I thought he'd jumped, but in actuality, he was climbing down some ladder-like rails attached to the hull. The boy saw the steward spring into action. When he was level with the shoreline, the steward held out a single arm so that the boy could throw him the bag. The boy hesitated.

'Now or never!' the steward cried. The boy looked up to me, and I gave him the nod. He threw the blue bag with some force, and my heart remained in my mouth as the steward fumbled it over the ocean. Nonetheless, he somehow managed to maintain a grip, and began to make his way back up to the deck. The young boy cheered, and I gave him a small round of applause, before reaching over to grab the bag.

'Thank you, thank you!' I cried.

'Your fiancée's, is it?' he asked.

'That's right,' I replied.

'Well, seeing as it was right by the dock, hopefully that means she's on board, sir.'

'Yes. Thank you again.' I forced my way back through the humming deck, a cacophony of human emotion as passengers bade farewell to their homeland—some for many months, others forever.

Eventually, I reached the ship's aft, where there was enough space to open the bag. From within, I pulled out a white satin dress. At the bottom of the bag, I noticed two small pieces of paper. My stomach turned as I laid eyes upon the charcoal drawing I had done the day before. Accompanying it was a note.

Knowing you was the privilege of my life.
Rest easy without the burden of having to keep me safe.
Ever yours,
Elle xx
(Go and live your life, as I must live mine.)

I felt numb. Nothing seemed real. The note implied that Elle had *chosen* not to get on the boat. She had *chosen* to leave me. 'No,' I whispered. 'It can't be…' My mind raced through the events of the last twenty-four hours. It had all seemed so perfect…

Without warning, my legs failed me and I collapsed to the floor. I expected tears, but none came. My body did not possess the power to produce them. At that moment, my inner light was extinguished.

"Scuse me, mista. You doin' all right down there?' I looked up to see a bright-eyed, painfully thin young girl with sallow skin and lank brown hair. She could have been no more than fifteen years old. "Ello, mista? Oh, bloody hell, he looks a bit peaky. Eddie, go and get someone in a bleedin' uniform, would yer?' A young boy beside her, aged perhaps five or so, ran off. "Scuse me, could someone help, please? This bloke's taken a bit of a tumble. 'Ello? Can you 'ear me?' The girl knelt down beside me.

'You shouldn't be on deck, you filthy toerag,' came a deep, plummy voice from above. 'You should be down below in ratbag class.'

'Yeah, sorry, mista, we was only coming up to 'ave a look at England for the last time. But this man's a bit poorly. Can you help?' the cockney girl replied.

The plummy-voiced man looked irritated. 'Get a steward. It's what they're paid for,' he sneered, before strolling nonchalantly away.

The girl threw her hands up. 'Right, thanks for nothin'. 'Ello, mista,' she said to me, producing an enormous grin and revealing a yellowing set of teeth. 'Don't worry, Eddie's gone to fetch someone.'

'I don't, I can't…' I vaguely remember mumbling.

The young girl took my hand, and began to shake it vigorously, I think in an attempt to revive me. 'It's all right, mista. What's your name? I'm Sarah.'

'Sarah…' I stumbled.

She nodded at me. 'That's right, mista. Feel a bit overwhelmed, do yer? Me too. But it'll be good in Australia. It'll be nice and 'ot and they say we can go swimming in the sea every day.'

I looked into Sarah's brown eyes. 'Elle,' I managed. 'Elle…'

She looked perplexed. 'Elle?' Sarah frowned. 'Who's that then?'

I groaned. 'She's gone, she's gone.'

Sarah looked around. 'Gone? Gone where, mista?'

'Gone away…'

She rolled her eyes. 'Oh blimey, he's gone loopy. You'll be all right, mista. Look, 'ere's a bloke who knows what to do.' A uniformed steward approached from across the deck. As he got closer, I noticed the annoyed look on his face.

'What are you doing up here?' he hissed at Sarah.

She laughed indignantly. 'We wanted to say ta-ra to England. Never mind about that, though, this poor bloke needs some 'elp!'

The steward knelt down beside me. 'I'll deal with it. Now take the boy here and get back downstairs. You know you're not supposed to be up here. We'll have complaints.'

Sarah sighed. 'Yeah, all right. Come on, Eddie.' The little boy gave me a small wave, and I did my best to reciprocate. ''Ope you feel better, mista,' said Sarah. 'See you in Australia.' She took Eddie by the hand and led him away. Before she disappeared from view, I saw her run to the edge of deck and lift the little boy up so he could see over the side. Then she waved her spare arm. 'GOODBYE, ENGLAND!' she cried. 'Give 'er a wave, Eddie!'

'Downstairs!' the steward barked. The children obeyed. 'I'm terribly sorry about that, sir, it won't happen again.'

I was beginning to recover my senses. 'No, I must thank her... Who is she?'

The steward rolled his eyes. 'They're orphans. There's about a hundred of them down in third class. They're being shipped out from England to find new families in Australia.'

'Orphans?'

'Yes, and I'm sorry, sir, I will ensure they don't bother you again.'

I was becoming frustrated by this man's attitude. 'No, I—'

'You've taken a fall, sir. Don't worry, we'll make sure you're all right.'

I tried to stand up. 'I...need...to get off.'

The steward held me down. 'Easy, sir. There's no getting off now. The next stop's Egypt.'

I tried to resist the steward, but the exertion proved too much. 'No, I...' was all I managed, before my world descended into darkness.

I awoke in my cabin, a man in a tweed jacket looking over me.

'Hello, Mr Tanit. Feeling better, are we?'

I blinked hard. 'Yes. What's going on?'

The man in the jacket smiled. 'I'm Doctor Lyons, the ship's medical officer. I have to say, I didn't expect to be called into action so early in the trip, but there we are. You had a bit of a fall on deck, Mr Tanit, do you remember that?'

'Yes.'

The doctor took out a small torch from his pocket and shone it in my eyes. 'It's quite understandable, I think. You seem to have had a bit of a day of it.' He raised an eyebrow at me. 'The steward on your floor says that you'd asked about the captain performing a wedding?' I nodded, still in a daze. 'I read the note that was in your hand. Hard luck, old man. That's very difficult to accept, I'm sure.'

A surge of dread ran through me as I recalled the events that had led up to my collapse. 'Oh no. Oh no!' I sat bolt upright in bed.

The doctor put a comforting hand on my shoulder. 'It's all right, Mr Tanit. Here, take this.' Doctor Lyons offered me a pill and a glass of water. 'It's a mild sedative which will put you to sleep for a few hours.'

I didn't want to sleep. 'I need to get off this ship!'

Dr Lyons gave me a sympathetic shrug. 'That's not going to be possible, Mr Tanit, which is why I suggest you take the sedative. I promise you, it will make the time pass quicker.' He practically forced the pill into my mouth, and I gulped it down. 'There's a good chap. That should knock you out for a while. I'll be in to check on you later.'

Dr Lyons stood up, and before he was out of the door, my eyes had closed.

When I awoke, I turned here, to my diary, to record my final thoughts.

For the sake of my own sanity, I have to believe that my life has not been a lie, and that Elle did truly love me. As for why she didn't board the ship… I can only surmise that she felt unable to continue her life plagued by the constant threat of Kreeg Eszu and his mission to do me harm. In this regard, who am I to blame her? Our lives have been spent living under a cloud, with the heavens threatening to open at any moment. She deserves so much more. I know that I truly love her, because in this regard, I am glad.

But I know that without her, there is nothing left for me here.

And so concludes the story of Atlas Tanit, or Bo D'Aplièse, or some amalgamation of the two—however you have come to know me, reader. I will put my pen down, and walk up to the deck. I hope my Seven Sisters shine for me one final time.

I do not fear death, but I hope the process itself is relatively quick, and that the cold of the Atlantic envelops me to save me many painful hours floating in the nothingness.

What will I do with the diamond? Should I…bequeath it to someone? Is there a way of getting it to Mr Kohler in Switzerland, perhaps for young Georg and Claudia, I wonder? But if Kreeg ever discovered its location…

I will pen a will before I jump, leaving my estate to the Hoffmans, with the proviso that the two young children are cared for. Perhaps it is best that the blasted diamond accompanies me to a watery grave. That way, it cannot cause more harm than it already has.

Before I finish these pages, something has begun to nag at me, reader. This diary begins in Paris in 1928. It is amusing to me, now, how cautious I was when penning those initial pages. I would not even record my name. Of course, such protections became moot when I was discovered by Eszu in Leipzig. If you have stuck with me this far, I believe I owe it to you to present you with the full picture of my life, and the precise events that led to the chaos which has tainted my existence.

Kreeg, if this diary ever finds you, I will, once again, address below the exact circumstances of your mother's death. Please, I beg of you, accept that the following account is given by a man at the end of his life, with nothing to hide, and nothing to gain from lying.

~~Tyumen, Siberia, April 1918~~

~~On reflection, my birth was an auspicious day, not that I was aware of it at the time. The end of the Romanov dynasty caused great unre~~

Apologies, reader. During the writing of that sentence I was interrupted by a knock on my door—Dr Lyons, who had come to check on me. He told me that a young orphan girl named Sarah from third class had enquired about my well-being during his visit to assess the health of the children below.

'She was very kind to me,' I said truthfully. Suddenly, I had a thought. I felt the diamond, still secure against my chest. 'I would like to thank her. Would you happen to know how I get to third class?'

'Yes, if you're sure you want to brave it. All our orphans are in fine fettle, but I'm rather afraid that personal hygiene is not a priority for them, Mr Tanit.'

I managed a slight laugh. 'It's really not a problem, Dr Lyons. Which way, please?'

I made my way down into the belly of the RMS *Orient* through a labyrinthine arrangement of corridors and quarters. Eventually, several decks below my own, I entered third class. The most striking thing was the lack of any natural light. The whitewashed walls glared with the reflection of clinical artificial illumination, which had a bewildering effect on one's sense of time.

The communal area in third class consisted of a room full of battered tables and chairs of various sizes, and was heavy with cigarette smoke when I entered. Around the largest of the tables sat a rag-tag collection of children. Among them, I spotted Eddie, the little chap who had been on deck earlier, but there was no sign of Sarah.

I approached the group. 'I'm sorry to interrupt. I was just wondering if Sarah was about?'

'She's snuck off again,' said one of the boys, before looking horrified at his admission. 'But don't be too hard on her, mista, she just likes to look at the ocean.'

I gave him a reassuring smile. 'Oh, that's all right. I like to do the same.'

'You won't beat her then?' he asked.

'Beat her?! Heavens no. Quite the opposite actually. I was hoping to thank her for something.' I gave Eddie a thumbs up, which he returned. 'I don't actually work for the ship. I'm just a passenger.'

'A posh one? You sounds posh!' said another boy, to sniggers from around the table.

'Oh, not as posh as some of the people on board. Would I find Sarah up on the viewing deck then?'

'Prob'ly, yeah,' replied the boy.

The viewing deck was silent, with only the infinite blackness of the water and the fierce chill of the January air for company. Sighing, I held on to the railing and looked up to the sky. Celaeno was especially bright tonight. The sound of the steamer cutting through the water was soothing, and the cold, crisp air felt invigorating on my skin.

'It's you, innit, mista?' came a familiar voice from the shadows. I looked round, and Sarah emerged from behind a life-ring housing. 'The bloke who pulled a whitey earlier?'

'Hello, Sarah. I wanted to thank you for your kindness this morning.'

'Shh, keep yer voice down. I'm not s'posed to be up here!' She raised a finger to her lips.

I sighed. 'What a ridiculous ruling. Listen, come and stand by me, and no one will be any the wiser.'

She came forth and joined me at the railing. We stood for a moment, taking in the salt-scented night air. 'You feeling better then?' she asked.

I nodded. 'Much improved, thank you. You were the only person to come and help me. That was very good of you.'

'That's all right, mista. It's just 'uman decency, innit? But all these poshos up top are more worried about getting their knees dirty than lendin' a helpin' hand.' She tutted comically.

The sound of the *Orient* surging through the water was relaxing, and I felt my blood pressure starting to lower. I really did enjoy being out on the ocean. 'Might I ask how many orphans are travelling to Australia?' I asked Sarah.

She took a moment to calculate. 'Probably a hundred. I'm fifteen, see, so I'm all right. But there are little 'uns down there not much older than three. Them's the ones I feel sorry for.' She stared out into the darkness. I was touched by her caring nature. After all, she was only a child herself.

'May I ask what happened to your parents?' I enquired gently.

Sarah looked around at the empty deck, as if to check no one was listening in. I suspected that the memory was painful, and as a consequence was not discussed often. 'In the war there were a lot of bombs that fell on the East End. The last one did for ten of us in our street, including me mam. We was in the cellar, see, 'cos the sirens had gone off, then she realised she left 'er knitting upstairs and went to fetch it just as the thing fell on our roof. I were dug outta the rubble without a scratch. I were only six years old at the time. Chap that heard me caterwauling said it was a blimmin' miracle.'

I went to put a hand on Sarah's shoulder, but feared it would be inappropriate. 'How awful. I'm so sorry for your loss. Where did you go after that?'

She took a deep breath, then exhaled slowly before continuing. 'Me auntie took me in to 'er house down the road. Was only s'posed to be till me dad came back from soldiering in France. Except 'e never did come back, and me auntie couldn't afford to keep me, so I was put in an orphanage. It were all right there, 'cos we stuck together. Then one day they told us we was going to Australia to get new lives. And 'ere we are.'

The *Orient* encountered a rogue wave, and Sarah and I were hit in the face by some fine sea spray. Sarah gave a throaty cackle, which in turn elicited a small laugh from me. Her positivity was inspiring, and a little infectious, too.

'Did you lose anyone in the war, mista?' Sarah asked.

Karine, Pip and Archie Vaughan all passed through my mind. 'I did, yes.'

Sarah nodded wisely. 'I thought so. You 'ave that sad look in your eye.'

'Do I?' I asked. Sarah gave me a sympathetic grin. I turned away to face the ocean. 'I actually lost someone very recently, not because of the war.'

'Who was that then?'

'Her name is Elle.' I shut my eyes. 'She was the love of my life.'

Sarah put her hands on her hips. "Er name *is* Elle? You mean, she's not popped her clogs?'

I couldn't help but smile at Sarah's brazen manner of speech.

'No, not at all. She's just...not on this ship.'

Sarah threw her arms out. 'Well, what are you so down about then? Just turn round and go get her back!'

'I wish it was as simple as that, Sarah. She doesn't want to be with me.' I felt for the diamond hung around my neck. 'Anyway, I want to thank you once again, Sarah. I have something here for you, actually.' I began to lift the string from around my neck.

Sarah put a hand out to stop me. 'Oh no, I won't take yer money, mista. Not for doing a kind thing. That's not right. I mean, if you need yer socks darning, or yer trousers stitchin' up, I'd be glad to take payment. But not for earlier.'

I was a little taken aback. 'I don't think you understand, Sarah, this is a life-changing amount of mon—'

'Mista, I'm on a boat to the other side of the world. Trust me, that's enough of a change for the time being. As I said, I'm useful with me 'ands, I'm 'oping I'll get a job and make some money of me own. And find a fella!'

I tucked the string of the pouch back beneath my shirt. 'In which case, I will leave you to enjoy your evening. Thank you again, Sarah.'

I started to make the journey to the other side of the deck. 'Do you believe in God, mista?' Sarah called to me.

The question caught me off guard. I turned back to face her. 'What do you mean?'

'I've been thinkin' a lot about all that recently, and you seem like a clever bloke. I just wondered what you thought?'

I strolled slowly back towards Sarah, pondering the question. 'I think it depends what you mean by "God". I believe in the power of the universe. Maybe that's the same thing?'

Sarah sniffed. 'So you don't think it's an old geezer with a big white beard?'

I chuckled. 'That sounds like you're describing Father Christmas to me. And I most definitely believe in him.'

'Ha. Well, 'e didn't make many visits to the orphanage, I can tell yer that.'

'No.' I cast my eyes heavenwards and took in the stars. 'Elle was an orphan, you know. I suppose I am too. Sort of.'

Sarah screwed up her face. "Ow can you be *sort of* an orphan?'

I smiled. 'That's a very good question. It's difficult to explain.'

'Well, one thing we ain't short of is time. I'm gonna do me best to escape up 'ere every night to get out of the smog from all that fag smoke downstairs. You can meet me up 'ere, and you can tell me your story.'

'My story, eh? I've never told it to anyone in full, apart from Elle. It's very long. And quite sad.'

'Sad *so far*, mista. It ain't over yet, is it?' I hesitated, unsure of how to respond. Sarah's face dropped. "Ang on a minute. I know that look. You're not thinking about chucking yerself over the edge, are yer?'

'I...'

Sarah was furious. 'Don't be so bleedin' selfish. You know who'd love to be 'ere right now? Me mam. But she can't be, because a bomb dropped on 'er head. Same goes for all the parents of them little 'uns down there. The kids would give anything to 'ave 'em back when they were so cruelly taken. And 'ere you are, thinkin' about snuffin' yerself out.'

I took a step back. 'Sarah, I didn't mean to upset you...'

'Upset me? Nah. I'll be all right. But you know who won't be? People who know yer. What about when this Elle finds out you killed yerself because of 'er? 'Ow d'you think she'll cope with that on her conscience?' She stared at me, eyes wide and eyebrows raised. In truth, I hadn't even considered Elle discovering the circumstances of my death. Sarah continued. 'What's more, if she did love yer, and it sounds like she did, the last thing she'd want is for you to top yerself.'

I was scrambling for a response. 'Well...no,' I conceded. 'Again, I'm very sorry to have caused distress. Particularly because I lost my parents myself at a young age.'

Rather than placate Sarah, it seemed to incense her further. 'Well, there yer bleedin' go then! Yer think they'd be 'appy tonight watchin' their son hit the ocean?' She pointed to the sky. 'I don't bloody think so.'

The young woman's straight-talking manner had a sobering effect on me. 'You're quite right, Sarah.' I was suddenly feeling very ashamed of my intentions.

Sarah took a step towards me and softened her tone. 'You've got to remember that life is a gift, mista. Whatever the circumstances.'

Tears filled my eyes. I nodded. 'Elle told me that once.'

Sarah shrugged. 'She was right.' She gave me a light push on the chest. 'And anyway, when we get to Australia, you can find a nice new girlfriend who doesn't abandon yer on ships. All right?'

I gave a chuckle through my tears. 'All right Sarah. Point taken.'

'Anyway, mista, I really do want to hear your story, starting tomorrow night. You won't let me down, will yer?'

I shook my head. 'I won't, Sarah.'

I bade her goodnight and returned to my cabin, and to my diary. I will keep my promise to Sarah. She somehow has managed to rouse me from the depths of my dark thoughts. Despite her difficult life, she strives to see the brighter side, and what's more, finds the capacity to care for others too.

She reminds me a little of Elle.

38

Once more, reader, the universe seems to have thrown me a lifeline. The next night, and all the nights after that, I have met with Sarah on the viewing deck of the RMS *Orient*. As a result, I have shared with her my story in full. She was glued to every word. I even felt compelled to show her the diamond.

'Bloody 'ell! Well, I regret turnin' that down the other night! Cor, it's the size of a bleedin' rat!'

'Do you promise not to tell anyone aboard that I have it, Sarah? Money and diamonds can make men mad, as I think I've managed to convey.'

She tapped her nose. 'Don't you worry, Mr T, your secret's safe with me.' Sarah folded her arms and leant back on the viewing deck's wooden bench. 'You know the thing I can't get me 'ead round? If you was plannin' on doin' a runner, why would you buy a wedding dress?' I considered Sarah's point. It was very astute. 'Did she take her time choosing it?'

I cast my mind back. 'She did, yes.'

Sarah sucked her teeth. 'Very strange, Mr T. As is the way the bag was just left on the dock, as if she'd disappeared into thin air.'

'I agree, Sarah. It has to have been a last-minute decision.'

She nodded. 'Must 'ave been, yeah. Do you reckon you'll go lookin' for her?'

It was a question I had spent many sleepless nights contemplating. 'I always promised to keep Elle safe. I worry that going back will only endanger her again. I'm trying to accept that Elle distancing herself from me is the safest outcome,' I replied sadly.

Sarah slapped a hand on my back. 'I feel for yer, Mr T. Will you be getting off tomorrow when we dock at Port Said?'

I tried to rally myself. 'Absolutely. I'd never miss an opportunity to set foot in an entirely new land. I'm assuming that your "captors" will let you and the other children off the boat for a visit?'

Sarah laughed. 'Yeah! We can't wait. Apparently, there's this rich old Scottish woman—even richer than you, she's in first class—who's going to treat us all to sweetmeats and Turkish delights. Fancy that!'

I was pleased to hear it. 'Oh, really? That *is* exciting news. What's her name?'

Sarah narrowed her eyes in thought. 'I'm pretty sure someone said it was Kitty Mercer. Apparently 'er 'usband died. Or left 'er or something. I'm not really sure. But she's got bags of cash.'

I thought for a moment. 'You know, I wonder if she's connected to the Mercer pearling empire that's run out of Australia? I've read about them in the newspaper.'

'Prob'ly is, I reckon. Apparently, she's got a massive mansion out in Australia, even though she started out like one of us—no money, I mean. Everyone says you can make a new life for yourself in this place. What do you think it will be like?'

Without my love...empty, heartbreaking, vast, cruel.

'Oh, I imagine it will be fantastic, and most importantly of all, you're going to do wonderfully there.'

The next day, I watched Kitty Mercer lead a small army of children off the ship and into Port Said. When I laid eyes on her, it occurred to me that I had seen Mrs Mercer before, on the day we left Tilbury. She had been one of the individuals I had desperately begged for information about Elle.

As the *Orient* was constantly in motion, the resulting breeze meant that nobody on board had a real appreciation for the air temperature. However, since docking, the African heat had hit us all, and I passed through a sea of red faces as I made my way to the gangplank. Walking off the ship, the smell of unwashed bodies and rotting fruit accosted my nose. I made my way through the busy port, observing a steady stream of crates and animals being moved to and from the docked steamships.

Leaving the port, I headed into the old town itself. I soon came across a well-stocked market boasting spices, fruit and flatbreads baking in scorching-hot ovens. The air around them quite literally rippled with the heat. Local residents swirled around me in their bright-coloured robes and fez hats. I did my best to take it all in.

As I did so, I was consumed by negative thought. How much sweeter this experience would have been if I were sharing it with Elle. Suddenly, the Turkish delight I purchased had no taste, and the vibrant colours of the stalls may as well have been grey.

That evening, when we were back on the ship, Sarah didn't meet me for our usual night-time chat. I could not blame her. Mrs Mercer had been able to show her and her fellow orphans a better time than I could ever manage in my current state. Nonetheless, I returned each evening, out of habit, and talked to my Seven Sisters instead. Five nights later, Sarah bounded up to me.

'Ello, Mr T!'

'Sarah! Hello. I thought you'd forgotten me.'

'Forgotten *you*? Don't be silly. I've just been helpin' Mrs Mercer scrub the little 'uns in her bath, and making them some new clothes. She let me cut up all 'er expensive dresses. Can you believe that?!'

'She sounds like a very good woman,' I replied.

'She is, Mr T. Just like you're a good bloke. I'm lucky to 'ave met you both, I really am.'

'On the contrary, Sarah. I'm lucky to have met you,' I said, speaking truthfully.

She gave me a wink. 'Actually, Mr T, I reckon you might be right on that one. I've spoken to Mrs Mercer about yer and she wants to meet.'

My heart skipped a beat. 'You've *spoken* to her about me?'

'Calm yerself, Mr T. I ain't said nothin' about that Kreeg, or that big rock you keep on your person. I just said you was a good bloke who was down on his luck and needed a bit of a helpin' hand.'

I felt uneasy about the situation. 'I don't wish to be a burden to anyone.'

Sarah rolled her eyes. 'Mr T, someone's only a burden when they don't need no 'elp but ask for it anyway. Seems to me you're due a bit of assistance. She's very well connected in Australia. And what do we 'ave? Nothin'! So, the way I sees it, if she's willing to give us a bit of an 'ead start, who are we to turn 'er down?'

I couldn't find fault with Sarah's reasoning. 'You're right about her connections in Oz,' I conceded. 'It would be nice to have somewhere to start.'

She clapped her hands together. 'Good. I'll see yer in her cabin at seven p.m. tomorrow evening. Just go to first class and ask for Mrs Mercer. I doubt the purser will look at you with as much venom as 'e does me and the orphans when we're up to visit.'

The next evening, I made my way along the thickly carpeted corridor to first class, and was directed by the purser to Kitty Mercer's door. After knocking, it was opened by a man in what appeared to be a dinner suit.

'Good evening, sir. My name is McDowell, I'm Mrs Mercer's valet. Do come in.' I followed him into the elegantly decorated cabin.

'Goodness me. What a wonderful room,' I remarked. The chandelier, silk-covered sofas and picture window gave the impression of the finest land-based hotel. 'But, if I might be so bold, where does one sleep?'

'This is the drawing room, sir. The bedroom is next door,' McDowell replied. 'Mrs Mercer will be out in just a moment. Might I offer you something to drink?'

'An English breakfast tea, please.'

'A good choice,' came a well-spoken Scottish voice from behind the bedroom door. When it opened, Kitty Mercer emerged in a distinguished purple evening gown, complete, as one might expect given her family business, with an impressive string of pearls. 'But, Mr Tanit, will you not join me in something slightly stronger? James here makes an excellent gin and tonic.'

'Good evening, Mrs Mercer,' I replied. Considering her offer, I could find no harm in sharing a drink with my kind host. 'If that is your recommendation, I shall be happy to join you.'

'Wonderful. Thank you, James.' McDowell nodded, and walked over to a drinks cabinet that appeared better stocked than most bars I had been to. 'Please, take a seat, Mr Tanit,' Kitty said with a soft Scottish lilt. I perched on the end of one of the grey silk sofas, and Kitty placed herself on its matching counterpart opposite.

'It's so wonderful what you've been able to do for the children downstairs, Mrs Mercer. Thank you for looking after them,' I said.

Kitty smiled. 'I merely do what anyone in my position ought to. I know you've bonded with Sarah. She's a very special young woman.'

I quickly agreed. 'I've enjoyed my conversations with her very much.' I tried to phrase my next question tactfully. 'Might I ask what she's told you about my…situation?'

'Merely, Mr Tanit, that you are a good man who has treated her with dignity, kindness and respect, when most others in the higher classes would do no such thing. When I asked her what you did for a living, she said that due to a personal tragedy, you were seeking a new start in Australia. Would that be an accurate summary?'

I gave a small chortle. 'I suppose it would be, yes.' James placed the gin and tonics on the glass table that separated the sofas.

'Cheers,' Kitty said, picking up her glass.

'Cheers,' I replied, and took a healthy sip. The drink was bitter, but very refreshing. 'Goodness, you weren't lying. James, that is a triumph.'

The valet nodded. 'Thank you, sir. I'll leave you to it. Please ring the bell if you need anything, Mrs Mercer.' He made his way to the door.

'Your pearls are incredibly beautiful, Mrs Mercer. I hope you do not find it too alarming that I am aware of your family business in Australia. The *Financial Times* in London has often reported its successes.' I raised my glass to toast her.

'Thank you. Although I've always been amused by the fact I have found myself head of a "family" business. I merely married into the Mercer family. Then, due to circumstances completely outside of my control, I became custodian of an empire I did not build.'

'Has it proved a burden?' I asked.

Kitty thought for a moment. 'No. It has been an honour. But this will be my final voyage to Australia. I intend to hand over the business to my brother, Ralph Mackenzie. During the past three years, Ralph has proved himself to be a talented manager, with an excellent head for business. Not forgetting that he is blood of my blood, which is in short supply these days. I can think of no one better to care for the business in the future.'

Over the course of the next hour, Kitty told me a complex tale of heartbreak, new beginnings and, most jaw-droppingly, of her relationship with a pair of identical twins—Andrew and Drummond Mercer.

When she had finished, I was silent for a while. 'I have not yet met an individual whose story rivals my own, Mrs Mercer, until today.' As the extraordinary events of Kitty's life danced around my mind, there was one aspect I found particularly bewildering…a detail that intrigued and shocked me beyond any other. 'The Roseate Pearl…do you truly believe it is cursed?'

Kitty took a slow sip of her gin. 'When Andrew forced Drummond to disembark the *Koombana*, it sank, taking Andrew with it. Then my maid's daughter, young Alkina, perished after digging it up in the outback.' Kitty stared at me. 'Tell me, Mr Tanit, after all I have told you, would you be willing to take ownership of that pearl?'

I needed no time to consider. 'No, I would not.'

Kitty managed a grim chuckle. 'Nor would I.'

'Do you know where the pearl is now?' I enquired.

'No,' Kitty replied. 'I haven't a clue. I think that's for the best, don't you?' I nodded emphatically. 'Anyway, now you know of my plan to hand over the business to Ralph, I am quite sure he is going to need some wise heads around him, to help with the day-to-day decisions that must be taken. I wondered if you were perhaps looking for employment? I would have no hesitation in recommending you to Ralph. Although, of course, the final decision would be his to make.'

I was touched by her kindness. 'Thank you, Mrs Mercer. But we've only just met. How do you have enough confidence in me to offer such help?'

Kitty smiled warmly. 'Young Sarah is very fond of you, Mr Tanit. It strikes me, from what she has said, that your only crime is heartbreak. After my story, you know that it is a topic I am quite familiar with.'

'Indeed. I really can't thank you enough, Kitty.'

She stood up and walked over to the mahogany writing desk in the corner of the room. 'This is the address of Alicia Hall in Adelaide. It is the grandest of the houses on Victoria Avenue, and it is where you will find Ralph and his wife Ruth. After we dock, Mr Tanit, that is where I will go, to inform Ralph of my position, before travelling on to Ayers Rock.' She stared wistfully out of the cabin window. 'I've always intended to make a pilgrimage there since I was a little girl, but life had other plans. As this will be my final time on Australia's shores, I'm finally going to visit.' Kitty's eyes shone with excitement. 'If you wouldn't mind giving me a few days to sort out my affairs before you make your appearance at Alicia Hall, that would be appreciated.

'Of course,' I replied. 'I'm so happy that you'll finally make it to Ayers Rock. Don't the indigenous people know it as Uluru?'

She looked surprised. 'That's right, Mr Tanit. I didn't realise you were interested in Aboriginal heritage.'

I finished the remnants of my drink. 'I must confess that I'm not as knowledgeable about it as I should be. But my father once told me Uluru was a deeply spiritual place.'

Kitty nodded. 'It is, particularly for the Aboriginal people. They say it dates all the way back to the "Dreamtime".'

'The Dreamtime?'

She returned to the sofa opposite me. 'Sometimes called the "Dreaming". Fear not, Mr Tanit, it isn't well understood by non-indigenous people. But Aboriginals believe the Dreamtime was the state at the very beginning of the universe. In their culture, the land and its people were created by spirits, or ancestors, who made the rivers, the hills, the rocks…'

'And Uluru,' I added.

'Exactly. That is why the rock is so special.' We both took a moment to picture the great sandstone formation in the middle of the outback, which can be seen from miles around. 'Do you know, it even changes colour at certain times of the year, glowing bright orange with the sunset?'

'How magical.'

'I've always thought so, yes.' Kitty's eyes sparkled as she thought about the special place that had eluded her for so long. It took her a while to speak again. 'Forgive me, Mr Tanit. Now you have the details of Alicia Hall, I will inform Ralph that you'll be showing up sooner or later.'

I stood up and gently shook Kitty's hand. 'Thank you, Mrs Mercer. I am deeply grateful to you, and to Sarah, of course. I wonder…' I said with trepidation, 'might you be able to offer her any assistance in Australia? Not that you haven't already done enough.'

Kitty gave me another wry smile. 'I have the strangest feeling that young Sarah and I may end up knowing one another for a long time to come.'

With that, I thanked her again, and made my way back to my cabin.

39

Alicia Hall, Adelaide, Australia

I have never experienced a heat quite like it. The Australian sun has the ability to stifle and suffocate, not like the pleasant warming rays of the Mediterranean. Here, in this new land, the earth itself is baked, and the strange creatures that inhabit it have adapted to manage the temperature over many centuries. I, alas, have not had that luxury. I am cold-blooded, accustomed to keeping heat in, rather than expelling it with ease.

Weather aside, my limited experience of Australia is that it is stunningly beautiful. The ochre-red outback is punctuated by primal rock formations and verdurous shrubs. Much of the ground is caked in orange mud, which dries out in the sun to form a powder, and blows across the roads in the wind like fairy dust.

As for Alicia Hall itself, I have rarely seen an oasis more delightful. After a few days spent around Adelaide's port, I eventually travelled down roads of tin-roofed shacks, which graduated to rows of bungalows and, finally, to a wide street lined with grand houses. Alicia Hall is the most impressive of them all. A white colonial mansion built to withstand the heat of the day, she is surrounded on all sides by cool, shady verandas and terraces fenced with delicate lattice work.

The lush garden is laid out by sections, with paths mown

into the grass, some of them shaded by wooden frames covered in wisteria. The dark green topiary bushes are perfectly pruned, as are the herbaceous borders that contain brighter specimens— fiery pink and orange flowers, glossy green leaves and honey-scented purple blooms. I have spent hours marvelling at the large blue butterflies which dip in to drink their sweet nectar. The boundaries of the garden are lined by towering trees with unusual ghost-white bark, which produce a fresh herbal scent that wafts into the house on the evening breeze, when a chorus of insects produce a cacophony of sound.

Ralph Mackenzie had charismatic blue eyes, a strong jawline and thick auburn hair. To my surprise, he was significantly younger than Kitty—perhaps twenty years or so. When I knocked on his door a week after arriving in Adelaide, the reception could not have been warmer.

'Mr Tanit? Welcome to Alicia Hall.' He greeted me with an enthusiastic handshake and welcomed me in through the grand hallway. After sitting me down in the drawing room, he asked his housekeeper, Kilara, for a cup of hot tea.

'I think a water would serve me well, actually, Mr Mackenzie,' I interjected.

'Aha! Clearly, like me, you come from the cold, Mr Tanit. I also could not picture anything worse than hot tea in this climate when I first arrived. However, my wise sister assured me that the hot tea makes you sweat, activating the body's natural cooling system.'

I shrugged. 'I had never even considered such a thing.'

Ralph gave me a grin. 'Australia is full of surprises, Mr Tanit. You'll find a new way of looking at the world.'

'I hope so.'

'Now, my sister tells me you're in need of employment. I should like to say straight away that Kitty's recommendation is enough for me. You are welcome to the job I have in mind for you…should you wish to take it.' Ralph looked hesitant. 'I'm sure she has made you aware of what she has done for me, so I am desperate to return the favour in any way possible.'

'I should be grateful for any work you are able to provide, Mr Mackenzie. I'm not put off by a lot,' I replied honestly.

Ralph leant forward on the old wooden chair he was sitting on. 'What do you know of opal, Mr Tanit?'

I thought back to the pendant necklace worn by Kreeg's mother. 'Only that it is a fine and rare material, prized by jewellers.'

'Quite right, Mr Tanit. Due to an unlikely combination of geology, Australia has been the world's primary source of opal since the eighteen eighties. We produce over ninety-five per cent of the stuff here. Now, to be quite honest, the pearling business in Broome has gone belly-up after the war. It's recovering, but slowly.' He sat up again and, perhaps unconsciously, adjusted his waistcoat. 'As the new head of the corporation, it is my intention to restore the Mercer reputation to its former glory in that field.'

'I see.'

'My nephew, Charlie, was a wise young chap, taken from us too soon during the war. He saw which way the wind was blowing, and invested in vineyards and an aforementioned opal mine in Coober Pedy. The profits are healthy enough, but we're not operating at full capacity. I've just come back from the place.' Kilara returned with the tea, served on an ornate silver tray. 'Kilara, Coober Pedy is Aboriginal Australian, isn't it?'

'Yes, sir,' Kilara nodded. '*Kupa piti*. Means "boys' waterhole".' She proceeded to pour the tea out. 'Lemon, milk, sir?' She looked at me, and I was struck by her amazing brown eyes, which sparkled like moonlight.

'Milk, thank you.'

Ralph continued. 'As I was saying, Coober Pedy is the home of the opal. I am quite convinced we haven't even scratched the surface of what's beneath the earth. Whilst I was up there, I was offered some more land that's going cheap. I'm going to invest in it.'

I took a sip of my tea. 'It all sounds very intriguing, Mr Mackenzie. What did you have in mind for me?'

'I'll need a man to run the operation there. It's…not going to be an easy position to fill. As with any mining, there are inherent dangers. And you'll find that over here in Australia standards of health and safety are not quite as high as in Europe.'

'Well,' I said, 'at least it might be cooler underground than it is above ground.' I smiled, placing my teacup back on its saucer.

Ralph looked hopeful. 'Might I take that as an expression of interest, Mr Tanit?'

'You may, Mr Mackenzie. Thank you.'

'Wonderful. But I do not wish to undersell the dangers of the role. We already have deep shafts, and it is my intention to build many more.'

I moved to reassure him. 'Mr Mackenzie, I recently lost the love of my life. I can confidently tell you that I consider it a miracle I am still here and breathing at all. What's more, I no longer possess any sense of fear. In truth, my life does not matter all that much to me anymore. I am glad of the opportunity you are kindly offering me.'

Ralph looked a little awkward. 'Sorry to hear all that, Mr Tanit.'

'Please, call me Atlas.'

'Atlas. What a superb name. And quite appropriate, given you'll be heading underground and holding up those opal mines on your shoulders!' He reached over to shake my hand. 'I'll make sure you're well recompensed, Atlas.' He raised an eyebrow. 'In fact, here's an idea. In addition to your salary, why don't I offer you a percentage of the opal we sell on? Shall we say…ten per cent of profits?'

I was shocked. 'That's very generous, Mr Mackenzie. But there's no need to—'

Ralph cut me off. 'In Scotland we have a saying, Atlas. "Don't look a gift horse in the mouth."' He smiled widely. 'I want to incentivise you. I really think this could be pretty big stuff. If you do the job as I believe it can be done, I hope it can make you a lot of money. You'll be in charge of increasing and maximising operations, exporting the opal, winning contracts… There's a lot to do. You'll be glad of the ten per cent, I assure you.'

I gave him a nod. 'Thank you, Mr Mackenzie. We have a deal.'

'Wonderful! I'm going to send confirmation that I wish to buy the land at Coober Pedy immediately.' He stood up. 'Now, I'll wager that with that suitcase…'—he pointed to my beaten bag, caked in dust from the road outside—'you'll need somewhere to stay until we can send you northwards?'

'It's true, I don't have anywhere to go,' I admitted.

'You're most welcome at Alicia Hall in the meantime.'

'Honestly, Mr Mackenzie, your kindness knows no bounds. I am eternally grateful.'

'In all honesty, you're going to need all the comfort you can get.' Ralph looked a little sheepish. 'There's one thing I haven't yet mentioned about Coober Pedy.'

'No?'

'You were quite right in assuming that it is far cooler underground than above ground. As a result, in order to avoid the punishing desert heat, the small population lives underground. They have quite literally burrowed into the hills. The chap I'm buying the land from will be handing over his house, too. It's where you'll live.' He stared at me with concern, as if I was going to be put off by the proposition.

'Mr Mackenzie, burrowing underground away from the rest of the world sounds oddly perfect.'

Ralph looked relieved. 'It's a match made in heaven! Now, I'm off to make some arrangements. Kilara will make you feel very welcome.' I finished my tea and got to my feet. 'Kilara, would you show Mr Tanit up to the master guest room?'

'Yes, sir.' She bowed her head.

'Thank you. I shall see you at dinner, Atlas.' Ralph turned to leave the room and immediately collided with a small boy, whom I recognised as little Eddie from the ship.

'Woah, steady, Eddie!' said Ralph, ruffling his hair.

'Eddie!' I exclaimed, with a huge smile on my face. 'What on earth are you doing here?!' The young boy grinned back at me and buried his head in Ralph's trouser leg.

Ralph's confusion was momentary. 'Of course, you must know each other from the ship!'

'We do indeed. It's very good to see him here at Alicia Hall, Ralph.'

'It's our honour to have him.' Ralph put his arm around the boy. 'He and Tinky the King Charles spaniel have become the firmest of friends, haven't you, Eddie?' He gave an enthusiastic nod. 'Hang on, I suppose you don't know that he and Sarah turned up here to find Kitty a couple of days after she'd arrived?'

'No, I didn't. As I recall they were due to meet their new families soon after we docked?'

Ralph sighed. 'That was the plan, apparently. But no one came for either of them. He and Sarah were taken to this godawful orphanage. But they did a runner, and made their way to Alicia Hall.' He looked down rather proudly at Eddie.

'Is Sarah all right?' I asked nervously.

'Absolutely, Mr Tanit. Kitty has taken her on as her maid. They're together as we speak.'

A wave of relief washed over me. 'Oh, that *is* good news.'

Ralph chuckled. 'They actually make quite a team. But my God, I'll see the demise of the St Vincent de Paul orphanage in Goodwood if it's the last thing I do, Mr Tanit. Apparently, the nuns worked the children like slaves. But Eddie's safe here now, aren't you, old man?'

'Yes!' Eddie squeaked, before turning and sprinting out of the room.

'Do you know, Ralph, that's the first time I've ever heard him speak.'

'He's a special boy. I hope perhaps one day to… It's silly, he's only just entered our lives, but it would give me great pride to make him into a Mackenzie. Officially.' Ralph cleared his throat. 'Anyway, I'm not a great believer in much, but I must admit that the healing powers of Alicia Hall are not insignificant. I have found it to be an oasis for reflection and still meditation. It might prove to be just the tonic for you.' He gave me a pat on the shoulder and made his way out of the room.

'Bag?' Kilara asked with a kind smile.

'Oh gosh, I'm sure I can manage. You lead the way, thank you.' Kilara shrugged. I picked up my suitcase and followed her up the resplendent, winding staircase. As I was taking it in, I managed to stumble on the second step. Quick as a flash, Kilara had turned around, grabbed my arm and whipped the suitcase from my hand as if it were filled with feathers.

'No worry, sir, I can carry for you.'

'That's awfully kind. I'm not usually so clumsy.' Kilara led me across the mezzanine, to a stately room with beautiful views of the garden.

'Here sleep, sir.'

'Thank you, Kilara.' She nodded, and went to leave. As she passed me, she took a moment to look me square in the eye. I was once more entranced by their sparkle.

'You know the Dreamtime?' she asked.

The question took me aback. 'Yes. No. Well, I know *of* the Dreamtime. It sounds very special indeed.' I chastised myself for the patronising way the sentence had materialised.

'You from the Dreamtime, mister. Ancestors know you.' Kilara put a soft hand on my elbow. I am unable to explain why, but Kilara's warm face and gentle touch brought tears to my eyes. 'Rest here. Rest now.'

She removed her arm and silently closed the bedroom door.

Suddenly exhausted, I collapsed onto the bed. I must have fallen asleep immediately, as I endured a cluster of awful dreams. In one, I was face to face with Elle. We were holding hands, when some dark, malignant presence arrived to pull her away into the shadows. In another, I was at a church, seemingly on the day of my wedding. I turned to see Elle walking down the aisle, but when she arrived at the altar, it was as if she could not see me. She said her vows, but would not meet my gaze. Then, when I eventually stepped off the altar, I could see that she was talking to another man, though I could not see his face.

The final dream involved a swirling night sky, with the Seven Sisters of the Pleiades taking human form and dancing above me. They joined hands, and I found myself encircled by them, as they laughed and skipped. They became faster and faster, until I became dizzy and could not watch anymore. When I opened my eyes, in front of me was a baby in a basket, mewling and crying out. All I wanted was to take it in my arms and comfort it, but when I reached inside, the baby disappeared from view. Then, when I looked around, briefly, I was met by a familiar face. It was the woman in the red dress with the long flowing hair... She vanished, and the world began to spin once more. This time, my field of vision exploded into an array of vivid colours. Swirling galaxies and patterns were created before my eyes, becoming brighter and brighter, until my entire world burnt a burning white.

When I awoke, the sun was shining brightly onto my face.

40

Coober Pedy, 1951

The desert of Coober Pedy is the driest and most arid place I have ever known, but undoubtedly produces the finest opal in all the world. The great irony is that the key to forming the precious stone is rain. When it does fall—once in a blue moon—and drenches the dry ground, the water soaks deep down into the ancient rock, carrying a dissolved compound of silicon and oxygen. Then, during the endless dry spells, the water evaporates, leaving deposits of silica in the cracks between layers of sediment. These deposits cause the rainbow colouring in the opal. That's what people pay for. The men I hire often ask me what sort of magic occurs to create our product. I give them the science, but they rarely choose to believe me, opting instead for the Aboriginal legend.

It tells of a stunning, butterfly-like creature named Pallah-Pallah, who possessed a pair of beautiful, shimmering wings. One day, Pallah-Pallah flew up to the peak of the highest mountain. But it soon began to snow, and she became buried. When the snow eventually melted, it stripped Pallah-Pallah of her wondrous colours, and they dissolved deep into the ground.

I think, in time gone by, I would have preferred that story too. But now all I see when I examine the fruits of the mines are submicroscopic spheres which refract light. It is merely logical, explicable science. Much like the stars that light the night sky. I have come to accept that they are not mystic beacons of hope and majesty, but burning balls of gas held together by gravity. Truly, it is better to think of them as such, rather than imagine that my Seven Sisters—my former guardians—would forsake me in such a way.

In this respect, I have come to like living underground. The 'houses'—if you can call them that, for they are more like burrows—are created by blasting into the rock, which is then excavated with pickaxes. We must ensure that the ceilings are four metres tall to prevent collapse, but rarely go higher. The result is, essentially, an underground cave. Some of the men create light wells, but I have not bothered. I like the dark now.

The skilled men have turned their homesteads into passable replications of overground housing, spending hours carving out arches, shelving, doorways and even art pieces. I have found that I have no desire for such home comforts. I sleep on an ageing, dusty mattress, and keep my clothing in my old suitcase on the floor. I have not even permitted myself a desk. During these last two years, I have found no desire to write in this diary.

When I first arrived, it was a small operation. I hired a team of five miners who were working for another corporation. With the handsome funds of the Mercer empire behind me, I was able to offer them more money in exchange for their expertise. Those early days were hard. We were faced with a vast expanse of land, and it was desperately slow-going.

It was in the winter of 1949 that I had my brainwave.

To expand the mines at the rate Ralph Mackenzie wanted, we would need men that were accustomed to working in difficult underground conditions. I sent one of my miners back down to Port Adelaide to scout for young male arrivals from Europe who had faced the perils of the last war and were looking for a new start. My man would approach them and offer immediate employment on a decent wage.

The plan worked. One year later, we had over one hundred men mining for opal in Coober Pedy.

Ralph Mackenzie simply did not believe the numbers I was reporting, so made a trip up to CP himself. I do not take pleasure from much these days, but the sight of his jaw dropping at the vast array of deep working shafts was a treat.

'Good Lord, Atlas! I can't quite believe what I'm seeing. I assumed that there was an accounting error. Or, perhaps...' He hesitated.

'That I was trying to con you,' I said icily. As the words came out of my mouth, I knew that I was a changed man. One year without Elle in the hellish landscape of the desert had hardened me.

Ralph laughed nervously. 'Well...yes.' He hung his head. 'But here I am, and the evidence is hard to contest.' He extended his hand to me. 'You're a titan of industry, Atlas Tanit.'

'Thank you, Ralph.'

'I say, I know how rotten it must be out here every day. How do you fancy a few weeks' break at Alicia Hall to relax? Fully paid, of course. I think it's the least I can do.'

I shook my head. 'There's no need. There's work to be done here and I'm happy to do it.'

'Well, that's as may be, but it's important to step back and appreciate one's achievements, too.'

'No,' I replied sternly, noticing that Ralph looked perturbed. 'Thank you.'

He shrugged. 'Very well. Now, I'm not the expert that you are, but from my layman's perspective, our plot of land seems rather full.'

'You are correct. There are few spaces for new shafts left. We would benefit from further areas to mine.'

'Understood, Atlas. I'll get you more. The money you've returned to the corporation alone will be more than enough to purchase double, perhaps even triple the plot we currently have.' He gave me a nudge. 'You'll soon be a millionaire with your ten per cent. How do you feel about that?!'

I met Ralph's gaze. 'I enjoy the work. I'd be doing it for less.'

He sighed. 'Lord, there really is no cheering you up, is there? Frankly I'm worried about you. When we met over a year ago, I saw a man who was downhearted and broken. But the man I see before me today is...hardened. You have done a fine job here, Atlas. But you would do well to remember that life is meant to be lived above ground, not under it.'

I narrowed my eyes. 'As I said, the lifestyle suits me.'

Ralph persisted. 'Forgive me if this is a little crass, Atlas, but this is a heavily male environment. There are hardly any opportunities for fraternising with the opposite sex. There are plenty of eligible young ladies I know in Adelaide who would be ever so glad to meet you at Alicia Hall.'

I slowly turned to him. 'Mr Mackenzie. Please never suggest such a thing again. I have no interest in *that* whatsoever.'

'Very well.'

Ralph Mackenzie left, and within one month had purchased ten hectares of new land. For this reason, I increased the presence of men at the port in Adelaide, and very soon, the Mercer opal mining operation at Coober Pedy was the talk of the industry. The operation is all I think about. Each day, I wake up and concentrate on the task at hand. My brain is full of axes, and shovels, and timber and darkness. There is, therefore, no danger that my mind may stray into any other territory which I do not wish to enter.

41

I nearly died today.

This morning, as I was preparing export documents in my tin shack of an office, the foreman, Michael, came running in with a look of intense panic.

'Sir! We've got a collapse! Three men under the rubble in shaft seven!'

Instinctively, I jumped to my feet. 'Are they alive?'

'Not for long, sir. I reckon the whole thing's going to go.'

I made for the door. 'Round up as many men as you can and bring them down to seven. Quickly!'

'Yes, sir,' replied Michael, and sprinted ahead of me. Then a sickening thought crossed my mind. I called out to him.

'You say it will collapse?'

'It's making a terrible groaning sound, sir. I think the timber might have got the rot.'

I inhaled deeply. 'Cancel the men, Michael. I'm not risking anyone's life unnecessarily. I'll go down by myself.'

'With respect, sir, there's no way you'll be able to do anything on your own. They're under a mountain of earth and wood.'

I accepted his assessment. 'You may ask for volunteers. Explain the situation carefully. No orders. It must be their choice.'

'Sir.' Michael nodded, before continuing at a pace. I ran across the orange earth until I reached the entrance of shaft seven, which, as Michael had described, was producing an awful moaning sound. Without hesitation, I began to descend using the steel railings fixed to the rock. When I reached the pit, I was greeted by a storm of mud and dust. I could just make out the flashes from oil lamps, and I followed them into the dust cloud. With my hands spread out in front of me, I soon felt the presence of a miner.

'Who's that?' he cried.

'Atlas Tanit! And you?'

'Ernie Price, sir!'

'Show me where the men are buried.'

'Right in front of us, sir!' He grabbed my shoulder and directed me to the ground, where I became aware of five or six men scrabbling at a pile of earth. 'There was an enormous cracking sound, so I ordered everyone out. But these three weren't quick enough.'

'The whole thing's going to go!' I cried. 'You have to save yourselves!' I pleaded.

'This is my mine, sir, and they're my men. I have to try!'

I became aware of a muffled screeching from beneath the earth. It focused me. 'Stay if you want. But think of your family.'

'You lot!' Ernie cried, addressing the men trying to move the dirt. 'Get out of here. Up the rails, now!' They hesitated. 'That's a bloody order! Go! Now!' They followed the instruction, dropping their pickaxes and shovels. Ernie stoically remained, and passed me a pickaxe. 'Just keep digging, sir. It's all we can do.'

The moaning and creaking intensified as we ferociously hit at the solid earth. 'Hang on!' I shouted. 'We're hitting timber, that's why we're not making any progress! The mud is piled on top of the wood! We have to dig from above, not below!' Ernie nodded at me and followed my lead as I began to attack the pile from chest-height downwards. To my delight, the cries of the men became louder as we were able to clear more earth. 'Keep going! We're getting closer!' After what seemed like hours, but in reality was probably no longer than two minutes of ferocious digging, I saw something move. 'It's a hand! Grab it and pull, Ernie!' He followed my instructions as I continued to dig. Eventually, a face emerged from the rubble and spluttered. Ernie pulled the man clear, and he groaned.

'Can you walk, Ron?' he asked. Ron shook his head. Suddenly, from the dirt storm at the shaft entrance, Michael emerged with three volunteers.

'Get him out of here!' I cried. 'We've got two more to free!' I put my ear to the pile of earth and listened. I heard a screech. 'He's here!' To my amazement, a stray leg was protruding from some ground we had already cleared. Although the removal was speedier than the last, the man looked in worse shape, and was fading in and out of consciousness. The mine emitted its most sickening groan yet, and the ground began to shake.

I knew which way this was going, and addressed the men.

'He'll be harder to get up to the surface. All of you will be needed. I'll find the last miner.' The volunteers began to drag the casualty towards the shaft's entrance, and Ernie picked up his shovel once more. 'Ernie,' I said, putting my hand on his shoulder. 'Thank you. But they need you. I'll find the final man. What's his name?'

'Jimmy, sir. He's only young. Nineteen years old!'

'I understand. Now go.' Ernie spun on his heels and ran into the dust. I put my head to the earth once more, but this time, there was no muffled cry to follow. Instead, I wildly hit at the pile of earth in front of me. I had accepted my fate. The mine would collapse, and I would be buried alongside Jimmy. In the hope of letting him know he wasn't going to perish alone, I cried out, 'Jimmy! We'll be all right! Do you hear me, Jimmy? We're going to be just fine!' To my utter surprise, I received a distinctly audible groan in reply. 'Jimmy?! Jimmy is that you?!'

'Uhhhhhh,' I heard again. I followed the voice, and to my shock, I came across a semi-conscious man whose torso was completely visible. His legs, however, were trapped directly under a timber support. I grabbed his hand, my heart beating out of my chest.

'Jimmy! Hold on tight!' I cried, yanking him as hard as I could muster. He cried out in pain, as it became evident that he was well and truly stuck. I began to dig around his waist, but it was no good. I grabbed the oil lamp and confirmed that the support beam had fallen against the shaft's wall at an acute angle, which is why it had not crushed Jimmy to death, but had trapped him instead. I grabbed the beam and tried to shift it. I could not.

'Please,' Jimmy mumbled. 'Please, please…'

I ran my fingers along the timber, feeling for any cracks in the wood. If I could somehow cause the beam to split, it might be enough to release Jimmy below, whilst keeping the earth above from crushing him. After a few moments of fumbling, I came across the required fissure. With renewed hope, I grabbed the pickaxe again, and began to attack the beam. The ground beneath my feet was now moving so much that my swings lacked the required accuracy. 'Damn it!' I yelled. If only I had something sharp to force into the split to help force it apart. As I felt around the floor for rocks, I remembered the object I had in my possession.

'The diamond,' I breathed. I whipped the leather pouch over my head, and prized the precious contents from inside. Then I felt for the largest part of the fissure, and forced the diamond inside. I took a step back and swung the pickaxe behind my head. With a silent prayer, I brought it down with as much force as I could muster. The clunking 'thud' reassured me that I had made contact. A cracking sound followed, as the lower half of the beam split away from the top. Dropping the pickaxe, I grabbed the timber and pulled with all my might. Against the odds, my plan worked. The bottom section of the beam came away, and the top continued to support the earth above. I grabbed Jimmy's hand and pulled him free.

It was fortunate that I was able to act so quickly, as the remaining timber soon split in two. Dragging Jimmy along the floor by his arms, I made my way through the rubble and dust.

'Help!' I cried at the top of my lungs when I reached the mouth of the shaft. 'Help, please!' I concluded that no one could hear me above the terrible rumble. Summoning every ounce of life I had left, I grabbed hold of Jimmy's limp body and flung it over my shoulder. Then I grasped the iron railings and began to climb up and out of hell. It was sheer agony. But I had come this far. After a few metres, I began to hear voices.

'Hey, someone's coming up!'

'There's no way. You're seeing things!'

'Just look down there!'

'Bloody hell, get down there and help him! We're coming, sir, just hang on!'

I continued to force my way up towards freedom, when I felt Jimmy's weight begin to lift from my shoulders.

'We've got him. Pull him up, Michael!' said Ernie's voice.

Removing Jimmy from my shoulders had the adverse effect of destabilising me, and my feet slipped from the railings. As I hung freely, I saw Jimmy being hauled over the entrance to the shaft. Then the rumbling from below me became a shrill howl, and debris from above began to fall onto my face.

'It's going!' Ernie shouted. 'Quick, grab him!'

I looked below and was faced with a collapsing vortex of earth and wood. The shrill howl turned into a deafening roar, and as I looked up, the last thing I saw was Ernie's hand, desperately reaching down for my own. I went to grab it, but the iron railing succumbed to the collapsing ground. I felt myself fall for a moment, before the world around me faded from view.

When I awoke, to my surprise, I was in one of the makeshift shacks above ground, lying on top of a pile of discarded work clothes.

'He's awake!' Ernie said. I blinked hard and he came into focus. 'Mr Tanit. You're alive!'

I became aware of the immense pain that breathing was causing me. 'My chest,' I groaned.

'It's your ribs, sir. We reckon they're well and truly smashed up. How're your legs?' he asked. 'Can you wiggle them?'

I tried, successfully. 'Yes. The men from shaft seven…'

'All fine, sir, apart from a few broken bones alongside being a bit shaken up. And it's all thanks to you.'

I put my hand to my throbbing head. 'The mine collapsed on me.'

'Yes, sir, just as you were about three metres from the surface. Thankfully, we had eyes on you and we started digging straight away. Near enough the whole workforce was involved in getting you out. Many hands make light work.'

'Thank you,' I said, trying to extend my arm to shake Ernie's hand. 'Ouch,' I said, as a jolt of pain seared through my joint.

'Try not to move too much, sir. We've informed Mr Mackenzie in Adelaide, and he's assured us that the finest doctors are on their way to you and the other men. But until then, well…Michael's had an idea.' He gestured to the foreman stood by the door.

Michael cleared his throat. 'Would you be open to seeing a member of the Ngangkari?'

'Ngangkari?' I asked.

'An Aboriginal healer, sir. I've heard of their presence in a village a few miles away. The doctors from Adelaide will be a few days, but one of the Ngangkari could be here later this afternoon.'

I managed a nod. 'Anything for the pain in my chest.'

Michael looked relieved. 'Don't you worry, Mr Tanit. I'll be back later on with help. You're a very brave man.' He ran out of the shack door.

'Is he awake?' asked a voice from outside.

'Hang on, Mr Tanit,' said Ernie, standing up to investigate. I heard some conversational mumbling, and he returned. 'I know you've only just woken up, sir, but you've got a very keen visitor outside, who wants to make sure you're all right.'

'Who is it?' I asked.

'Jimmy, sir. He wants to thank you.'

'Please, send him in.' Ernie left and was replaced by a fresh-faced individual who looked no older than a boy. He entered with a limp, and removed his sun hat, holding it humbly in front of his stomach. 'Jimmy,' I said. 'How are you?'

'I am alive, sir. And it is because of you and you alone. The other men have told me that you stayed down there to dig me out, and carried me up on your back. I owe you everything.' He looked down at the floor.

'You all work for me, which means your safety is my responsibility. I was just doing my job.' The young man shuffled uncomfortably. 'Is everything all right?'

'Yes, sir.' He turned around to look at the door. 'I just have something to return to you.'

'What do you mean?' I asked. Jimmy tentatively put a hand in his pocket, and took out a familiar object. I couldn't help but laugh, which sent an excruciating pain through my chest. 'Ouch,' I mumbled. 'Well, I didn't think I'd be seeing that again, Jimmy. Do you know what it is?' After all, the diamond was still covered in glue and boot polish.

'Yes, sir. I used to work the diamond mines of Canada when I was a boy. I could spot one anywhere. But'—he shook his head—'I've never seen anything like this before.'

'No, I can't imagine you have.' I tried to sit up a little on the pile of clothes. 'How on earth did you end up with it? I readily kissed goodbye to it down there.'

'I saw you take something out of a pouch from over your head. Then, when you hit the beam with the pickaxe, it literally dropped onto my chest, sir. I held on to it for you.' He approached my bedside. 'Here.' He placed the diamond in my hands.

I stared at it for a few moments. 'I thought that the last act of its existence in my possession would be to save a life. But here it is. Back once more.' I rotated it in my hands, then looked up at Jimmy. 'Why didn't you keep it? It could have taken you away from all this. You could have gone anywhere you wanted, done anything with your life... And yet you've chosen to return it to me.'

Jimmy shook his head ferociously. 'I wouldn't dream of it, sir. It's not mine.'

'Well,' I said, 'thank you for giving it back to me.'

He looked at me timidly. 'I could ask you the same question, sir.'

'I'm sorry?'

'You said it yourself. With a gem like that, you could be whoever you wanted to be. But instead, you're here with us, a pile of broken men in the desert. You nearly died today. Why don't you sell it and start a new life?'

I reflected on how strange the concept must be for this young man. 'You said, "it's not mine," didn't you, Jimmy?' The young man nodded. 'Well,' I replied. 'I would give the same response. Thank you again for returning it.' Jimmy turned to leave the shack. 'Jimmy?' I called out. 'There's no need to tell any of the others about this, if you don't mind.'

'About what, sir?' Jimmy replied. I gave him a nod, and he limped out.

I stared at the diamond. 'Even when I tried to get rid of you, you came back. Have you not served your purpose?' I delicately moved the stone into my pocket. Then I closed my eyes and slept.

I was awoken by Michael. 'Mr Tanit? A member of the Ngangkari is here.' I rubbed my eyes, and next to Michael stood a tall man in a skirt made of long, dry grass, and a body painted with striking, colourful patterns. He stared down at me, and gave me a wave.

I returned the greeting. 'Hello. Thank you for coming.'

He pointed to himself. 'Yarran.'

I pointed to myself in return. 'Atlas.' He nodded. 'I have a very bad pain in my chest. I think that my ribs are broken, and I wondered if you might have any remedies for the pain?' Yarran stared blankly back at me.

Michael stepped in. 'He doesn't seem to speak a lot of English, Mr Tanit.'

Yarran pointed at my chest. 'Yes. Pain,' I said. Yarran nodded his head, and patted Michael on the back. 'I think that might be your cue to leave, Michael.'

He looked wary. 'Are you sure that's all right?' he asked.

'Yes, quite all right. Thank you.'

Once Michael had left, Yarran went to place his hands on my chest. 'Careful!' I cried, fearful of the pain he could inflict with even the lightest touch. He paused and smiled down at me.

'Ouch,' he said.

'Yes, ouch. Painful,' I replied.

Yarran nodded again, then inhaled deeply, before once more bringing his hands towards my centre. I braced myself, but his touch was light, and his palms moved softly across my ribs, as if he were gently stroking a cat.

'Um, please,' said Yarran, pointing at my mud-caked shirt. I gingerly unbuttoned it and looked down at my skin, which was black and blue. 'Ouch,' Yarran repeated. He returned his hands to my chest. He closed his eyes, and his breathing became deeper and deeper.

'Mmmmm,' he started to chant, in his deep, melodic timbre. I looked up at him again, and saw that he was frowning.

'Is everything all right?' I enquired.

'Inside, ouch,' he said once more.

'I know. Broken ribs, I think.'

'No. Inside. Deep. Ouch.'

A light wave of panic went through me. 'Deeper? You think there's a problem with my heart?' I pointed to the centre of my chest.

'Body gonna fix,' Yarran said to me. 'Spirit is broken.' He stared at me with his deep brown eyes, which sparkled like Kilara's. 'Ancestors,' he continued, pointing upwards. 'Ancestors care.'

'I don't know what you mean. I...' Before I could complete my sentence, Yarran had placed his hands on my head, and begun to massage my temples with his thumbs. His fingers gripped my cranium tightly, but I did not feel pain.

What happened next is very difficult to describe, but I will do my best. Yarran's fingers seemed to grasp harder and harder, until it felt as though he had penetrated my skull and reached into my mind itself. I stress again, the feeling was not at all painful, more like I was somehow being cradled from the inside. The sensation continued to pass down from my head, into my neck, and then into my chest. Suddenly, I felt I was able to breathe easier, as if my lungs had unlocked some extra capacity of which I was previously unaware. The room in front of me faded into a brilliant white. I felt soft, and peaceful. Then I heard Yarran's voice, which danced and echoed around my head.

'Your soul is in deep pain,' he said. 'The ancestors and I will help you to mend.'

'You're speaking perfect English, Yarran!' I replied euphorically.

'We are only limited by the world of the physical, Atlas. As I worry you have forgotten, there is much more to this existence than that.'

'Where are we?' I asked.

'Wherever you wish to be,' he replied.

I thought for a moment. 'I want to be with Elle. But she's gone, Yarran. I still don't fully understand why.'

'She is missing,' said Yarran softly.

'Missing from my life, yes.'

'Missing from…everywhere,' he countered. 'Hmm.'

'What do you mean?'

'There is a line which connects us to those we love, even if they are far away. Though we cannot see the line, it makes sure that wherever we are, we are always tied to them. You are still tied to her.'

My heart fluttered. 'Even though she didn't get on the boat?'

'Yes. I cannot see where the line which connects you ends. But she wishes to be found.'

'She does?' I asked, a little stunned.

'Hmmm,' Yarran mused again, melodically. 'You have much to do. Much to do.'

'Do you mean that I should go looking for Elle?'

Yarran paused, as if contemplating his next words carefully. 'The ancestors believe you have a destiny to fulfil. They will protect you, Atlas.'

'Yarran, I really don't understand.'

'Sleep now. The ancestors will watch over you.'

The white light slowly turned to black, and I drifted into a blissful slumber. When I awoke, the room was dark. Inhaling deeply, I noted significantly less pain in my chest. I was in no doubt that my ribs were still very much broken, but I was able to breathe freely. I even found I could sit up and stand with relative ease. Buttoning up my shirt, I opened the door to the shack, and was greeted by the still of the outback night. The full moon shone brightly down onto the sea of shafts in front of me, depicting an alien landscape filled with vast craters.

The high-pitched squeaks and chirps of desert frogs echoed across the plain, punctuated only by the rare sound of a dingo howling. I felt a hand on my shoulder, and turned to see Yarran.

'Yarran. I feel much better. Thank you!' I gave him a thumbs up.

Yarran nodded and held out a pile of what looked like freshly picked herbs and flowers. 'Drink down,' he said, handing them to me.

'Thank you. I shall.' I dithered for a moment. 'It was very good to talk to you earlier.' He stared blankly back at me, and I berated myself for ascribing my dream to Yarran's spiritual powers. 'Anyway. I really do feel a lot better.'

Yarran turned and waved back over his shoulder. 'Come,' he said, and started to walk out into the open desert behind the shack. I followed him, and we must have walked for ten minutes or so, with the ground lit up before us by the brightness of the moon. Then Yarran stopped, and sat cross-legged on the dusty ground. I mirrored him. He pointed to the sky. 'Ancestors,' he said.

I looked up, and the sight that greeted me took my breath away. The stars shone down as I had never seen them before. An array of brilliant, twinkling majesty hung above us. Orion, Taurus, Perseus, Pleiades… The constellations themselves were ablaze with wonder.

'Yarran…the stars…I have never seen them like this…'

'Always here,' Yarran replied. 'But you don't see. Spirit broken. Getting better.'

I was humbled by the sheer breadth of the shimmering sky. In that moment, I saw life in the dark and warmth in the cold. I turned my eye to the Seven Sisters.

'Hello, old friends.'

I absorbed their splendour, silently apologising for forgetting all they had done for me during my life's journey. After all, it was they who had delivered me to safety during my impossible journey as a young boy. Without them, I would be lying dead on a bed of Siberian snow. I still believed that the sisters had sent me Elle, and Landowski, and Brouilly, and Pip and Karine and Archie Vaughan. Not to mention Kitty Mercer and her brother Ralph.

'All right,' Yarran said, standing. 'Home.' Without so much as a goodbye, he continued walking away from the mines.

'Hang on a moment, Yarran, the village is back this way.' He waved me away. 'Please, come back and stay the evening. We'll take you home on horseback tomorrow!'

Yarran turned back to me. 'No, *you*, home.' He pointed up to the sky again.

'Wait, you mean I'm supposed to go home? To Coober Pedy? Or did you mean *home* home? Switzerland? Yarran!' I cried.

He paused and turned to me once again, a broad smile on his face. 'Much to do.'

Those three words…he'd said them in the dream. 'I knew it… Am I to go looking for Elle, Yarran?' He continued to walk away from me, and did not turn around this time. 'Please stop. I can't let you disappear into the outback! It's not safe!'

Yarran laughed loudly, and wandered off into the still Australian night.

Knowing it was a lost cause, I made my way back to my underground abode.

After my encounter with a member of the Ngangkari, I feel enlivened…dare I say, even hopeful? There is air passing through my lungs, which is more than can be said for those who I have lost. Father, Pip, Karine, Archie… I owe it to *them* to get up and live my life.

And now I know what I have to do.

I have to find Elle.

And win her back.

For that is all there is.

The Titan

June 2008

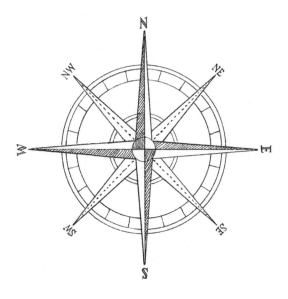

42

Star put the page down and turned to CeCe, who had tears in her eyes. It was still unusual for her to see, since her sister had always been a tower of fiery strength.

'Oh Cee, come here,' Star said, enveloping her in an embrace. 'It's so emotional reading about our families, isn't it?'

'Yeah,' CeCe sniffed. 'Just in case you were struggling to follow along, Sarah—the orphan girl on the ship—is my grandmother. I had no idea that she and Pa had ever met.'

'More than that, CeCe. She saved him. Without her, he would have ended up throwing himself into the ocean. Without your granny, Pa wouldn't have lived as long as he did. And none of us would be here either.' Star squeezed her sister's hand. 'That's amazing.'

CeCe managed to smile back at Star. 'You're right. It is pretty cool. But I could say exactly the same thing about the Vaughans. It sounds like Pa was so happy at High Weald.'

Star giggled. 'Yes, that's true. Flora in particular was amazing. But Grandpa Teddy nearly cost him everything! What a...' —Star contemplated her next words carefully—'...bloody bastard!' she squeaked, much to CeCe's surprise.

CeCe began to chuckle too. 'Yeah, sorry, Star. We can't *all* have hero ancestors.' CeCe stood up and rubbed her eyes before crossing her cabin to the mini fridge, where she retrieved some bottled water. 'Want one? You've been narrating solidly for over a couple of hours.' Star nodded, and CeCe threw a bottle across the room. It landed next to her sister on the double bed. 'So. What do we think happened to Elle?'

Star cracked open her bottle. 'I have no idea. It seems so strange. They were clearly deeply in love.'

CeCe perched herself on the edge of the cabin's writing desk. 'Unless Pa got it wrong.'

'What do you mean?' Star queried.

'We're accepting everything Pa says in the diary as fact. But it's only his side of the story. Do you think it's possible that Elle's feelings weren't as strong? Pa did have this psycho Kreeg guy chasing him across the world trying to kill him. I think even if you did love someone, it'd be a little much, you know?' She took a glug from her water bottle.

Star considered CeCe's observation. 'They'd been through so much together. I don't understand why she'd just abandon him on the dock. It's all a bit weird.'

CeCe laughed. 'That's Pa Salt all right. A bit weird.' She stood up and sprawled out on the bed next to Star.

There was a knock on the cabin door, and Electra appeared in an orange kaftan. 'You guys done?' she asked.

'Yeah. Star's just finished reading to me,' CeCe replied.

She rushed in and joined her two sisters on the bed. 'Holy shit. There's so much to take in. You know that woman he met in NYC at the protest? That was my great-grandma! Well, kind of. She took care of my granny when she was little. What are the chances of that?'

'Wow, Electra. We wondered if that was connected to you in any way.' Star took her sister's hand.

'Oh, it is, big time. And can we just take a moment to discuss Georg and Claudia? What the hell?!'

Star shook her head in disbelief. 'Yes, what a revelation that was. No wonder Georg's always been so loyal to Pa. He saved them both.'

'Thanks to his super-rich grandmother,' Electra snorted. 'What a stroke of luck that was.'

CeCe was spiky in her reply. 'I mean, I think Pa was due some, Electra. I've never known a person have so many bad things happen.'

'Yeah, I guess,' Electra conceded. 'I don't know about you guys, but I'm most curious about Russia.'

Star clapped her hands together in excitement. 'Me too! We got a little snippet of it, didn't we? Pa's father worked for Tsar Nicholas II. Just wait until Orlando gets a load of that. He'll probably explode.'

Electra sighed. 'I won't lie to you, Star, I've got no idea about any of that stuff. What does it mean?'

'I'm definitely no expert. But I remember some bits and pieces from school. Tsar Nicholas II was the last Emperor of Russia. He abdicated in 1917.'

'Why?' asked CeCe.

'Revolutions, basically,' Star continued. 'The Russian tsar was hugely powerful. He was the principal authority in the country, and controlled all the wealth too.'

'So, he was, like, a dictator?' Electra asked. 'A bad guy?'

Star shrugged. 'I suppose, yes. It was certainly an autocracy. The Russian people were unhappy. They faced food shortages against a backdrop of bitter cold. So they overthrew him.'

CeCe and Electra took a moment to absorb the information. 'What did he do after that?' Electra enquired.

'He and his family were executed. Vladimir Lenin and his Bolshevik revolutionaries took over the government.'

'Why did they hate him so much?' CeCe asked.

'The Bolsheviks thought that the monarchy was a cancer that made it impossible for the working class to rise. And what do you do with a cancer?'

'Cut it out,' Electra replied. Star nodded.

Maia leant back in her chair and stretched. 'Oh Pa,' she whispered to herself. 'What a mess you found yourself in.' She stood up and crossed the salon to the viewing window. The ocean seemed to be getting choppier as the *Titan* raced towards Delos.

'Hello? Maia?' came a voice from the salon door.

'Hi, Merry. How are you doing?'

Merry walked towards her newfound sister and put a hand on her back. 'Ah, I'm not too bad. I can't believe that Atlas lost Elle in such a sudden way. It seems to defy all logic.'

Maia pondered the situation. 'Yes, it does rather. I thought they were so happy together.' She noticed that Merry had shifted her gaze down to the floor. 'Gosh, I'm sorry, Merry, I didn't even think—that's your mother you're reading about too. It must be doubly hard.'

Merry waved her hand. 'Oh, go on with you. I didn't even know her. You're the one I worry about, Maia. I know that this villain Eszu's son has treated you very poorly.' She pulled Maia in for a hug. 'I can't imagine how bloody awful you're finding this.'

Maia nestled her head into Merry's shoulder. 'Thanks, Merry, I needed that.'

'I know you did, my darling.' Merry smiled, then put her hands on her hips. 'Now, there is something I wanted to mention to you.'

'Go ahead.'

'As you know, my coordinates on the armillary sphere pointed to this house in West Cork, which seems to have been owned by the Eszu family.'

'Yes,' Maia confirmed.

'Well, I told my friend Ambrose about it, and he promised to do a little bit of investigating. He was able to ring around half of West Cork, being passed from one household to another. Eventually, he managed to get in touch with a family in Ballinascarthy.'

Maia stared back blankly at Merry. 'Sorry, I don't know where that is.'

'Oh.' Merry tutted and grinned. 'Of course you don't. It's a village that's pretty close to Argideen House.'

'I'm with you.' Maia nodded.

'It turns out that the grandfather of the family, Sonny, used to work up at the house as a gardener in the fifties. The old boy's nearly a hundred now, but was happy to talk about his time at Argideen.'

Maia's eyes widened. 'What did he say, Merry?'

Merry shrugged. 'Not too much. Just that he rarely saw the owner as he was always off travelling. Apparently there were two other gardeners, and none of them were allowed in the house under any circumstances. He also remembers a housekeeper, too.'

Maia raised an eyebrow in thought. 'Do you know what her name was?'

'Sonny couldn't recall. He said that she hardly ever left the house, and never spoke a word to anyone. Then one day, she disappeared. After that, they didn't see the owner for months on end, but they kept receiving payment, and so the gardeners continued to work on the gardens.'

Maia did her best to connect the dots, but found herself struggling. 'But what on earth does it have to do with you, Merry? Why did your coordinates lead to Eszu's house? That's what I can't get my head round.'

'Me neither, Maia.' Merry sighed.

The two women looked out at the ocean, lost in their thoughts.

They were startled by a loud crash from outside the salon door, and the pair headed over to investigate. To their shock, they saw Ally pinning Georg into a corner in the corridor, her finger pointed right in his face.

'I'm serious, Georg. We're going. Right now. I don't care what the precious instructions are. Do you realise that there are people on this boat who—'

Georg spotted Maia and Merry. 'Hello, girls,' he said calmly. Ally spun round.

'Ally? Is everything all right? What on earth is going on?' Maia asked.

Ally was flustered. 'Yes. It's fine. Everything's fine, isn't it, Georg?'

'Oh yes,' the lawyer replied. 'Ally and I were just discussing…the…future of the *Titan*. That's all,' he said smoothly.

'Yes,' Ally agreed, regathering some control. 'Georg thinks that perhaps we should hire it out in the winter season, seeing as we don't use it.'

Maia knew her sister was lying. 'I wouldn't have thought you'd get so heated about that, Ally.'

Her cheeks reddened. 'No. Sorry. You know how passionate I am about boats, Maia, that's all.'

Maia eyed her sister for a moment, before turning to Georg. 'Come here, you.' She went to hug him. 'Why did you never tell us about you and Claudia?'

Realisation dawned on Georg's face. 'Ah, the diary. Your pa has met us?'

'He certainly has,' Maia replied.

'You've moved in with Agatha's old housekeepers,' added Merry.

He smiled at the memory. 'The Hoffmans were very good people.'

'No wonder you and Pa were so close,' Maia continued. 'You've known him practically your whole life. Isn't it amazing, Ally?'

She looked genuinely confused. 'Yes, uh... I...' she floundered.

'You have read the last one hundred pages, haven't you?' Maia pressed. 'We all agreed to it.'

'Sorry, Maia. No.' Ally sighed. 'Georg and I have been having this chat about...the *Titan*.'

'Oh.'

Merry cut in. 'Well, sounds like you've got a bit of catching up to do there, Ally. Shall we leave you to it? Come on, Maia, let's track down a coffee.' She took Maia's hand and led her down the corridor. 'I wonder what all that was about?'

'It was strange, wasn't it?' Maia replied. 'Something's most definitely going on there. And I don't think it's anything to do with renting out the *Titan*.'

'It's so awful, what happened with Elle, Ma.' Tiggy wiped a tear away as she sat next to Marina on the plush seating on the bow of the upper deck.

Ma rearranged Bear, who was dozing in her arms. 'I know, *chérie*, I know. But I try to remember that without such events, he might never have found you. Or me!'

Tiggy rested her head in her hands. 'Did you know about Georg and Claudia? That he found them as children?'

Ma nodded. '*Oui*, of course.'

'And everything with Kreeg?' Tiggy looked sorrowful.

'Yes.' Ma lowered her voice. 'I don't need to explain why I never said a word. You've read about how dangerous he was. And after all that happened with Zed…'

'I know. So when are you going to appear, Ma?' Tiggy questioned. 'Pa's just left Australia to search for Elle. When does he meet you?'

Ma looked down at her snoozing de facto grandchild. 'Soon enough, *chérie*, soon enough. I hope that you do not judge me too harshly. As you have learnt on this trip, there is much you do not know.'

Tiggy moved closer and put an arm around her. 'Oh Ma, whatever we learn, nothing will change. Ever. I love you.' Tiggy planted a gentle kiss on Marina's soft cheek.

'Thank you, Tiggy. I love you too.'

They looked into each other's eyes for a moment, before Tiggy spoke again. 'Can I ask you a personal question?'

'You know you can ask me anything.'

'You lived with Pa for so many years. Did you ever…you know…?'

'What, my darling?' Marina looked perplexed.

'Did you ever fancy him?!' Tiggy giggled.

'Ooh! You did not tell me that the question was going to be cheeky!'

'Haha, I'm sorry, Ma. But you know that I've always been able to *feel* things. I've just always sensed that you had a great longing in your heart.'

Ma raised her eyebrows. 'Have you now, my little hedgehog?' Tiggy nodded slowly. Marina sighed. 'Your father was a very good-looking man. In many ways he was perfect. Handsome, kind, intelligent…a truly good human being. But you may rest assured that not ever in my life did I think of him in *that* way.'

Tiggy was a little perturbed. 'Really?'

'I speak God's honest truth,' Ma swore firmly.

Tiggy frowned. 'I'm not normally wrong about these things.'

Ma's cheeks flushed with embarrassment. 'Stop it, *chérie*, you are making an old woman blush.'

'Don't be ridiculous, Ma, you mustn't call yourself old! But I have to know, who is this mystery man you're pining after?' Tiggy whispered.

Marina tutted, and just as it looked like she was about to say something, Charlie's elegant figure rounded the corner.

'There you are, my darling.' He grinned at Tiggy.

'Hello, Charlie. Is everything all right?'

'Yes, thanks. All ship-shape. No pun intended.' Tiggy rolled her eyes. 'All right. Maybe it was slightly intended. I've been sent on a mission by Ally to make sure everyone finishes the whole diary before dinner this evening.'

'Oh, really?' Tiggy asked. 'We've still got plenty of time before we get to Delos.'

'Don't shoot the messenger!' Charlie held his hands up. 'In all seriousness, she really did seem quite keen that everyone's on the same page...' Tiggy raised her eyebrows. 'All right, that one was pushing it.'

'Thanks, Charlie. I'll crack on now. Is everyone else doing the same?'

'No complaints so far.' Charlie bent down to look at Bear in Ma's arms. 'The little chap's really growing, isn't he?' He brushed the baby's cheek with his finger. 'Anyway, I'll leave you to it. Speak to you later.' He headed back inside the boat.

Tiggy frowned. 'There must be a reason Ally wants us all to finish the diary as quickly as possible. Do you know why that might be?'

Ma's face reddened once more. 'No.'

Tiggy pushed her. 'You'd tell me if there was something... going on here, wouldn't you, Ma? It's a horrible feeling to be left out of the loop.'

'I would not lie to you, *chérie*,' Ma replied tactfully.

'All right.' Tiggy slapped her knees and got to her feet. 'You know, everything inside me is…parking and bubbling. It's like I can *feel* something, but I'm not quite sure what.'

'Perhaps it is Merry?' Ma theorised. 'Your pa's own blood, here on the boat. That would make sense, wouldn't it?'

Tiggy shrugged. 'I suppose so. Well, I'd best go back down to my cabin and finish the diary off.'

'Okay, *chérie*. I will speak to you later.'

Once Tiggy was out of sight, Ma hurriedly laid Bear down on the soft cushions and sent a text message to Georg Hoffman.

The Diary of Atlas

1951–93

43

I spent the return journey to England planning out a list of where Elle might be. I knew the task would be a mammoth one, as it would involve retracing our steps across Europe—not that there was any guarantee that she was in a location we had been to before. But I had to start somewhere.

Ralph Mackenzie had been nothing short of exemplary when I contacted him to say I was leaving Australia. He came to wave me off in Adelaide as if I was an old friend or brother.

'Thank you, Atlas. You've resurrected the Mercer empire almost single-handedly. The opal mine has allowed us to do so much, not least restore the rather dilapidated Hermannsburg Mission, which means so much to Kitty. From the bottom of my heart, I truly appreciate everything you've done.' He hugged me.

'Likewise, Ralph. Thank you.'

'I hope you're travelling back first class?' I laughed and held up my second-class ticket. 'But Atlas…you're a multi-millionaire. Your ten per cent has seen to that.'

'I suppose old habits die hard. That reminds me, I might need your assistance transferring my funds back to Europe.'

'Absolutely. I'll do anything to help. I'm so sorry to lose you, as I know the men in Coober Pedy are. That day you saved the miners from the collapsing shaft will live in their minds forever. You're a hero.' Ralph genuinely looked a little overcome with emotion.

'Actually, Ralph, I rather think it was they who saved me.

Plus, Michael will do a fine job in my absence.'

'Until we meet again.' He put his hand out, and I shook it, before turning and walking up the gangplank of the *Orient* once more.

The crossing itself remains a haze to me. You see, I am rather afraid that, for the first time in my life, I heavily indulged in the numbing qualities of alcohol. On my first night, I entered the bar to toast my time in Australia with a whisky, and ended up spending the entire evening there. I returned the following evening. And the evening after that. Then, soon enough, I was there in the daytime too.

What can I say? It seemed to make the time pass quickly and the days without Elle less difficult. It was true enough to say that I had a renewed purpose, but until I found her, the pain of the journey was going to be intense. Regrettably, I didn't leave the bottle on the *Orient* when I came ashore after my two-month voyage. I knew that I was going to be reunited with ghosts from my past, and I continued to drink to help me face them.

Upon my arrival back in England, I returned to Arthur Morston Books, where Rupert was so shocked to see me that he spilt his cup of tea over a box of new stock.

'I say, old man! You could blow me over with a feather! Good Lord! How are you?'

I explained the events of the last two years as concisely as I could.

'My word. You poor, poor chap. I wish I could give you some good news and tell you that she's been here. But alas, I cannot.'

'Oh well. It was worth a visit.' I turned towards the door.

'Hang on, old boy, you look like you could do with a strong coffee, and perhaps a cosy bed for the night. You know, Louise and I would be happy to—'

'When we parted, Rupert, you said that you'd look into Kreeg for me.'

He looked chastened. 'Yes, I did, and I kept my word. Just as you predicted, the bugger hardly seems to have existed at all. There's neither hide nor hair of him in any of our records. My pals at the Circus did find mention of a Kreeg Eszu in an old Russian census, but it doesn't do you a lot of good.'

'No,' I sighed. 'Did he ever come back here?'

'Never, old chap. We watched the place like hawks for weeks after you'd left, but there was no sign of the man.'

I looked around the shop. The shelves had been painted white, which made the whole place appear brighter. Elle would have approved. 'Thanks, Rupert.' I had a thought. 'I wonder if it might be possible to contact Flora to see if Elle has been in touch with her?'

'Of course,' Rupert replied, making his way to the back of the shop. 'I'll telephone right away. She's back up in the Lakes these days.' He jogged up the stairs, but eventually returned shaking his head. 'Sorry, old chap, Flora hasn't heard a peep from her. But she would love to see you. She said it's an open invite.'

'Right. Thanks, Rupert,' I inevitably slurred, shaking his hand.

'Are you sure we can't get you a nice cup of strong—' I had shut the door to Arthur Morston Books before my old friend could even finish his sentence. I made my way back to Claridge's Hotel, where I had booked myself in, and instructed the concierge to arrange the next leg of my journey to Switzerland.

Without a doubt, Mr Kohler was less pleased to see me than Rupert. When I walked into Kohler & Schweikart on the Rue du Rhône, the secretary did a double take.

'Monsieur Tanit?' she gasped, struggling to work out if the haggard man with the beard in her lobby was really me. I nodded, and she hurriedly picked up the phone. Eric Kohler came running out of his office in disbelief, before pulling me inside.

'Atlas! Where on earth have you been, man?! What was the one thing I begged of you at the start of this process? Not to disappear from the face of the earth! And you, my friend, saw fit to do just that. Really, I've a mind to pass you on to a new younger lawyer, for the Tanit family will be the death of me—'

I held my hand up so that Eric would stop talking. 'Elle. Has she been in contact with you?'

'No,' he continued angrily. 'She certainly has not. Now, you've got a great deal of explaining to do, not least to the Swiss Citizenship Bureau, who have been holding your application for two years. Atlas, where have you been?' I sank into the sofa at the back of the room and told the lawyer my tale of heartbreak and Australia. Eric listened intently, but was unsatisfied. 'I'm sorry to hear all that, Atlas, but what on earth possessed you to make for Australia in the first place? If you wanted a change, why not return to the country of your birth, with your citizenship and your fortune?!' I remembered that at no point had I informed Eric about Kreeg, and I was too exhausted to do so at this moment.

'I'm going to visit the Hoffmans to see that all is well with the children. Please would you telephone ahead?'

He sighed. 'That sounds fine, and I'm sure they would be happy to receive you. Georg in particular is doing very well. In fact, we have become firm friends, as he shadows me once per week. He has a fine brain, and wishes to become a lawyer.'

'In which case, I can sack you and hire him!' I mumbled.

'Well, perhaps one day. But Atlas…'

'Yes, Eric?'

'I know that you're still my client, and I don't wish to speak out of turn. But it might be an idea to have a cold shower first. Perhaps a shave too. And make sure to drink plenty of water. Remember, you are a saviour to these children.' He looked at me sternly. 'Do not sully their view of their guardian angel.'

Eric Kohler's words hit home. 'Very well. I will go first thing tomorrow. Please ring my hotel later to let me know if that suits the Hoffmans. I'm at the Beau Rivage.'

'As you wish, Mr Tanit.' Eric gestured towards the door.

I crept back to the hotel steeped in shame, and didn't touch a drop of alcohol all night. The next morning, I took a cab to Agatha's tall town house, still easily identifiable by the pink paint that coated the exterior. The inhabitants greeted me very warmly.

'Thank you for coming back, Mr Tanit! Mr Kohler tells us how busy you are, with all your businesses,' Mrs Hoffman exclaimed. I realised that Eric had clearly chosen to share a lie with the family so as not to upset the children. A pang of guilt coursed through me. 'Georg and Claudia will be so happy to see you!'

'Do you have everything you need, Mrs Hoffman?' I asked. 'I want to make sure you're not a penny out of pocket.'

She nodded enthusiastically. 'Absolutely, thank you, Mr Tanit. Agatha would be very, very proud of your philanthropy. It's in your genes.'

The children welcomed me like a long-lost uncle. I was taken aback at how much both had grown in the years I had been away, forgetting that they were in their formative shape-shifting phase. The Hoffmans had clearly insisted that the pair dress up for the arrival of their benefactor, and I was flooded with remorse that I had not been more present in their lives.

'Hello, Mr Tanit!' Georg said in a broken voice, now nearly meeting my eyeline as he shook my hand.

'Goodness gracious. Is this young Georg, or his father?!' I said in an attempt at humour, before remembering the fate that had befallen his parents. Georg saw my mortification, and he smiled kindly.

'You remember my sister Claudia, too?' He signalled towards the young girl who was also noticeably taller, but with the same sweet face I remembered from before.

'Nice to see you again, Mr Tanit.' She curtseyed. 'My brother and I really cannot thank you enough for your kindness.'

'It's very nice to see you too, Claudia. There is no need to thank me. It is Mr and Mrs Hoffman who you need to be grateful for. Are you both enjoying life in Geneva?' They nodded heartily. 'And how are your studies?'

'Mine are going very well, thank you, Mr Tanit,' Georg replied.

'I hear you have been visiting Mr Kohler. He says you wish to be a lawyer?'

Georg shuffled where he stood. 'It has become a dream of mine, yes. I wish to influence the way the world runs so that people may live a fairer existence.'

His words brought a smile to my face. 'I cannot think of anything more noble or appropriate. I am happy for you, Georg. Make sure you pursue your dream with your whole heart.'

'I will, Mr Tanit.' He hesitated, and looked to Mrs Hoffman

in the corner of the room, who seemed to give him a stern gaze in return. 'But Mr Kohler says that the fees for universities and law schools are very high.'

'Georg!' cried Mrs Hoffman. 'Mr Tanit has been here no more than five minutes, and you have the audacity to pester him for more money, when he already funds your entire existence!'

I chuckled. 'Please, no need to shout, Mrs Hoffman. A lawyer must be brave, resourceful and ask leading questions. I believe young Georg managed all three simultaneously.' I raised my eyebrows.

'I promise to return the money one day,' Georg said. 'Every penny!'

I placed a hand on his shoulder. 'I do not doubt you would, given the opportunity. But there is no need. If you continue to work hard and please Mr and Mrs Hoffman, I assure you that there will be no financial barrier to you furthering your education.'

'Thank you, Mr Tanit! Thank you!' Georg squealed in delight.

'The same, of course, applies to you, Claudia. Are you enjoying school?'

She looked a little diffident. 'I find some of the lessons a bit difficult. My French is not as good as my brother's.'

'*Yet*,' I told her with a wink. 'Keep going.' I put my hands out. 'It has been very good to catch up and see you all, but I'm afraid I must leave now. Continue to behave for Mr and Mrs Hoffman, children.' I shook Georg's hand, and Claudia rather surprised me by enveloping me in a hug.

Mr and Mrs Hoffman walked me to the front door. 'What you do for the children really is wonderful, Mr Tanit,' Mr Hoffman said, putting a steadying hand on my back.

'Please, do call me Atlas. And I cannot stress it enough, you are the ones who should be thanked.'

'Well, that's as may be, but I think there are few in this life who would use their inheritance to finance the lives of two orphans. Two complete strangers. You were motivated by nothing other than kindness, and that is something to be celebrated.'

'Thank you,' I said, a lump coming to my throat.

After settling my affairs with Eric Kohler, which involved putting him in touch with Ralph Mackenzie to organise the secure transfer of my well-stuffed Australian bank account, I finally signed the last documents which would grant me citizenship.

The reader may well ask themselves about my fear of bumping into Kreeg Eszu during the retracing of my steps across Europe. However, I must confess that the fear was virtually non-existent. You will already know from these pages that without Elle, I hold no regard for my own life. I am totally driven by my quest, and nothing else. I will succeed, or I will die trying.

The Newcastle to Bergen ferry was a choppy experience, but mercifully quick, and we were docked within twenty-four hours. Of all my return visits, this was the one I had been dreading most. What could I possibly say to Astrid and Horst after the unimaginable tragedy they had experienced? This worry was compounded by the prospect of looking once again into little Felix's eyes and seeing his pain. As a result, I had ensured to medicate with a bottle of whisky during the crossing.

I knew I had to stick to my task. If Elle had returned anywhere, Bergen seemed the most obvious choice. Karine had been her best friend, and the Halvorsens like a family to us. I made the familiar trudge up from the harbour to the hills, where the cottage which had once housed us still stood.

I knocked on the door. '*Ett minutt!*' came the reply. I waited for a moment, bracing myself for a difficult interaction.

Astrid soon appeared. She looked so much older. Her once rosy cheeks had sagged, and the thick blonde hair I remembered was now scraggly and grey. As she slowly recognised me, her eyes widened, and began to glisten with tears.

'Hello, Bo,' she said.

'Astrid—words will never be able to describe how sorry I am that—' Before I could finish my sentence, Astrid had thrown her arms around me, and squeezed me so tightly that the air left my lungs.

'Horst! Horst!' she cried, dragging me by the hand into the

house.

Pip's father appeared from around a corner at the end of the hallway, and did a double take. 'Could it be... Bo D'Aplièse?' he stuttered.

'Hello, old friend.' Horst now walked with a stick. He slowly made his way over to me and embraced me too. He tapped my chest with his cane. 'It is good to see you, not-so-young man!'

'Please, sit down! I will brew some tea! Do you still like English breakfast?' Before I could reply, Astrid had pottered off to the tiny kitchen. I followed Horst into the living room, which had not changed even slightly in the decade I had been away.

'Horst,' I began, 'I am unable to express my sorrow for—' He raised his stick in the air to stop me.

'Please. We do not talk of it. Everyone in Bergen knows what we have been through. When we pass them in the street, their faces are filled with pity and sorrow. We have had enough of that for one lifetime.'

'I understand,' I replied apologetically.

Horst eased himself into his armchair, and gestured for me to sit too. 'So, tell me of your life, Bo! How is that arm of yours? Are you now a cellist for the London Symphony Orchestra?'

It had been so long since I had even thought of my cello. 'Alas, no, I regret to say that I am not. I am without pain now, but after only a few minutes of sustained activity, the arm becomes stiff. I have accepted that I will never be a virtuoso.'

Horst looked downhearted. 'What a terrible waste. I had high hopes for you. So, how have you spent the last decade?' I told him of High Weald, and Arthur Morston Books, and Australia. 'My goodness, Bo! Opal mining! I never would have guessed that the sweet, timid boy I knew ten years ago might become the head of such a big operation! But life provides interesting twists and turns. As long as you and Elle are happy. Where is she, by the way? Here in Bergen with you?'

I cast my eyes to the floor. 'No, Horst, she is not. It is the reason I am here—to look for her. I am guessing by what you have just asked that she has not been to Bergen in the last two years?'

'No,' he said with concern. 'Has something happened

between you? When you were here with us, you seemed so in love. We were sure that marriage was not far away.'

I swallowed hard. 'I thought that too. But I have had no contact with her for two years now.'

Horst was unsure of what to say, but thankfully Astrid returned with the tea. 'I feel I have caught the tail end of that conversation,' she said with a sad smile. 'You and Elle are no longer together?' I shook my head. 'I did think it unusual that you were not mentioned in the letter she sent.'

My head shot up. 'A letter? When did you receive it?'

'Gosh, it would have been about six months ago.'

'Only six months ago? That's fantastic! May I see it?' I enquired, my heart rate increasing.

'By all means, Bo,' replied Astrid. She crossed the room to a desk, opened the top drawer, and flicked through a variety of papers before selecting one. 'Here it is. It's only very short, but it was lovely to hear from her.'

Astrid handed it to me. It was comforting to see Elle's neat, elegant handwriting once again.

Dearest Horst and Astrid,

I hope this letter finds you well. Please know how terribly I miss you and Bergen, and my darling friends Pip and Karine too.

Recently, I have thought a great deal about you, and the nights we used to spend together playing music on the hilltop.

Evenings in Norway were magical, and I find myself yearning for what once was, but now is gone.

Listening to Grieg makes me think of you and the beautiful land which I was so lucky to call home for a little while.

Another lifetime has passed, but I wanted you to know that you are still so close to my heart.

Never forget the memories we all have together; I know I shan't.

Darling Felix must be getting tall now!

Bonny babe no longer!

All is ahead of him.

But I wish his parents were here to see him too, how proud they must be.

Yours,

Elle

I let the letter rest on my lap, and furrowed my brow. 'It's an unusual letter, would you not agree?'

Astrid shrugged. 'Is it? A little broken perhaps, but I put it down to the fact that Norwegian is not a first language for either of you.'

'No. But she was fluent by the end of our time here, as am I. I can't put my finger on it, but something about the way she writes is odd. It doesn't sound like the Elle I know.' I looked to Astrid. 'You have every right to say no, but might I be able to keep this?'

'Of course,' she smiled kindly.

I had a brainwave. 'Astrid, do you have the envelope this letter arrived in? I've just realised it will have a postmark!'

She shook her head. 'I'm sorry, Bo. It has been thrown away. I only kept the letter.' My heart sank. 'I do remember that it came from abroad...'

'Where? From England?'

'No, it wasn't England.' She closed her eyes and thought deeply. 'Or was it? I do recall the postmark being *in* English. I think. Oh, I can't be sure. I'm sorry not to be of any use to you.'

'That's all right, Astrid,' I replied, hiding my disappointment. I changed the subject. 'How is Felix? he must be, what...eleven years old?'

Horst and Astrid looked at each other. 'He's thirteen now,' Horst replied solemnly.

'Goodness me, how time has flown. Is he well?'

'As you know, Felix has had a difficult life. He is...a little disruptive,' Horst said diplomatically.

'Well then, he is his father's son!'

A faint smile played on Astrid's lips. 'He is indeed. But young Felix is much more of a troublemaker. It's not his fault. He misses his mother and father very much.'

'I can only imagine,' I said truthfully.

As if on cue, I heard the front door to the cottage swing open, and loudly slam. A young man, who was the spit of Pip— but with Karine's dark hair and deep brown eyes—peered into the living room.

'Felix Halvorsen! You're not even halfway through the

school day. What are you doing home?' asked Astrid.

Felix gave a nonchalant shrug. 'I didn't want to stay. The lessons today are so boring.' He locked eyes with me. 'Who are you?'

'Felix!' snapped Horst. 'Don't be so rude!'

'That's quite all right,' I replied. 'This young man has a right to know who is in his house!' I stood up and went to shake his hand. 'Hello, Felix. My name is Bo. I was a close friend of your parents. I remember you from when you were just a little baby.'

He eventually took my hand. 'You knew Pip and Karine?' he asked.

'Yes, very well. They were exceptionally kind to me when I needed it the most. I will never forget them. Not to mention your grandparents here, who agreed to house and feed a complete stranger.'

He eyed me. 'If you were so close to my parents, why have I never met you before?'

'For goodness' sake, Felix. Be polite to our guest, will you?' chastised Astrid.

'What? I'm just remarking that clearly he wasn't that close to Mum and Dad if I've never seen him before.'

I accepted his anger. 'You're right, Felix. I should have been back in the intervening years, and I have not. I sincerely apologise. I am glad to see you have grown up to be a forthright, opinionated young man. Your parents would be very proud of you.'

'Not if he keeps skipping school, they wouldn't be,' quipped Horst.

Felix frowned. 'Oh shush, Grandpa. I can learn more from an afternoon with you on the piano anyway. I'm going to practise.' He stomped off up the stairs to his bedroom. I couldn't help but smile at the attitude of Pip and Karine's son, so full of the spirit they had once possessed. I meant what I said to him. His parents decidedly *would* be exceptionally proud.

'Young Felix is a musician too?' I asked.

Horst shrugged. 'What can I say? It is in the genes. I tell you, even though he is a little tearaway, he is a supremely talented pianist. I think, musically, even better than Pip.' Horst suddenly looked deeply sad. 'And that is saying something.'

I walked over to my old friend and put a hand on his arm. 'I know how thankful he would be for what you and Astrid are doing for his son. Karine, too.' Horst's eyes twinkled with tears. 'It was so good to see you both again. Thank you for the tea, Astrid.'

'You're really going so soon? You've only just walked in the door!'

'I wouldn't want to impose upon you,' I replied. 'I've done quite enough of that for one lifetime.'

'Don't be silly, young man!' Astrid said sternly. 'In fact, we will not debate this. You will be staying for dinner. Where are your lodgings?'

'I…'

Astrid wagged her finger at me. 'For goodness' sake, Bo! Don't tell me you have nowhere to stay?'

'I planned to check myself into the Grand Hotel and catch a ferry to France tomorrow morning.'

'France?' Horst enquired. 'Why France?'

'It is Elle's home country. I think it is feasible that she could have returned to Paris, where we met.'

Astrid approached me and put both hands on my elbows. 'Fine, go to France if you must and continue with your mission, but for a few days, Horst and I insist that you stay with us.' She looked up at me with pleading eyes.

'Thank you,' I replied. 'I would be delighted to.'

The few days I spent in Bergen were blissful. I took luxurious strolls through the Bergens Fjellstrekninger, warmed myself by the log fire in the evenings, and filled up on Astrid's famous mutton and cabbage stew. By the end of my stay, I think even Felix had warmed to me—particularly after I tuned the upright piano which had once belonged to Pip.

When it was time to leave, I boarded a ferry from Bergen to Amsterdam, and from there used the train network to get me to Paris. If Elle had returned to the city, who would she have chosen to contact? Landowski? Brouilly? Perhaps Madame Gagnon? Part of me longed to speak with Monsieur Ivan, but I knew that returning to the Conservatoire de Paris was inadvisable, given what had transpired between myself and Monsieur Toussaint all those years ago. Landowski's atelier in Boulogne-Billancourt was where I had to start.

The house looked just as it did in my memories. The white stone exterior was perhaps a little faded, but was still covered by thriving purple wisteria. I stood there for a while, drinking in the place that had been my home as a boy. My eyes fell onto the bench that I used to play my fiddle on. I strolled over to it and sat down, closing my eyes, and drifting back into the past...

'What do you think you're doing?!' shouted a familiar French voice. I opened my eyes, and turned to see a greyer, plumper Evelyn storming towards me across the grass. 'This is private property!' My face had broken out into a huge smile at the sight of one of my kindliest saviours. Oh, it was *so* very good to see her again. 'I say again, what on earth do you think you're doing? Don't make me get the broom!' I continued to sit motionless on the bench, staring back at her. 'Who are you?'

'Hello, Evelyn,' I said, standing up. I now towered at least a foot over her. As she looked into my eyes, I saw a flicker of recognition. Her expression immediately softened.

'It cannot be...' she whispered. 'Bo?' I held my arms out to her, and she grabbed me tightly. 'Bo! Oh Bo! I never thought I would see you again.' She detached herself for a brief moment to look back up into my face. 'Oh, my sweet boy. You're all grown up! What a happy day!' Once again, tears formed in the eyes of an individual who appeared very pleased to see me. If I might take a moment to flatter myself, a pattern was beginning to form.

'I have missed you very much, Evelyn.'

'And I you! You must come inside! Monsieur Landowski is here. Careful, little Bo, you might give him a heart attack!' Evelyn took my arm and walked me in through the familiar hallway. 'It is still just me here most of the time, with Monsieur Landowski's work taking him all over the globe. What has become of your life? Are you a famous musician now? What about that boy who was chasing you? Did you make up? And what about little Elle?! What has become of her?'

Her avalanche of questions revealed that she and Elle had not crossed paths since we left France all those years ago. I tried to hide my disappointment. 'Much has changed, Evelyn.'

'Clearly. For one, you speak more than you used to!'

'What's this racket?' Monsieur Landowski's booming (but now slightly croaky) voice echoed through the corridor. He appeared from around the corner, in the same smock he had worn twenty-five years ago. The little hair that remained on his head was a wispy white, as were his trademark moustache and beard. We stood face to face in the corridor for a moment. 'Boy!' he said eventually. 'Ha!' He shook his head, before turning and gesturing for me to follow. 'Come. I could use some help. Evelyn, would you put some tea on? Then perhaps you can join us in the atelier.' She squeezed my arm and disappeared off to the kitchen. I followed Monsieur Landowski into his workshop, where, on the table, was a near-finished stone sculpture of a dancing woman. Her arm was thrown up elegantly above her head, and her face cast down towards the floor.

Landowski picked up his chisel and began to delicately tap at her flowing hair. 'Pass me the finer instrument from the workbench, would you?' Without skipping a beat, I did so. 'Well, what do you think?' He nodded to the sculpture.

'You have not lost your touch, Monsieur Landowski. Is she a flamenco dancer?' I asked.

'Indeed.' He took a moment to step back and admire his work. 'I am quite proud of this one.' He turned to me. 'Now then, boy, you are back. Does that mean you are finally safe?'

I sighed. 'It's a hard question to answer, Monsieur Landowski.'

'Hmm. Well, don't worry about that rogue Toussaint from the *conservatoire*. Your old teacher Monsieur Ivan dealt with him.'

The mention of Monsieur Ivan's name brought a smile to my face. 'He did? How?'

Landowski chuckled. 'Ivan was from Moscow, and was angry. Need I say more?'

I shrugged. 'Probably not.'

'Toussaint ended up leaving Paris. We never heard from him again. The rats crawl back to the sewer in the end.'

'How is Monsieur Ivan? I would dearly love to see him.'

Landowski leant on his workbench. 'I'm sorry, Bo. He died several years ago now. We kept in touch after you had gone to Germany. He often spoke of you, and predicted great things.'

Landowski looked me up and down. 'But clearly you do not play anymore.'

I was bewildered. 'How did you know, Monsieur Landowski?'

'You look joyless. Soulless. Therefore, I wager you do not play.' Evelyn returned with the tea. 'Thank you, Evelyn. I do not know what I would do without this one, boy. She runs my entire life in France, from bedsheets to scheduling. My memory is not what it once was, is it, Evelyn?'

Evelyn laughed. 'You are still sharp as ever, Monsieur Landowski.'

'You have to say that, I pay your wages! Anyway, please do take a seat as our old friend tells us everything about his life.' Evelyn made her way to the dusty old sofa at the back of the atelier.

'Before I begin, may I ask where the rest of the family are, Monsieur Landowski?'

'Most of them are still in Rome.' He pointed to his sculpture. 'I'm only in Paris because I have to finish this commission. I began it here when I was bored of my ailing mother-in-law's prattlings last Christmas.' He delicately stroked the stone face. 'It's for a private client from Spain. I hope you don't mind if I continue to work whilst you speak, Bo. I'm already delayed on this piece. I have to finish it off today.'

'Not at all, Monsieur Landowski.'

'Thank you.' He picked up his chisel again. 'Oh! Marcel made it into the *conservatoire* by the way.' He chuckled. 'He studied under Marguerite Long, and now composes professionally.'

I gave a small round of applause. 'Very well deserved, too. Please pass on my sincere congratulations when you see him next.'

Monsieur Landowski gave me a wry smile. 'I'm sure he'll be very glad to receive them.'

As I told my story, Monsieur Landowski sculpted, and I assisted him, somehow slipping back into the old routine of a quarter of a century ago. He hardly reacted to anything I said, from the pain of Kreeg breaking my arm and destroying my musical career, to the drama of saving the men from the mineshaft in Coober Pedy. He was focused intently on his work. Evelyn, on the other hand, gasped and gesticulated at every twist and turn.

'Oh Bo,' she said when I had finished my story. 'I'm so sorry for all that has happened. Life can be very unfair.'

'I suppose I need not ask if Elle has been in touch with either of you?' I asked. Landowski shook his head. 'What about Monsieur Brouilly? Do you think that's a possibility?'

'I converse with him regularly,' Landowski replied. 'He has progressed to Head of Sculpture at the École des Beaux-Arts. I assure you, he would have mentioned it.'

'Equally, I am still in touch with Madame Gagnon,' Evelyn added. 'She is retired now. But we go for tea occasionally. There has been no mention of Elle. I am sorry, Bo.'

'And what of Kreeg? Do you not fear him any longer?' Landowski asked.

'I do not know what he could take from me that I have not already lost,' I replied honestly. 'This was my last hope. I do not know where else Elle might be. I thought that if I revisited the locations of our past, she might have returned to one of them. But now, I do not know what I am to do.' I ran my hands through my hair.

Landowski stared at me. 'You are purposeless.' He clapped his hands together. 'So, would you like a job?'

His offer caught me off guard. 'Oh, Monsieur Landowski, you are very kind, but I am not sure I could assist you here in the atelier as before.'

'I meant something much more temporary. This commission needs to be transported to Sacromonte in Granada. As I mentioned, it's late. You could take it via train to get it there as quickly as possible. Otherwise it will have to travel by boat, which will take far longer.' He raised an eyebrow. 'You would be doing your old friend a favour.'

I thought about his proposal, and was unable to fathom a reason why I could not do as he asked. 'Very well, Monsieur Landowski. I would be glad to accompany your piece.'

'Good. I can't imagine that sitting alongside it in a freight train will be particularly comfortable, but I'm sure you will cope.' He looked out of the atelier window at the bench. 'You know, a sculpture of mine hasn't had a personal escort since Brouilly took the *Cristo* across the waters to Brazil.'

'It seems a lifetime ago,' I replied.

'Because, boy, it was.' He returned to his work. 'Anyway, go down to Sacromonte, enjoy the Spanish sunshine. Rest and reflect. I predict it will be just the thing.'

'Who is the commission for?'

'The trustees of the Alhambra Palace. Apparently, it is famous for some sort of dancing competition. What was the name of it, Evelyn?'

'The *Concurso de Cante Jondo*,' she replied.

'Yes, that's it. Anyway, there was a young Gypsy girl who won the competition and went on to achieve fame. She has become somewhat of a symbol for the region after the Civil War.' He shrugged. 'One thing is for sure. She is very beautiful. Here.' Landowski handed me a photograph from his workbench. 'This is what I have been working from.' The image was of a stunning, dark-haired woman in a red dress, captured mid-twirl by the camera.

'What was her name?' I asked.

'You embarrass me, boy! My mind is as firm as a plate of jelly.' He clicked his fingers in rapid succession. 'What was the woman's name, Evelyn?'

'Lucía Amaya Albaycín'.

'That's it. She's very big in South America, apparently.'

'How interesting. Well, it will be an honour to escort the stone version of Lucía to her permanent home.'

'Good. You will be paid for your efforts, of course.'

I held my hands up. 'No, Monsieur Landowski. I could never accept payment for this. As I told you, I am not short of money these days. Please, allow me to pay you back for my conservatory tuition, and the cost of housing me for all those years.'

Landowski sighed and rolled his eyes. 'Don't be ridiculous, boy. You had nothing! Now, Evelyn, would you telephone the freight train companies and make the appropriate arrangements?'

'Yes, Monsieur Landowski.' Evelyn looked like she was struggling to lift herself out of the ancient sofa, so I provided a hand. 'Evelyn, forgive me. I realise I have not asked about Louis. How is he?'

She gave me a sad smile. 'He achieved his dreams, and is now high up in the Renault manufacturing business.'

'Superb! What about family? Did he ever take a wife?'

Evelyn sighed. 'Yes. Her name is Giselle.' I notice her eyes dart over to Monsieur Landowski, who gave her a sympathetic look in return. 'She is a very temperamental lady, who has never approved of my close relationship with my son. Over the years, I have seen less and less of him.'

I was heartbroken to hear it. 'Oh Evelyn. How terrible.'

She nodded. 'What's worse is that I am yet to meet my granddaughter. She is already five years old, but Giselle will not let me see her.'

I was perplexed. Louis and his mother had been so close. 'But your son adores you. Surely, despite whatever Giselle says to him, he would not allow your relationship to become damaged?'

'A man in love is a man intoxicated. And, unfortunately, Giselle is my Louis's poison.' She emitted a sad sniff.

'What is your granddaughter's name?'

'Marina,' Evelyn replied wistfully.

'What a beautiful name.' I didn't know what else to say. 'I hope you will meet one day.'

'As do I, Bo. Anyway, will I make up your bed? Your room is much the same as it was twenty years ago.'

Landowski baulked. 'I'm sure we can upgrade him from the attic bedroom to the guest suite, if that would suit, boy?'

'Oh, I do not wish to trouble you. I will happily stay at a hotel if—'

Landowski burst out laughing. 'We housed you for all those years! I'm sure we can cope with one more night, can we not, Evelyn?'

The evening was spent drinking bottles of wine from the Côtes du Rhône, and discovering how those I had once known had gone on to spend their lives. Landowski and Evelyn still had the same sparkling energy inside of them, even though their bodies, like mine, had aged. After dinner, I walked up the stairs to my old bedroom at the back of the house. The bed, which as a child I had found the height of luxury and comfort, now felt miniscule and lumpy. Nonetheless, I slept dreamlessly, helped by the copious amounts of *vin rouge* I had consumed that night.

The next morning, three men arrived to box up the statue of Lucía and transport it, along with myself, to Paris's Gare de Lyon.

'I have sent word to the Alhambra that you are on your way, and should be there within five days,' Evelyn explained. 'There is one change in Barcelona, where the freight employees will move the statue for you. They will also arrange transport from the station in Granada to the Alhambra Palace.'

'Thank you, Evelyn. You are still organising my life, all these years later.' I hugged her tightly, then went to shake Monsieur Landowski's hand.

'It was good to see you, boy. The question I must inevitably ask is…will you ever be back?'

'With a fair wind, Monsieur Landowski. I very much hope our paths will cross again.'

He laughed. 'Indeed. I am glad that your time in the Landowski household has taught you well.' He put a slightly frail hand on my shoulder. 'Love is all there is. Now, go and find her, boy. Whatever it takes.' He raised a finger, as if remembering something, and disappeared into the house. He returned with a straw bag that clanked with every footstep. He handed it to me, and I looked inside to see four bottles of the Côtes du Rhône we had been enjoying last night. 'For the trip,' he winked.

'Thank you.'

'But be careful.' He put his hand to my cheek and looked me dead in the eye. 'Everything in moderation, eh?'

I nodded. 'Goodbye, Monsieur Landowski.'

The *vin rouge* made my journey across Europe a fairly painless experience, and it has since rolled into a hazy blur in my mind. I became quite friendly with the train guards. We traded stories and sips of alcohol, and played cards too. Conveniently, I was able to win some pesetas from them, for I realised that I was heading to Spain with no local currency. I actually became quite accustomed to the idea of such an existence—always on the move, with no need to think too hard about things. Perhaps this was the future for me.

The change at Barcelona was smooth, just as Evelyn had promised. I slept for the final leg of the journey, rocked gently by the movement of the carriage on the tracks and the darkness of the enclosed space.

I was woken by a bright, searing light which covered my face, as two members of station staff in Granada pulled the side of the carriage open. My head was pounding.

'*Señor? Por favor apártate del camino.*'

I hardly spoke a word of Spanish. And, unlike the first time I set foot in Norway, I didn't have two multilingual friends to assist me.

'*Salga, por favor,*' they gestured for me to leave the carriage.

I hauled myself up, and stepped out into the morning heat, which made me feel sick and dizzy.

'*¡Tiene Resaca!*' cried one of the men, and the other looked at me and laughed.

My mouth was hideously dry. 'Water?' I asked, which elicited no response. I mimed drinking from a bottle.

'*Agua? Sí.*' One of the men pointed to a drinking fountain on the station's platform, and I nodded gratefully.

By the time I had drunk my fill, the men had removed the statue and were in the process of wheeling it off the platform. I followed them, and stood pathetically by as they loaded the wooden crate onto a battered old truck with an open back.

'Alhambra?' I asked.

'*Sí, señor. Alhambra. Treinta minutos.*'

'*Gracias,*' I managed to muster, before climbing up onto the truck.

Granada was a striking place. The city, made up of hundreds of whitewashed buildings, shone a brilliant white in the morning sun. Beyond the city walls was a towering mountain range. Upon closer inspection, the nearest hillside appeared to be punctuated by a vast number of caves in the rock. I held my gaze, and noticed some little figures, which moved about in front of them. Were the caves abodes?

Soon enough, we were on the approach to the mighty palace. The Alhambra's ancient red towers rose up out of the dark green forest, and I was in awe of the architectural vision. The truck approached the great gate and stopped. The driver left his cab to speak to me.

'*Esto es lo más lejos que puedo ir,*' he said, shrugging. 'No further,' he managed in English, pointing to the keyhole-shaped entrance, which led to a bustling square. I nodded, and jumped to the ground, my head still pounding due to the bottle of wine I had thirstily gulped down last night. As I walked through the gate, I was accosted by locals touting their wares, selling water, oranges and roasted almonds. Amongst the chaos, I saw a man in a linen shirt jogging towards me from another gate across the square. He pointed towards the truck.

'Statue?' he asked in French.

'*Sí, señor*, statue. Monsieur Landowski.'

Two men in boiler suits helped to carry the statue into the centre of the square and remove the crate. After the layers of cloth had been taken away too, the Landowski statue stood proudly in the Alhambra.

'She is superb! Better than I could have imagined,' said the man in the linen shirt. 'Monsieur Landowski is a genius. It is as if the young Lucía is here amongst us.'

'Forgive me, I am not local to the area. Monsieur Landowski mentioned that Lucía won a dance contest? Is that right?'

The man chuckled. 'The *Concurso de Cante Jondo* was much more than a dance competition, *señor*. It was a *fiesta* of music, flamenco and *life* which took place in 1922. Four thousand people came to celebrate with us. It was a very special time.'

'Clearly,' I mumbled. 'You're still talking about it thirty years later.'

'*Señor*, that night four thousand citizens witnessed before their very eyes the raw power of the *duende*. It lives inside Lucía,' he said, touching the statue's cheek.

'The *duende*?' I asked.

'Such a thing is hard to describe for those who do not understand our culture. The *duende* is a quality of passion and inspiration, which manifested itself in Lucía through rhythm and dance.'

Lucía sounded quite astounding. 'I should love to meet her and tell Monsieur Landowski of her reaction to the statue.'

The man in the linen shirt sighed. 'The last we heard, she had returned to America to dance and provide money for her family. Things have been so difficult after the war. No mercy was shown to the *gitanos* of Sacromonte.' He shook his head sadly. 'It is why my fellow trustees wished to commission this statue.'

'Forgive me,' I said, embarrassed that I had to question another Spanish word I did not understand. '*Gitanos*? What does that mean?'

'The Gypsy people, sir, once cruelly driven from the city walls.' He pointed to the landscape beyond the gate. 'Perhaps you have noticed their caves on Sacromonte mountain.'

'Ah,' I nodded in realisation. 'By the way, *señor*, I wonder if you have any recommendations for a tourist in Granada? Now Lucía has been safely delivered, I find myself at a loose end.'

The man thought for a moment. 'A trip to the central plaza is essential. There is always something going on there.' He shook my hand.

'*Gracias, señor.*' I turned and walked back out of the Alhambra, hoping the journey down the hill would begin to cure my significant hangover. The smell of the cypress trees and the light breeze on the hillside transpired to be just the ticket, and by the time I arrived at the plaza, my head was finally beginning to recover.

I took a moment to appreciate the most impressive of the plaza's buildings—an old cathedral with an open bell tower—then I walked across sleek, shiny tiles to the grand fountain in the middle of the square. Peering within, I saw that the bottom was covered in pesetas, each representing a wish of its former owner. I reached into my pocket, faced away from the fountain, and threw a coin over my shoulder. Needless to say, I silently prayed that I would find Elle.

The day was getting hotter and hotter, and I was in need of something cooling. I wandered down one of the alleyways leading away from the plaza in search of a cafe. Sure enough, I came across a little place which sold ice creams of every conceivable colour, and seemed to be doing a roaring trade with passing tourists. As I approached, I spied a dark-haired young girl leaning against the wall, kicking her heels and staring dreamily off into the distance. I think I managed to catch the general gist of the conversation that followed:

'You want one, *señorita*?' asked the cafe's proprietor from behind the big freezer that displayed the ice creams.

'*Sí*,' the girl replied. 'But I have no money, *señor*.'

'Then go away,' he shouted at her. 'You are putting other customers off.'

The girl shrugged and turned away. I felt moved to defend her.

'She's not putting me off,' I said, and walked over to the freezer, where I surveyed the rainbow of colours which were on offer. The green ice cream looked the most enticing, and I pointed to it. 'I would like two of those,' I said.

'*Sí, señor*,' replied the bad-tempered cafe owner.

Behind me, the bell in the plaza rang, and I turned to see crowds flooding out of the cathedral. I guessed that morning mass must have just finished. I handed over a few pesetas to the cafe owner, and took the ice creams. I looked down at the little girl, who was staring up at me with wide eyes.

'Here, *señorita*,' I said as I handed one of the cornets to her. She looked surprised.

'For me?' she asked.

'*Sí*.' I nodded.

'*Gracias a Dios*,' she said as she took a lick of the ice cream that was already melting in the sun and dribbling down her hand. '*A usted le gustaría que dijera su destino?*'

I think she was asking me a question. '*No comprendo*,' I replied with a smile. '*Hablo...Inglés?*' I thought she had a better chance of understanding English than French.

'You like fortune tell?' she asked sweetly.

'You can tell my fortune?' I looked down at the girl, who returned my gaze quizzically.

'*Mi prima*, Angelina.' The girl pointed back towards the plaza. 'She very good,' she said, as she stretched out her palm and mimed the reading of it.

'Why not?' I shrugged as I licked my ice cream, and indicated to the girl that she should lead the way. We walked back down the narrow alleyway to the now buzzing plaza. I followed the girl towards a slightly older young lady in a bright red dress. She was sitting on the steps of the cathedral, and was finishing a reading for another client. When the money had been exchanged, it did not pass me by that the woman who was leaving looked a little shaken, and I wondered what was in store for me.

'*Toma, tengo un hombre para ti. Su español no es bueno,*' said the younger girl.

'*Hola, señor,*' said the fortune teller, who turned towards me.

I nearly fell where I stood. I knew this person. I had seen her before, several times. My jaw dropped as I observed her heart-shaped face and huge, blue opalescent eyes, framed by dark eyelashes. She had a long glossy mane, and wore a garland of flowers.

She looked just as she had the night she appeared to me the first time.

In the fire.

In Leipzig.

She gave me a bright smile. 'I see your hand?' she asked me. Hypnotised by the face I swore I recognised, I gaped at her as she grabbed my arm and examined my palm. 'Then I tell you about your daughter.'

My stomach turned. 'My daughter?'

'*Sí, señor,*' she replied. 'Please, sit with me.'

The younger girl gave me a nod, and skipped away to finish her ice cream in the shade of an awning across the plaza.

'Your face…' I stuttered. 'I know it. You've appeared to me…in my dreams…'

The girl giggled. 'I assure you, *señor*, this is the first time we have met. But you are not the first to say that you know me. Sometimes this can happen. It is the way of the *bruja*.'

'The *bruja*?' I parroted.

'*Sí*, yes. My spiritual ancestry.' She sighed. 'It is difficult to explain to a *payo*, *señor*, but I will try.' She looked up at the cathedral, seemingly for inspiration. 'You and I were always going to meet. Our destinies are entwined, if only in a very minor way.

Because of this, our souls may have already done a dance together. Do you see?' My mouth continued to gape open. 'No,' she laughed. 'I thought not.'

'I don't understand it. You've spoken to me. I've heard your voice.'

'If I have, *señor*, it is not consciously. I am sure that my form was merely a vessel for whatever message the universe needed to send you.'

Comically, the remainder of my ice cream fell out of its cone, and plopped onto the steps. 'You mean to say you do not recognise me at all?'

'I do not, no.' The girl took my palm once again. 'Dreams and visions are wildly powerful things, *señor*. We cannot control them, yet we manifest them. When we met before, what did I say to you?'

I closed my eyes and recalled that terrible night. 'You told me that I had to live…that I had a purpose.'

'How interesting,' the girl mused. 'Let us see if I was right.' She scrutinised my hand. 'It is nice to meet you in person, Atlas. I am Angelina.'

My heart was racing. 'How do you know my name?'

'I can see it. It is engraved in the stars. As is so much of your destiny.' She looked up from my palm and stared into my eyes. 'Do not be fearful of what I am telling you, or what I know.' She flashed me a reassuring smile. 'The *bruja* can see everything that ever was, is and could be. It is a gift passed down through our bloodline.'

I was simply dumbfounded. 'I'm not even supposed to be in Granada. I was merely delivering a statue. It was pure chance I ended up here.'

'A statue?' asked Angelina. 'To the Alhambra Palace?'

'That's right.' I nodded.

'Lucía Amaya Albaycín. My aunt.'

'Your aunt?'

Angelina giggled again. 'That is correct, *señor*. Now do you see what I mean when I say that our destinies are entwined, and we were always going to meet? To you, it appears as pure chance. But to me, it is part of a greater plan.'

'Good Lord,' I said breathlessly.

'Regrettably, Aunt Lucía is no longer with us on earth. But she is truly free now, and dances amongst the clouds.'

'The gentleman at the Alhambra believed her to be very much alive.'

'Yes, as does her mother, and her daughter too.'

'Her daughter?' I asked with concern.

Angelina pointed towards the little girl I had bought an ice cream for. 'Isadora, my cousin. They are not *bruja, señor*, so they cannot feel that Lucía is gone.'

I stared over at the innocent child, who was blissfully unaware that her mother was dead. The heartache she would have to endure pained me. 'Why do you not tell them?'

Angelina sighed. 'What is better, to learn the truth and be empty, or to live in hope? After all, it is the only thing that keeps us alive, *señor*.'

A pleasant citrus smell filled the air, and an elderly gentleman wheeling a wooden cart full of fresh oranges passed by.

'Very unusual, *señor*. Very unusual.' Angelina's eyes flitted between my palm and face. 'I have never met another like you here in the plaza. You are something different.'

'What do you mean?' I said, hanging on her every word.

'Often, I can advise people, and give them the power to change their destinies. But your path is fixed, Atlas. Unchanging.'

'What does that mean?' I asked, unease growing inside me.

A smile from Angelina went a long way towards reassuring me. 'It means that you will do great things. Your name is appropriate. Atlas is a man who carries the weight of the world on his shoulders, is he not?'

'So the myth goes,' I replied.

Angelina narrowed her eyes. 'Myths are just what stories become when there is no longer a soul alive who witnessed the events first hand.'

'I see,' I replied. The cathedral bell rang to signify midday, and I nearly jumped out of my skin.

Angelina squeezed my hand tightly. 'Know this, Atlas. The weight of the world is only ever given to those who have the strength to carry it.' She closed her eyes, and I watched her grimace as she apparently saw something painful in her mind. 'The little boy in the snow, who had to run from a crime he did not commit...'

'You know so much,' I whispered.

She reopened her eyes and gazed at me. 'Your journey has been wretched. But you have endured. Because, despite everything, many have shown you kindness. Am I correct?'

'Yes,' I said, my voice cracking under the emotion I was beginning to feel. I didn't wish to cry in front of Angelina, so tried to focus on the activity taking place within the square. I watched two young boys kicking a football to each other, a pair of lovers holding hands by the fountain, and a man shooing some starlings away from his shopfront.

Angelina continued. 'The universe is readying you for the task that is to come.'

'Task?' I asked, looking back at her. 'What task?'

'The task of raising your daughters.'

Suddenly, Angelina's magical aura was broken. 'Angelina, I think you're mistaken. I'm afraid I don't have any daughters.'

She grinned once more. 'Oh, you do. They are just not on earth yet.' Her brow suddenly furrowed, and she looked up at the clear blue sky. 'Except...for one.' Angelina nodded, as if confirming her thought to herself.

My heart felt as if it might explode out of my chest at any moment. 'Please, tell me what you mean.'

Angelina looked deep into my eyes. 'You already have the first of your daughters, Atlas. She walks this earth as you or I do.'

The plaza began to spin. 'Elle...' I breathed. 'Elle has borne our child? Is that why she left? She was afraid for the safety of our baby? My God... My God! Why wouldn't she tell me?!'

Angelina grabbed my shoulders. 'Be calm, Atlas, be calm.'

'Where is she? Please, Angelina, tell me! I must know!'

Angelina shook her head, and spoke firmly. 'I do not have that answer. All I know is that you will father seven daughters, and the first one already lives.'

I didn't know whether to collapse to the floor or stand up and dance a merry jig. 'That's...that's wonderful news! So I will find Elle? And together we will have six more children?'

The starlings the man had shooed away from the shopfront landed on the steps of the cathedral, and were staring expectantly up at Angelina. She reached into her pocket, produced a small piece of bread, and threw them some crumbs. 'As I said,' she eventually replied. 'You will father seven daughters.'

'You *must* mean I find Elle. You have to! She is the only woman I will ever love.'

Angelina gave a secretive smile. 'You are capable of deep love, Atlas, despite everything. That is what makes you special.'

I watched the starlings fight over the offering Angelina had thrown them. 'I have another question for you. A moment ago you called me "the little boy who ran from a crime he did not commit". I must know about Kreeg Eszu.'

Angelina inhaled deeply. 'Your pursuer?'

'That's right. If Elle left to protect our child from his grasp, then I have to know if he is still out there.'

Angelina's eyes travelled across to Isadora, who was staring back at both of us, no doubt waiting for her cousin to be free. Angelina gave her a small wave, which Isadora returned. 'I cannot see, Atlas. Some things are impossible to discern.' She saw my shoulders drop. 'But,' she continued, 'I predict that your daughters will benefit from a place of safety and shelter. Their seas will prove to be as stormy as yours. They will require—'

'A hidden corner of the world?' I cut in.

Angelina looked impressed. 'Precisely, yes.'

A shiver travelled down my spine, as I thought of Agatha's plot on Lake Geneva. In her letter, she had predicted such a place would be required. 'What shall I do now, Angelina?'

Angelina gestured out towards the square. 'Find your daughters, Atlas.'

I nodded. 'That means finding Elle, of course.' I looked at her expectantly. 'You can see so much…can you not tell me where she is?'

The starlings chirped and demanded more food. Angelina obliged, and I watched her face closely. She wore a slight frown, and seemed to be considering her answer very carefully. After a while, she shook her head. 'No. As I have told you, your path is preordained, and you will walk it with no need of assistance from me.' She looked at me, and we stared at one another for a while. I was hoping it might serve to prise out some additional detail from Angelina, but it proved to be wishful thinking. 'That completes your reading, *señor*.'

'All right.' Unthinkingly, I wrapped my arms around her, an ecstasy rising inside of me. 'Thank you, Angelina. You have saved me!'

'It is my pleasure, *señor*, but…'—she looked cautious— 'please, go carefully into the world, with open thoughts and open arms.'

'I promise I will, yes. I feel like Ebenezer Scrooge on Christmas morning! Oh, and don't worry. I'll stop the drinking.' I gave her a wink. 'I'll need to be ship-shape for my reunion with Elle. And my daughter!'

She sighed. '*Señor*, I—'

I jumped to my feet. 'I can't quite believe it. I'm a father. I'm a *father*! Ha!'

'You are, but I—'

'Perhaps I'll name her Angelina. Oh, what am I talking about? Elle will have already given her a name. I wonder what it is?!' I saw Isadora approaching us. She had somehow acquired a black and white kitten, and was carrying it over to the cathedral.

'Please thank your little cousin. Without her, we never would have met.' Angelina gave me a nod, and I began to walk away. 'You're absolutely right,' I called back. 'You have no need to tell me where to go next. I know I must build a safe space for Elle and my child before anything else. Fear not! I know what to do!' I was so full of renewed energy that I broke into a jog. 'Thank you, Angelina! I will never forget you!'

With that, I bounded away, millions of possibilities, parallels and dreams spiralling through my head.

44

1965

I am very proud of Atlantis. As I sit on the edge of the jetty watching the golden sun set on the house, I find myself admiring my design. Mr Kohler introduced me to more than a dozen architects before I was able to confidently select one to deliver the project. There was certainly no shortage of interest—the opportunity to build on a secluded patch of Lake Geneva was an attractive prospect to many. Although several men had exciting visions, there was one thing above all else that I required in my chosen contractor: a bond of trust.

Safety and solitude were at the forefront of my brief. The plans were ambitious and would need to be executed flawlessly. Firstly, I wanted the house to look as though it had stood for centuries. I was aware that word might spread about the eccentric man who was building an enormous property on the lake, and the last thing I wanted was for it to look like it might be owned by one of Mr Fleming's Bond villains. As a result, I had the house built in the style of Louis XV. In fact, I should mention that as far as anyone who wishes to investigate the land registry is concerned, Atlantis has been standing since the eighteenth century. It is amazing what men will do for you when you offer them large sums of money.

The land registry would also inform any prying eyes that the property is owned by Icarus Holdings—a shell company under the stewardship of two directors: Eric Kohler and Georg Hoffman. Over the last fifteen years, Georg has developed a fine legal mind. As per my promise, I paid for him to attend university and law school. Mr Kohler hired him almost as soon as he had graduated, clearly seeing him as a protégé whom he had nurtured from a young age. Eric retired five years ago, and Georg now oversees my affairs.

If Kreeg ever did come sniffing around Switzerland, I am confident that I have taken every reasonable precaution to throw him off the scent.

The casual observer could not, in fact, discern that this property is entirely new. I took great pains to ensure that period materials were used, down to each doorknob and flagstone. Thanks to this, Atlantis boasts an elegant grandeur. Four storeys high, its pale pink walls are punctuated by tall multi-paned windows, and topped by a steeply sloping red roof with turrets at each corner.

The house's interior boasts every modern luxury; thick carpets and plump sofas adorn the twelve bedrooms which lie within. My favourite floor is the very top, where I specified seven bedrooms should be built. Each has a superb view of Lake Geneva over the treetops. I had hoped, prayed and naively *assumed* that by now each would be occupied by the daughters promised to me by Angelina all those years ago. However, they remain empty.

One would never know that Atlantis holds many secrets, which I have ensured are completely invisible to the naked eye. Perhaps now it is clear why trust was the key quality I looked for in my architect. Should I or any of Atlantis's occupants come under threat from an unwelcome visitor in the form of Eszu, measures have been taken to ensure escape is possible. For obvious reasons, I will not state the exact nature of the house's secrets, but if someone needed to swiftly disappear from the property, a network of hidden lifts and tunnels exist within to guarantee safety can be reached.

I wanted to ensure that the house boasted gardens which would make Flora Vaughan proud, too. Atlantis now benefits from sweeping lawns which sprawl out in front of the house and continue down to the water's edge. I have planted myriad shrubs and trees which form hidden pathways and secret grottos, produced by over a decade of growth. In the springtime, when the flowers are in bloom, I do not believe there is any more beautiful place on earth.

I only wish I had someone to share it all with.

When I left Granada in 1951, I vowed that the next page in this diary would tell of my happy reunion with Elle and the child which I knew had been born. That is a promise I have broken today.

After my meeting with Angelina, I travelled back to Geneva to begin the process of building Atlantis. When construction was fully underway, I resumed my search of the globe for the woman I love, and my baby girl.

That was fourteen years ago. My daughter is fast becoming an adult, wherever she is.

I began methodically, travelling first around France, visiting towns and villages Elle had mentioned during our time together. In Reims, I met a waitress who told me about a woman with a baby who was making her way to southern Italy for a new start…so that is where I travelled next. I followed vague sightings around the continent, to Spain, Portugal, Germany and Belgium.

To help me, I instructed Eric Kohler to search records in every nation for the names 'Leopine', 'Elle', 'Tanit', 'D'Aplièse'… and any variation I could think of. When Eric re-tired, the responsibility shifted to Georg. I cannot credit the young man enough. He has been nothing short of determined in carrying out what must be very tedious work. Each time he discovers a lead, no matter how tenuous, I board a plane and travel to that location. Then I painstakingly interview confused residents, until I am convinced that the trail is dead. On my quest, I have seen parts of the world I had never anticipated. Kenya, South Africa, India, China…

Reader, I have never stopped searching for them. I have been to every corner of the globe, convinced that one day, as I round a street corner or stroll onto a beach, I will see Elle's beautiful face once more. But my task has been fruitless.

No doubt you are asking, then, why I have returned to my

diary. This morning I received a letter from an old friend, forwarded to me by Georg. I enclose it here:

> *Dear Bo,*
> *I hope this letter reaches you via the law firm. Monsieur Landowski passed on the contact details to me alongside his chisel when he died. 'In case you need one another,' he wrote. He was perceptive like that.*
> *Do you think you might be able to meet me in Paris? I am guessing, by the lawyer's address, that you are residing in Geneva these days, so hopefully the trip would not prove too strenuous. I would offer to come to you, but my sixty-year-old bones will not allow such a thing.*
> *It would be good to see you, Bo, one last time.*
> *Your friend,*
> *Laurent Brouilly*

I stared down at the page. I had provided Mr Kohler's contact details to everyone from my past, from Monsieur Landowski to Ralph Mackenzie, in case Elle ever turned up on their doorstep. It has been one of the small joys in my life to occasionally receive updates from those who have meant so much to me over the years.

Monsieur Landowski had died in 1961. To my eternal shame, I had not attended his funeral, as I thought it would be the perfect location for Kreeg to ambush me. Knowing that I had a daughter in this world had galvanised my desire to stay firmly on it, and I had returned to a state of overt caution. Instead, when I received word from Marcel, I had wept alone for three days, and asked the stars to care for him in his new life.

As for Laurent Brouilly, I have not laid eyes on him since that fateful day in Paris when Elle and I were forced to flee.

I followed the address on Brouilly's letter, and knocked on the door of his quaint town house on the quiet, cobbled avenue in Montparnasse. I heard a fumbling, and the door was opened by a young lady in a blue medical smock. She looked at me quizzically.

'Hello, madame. Am I right in thinking that Monsieur Brouilly lives here?'

She smiled at me. 'Yes, this is Professor Brouilly's house. Is he expecting you?'

I thought for a moment. 'Do you know, I'm not entirely sure. Could you let him know that his old friend Bo is here to see him?'

'Of course.' She put the door on the latch, and returned quickly. 'He seemed very excited when I mentioned your name, Bo. Please come in.' I entered Brouilly's charming home, which was just as cluttered as his tiny apartment had been all those years ago. Strewn about the hallway were discarded canvases, dust sheets, half-finished sculptures... It was the den of a true *artiste*.

'He's a little frail these days, Monsieur Bo, despite what he might tell you. Do go carefully with him.' I nodded. 'Just through here.' The young girl gently opened a door to a living room populated by a mass of green plants. In amongst the foliage, a painfully thin and aged Laurent Brouilly was perched upon a large velvet sofa. In truth, he looked as though a small gust of wind from the open window might blow him onto the floor.

'I can't remember,' he said. 'Do you speak now?' I opened my mouth, unsure of what to say. 'I'm joking!' cried Brouilly cackling.

Relief flooded my body. 'Hello, Laurent.' I crossed the room to shake his hand, which felt light as a feather.

'Regrettably, my grip is not as strong as it used to be,' he said. 'The sculpting went out of the window a few years ago. I paint, though. Please, have a seat.' He indicated the unoccupied space on the sofa. 'Do you still play the violin? Or the cello?'

'Sometimes. I can manage about fifteen minutes before my arm begins to ache from an old injury.'

'Ah, yes, Landowski mentioned it.' He stared intently at me, and I was heartened to see that despite his thin grey hair and fragile body, his eyes had not changed one iota. 'Thank you, Hélène,' he said to the young girl at the door.

'Just shout if you need me, Professor Brouilly.' She left the room.

I raised my eyebrows at my old friend. 'Professor, eh?'

'I rose through the ranks to become Director of Sculpture at the Beaux-Arts, would you believe?'

'Do you know, Laurent, I would.' I paused before asking the difficult question. 'You wrote in your letter that you would like to see me "one last time". What on earth did you mean? How old are you? Sixty-one?'

'Sixty-two now, Bo. But you are not blind. I am sick. The blasted doctors have told me that I will not recover. They cannot accurately predict how long I will last, but it will not be more than a few months.'

'Laurent... I'm so sorry.'

He shrugged valiantly. 'Cancer is still easier to accept than losing Bel all those years ago.'

I put a tender hand on his leg, and it distressed me to feel the bone. 'Do you still think about her?' I asked.

'Every minute of every day,' he replied nostalgically. 'But...' A smile played on his lips. 'Despite it all, I have lived a blessed life. I will now tell you a story, which even you might find difficult to credit...' He closed his eyes. 'Many years ago, I had just finished teaching a class on Donatello. As I was packing my books, a student walked up to me. Bo, as soon as I laid eyes on her face, I knew...for it was like looking into a mirror. She introduced herself as Beatriz Aires-Cabral.' Brouilly shook his head.

'Aires-Cabral?' I replied. 'Wasn't that Bel's surname?'

He met my eye. 'Precisely.'

I was in a state of disbelief. 'My word.'

'She asked if I remembered creating a sculpture of her mother for her father, Gustavo, which was shipped over to Brazil as a wedding present.' He chortled. 'If only she had known. Stood in front of me, in my classroom, was my own daughter.'

We sat in silence for a while, both choked. 'I...don't know what to say...'

'Quite. She told me that her mother had died when she was only eighteen months old. There was a yellow fever outbreak in Rio, and...' His voice cracked and his eyes glazed over. 'She was only twenty-one. After all that turmoil and tragedy, to die so young... Forgive me.' A tear fell down Brouilly's ashen cheek. 'Anyway, I enquired about her *father*, as she knew him. She told me that their relationship was difficult and that he had sunk deeper and deeper into the bottle as the years passed by. Gustavo forbade Beatriz from pursuing her artistic passions, but died himself when she was seventeen. She enrolled at the Beaux-Arts after his death, as she knew her mother had done before her.'

'And she ended up in your class,' I whispered. Brouilly and I stared at one another, before both breaking into smiles.

'The universe works in magnificent ways, does it not, Bo? Anyway, Beatriz stayed in Paris for five years. Naturally, I took her under my wing. She often visited my house here in Montparnasse. We even used to have a weekly lunch at La Closerie des Lilas, where I used to take her mother.' He chuckled. 'Oh, what a blessing! You know, I even took her to Landowski's atelier. He proudly showed her photographs of our work on the *Cristo* and told her stories about my youth.'

I was desperate to ask my next question. 'Did…you ever tell her the truth of her parenthood?'

Brouilly looked down and shook his head. 'What right would I ever have to tell her that Gustavo was not her real father? No, monsieur, no.'

I leant back into the sofa and looked up at the dusty ceiling. I was finding it difficult to keep my emotions in check. The sight of the dying Laurent and the story of his daughter had created an enormous lump in my throat. How anyone could doubt the power of the universe after such an event, I do not know. After a minute, I managed to regain composure. 'Do you still speak with Beatriz now?'

'We write to each other every month! I know all about her life, Bo. She has married a good man who treats her well and loves her dearly.' Brouilly sighed. 'Tragically, her first child died. But she had a second baby.'

'What's the name?' I asked.

'Cristina,' Laurent said quietly. He suddenly seemed troubled. 'From what Beatriz has told me, she is a very difficult child. Even though she is only seven years old, she treats her mother very poorly.' Laurent turned to look out of the window, formulating his next sentence. 'Cristina is ferociously intelligent, but appears to have no sensitivity or empathy when it comes to her fellow human beings. It makes her almost impossible to deal with.'

'How awful for Beatriz,' I replied. She's already been through so much.'

'Yes.' Brouilly slowly turned to me. 'Which brings me to why I asked you here today.'

'Please, go on,' I encouraged him.

Brouilly inhaled, and I noted the slight rattle in his chest as he did so. 'I want to provide my daughter with all the assistance I can, but I am not long for this world, Bo. I will leave her what money I have, but it is not a great deal. I wonder, if...' His voice cracked once more, and I placed my hand on his. 'I wonder if you might look in on the family from time to time. There is no one else I can ask, without the risk of exposing the secret of Beatriz's parenthood, which I most certainly do not wish to do.'

I nodded. 'Of course, Laurent. Do you wish me to contact Beatriz?'

'No. It will only cause more questions to be raised. Perhaps you could...observe from afar, and if the family is ever in dire need of help, it would be a tremendous comfort to know that someone could give it.'

'I understand.' My mind raced at the gravity of the task Laurent was endowing me with. His family lived in Brazil, and I resided in Switzerland. There would be numerous practicalities to overcome, not to mention the interference it might cause to my own search for Elle. I gazed at Laurent's pleading eyes. His only crime was loving another too much. I was familiar with the phenomenon. I decided then that I would not let him down. 'Please rest assured that I will do as you have asked.'

His face radiated warm gratitude. 'Thank you, Bo. Thank you.' He patted my hand. 'Now, I am growing tired, but before I go, is there anything *you* wish to know?'

I took a moment to think. 'Evelyn,' I replied. 'Do you ever hear from her?'

Laurent winced. 'I'm sorry, Bo. Evelyn died soon after Monsieur Landowski.'

My heart ached. She had been so very kind to me, and in the ferociousness of my quest to locate Elle, I had failed to stay in touch. 'When I spoke to her fifteen years ago, she mentioned that she hadn't even met her granddaughter. Tell me, Monsieur Brouilly, was that ever resolved?'

Brouilly shook his head. 'No. I saw Louis at the funeral. But there was no sign of Giselle or Marina.'

'Marina,' I recalled. 'That was her name. She must be in her twenties now?'

'Yes. It is a sad story. As you heard from Evelyn, Giselle was a force of nature. The rumours were that she was fuelled by drink. Things went sour in the relationship between her and Louis. One day, she simply took Marina and left her husband behind. He has told me since that he often tried to contact his daughter, but Giselle did a thorough job of brainwashing her against him.'

'How terrible.'

'Indeed. But then, according to stories I have heard, Giselle fought viciously with her own daughter, and kicked her out of the house. Since then, apparently…' Brouilly hesitated.

'Please, say, Laurent.'

'I have recently heard tell from Marcel Landowski that Marina frequents the Rue Saint-Denis.' I stared back blankly at him. Brouilly sighed. 'Apparently she is selling her body to pay her way.'

I put my hand to my mouth. 'Oh Laurent.' I rubbed my temples. 'I have to do something to help. For Evelyn.'

Brouilly nodded. 'I would like to think that I would have acted, were I in a position to.' Laurent inhaled deeply, and flinched when breathing out. He put a hand to his chest. 'Do you think you could fetch Hélène?'

'Of course, Laurent,. I stood up, and he grabbed my hand.

'You will keep your promise, won't you? You swear?'

'On the stars, Laurent.'

He gave me a final smile. 'Then I know you are telling the truth.'

45

The rain made the street slick on the Rue Saint-Denis, and flashing red lights were reflected on the ground beneath me. Burly men puffed away on cigarettes under dilapidated awnings, and I felt their eyes following me as I made my way up the pavement. Not far ahead, a glamorous-looking woman in a fur coat was huddled in the door of a run-down cafe. I gritted my teeth.

'Excuse me,' I said, approaching her. 'I'm looking for someone.'

'Look no further, monsieur. A hundred francs, you can do anything you want to me.' She winked.

'No, you misunderstand, that's not what I meant. I'm looking for a woman called Marina.'

The woman rolled her eyes. 'What would you want a little girl like that for, when you could have a woman like me...' She grabbed the lapels of my coat.

'No, I'm not here for *that*. I'm just an old friend of her family. I was told that I might find her here. Do you know where she is?'

She frowned and gave a snort. 'Whatever you say, monsieur.' She pointed further up the road. 'Marina's at Le Lézard.'

'Thank you. I really appreciate it.' The woman shrugged and turned away, and I continued towards the glowing neon sign ahead.

As I attempted to enter the premises, an enormous man in a

leather coat put his arm out to stop me. 'Can I help you, monsieur?'

'I'm here to see someone,' I replied.

'Sorry, monsieur. You need to make an appointment with me. But don't worry, I'm very amenable.'

I involuntarily turned my nose up at the man. 'I don't want anything like that, thank you. I just want to talk to Marina.'

He looked sceptical. 'Marina?'

'Yes.' The man looked me up and down. 'Fine. Don't know why I keep her on my books. She's choosy. And beggars can't be choosers, monsieur.' It took nerve to restrain myself as the man spoke with such little regard for a desperate human being. He pushed the club door open. 'She's right at the back.'

I walked into the dimly lit club, which was sparsely populated by men in suits with girls in short skirts draped over them. The musty air stank of cigarette smoke and bleach. I made my way to the back of the room, where a long leather banquette was positioned against the wall, next to a winding staircase. A slight woman sat cooing over a baby, who couldn't have been more than six months old.

'Shh, *chéri*,' she comforted. 'All will be well. Mama will be back soon.'

'Hello,' I said. 'Are you Marina?'

The woman looked up at me with fear in her eyes. 'Pierre is supposed to tell me when someone wants me.'

I put my hands up. 'Please, that's not why I'm here. I'm an old friend of your grandmother's.'

Marina looked perplexed. 'I don't have a grandmother. Both died before I was born.'

I took a deep breath, realising this would be a difficult task. 'Ah. Actually, Marina, that might not necessarily be the case.'

She furrowed her brow. 'What do you mean? Who are you?'

The baby began to cry, and a loud male voice shouted from across the room. 'Shut that bloody thing up. Jesus, I come here to get away from that racket!'

Marina shook her head. 'Come on, *chéri*, not much longer now.' She rocked the child gently, and hummed a quiet lullaby until it began to settle. 'There now, that's better.' She looked back up at me. 'Just tell me what you want.'

'May I take a seat?' I asked, and she nodded. 'Is the baby yours?'

'No. He is my friend Celine's.' Marina looked up at the clock which hung on the wall above her. 'She is busy at the moment. Probably for another ten minutes.'

'I see.' I shifted awkwardly. 'Well, as I mentioned, I knew your grandmother, Evelyn. Believe it or not, she actually looked after me when I was a little boy.'

'Huh. So what does that have to do with you being here?'

I folded my arms. 'I recently learnt about your family circumstances from an old friend of mine, and I wanted to say how sorry I am. It must all be very difficult for you.'

Marina pursed her lips. 'I don't need your pity, monsieur.'

'You don't have it, merely the offer of assistance should you want it.'

She looked me in the eye. 'I've heard about men like you, coming in and promising the world. Girls leave with them, and then are treated as property. I'm fine where I am, thank you very much.'

I was mortified to hear of such a thing. 'No, Marina. It's nothing like that. Your grandmother—your father's mother—loved you very much. She didn't die before you were born. In fact, she was desperate to meet you, but your mother didn't want that. I think perhaps that she was jealous.'

Marina held my gaze for a while, before returning her attention to the baby. 'I can believe it.'

'Evelyn was once very, very kind to me. And I should like to repay the favour, in any way I can. Marina, what do you need? If it's money, or a listening ear, I can help with both.'

The young woman rolled her eyes. 'I am not naive enough to think that there are no strings attached here, monsieur. I definitely do not want your money.'

Short of other options, I pushed on. 'I am just a friend, here to help…and, yes, to repay a great debt I owe.' Suddenly, a portly man—bright red in the face and dripping with sweat—stomped down the stairs, tipping his hat at Marina as he left. Following him was a tall, slender woman with red hair and fishnet tights.

'Eurgh, he stank,' she said to Marina when he was out of earshot. 'Hello, little one! Were you good for Aunty Ma?' she went on, taking the baby from Marina's hands.

'He was as good as gold. He's so adorable, Celine.'

'He's a terror is what he is, aren't you, little one?' she said, giving her baby a tender kiss on the forehead. 'Here.' She reached into her pockets and gave Marina some francs. 'Your cut.'

'Thank you, Celine.'

Celine eyed me. 'Got yourself a customer, have you, Ma? You're very lucky, sir. You're the first she's accepted in weeks.'

'Celine, please,' Ma replied coyly.

'There's no shame in it. Ma mainly runs a crèche service back here, don't you? There's a few of us with little ones. She looks after them whilst we make our money.'

I nodded. 'That's very good of her to do.'

Celine laughed. 'She loves it. I don't know why you don't become a babysitter, Ma!'

'No one would want me,' she whispered.

The large man in the leather jacket entered the club, walked over and nodded at Celine.

'Another already,' she groaned. 'It's my lucky night.' Celine handed the baby back to Marina, and returned upstairs.

'Marina, I won't impose upon you any longer. But trust me, I am here to help.' I reached into my pocket. Here's a card with the details of my friend Georg. Call the number any time, and he'll put you through to me.' Marina nodded, before devoting her attention to Celine's child, which she looked at with so much love. I walked out of Le Lézard praying she would one day make contact.

Upon my return to Geneva, I instructed Georg Hoffman to liaise with a law firm in Rio de Janeiro, so that I might receive regular updates on Beatriz Aires-Cabral and her daughter. He was most perplexed when I made the request of him, but was as obliging as ever when I spoke with him at the offices of the newly named

Schweikart & Hoffman on the Rue du Rhône.

'I am happy to arrange this for you, Atlas, but I wonder if it is the most efficient use of funds. It would be infinitely cheaper for you to fly out to Brazil once or twice a year, so that you might look into things personally.'

'Thank you for your concern, Georg, but I was instructed to keep my distance. Plus, there is no shortage of cash in the coffers, is there?'

Georg chuckled. 'No. In fact, I received a phone call from our New York stockbroker this morning. Your investments are growing at an unprecedented rate.' He took a notepad out from the top drawer of Kohler's old desk. 'Telex, Control Data, Teledyne, University Computing, Itek…technology is booming. The pot is growing and growing.' He passed me his notes for me to examine.

'And there you were, Georg, trying to convince me to put my money into gold and silver.'

His cheeks reddened. 'Yes. I'm afraid my instincts for the financials are not yet as strong as they could be.'

'Neither are mine, my young friend. You know why I invest in technology.' I sank into the chair opposite Georg. It was still a little odd to see him occupy the room once inhabited by Eric Kohler.

'Yes,' he replied. 'In the hope it might one day help us to find Elle.'

'Precisely,' I said, pointing my finger at him for emphasis. 'As safe as gold may be, it cannot provide me with computer databases and global tracking equipment.' I shrugged. 'Even if my stocks make no return, it is better to give clever people my millions to advance the landscape.'

'Absolutely. Now, what am I asking this Brazilian firm to keep tabs on when it comes to the Aires-Cabral family?'

Georg raised a good point. Laurent had been vague. I folded my arms and looked out at the lake. 'Just have them monitor the family's health, and their financial situation too.'

He nodded. 'Consider it done, Atlas.'

'Thank you, Georg. Also, if you could stay alert for a call from Paris. There's a young lady I met called Marina. She's

Evelyn's granddaughter.'

Georg looked surprised. 'Oh.'

'I have given her your telephone number. If she rings, and I hope that she does, please patch her through to Atlantis immediately. No security screening needed.' I returned Georg's notebook, and he scribbled something down. 'How is Claudia, by the way?'

'She's still working at the bakery. Actually, she's recently met a young man—a customer—and is really rather sweet on him...' Georg looked pleased with himself. 'No pun intended,' he lied.

I chuckled. 'And how do you feel about that, big brother?'

He put his pen down to reflect. 'If she is happy, then I most certainly am too.'

'Excellent. Please send her my love.' I stood up to leave. 'Oh, by the way, are there any other names that have cropped up in the last week?'

He raised a finger, and opened another drawer in the desk. 'I've managed to find an "Eleanor Leopold" residing in Gdansk. As far as I can tell, she's lived there since birth, but you of all people know that records can be changed if you are clever.' He handed me the piece of paper with the new information.

'Gdansk it is,' I replied. 'I've never been to Poland. Are you all right to book the flight?'

'Of course.'

'Jolly good. Thank you, Georg, I think that completes this marathon meeting. I'll check in with you next week.'

'There was just...one other thing.' Georg, normally so calm and measured, looked hesitant and nervous. He opened his briefcase and slid another piece of paper to me over the table.

'What's this?'

'In addition to Elle, we also keep tabs on any mention of the name "Kreeg Eszu", as per your instruction.'

I stared down at the piece of paper, and the blood drained from my face. Georg had handed me what seemed to be a certificate of incorporation for a new company, called Lightning Communications. On the sheet, under 'Director', was Eszu's name.

46

May 1974

Many days were taken up with the investigation of Lightning Communications. It was incorporated in Greece, with a registered address in Athens. Georg and I took swift action, hiring legal firms and private investigators. What they were able to discover was infuriatingly minimal. The company itself was inactive (and has been for the last decade). Accounts are nonetheless filed each year, showing no income or expenditure.

As for Kreeg himself, the teams have established that Eszu now resides in a large, gated compound at the edge of the city. I have been sent blurry photos on the rare occasions he is seen leaving, and there is no doubt in my mind that it is the man who has tried to end my life on several occasions. During the past ten years, since I last wrote in this diary, Kreeg has made no attempt to contact me, or, as far as we are able to ascertain, attempted to seek me out. He merely stays in his enormous estate, keeping himself very much to himself.

As the years have passed, and my team have observed Kreeg's movements, my initial panic turned to unease, which turned to confusion, and a decade later, I have found solace in knowing exactly where he is on the globe. We discovered that he had married an incredibly wealthy Greek woman named Ira, who inherited *her* money from an ex-husband, an oil tycoon. Ira Eszu died last year, in 1973, during the birth of the couple's only child. Records state that Ira was born in 1927, making her forty-five years old. It was no surprise, therefore, that there were complications during the birth.

Nonetheless, the baby boy lived. His name has been registered as Zed Eszu. We continue to monitor the situation closely.

Perhaps it will please you to know that Evelyn's granddaughter, Marina, did eventually reach out to me. Nearly two years after I had left Paris, Georg patched her call through to Atlantis. I listened with concern as she explained a run-in she had suffered with an aggressive 'client' at Le Lézard which had caused her to flee the Rue Saint-Denis. I assured her that I would have money wired to her immediately, but she would not accept it. Rather, she asked if I was able to provide her with some work, so that she might both leave Paris and pay her way without assistance. I invited her to Atlantis and offered her the position of housekeeper. It was inevitably a dull affair, with just me rattling around the place. Marina dutifully vacuumed and ironed for a time, but I could tell she was unfulfilled.

'I miss the children, Atlas,' she confided in me over a glass of Provençal rosé one evening.

I asked Georg if he could help Marina to secure some part-time work in his old school, and that he should offer a donation from me as an incentive. I have found that young Monsieur Hoffman trips over himself when it comes to doing anything for Marina. He looks at her like a puppy looks at its master: dedicatedly, obediently, adoringly. Needless to say, Georg ensured that he was successful in his venture. For the last few years, Marina has run after-school clubs for children in Geneva whose parents work late. She is loved dearly by all who attend.

Marina resides in the Pavilion here at Atlantis, and continues to run the main house as a means of thanks. She cooks for me, cleans, and generally keeps my domestic life ticking over. Her company has come to mean a great deal to me over the years. There is nothing which she does not now know about my life, and vice versa. I have told her about my origins, my search for Elle, and the reason I fear Kreeg Eszu. Along with Georg, the three of us have become a bizarre little family unit, which I treasure.

Speaking of family units, the dedicated reader of this diary will recall that I was entrusted with looking in on the Aires-Cabrals of Rio de Janeiro. Laurent Brouilly sadly died only a few weeks after I visited in Montparnasse. I was determined not to let him down.

As the years passed, Laurent's granddaughter—Cristina— became ever more troubled. Our Brazilian team informed us that she put her parents through hell. As a teenager, she began to frequent some of the seedier bars in Rio, and fell in with a bad crowd. I was faxed police reports filed against her, which ended in Cristina being returned to her parents drunk and dishevelled. She was eventually expelled from school, and started spending vast amounts of time in the city's *favelas*. The law firm guessed that she had become addicted to some sort of drug.

Eventually, the team in Rio informed us that Cristina had stopped coming back to the family home in any capacity, electing to live her life up in Rio's hills. It was soon established that there was a young man in a *favela* whom she had fallen in love with. That, I thought, might have been that. Both Beatriz and Cristina were free of one another, and could live out their lives without the burden of causing the other pain. That was until we received a photograph of Cristina, taken on a long lens. She was sat on a dirty street, stroking a dog. The most notable thing about the image was the size of Cristina's belly. She was clearly pregnant.

Yesterday morning, I received a frantic call from Georg.

'Atlas, there is something you should know.'

'Go on, Georg.'

'Cristina has given birth early. As far as we can tell, she didn't even attend a hospital. The child was born on the streets of the *favela*.'

'Goodness. We must help her out of the *favela* immediately. It's no environment for a newborn. Could you have the Brazilian team find a suitable property we can rent for them?'

Georg sighed. 'There's more. I'm told that Cristina has taken the baby to an orphanage. Apparently, she simply left her and ran.'

My head whirled as I contemplated my next move. This fresh new life had just been handed the cruellest possible start to existence. 'I think we should contact Beatriz. Let her know that she has a granddaughter. I'm sure she would be overjoyed.'

'I do not doubt it, Atlas, but it is my job to remain practical and remind you of the consequences of such a course of action.'

'Go on then.'

'Firstly, Cristina is deeply unstable. You know that she had a falling out with her parents. Apparently, she stole her mother's jewellery to fund her narcotics habit—which itself has only deepened her neurological problems. I worry that if she were to one day discover that her mother had taken her child, she might…'

'I understand what you're saying. It might not be safe for the baby. Imagine if one day Cristina turned up and tried to reclaim her child because it suited her.' I began to pace frantically around my office. 'Plus, if I contact Beatriz, it will raise questions about her lineage which I swore never to reveal.'

Georg spoke solemnly. 'It is difficult to know how to advise you. I can attempt to locate a suitable family in Brazil that might take her in. But it won't be easy. The orphanages in Rio are full of newborns from the *favelas*. Most struggle to find permanent families.'

I shuddered as I thought of Elle in the *Apprentis d'Auteuil*, unable to find a family. My heart broke into pieces all over again. Inaction was unacceptable. 'No, Georg, I need to take personal responsibility for the baby. I will find her someone.' I looked out onto the lake, which shimmered in the morning sun. 'We'll bring her back here to Geneva, and I will find her a suitable family. Just as I did for you. I want to fly tonight.'

'I will arrange the ticket,' Georg confirmed.

'Tickets, plural. Marina should accompany me. I don't know the first thing about babies. And do whatever is necessary to ensure we can collect the child as soon as possible.'

Within two hours, Marina and I were on my personal jet to Paris's new Charles de Gaulle airport, where we boarded the jumbo to Rio. My travelling companion's jaw positively dropped as we approached the Boeing 747 on the tarmac. 'Are you sure this thing will fly, *chéri*?! It is bigger than the Arc de Triomphe!'

'I assure you, I have flown in the belly of this bird many

times, and she has never failed to get me to my destination in one piece. Plus, we're going to be travelling in the first-class cabin. You'll hardly even notice that you are in the air.'

During the flight, I told Marina stories of my childhood, and the kindness both her grandmother Evelyn and Laurent Brouilly had shown me.

'How long do you think the little *bébé* will be with us?' Marina asked. In the years she had been in my employ, I had never seen her so excited.

'Until I can find her a suitable home. It could take a few weeks. Perhaps a month.' She struggled to suppress a smile.

Upon landing, we were met by a representative of the legal team I had hired in Rio de Janeiro, who escorted us to the Copacabana Palace Hotel. It cut an impressive figure on the Avenida Atlântica, towering over Rio's most famous beach. The exterior reminded me a little of the Presidential White House in the United States. I did not doubt that the elegant, air-conditioned lobby would prove quite a contrast to the *favela* we were due to visit tomorrow.

'I am very glad to say that all has been arranged, sir,' said Fernando, the lawyer. 'We are a highly respected firm here in the city, and as such, your documentation, alongside our recommendation, have been sufficient for the director of the orphanage to quickly accept your application to foster. To be frank, it is a struggle for many children to find homes, and they will be grateful for the space.' He shook his head. 'Anyway, the orphanage is expecting you tomorrow, and you will be free to leave with the child.'

'Thank you for your assistance, Fernando. And please extend my appreciation to the entire team for the stalwart job you have done for me during the last decade.'

'I shall, Mr Tanit.' He bowed and walked out of the lobby.

That afternoon, Marina led me around the sticky streets of Rio, as she tracked down babygros, bottles, formula, muslin cloths, and all that we would need to return the child to Europe. I followed her around cluelessly, providing the funds for whatever she decreed was required. The mission was so exhausting that despite the significant jet lag I was experiencing, I slept like a baby that night, the sound of the ocean waves from the open window lulling me into a deep slumber.

The next morning, Marina and I took a cab to the *Rocinha favela*. The driver was reticent about taking tourists into the enormous urbanised slum, but I assured him I knew the risks.

'Look,' he remarked a few minutes into the journey. The driver pointed upwards to Corcovado mountain—on which a familiar white statue stood, arms open wide, embracing the city. 'There is our *Cristo Redentor*. Perhaps you have seen him in photographs before now.'

I gave a smile and replied, 'Yes.' I gazed up at Landowski's pale, elegantly sculpted figure, who seemed to be hovering amidst the clouds like an angelic apparition. Even though I had seen him up close in the Parisian atelier, the reality was breathtaking. Laying eyes on my old friend in his permanent home, I found myself overwhelmed by surges of pride and awe.

As we drove higher up into the hills, concrete and brick were replaced by wood and corrugated metal. Unsettling-looking liquid flowed in the cramped streets, with most of the settlement seeming to lack even basic sanitation. After a fifteen-minute drive—for that is all it took for opulence to become poverty—we were greeted outside of the orphanage by an exhausted-looking woman. She had dark rings under her eyes, and her shirt was covered in stains of various colours and sizes.

'Baby? *Europa?*' She asked as we approached.

'Yes...*sí,*' I replied.

She nodded, taking a moment to look us up and down. Seemingly satisfied, she invited us in. 'Okay. Come.'

We were led inside a rudimentary building. The floors and walls were concrete, and the atmosphere was dark and dingy. In truth, the place reminded me a little of a prison. We followed the woman through a second door, and I was shocked by the sight that greeted us. Thirty or more children of different ages were crammed into a single room. Overwhelmed staff were struggling to remain calm in the heat of the day, berated by a cacophony of screaming and crying. To my eye, the main issue appeared to be that there were simply not enough toys to go around.

'*Mon dieu,*' Marina breathed. 'Poor, poor children.'

As we walked through the room, dozens of wide eyes followed us. I am ashamed to say that I tried not to meet their gaze, for fear that my heart would simply break in two. It had been over forty years since I had set foot in an orphanage. I had, naively, assumed that conditions would be better after all this time. More money, more resources, more knowledge…more love. But here, in the middle of Rio, it saddened me immeasurably to see that things were even worse than they had been in the *Apprentis D'Auteuil* forty years ago.

Marina and I were taken into a separate room which housed approximately ten babies. It was staffed by one woman, who was attempting to make sure each child was adequately swaddled. We were led to a crib at the end of the room.

'You baby,' said the lady we had been following.

Marina and I peered down into the cot. I was taken aback by the shock of dark hair on top of the child's head, alongside the pair of huge, startled eyes which blinked at the two new faces they were observing for the first time.

'Oh, *bonjour*, little girl, *bonjour*!' said Marina. 'Or should I say *olá*? Look at her eyes, Atlas. They are enormous! And so open for one so young.'

'She looks like her great-grandmother,' I said, honestly.

'Really? How beautiful.' The lady gestured to the baby, and Marina gently took her in her arms.

We walked back through the overcrowded room. Just as we were about to leave, the lady clapped her hands, as if remembering something. '*Um momento, por favor!*' She ran back through the door.

The baby began to cry, and what started as an uncomfortable gurgle soon turned into full-on bawling. 'Oh, shhh, *chérie*, all will be well, I promise.'

'Do you need a bottle, Marina?' I hurriedly dived into the leather satchel that was slung over my shoulder.

'I actually feel a little faint,' Marina said. 'It's the heat and the sight of all those darling children. Would you mind taking her a moment?'

'Oh, I haven't held a baby for many years. I'm not sure…'

'It's very easy, everyone can do it. Here…' Marina gently passed the child to me. 'Be careful of her head. Rest it still on your elbow. There we are.' She quickly made her way to the sole, rusty chair in the corner of the room.

I looked down at the baby, who stared up into my eyes. Out of some sort of primal paternal instinct, I naturally began to rock her back and forth. To my surprise, the little girl stopped crying, and her face wrinkled itself into a gaze of bizarre contentment.

'There you are, Atlas. You're a natural,' Marina said with a wink whilst fanning herself vigorously.

'She is very beautiful,' I replied.

The lady returned, clutching something in her hand which looked like a pendant. She tried to give it to me, but as a novice baby holder, I simply shuffled awkwardly. Marina valiantly stood up and walked over to claim it.

'What is this?' she asked me. I looked vacantly back at the woman.

'For baby. From mama,' she said.

'Ah,' I replied, understanding. 'Thank you. *Obrigado*.' Marina slid the pendant into my back pocket. 'We'll leave now. Goodbye.'

The woman nodded at us again. 'Take good care. Please.' She put her hands together in a pleading gesture.

'I promise, we will.'

Our time in Rio was all too short, and before the day was over, the three of us were back in the first-class cabin of the jumbo jet. Marina cradled the baby, who had slept contentedly in her arms for the majority of the afternoon. As we climbed into the Brazilian sky, I had a thought.

'Marina…is it our responsibility to name her?'

She sighed, and gave me a weary smile. 'I am not sure. This whole thing has been such a whirlwind that I have not even considered it.'

About an hour into the flight, just as the cabin lights had been dimmed for passengers to get some sleep, the baby began to become unsettled, no doubt because of the discomfort of cabin pressurisation. As I shifted in my seat, I felt the pendant in my pocket. I reached inside and pulled it out.

It really was the most amazing piece. I examined the central gem's opalescent hue, admiring its blueish, billowy glow. I was almost certain it was a moonstone. The gems have acquired a certain amount of romantic lore about them, much like their namesake, becoming associated with love and protection. Without warning, a lump arrived in my throat at the thought of Cristina leaving the necklace with her child as a link to her past.

Despite Marina's best attempts to feed, rock and coo, the baby's screams were becoming louder and louder. Even with all her experience, Ma was looking somewhat frazzled.

'Shall I have a go?' I offered.

'Please,' she replied.

I stood up, and Ma passed her to me. 'Come on, little one. It's all right. I was nervous the first time I flew on an aeroplane, too.' I left first class, and walked her to the back of the aircraft. Gladly, she responded positively to the motion and the change of scenery. When we reached the rear of the 747, some of the stewardesses were preparing coffees in a dimly lit crew area. 'I'm sorry. I didn't mean to bother you.'

'Not at all, sir,' a young blonde girl replied. 'Aw, look at her! She's adorable.'

'Oh, thank you,' I said, returning her smile.

'It's so nice to see a father helping with the newborns. Most just turn their noses up and wait until they can move themselves about.' The stewardess leant over to gaze at the baby's face. 'Look at the way she stares at you. She loves her daddy so much.'

When she had finished fussing over my ward, I returned to the front of the aircraft with a quiet, if very awake, baby. I noticed that Marina had curled herself up and was snoozing happily in her seat. I certainly didn't blame her. The last two days had been positively draining, physically and mentally. I gingerly stepped over her and shuffled back into my own seat, before looking down at the child.

'Now then, we're both going to be very quiet, so that Marina can have a sleep. Is that agreeable to you?' I whispered. The baby blinked pointedly, and I chuckled. 'Good girl.' I had become aware of the sense of peace that holding the baby was giving me. The little bundle represented new beginnings, hope, opportunity... I wished for her an existence filled with love and joy. She gurgled at me. 'Shh, shh, little one,' I whispered.

Facing a long ten hours ahead, I looked around me for

inspiration, and my gaze landed on the window to my left. The moon was shining brightly onto the clouds below, filling the sky with a brilliant luminescence. 'Shall I tell you the story of the stars, little girl?' I gently shifted her head from my left elbow to my right, so that she was angled towards the window. 'There are more stars in the sky than grains of sand on all the world's beaches. I have always found that impossible to believe, but it is the truth. Since I was a boy, I have been fascinated with the infinite constellations, each one a symbol of possibility. You see, little one, stars are the givers of life. They provide light and warmth in the lonely dark sky.' The baby began to blink more slowly, my voice having the desired soothing effect. 'But there is one constellation out there which I find to be more magical than all the others combined, called the Pleiades. The story goes that there were seven sisters. Their father Atlas—with whom I share a name—was a Titan commanded by Zeus to hold up the earth. The sisters, though very different, lived happily together on the fresh new earth in its earliest days. But, after a chance meeting with the brutal hunter Orion, the girls became the objects of his relentless pursuit. So the sisters fled to the sky itself. You can see them tonight, look!' I bent my head to peer up at the heavens from the bottom of the small plane window and managed to sneak a view of my eternal companions. 'For my entire life, I have looked up at them for comfort and guidance. They are my protectors and my guiding lights. It is interesting that Maia appears brightest tonight. They say she used to outshine her sisters every night, but then, one day, Alcyone grew brighter. Actually, "Maia" means "Great One" in some translations. She was even seen by the Romans as their spring goddess, which is why our fifth month is known as "May".' I looked down at the baby, who had fallen asleep in my arms. 'Oh, did I bore you, little one?' I chuckled.

'Perhaps, *chéri*, but you did not bore me.' I turned around to see Marina gazing at me from the next-door seat.

'I do apologise, Marina. I didn't mean to wake you.'

'I was just dozing.' She glanced down at the baby. 'My goodness. You really do have the magic touch. She loves you.'

A smile crossed my lips. 'Do you think?'

'I know, *chéri*. You have saved her from a difficult and sorry existence.'

'We both have.'

Marina smiled. '*You* took on the duty of observing her family for years, and then sprang into action when someone faced danger. I do not know of anyone who would do what you have done. You are incredible, Atlas.'

'Thank you, Marina. That is generous of you to say.'

She looked past me and out of the window. 'Earlier, you asked me if it was our responsibility to name her. I think you already know what she is called.' She pointed out of the window to the moonlit landscape.

'Maia…' I replied.

47

Those first few weeks were a maelstrom of nappies, burping and long nights of feeding. I had insisted that Marina move into the main house so that I might provide support during the small hours. I think those were some of my favourite moments—when Maia and I were alone, in the still of the night, with only the sound of the lapping lake for company. She has taught me so much, without ever uttering a word. For thirty years, I have been so focused on finding Elle and chasing the prophecy given to me by Angelina that I have become closed off to others. I was self-absorbed, single-minded and obsessed. Baby Maia has opened my eyes. I am alive in a way which I have not been for years.

Marina says she knew the moment I laid eyes on Maia that I would never be able to part with her. Indeed, I had accepted my destiny before the wheels of the plane touched down at Charles de Gaulle. Maia had been as good as gold for the entire flight, and listened to my entire repertoire of Seven Sisters mythology to boot. To cradle such an innocent, fragile human in my ageing hands reminded me of this world's most comforting lesson: that whatever may happen, life prevails.

I had been nervous about telling Marina of my decision, worried that she would think me ill-equipped for the position of parent. I needn't have been so concerned. In fact, her face flooded with joy.

'Oh, this is truly wonderful news, *chéri*! Of course it is right that you legally adopt Maia. You need her as much as she needs you.'

I embraced her, before stating the inevitable. 'I cannot do it on my own, Marina.'

She laughed. 'Nor should you! I've watched you trying to put on a nappy. I think an orangutan could do it with more precision!'

'You're saying that you will stay and care for Maia?' I asked with excitement.

'Yes, *chéri*. Of course.'

Georg finalised the adoption papers. At his suggestion, Maia's surname has been registered as 'D'Aplièse' to prevent any unwelcome attention that may arise as a result of her being a 'Tanit'.

And just like that, I am a father.

As I approach the age of sixty, I have come to realise that Angelina's prophecy is unlikely to come true. Of course, I still have Georg search the databases of the world for Elle's name, but the physical trips to follow up on tenuous leads have become less frequent. Whenever I *am* away, I simply cannot wait to return to Atlantis and spend time with little Maia. I love nothing more than to take her toddling around the gardens and down to the shoreline, and to tell her lengthy bedtime stories about my adventures.

This does not mean, of course, that I am not deeply pained by the concept that I already have a biological daughter living in the world—one who needs me as much as little Maia does. I simply try not to think about it too much. For so long, I have put my faith in stars and prophecies. Perhaps it is time to live in the real world.

I was given a sharp reminder to do so earlier this evening, when I received a telephone call. Normally, when I pick up the receiver, it is Georg. My calls are screened through his firm, to prevent any unwanted contact from Eszu (who, by the way, has been as quiet as a mouse).

'Good evening, Georg,' I said, answering the call.

'Hello?' replied a voice in a Norwegian accent.

'Horst?' I asked. He and Astrid, along with the Forbes family and Ralph Mackenzie, are the only humans I permit to have a direct line to Atlantis.

'Good evening, Bo. I hope I'm not troubling you?'

'Not at all, my dear friend. How are you?' I asked, slipping back into Norwegian—effortlessly, if I may brag.

'Oh, physically, I am well, as is Astrid.'

I picked up the telephone unit and took a seat in my leather office chair. 'I read about Felix's latest composition in *The Instrumentalist* magazine. Bravo! You must be very proud.'

When he replied, Horst sounded grim. 'Proud is the last thing I am of my grandson.'

'Oh.' I was taken aback.

'Before I get into that, tell me, *Papa*, how is young Maia?' he asked.

'Incredibly well! Thank you for asking, Horst. Just this morning I caught her reading *Winnie the Pooh* aloud to herself. Not *actually* reading it—she's still only three. But she was adjusting her voice for different characters, just as I do when I narrate it to her myself...' I had to stop myself gushing.

Horst chuckled. 'Children are a blessing.'

'She teaches me something new every day,' I said, mindlessly curling the wire of the phone around my finger. 'Even if that thing is how to scrub chocolate out of a shirt.'

'I'm very happy to hear that the both of you are getting along so famously.' There was a pause on the line. 'Dare I ask about Elle?'

'There is nothing to report, I'm afraid to say, Horst. As each day passes I lose more hope. As you know, I will never stop my search, but I have Maia to focus on now.'

'I know you do.'

I was struggling to hear my old friend down the line. 'Sorry, Horst, it's a little difficult to hear you. Is there any way you could speak a little louder?'

'Uh...no, I'm afraid not. Astrid's asleep upstairs, and the matter I wish to discuss should remain private between you and me.'

I sat up in my chair. 'Is everything all right?'

Horst exhaled. 'Frankly, my old friend, it is not.' He tutted. 'It's Felix. He's got himself into a rather difficult situation.'

'I see. Well, I'll provide any advice I can.'

'As you know, Felix has become famous here in Bergen. In fact, in all of Norway. People know him as the orphan of the great Pip Halvorsen and his beautiful wife Karine, who died so tragically when their son was an infant. There have been articles on it, and I dare say that the prodigal son has begun to believe in his own myth.'

'I see,' I replied, not entirely sure of how to respond.

'All this has been compounded by the fact that he has been given a teaching role at the University of Bergen. There are many young women there...'

I didn't like where this conversation was going. 'Young women?'

'Yes. Whenever Astrid and I see him, which is rare these days, there is a new one on his arm. And he drinks far too much.' Horst gave an exhausted sigh.

I thought for a moment. 'He is a young man with a little fame and notoriety. I think it would be naive to expect anything else,' I encouraged. 'Hopefully it is a phase he will grow out of as the years pass.'

Horst guffawed. 'Not if he keeps drinking. He will simply disintegrate.'

I considered the help I could offer. 'You know, there are some highly reputable rehabilitation clinics available across Europe. As you know, my friend, there is no problem when it comes to money. Perhaps you would allow me to finance a treatment plan for Felix?'

'Thank you, Bo. But I understand the key to successful rehabilitation is to want to be rehabilitated, which I can most emphatically confirm Felix does not. Anyway,' Horst continued, 'the matter at hand is more complex.'

I stood up in anticipation. 'Please, tell me exactly what you mean.'

'Two days ago, whilst I was out shopping for groceries in Bergen, a young woman approached me. She looked pale and ashen, as if she had been deprived of sleep for many weeks. She said her name was Martha, and that she was pregnant with twins.'

'Ah,' I said, beginning to understand.

'I wished her well, and asked her what it had to do with me. Then she told me that Felix was the father.'

'Oh Horst.'

'She said she was a student of his, and that they were deeply, deeply in love. But apparently my grandson will not respond to her requests for support.'

I felt deeply for the man who had shown me such kindness. 'This is the last thing you and Astrid need, Horst.'

'Quite. But it gets worse. When I met her, Martha seemed somehow...troubled. The way she spoke and the frantic look in her eye... So I told her not to worry, took her telephone number, and told her I would contact Felix, to buy me a little time. Despite everything, I was giving my grandson the benefit of the doubt. I went to see him in his cabin that evening. He was shocked when he opened the door to me, and desperately tried to hide the empty bottles as I walked inside. I told him about the woman in the supermarket.'

'How did he respond?'

'Angrily. He said that Martha had taken one look at him at the university and immediately fallen head over heels in love, to the point of obsession. I asked him if he had slept with her, and he admitted to it. So, naturally, I told him he was to come with me and take responsibility for his actions.'

'What did he say to that?'

'He flat out refused. He said that Martha had a long-term partner, and it made logical sense that the pregnancy was his doing, rather than his own.'

I rubbed my eyes with my free hand. 'I see.'

'Felix told me that Martha suffers from mental health issues too numerous to mention. He begged me to believe that she is a danger to him.'

I pondered the situation. 'Do you believe him?'

Horst sighed. 'After my confrontation with Felix, I met up with Martha at a restaurant outside of the city. She described her romantic encounters with my grandson in a little too much detail, including dates, and it seems to me that there is little doubt. Felix is the father.'

It was very difficult to know how to advise Horst. 'Right,' was all I managed in response.

'But…' Horst was clearly finding every second of this painful. 'I think Felix is right about Martha. She does seem to be completely obsessed with him, despite the fact they were only together twice. Not that it excuses Felix's actions, but I at least take his point about the young lady's mental health.'

I crossed over to my bookshelf, and picked up the lucky frog that Pip had gifted me on the *Hurtigruten*. 'Is the child well in the womb?' I enquired.

'Children,' Horst replied sullenly. 'She's having twins. The ultrasound confirmed it.'

'Forgive me, is that where they are able to bring up an image of the baby? Or babies in this case?'

'Yes.' Horst took a moment to gather himself. 'This is where things become absurd. I asked Martha if she knew the sex of the children. She nodded, and proudly told me that she was expecting a boy. But when she informed me the other was a girl, she rolled her eyes and grimaced.'

I frowned. 'So she was pleased to learn about her son, but not her daughter?'

'Precisely. Martha said that she and Felix were going to have a perfect boy, the next great Halvorsen man.' Horst groaned. 'When I asked about her daughter, she simply shrugged, as if totally dismissing her existence.'

I gripped the lucky frog tightly, as if willing it to somehow improve the situation. 'Good Lord. Why?'

'As I told you, this young woman is deeply mentally troubled.'

'Does Astrid know anything of this situation?'

'No. I won't burden her with it until I have to. And rest assured, I will have to. These are my great-grandchildren…my dear son's grandchildren. I cannot ignore Martha and the situation which has presented itself.'

I understood Horst's sentiment. It's doubtless that I would have felt the same were I in his shoes. 'What do you plan to do?'

Horst took a deep breath. 'There is no chance of Felix

accepting responsibility and doing the decent thing. I feel ashamed of his behaviour.' His voice cracked a little. 'And so would his father.' Horst cleared his throat and regathered his composure. 'Apologies, Bo. Anyway, I have concluded that we must take Martha in after she gives birth. I am not convinced that the babies will be safe on their own. I owe it to my son, and to Karine, to make sure their bloodline is unharmed.'

Did this man's kindness know no bounds? 'That's...very noble of you, Horst,' I replied.

'But...Bo. I am a ninety-three-year-old man. My days are severely numbered. Astrid is seventy-eight, and will live longer, but who knows. We have very little money, most of it gone on Felix's education, and getting him out of the sticky situations in which he has found himself.'

'Say no more, Horst. I will write a cheque...'

'Thank you, but it is not your money I wish to ask you for.'

'Then what is it, my friend?' I heard Horst shifting down the line.

'Your love. I know the joy that Maia has brought you over the last three years. There is a lightness in your voice, a song from deep within which I had not heard since our evenings playing music together in my cottage. With one child, I believe Astrid and I will just about manage. But with two, quite simply, we will not.'

My pulse had begun to quicken. 'What are you asking, Horst?'

'The little girl. Would you take the little girl?'

I sank back into the chair in shock. What was I supposed to say to such an enormous request? 'I... Horst...'

He continued his plea. 'I know it is more than any one man should ever ask of another. But in truth, I do not know what else to do, Bo. Martha is ill, and her daughter will not receive the love and care she deserves as long as her twin brother exists.' Horst's breath suddenly quickened, and he let out a sob. 'There is no doubt in my mind that she will give the girl up for adoption. Astrid and I would gladly try to make up the shortfall, but we are aged and frail.'

We sat in an uncomfortable silence for a minute or so. 'I don't know what to say,' I eventually managed.

'No need to say anything now, Bo. Please take as much time as you require to give my proposal due consideration. I ask you because I know what a good man you are. Moreover, you are the only connection I have left to Pip and Karine. I know just how much they admired you, and how proud they would be if you would care for their grandchild.' Horst sobbed again.

'Those are very kind words, Horst.' It was devastating to hear him so distressed.

'For what it's worth, we always regretted not giving Pip a sibling. I have no doubt it would make little Maia's life even better if she had a little sister to play with.'

'I will…certainly give it plenty of thought.'

'Martha is due any day now. I will tell Astrid about everything once the children are born, and she will move into the cottage with us so that we may keep an eye on her.' Horst gathered himself. 'If…Astrid did not have to know about her granddaughter, that would be best. You know how kind she is. No doubt she would try to take on both, and I fear the consequences of that for all involved.'

I put the receiver down, poured myself a glass of Provençal rosé, and went to sit on the grass by the water's edge. It was hard to take in the gravity of the request Horst had just made of me. My mind was flooded by images of Pip, Karine, Elle and me in Bergen, and the happiness which we experienced there. I remembered the way Elle had looked at little Felix, a yearning in her eyes to mirror the family unit which her best friend had built.

I had once sworn that I would do anything to repay the kindness of the Halvorsen family.

I looked up to the heavens. 'Guide me, Pip. Tell me, Karine. Is this what you want?'

'Pa, pa, pa, pa, pa!' came a high-pitched squeal from behind me.

I looked over my shoulder to see Maia toddling towards me at speed, followed closely by a smiling Marina.

'Hello, my darling daughter!' I picked her up and held her in my arms. 'Have you had a good day?'

'Yes!' replied Maia enthusiastically.

'I can't quite believe it, but she managed to read the first few lines of *Madeline* to me,' said Ma, putting a hand on my shoulder.

'Goodness gracious me. Perhaps we have a little scholar on our hands, Marina!'

'Indeed, we might.'

I looked down at my daughter, who sat clapping in my lap. 'Maia?'

'Yeees,' she replied.

I tipped her chin up to meet my eyes. 'Would you like a little sister?'

I felt Marina's hand drop from my shoulder, but Maia's tiny face lit up. 'A sister? For me?'

'That's right.' I smiled. 'Just for you.' Maia looked up at Marina, and I followed her gaze. She stood quizzically above me, hand on her hips.

'Will she live in Ma's tummy?'

Her intelligence never failed to amaze me. 'No, she won't. She'll arrive magically, from the stars. Just like you. Would you like that?' Maia's eyes grew wide and began to shine. 'Can we read stories together?' she asked.

'Of course, my darling.'

'Then yes please!'

I chuckled. 'All right then. Ma and I will think about it.'

'Yes, that's right, Maia,' Marina interjected hurriedly. 'We will *think* about it. Come on, *chérie*. It is time for your bath.'

That night, I invited Georg to Atlantis, and he, Marina and I discussed the developing situation on the terrace.

'I know you feel compelled to do this, Atlas, but are you certain you can take on the responsibility? A second adoption will surely mean even less time for trips to look for Elle,' Georg pointed out.

I shook my head. 'I doubt that our new arrival will impact that side of things any more so than caring for Maia already does. The real question is for you, Marina. Could you cope with another newborn?'

'Atlas. You could give me one hundred babies to feed and care for and I would be happy. You know how much I love them, *chéri*.' She raised a critical eyebrow. 'Although next time, please talk to me before introducing such an idea to Maia.'

I held my hands up. 'I apologise. I just had to know what her reaction was. If she had been anything but overwhelmingly positive, I would not be giving Horst's request so much consideration.'

Ma nodded. 'I understand.' She cast her eyes out onto the quiet lake. 'For what it's worth, I think your friends would be eternally grateful to you,' she said quietly.

The next morning, I called Horst to confirm that I would do what he had asked. He cried with appreciation. Later that day, he contacted me again to say that Martha had been overjoyed at the plan. I asked if I could meet her to confirm that for myself, but Horst advised me that it would be better for the baby if Martha did not know who I was, given her mental state. Three days later, I received word that Martha had given birth, and Marina and I took the jet to Bergen.

The little girl we took home to Atlantis was notable for the tuft of bright red hair which adorned her head. For the entire journey, I noticed her fists were clenched in steely determination of something. Of what, I am not entirely sure.

The sight of Maia peering over the cot to look at her new baby sister melted my heart, and confirmed that my decision had been the right one. She was so quiet and gentle in her approach.

'Her name is Alcyone. After the star,' I whispered.

'Hello, Ally,' said Maia, doing her best to pronounce her sister's name.

'Yes,' I whispered. 'Hello, Ally.'

48

May 1980

Aside from a new lick of paint, Arthur Morston Books hadn't changed a bit in the thirty years I had been away. It was tremendously good to see Rupert Forbes again. He greeted me with a firm handshake and a hearty hug. 'By Jove, you hardly look a day older, old man!' he said with a broad grin across his face.

'I can only say the same of you.'

'You flatter me, Atlas, old bean, but you're lying through your teeth.' He pointed to his temple. 'Look at this bloody grey hair. I look like my grandfather!'

'Well, I don't know how to tell you this, Rupert, but you *are* a grandfather these days.'

He smiled. 'Gosh. Am I?! Don't spread such vile rumours!'

I laughed. 'How are the boys?'

'Oh, grand, thank you. We just celebrated Orlando's fifth birthday. Louise gave him the complete works of Dickens. I said she was crackers, but apparently he's already finished *A Christmas Carol*. At five!'

'Goodness me. You've a genius in the ranks! And how is... um...forgive me, Rupert...Owenmus?'

'Not to worry old sport, I can hardly remember myself. Oenomaus. Poor bugger. I tried to tell Laurence he'd suffer with that name, but Vivienne was set on it apparently. Although I'm proud to say he hasn't let it hold him back. He's captain of the prep school rugby team.'

After all these years, Rupert's chipper British demeanour could still lift my spirits. Nonetheless, I had not made the trip without trepidation. He had invited me to London to 'share some important news', which I assumed was related to Kreeg. Although he was now retired, Rupert still maintained connections within British intelligence. He would kindly liaise with Georg if anything significant cropped up…but had insisted that I made the trip for this matter.

Rupert locked the door to the bookshop and turned the *closed* sign around to face outwards. 'How are the family? I imagine those little girls give you quite the runaround!'

'Oh, they do. They're three and six now, would you believe! Marina and I have taken to calling them "the terrible twosome"!'

He handed me the cup of tea he had prepared in the flat upstairs. 'Is that right? You know, I really admire you. What are you now, sixty?'

'Sixty-two,' I confirmed.

'Gosh. Sixty-two and the adoptive father of two girls. I don't know how you have the energy, old boy!'

'I know it's a cliché, but I really mean it when I say they've given me a new lease of life. I feel as young now as I ever did.'

'That's wonderful to hear, Atlas, it really is.' He gestured to a pair of plush chesterfield chairs nearer the back of the shop. 'Come and take a seat.' I followed him over, past the *Poetry* and *Philosophy* shelves.

'It's the oddest thing,' I remarked, 'but it still *smells* the same in here.'

'That's books for you, Atlas. Dependable and unchanging. I find it bizarre to think that there might well be some volumes you and Elle put on the shelves thirty years ago which haven't sold.' We sank ourselves into the wing-backed chairs.

'Is that why I'm here, Rupert?' I asked nervously. 'Have you discovered something about Elle?' After all these years, my greatest fear is to be told that her location has been found, and she is no longer living.

Rupert shook his head. 'Sorry, old sport. Still nothing on that front.' He sighed. 'I'm terribly ashamed that I haven't been able to come up with the goods there.' He took a sip of his tea. 'Wherever she is, she is well and truly hidden.'

I nodded solemnly. 'I know. Please don't blame yourself, Rupert, Georg's had PIs and intelligence firms across the globe search for her. No one has ever found anything.'

He furrowed his brow. 'It's awfully unusual. Normally when a person disappears, there's *something* that gets left behind which helps us to find them. But it's as if your Elle has vanished into thin air. I admire you, Atlas. You've been searching for her for what, thirty years now? And you have never given up.'

'I could never forgive myself if I did,' I said quietly.

'I know. As for that thorn in your side from years gone by, Kreeg Eszu...' He shrugged. 'The man still seems to be holed up in that enormous compound of his.'

'Yes.' I stared at the door that led to the flat, which Elle and I had cowered behind three decades ago. 'I can only assume that when his wife died he lost the will to live himself. He just...gave up the hunt.'

Rupert narrowed his eyes as he contemplated the possibility. 'I think that's a fair bet. How old would the son be now?'

It took me a moment to calculate. 'I think he's roughly the same age as Maia. Perhaps six or seven?'

'Poor little chap. Rough to lose a mother. And to have that psychopath as a father... I can't imagine what it's like for the boy.'

I hadn't really given it due consideration. 'I suppose you're right, Rupert, yes. I do not envy Kreeg Junior.'

'No, indeed not.' He set down his cup and saucer. 'Now, on to the matter at hand, if it's all right with you?'

'Yes, please proceed. I'm intrigued.'

'Righto,' Rupert said, putting the tips of his fingers together. 'Where to begin... Do you recall the Vaughan-Forbes split in the forties? When Louise's father Archie died, and Teddy inherited High Weald?'

'Pretty clearly, yes.'

'Good, that's helpful. Are you aware that Teddy went on to marry an Irish woman name Dixie? And together they had Michael?'

'Vaguely.' In all honesty, Teddy Vaughan's lineage had hardly been on my list of priorities.

'Not to worry, the details aren't important. Going a little further back, do you have any memory of a woman named Tessie Smith from your time at High Weald?'

Now there was a name I hadn't heard for a long time. But I had not forgotten the poor woman's difficult circumstances. 'I do indeed. She was a Land Girl.'

Rupert looked pleased. 'Perfectly correct, old sport.'

I took a moment to sip some tea and recall her in my mind. 'As a matter of fact, Tessie was pretty friendly with Elle.'

Rupert nodded sagely. 'I thought that may have been the case.' He inhaled deeply. 'Now, prepare yourself. I'm in possession of a bit of a Vaughan family bombshell here. Basically, there's no delicate way to put this, but—'

'Tessie fell pregnant with Teddy's baby, and was paid off by Flora,' I replied, coldly defusing his bombshell. Rupert looked a little crestfallen.

'Righto, so it was common knowledge amongst the staff...' I gave a small laugh at his indignant response. He looked mortified. 'Sorry. I didn't mean to offend you...'

I put a hand up to reassure him. 'You didn't at all,' I replied honestly. 'In answer to your question, yes, it was, I'm afraid. We all knew. Tessie hardly kept it a secret.'

Rupert put his head in his hands and managed a chuckle. 'Dear, dear. That Teddy, eh? What a wild soul.' He regathered his thoughts. 'To bring you up to date, Tessie died five years ago now, in nineteen seventy-five.'

'I'm sorry to learn that. Do you know if she went on to birth Teddy's child?'

'She did indeed. Her name is Patricia Brown.'

'Brown?'

'The surname of her eventual husband. Also now deceased.'

'I see.' It was a little difficult to keep up, but I was doing my best.

'Now, to be absolutely clear, I knew nothing of the situation I am describing until the last few weeks. Apparently, Louise was fairly clued up on it all, but never thought to tell me, as it was

Tessie's private business.'

I smiled at Louise's loyalty. Her mother would be proud. 'Why are you telling me all this, Rupert?'

He looked around the empty bookshop, as if to check for any unwelcome ears. I do not doubt that this was a habit he had picked up from his years of service. 'A few days ago now, I received a telephone call from Buckingham Palace.'

'Buckingham Palace? As in the British royal family?' I asked, stunned.

Rupert looked satisfied at my response. 'Correct…although it was not Her Majesty herself making the call! It was a member of the royal intelligence team.' He paused for a moment, and it was difficult not to attribute it to dramatic effect. 'Anyway, to cut a long story short, I have a little piece of news of which I dare say you were *not* aware.'

I was on tenterhooks. 'And what is that?'

'Louise's mother, Lady Flora Vaughan—née MacNichol— was the lovechild of King Edward VII.'

To be fair to Rupert, his dramatic pause had been earnt. I shook my head in disbelief. 'What on earth?'

Rupert grinned widely. He was enjoying this. 'I know. It's the truth, so I am assured.'

I gave a shocked guffaw. 'How incredible. Did Louise know *that* part of the story?'

'Most emphatically not, dear chap, and it must remain that way.' Rupert suddenly looked stern.

'She *still* doesn't know?'

'No. As a member of the British intelligence family, I am trusted, nay *duty-bound*, to keep such sensitive information to myself, as the palace are aware.'

I put my arms out and looked around the bookshop. 'Well, Rupert, it's a good job I'm not working for the Soviets then, isn't it? Considering you haven't even shared this information with your wife, why on earth are you telling me?'

'I'll get to that in a minute.' He took a moment to formulate his next sentence. 'If you are the direct descendant of a British monarch, it transpires that the royal family…keep tabs on things.' He shuffled awkwardly in his chair. 'To, you know, avoid any *embarrassment* down the line which might...'

'Damage the brand?' I suggested.

'That's right,' Rupert confirmed. 'To that end, the palace have followed the MacNichol dynasty with interest. And so, they observed Tessie Smith, who by all accounts led a quiet and largely uninteresting life.'

'So why did they feel the need to get in touch with you?' I enquired.

Rupert cleared his throat. 'Tessie and Teddy's daughter, Patricia, is not the shy and retiring type of which the palace approve. She is staunchly Catholic, to the point of detriment.'

'What's the expression...'—I searched my head for English phraseology—'fire and brimstone?'

Rupert snapped his fingers. '*Precisely*. From what the palace have told me, Patricia herself has two daughters. The first, Petula, was born eighteen years ago. She's apparently doing very well these days, and is a student at my own *alma mater*—the University of Cambridge.'

I was pleased to hear it. 'What a wonderful achievement considering the challenges she must have faced in her life.'

'I couldn't agree more. Now, in terms of the second child...there is a significant age gap. In fact, it seems that Patricia has only just given birth.'

I was doing my best to keep up. 'Didn't you mention that her husband had died?'

Rupert nodded. '*Precisely*. The palace can find no record of the new baby's father. We can therefore surmise that the child was conceived and born out of wedlock, which would disgust Patricia's Catholic community.'

'So what's happened to the baby?'

Rupert stood up. '*That*, Atlas, is the reason I got a call from the palace a few days ago. It seems that Miss Patricia has given away her new baby to an orphanage in the East End to cover up her perceived shame.' He crossed over to the old wooden desk which had once been mine.

'I'm still struggling to understand why the palace saw fit to phone you. If they're concerned about reputational damage, how on earth could a baby who knows nothing of her own history possibly tell the tabloids that she has a distant claim to the throne?!'

Rupert gave a shrug as he rifled through some papers. 'I asked this very question myself. The palace said to me that the late king cared greatly about his family, and that they were simply doing their duty by informing me.' He paused and looked out onto the bustling Kensington Church Street. 'I suppose the idea in this particular instance is that the baby should be adopted and properly cared for.'

I stood and walked over to the desk myself. 'But they wouldn't inform just anyone, I'm assuming...'

'No. You're quite right there. It is because I am formerly of MI5.'

'So, are the palace expecting you to act upon their information?'

Rupert wouldn't meet my eye, and continued to shuffle through documents. 'There is a certain element of that, yes.' He came across what he had been searching for. 'Now. I have something for you.' He handed me a white envelope.

It was labelled, in scraggly handwriting:

Eleanor Tanit c/o Louise Forbes at the bookshop

'A couple of weeks ago, that was dropped through the letter box here, along with a letter for Louise, and a note from Tessie's solicitor. The note apologised for the time it took to work out who 'Louise Forbes at the bookshop' was.

I examined the envelope, which appeared unsealed. 'Have you read it?'

'No, old boy. But I've read Louise's, and I'd imagine the content is quite similar.'

I opened the envelope and scanned the contents.

Hello Eleanor,
Hope you're well, my dear. Sorry I ain't been in touch in all these years. I hope you remember me!
I've been a bit poorly of late, and I just wanted to make sure I wrote to everyone that was kind to me back in them days at High Weald.

You in particular was always lovely. As you know it was hard back then, and not everyone thought I'd done right in telling people about me and Teddy and the baby.

But you told me to stick up for myself and that I'd be all right.

And do you know what, I was! I went on to have a lovely little girl, Patricia, who has given me a lot of joy over the years. Even if she is a bit prickly on occasion, she means well. She and her husband also gave me a lovely granddaughter too.

I've done all right for myself in the end.

Anyway, I'll wrap up now to save me rambling. Just wanted to say thank you while I've still got breath in me lungs. Send my love to that feller of yours, too.

Love your friend,
Tessie x

I put the letter back in the envelope. 'I didn't know Elle's friendship meant so much to her.'

'Nor I Louise's,' Rupert replied. 'She was ever so emotional after reading hers. It was very good of Tessie to send those, isn't it? It says a great deal about her character.'

'It does,' I said quietly.

'I'm only sorry that we haven't been able to get the letter you've just read to Tessie's intended recipient.'

'So am I,' I whispered. A pregnant pause hung between us, as I stared at my old friend. 'I know what you're going to ask of me, Rupert.'

He nodded slowly. 'Before you say anything, I've considered all the options. I'm a decade older than you, and Louise isn't far behind. Of course, I thought about asking Laurence and Vivienne, but they're hard up spending all their cash sending the boys to a boarding school which they cannot afford. To make matters worse, they've just found out young Orlando is epileptic. They couldn't handle another child.'

I took a deep breath. 'What about Teddy's side of the family? You know, the ones that live in the enormous country estate? Is there not enough room for the baby there?'

Rupert ran his hands through his hair. 'You're right. Teddy and Dixie still inhabit High Weald. Their son Michael is a decent sort. In fact, just had a daughter of his own, Marguerite.'

'Wouldn't she like a playmate, Rupert? She's literally a blood relative!'

Rupert put a hand on my shoulder. 'Please believe me when I say I've given it consideration. But the knock-on effects of sharing information about the situation with Michael might upset the palace.'

His comment served to annoy me. Why was the indiscretion of a reprobate being made my problem? 'Well, we wouldn't want that, would we?' I took several steps away and tried to calm myself by looking at the illustrations on display in the children's section.

'To be very honest, old boy, no. The firm can be quite aggressive when they want to be, let me tell you. There's a reason they've survived as long as they have.' I heard him take a nervous gulp of tea.

I stared at the beautifully arranged volumes of *Alice in Wonderland* which had no doubt been delicately placed by Louise. I picked one up, cracked the spine and inhaled its vanilla-like essence. Turning around, I took in the shop, and was transported back to the heady days when Elle and I did little but read and restock the shelves. We had nothing but each other, and we were happy. None of it would have been possible without the kindness of Rupert and Louise, and before them, Archie and Flora. Just as with the Halvorsens, I had vowed to myself that I would do anything to repay the Vaughan family.

I already knew what my answer was going to be, but I wished to watch Rupert squirm a little more. 'So. It's not appropriate for Teddy's family to bear the burden of his "mistake". But it's all right for me, Mr Tanit the gardener?' I raised my eyebrows at him.

My question had the desired effect, and the normally measured Rupert looked as though he might combust. 'Of course it's not, dear chap. I'm not here to strong-arm or force this. But the simple fact is you've recently adopted two marvellous little girls and given both of them more love than they could ever have dreamt of, plus the most amazing lives. When I heard about this baby in need of a family, my mind immediately turned to you. Of course it did.'

I nodded. 'Yes. When you put it like that, I suppose I am a

logical solution.' I eyed him pointedly, declining to speak.

'Well?' Rupert floundered. 'Is there room for one more little princess in that magical palace of yours?'

I crossed over to him. 'Flora and Archie Vaughan took care of me and Elle when we were in need. As for you and Louise…without your help, I do not know if I would be alive today.' I gave him a wide smile and shook his hand. 'It would be my privilege to repay the favour.' Rupert looked like he might collapse with relief.

Later that afternoon, we found ourselves at the Metropolitan and City Foundlings Orphanage in the East End of London. Rupert had made the requisite telephone calls to ensure that the little girl would be able to travel back to Geneva with me later in the evening.

'The palace are very happy about the resolution,' he informed me in a discreet voice.

'I don't give a damn about the palace in all honesty, Rupert. This is about your family.' I looked down at the sleeping baby in my arms. 'And my own.'

49

August 1980

The peril of growing older is that we must watch those we love slip away one by one.

In July, my youngest companion from the RMS *Orient*, Eddie, rang me. He had been an official member of the Mackenzie clan for over twenty-five years, but his reason for contacting me at Atlantis was not a happy one. With a shaking voice, he informed me of his father's—Ralph's—passing.

I spent an hour on the telephone comforting Eddie and reminding him of all his family had done for me. I was profoundly upset by the news of Ralph's passing, and mourned a dear friend who had been trustworthy and steadfast to the last.

One week later, I found myself outside Alicia Hall in Adelaide for Ralph's memorial service. Far gone are the days where I would have to embark upon an epic sea voyage to reach Australia. Anyone could, in fact, be on the other side of the world in twenty-four hours. From the outside, the grounds of the hall appeared as opulent and luscious as ever, and as I walked through the gate, a well-dressed young man with blond hair approached me and shook my hand.

'Mr Tanit?' It was Eddie Mackenzie. 'Thank you for coming.'

'Eddie! I'm so sorry for your loss.'

He bowed his head. 'Thank you.'

In that moment, Eddie was a five-year-old child again, and I felt moved to put a comforting arm around his shoulder. 'I can't tell you how good it is to see you again. I'm sure you won't recall, but I remember you as a little boy. I was on the boat that brought you over here.'

Eddie smiled. 'So my father told me. He really thought very highly of you, Mr Tanit. He'd often tell stories of how you saved those men in the opal mines.'

That dramatic day seemed a lifetime ago. 'Well, without your pa, I'm not sure where I'd be. I owe him a great deal.'

The memorial was very well attended, with well over one hundred people present to watch the priest inter Ralph's ashes in the gardens of the hall. After the ceremony, I tracked down Ruth Mackenzie, who seemed very touched that I had made the effort to come to Alicia Hall to honour her husband.

There was, however, one individual that I had been desperate to reconnect with in Adelaide today—Sarah. Arguably, I owe all I am today to her caring nature. During the darkest time of my life, her optimism and warmth literally dragged me out of the depths of my despair. But there had been no sign of her.

'Do you remember her, Ruth?' I asked.

'Of course I do, Mr Tanit! In fact, she and her husband have visited Alicia Hall on several occasions over the years. She's even married to a Mercer!'

'Is she?' I asked, my heart soaring for her.

'Yes. He's a gentle man called Francis Abraham—the son of Kitty's boy, Charlie, and her maid's daughter, Alkina.'

The universe truly did work in mysterious ways. Never could I have predicted that Sarah the orphan would one day become a member of one of the world's wealthiest families. I recalled her ambitions from our first conversation: 'I'm 'oping I'll get a job and make some money of me own. And find a fella!'

Ruth continued her story. 'It's a very sweet tale, actually. Sarah met Francis at the Hermannsburg Mission when she visited with Kitty. And never left!'

I clapped my hands together in joy. 'I'm so thrilled she had a happy ending, Ruth. Goodness knows she deserved one.' I noticed Ruth wince slightly at my words. 'Might I ask why she and Francis are not in attendance today?'

Ruth sighed. 'I know that Eddie tried very hard to contact them. Sarah meant a lot to him in particular. But they proved very difficult to track down.'

'Why so?'

'The last address we had for them was Papunya. It's a great little village, full of creative types. It's where Francis and Sarah had their daughter, Lizzie.'

'Named after Queen Elizabeth, I bet! Very Sarah,' I reminisced with a warm smile.

'Spot on, Atlas. But Lizzie grew up to be a bit of a tearaway. She met a man in the village, who was a painter. Toba, I think his name was? He was a very talented Aboriginal artist, but I'm afraid to report that he was also a drunken reprobate. Sarah and Francis wouldn't give permission for their marriage. So Lizzie and the man eloped.'

It didn't escape my attention that Lizzie shared her mother's headstrong personality. 'I see. Where did they go?'

Ruth sighed. 'That's just the thing. No one knows. Apparently, Francis takes Sarah on enormous treks through the outback to try and find their daughter. They've basically become uncontactable.'

Poor old Sarah. She deserved nothing but happiness, and it seemed her own flesh and blood was denying her that. 'I would have dearly loved to have seen her,' I said to Ruth. 'Please say when you see her again that I asked after her, and send my very warmest wishes. I'd love to get back in touch after all these years.'

'I'll make sure to, Mr Tanit. Thank you again for coming.'

I spent the remainder of the afternoon milling around Alicia Hall, making conversation with employees of the Mercer empire, who all harboured immense admiration and respect for their former boss. Some still worked in the opal mines, and I greatly enjoyed exchanging stories about the old days and methods with them. As the sun began to dip lower and lower in the burning sky, I said my goodbyes to my hosts, and to Alicia Hall itself. It had been an honour to revisit one final time. Before I left, Eddie came jogging up to me.

'Mr Tanit, Mum said you were asking about Sarah?'

'Yes. I understand you can't contact her.'

'No, but…I had a thought. The other day I was sorting through some of Dad's documents, and I found Kitty Mercer's will. Apparently she owned a house in Broome, which she left to Sarah and Francis, to pass to Lizzie when she got older. If I had more time, I'd investigate it as a lead to their whereabouts. But I've got the businesses to run now, and everything's pretty turbulent.' Poor Eddie looked terrified at the prospect.

'How interesting. Broome, eh… Whereabouts is it?'

'It's a little mining town in the north-west of the country,' Eddie informed me. 'You'd need to hop on a plane to get there. But it's where Kitty spent a lot of her time in the early days. So there's that, if nothing else. Here, let me write down the address.'

'Thank you, Eddie.'

The following afternoon, I disembarked the propeller plane at Broome's tiny airport, having hopped on a connecting flight from Darwin. I took a bus along the port and into the town centre, which was small and dusty. The main road—Dampier Terrace—boasted a courthouse, a rickety tourist information centre and a pearling museum. I realised that the town was where it had all begun for the Mercers many years ago. I looked down the orange, barren road, and pictured the young, fair Kitty melting in the Antipodean sun and longing for the chill of the Scottish wind.

I made for the tourist information centre and asked for directions. 'Do you know how I find this address, please?' I asked, handing the attendant the piece of paper I'd received from Eddie.

'Of course, mate, just follow the main road out of town for about a mile. You can't miss it, unless you decide to have a walkabout in the bush!'

I followed the man's instructions. My trek up the road took me the best part of an hour in the punishing heat, and I was grateful to finally see what I was surprised to find was a relatively modest construction. The Broome house was a far cry from Alicia Hall. The house's wooden frontage was old and worn, and the beams which held up the awning looked like they might snap at any moment. Next to the house was a small tin-roofed bungalow. Given the choice, I'm honestly not sure which I would have chosen to inhabit.

The place was silent, and I didn't hold out much hope for the presence of any occupants. Nonetheless, I'd come this far, and went to knock on the door. As I climbed the creaking steps up to the porch, I noticed that the front door was ajar. I pushed it open ever so slightly.

'Hello? Is anybody at home? Hello?' The house remained silent. 'Sarah? Are you in, Sarah? Francis?' I took a step inside.

I made my way through the hallway and called up the stairs but received no response, so I resigned myself to returning to town. As I walked back to the front door, I glanced into the messy kitchen. The tap was dripping into the sink, so I went to tighten it. As I did so, I noticed a half-drunk cup of coffee on the kitchen table with a small amount of mould growing on top. This piqued my curiosity, and I opened the fridge. Sure enough, there was a pint of off milk, along with some stale bread and cheese.

Someone had been here recently. Judging by the state of the perishables, perhaps only a few days ago. With renewed hope, I made my way back into Broome and entered the first bar I came across to quiz the locals.

Luggers was dark and gloomy, but acted as a retreat from the soaring temperature outside. I took a seat on the decrepit bar stool and ordered an orange juice. Once I had built up enough courage, I asked the barman if he knew Sarah or Francis Abraham.

He momentarily stopped polishing glasses to think. 'Those names don't ring any bells, mate. Sorry.'

I sighed. 'No problem. They own the old house just out of town. I thought they may have been here recently.'

A man at the other end of the bar, who was nursing a tall, frothy beer, spoke up. 'What, you mean the old Mercer place?'

I turned to face him. 'Yes, that's exactly right.'

The man scratched his chin. 'Hmm. Strange. There was someone at the house recently. But not the couple you've just described.'

I left my stool and moved closer to him. 'May I ask who it was?'

He frowned. 'A young girl. She was up the duff, actually.'

'She was pregnant?'

'That's right, mate, looked like she was about to pop.' He sniffed and took a swig of his beer. 'My wife runs the grocery store over the road. She dropped a few bits and pieces round for her a while back.'

'That's very helpful, thank you.'

The man shrugged and returned his attention to his drink. Who had been in Kitty's old home? I would have been inclined to think it was a criminal, but everything looked to be in relative order. Plus, I didn't know too many pregnant thieves who ordered groceries and made themselves coffee. Could it be...

I downed my orange juice and walked out of the bar, the bright sun stinging my eyes. I returned to the visitor information centre, and asked for directions to the nearest hospital. It was a very long shot, but I hoped that the individual I'd just missed at the house had stopped drinking her cup of coffee because she had gone into labour.

I must note, reader, that barrelling into Broome Hospital to ask about a stranger I had never met was one of the more bizarre things I have done in my life. Within fifteen minutes, I had reached a building that looked small and pedestrian. Nonetheless, when I stepped inside, I was pleased to learn that it was indistinguishable from any medical centre in Geneva.

I hurried over to the receptionist. 'I'm terribly sorry, but I'm looking for a woman who's recently had a baby. Or maybe even is *having* a baby as we speak.'

She chuckled. 'You'll need to be a bit more specific than that, mate! What name?'

I paused for a moment. 'Elizabeth.'

'Elizabeth who?'

'Umm,' I put my head in my hands. 'Mercer. No, *Abraham*, I think. Wait, sorry, she got married, didn't she? I apologise, I don't know the surname.'

The woman looked at me like I was mad. 'Are you family,

sir? We don't let just anyone in. Particularly people who aren't even sure of the patient's name…'

'No, of course not, I perfectly understand. I won't ask to come in. I just wondered if you might be able to tell me if anyone by the name of Elizabeth has given birth here recently.'

The receptionist looked reticent to provide me with any details. 'I really shouldn't be doing that.'

'I appreciate that. I'm only asking because she's the daughter of a friend of mine, and hasn't been seen in quite a while. I'd just like to make sure she's all right. Once I've done that, I'll leave, I promise.'

She eyed me up and down. 'Fair enough, mate. Take a seat, I'll give maternity a ring.'

I spent a good half hour staring at the wall in the sterile white reception, wondering just what I would do if Lizzie was confirmed to be a patient. My train of thought was broken when I was approached by a woman with nut-brown skin and hazel-flecked eyes. She was dressed in a blue nurse's smock. 'Were you the gentleman asking about Elizabeth?'

'Yes, that's right.'

The nurse gave me a smile. 'Please follow me.' She led me down a corridor and into a private room with a bed and two chairs. 'Please have a seat. My name is Yindi.' She extended a hand.

'And I'm Atlas. It's good to meet you, Yindi.'

'Are you a friend of Elizabeth's?'

I rubbed my eyes. 'That's a little bit complicated, actually. Elizabeth and I have never met. But I am a…relation of her mother, Sarah's.' I lied, but knew that as a family member, I would be entitled to more information.

Yindi looked a little sad. 'Lizzie talked a lot about her mother.'

'That's why I'm in town, actually. I'm here to look for Sarah. I went to her house, but found it empty. Then I heard a pregnant woman had been living there recently, which is what brings me here.'

'Okay, Mr Atlas,' said Yindi, giving me a pat on the arm. 'A few weeks ago Lizzie came here. She was in labour.'

'Did she have anyone with her? Her husband?'

Yindi shook her head. 'No. She told me about him. He had abandoned her a month or so before.'

'Gosh, poor Lizzie.'

'Yes. And her labour was difficult. Nearly forty hours.' Yindi all but shuddered at the memory. 'The baby, she was a stubborn one. Didn't respond to our medicines. So I called upon the ancestors.'

I raised my eyebrows. 'Ah, you have Aboriginal heritage then?'

Yindi giggled. 'Can you not tell, Mr Atlas? I asked the ancestors to help the baby. And they did. But they also told me...' Yindi sighed. 'They told me that the mother would not live.'

My face fell. 'No... So Lizzie is no longer...' Yindi shook her head, and my heart ached for Sarah. 'What about the baby?'

'The little girl is healthy, and full of spirit.'

'I am glad to hear it. May I ask what happened to Lizzie?'

'She had a very bad postpartum infection. I tried hard to help her fight it, but the only medicines she responded to were traditional, which cannot save a life, merely improve its quality. Lizzie stayed alive for seven days, and the ancestors granted her a week with her new daughter before they took her. I'm sorry, Mr Atlas.'

I sat in silence for a while. I had come to Broome to find an old friend, but instead, had discovered some news which would no doubt devastate her. 'Where's Lizzie's baby?' I asked. 'Has she gone into specialist care?'

Yindi gave me a wry smile. 'No. Lizzie's baby is here.'

'Really? Still?'

Yindi nodded proudly. 'That's right. I have kept her here for as long as possible. She is a very special child, sir, the ancestors have told me. Full of fire! We nurses have tried to find a family to take her in, but have had no luck.'

I was surprised. 'Really? As sad as it is, I thought potential adopters were most keen on newborn children.'

Yindi looked downhearted. 'Yes. But the child is mixed race. People here...do not want such a child.'

My stomach turned. 'Good Lord. How terrible.'

'It is why I feel particularly protective of her.'

'I can absolutely understand. I feel compelled to thank you for looking after her, Yindi.'

'I have done my best to ensure the baby remains under my supervision for as long as possible, just as the ancestors asked me to do. But she cannot stay here at the hospital forever.' Yindi narrowed her eyes and grinned at me, as if we both shared some cosmic secret. 'Just today, the paperwork is being processed to hand her over to a local orphanage. What are the chances of that? This *very* day. And in walks Mr Atlas,' Yindi said with a knowing wink.

'That is…interesting timing.'

Yindi threw her head back and laughed. 'The ancestors said you would come. They seem to know you, Mr Atlas.'

Based on the things I had experienced in my life, I was beyond questioning such matters, even if I did not fully understand them. 'I have enormous respect for the ancestors. I lived here in Australia many years ago. A member of the Ngangkari saved my life, in more ways than one.'

Yindi seemed shocked. 'Ngangkari?' she asked, open-mouthed.

'That's right, yes.'

'Mr Atlas… I am descended from Ngangkari. My grandparents were healers for the Anangu people. It is why I became a nurse.'

A shiver travelled down my spine. 'My word.'

'You know the gifts of my people. I try to marry them here with…'—she gestured around the room—'penicillin and blood transfusions!'

I gave a laugh. 'That's a very powerful combination.'

'It is no wonder that the ancestors spoke so clearly of you! We are connected by our pasts, Mr Atlas. You are with a Ngangkari once again!' She put her hands together in prayer a moment, then stood up and made for the door. 'Come on then!' she cried.

'Oh.' I stood. 'Where are we going?'

'I shall introduce you to the baby!' Before I could say

anything else, she had grabbed my hand and started to walk me through the clinical corridors of Broome Hospital. Eventually, we reached a room filled with newborn infants, swaddled and lying in Perspex cribs. Yindi entered and wheeled out a baby who looked a little larger than the others. 'Come,' she gestured. 'We will sit in here.' I followed her into a small staffroom nearby, complete with sofas, magazines and tea-making facilities. Yindi lifted the baby from the cot. 'Would you like to hold her, Mr Atlas?'

'Oh, I…'

'Come on, you're an expert. You are already raising three daughters.'

'How did you know that?'

Yindi shrugged. 'The ancestors. They know everything!'

I sank into the old yellow sofa in disbelief. 'I'm rather inclined to think they do.'

Yindi passed the child to me, and I cradled her in my arms. She had a searching, probing gaze. 'You were right, Yindi. She really is very striking.' I looked across to Yindi, who seemed to be beaming from ear to ear. 'I feel stupid for not asking before, but did Lizzie name her?'

Yindi shook her head. 'No, Mr Atlas. After the birth she was rarely fully conscious.'

'It just breaks my heart.' The baby whined a little, and I rocked her gently. 'I know that the papers for the orphanage were due to be completed today, but surely now I'm here and able to identify her grandparents, she does not have to go into care?'

Yindi sighed. 'I'm afraid that's not quite true. We have already significantly bent state laws by allowing the child to stay in the hospital for so long.'

'All right.' I thought through the other options. '*If* she goes to the orphanage, is there a way that they can guarantee that she will be able to stay until Sarah and Francis come for her?'

Yindi bowed her head in what seemed to me like exasperation. 'That would not be fair on the child, because there is absolutely no guarantee they *will* ever come.'

I stood my ground. 'I'm absolutely positive they will come

immediately when they are made aware of the situation.'

'How do you intend to make them aware? You said you were looking for them. Why have they proved so difficult to find?' I explained that Sarah and Francis were currently searching the outback for their daughter. 'Mr Atlas,' Yindi replied firmly. 'Do you know how big Australia is? Francis could be leading Sarah on this quest for years.'

'I take your point,' I conceded.

Yindi put her hand on my shoulder, and a warm sensation passed through me. 'Forgive me for being so bold, Atlas, but I think you already know that it was more than chance that led you here today.'

'What do you mean?'

'The ancestors say that you are to father seven daughters.' She looked down at the baby.

I stood up and placed the baby back in her cot. 'Yindi, as much as I would love to help, I cannot take this child away when I know her grandparents would be overjoyed to find her.'

'They will not find her, Mr Atlas.'

I gently put my head against the door and took a deep breath. 'How can you say that?'

Yindi pointed upwards. 'I told you. Ancestors.' She shrugged.

'I cannot simply take your word for it.'

Yindi crossed over to me and put a hand on my back. There was that warm sensation again. I realised that I had felt something similar when Yarran had run his hands over my broken ribs in Coober Pedy. 'You have seen for yourself the power of the ancestors. Trust in them. Do not doubt their path.'

'I…'

'Mr Atlas, if this child is released to the orphanage today, as she has to be, then there is no chance of Sarah and Francis ever finding her. They might not even learn of her existence. But you could whisk her away to a life of love, comfort and family *today*.'

'I came to Australia for the funeral of an old friend of mine, Yindi. That's all.'

'You do not see the greater plan. What appear to you as a series of remarkable coincidences were mapped out in the stars long before you or I were born. It is not chance that you returned to Australia when this child needed a home. You returned because it was the right moment.'

Yindi's words resonated with me. After all I had seen in my life, who was I to question the omniscient nature of the universe? I had a thought. 'What if I were to take temporary custody of the baby? I will leave the details of my lawyer, Georg Hoffman, here at the hospital, so that if Sarah and Francis do arrive, they will be able to contact me straight away.'

Yindi chuckled. 'If it makes you feel better, of course you may do that. I will have everything entered into our official records, so that contact may be made. But Atlas, they will not. Never. The ancestors have shown me. She is yours. Daughter number five.'

'Four,' I replied. 'Perhaps the ancestors don't know *everything*.'

Yindi looked confused. 'No,' she replied. 'They do.'

50

1981

I must applaud Georg for a clever invention. In addition to the girls' name being registered as 'D'Aplièse', he quite rightly advised me that we should be cautious about my young daughters publicly stating that their father's name is 'Atlas'. My moniker is unique, and I have found over the years that it is one which easily sticks in the mind. The security of my family is my top priority, and even though Eszu is still holed up in his Athenian compound, I won't hesitate to take any measure I can to strengthen our anonymity.

When Georg had suggested that I employ a different name for my daughters to use, I had played around with an anagram of 'Atlas', which somehow felt better than concocting a pseudonym once more. I love my daughters more than anything, and the idea of lying to them in any way was abhorrent. There was nothing particularly satisfactory that arose from my first name alone, and so I added 'Pa' (which is what the girls call me) to try and help. After a moment or two of playing with combinations and possibilities, I arrived at 'Pa Salt', and laughed out loud.

Shortly after young Ally had arrived in our lives, Maia had remarked as she sat on my knee that I 'smelt of the sea'.

'I'm not sure that's a compliment, little Maia!' I laughed. 'Doesn't the sea smell of fish and seaweed?'

'No,' she replied firmly. 'It smells of...salt.'

I chuckled. 'Well, that's not too bad then, is it? Maybe it's because I'm always travelling.'

How perfect. From thereon in, I was known to all at Atlantis as 'Pa Salt'. I asked Marina to use it whenever she addressed me around the children, in addition to the two new members of staff who have recently joined our odd little family here on the shores of Lake Geneva.

Claudia, Georg's sister, has been employed as a full-time housekeeper and cook, responsible for feeding an ever-increasing number of mouths. After the arrival of baby number three, it became necessary for Marina to become a full-time nanny to the girls. Claudia did not arrive alone, either. She brought with her a young son—Christian—too. His father had left the picture not long after his birth, and I insisted that he was very welcome at Atlantis. Since his arrival, Claudia speaks German around the house, to remind her son of their heritage—a decision which I fully applaud. It is good for my children to hear as many languages as possible.

After a few days of half-heartedly tending the lawns and watering the flowers, I noted Christian staring longingly at the boat which was moored on the jetty.

'Do you like the water?' I had asked.

He nodded. 'Yes, sir.'

'We've talked about this, there is no need to address me as "sir". Pa Salt will do nicely, I promise you.' He nodded. 'Have you ever driven a boat?' I asked.

'Never.'

'Well.' I shrugged. 'Would you like to?' Christian's eyes grew wide. 'The lake is very quiet around here. Let's go and have some fun.'

We spent the afternoon cruising about on the tender. I recognised the unparalleled joy the young man experienced out on the water, and I informed Claudia that I would like to employ her son to run and maintain the boats, and act as the official transport between Atlantis and mainland Geneva. It is not a decision I have regretted a day since. Christian is polite, hardworking, and an asset to my staff, just like his mother.

So far, Yindi's prediction has been proved right—I have not

heard anything from either Sarah or Francis about their granddaughter. As difficult as it is to write, I am at least a little thankful for this, because Asterope and Celaeno have formed an incredibly close bond. Perhaps it is because they are so close in age, but they appear to all around them as spiritual twins. The thought of breaking them apart now is anathema to me.

Ever since that day at the hospital in Broome, I have not been able to forget Yindi's assertion that Celaeno was to be my fifth daughter, not my fourth. Although I have long abandoned the assumption that Angelina's prophecy will come true, I have recently begun to wonder about my interpretation of her words. Perhaps she meant that my destiny was to *adopt* seven daughters…but, at the same time, the theory simply did not tally with her assurance that my *first* daughter was already alive in 1951.

Eventually, the questions that ran through my head in the night became too much, and I booked a flight to Granada. Of course, I had no way of knowing if Angelina was still in the area, and if she was, exactly how to find her. So, when I got off the plane, I did the only thing I could, and returned to the plaza where I had met her all those years before, in the hope that she was still giving readings. I knew I would recognise her. After all, her face was imprinted on my subconscious after she had appeared to me in my dreams.

Even though the cloak of autumn was beginning to fall in Sacromonte, the Spanish sunshine was still blazing. I treated myself to a fresh lemonade from a local vendor, sat on a bench in the half-shade, and resigned myself to watch. The plaza had not changed in my thirty-year absence, like so much of the modern world. The cathedral bell shimmered in the golden light, just as I remembered, and the fountain spluttered and spurted in much the same pattern too. I even wagered that some of the pesetas in the bottom had been present at my last visit.

Hours passed in the square, and I began to reflect on how stupid I had been to return with no plan. I asked several locals, but my poor Spanish and general description of a younger Angelina got me nowhere. So I remained on the bench, and afternoon turned into evening. Eventually, the sound of the trickling water and the pleasant warmth of the setting sun relaxed me into sleep.

I was woken by a hand on my shoulder. Startled, I cursed myself that I had been so careless. Angelina could have strolled past, and I would never have known. I looked up at the stranger who had woken me, and did a double take.

'Hello again, Atlas.' Angelina's kind eyes met my own.

'Angelina! Good Lord!' I rubbed my eyes to confirm that I really was awake. After, Angelina was still present before me. It was most remarkable. Thirty years had passed, and although she was now the owner of one or two crow's feet, she hardly seemed to have aged a day. I jumped up and put out my hand. She smiled, took it, then pulled me close and kissed me on both cheeks. 'Angelina,' I was lost for words. 'You look almost exactly the same.'

'You're very kind, *señor*. I wish I could say the same for you. Look at that grey hair! It must be those *bébés* of yours, no?'

I still couldn't grasp that she actually stood before me 'I…just… Angelina, how did you know I would be here?'

She giggled, and sat down on the bench. 'You were expected.'

I slowly lowered myself back down. 'Expected?' I gestured up to the sky, and Angelina nodded. We sat for a while, taking each other in. 'It is very good to see you again.'

'I feel the same.' Angelina gave me a wide grin. 'Last time I saw you, the world which you carry on your shoulders was very heavy. Now, it seems it is as light as it ever has been. Would I be right…*Padre Sal?*'

I let out an exasperated sigh, as once more, the power of Angelina's insight was beyond my earthly comprehension. 'You would be, of course. Not that you need me to confirm that.'

Angelina smirked. 'You never know, Atlas. I am not able to interpret *everything.*'

I took a moment to compose myself. 'Angelina,' I began. 'Thirty years ago, you told me that I would father seven daughters. As I think you are aware, I assumed that I would find my Elle and we would have the children together.'

She shifted a little uncomfortably on the bench. 'I told you that you would be father to seven daughters. That was all I saw, nothing else. And now, you have five of them. My prediction is nearly complete, is it not?'

The assertion that Yindi had made in Broome was mirrored here. 'I have *four* daughters. Not five.'

Angelina was taken aback. She gave a frown, then edged closer to me. 'May I see your palm?'

'Of course.' I presented my right hand.

She studied it, then shook her head. 'I am surprised. I…' Angelina looked as if she was about to say something, but stopped herself. 'Sometimes the messages from the upper world can be confused.'

'How unfortunate,' I replied, noticing that Angelina had suddenly become awkward. I pulled my hand away. 'You told me thirty years ago that my first daughter was alive and already walked the earth, did you not?' Angelina looked hesitant, but closed her eyes and nodded. 'I know you cannot have possibly been referring to Maia, as she was not born until nineteen seventy-four. What exactly did you mean? I need to know, Angelina.'

Angelina inhaled deeply, and looked up to the cathedral bell as she formulated a response. 'I understand your frustration. Can I, just once more…?' she asked, gesturing to my hand. With a little hesitancy, I slowly returned it to her grasp, and she nodded in gratitude. After examining my palm more closely this time, she looked me dead in the eye. 'I was not wrong when I told you that your first daughter lived.'

My heart rate increased. 'You weren't?'

'No…' Angelina looked uncomfortable. 'I confess, it was my prediction that you would have found one another by now.' She looked down at the floor.

'So she *is* alive and…missing from my life?'

Angelina thought for a moment. 'That is a good way of phrasing it. Yes. She is "the missing sister".'

I put my head in my hands. 'I came here today in the hope that you would tell me that you had misinterpreted things. That, actually, my first daughter had not been born all that time ago.' I sniffed, as tears began to prick the back of my eyes. 'I have searched for half my life, and I have failed to find her and her mother.'

'But,' replied Angelina tentatively, 'you have found others

along the way.'

'My adopted girls?' I asked. She nodded gently. I leant back on the bench and craned my neck to the sky. The clouds burnt orange in the setting sun. 'Yes. I love them so much, Angelina. The universe brought us together through a remarkable set of circumstances.'

She contemplated my words. 'You say remarkable, I say inevitable.'

'Meaning?'

Angelina pursed her lips in thought. 'Humans are bound to one another, long before they meet in the physical world.'

My mouth had become dry, and I reached for the remnants of my lemonade which had been marinating under the bench. I took a gulp of the hot, sticky liquid and winced. 'Time is a cruel mistress, Angelina. Each day that passes the "missing sister" gets older, and my opportunity to be with her diminishes. I am becoming an old man. For God's sake, she'll be in her thirties by now.'

Angelina put a hand on my arm. 'Atlas, I have just examined your palm. I assure you, with a lifeline like that, I can confidently say that you have many years left on this earth.'

A group of young girls appeared on the plaza in front of us, and began to draw on the tiled ground in chalk. It reminded me of my first day at the *Apprentis d'Auteuil*, when some of the children had played hopscotch. A few moments later, that little villain Jondrette had tried to smash my violin…but Elle had saved me.

'I will never stop my search,' I resolved. 'Not until I find Elle and the missing sister.'

'I know,' Angelina replied quietly.

I was nervous about asking my next question. 'Do you think I will find her, Angelina? Be careful in filling me with false hope, as you have done before.'

'No hope is false, Atlas. Hope is a choice. Hope means hoping even when things seem hopeless. *Choose* to be hopeful, and amazing things can happen.' She gave me an encouraging pat on my knee.

'Then that is my choice.' I looked into the fountain. 'Perhaps I need to throw another peseta in.' My eyes drifted over to the alleyway where I had purchased the ice creams three decades ago. 'How is your little cousin, by the way? I'm so sorry, but I can't remember her name.'

Angelina's gaze momentarily lost its sparkle. 'Isadora. She is with the spirits now.'

'I'm so sorry, Angelina. Without her, we never would have met.'

Angelina ran her hands through her hair, which was as blonde and lustrous as ever. 'Do not be sorry, *señor*. Isadora lived a life full of love and laughter. She married her childhood sweetheart, Andrés, who she met right here in the plaza.'

'Were they happy together?'

'I have never known two people who brought so much joy to one another, *señor*.'

'Love is a beautiful thing.'

Angelina looked skyward, allowing the sun to warm her face for a moment. 'It is. But the upper world often has strange plans. Not even I can understand it all.'

'What do you mean?'

Angelina stood up and held her hand out to me. 'Come. We will take a walk up to the Alhambra, and I will tell you their story.'

I got to my feet, and Angelina took my arm. Together, we walked across the plaza in the direction of the setting sun. 'Andrés and Isadora tried for years to have a child, but could not conceive. Many times, they thought that they had succeeded, only for the baby to pass away in the womb after a few weeks.'

'Oh Angelina. How awful for them.' We left the plaza and made our way onto what used to be a very dusty road. In the intervening years, tarmac had been laid. It certainly would have made for a much more comfortable trip up from the station in 1951.

'I tried to help by consulting with the spirits, of course...but never received a response.' Angelina gave a sad shrug. 'I simply thought that it was not meant to be. Then, one day, twenty years into their relationship, a miracle occurred. Isadora found herself with child.'

'Wow.' I turned to her. 'That *does* sound miraculous.'

Angelina nodded, and her face brightened. '*Señor*, I have

never seen such happiness in a human as the day my beloved Isadora came to tell me she was three months pregnant.' She sighed wistfully. 'Andrés was exactly the same. We held a party in the caves.'

'Quite right, too.' The impressive Alhambra was just coming into view, and it appeared as magnificent as ever.

'After Andrés found out,' Angelina continued, 'he treated his wife like a precious china doll. He worked overtime, too, so that he could put away extra money for when the baby arrived. But then...' Angelina stopped and closed her eyes. 'Only a few months ago, Andrés perished after falling from his motorcycle. The roads were very slippery after a rainstorm, and his cargo was heavy.' She bowed her head, and I felt moved to embrace her. 'Isadora's heart was broken, as was her spirit. After Andrés died, she could not even eat or drink. I told her she must, for her baby's sake, but she began to slowly fade.'

'I'm sorry, Angelina.'

She stoically continued. 'The baby arrived a whole month early. I tried everything I could to save my cousin, but I could not stop the bleeding, and neither could the *ambulancia* when it eventually arrived in the hills.' A tear ran down Angelina's cheek. 'She died last week, only one day after the baby was born.'

'Angelina... I have no words. How awful.'

'Isadora called her baby Erizo. It means, how do you say...' She searched for the English translation. 'Pig from the hedge.'

'A hedgehog?' I queried.

'*Si*, yes. Hedgehog. Her hair sticks up, you see!' Despite everything, Angelina let out a laugh. 'So now we look after the little *erizo*, Pepe and I.'

'Pepe?' I asked.

'Our uncle...the brother of Lucía, whose statue you delivered to the Alhambra.'

I understood the connection. 'Got you.' We strolled for a little while longer, until we reached a fork in the road. One direction led straight up to the palace. From where we stood, about two hundred metres away, I could just make out the figure of Landowski's statue in the centre of the square.

'You know,' Angelina said, 'I think we will go this way.' She began to pull me towards the other road, which wound up towards the caves.

'Where are we going?'

'The day is growing old. We must go and meet Erizo. She will be happy to meet her new pa…'

I stopped in my tracks. 'What do you mean, Angelina?'

She gave me one of her winks. 'I told you, you were expected.'

Having resigned myself to Angelina's will, I followed her up into the hills of Sacromonte.

The caves which I had first glimpsed thirty years ago were most remarkable up close. I thought back to my time in the underground home in Coober Pedy, and there was no question—the Spanish equivalent was preferable by a long chalk. For one, they offered a breathtaking view of the world below. From the dusty road outside of Angelina's cave, I observed rows of olive groves, intersected only by the steep, winding paths that wove between the dwellings. In the valley beneath, the River Darro ran through verdurous trees, which were just beginning to turn from green to gold in the mellow September sunshine.

'Pepe?' Angelina called into the cave. 'He is here.'

I followed her inside, and saw a moustachioed man whose skin had been well baked and wrinkled by the Spanish heat over the years. He was bottle-feeding the baby, and humming a tune.

'*Hola, señor*,' he said, giving me an affirming nod.

'Pepe prefers to speak Spanish, I apologise.'

'No need, I am in his country with no knowledge of his language. I should be the one apologising. Please tell him that I'm so sorry for the losses he has endured in his life.'

Angelina did so. '*Gracias por su simpatía, señor*,' he said, bowing his head to me.

'Well, no time like the present, as they say. I will begin to pack Erizo's blankets. She has one which her mother and grandmother used. It would be nice if that could travel with her—'

I grabbed Angelina before she could move a muscle. 'Angelina, stop, please,' I begged. 'I know that you are able to communicate with the "upper world". But I have no right or, more importantly, wish to take Erizo away from you. I simply came here for another reading from an old friend. That is ALL.'

Angelina sighed. 'You may think that is all, but the upper world returned you here just at the moment you were needed.'

My blood pressure was beginning to rise. 'That's merely your interpretation of the situation. Do you not respect that I am reticent to take away a child from her own family?'

Angelina took my hand and led me out of the cave again, so that Pepe would be spared my angst. 'Atlas,' she replied, 'your arrival here is not by chance. Pepe and I cannot give Erizo the life she deserves. You, however, can.'

I shook my head. 'Angelina…this is a conversation I have had many times across the years. Families have practically begged me to take their descendants from them. And when they do, I find myself in the centre of the most hideous moral quandary.' My head had begun to spin. 'I…' Before I could say another word, I involuntarily found myself sinking to the floor.

Angelina ran back inside. '*Agua*,' she called to Pepe.

With my back against the rock, I stared across at the Alhambra Palace. The setting sun cast a rich orange glow on the towers that seemed to rise magically out of the dark green forest opposite the caves. Angelina returned with a mug of water, and I sipped it gratefully. She joined me on the rocky floor.

'Angelina, I worry every day that people might interpret me adopting my daughters as somehow…*wrong*. Moreover, I *myself* panic that I have deprived them of a chance to grow up in their native lands.' I put my water down beside me, and sank my head onto my knees.

Angelina squeezed my shoulder. 'I understand, Atlas. You would not be the man I thought you were if you did not have such concerns. But the universe smiles on you for all you have done.'

I lifted up my head and met her eye. 'With respect, Angelina, for my whole life I seem to have been governed by a power that I myself do not understand. You told me that my path was fixed.'

'It is, my friend. But you could have chosen not to walk it. No one has forced you into adopting your daughters. You did it because of your desire to help others. Did you not?'

I ran my hands through my hair. 'I suppose so.'

Angelina gave me a sympathetic smile. 'You talk as if I was

the first person to introduce you to the powers of the universe. But we both know I am not. As a little boy, you had eyes for the heavens. They kept you safe and guided you on your impossible journey.'

'They did,' I whispered.

We sat in silence for a long while, watching the Alhambra grow darker in the disappearing light. After a while, Angelina spoke again, softly this time. 'You have spared your daughters lives filled with poverty and heartbreak.'

'I know, Angelina. But I still wonder if it was right to take them away from their countries. I could have merely funded their lives from afar.'

'I fear you sometimes forget that *you* are owed some happiness too, Atlas. With one hand, the universe has taken much from you, but has given you so much with the other. Your daughters bring you more joy than you ever thought possible, do they not?'

'Of course.' The evening was now punctuated by the sound of the swifts flitting over the trees. I closed my eyes to listen.

Angelina continued. 'Since we first met, I have thought of you often, and consulted with the upper world. You are a *good* man, Atlas. Special, even. Perhaps there are not enough people to tell you this. So I am telling you. Okay? Believe me.'

I tried to withhold my tears. 'Thank you.'

'And…' Angelina said tentatively. She took my hand. 'Atlas, you *will* find the missing sister. This I swear to you.'

I sat bolt upright. 'I'm sorry?'

'You two will meet. But…you will need the help of all your other daughters. Without them, your paths will never cross.' She looked at me with a stern face and I gawped back at her. 'The six girls will lead you to the seventh.'

'Angelina,' I replied breathlessly, 'how do I—'

She put a finger to her mouth. 'Shh. I have nothing more to say. It is a message to you from the upper world, so I cannot answer the questions you may have.' She squeezed my hand tightly and turned back to face the Alhambra.

My panic had been replaced by euphoria. I cast my eyes to the burning sky and 'thanked' the upper world. 'So, Erizo is her name?' I asked Angelina.

She chuckled. 'No, it is not official. Just a silly name. After all, someone cannot really be called "hedgehog"! May I take it that after your assurance from the spirits, you will be leaving Sacromonte with your fifth daughter?' I nodded, beaming from ear to ear. 'Good! This is a happy day indeed.' Angelina stood up and dusted herself down. 'She will be the fifth star in your sky. So you will call her...'

'Taygete, yes.' Angelina offered me a hand, and I took it. She led me inside the cave once more.

'Come and see her.' I followed Angelina over to Pepe, who gave me the warmest of smiles.

'Meet your papa, Erizo.'

Pepe held her up to me, and I took her in my arms. 'Hello, baby,' I said to her.

'She is a special one, *señor*.'

'I know.'

'Actually, I think perhaps you do not. This little girl has the powers of the *bruja*.'

'Like you?' I asked.

Angelina nodded. 'Precisely. She is the last in this family.' Angelina gave me a steely look. 'As this little one grows up, she will see the world differently, and you must pay reverence and respect to it.'

I bowed my head. 'I promise I will.'

'Good.' She thought for a moment. 'She will not understand the ways of the *bruja* herself...' Angelina looked at the child. 'One day, you must send her back to me. When you do, I will be able to help her unlock her spiritual lineage.'

I had my eyes on a wooden chair in the corner of the room and walked towards it. 'May I?' I asked. Angelina nodded, and I sat. 'In truth, I have not considered the possibility of telling each of the girls about the circumstances of their birth, and how they came to be my daughters.'

Angelina looked a little surprised. 'No?'

I looked down at the innocent young life. She had closed her eyes and begun to sleep. 'Each of the girls, in one way or another, is directly linked to my flight from Kreeg Eszu. I worry that if I were to tell them about their pasts, it might somehow endanger them. I have deliberately tried to build as quiet a life as is possible.'

Angelina folded her arms and narrowed her eyes, deep in thought. 'Yes… I understand. But irrespective of that decision, you must keep your promise. One day, when the time is right, send her back to me. Do you swear?'

I wriggled an arm free from underneath the baby and offered my hand to Angelina. 'I do.' She shook it.

'Thank you, Atlas. Then she is yours.' Angelina gently stroked her kin's fluffy hair. Then she began to sing a lullaby in Spanish, and her sweet voice travelled out of the cave and into the valley below.

51

1982

'There's nothing I can think of which signals danger,' Georg said, taking a sip of strong black coffee as we sat in his office on the Rue du Rhône.'

'They rang Arthur Morston Books?'

'Yes, and Rupert Forbes passed on my contact details.'

'Rupert has no idea what this could be related to?'

'None at all, no.'

Earlier this morning, Georg had informed me about a telephone call from an American woman named Lashay Jones. She had asked to speak to me, stating that the matter was of great importance. Georg had told her that he was my representative, and she was free to speak to him in confidence, but Lashay simply refused. For reasons already stated on these pages, I am extremely reluctant to take mysterious phone calls from strangers.

'She definitely asked for Atlas Tanit?'

Georg nodded. 'One hundred per cent. She told me that she thought you worked at Arthur Morston Books. But there's nothing which suggests that this is related to Kreeg Eszu. I am confident it would be safe to speak to Miss Jones.'

I mulled it over. 'The timing is unusual, though, would you not agree?'

'Yes. A little,' Georg conceded.

One month ago, Lightning Communications had suddenly become active as a company. They had begun to build a client base in Greece, and promised businesses an opportunity to transmit 'coherence, credibility and ethics'. When I had first read those words, I couldn't help but throw my head back and laugh. Quite how that man could offer expertise in credibility and ethics with a straight face was beyond me. They'd also given themselves a logo—a lightning bolt emerging from a cloud. It seemed that Kreeg was taking a hands-on approach, too. We had photographs of him giving presentations, hosting business lunches and various articles on the company in local newspapers.

If Eszu had been grieving for the last few years, it appeared that time was over, and he was starting to re-emerge into society.

'You're sure that this isn't some way of Kreeg obtaining my exact location?'

Georg shook his head. 'My instincts tell me this is something altogether separate.'

I trusted my lawyer's judgement. 'All right then. Let's set up the call for tomorrow.'

The next day, I sat in my study waiting for Georg to patch Lashay through to Atlantis. As I waited, I surveyed my shelves, which were filled with artefacts and trinkets from my travels across the globe. These were interspersed with framed photographs of the girls and me. I picked up one of my favourites: an image of the six of us enjoying ice creams on the jetty of Atlantis. At ten on the dot, my office phone rang. I put the picture down and picked up the receiver. 'Atlas Tanit.'

A soothing, velvety voice replied in an American accent, 'Oh, hello, Mr Tanit. This is Lashay Jones. I believe you were expecting my call?'

'Hello, Lashay. Yes, I was, although I must admit I have absolutely no idea what it could be about.'

She took a deep breath. 'I'm sorry about that, Mr Tanit. I'm phoning from the Hale House Centre in Harlem, New York.'

I scanned my memory banks. 'I'm sorry, Miss Jones, I don't know the name.'

'Perhaps you've heard of Mother Hale? Clara Hale?'

'I regret that I have not.'

There was a pause on the line as Lashay realised that this would require more explaining than she had anticipated. 'I appreciate that you're in Europe, so the name might not be as meaningful over there. The Hale House Centre is a children's home here in New York.' My heart skipped a beat. Was this the call I had been dreading? A children's home who, for some reason, wanted one of my daughters back? I tried to remain composed. 'We had a newborn girl left on our doorstep two nights ago now.'

I relaxed a little. 'Is that...unusual for Mother Hale's House?' I asked.

'Sadly not, sir. But the reason I'm calling you is we found something with the child. Specifically, a business card with your name and contact details on.'

I really didn't know what to say. 'That is unusual. I have no family in America...nor any friends to speak of.'

Lashay fumbled around on the phone. 'I've got it here. The card looks old. It's real torn and scuffed.'

'It would make sense. I haven't worked at the bookshop in over thirty years.' I racked my brains. 'I don't suppose you got a look at who left the child?'

Lashay sighed. 'No, sir. But we could make out a little writing on the old business card of yours.'

'You could?' I asked, genuinely intrigued. 'What does it say?'

'It says "kind man", sir.' Lashay replied. 'It's written right under your name.'

I gasped and sank into my office chair. In an instant, my mind was transported back to the Waldorf Astoria dining room in New York City, and Cecily Huntley-Morgan's smiling face.

Look! I even wrote 'kind man' on the back! I shall keep it with me forever, as a token of good luck.

'Are you still there, Mr Tanit?' asked Lashay.

'Yes,' I replied, exasperated. 'Uh, Lashay, I actually have a hunch about who the baby might belong to. I wonder...do you know *anything* about her family circumstances?'

There was a slight pause on the line. 'Well, we know one thing. The Hale House Centre isn't just for unwanted children.' I winced at the term. 'Mother Hale provides support for children who are born addicted to drugs. I'm sorry to tell you that we strongly believe that this baby is addicted to crack cocaine.'

I put my hand over my mouth. 'Good Lord.'

'A lot of people find it shocking. But that's the reality here, sir. Drug dens are rife in Harlem. If I were to bet, I'd say that this child came from the one off of Lenox Avenue.'

Lenox Avenue. I'd heard the name before. 'Listen, I'll make arrangements to fly over tomorrow.'

The very next day, I found myself standing in front of Mother Hale House—a crumbling brownstone—in Harlem. I knocked on the door, and was greeted by a woman dressed in a blue tracksuit with a magnificent afro haircut. 'Are you Mr Tanit?' she asked.

'That's right.'

'I'm Lashay Jones, we spoke on the phone.'

'Hello, Lashay, it's a pleasure to meet you.' I put my hand out to shake hers.

'Nuh-uh. We do hugs around here,' she said, pulling me down to her and wrapping her arms tightly around me.

I gave a chuckle of surprise. 'Oh, that's very nice.'

'You just flown in from Sweden?'

'Switzerland, actually.'

She put her hands on her hips and raised an eyebrow. 'That near Sweden?'

'It's…on the same continent.'

Lashay burst out laughing. 'I'm joking, I'm joking. Sorry, busy morning. We've got a lot of hungry bellies in here today.' I instantly warmed to Lashay and her charming self-deprecation. 'Come on in.' I followed her into the Hale House Centre, and was directed towards a door on the left of the hallway. 'She's just in here.'

'Who is?'

'Mother Hale, of course!' Lashay opened the door and revealed a small office. Behind a large desk in front of a window was a slight old woman with grey hair, dressed in a white cardigan. She turned around as I walked in.

'This is the gentleman from Europe?' she asked Lashay, who nodded. The woman stood up gingerly, and made her way over to shake my hand.

'Clara Hale.'

'Atlas Tanit. It's an honour to meet you.'

'Likewise, I'm sure.'

'I'll leave you to it,' Lashay said with a smile, before backing out of the room.

'Please, won't you sit?' The older woman indicated a beaten leather sofa.

'Thank you.'

'So,' Clara said. 'The mystery of the business card.' She opened a drawer in her old wooden desk and picked out a small scrap of paper. 'Here you go, Mr Tanit.'

'Thank you.' I took the card from Clara and examined it. 'Yes, it's definitely one of mine,' I confirmed. 'But as I said to Lashay, I haven't used these for decades, since I was managing the bookshop.'

'And yet it came to be that the card arrived on my doorstep along with a little bundle of joy. Now, I wonder, how on earth that could have happened?'

'You and me both, Clara. Sorry. Miss Hale. Mother Hale.'

Clara wrinkled her nose, then, just as Lashay had done moments before, burst out laughing and smacked her knees. 'Clara's just fine. I only adopted the "Mother" because…well…' She shrugged and gestured around her.

'Of course. Lashay was able to tell me a little bit about what you've done. It's incredible.'

'Incredible is one word for it. I shouldn't have had to live the life I have. Children are gifts from the Lord above. How anyone could bring themselves to part from their own, I do not know, Mr Tanit.'

'It is a curious question. But I suppose that there are certain circumstances where the children are better cared for by others.'

Clara tapped the ends of her fingers together. 'How interesting.'

'What is?' I asked.

'I've been looking after the children of others for forty years now, and I've never heard anyone raise that point. Usually they agree with me, and say how *awful* it is.' I felt Clara's scrutinising gaze, and tried not to let my nerves get the better of me. 'So, Mr Tanit. *you* clearly have a different experience to most. What is that?'

I was staggered by Clara's wily intelligence. 'You're incredibly perceptive.' I laughed. 'I actually have five adopted daughters.'

Clara's eyes widened. 'Lord Jesus, you do not?!' I nodded in affirmation. 'Well, well, well,' she laughed. 'You're another one of me.'

I gave her a quizzical look. 'How do you mean?'

She shrugged. 'Oh, you know. Big-hearted. Probably a little foolish, too. You have to be to do what we do.'

'Honestly, Clara, I don't think we compare. I have only five daughters, and am able to give them a very comfortable life. Just how many children have passed through your doors?'

She inhaled deeply. 'Hundreds. I fostered damn near fifty in my own home before I went official and got a childcare facility licence in 1970. But one, or one thousand, it doesn't matter. The act of giving love to an unloved child is one of the noblest things a human can do.'

Her face was so very…warm. Although her presence was intimidating, she radiated kindness. 'I used to think that, Clara. But the love I have received from my daughters has been tenfold.'

Clara laughed again. 'That's the secret, isn't it?' She leant back in her leather office chair. 'You know, my husband died when I was only twenty-seven years old. I was heartbroken, and so were the three children we had together. I moped around for a while, and made the decision that no matter what, I'd just…keep…breathing.' She smiled wistfully. 'I ended up working as a janitor to get us through the Great Depression. It was an awful job. But I loved the smiling faces of the kids. They gave me hope. So, I turned my home into a day care. And suddenly, one day, I found that I wasn't just breathing, I was *living* again.'

Clara's tale was familiar to me. 'Children can do that for you.'

'They sure can, Mr Tanit.' Clara stood up from her chair, and turned to look out of the window. 'Soon after I opened the day care, I started heading out into the streets to help homeless kids. That's when I began to foster. I'd take seven or eight at a time.' She put her head in her hands. 'And it was just little old me. Imagine that!'

'How did you manage?'

'Simple! I loved each one of those children as my own. I became a mother to those who did not have one.'

What a remarkable human being. 'Lashay mentioned that you...specialise in the care of those children whose parents were addicted to drugs.'

Clara turned back to face me, looking a little sad. 'That's right. One day, about a decade ago now, Lorraine—that's my first daughter—brought a mother and child into my home who were dependent on heroin.' She perched on the edge of her desk. 'They needed a special kind of care, you see. That's when I got the official licence and I bought this bigger building. It's got five stories, and we need each and every one of them, with this new thing that's going around the place.'

'New thing?' I enquired.

Mother Hale shook her head. 'The AIDS virus.'

I had read about it in the newspapers back home. 'Is it a big problem here?'

'You betcha. It's spread through blood, as best we can tell. And when people share needles...well. The babies are born with it, you see. Not that anyone seems to want to talk about it. President Cheesecake won't even mention its name. These people need help, Mr Tanit. And they're not gonna get it if we don't start discussing the damn thing.'

'Can I ask how you care for these children who have had a particularly difficult start to life?'

'It's simple. You hold them, rock them, love them, and tell them how great they are. I nurse them through their inherited addiction. Then, when they're healthy—and many, many do get healthy—you go out and find them an amazing family. I personally make sure each one is a good fit.' Clara stiffened, and looked proud. 'I'm not ashamed to say that I've turned people down if I thought that they couldn't provide a good enough environment for the child. So'—she exhaled—'that's my story.' She pottered over and joined me on the leather sofa. 'What's yours, Atlas Tanit?'

I gave Clara a brief outline of my life, focusing on how I had become the adoptive father of my five wonderful daughters. I also mentioned my brief trip to New York in the forties, and my encounter with Cecily Huntley-Morgan…who I was sure the business card had once belonged to.

'Cecily…was she black?' Clara asked.

'No,' I replied. 'She was a white English woman.'

Clara looked surprised. 'It would have been quite a thing for a young white woman to come to Harlem to support black rights in the forties. I only ask as the natural assumption is that the little girl who was left on our doorstep a few days ago is a descendant of this woman you met.'

I gave a confirming nod. 'It would be the logical explanation.'

'Maybe one of her kids fell in love with a black man and someone in her family didn't like it. Who knows. In any case, is there any way you can contact her?'

I shook my head. 'I'm afraid not. I had my lawyer investigate the possibility but…she died of malaria in 1969.'

'Huh,' Clara said, pondering the situation. 'Did you find out if she had any children?'

'The thing is,' I continued, 'Cecily *did* have a daughter. She told me when we had lunch all those years ago…but she was never registered under her own name. From memory, she had taken in the abandoned baby of a Kenyan woman. Legally, the child belonged to someone else, so it isn't possible to trace her.'

Clara began to fiddle with her hair as she took in the details. 'So.' She looked at me with her shrewd brown eyes. 'What next?'

'What do you mean?'

'I mean, what do you wish to do about the child who was left on my doorstep, Mr Tanit?'

'Oh.' There was an uncomfortable silence.

Clara slapped a hand across her knee and gave me a grin. 'Oh, come on! Are you seriously telling me that you get a call, drop everything and fly halfway across the world just to satisfy some curiosity about a business card?'

Clara's burst of energy rendered me speechless. 'I...'

She shuffled closer to me. 'You've spoken about these five beautiful adopted daughters, all of whom seem to have arrived in your life through mysterious happenstance. So, when you get a call about a newborn baby girl who has your details from thirty years ago attached to her basket, are you seriously telling me that you're not here to take her home?' She raised her eyebrows at me.

'I hadn't really—'

She gave me a friendly shove on my shoulder. 'Of course you have, Atlas! May I call you Atlas?' I nodded fervently. 'There's no need to act coy or shy about it. Not with me. Not with what I do.'

'I suppose that...yes, I have contemplated that the universe is trying to tell me something.'

'Maybe it is, honey. And just so you know, I would have done exactly the same thing. Thirty years that business card of yours has survived somehow. Isn't that incredible? Cecily thought, *I'll keep this thing, in case one day I need it.* And guess what? One day she did... I think we'd better go and meet this baby.'

I followed Mother Hale up the steps of the brownstone, which she took carefully but purposefully. As we climbed higher, a sound of crying became louder. When we reached the third floor, Clara turned to me, looking a little grim. 'You might need to brace yourself. This part can be tricky for first-timers.' She led me into a room populated by about a dozen very young babies in cribs, some of whom were being tended to by women in smocks.

'They all seem so distressed.'

'That, my dear, is because they are. These are the babies we think have been born addicted to drugs. It's heartbreaking.'

The children seemed to howl and screech. It was a sound that came from their very core, and it distressed me greatly. 'Their crying... I can't explain it. It's different to what I'm used to.'

Clara met my eye. 'I know. As difficult as it is to comprehend, they're begging for a hit of whatever it was their momma was taking.' I shuddered.

Clara led me past one baby who trembled in her crib. The entirety of her tiny body was physically shaking, and her little limbs flinched and jerked violently. 'Is she all right, Clara?' I asked nervously.

Mother Hale took her glasses from her pocket and peered into the cot. 'There now, child.' She reached her hand into the crib and gently stroked the baby's hair. 'You stay strong now, my girl, you stay strong.' She gently tucked the baby's arms back into the swaddling cloth, and tightened it up. 'Babies suffering from withdrawal are naturally irritable. We try to wrap them up all snuggly to help.' She moved her hand to the baby's neck to feel her pulse. She waited for a moment before nodding at me. 'She'll be okay. These are the hardest times for them. Hilary?' Clara addressed one of the women in smocks, who was rocking a baby with a particularly high-pitched wail. 'How are Simeon's seizures?'

'Not a single one today, Mother Hale,' Hilary replied.

Her face broke out into a broad smile. 'Now that *is* good news. And Cynthia?' Clara addressed another woman, who was looking into a different crib. 'Has Grace managed to keep the food down?'

'Four out of five times today, Mother Hale.'

'Good!' she said, clapping her hands together in genuine joy, before looking up at me. 'These babies need extra calories because of all the wiggling and jiggling. When they start keeping the food down, that's when you know you've turned a corner.' Mother Hale walked me over to the last crib on the row. 'Well, here she is,' she said, pointing to the tiny occupant.

I stared down at the little girl who was writhing with as much force as she could muster, as if trying to break out of her swaddling. 'I notice that the other babies have been given names. Has she got one, Clara?'

'Of course. We call her Kindness, after what was written on the business card.'

'Lashay mentioned that you think it's…crack cocaine her mother was using?'

Mother Hale shrugged. 'We'll never know for sure. But her pupils are a little dilated and her breathing rate is particularly sharp. It tallies. There's a lot of it going on around here I'm sorry to say. When was this one last fed, Hilary?'

'About two hours ago now, Mother Hale.'

'Perfect timing.' She walked over to a wooden cupboard in the corner of the room and pulled out a few sachets of powders before mixing them together in a fresh bottle. She handed it to me. 'There you go.'

'You'd like me to feed her?'

Clara nodded. 'That would be most helpful.'

I placed the bottle in the crib, and went to pick the baby up. When I touched her, she began to scream ferociously and, considering she was a newborn, wriggled around with the force of one much older. 'It's okay. Shh, shh, little girl.' Instinctively I began to rock her back and forth, as I had done with my other children. 'Would you mind passing me the formula?' I asked Clara. She handed it to me, and I gently guided the bottle into the baby's mouth. I was shocked at how forcefully she began to suck, as if she was starved and desperate for nourishment.

'Well, you weren't lying,' Clara said. 'You've done that before.'

'You doubted my story?'

'No. I just didn't know if you'd be any good with the babies themselves. But you have the touch.' She tapped her nose.

Kindness, as she was currently known, was visually striking. Her stunning yellow-gold eyes and ebony skin would fool the casual observer into thinking she was completely healthy. 'I know that she's going through this awful period, Clara. But she feels so full of life.'

Clara nodded. 'Yep. Hil said something similar. What was it, Hil?'

'She's full of electricity, that one.' Hilary chuckled, before turning her attention back to another baby.

'That's very well put,' I replied.

Within minutes, the bottle was drained, and I handed it back to Clara. 'So. Back to my earlier question,' she said. 'What next?'

Cecily had written *kind man* on my old business card. I knew I could not betray that moniker. 'I can fly her home this evening,' I confirmed.

Mother Hale's mouth dropped open, and her nose wrinkled once again, so I knew what was coming. She laughed heartily, nearly doubling over this time. 'You'll do no such damn thing, Atlas Tanit! Have you not listened to a word I've been saying?'

I was mortified. 'I'm so sorry, Clara. I thought you were

implying that you wanted me to take her.'

'I do, I do! But fly her home his evening? Are you out of your damn mind? Did you hear him, Hil? Cynthia?' The other two ladies in the room began to laugh along with Clara, and my cheeks flushed a hot red. 'Firstly, I don't care if you've done this five times before, I need to perform the requisite background checks on you and your family, to make sure that Kindness will be moved to a loving home.'

I looked down at the floor, well and truly admonished. 'Of course.'

'Plus.' Clara paused. 'I hate to highlight the obvious, but this little girl would be growing up with five white sisters. I don't want her to feel alienated by that in any way.'

'Gosh, no. But to be factually accurate, only four of my children are white. I told you about Celaeno—CeCe—my daughter from Australia?'

Clara eyed me. 'You did.'

'Her father was indigenous to Australia, and her mother was mixed race. She isn't white.'

Mother Hale paused to reflect for a moment. 'Huh. A lot of folks, even if they adopt, choose children with the same skin colour. But it doesn't matter to you?'

'Not one bit, no,' I stated honestly.

Clara nodded, seemingly in approval. 'Good, good. There's still the question of helping Kindness overcome her addiction. She's a few weeks away from not needing our expertise, and then after that, she'll need special attention at home.'

'I can have the finest doctors at my beck and call,' I assured her.

'Well, I'm very glad for you, but I'll be needing to speak to them, too. Having a degree in medicine from a fancy university is all well and good, but most won't have any practical experience in dealing with such a situation.'

'Of course, Clara. In fact, I would insist.' I manoeuvred the baby into a vertical position and began to burp her. Clara smiled.

'All right then. We can get the ball rolling.' She put a hand on my back. 'Congratulations, Daddy.'

52

1993

Dear reader, if you have made it this far, you will have naturally begun to question the immense gaps in this diary. When I first began recording my thoughts in the 1920s, the purpose was to articulate my feelings, for at that time, I did not speak. I found it such a successful exercise that I continued it throughout my life. When I first met Angelina in Granada, I resolved to dedicate my life to the search for Elle, and my first daughter. The diary lay on my study desk, forgotten. I was a man driven by a single purpose.

Then, when I adopted Maia, I felt it such a significant moment that I owed it to the 'reader' to record it. The same, of course, went for Ally, Star, CeCe, Tiggy and Electra, too. It has not escaped me that the last few chapters serve to chronicle how I met my children, and I should like to think that one day, they will read these pages. Know that the gaps in the diary were filled with love, laughter and family. My children have given me more than I can ever express on paper. Whenever I have left Atlantis to continue my search for the missing sister, I have felt a deep longing in my heart for the company of my girls.

Speaking of the missing sister, I should inform you that I have not today picked up my pen to celebrate our long-awaited meeting.

Forgive me, reader, I appreciate that the writing here is a little sloppy. But I am unable to stop my hand from trembling. Earlier today, I had a conversation with my eldest daughter which chilled me to the bone.

This evening, we have been celebrating the end of Maia's second year at university at a special dinner with all the girls. She still has half a term to go, but has blessed us with a visit during her reading week. At around three p.m. this afternoon, I walked out onto the jetty to watch for the sight of Christian ferrying Maia home across the lake. When she came into view, I couldn't help but feel my heart strings tug a little. My little girl is a woman now. No doubt the occasions she returns here to see her old pa will be few and far between.

As the boat lightly buffeted the wood at the end of the jetty, she practically leapt off, and jogged towards me.

'Hello, Pa!'

'Maia, my darling!' I embraced her tightly for the first time in very nearly three months. 'It is so very good to see you. Welcome home.'

She gave me a light kiss on the cheek. 'You too. Oh look, here they come!'

I turned and looked up towards the house to see a trickle of D'Aplièse girls heading down the slope to greet their eldest sister. CeCe was practically dragging Star, Tiggy skipped freely and Ally followed behind, arms folded. Electra was, of course, leading the pack in a full-on sprint.

'MAAAAIIIIAAAA!' she screeched.

'Hello, Electra!' she said, as my youngest daughter knocked the breath out of my eldest. 'Oh, I've missed you.'

'Yeah, us too,' Electra continued. 'You know, Tiggy found a stray cat, and it lives upstairs with her, but Ally's allergic and CeCe said that wasn't fair so—'

'Woah, E, slow down. I can't wait to hear all the news. Come on, let's get up to the house. You can help with my bags!'

Claudia had prepared Maia's favourite—chilli con carne—and the conversation at dinner had focused on my eldest daughter's exciting new life. Initially, I had been thrilled to hear of her experiences away from Atlantis. She has grown up to be a somewhat reserved young lady, but I know she has so much to offer. During her first two years at university, Maia has really begun to blossom.

'Do you go out at night?' CeCe asked.

'Sometimes we do,' Maia replied. 'My flatmates Samantha and Tom are more party animals than I am, though.'

Electra sat up in her chair. 'When I go to university, I'm going to go out *every* night,' she proudly exclaimed.

'I don't think that's unlikely,' Ally said with a smirk.

Tiggy frowned. 'Can you have pets there?'

'Ooh, I'm not sure actually, Tigs. I know a girl who has a goldfish. But I'm not sure that Bagheera the cat would be too welcome.' Maia giggled.

Tiggy shrugged. 'Oh. Well, maybe I won't go to university then.'

'I'd look after him for you,' Star offered quietly.

'Ew, no you won't,' CeCe snapped back. 'He's not sleeping in our room, Star. He smells weird.'

'Please, CeCe. Do not speak to your sister like that,' I interjected. 'Now, I would like to propose a toast. Firstly, to your eldest sister, Maia, who is on track to receive a first-class result at the end of this year. And secondly, to Ally'—my second-eldest daughter shot me a look—'because, and I'm sure she won't mind me sharing this with you, she has today received an early offer from the Conservatoire de Musique de Genève to study the flute. They wish to give her a scholarship.'

Ally reddened. 'Pa, tonight's about Maia!' she hissed.

'Ally!' Maia said with genuine enthusiasm. 'Don't be ridiculous! That's amazing news!'

'Wow! Ally! Well done!' Tiggy beamed.

'Thank you,' she replied sheepishly.

'I am so proud of my two eldest daughters, as I am of you all. So let's raise our glasses to one another tonight. We are the most amazing family. Hip hip...'

'Hooray!' replied the table.

Ma began to pour out some more wine for myself and the two eldest girls. 'You are all so like your pa, in your own ways.'

'Don't insult the poor girls, Ma. They're far more interesting than I am.'

'Speaking of interesting,' CeCe said, 'do you have a boyfriend yet, Maia? Ma thinks you do.'

'CeCe!' Ma shouted.

'What? You were talking about it the other day.'

Maia raised her eyebrows at Marina. 'Were you indeed, Ma?'

'I…was just making conversation with your sister.' She eyeballed CeCe. '*Private* conversation.'

'So what gives you that idea, Ma?' Maia asked, taking a deliberately slow sip of her wine.

Marina blushed. 'Well, whenever we talk on the phone, you sound sort of…happy. I thought that, just maybe, you might have a young man in your life…' She shrugged.

'Yeah! So do you?' CeCe pushed.

'CeCe!' Star admonished her outspoken sister.

'What?' she replied. 'We all want to know! Don't we?'

This led to an emission of giggles around the table. 'I'm not sure *I* want to know, girls!' I groaned, which led to even more laughter.

'Oh, tell us, Maia, go on!' begged Tiggy.

'Yeah, tell us! Tell us, tell us!' Electra began to chant.

Maia looked to Ally, who shrugged at her, as if to say, *the cat is out of the bag.*

'All right, all right. Pa, cover your ears.'

I laughed. 'It's all right, my darling, I'm sure I can take it. As long as he doesn't have tattoos. Or ride a motorcycle.' There was an awkward pause, and Ally exploded with laughter. 'Oh no,' I replied, putting my hands over my eyes in a display of melodrama. 'Come on then, give me the bad news. How many tattoos does he have?'

'Just one, Pa. I think it's pretty tasteful,' Maia replied coyly.

I sighed. 'I'm sure. Dare I ask what of?'

'It's just a little lightning bolt,' Maia said.

'I knew it!' CeCe said. 'She *does* have a boyfriend!' The table erupted in a cacophony of squeals and cheers.

Maia put her hands up to quell the excitement. 'Well, I don't know if he's my *boyfriend*,' she qualified.

'But are you going out?' Tiggy asked, eyes agog.

'We're...seeing each other, yes,' Maia said quietly.

CeCe folded her arms. 'If he's not your boyfriend, then what is he?'

'He's just...you know...he's just a boy!'

Ally tried to stick up for her elder sister. 'Come on, girls. Stop torturing her!'

'What does he look like?' Star asked.

'Well,' continued Maia, 'he's from Greece. So he's very attractive.'

'You've nabbed yourself a Greek god then, Maia?' I asked, taking a sip of my wine. 'Now, I must ask, when can we all meet him?'

'Pa, I'm not bringing him here to the lion's den. He wouldn't even last five minutes with this lot! You haven't even asked his name!'

'Yes, forgive me, my darling. Please, tell me. What is my future son-in-law called?'

Maia smiled shyly, and looked down at her plate. 'Zed.'

My stomach dropped. 'I'm sorry?' I asked.

'Zed,' Maia repeated.

'What, like the letter?' Electra asked.

'I guess.' Maia giggled. 'It's spelt Z-E-D.'

I made eye contact with Marina at the opposite end of the table. She gave me a nod as if to encourage the question she knew I was desperate to ask.

'And his surname, Maia?' I enquired.

'It's Eszu. E-S-Z-U.'

I thought I might pass out.

'Maia Eszu!' Star said. 'I think that's a very cool name.'

'It's *not* as nice as D'Aplièse, though, is it?' added Electra.

I stood up, keen to get away from the table before I fainted. 'Excuse me, girls, I'm not feeling too well. I'm just going for a little lie-down.'

'Are you all right, Pa?' Ally asked.

'Oh yes. I'm sure I'm fine. I was out on the Laser for a little too long today. I think I have a bit of sunstroke.'

'I don't think Pa likes the fact that you have a boyfriend, Maia!' CeCe squealed.

'No, it's not that,' I replied firmly. 'It's not that at all.'

I left the dining room and made straight for my study, where I locked the door and collapsed into my armchair. *Oh God. Oh God. This cannot be. It cannot!* My heart was banging so ferociously that I thought it might beat its way out of my chest. I went to pick up the phone to call Georg when there was a knock at the door.

'Sorry, girls, just having a little rest.'

'It's Marina.'

I opened the door to her. 'Come in, Ma.'

She shut it behind her and threw her arms around me. '*Courage, chéri. Courage.*'

'I don't know what to say,' I panted.

'Neither do I, Atlas. Let me get you a drink.' Marina crossed to the decanter which contained a Macallan single malt, imported especially from the Scottish Highlands. 'I do not suppose there is much point in wondering if it is a coincidence.'

'No. Think of all the universities on the planet. Kreeg's boy just *somehow* ends up at Maia's, and becomes her boyfriend? It cannot be chance. This is targeted, I am sure of it.' I sat down in my chair, and Marina handed me the whisky. 'Cheers.' I clinked her glass, and we both took a swig. The warm mellow spirit helped to fortify me. 'What's the purpose of it, Ma? To send a message? To let me know that he's watching me? Or worse. What if he intends to harm the girls? Oh dear, my little Maia…' I put my head on my desk. Marina rubbed my back.

'Please try to remain calm, Atlas. We do not have the full picture yet.'

'I was about to call Georg to get an update on Kreeg himself.'

There was another knock at the door, and I looked up. 'Are you all right, Pa? I just wanted to check on you.' The voice belonged to Maia.

'Let her in,' Marina mouthed to me. I crossed to the study door, breathed in deeply, and smiled widely before opening it.

'Hello, Maia!' I said, with probably a touch too much enthusiasm. 'I'm so sorry I had to leave the table on your first night back. I just began to feel a little wobbly, that's all. As I said, it's only a bit of sunstroke.' She entered the room, and I closed the door behind her.

'If you say so, Pa.' She looked at the whisky glasses on my desk. 'But everyone really does think it's because I mentioned my...boyfriend.'

I vehemently shook my head. 'No, Maia, absolutely not. I encourage all of you to find love. As I have told you before, it is the only thing that makes life worth living.'

'It's just...you seemed fine, then I mentioned Zed, and suddenly you were standing up to leave.'

I gave her a hug, but she was an unwilling recipient. 'It's just a funny turn, my darling, that's all. I'm all right, aren't I, Ma?'

Ma nodded. 'Oh yes, your pa will be right as rain. Please go back and enjoy your chilli. Claudia made it especially for you.'

'All right, Ma.' She went to leave, but turned to me before reaching the door. 'I promise you, Zed is the sweetest man I've ever met. He asks so many questions about my sisters, and you, and Atlantis... I never thought someone could be so interested in my life!' She giggled and left.

'Oh dear,' was all I could muster.

'Come on, sit back down. You look as white as a sheet,' Ma said, guiding me back into the chair, where I sat for a while, my head in my hands.

'No doubt Kreeg has asked him to probe Maia for info on Atlantis. I just hope she hasn't given Zed the exact details of its location.'

'Even if she has, please remember that you have prepared for such an event.'

'You're right,' I replied. 'But I haven't had the escape routes checked in over a decade.' I shook my head. 'I thought he'd let me be.'

'I too, *chéri*.'

I drummed my fingers on the desk. 'It's no good sitting here and panicking. Firstly, I want us to inspect all the hidden areas of the house. I need to make sure the lifts are in working order, and the lights in the tunnels which lead to the boathouse are working too.' I stood up and poured another whisky. I offered to do the same for Marina, but she declined. 'I'll have

Georg increase the surveillance on Kreeg himself, too. I don't want us to be sitting ducks. I'll also put my search for Elle on hold for a while. God forbid that Eszu arrives at Atlantis and I'm not here to protect the girls.'

'Do you really think he would hurt them? Your innocent children?'

'I don't know what he's capable of. I worry that for him, nothing is off limits.'

'Then you are wise to be as cautious as you are.' Marina took my hand. 'We will protect them, Atlas. Together.'

53

Over the course of the next few weeks, all of Atlantis's secrets were investigated and reinforced. With Ma, I ran through various scenarios in which Kreeg might arrive at the house, and how we could best organise the girls. It is a situation I dread. How would I even possibly begin to explain to them what was happening? They would start to question and doubt their own father. It is a reality which I find too difficult to contemplate just at the moment.

The night before Maia was due to return to university, I spied Marina emerging from my eldest daughter's bedroom looking pale-faced.

'Everything all right, Ma?' I asked.

She hadn't seen me in the corridor, and nearly jumped out of her skin. 'Sorry, I was in another world,' she gasped, clutching her hand to her chest.

'Evidently. Is everything okay?'

'Hmm? Oh, yes, fine. Everything's fine.'

Lying was not Marina's strong suit, but I did not wish to push her. Reluctantly, I let it go.

Georg Hoffman has been as reliable as ever, hiring a team in Greece to study Eszu's every move. Almost to my frustration, nothing seemed to have changed, save for Lightning Communications growing into a multibillion drachma business. It has even spawned a parent company to cater for Eszu's expanded interests—Athenian Holdings. There was no doubt in my mind, the name was chosen to needle me. When we were children, he would often tease me about my passion for Greek mythology. Why else would he have selected Athena, the goddess of war, other than to make his position clear?

But as for the man himself, Georg assured me nightly that there was no suggestion he was about to make a journey to Atlantis to seek revenge. Instead, he seemed to be doing that via the next generation.

For this reason, I had Georg look into Zed himself. There was little we discovered that surprised me. The young man was arrogant, privileged, and spent his father's money as if there was no tomorrow—the opposite of what I insisted on for my girls. Each had enough private finances, provided by me, to make sure they were comfortable, but I would not allow them any ludicrous extravagances. Certainly not the several Lamborghinis which Zed Eszu used to bomb around the streets of Athens.

It had been a month since Maia's revelation when Marina knocked on my office door. As soon as she entered, I could tell that something was off. Her shoulders were hunched over and she struggled to maintain eye contact.

'What is it, Ma?' I asked. She poured me an enormous brandy from my decanter. 'Good Lord. That's a large one. This *must* be bad news.'

'It will be a little difficult to accept, yes.' Marina hesitated.

'Out with it, please.'

'I have been fighting with myself about whether or not to reveal this information to you, Atlas. But I have concluded that I owe it to you. I must tell you that…' She couldn't bring herself to say the words.

It was my turn to pour a brandy for Marina. I handed it to her. 'Drink that down.' She followed my instruction and gulped it.

'Maia is pregnant.'

I drained my own brandy glass. Then I tried to remain as still as possible, allowing the wave of dread and fear to wash over me before I regathered my thoughts. 'Thank you, Ma. That is very useful information.'

'Atlas, I'm so sorry. I can't possibly imagine what you're

feeling.'

'No,' I whispered. I noticed that my fists were clenched together. 'It leads me to wonder, of course, whether *this* was a deliberate act. The ultimate humiliation.'

Ma swallowed hard. 'I do not think that would be out of the realms of possibility, I admit.'

I erupted. 'How could they be so very cruel?!' Without warning, streams of tears began to fall down my cheeks, and I sobbed heartily. Marina put an arm around my hunched form.

'Because for every angel, there is a devil that must be endured.'

I wiped my tears away with my handkerchief. 'Obviously this is why you looked so awful the night before Maia returned to university.'

Marina nodded. 'It's true. She had confided to me about her symptoms, so I made her take a test. Oh, *chéri*, when it came back positive, I nearly died. But I could not show any weakness to precious Maia. I had to be strong for her.'

'Of course you did, Ma. And I cannot tell you just how grateful I am to you for that.' I gave her a reassuring pat on the shoulder. 'None of this is Maia's fault, in any way, shape or form.' I closed my eyes momentarily. 'But we must accept that these circumstances are particularly troubling. How is my daughter?'

Ma sighed deeply and gave a shrug. 'She is experiencing what any teenager who becomes unexpectedly pregnant does, I imagine. Fear. Shame. Guilt.'

My heart ached for her. 'My poor little girl. How awful. I just wish I could take her in my arms and give her a great big hug.'

Ma looked suddenly panicked. 'She cannot know that you are aware of her situation, *chéri*! You mean the world to her, and she believes that if you find out, your opinion of her will plummet. She could not take it.'

I nodded. 'Yes, Marina, and that simply breaks my heart.' A further lump arrived in my throat. 'I hope you know that is not how I would ever feel about any of my children. I just wish there was something I could do to help. She needs more love, support and help from her pa than ever. And I am unable to give it to her.' Ma squeezed my hand. 'Does Zed know about the baby?'

Marina shook her head. 'No. And Maia is adamant that he must not.' Ma rubbed her forehead. 'Zed has hurt our young Maia very deeply. As he is about to graduate, he informed her that their relationship had merely been a meaningless fling, and wants nothing else to do with her.'

I put my head in my hands, my nightmares materialising before me. 'Please reach out to her, Marina. Assure her that whatever she wants to do, she has your full and unconditional support.'

'I will go and telephone her.'

'Please do. And report back to me.'

Maia finished the final term of her second year of university in the summer of 1993. She returned to Atlantis wrapped in layers of clothing to hide her bump, even though it was the height of the hot weather. A week before, I had suggested to her that as she was the eldest, she should be given the Pavilion. It is a private residence which lies about two hundred metres away from the main house—the building Marina used to inhabit.

'I think you deserve your own space, my darling,' I had told her.

She had looked as if she might cry. 'Really, Pa? Oh, thank you, thank you. I would adore it.' As she had moved to hug me, I noted that she kept her belly away from my embrace, so I could not feel what was growing inside her.

It will not surprise the reader to learn that Maia did not return to university to begin her third-year studies. She conveyed to me that she was experiencing a nasty bout of glandular fever, and that she would resume her course as soon as she felt able. As she grew larger and larger, I saw her less and less, and my heartache increased. In truth, I longed to wander down to the pavilion, wrap her up in my arms, and tell her that everything was going to be all right. But I appreciated that her autonomy had to take precedence. I frequently reiterated to Marina to convey to Maia that, if she told me, I would be nothing but sympathetic and loving. But that day did not come.

Ally must have known. Maia's eldest sister would spend long hours in the pavilion with her, and I was glad that Marina did not have to bear the burden alone.

I thought perhaps that another member of the family had worked it out, too—Tiggy. I caught her, once, staring at Maia's belly when I had taken my eldest a cup of tea and a slice of cake to the Pavilion. Due to her 'glandular fever', we were never permitted to come too close. But even from several metres away, little Tiggy's eyes were totally fixated on her sister's stomach.

One evening, when Maia would have been about six months pregnant, Marina told me of my eldest daughter's decision about the future. 'She wishes to give the child up for adoption.' I was unsure of how to respond.

'Is that what she truly wants?' I asked. 'Because if she is making this decision out of a sense of shame or guilt, I'll simply have to say something, Ma.'

Ma nodded. 'It is what she desires, Atlas. Wholeheartedly. She does not believe that she is ready to be a mother, and thinks that her baby will be better cared for by someone else. She said she thought of her own mother, and her decision. Because of that choice, she ended up with you as a father.'

I shook my head in disbelief. 'What a tragedy. What a great, great tragedy.'

Ma hugged me. 'I know, *chéri*. But if you take away one thing from this awfulness, it is that you should be so proud of your eldest daughter. She has been braver and more resilient than I ever thought possible. She is amazing.'

'She is,' I agreed. 'Being practical, as you know I always must be, Georg is the man to speak to about where Maia's child should be placed. I expect he'll even be able to arrange a private adoption, by a family who will love and care for…my grandchild.' The word pierced my heart. 'Because, despite absolutely everything, that is who they are. We must ensure that they are given the best life possible.'

'We will, Atlas, we will.'

'I will transfer you a few thousand francs. Please offer to pay for any hospital or method which Maia chooses to give birth. As usual, money is not an object.'

The child, a boy, was born three months later at a private hospital in Geneva, and Marina was with Maia every step of the way. Unbeknownst to anyone else, I had worked very closely alongside Georg to ensure that the adoptive family were well placed to give the boy all the love and care he could ever wish for. I hoped that Clara Hale would be proud.

I did not see my daughter, nor Marina, for three weeks after the birth, under the pretence that they were on a mother-daughter holiday, as Maia had finally 'recovered' from her long bout of glandular fever. When she did eventually step back onto the shores of Atlantis, I held her in my arms for a very long time. I wonder if she knew that *I* knew. Something tells me that, perhaps, she did.

'I'm well enough to go back to university now, Pa. I'm feeling so much better.'

'That is wonderful to hear, Maia. But only return when you are ready. The Pavilion will always be here for you, whenever you need it.'

'Thank you, Pa. I love you.'

'Not as much as I love you, little one.'

The Titan

June 2008

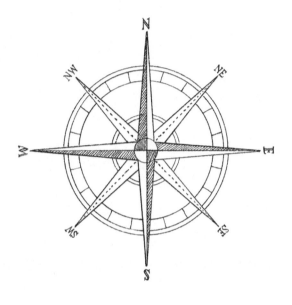

54

'He knew all along. Oh God,' Maia cried, allowing the final pages of the diary to fall to the floor of her cabin.

'Knew what, Maia?' Floriano asked quizzically.

'My baby that I gave away. Zed Eszu's baby.' Maia saw Floriano involuntarily bristle at the mention of the situation. She did not begrudge him that. When she had first told him of her past, he had been so sweet and understanding. But the last few days had added a lot of new context to what had happened all those years ago.

'I'm so sorry, my darling Maia.' He wrapped her in his arms.

'It all sounds stupid now, reliving it from his perspective. All those months I spent cooped up in the Pavilion at Atlantis, pretending I had glandular fever. Of course he knew.'

'But he never mentioned it, because he loved you. So much.'

'That's the worst thing about it, Floriano. I let him down. He was my world, and I let him down.'

'No. Do not talk like that, my love. You knew nothing of the past he shared with this Kreeg. You were targeted. An innocent victim. Nobody could ever possibly blame you.'

Floriano stood and went to draw the curtains of the cabin, as darkness had begun to descend on the *Titan*.

'Pa and Georg worked together to find a suitable family. I could find out who my son has become.'

Floriano bent down to the miniature fridge and pulled out a

beer. 'It is as if the winds of coincidence are swirling around the ship. Would you like anything?' he asked Maia.

She shook her head. 'I really appreciate you sitting in here with me for the last few hours, Floriano. It must have been very dull just watching me read.'

'My love, I would stay awake whilst you slept for a week if it made you feel safer.' He planted a tender kiss on her forehead. 'Have you all the answers you were hoping for?'

Maia rubbed her eyes. The answer was a most definite 'no'. She still knew nothing of Pa's time in Russia, or the mysterious circumstances surrounding the death of Kreeg Eszu's mother. 'The diary ends over a decade ago, in 1993.'

Floriano perched beside her on the bed and took a swig from the beer bottle. 'Do you know what happened to the diamond?' he asked.

Amongst all the other drama, the location of the gem had slipped her mind entirely. 'Do you know, it's hardly mentioned after the 1950s. Who on earth knows where that ended up.'

Floriano stretched out as he pondered the diamond's fate. 'How curious. I wonder if it ever made its way back to Kreeg?'

'Perhaps we'll never know. Anyway.' Maia stood up. 'I want to go and check on the others before dinner.'

Floriano grabbed her hand and kissed it 'All right, my love.' Maia went to leave, but he pulled her back and planted a final, tender kiss on her stomach. 'Your boys are proud of you.' Floriano's words caught her a little off guard, and she swallowed the lump in her throat.

'Thank you. I'm a little worried about Electra. The diary confirmed she was addicted to crack cocaine from birth.'

Floriano's eyes widened. '*Meu Deus!* How awful.'

'Oh, and then there's CeCe,' Maia continued, 'whose mother was abandoned by her father and died alone. Or Ally, who was separated at birth from her twin because her mother wanted a boy.'

'Maia, I—'

'Or Tiggy, actually, whose family prophesised our individual arrivals in Pa's life.' Floriano's jaw was practically on the floor. 'So yes, I suppose there is a lot to unpack.' She made for the door, opened it, and just before she left, added, 'And Ma was once a prostitute.'

Ally D'Aplièse and Georg Hoffman descended the *Titan*'s main staircase, making for the lower deck on which Atlas's private onboard study was located. As they approached the door, Georg removed the only existing key from his pocket.

'If you wouldn't mind, Ally, I will go in alone. I want to make sure that at least some of his wishes are respected.'

'That's fine, Georg. I'll just be out here,' Ally replied.

'Thank you. Back in a moment.'

Georg entered the study, and Ally took her mobile phone out of her pocket. She was glad to see Hans had anchored them within range of a mast, and that a text had come through from Jack.

Hey, you okay? You looked a little stressed earlier. Here if you need me. X

In spite of everything she had recently learnt, Jack's kindness relieved some of the pressure she was under. She pondered how to reply... This was not something she could explain in a short text, nor should Jack know about the situation before her sisters.

Sorry, just a bit frazzled. Will explain later, if you want to meet in my cabin after dinner? x

The response was immediate.

It's a date x

Inside the study, Georg inhaled the smell of the leather-bound books that lined the shelves which he so closely associated with his employer. His eyes travelled around the room, glancing at various trinkets Atlas had picked up from his explorations of the globe: a Stetson hat from Mexico, an ice hockey puck from Finland and a fortune cat from China, which still waved jovially from its position on the desk. All were painful reminders of the fact that, ultimately, Georg had failed his best friend. Each time he or his team had managed to sniff out a trace of Elle Leopine, Atlas had never failed to follow the scent, however faint it may have been.

Georg took another, smaller key out of his breast pocket. Unlocking the desk's central drawer, he retrieved an envelope, which he had certainly not anticipated doing on this voyage. He closed his eyes and thought back to the last time the pair of them had been together in this room.

'The final pages are complete, Georg,' Atlas said quietly. His breathing was heavy, and becoming more laboured by the day.

'Well done, old friend. Your story is finished.'

Atlas gave a wheezy chuckle. 'Well, very nearly, I imagine. The doctors say it could be any time from now. They predict no longer than three months.'

'You have spent your entire life defying logic, my friend.'

'True. But immortality is perhaps one hurdle too far.' He smiled. 'In any case, it is all done now. The loose ends are very nearly tied up. But, Georg...'

'Yes, Atlas?'

'I still have deep concerns about Zed Eszu. Although I tried to make a bargain, he will remain a threat as long as he walks the earth. Even though my girls are strong, and will be even stronger after they learn the truth about their pasts, you must promise me you will do your best to mitigate his influence,' he implored. 'Protect my daughters from him as best you can.'

'I swear, my friend.'

'Thank you, Georg. You have been...exemplary. I owe you so very much.' Atlas gently bowed his head.

Georg was choked. 'It has been the honour of my life. All that I have done has been in grateful recompense for your kindness.'

'You've made me very proud. As has Claudia, of course. There is no one in the universe I trust more than you.'

'The feeling is a mutual one, Atlas.'

'Good. Now, are you absolutely sure that you are clear on my instructions? Given this unexpected turn of events, I just want to run through everything one more time.' Atlas went to stand, and Georg extended a hand to help. 'Thank you.' He tottered over to the bookshelf and cast an eye over his collection. 'Repeat the plan back to me, please.'

Georg nodded. 'Of course. Firstly, I am to give the missing sister your original diary when she is found. We have all the information we need now. I will find her.'

Atlas raised a questioning eyebrow. 'You've definitely got the drawing of the emerald ring?'

'Yes.'

He continued his mental checklist. 'And the coordinates to Argideen House?'

'Absolutely.'

Atlas picked up the charcoal drawing of Elle, and stared at it for a while. 'Are my letters to the girls in place at Atlantis? Alongside the physical clues?'

'They're in my office. All are sealed and ready to be handed over as soon as I return.'

Atlas seemed to relax a little, before remembering something else. 'What about the armillary sphere? Has that all been seen to?'

'Yes. The engraver is finishing off his work this afternoon. I will double-check the inscriptions and coordinates myself.'

'Excellent. And the surprise?'

'Seen to, Atlas.'

Atlas gave a weak smile. 'I'll look forward to seeing everyone's faces, from wherever I am. Thank you, Georg.' He walked back over to the desk and shuffled his papers together. He looked at the pages ruefully. 'I only wish I could be there to guide them through all this.' He shook his head. 'Maia, Ally, Star, CeCe, Tiggy, Electra…they have so much to learn about their origins.' A slightly haunted look crossed Atlas's face. 'Have I done the right thing, Georg?'

'I believe that you have. With all my heart.'

Atlas gently eased himself back into his chair and looked out of the *Titan*'s window at the open water. 'I worry that I should have told them all the truth years ago.'

'It is only natural that you would fret. But remember, if you had told them everything before now, it could have endangered them all.'

Atlas nodded slowly, and took a sip of his water. Georg was distressed to see just how much his hand trembled whilst he held the glass. 'Now, when I am gone, and only then, you will give my daughters these.' With a frail hand, Atlas pointed to the fresh pages which lay on the desk, the ink still drying. 'If the girls think that I have in any way deceived them…'—he paused and put a hand to his chest—'it would ruin it all.' A long pause hung between the two men. Atlas looked up at Georg. Although his skin was wrinkled and his hair white, Atlas's brown eyes were as searching as they had always been. 'You know exactly what I set out to do. I could never have predicted I would survive.'

'No. Neither could I,' Georg replied quietly.

Atlas opened a drawer in his desk and produced an A4 manila envelope. He delicately placed the new pages inside, returned them to the drawer and turned the key in the lock. Then he removed it and handed it to Georg.

'Only when the time is right. When I am gone.'

Atlas went to stand again, but struggled this time. Georg immediately offered his arm, and his old friend hauled himself to his feet. Then he embraced him, an action which produced tears in the eyes of both men. 'I am glad we had this extra time, old friend. It gives me the opportunity to say something I did not the other day.'

'What is that?'

Atlas smirked. 'Will you hurry up and tell her?'

'I'm sorry,' Georg replied quizzically 'I'm not sure what you mean.'

His employer rolled his eyes. 'For God's sake, man. I mean *Marina*.'

Georg immediately turned a bright shade of red. 'Ah.'

'You've loved her for the last thirty years. Let me be proof that you must seize the day, Monsieur Hoffman.'

That had been the last time Georg had seen Atlas Tanit. Now he produced a handkerchief from his pocket and dabbed his eyes. Placing the envelope under his arm, he locked the desk drawer and left the empty study.

'Are those the pages?' Ally asked, putting away her mobile phone and pointing to the envelope.

Georg nodded. 'I'll have them copied, just like the original diary.'

'Good. We'll tell them at dinner. Then everyone can read.'

'Ally...' Georg shuffled nervously. 'I must tell you that I am scared. I have no idea how your sisters will react. If you are anything to go by, each one might wish to throttle me, individually. Marina, too. I want to make sure she's protected.'

'Slow down, Georg. Yes, people are going to be distraught, as I was. But you know very well that the pain can be quickly remedied. I assume you've spoken to Captain Hans?'

'Yes. He's made the necessary navigational adjustments.'

'Good. Right.' Ally inhaled deeply. 'I'll see you at dinner.'

That evening, the Seven Sisters and their partners gathered on the top deck of the *Titan*, joined, as ever, by Ma and Georg Hoffman. Each had made a special effort to dress for the occasion. Tonight, they were due to honour Pa Salt's life by telling favourite stories from their childhoods.

'Oh, my darlings!' Ma cooed. 'You all look wonderful. It is rare that we are all together in one place these days. I shall treasure tonight, despite the circumstances.'

The girls had made sure to surround Ma with love and support, after what had been revealed to them in the diary. She needn't have worried for a moment that her wards would judge her for what she had been in the past.

'What I want to know, Ma, is did you ever reconcile with your father, Louis?' Star asked.

'I did, my sweetheart.' Ma nodded at the happy memory. 'Your pa, and of course, Georg, were so helpful in facilitating a reunion. Atlas flew me over to America, and my father met me at the airport. He was so nervous. As you will have read, my mother, Giselle, was a force of nature and tried to keep my father and me apart from one another. But we had a wonderful week in Detroit, and we visited each other at least once per year until his death in 1987. I gave the eulogy at his funeral,' Ma said.

'That's so wonderful. I'm sure he would have been so proud,' Star replied.

'I hope so, *chérie*. I'm only sorry that I never met my grandmother Evelyn.'

'She sounded so wonderful, Ma,' added Electra. 'She really did.'

'She looked after Pa like a mother,' said Maia.

'He always did speak so fondly of her, yes,' continued Ma. 'So, in a way, I feel like I did know her. Every year, on the anniversary of her death, we would light a candle.'

Maia had made significant efforts to show the table that she was feeling all right after her sisters had read, in detail, about the son she gave away. She had led the conversation, and was effervescent in her responses. 'To be honest,' she told the table, 'I'm much more worried about Zed's "Atlas" project. It's going to be world-famous.'

'With that scumbag, it's always been about having power over us, hasn't it?' Electra spat. 'What an asshole.' She looked at Marina apologetically. 'Sorry, Ma.'

'I think, on this occasion, I have no choice but to agree, *chérie*.'

'It was odd to read about his mother,' Tiggy mused. 'I remember Zed telling me that she was a lot younger than his father. And that she died when he was a teenager.'

'He told me that too,' Maia agreed.

Marina sighed and gave a shrug. 'Mere fantasies, it would seem. I suppose it is the one thing he cannot be blamed for. The loss of a parent is a traumatic event, and to have that blaireau for a father…it is no wonder he longed for a youthful mother who was with him as he neared adulthood.'

'Is there anything we could do to Zed from a legal standpoint, Georg?' Tiggy asked. 'I know you can't trademark a human name, but if we could somehow prove that it was a malicious act… I don't know. What do you think?' Georg was staring down at the floor, and failed to respond. 'Georg?'

'Hmm?' he replied. 'I'm sorry, Tiggy, I was a million miles away.'

'That's all right, Georg,' she chuckled. 'It can wait until another day.'

'I have a question actually, Georg,' said Star. 'But I'm a little bit nervous about the answer.'

'No problem, Star. Please, ask away.'

'Well, when I was adopted, Pa didn't know about my birth mother, did he? Sylvia—who left me with her mother?'

Georg shook his head. 'Of course not, Star, no. The palace had informed Rupert that a baby had been delivered to an orphanage by Patricia Brown. The revelation that you weren't her daughter after all, but her granddaughter, only became apparent during your own investigation of your past. Your pa genuinely had no idea.'

'Okay, just checking,' Star said, clearly slightly relieved.

'It probably would have taken the shine off your miraculous adoption if Atlas had known you had a loving mother who didn't want to give you up,' Mouse chipped in. Star glared at him, and he looked apologetic.

'I guess I have a similar question,' said CeCe.

'Please, ask it,' Georg urged.

'Did Pa definitely leave your details at the hospital in Broome? So that if Sarah or Francis had arrived, they could have gotten in touch?'

'Absolutely. I even telephoned Broome Hospital on several occasions over the years to check if anyone had enquired about you.'

'That's good to know, thank you, Georg,' replied a reassured CeCe.

'What about my grandmother, Stella?' Electra asked. 'I know that she and Pa went on to meet. In fact, he was the one that ended up telling her half of my story.'

'You're spot on, Electra, yes. My team and I discovered that Cecily went on to be a teacher at a Harlem school, established specifically with the aim of sending underprivileged black children to Ivy League colleges. As you might imagine, she was the only white teacher. She was famous. People really remembered her.'

'I bet they did.'

Georg continued. 'Eventually, we managed to get in touch with Rosalind—Cecily's friend who was, eventually, *legally* registered as Stella's mother. She was able to tell us all about your grandmother… Columbia University, civil rights organisation, a career at the UN…not to mention her daughter, Rosa.'

'My mother,' confirmed Electra, for the table's benefit.

'Right. Your pa told Rosalind about the business card they had found with the child at Mother Hale's house. Rosalind couldn't believe it. She told him that Cecily had kept the card as a token of good luck for many years, and passed it on to Stella when she returned to Africa. Stella must have given it to Rosa.'

'My brain is beginning to ache,' laughed Chrissie.

'Yeah, this is a movie in itself!' gasped Mary-Kate, taking a swig of her rosé.

'When we asked what had happened to Rosa, Rosalind confirmed that she had died of a drug overdose.' Electra cast her eyes down to the floor. Tiggy put an arm around her sister. 'I had some contacts in New York look into it. They found the…'

'Crack den,' Electra interjected, sparing Georg his awkwardness.

'Yes, *that place* which Rosa frequented. We were told that someone had snatched you away when you were crying, so that the police wouldn't come to investigate. It appears that as her final act, your mother pushed Pa's card into the assailant's hand. He must have left it in the basket with you. When you think about it, she saved you.'

The table took a moment to reflect on the poignancy of Rosa's decision. The silence was broken by the first steward, who appeared from the salon and asked if her team could clear the dinner plates. 'Yes, thank you,' Ma confirmed. As the *Titan*'s finest crockery was collected, Maia could have sworn she noticed Jack's hand subtly move across to Ally's knee under the tablecloth. She caught her sister's eye, and raised an eyebrow. Ally's blush confirmed Maia's suspicion. She smiled to herself.

'Anyone for more vino?' Charlie asked, receiving several nods. 'Smashing. I'll top up the reds. Would you mind doing white, Miles?' Miles stood up to oblige, and Charlie's eyes widened. 'Bugger, sorry. You don't drink, do you? Floriano, would—' Miles put a hand up to quiet him.

'No worries, Doc. Thankfully my teetotal status doesn't prevent pouring for others.' Charlie laughed nervously.

As the pair went around the table with the bottles, CeCe began to frown. 'The diary finished in a really weird place, didn't it?'

There was general agreement from the sisters. 'Yes,' said Star. 'Georg, why did the diary stop in 1993?'

He looked nervous. 'Your father intended it to stand as a definitive record of how each of you came into his life. And, of course, as an explanation for some of the odd circumstances you endured whilst growing up.'

'Cheers to that.' CeCe raised her refilled glass.

'Do you know what happened to the diamond?' asked Tiggy. 'The first half of the diary mentioned it frequently. But as soon as Pa settled in Atlantis, he stopped talking about it.'

'Good point, Tigs. Was it handed back to the Eszus?' Electra asked.

'Your father was very protective over the location of the jewel, even with me. He hated talking about it, seeing it as a symbol of all that he had lost in his life. As for its current location...' Georg merely shrugged.

'Maybe he just...threw it into the ocean?' pondered Star, sipping her white wine.

The table was quiet once again as each member of the extended D'Aplièse family drew their own conclusions about the fate of the mysterious diamond.

Merry spoke next. 'Did he continue to search for my mother after 1993?' she asked. 'Did he keep travelling when you gave him a new lead, Georg?'

'Yes, Merry. He never, ever stopped, until his failing health prevented him from taking so many flights in the mid-2000s. It is only as a result of his tireless efforts that you are sat here today.'

'But, to confirm, he never successfully located Elle?' Maia asked.

Georg swallowed hard. 'Your father never found her.'

Merry gave a large sigh. 'I wonder what happened to her.'

'One thing I still don't understand is how you found the coordinates that led us to Merry,' CeCe mused. 'The dots don't connect. You must have received some new information a year ago that led to you engraving the armillary sphere.'

Georg nodded. 'That's true.'

Star leant in. 'So, don't leave us in suspense, Georg. What was the information?'

He hesitated, and took a moment to dab his brow with his handkerchief.

'Was it something to do with Zed?' Maia pressed. 'Seeing as the coordinates lead to a house his family owned?'

'No. It was nothing to do with Zed. Girls...' Georg took a deep breath. 'I'm sure there is a better way of doing this. But for once, on this occasion, I find myself a little unprepared. As you know, your father's diary ended in 1993. He did not write in it again, largely because of the fact that his life quietened down. I truly believe that the last two decades of his existence were his happiest.'

'Is there a "but" coming?' asked Electra.

Georg continued. 'After that first appointment with his doctor, when we knew his health was beginning to fail, I asked him if he wanted to write down the tale of his early years, before the diary began in Paris.' Georg paused to take a sip of water. 'He told me that, although he had considered it many times, the memories of Russia caused him too much pain. Nonetheless, he ensured that I was ready to fill in any blanks, and answer the questions that you might have.'

'That's good, because I still feel like there's so much we don't know,' Star lamented. 'We don't even have an account of what happened between Pa and Kreeg as children.'

Electra folded her arms. 'Okay, Georg. Tell us about Russia.'

'That was certainly my intention. But, as things have turned out, he will be able to tell you in his own words.' He stood up and briefly disappeared inside the salon.

Maia turned to Ally. 'Do you know what's going on? Merry and I saw you haranguing Georg in the corridor earlier.'

Ally was resolute in her response. 'After we watched Zed on

television earlier, I saw Georg losing the plot on the deck outside. Long story short, I demanded to know why.'

'Hang on, is this why you wanted all of us to finish the diary before dinner this evening?' Electra asked. Ally nodded.

Georg returned with a big chunk of white paper, which he began to distribute evenly amongst the sisters.

'What are these? Extra pages of the diary?' Tiggy asked.

'Not quite, no,' Ally said.

Star was scrutinising the paper. 'Look at Pa's handwriting here. It's nowhere near as good. He had arthritis in his wrists from the sailing in his later years,' she theorised. 'Therefore… this was written much more recently. I'm right, aren't I, Georg?'

The lawyer gave a solemn nod.

'When did he write this? Just before he died?' Merry asked.

Georg didn't answer her question. Instead, he took a moment to steel himself, and separate his feelings from his duty. 'What you have before you is the true story of your father's final days, and how they relate to his beginnings. I must warn you that as soon as you begin to read, you will be faced with information that *will* differ from the account given to you by myself, and by Marina.'

'Ma?' Tiggy asked, sounding wounded.

'Please, *chérie*, listen to Georg.'

'I wish you to know that Ma and I never set out to deceive you. Everything we have done over the course of the last year was designed by your pa, and Marina and I have merely executed his plan.'

'Oh God,' moaned Electra.

The tension at the table was palpable. Georg continued resolutely. 'You have all read his diary, and are aware that Marina and I owe everything to him. He inspired in us an…'—Georg considered his next words—'…unending loyalty. As you will shortly read, everything we have done was in an attempt to ensure your continued safety.'

'It's one twist after another,' whispered Maia, shaking her head.

'I know, *chérie*, I know,' said Ma, tears in her eyes. 'But this is it. The ultimate truth is within these last pages.'

Georg exhaled deeply. 'I must tell you that I was under strict instructions from your pa not to present you with these final pages until...a particular moment...but, after conversing with Ally earlier, I decided that this would be the right thing to do instead.'

Star looked distraught. 'Georg...what are we going to find out?' she asked. Georg simply shook his head. 'Ally?'

'I haven't read any of this. I just have an outline from Georg,' she replied. Boldly, Jack put his arm around her, in a show of protection.

Georg put his hands behind his back and formulated his thoughts. 'As you now know, your pa's heart began to fail in his mid-eighties, a fact of which you were all then largely unaware. The last thing on earth that he wished to do was cause any of you pain.' The entire table was on tenterhooks, hanging on his every word. 'Having read his diary, you also now know of the lifelong threat Kreeg Eszu presented, which...'—Georg bowed his head—'seems to have continued down the generations. When your father realised that his time was getting short, and that he would no longer be on earth to protect you himself, he devised a plan to save his girls from future persecution by either Kreeg himself, or his son Zed.'

'What was that plan, Georg?' Tiggy asked nervously.

'To confront him.'

'Oh my God,' Merry murmured.

'They died on the same day...' Maia breathed. 'Ally, when you saw the *Titan* that day, you said there were reports of the *Olympus* nearby?' Ally nodded.

'So wait, he didn't die at Atlantis like you said?' CeCe asked frantically.

'No, CeCe, he did not.'

'Holy shit, Georg! And I suppose you knew about this too, Ma? How could you betray us like this?' cried Electra.

'I know it's upsetting,' said Ally, 'but you mustn't blame them. There's much more to the story.'

'Did Kreeg kill him? Did *he* kill Kreeg? Jesus!' cried CeCe.

'Please, girls, you must read,' Georg pleaded.

'We can't all just sit here and read, that's ridiculous,' said

CeCe. 'Star'—she turned to her sister—'would you read these pages to all of us? As you've been doing for me?'

'Oh. Is that what everyone wants?'

There was general agreement around the table.

Star looked terribly nervous at being handed such a responsibility. Mouse placed a gentle hand on her back. She took a deep breath and swallowed hard. 'All right then,' Star replied.

'Are you girls all right with the other halves here?' Chrissie asked. 'Or shall we scarper?'

'No, stay. All of you,' Maia said, making sure to look at Mary-Kate and Jack, too. 'Everyone here is part of the story, in one way or another. I think we should all be here to understand its ending.'

'Agreed,' said Ally, leaning into Jack's shoulder. The table didn't possess the mental capacity to comment on that particular revelation in the middle of the whirlwind.

'Before we start,' Electra said. 'Miles, make yourself useful and grab a few more bottles of wine from downstairs.

'I might have a gin and tonic,' Tiggy added. 'I think it's what Pa would have chosen at this moment.'

'Me too,' said CeCe.

'That sounds good.' Star nodded.

'Right,' said Mouse, standing up, 'I'll do a round of strong G&Ts. Come on, Miles!'

Each of the seven sisters began to prepare themselves for what lay ahead. In their own ways, every one of them had held suspicions about the circumstances surrounding their father's death. Would the man that cared for them all so much really rob his daughters of an opportunity to say goodbye? It had never truly made sense.

Once drinks had been replenished, and every seat at the table once again occupied, Star cleared her throat. 'Are we ready?'

'Yes, Star,' Ally said. 'We're all ready.'

Star turned her attention to the papers in front of her. 'Here we go then. "My girls. My precious, precious girls…"'

Pa's Final Pages

The Titan

June 2007

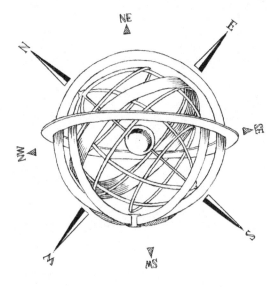

55

My girls. My precious, precious girls. If you are reading this, then Georg has done his duty. By now, you will know that I am truly gone, and you are ready to know the full circumstances of my departure from this earth. Rest assured that I am looking down on you from the next life, which, as you know, I believe in with my whole heart.

If Georg has followed my instructions, then each of you will have been on quite the journey recently, discovering your pasts, and how I came to adopt you. I imagine some of it was painful, but I hope that it brought you great amounts of joy, too. No doubt you will have read my diary by now, and any blanks in the stories of how we all came to meet have been filled in. Your birth families were all very dear to me, and everything I was able to become, I owe to them.

I wish to be clear with you. The following pages were not part of my original design. As I hope to explain, the course of events I predicted did not unfold as expected. Far from it.

My diary will have told you that my whole existence has been burdened by the life of another. Kreeg Eszu believes that I, Atlas Tanit, killed his mother and stole a priceless diamond from her body when we were starving in Siberia in the 1920s. For this reason, as you know, he has pursued me for my entire life.

In the autumn of 2005, I suffered a small heart attack, which I did not wish to worry you with unduly. However, as the doctors in Geneva investigated, I was given the news that my most important organ was failing, and that, although they could not say for certain, I would be lucky to make it past my ninetieth birthday. The news was not at all devastating to me. I have lived a long, long time—longer than I had any expectations of. It has been the greatest privilege of my life to watch each of you grow into a remarkable individual, and I thank my lucky stars that I have been permitted the time I have here on earth.

Nonetheless, the news of my failing health prompted me to take urgent action. Without my protective presence, I worried that you would be vulnerable to persecution by either Kreeg himself, or his son Zed. Therefore, working alongside Georg and Ma (as it has been my honour to do for most of my life), I devised a scenario which I believed would prevent Kreeg and his son from ever darkening your doorstep again.

As you will have surmised, the justice Kreeg Eszu seeks above all else is retributive. It is retribution for an act which, I'm sure I do not need to stress, I did not commit. Nonetheless, I calculated that if I allowed Kreeg to finally exact the revenge he had been seeking for eighty years, by taking my life, then we might be able to strike a deal to ensure that you were left alone. In the spring of 2007, I contacted Eszu via a letter sent to Lightning Communications. In this letter, I told him of the regret I harboured for all that had happened between us, and that I wished to give him the opportunity to 'make things right'.

It did not surprise me that within twenty-four hours, Georg had received a phone call from Kreeg's private secretary, and a destination for our encounter was set—a secluded cove just off the coast of Delos in the Aegean Sea.

To protect you from the awful truth of the situation, knowing I was heading to my death anyway, I arranged for you to be told that I had suffered a final, fatal heart attack. I asked Ma to inform you that my body had been removed immediately, placed in a lead coffin and taken out to sea on the *Titan*, where a private funeral had taken place.

Without a doubt, this part of my plan was the hardest to navigate. I am aware of the pain and confusion that such an announcement will have caused you, and for that, and so much else, I am deeply, deeply sorry. But I hope you are able to see that it was the only thing I could think of to avoid you discovering that I had been killed by Kreeg Eszu.

On 19th June, I took control of the *Titan* from Hans Gaia at its port in Nice, informing him that he was to pick it up from the cove in Delos in four days' time. Hans tried his best to convince me of the dangers and, indeed, the laws against crewing the yacht by myself, but I stood my ground, and as the owner, ordered the engineers and officers off my vessel.

Despite everything, my gentle cruise to Delos was a peaceful experience, filled with memories of our lives together. I assure you, I felt nothing but tranquillity on what I was certain would be my final journey.

On the third day of the voyage, I carefully navigated the *Titan* into the agreed bay, and saw that the *Olympus* was waiting for me. On its bow was a lone figure. I brought the yacht around so that the boats were parallel, dropped the anchor and walked out onto the bridge deck.

Opposite me was the face that has haunted my nightmares for eighty years. The face I had seen on the worst day of my life in Siberia, in a cafe in Leipzig and outside Arthur Morston Books. For a while, we said nothing, simply absorbing one another, in anticipation of what was to come next.

'Hello, Kreeg.'

'Hello, Atlas. I've been waiting a very long time to see you.'

'I know. May I come aboard?' Kreeg smiled, and grabbed a metal gangplank from his deck. He passed one end over to me. 'Thank you.' I warily climbed up onto it, and crawled from the *Titan* to the *Olympus*.

'I see you've lost a little of your speed,' Kreeg sneered.

'I never really had that much to begin with. I remember you were always faster when we played football in the snow.'

'Inevitably,' he cackled. 'You spent too much time with your head buried in books.'

I lowered myself down onto the deck. 'Maybe so. May I ask if we are alone?'

Kreeg nodded. 'We are.' He slowly reached behind his back. I knew what was coming. Eszu produced a small metal pistol, and pointed it at my stomach. 'Do you recognise this, Atlas?' he asked.

I shook my head and replied calmly. 'I'm afraid I don't, no.'

'It's a Korovin pistol.'

I raised my eyebrows. 'Of course. The first Soviet automatic pistol, if I'm not mistaken? All the guards had them when we were children. The Bolsheviks, too.'

'I am pleased your memory is still intact.' Kreeg approached me slowly, until he was only inches away. He pointed the barrel firmly into my abdomen. 'I have kept this one with me. I took it from the body of a dead soldier. Over the years, I have carried it in the hope that we might be reunited.'

'Before you kill me, Kreeg, would you like to know the truth?'

'Truth?' Kreeg parroted, before erupting into a deep, throaty laugh. 'Such an interesting word. Do not worry, Atlas. I have not waited this long to shoot you on sight. There are some things I wish to share with you, also. Now, turn around.' I followed his instructions. 'Put your hands up, too.'

'As you wish, Kreeg.'

He jammed the pistol into my back. 'Walk to the aft deck. I have placed a table and two chairs so that we might have our final conversation.' We slowly walked along the *Olympus* until we reached the back of the yacht. A mahogany table was placed between two dining chairs. 'Sit.'

I pulled out a chair, as did Kreeg. Still grasping the gun tightly, he placed his wrist on the table between us, so the pistol was aimed directly at my chest.

'It's a beautiful yacht you have, Kreeg.'

'Not quite as grand as yours,' he spat.

We stared into one another's eyes. His were so full of rage. I tried to calm him. 'So, here I am, unarmed and sat in front of you after all these years of running. I wait for you to extract what you have always believed is your rightful revenge. I ask only one thing, Kreeg—that after I am dead, you will consider the feud over. And ask you—and your son—to leave my precious daughters alone.'

Kreeg gave me another smile, this time revealing a set of whitened teeth and a menacing aspect. 'For me, Atlas, it has been over for many years.'

'It has?' I queried.

Eszu shrugged. 'You believe that I could not have come to your door at any time during the last forty years? Atlantis. A personal palace named with characteristic pomposity.'

'You've known where I was for the entire time?'

'Of course I have. Since the nineteen seventies.'

'Then why did you not come?'

Kreeg grinned again. 'All in good time.'

'Is it because you were using your son to prey on my daughters?'

'Your girls obviously have a certain…charm for him.' Kreeg cocked the pistol. 'Now tell me, what is it you have to say to me before you die?'

I shook my head. 'I'm beginning to wonder what the point would be. I told you the truth more than eighty years ago, as we stood together over the body of your mother.' Kreeg's jaw tensed, and he narrowed his eyes. 'We were brothers, Kreeg. You didn't believe me then. Why should you believe me now?'

'What is there to *believe*, Atlas? I will never forget you standing there, with her precious icon in your hand. It was covered in her blood. You used it to beat her to death. The leather pouch containing the diamond slung across your body confirmed your motives.'

I shuddered at the memory. 'I told you what had happened.'

'As you well know, your mother was sleeping with a senior officer of the Red Army to put food on our table.'

Kreeg baulked at the memory.

'I didn't even know it was a diamond she possessed. She only told me that she had something of great value and had pleaded with the officer to sell it on her behalf, so that we could eat, Kreeg. Do you not remember how hungry we were? How cold…'

'NO MORE!' Kreeg screeched, banging his free fist on the table.

'Just listen. That night, I tried to give you proof that your mother had realised her mistake and had asked me to take a "thing of value" to her relative in Tobolsk for safekeeping. So that if the Bolsheviks came to search the house, it would not be there. I had a letter in my hands, from your mother. She'd written it so that I could pass it on to her relative. But when you saw the scene, you didn't even read it.'

'I didn't need to,' he snarled.

'You just screwed it up and stuffed it in my mouth…'

'You were LYING to save your sad skin. You *knew* about the diamond! Don't tell me you didn't! You wanted it for yourself. So you waited until she was vulnerable and you…' Kreeg wavered, and his eyes filled with tears.

I spoke coolly but firmly. 'I knew nothing of the diamond until that night, as I ran from the house when you tried to kill me. But what does it matter now? You will never accept my word. Please, I beg of you, extract the revenge you have always dreamt of.'

Kreeg had begun to breathe heavily. Maintaining eye contact, he reached into his pocket with his spare hand and produced a pill. He swallowed it without water, and winced. 'I'm sure you have heard of my diagnosis. It has been reported in the news.'

I nodded. 'I have. I was sorry to learn about it. Cancer is the cruellest of illnesses.'

He shrugged 'The cancer is nothing compared to what you took from me that day.'

I sighed. 'I took nothing from you, I swear. But if you mean to say how cruel it is to never know the love of a mother, then you are right.'

Kreeg jeered. 'Excellent point, Atlas. You didn't just kill *my* mother. You killed your own, years before!'

His words caused me visceral pain. 'I know,' I said. 'I have thought of it often, and wished that the universe had taken me and not her on the day I was born.'

He leant back in his chair a little, clearly enjoying my pain. 'Ironically, you would not be alive without my mother. She delivered you.'

'I know. She told me many times, and I hope that I was able to repay her by acting as a dutiful child, particularly after my father left.'

Kreeg held my gaze. 'This letter you speak of. The one from my mother. It is a shame you don't still have it, Atlas.'

'I do.'

'What?'

'I have held on to it for dear life. Would you like to read it?'
Kreeg nodded slowly. 'May I reach into my pocket?'

'Slowly.'

I cautiously retrieved the letter from my trousers and placed it on the table. 'There you are. Still battered and covered in teeth marks from that awful day.'

Kreeg peered down at the envelope. 'It is addressed to Gustav Melin.'

'Your mother's cousin.' I nodded.

'You open it, Atlas. If you think I'm putting this gun down, you are mistaken.'

'As you wish.' I took the envelope and gently removed the ancient piece of paper from within, before sliding it back across to Kreeg. He observed the contents.

Dear Gustav,

I hope you and Alyona are as well as can be. I regret that I have not been in touch as often as I would have liked. Things have been hard since Cronus died.

As you know, the Red Army are monitoring us very closely. For this reason, I wonder whether I might ask a favour of you?

If you are reading this, then young Atlas is standing before you. He is a trusted messenger, and carries upon his person a package of immeasurable value.

Gustav, you are the only family I have left. I must ask you to keep the package safe until tensions have eased, and we are no longer under such scrutiny.

I would ask you not to unwrap the package, but if you do, then I know it will be tempting to sell the item for yourself. Please, Gustav, however tempted you may be, remember that I have two starving boys in my care. When I am able, I will sell the item, and reward you with a handsome commission.

I must ask this of you for I have made a mistake. I informed a Bolshevik soldier about its existence. I am worried that they will come for it.

Please confirm with Atlas that you are a willing recipient, and he will transfer the package.

Thank you, Gustav. I believe you will prove yourself a loyal cousin.

Yours, with love,

Rhea Eszu

'Are you still able to recognise your mother's handwriting?' I asked, once Kreeg had finished reading.

He nodded. 'I am. I do not doubt that the letter is hers. But it does not absolve you in any way. This changes nothing.'

'I hope it lends context to the truth of what happened that day. That morning, your mother handed me the letter, and then a leather pouch, which she hung around my neck. I swear, Kreeg, I did not know what was held within.'

'Nonsense! Why would my mother trust you with such an important task? As you have already admitted, I was physically stronger. And her own flesh and blood.'

'That is precisely why she chose me. The journey was over twenty miles through the frozen conditions. There was no guarantee I would even survive the trip. She was protecting you.'

Kreeg narrowed his eyes. 'A convenient excuse.'

'Merely the truth. As you'll recall, you were out of the house during those days anyway, receiving your academic tuition in the neighbouring village. It was only made available to one of us. If that does not assure you that your mother had only your interests at heart, I do not know what will.'

He raised his gun a few inches off the table. 'Continue with your account.'

I swallowed hard. 'I remember opening the door to the house to begin my journey. The wind practically forced me back into the hallway. But I struggled outside, and closed the door behind me. I made it about thirty feet away from the house before I saw them.'

'Them?'

'The soldiers. Bolsheviks. There were five of them. I knew that their presence meant trouble. I was scared…so I ran for the coal shed and hid myself there. As they approached the house, I saw that they were being led by the man your mother was sleeping with. They banged on the door, but your mother didn't answer. So they shot the handle and forced entry. I heard her scream…' I had to pause for a moment and regather myself, as I replayed the sound in my mind. 'Then they ransacked the house. They smashed vases, lamps, dismantled beds…you remember the devastation.'

Kreeg stayed silent for a moment. 'I do.'

'It felt like their search lasted for a long time. But they could not find what they were looking for, because it was hung around my neck. When they didn't get their prize, the men became angry. They began to shout at their leader, calling him a liar, cursing him for bringing them all here. That caused him to turn on your mother. She protested her innocence vigorously, but he didn't accept it. I heard her pleading... She said she had a son, that they would make him an orphan...' Tears were in my eyes as I recounted the events. 'There was a series of thuds, and your mother's cries grew quieter and quieter, until there was silence. Then the men simply left, returning to the snow from where they had come.' I took a moment to gather myself, not wanting to leave out any detail. 'After a while, I dared to emerge from the coal shed. I was so scared... I walked inside and saw all that they had done. Destroyed our home. I called out for your mother, but no part of me expected her to return my cry. I found her next to the bloodied wooden icon which the tsarevich had given to your father in recognition of his loyal service. That was the weapon the men had used, no doubt as a final message to express their hatred for the tsar and his associates.'

Kreeg drummed his fingers on the table. 'You had it in your hand when I entered the room.'

'Yes. I'd merely picked it up to move it away from her. That was all, I swear on the lives of my daughters.'

Kreeg dared to look away from me, and out over the water. 'I knew something was amiss as I approached the house, because the door was open. I crept inside as quietly as I could, not knowing who I would find. But it was just you.' He turned back to meet my eye. 'Do you remember what you said to me, Atlas?'

I swallowed hard. 'I'm sorry,' I whispered.

'I didn't think you were sorry for what you had done. I thought you were sorry that you had been caught.'

'You launched yourself at me, Kreeg, without pause. I remember to this day the force with which you ripped the icon out of my hand. You were so strong.'

'But you wrestled it back...'

'And you forced me to the ground.'

Kreeg licked his lips at the memory. 'In the struggle, your shirt ripped open. That's when I saw the leather pouch. I'd observed it around my mother's neck many times. I knew then what you had done. Murdering thief.'

'The difference between us, Kreeg, is that you knew precisely what the pouch contained. I did not.'

'So you say, Atlas. Yes, I knew of the diamond. I too had heard her talk of it, in less veiled terms than you claim. It was my way out. My ticket to salvation. And you took it from me. You took it all away.' Kreeg slowly shook his head.

'That's when I managed to reach into my pocket and wave the letter in front of your face. And you tried to choke me with it.'

'It nearly worked.'

'Yes. If I hadn't managed to grab the icon...'

'And attack me with it.'

'*Defend* myself with it... I would be dead.'

Kreeg bristled. 'We'll remedy that soon, Atlas.'

'We both know what happened next. Whilst you were disorientated, I ran out into the snow. I was already dressed for a long journey.' I gave a small shrug. 'Little did I know how long that journey would last...'

'When I regained my wits, I followed you to the door.'

'And the words you shouted have haunted me ever since.'

'I will find you, Atlas Tanit, wherever you may hide. And I will kill you,' Kreeg repeated.

I nodded. 'I ran for as long as I could, to put as much distance between you and me as possible. Eventually, I collapsed in a disused barn.' The memories were so clear in my mind. It was as if I was reliving every painful moment. 'I was scared beyond belief, Kreeg. I had no one. So I resolved to do the only thing I could think of—try to find my father.'

Kreeg stroked his chin. 'It is what I calculated you would do. I thought that, maybe, the Siberian midwinter would claim you...but you survived. I've never had the opportunity to ask how.' He gave me a quizzical stare.

'I don't know, Kreeg. My journey across Russia took me eighteen months. I knew that Switzerland was west of Tobolsk, so that is where I walked.'

'How did you know in which direction you were travelling?'

I pointed up to the sky. 'The stars. My father used to spend hours teaching me about the Seven Sisters. It is how I navigated.'

Kreeg scoffed. 'Navigation is all well and good, but how did you keep the cold and hunger at bay?'

I closed my eyes. 'I believe the stars kept me safe. Always, when I was at my weakest, I would happen upon an empty cabin, or a kind stranger would take pity on me. But I am ashamed to say that I was forced into performing deeds that no one would be proud of.'

'You stole?'

I nodded. 'I stole. I lied. I manipulated people. But I lived.'

Kreeg scrutinised me. 'Nobody would believe that an eight-year-old boy could survive an eighteen-month trip across the Russian wilderness.'

I put my hands out to express my disbelief a little too quickly, and Kreeg's grip on the pistol tightened. 'I have experienced things in my life which have confirmed that the realm of the physical is only part of the human story. I cannot explain how I lived. But live I did.' Kreeg huffed, not satisfied with my answer. 'In the end, I managed to overshoot Switzerland. I ended up under a bush in a Parisian garden, where I finally collapsed.'

My enemy continued with his own narrative, despite the truth of the situation. 'So, you were trying to find your father to give him the diamond. He knew of its existence and instructed you to steal it! The pair of you plotted together.'

I rejected his assertion. 'I do not blame you, Kreeg, but you are blind to reason. I swear on my daughters' lives, I never knew about the diamond. I did not even know it *was* a diamond until I was in that barn and looked inside the leather pouch your mother had given me. And even then, I believed it was made of Onyx or some such semi-precious stone, for your mother had smeared it in black boot polish and varnished it with the glue she used for her bone carvings. It was only when it began to leave marks on my fingers that I took a rag to clean it and realised what was hidden beneath. Here.' I slowly undid two buttons on my shirt, and removed the battered leather pouch from around my neck.

'What is this?'

'What do you think, Kreeg? I wish you had given me a chance to return it eighty years ago, but you were intent on killing me first, and back then, I did not wish to die. Nor on the other occasions you have hunted me down and I have yet again run for my life. In Leipzig, when you set the building containing my lodgings on fire, or in the bookshop in London… Nevertheless, I have kept it safe for all these years. I hoped that if it came to it, I would be able to return it to you in exchange for my life, and the safety of my daughters.' Kreeg picked up the pouch, and attempted to undo the drawstring with one hand, which proved an impossibility. 'There is no need to keep the pistol trained on me, Kreeg. I am eighty-nine years old. Even if I wanted to, I could not run. Remember, I am here willingly.'

Kreeg considered, and after a moment, slowly placed the gun on the table. Then he undid the pouch, and gently removed the contents. He examined the rock closely, and began to scrub away the boot polish on his trousers. Having done so, he held it up to the light, where it sparkled magnificently in the Mediterranean sun.

Kreeg looked genuinely perplexed. 'Why would you not sell it?'

'It was not mine to sell.'

'So you acknowledge you stole it!'

'No. I acknowledge that through circumstances beyond my control, I came into its possession.'

Kreeg paused, and for the first time, I saw a small flicker of doubt pass across his tanned face. 'So, you have kept the diamond. But you can never return my mother.'

'I cannot, brother, no. But if it was not for the diamond, please tell me why I would have wished her dead? She was all we had. Believe me when I say that I loved her.'

Kreeg rolled the diamond around in his palm. 'You loved the thought of food in your belly more.'

I put my head in my hands. 'Who can ever prove their love for another? It exists in the soul and is based on trust. If you trusted me the way I believed you did, you would know I could never harm her.'

'Fine words, Atlas. You always had those.'

'A fine diamond, which…I have now…returned.' I closed

my eyes. The air from the fresh, salty sea filled my lungs, and I felt the warmth of the sun on my face. Involuntarily, I stretched my arms above my head, and a heavenly peace descended on me. 'Kreeg…no longer do I hold the weight of the world on my shoulders. I am grateful to you for giving me the opportunity to tell you the truth of what happened, whether you believe me or not. And now… I am free. Pick up the pistol, brother. I have surrendered and am happy to die.'

Eszu hesitated. 'Is there anything you wish to ask me before you do?'

I thought for a moment. 'Yes, actually. There is. You are fixated on the idea that I knew of the diamond's existence. You mentioned moments ago that you believe my father had told me about it. Kreeg, he had not. So, please—tell me what you meant.'

Eszu nodded. 'As you wish, Atlas. You have told me your story. And now, I shall tell you mine. Let me begin with your birth.'

56

Tyumen, Siberia, 1918

Tsar Nicholas II's reign had been characterised by a growing discontent amongst his people, which he himself had failed to alleviate or quash. The anger, in the most part, had been caused by the distribution of land in the country, most of which was owned by the aristocracy.

The majority of Russia's deeply religious people attended church on a weekly basis, where it was preached that Nicholas had been chosen as tsar by God. But, as bellies went continually hungry, the congregations slowly began to question why their divine ruler required so much land and power to exercise his duties, when their families had so little. Thus, the social revolutionary movement began to gain momentum. It had culminated in February of 1917, where days of protest and violent clashes gave Tsar Nicholas II little choice but to relinquish the throne. He passed the tsardom to his brother, Grand Duke Michael Alexandrovich. But the duke had seen which way the wind was blowing, and refused to ascend—stating that he would only do so if warranted through democratic action.

As a result, a provisional government, led by Alexander Kerensky, was formed. The initial solution to the problem of the purposeless monarchy seemed to be exile. After February, opportunities for asylum looked relatively promising. But, after months of debate, Britain and France withdrew their offers of residency, as the tsar's wife, Alexandra, was regarded as pro-German.

The question of what to do with the family therefore raged on, but during Kerensky's premiership, the Romanovs existed in relative safety. After the revolution, the royal family were escorted to the Governor's Mansion in Tobolsk, where they were allowed to live in comfort, with a significant government subsidy provided to fund their existence. In addition, several members of the royal household had also been permitted to travel to Tobolsk with the Romanovs, with the tsar and tsarina choosing their most trusted companions to accompany them.

A few months later, the October Revolution came. The people were unhappy with Russia's continued involvement in the First World War, and the manner in which Kerensky had ruled with an iron fist. Because of this, the Bolshevik Red Army overthrew the provisional government and seized power. They installed their talismanic leader, Vladimir Lenin, as premier.

Suddenly, the situation for the Russian royal family looked bleaker, with their fate fiercely debated amongst Bolsheviks. Some had favoured extradition. Others wished for the family to face life imprisonment. Many wanted a straight execution, to eliminate what they believed to be the cancer that prevented true equality for the Russian people.

After Lenin took power, the amount of time the Romanovs were permitted to spend outside the Governor's Mansion was policed. The family was even prevented from walking to church on Sundays. Needless to say, the subsidy they had been granted by Kerensky's government was cut, and 'luxuries' such as butter and coffee disappeared overnight.

The leaders of the party eventually agreed that the best course of action for Tsar Nicholas was a show trial in Moscow, so that the Bolsheviks might demonstrate their grip on power. But in order for that to happen, they needed the tsar alive.

This could not be guaranteed. Amongst the lower ranks, discontent about the tsar's fate was increasing, and in March of 1918, rival factions of Bolsheviks descended on Tobolsk. Fears grew for the safety of the royal family, and the government appointed a special commissar to move the family 350 miles west of the settlement to the city of Ekaterinburg.

Commissar Vasily Yakovlev and his men decided to begin the perilous journey in the dead of the night. Nicholas, Alexandra and their eldest daughter Olga were traipsed out of bed at two a.m., along with several members of the royal household. The party were forced to endure fording rivers, changing coaches and observing the narrow foiling of several assassination attempts. After 150 miles of perilous travel, the family and their entourage arrived in the city of Tyumen, where Yakovlev requisitioned a train to speed them to Ekaterinburg.

'You will board,' he barked at the former tsar.

'Very well,' Nicholas replied, and took Olga by the hand. Alexandra followed behind.

Lapetus Tanit, personal astrologer to the tsar and teacher to the tsarevich and his sisters, put his arm around his wife, Clymene—herself a lady-in-waiting to the tsarina. Clymene was heavily pregnant, and Lapetus had spent the entire journey fretting about her welfare. Nonetheless, they had no choice but to follow the orders of Commissar Yakovlev. If they had remained in Tobolsk, the Red Guards would have seen to them.

Clymene went to follow Alexandra, but grimaced in pain after a single step.

Lapetus held her arm tightly. 'Are you all right, my darling?'

'Yes,' she gasped. 'He's very active today.'

'Oh, we're calling the baby *he* now, are we?' Lapetus asked, mustering a smile.

'Stop!' Yakovlev cried as the couple approached the train. 'Family only.'

'What would you like us to do?' Lapetus asked.

'You will go in this carriage.' Yakovlev pointed to a separate train car with no locomotive.

'Is… His Majesty aware of this?'

Yakovlev laughed. 'It matters not what he is aware of. Now,' he said, raising his weapon. 'Get in that carriage.'

Lapetus stood firmly. 'Is it necessary to point a gun at a pregnant woman?'

'Absolutely, because, like you, she blindly serves an evil

autocrat.'

Lapetus felt a hand on his shoulder. 'Come on, my friend. Let's go.'

Cronus Eszu was a Prussian count, and had been a loyal member of the royal household since the ascension of Nicholas's father. He was responsible for teaching the royal children languages and foreign culture. As Lapetus was responsible for music and Classics, their lessons often shared aspects, and Cronus and Lapetus had become firm friends over the years. Cronus was married to Rhea—also a lady-in-waiting to Alexandra—and together they had a four-year-old son, Kreeg.

It had been speculated by many that Tsar Nicholas II was not as fond of Cronus as his father was, but had elected for him to remain in the household post revolution due to his young son, to whom he did not wish to pass on a death sentence.

'You're right, Cronus,' Lapetus replied. 'What choice do we have?'

He helped his wife up into the neighbouring carriage, which was dark, damp and altogether miserable. Lapetus took Kreeg from Cronus's arms and lifted him up inside. 'There we go, little man.' Lapetus surveyed the surroundings. 'Good Lord, it's *biting* in here, isn't it?'

'Yes. Somehow it's worse inside than out,' Clymene replied.

All in all, there were seven members of the royal household ordered into the carriage, including Alexandra's dressmaker and two other ladies-in-waiting. Once the last of the party had climbed in, a guard slammed the door shut.

From outside, Yakovlev screeched, 'Let's go!'

The locomotive hissed as it built up a head of steam. Both the Tanits and the Eszus watched through a carriage window as the large wheels began to turn, and the Romanovs were moved on from Tyumen station.

'Do you really think they're going to Ekaterinburg?' Rhea asked.

'Who knows, my darling,' Cronus replied. 'They're all so busy fighting and disagreeing amongst themselves.'

'Will we see them again, Lapetus?' Clymene asked her husband, a hint of a tear in her eye.

'I fear not, my love. I fear not.' He took his wife's hand.

'Those poor, innocent children, Lapetus. I can't even comprehend it.'

Suddenly, the occupants of the carriage were thrown from their feet, as a great force hit them from behind.

'What's happening?' Rhea cried from the floor.

'They're shunting us!' shouted Cronus.

After an uncomfortable few minutes, the carriage came to rest against a buffer, and the door was wrenched open by a soldier. 'You will remain here,' he said.

'Is there any chance of some food for my wife?' Lapetus asked. 'Or a blanket? As you can see, she's pregnant. You might not approve of our association with the tsar, but you cannot blame an unborn child.' The soldier rolled his eyes, but returned moments later with some coarse woollen throws and a few pieces of bread. 'Thank you,' said Lapetus sincerely.

After a few hours with no further Bolshevik instructions, the occupants of the carriage resolved to get some sleep. Each was exhausted after their marathon journey. They huddled in the corner of the carriage and packed themselves in tightly against one another to share the little bodily warmth they had.

Soon enough, the Eszus began to snore, as they were often prone to doing.

'Lapetus?' Clymene whispered. 'Are you awake?'

'Of course, my love. Are you all right?' He reached for her hand.

'Yes. But I have something to tell you. Do you think everyone is asleep?'

Lapetus craned his head to observe Cronus and Rhea, whose chests continued to rise and fall slowly. To double-check, he gave a low whistle, which received no response. 'Yes. You can speak freely.'

'All right. The night before we left Tobolsk, the tsarina tasked me with something. It is a mission which I now worry I will be unable to fulfil.'

'Tell me.'

Clymene took a deep breath. 'She knew that Yakovlev was going to move us that night. I asked if there was anything she wished to take that would remind her of her past, and her rightful position as ruler. She crossed to her dresser, where she removed a small box from the drawer and unlocked it. Then...' Clymene was interrupted by a grunt from Cronus, who resumed his snoring after a few moments. 'Then she produced the largest diamond I have ever seen in my life. She told me that it had been in the royal family for generations, and was her favourite piece. She said that she could not transport it herself, as in all likelihood it would fall into Bolshevik hands. So she...'

'Gave it to you.' Lapetus completed his wife's sentence for her.

'Yes.'

'Where is it now?'

'Safely sewn into the lining of my skirt.'

Lapetus sighed. 'I can only pray that you are given an opportunity to return it to her.'

'No one can find out about it.'

'I understand, my love.' He squeezed her hand harder. 'And no one will.' Eventually, exhaustion caught up with the Tanits, and Lapetus and Clymene descended into sleep.

When Clymene woke, a shooting pain surged through her stomach. It felt as if someone had gained access to her insides, and was scraping and scratching at them. She cried out in agony.

Lapetus sat bolt upright. 'My darling. What's wrong?'

'It's the baby,' Clymene groaned.

He put a gentle hand on her belly. 'Is everything all right?'

'I don't know. It hurts...' Another jolt of pain passed through her abdomen, and she cried out once more.

'What's going on?' asked a bleary-eyed Cronus.

'The baby,' Lapetus replied, aware that his midriff had become wet. 'My love, I think the baby is coming.'

Clymene looked panicked. 'But he is not expected for another month!'

'I think your waters have broken. Cronus, could you bring an oil lamp?'

'Of course, there's one by the door.'

The whole carriage was now awake and sitting up. Clymene screeched again. 'It's going to be all right, my darling, you'll see. I am here,' Iapetus comforted her.

Cronus returned with the lamp, and after scrabbling around in his pockets for a match, handed it to Iapetus. As he peeled back his own blankets, and then turned his attention to Clymene's, to his horror, the liquid he observed was not clear, but red.

Clymene saw the look of shock on her husband's face. 'What's wrong?'

'Nothing, my love, nothing,' said Iapetus, flustered.

'Rhea!' Cronus cried.

His wife threw off her blankets and made her way over to Clymene. Iapetus pointed to the blood, and Rhea nodded. 'Vera, Galina!' she screeched at the other two ladies-in-waiting. 'Your assistance is required.' Both women obliged.

'Mama?' came a high-pitched voice. 'What's going on?'

'It's all right, Kreeg,' Cronus said, lifting his son into his arms. 'You're going to come over here with me, and we're going to play a game of cards.'

'I'm sleepy,' Kreeg replied.

'I know. But you won't be soon.'

'Iapetus, gather as many blankets as you can. We will need them for the blood. Vera, I require water, too.'

'But we barely have enough to drink…'

'Damn it, Vera, are you unaware of our surroundings?' Rhea snapped. 'Find a way to melt some snow.' Vera scuttled out of the carriage.

Rhea felt her way under Clymene's skirt, checking for any sign of the baby. What she found alarmed her.

'Clymene, you're going to be all right. Your baby is coming, but it is the wrong way round. It will come feet-first.' She inhaled deeply. 'This will not be easy, but we will all help you through it.'

'Is that why there is so much blood?' asked a worried Galina.

Rhea nodded. 'The feet have ripped her.'

Iapetus returned with a bundle of blankets. 'What can I do?' he asked.

Rhea turned her head so only he could hear. 'Hold her hand. Stroke her hair. Pray.'

Iapetus nodded and assumed his position.

The labour was long and painful. Many times, Rhea was

convinced that Clymene would pass out, which would mean the end for her and her child. But, against all the odds, whenever it seemed that she was close to giving up, the new mother found another surge of life within her.

'All right, Clymene. One more push and your baby will be here. But it will need to be a big one. You must give it all the strength you have.' Clymene nodded through her panting. 'Good.' She turned to Lapetus. 'When the head appears, the cord will be around the neck. When I pull the child out, act as quickly as possible and unravel it. Are you clear?' A shaken Lapetus did his best to nod affirmatively. 'Then we are ready. Here we go, Clymene. Ready?'

'Yes,' managed Clymene.

'Three, two, one, push!'

Clymene's screams pierced her husband's very soul. Suddenly, the baby was propelled forward, but skilfully handled by Rhea. Lapetus was in shock, staring down at the grey-blue infant which had just made its way into the world.

'Lapetus!' Rhea cried. 'Now!' After her instruction, he didn't hesitate. Lapetus grabbed the fibrous cord, which was entangled around his child's neck. 'No need to be gentle. Just get it off, quickly.' Against his instincts, Lapetus forcefully unwrapped the baby until he was free.

'Why…is there…no crying?' Clymene stammered.

Lapetus and Rhea stared down at the little body, which had failed to take its first breath.

'Oh God… Please…not this,' Lapetus whispered.

Rhea grabbed the baby by its leg as if it were a newborn calf, and gave it a firm smack on the bottom. Suddenly, the child seemed to stutter into life, and as first light broke over Tyumen, the cries of a newborn baby were heard from the railway carriage.

Rhea handed the child to Clymene. 'There we are. Well done, Clymene. You were superb.'

Clymene stared down at her new baby, her husband by her side. 'Hello, little boy.'

'You knew it would be, Clymene,' said Lapetus. He found his eyes filling with tears. 'I am so very proud of you.'

His wife smiled at him, as she had done when their eyes had

first met across the ballroom at Alexander Palace. 'You weren't so bad yourself. I could not have done it without you.'

'You have made something so very perfect, Clymene.'

'*We* have.'

'No. He is perfect because he came from you.'

Cronus approached, carrying Kreeg in his arms. 'Congratulations, my friends. The more the merrier in this rail carriage. And good news, Lapetus…' He pointed towards a storage cupboard. 'Our countrymen have not let us down. There is a bottle of illicit vodka stashed away over there. I will fetch us a glass to wet the baby's head!'

'You will do no such thing, Cronus Eszu! Bring it here now. Clymene needs her wounds sterilised. It's just what we need,' Rhea asserted.

Cronus chuckled. 'Oh well, Lapetus. It was worth a try!'

As the Siberian sun rose in the sky, a deep silence descended on the carriage. All but the new parents had collapsed with the exhaustion of the previous five hours, and the baby suckled contentedly at Clymene's breast.

'He's being so good,' Lapetus whispered.

'He's hungry,' smiled Clymene.

'I know we haven't allowed ourselves a moment to discuss names, for fear of what fate might befall us,' Lapetus said. 'But now he is here, what shall we call him?'

'Didn't you promise your mother that you'd name her first grandchild after her?' Clymene giggled.

'That's true, I did. But I don't think our son looks much like an *Agatha.*'

'Augustus?' Clymene asked.

'A little pompous, don't you think?' Lapetus replied. 'Augustus Tanit. I'm not so sure.' He craned his neck as he thought through potential names.

'It would be nice for it to start with "A" though. Alexei? Alexander, in honour of the tsar?'

Lapetus stared at his wife. 'Do you wish him to have a death sentence?'

Clymene shook her head. 'I'm only teasing you, my dear.' Suddenly, she winced. 'Ouch.'

'What's the problem?'

'I'm so sore...' Clymene put her hand down to feel the source of her pain. When she removed it from under her skirt, it was covered in blood.

Lapetus's face dropped. 'You're still bleeding...'

Clymene swallowed hard. 'Yes.'

'What do I do, Clymene?'

She looked into her husband's eyes, and put a tender hand to his cheek. 'I love you, Lapetus. With all my heart. It is the only thing I have been truly certain of in my entire life.'

'And I love you, Clymene.'

'Now,' she said. 'I am so tired. So...tired.' Clymene closed her eyes, and her husband began to stroke her hair.

'Rest now, my darling. You are safe, and our baby is safe, and we are here together.'

Soon after, mother, father and baby drifted into an unbroken sleep.

They awoke to shouting. 'Stand up!' The new family blinked in the bright light which streamed from the open door, and focused on the Bolshevik guard, with his rifle swinging in front of him.

It didn't take long for the occupants of the carriage to obey his instructions, all save for Clymene, who looked deathly pale.

'My darling?' Lapetus asked. Clymene blinked slowly.

'I said stand, by order of the Red Guard!'

The newborn child began to cry. 'Please, my wife is sick. She only gave birth last night. If you have any compassion, you will fetch a doctor,' Lapetus pleaded.

The guard slowly approached him. 'Compassion? Where was the tsar's compassion as his people starved in the fields?' he hissed quietly. 'She. Will. Stand.'

'It's...all right,' Clymene breathed. 'Here, Lapetus, take the baby. Her husband did so, and Rhea Eszu rushed to help her to her feet.

'I have a list of names,' barked the guard. 'The following will accompany me: Vera Orlova. Galina Nikolaeva. Clymene Tanit.'

'What do you want with the ladies-in-waiting?' Cronus asked. 'Are they to be reunited with the tsarina?'

The guard smiled slowly. 'One might say that, yes.'

Vera and Galina held on to one another, and began to sob.

An electricity began to course through Lapetus's veins. 'Sir, as I said, my wife gave birth to our child only last night. The baby needs his mother.'

The guard looked at Clymene and nodded. 'The child can come too.'

'No!' Clymene cried. 'No!'

Lapetus dropped to his knees. 'Please allow her to stay here. What harm can we do in this railway carriage? I beg you. Keep our family together.'

'Your precious Nicholas did not care about families, and neither do I. She will come.'

'Take me in her place.'

The guard began to laugh raucously. 'No, I don't think so. The men would be very displeased.'

Lapetus's muscles constricted. 'Please. She is sick.'

'Do you see this face?' the guard asked Lapetus quietly. 'Take a good, long look at it. This is the face of a man who does not care.' He moved towards the door. 'The choice is simple. You will come now. Or you will be shot.'

Lapetus returned to his feet and embraced Clymene. Unending tears started streaming from his eyes. 'Clymene…'

'It's all right, Lapetus,' she whispered. 'It's all right.'

'This can't happen,' he sobbed. 'We've come so far, my love. So far…' He gripped her tightly.

'You and I both know that I am not long for this world anyway. I cannot stop the bleeding.'

'If we can just get you to a doctor…'

'There is as much chance of that as our child standing up and walking today. To these people, we are an embodiment of everything they hate.' Gathering as much strength as she could, she grabbed her husband's head and kissed him. 'I have to go now, Lapetus. Be brave. For our child.'

'I will be,' Lapetus whispered.

'Protect him.'

'Always. I love you, Clymene.'

'And I love you, Lapetus. Now then, little one.' She focused her attention on her baby. 'We only knew each other for a short time. I'm sorry for that, for both of us. Your mummy loves you more than anything.' A single tear fell from her eye onto her son's cheek. 'I only have time for one lesson. Be kind, little one. It is the secret to happiness.' She placed a gentle kiss on her baby's head.

Then Clymene Tanit took a deep breath and staggered towards the door. She and the other two women were marched outside and bundled into a horse-drawn carriage. Lapetus watched on, holding his son in his arms and weeping desolately. The driver whipped the stallion, and the carriage lurched away, taking Clymene and the other girls away and out of sight.

Lapetus looked down at his son, who mewled gently in his arms. 'I am sorry, my son. So very sorry.' Then, for the first time, the baby opened its eyes, revealing two deep brown pools. 'You hold the weight of the world on your shoulders, my boy. I shall call you Atlas.'

57

As the day passed, the Eszus did all they could to comfort a distraught Lapetus, who had spiralled into a realm of despair.

'How will I feed Atlas? Oh God, I can't lose him too.'

'I saw goats with young yesterday,' Rhea said. 'Perhaps a mile or two away. Cronus will bring the mother back. Her milk will suffice.'

'Where did everyone go, Daddy?' Kreeg asked.

'Just for a little walk, that's all. Like the walk I'm about to go on, to make friends with a goat.'

Lapetus grabbed his friend's arm. 'Cronus, it will be dangerous. I don't know where the guards might have gone, but if they spot you…'

'Then they spot me,' Cronus replied softly. 'But your child needs sustenance, Lapetus. As do we all. We have no idea how long we're going to be here. It has to be done.'

'At least let me come with you,' Lapetus asked.

'You said it yourself, if I am spotted, in all probability I will be shot. Young Atlas does not deserve to lose two parents in a day.' He put a comforting hand on Lapetus's shoulder. 'I'll be fine. Now, help me rip up a blanket. I will require a leash.'

True to his word, Cronus returned two hours later with not just a mother goat, but a large male and kids in tow, too. 'It seems the family did not wish to be separated.' He chuckled.

Rhea milked the doe, and showed Lapetus the painstaking process of feeding Atlas by dipping his thumb in the milk and placing it in his son's mouth, which was gratefully received.

By the end of the day, the poor doe had been milked dry, with the five occupants of the carriage enjoying fuller bellies than they had for a while.

As the sun was beginning to set, the sound of distant horse hooves drifted into the carriage.

'They're coming back,' Rhea said, holding Kreeg tight.

The trotting grew closer and closer, and sure enough, the door to the rail carriage was wrenched open once again, revealing a soldier that the occupants had not seen before.

'You are free to leave,' he decreed.

There was a stunned silence. 'I'm sorry?' asked Cronus.

'You are of no concern to us. You may go.'

Cronus looked puzzled. 'May I ask what has changed?'

The guard sighed. 'The White Army is sending reinforcements to this area to confront us. You're the least of our problems.'

'Where do you propose we go?' asked Rhea. 'You took away our papers.'

The guard shrugged. 'That's your problem, not mine.' He turned to leave.

'One moment,' Lapetus said. 'Will trains run on this line again? Can we make use of the station?'

'The Trans-Siberian railway has been requisitioned by the White Army. How do you think they are sending reinforcements? They're travelling here as we speak.'

'Please, tell me where my wife is,' implored Lapetus.

The guard looked at him for a while, but did not say a word. Then he simply turned and left.

'I can't believe it,' Cronus whispered. 'They themselves don't even seem to know who is in charge anymore.'

'What do we do now?' Rhea asked.

'I'm not sure we have a lot of choice,' replied Cronus. 'Without any official papers, trouble looms. The White Army will assume we're Reds, and vice versa.'

'I think they want us to stay here,' Lapetus reasoned. 'That's the point of this. They know full well we can't go anywhere.'

'I fear you may be right, Lapetus,' Cronus said. 'Thank goodness for the goats. And…'—he crossed over to the storage cupboard and pulled something out—'the vodka.'

The next month was difficult, but a routine was formed. The goat was milked in the morning, and Cronus would set out hunting. Although rarely successful, on the odd occasion one of his traps had yielded a rabbit or, regrettably, a rodent, the occupants of the carriage devoured the meat. Lapetus had even been able to siphon fuel from an abandoned motorcar, so fire did not prove to be a problem.

After four weeks had passed, a Red Guard knocked on the carriage door, and handed some documents to Cronus.

'What are these?' he asked.

'Papers.'

A shocked Cronus began to rifle through what he had been presented with. 'There's only one set here. Surely we need five individual sets?'

'It's one set, authorised for five.' The guard shrugged. 'You must travel together.' The guard departed as swiftly as he had arrived.

That evening, they discussed their next move.

'This is deliberate,' Lapetus said. 'They want us to stay together so we're easier to keep track of.'

Cronus nodded. 'Where do we go?'

Lapetus sighed. 'Tobolsk. It's the closest settlement.'

'And when we arrive, what then? It might sound odd to say, but at least here we have shelter and can source food,' Rhea asserted.

'Opportunities will be better in Tobolsk. We will all have the chance to earn money. As for accommodation, we'll have to take anything we can find.'

The journey to Tobolsk was predictably horrendous. The five individuals wrapped themselves in layers of blankets, and Lapetus had managed to fashion a makeshift sling for Atlas, whom he carried beneath his fur coat on the front of his body. Cronus led the mother goat, too, who was milked several times to keep the baby fed. As for the male and the kids, they had been regrettably sacrificed to provide food for the others during the journey. After a punishing week of walking through the snow, the weary travellers arrived on the outskirts of the settlement, just as the sun was beginning to set.

'Look for the houses with no light from within,' Lapetus advised.

After hours of searching and scouting, they came across a small shack of a building which was decidedly unoccupied. To say it was in a state of disrepair would be an understatement. It suffered from smashed windows, crumbling brickwork and a door that had been battered in.

But it would do.

During the next few weeks, the men made gradual improvements, boarding up the windows and fixing the door. Then they turned their heads to finances. After Lapetus and Cronus had bickered over who to approach in the town for over an hour, Rhea suggested an alternative.

'You know that I have a talent for bone carving. We could try and sell my work at the market,' she suggested. 'Although I doubt that walrus tusks will be easy to come by.'

'No,' Lapetus conceded. 'Can you work on the leg bones of musk deer? The woods are filled with them.'

'And raccoon dogs,' Cronus added. 'Would the skulls suffice?'

Rhea nodded, and the trio took a moment to wonder how they had gone from the Throne Room at Alexander Palace to scavenging for animal bones to survive.

And so, Cronus and Lapetus would hunt for animals for Rhea to work from, which had the twofold benefit of providing sustenance for the household. Once a collection of pieces had built up, the makeshift family would descend on Tobolsk's weekend market to sell their wares. On one such weekend, a fiddler was playing in the middle of the square. Lapetus watched him for an hour or so, and yearned keenly for his former life. The man was talented, but his positioning was awry, and it irked the former tutor in him. In a moment of boldness, Lapetus approached the lone fiddler.

'Excuse me, sir,' he said. 'You are highly skilled. But if you improved the angle of your elbow, you would find it far easier to reach the difficult notes. May I?'

The musician cautiously allowed Lapetus to adjust his arm, before playing again. 'Goodness, that is better. Thank you.'

'My pleasure.' Lapetus flashed him a smile, and turned back towards his stall.

'Do you give lessons?' the fiddler asked. 'I'm not so arrogant as to assume my playing couldn't be improved.'

'I dare say it could, sir.' Lapetus sighed. 'I was a teacher once upon a time. But no longer.'

'That's a shame.' The fiddler shrugged. 'I'd have taken you up on some tutoring. I couldn't pay much, but you'd be welcome to a third of what I make on market days.' Lapetus broke out into the largest smile he had worn in many months.

A few weeks later, word of Lapetus's skill had spread throughout Tobolsk. He had begun to provide music lessons to whomever would pay him. So together, the five were just about able to scrape a living, and continued in this manner for no fewer than five years.

During that time, the Tanits and the Eszus did their very best to merge quietly into society. Uncertainty over who was in charge of the country—and therefore their safety—dominated their existence. Many times, plans to flee Russia were discussed, with the aim of being repatriated to their home countries— Switzerland for the Tanits and Prussia for the Eszus. However, any strategy which was concocted proved to be too dangerous, particularly with the two young boys to consider.

As young Atlas grew, his father spent many hours during the long, freezing winters teaching his young son to play a battered fiddle, which he had been given by a client. Atlas showed a quite unbelievable talent, and Lapetus would recurrently become emotional as he listened to his boy play.

'My word, Rhea,' Lapetus exclaimed after finishing a lesson. 'I have never known a child so naturally gifted in all my years of tuition. He could be a virtuoso! Clymene would be so proud of him.'

Rhea sniffed. 'He'd be better going out with Cronus and Kreeg learning to hunt. *That*'s a skill which will prove useful to us all.'

Atlas tried not to take Rhea's comment to heart. 'You know, I'd be happy to teach Kreeg. After all, Atlas receives language tuition from Cronus. Perhaps we merely need to find *his* instrument...' Rhea rolled her eyes.

Indeed, despite Lapetus's best efforts, Kreeg showed little interest in musicianship, or learning a language from his father. Lapetus thought it rather sad. He recognised the glint in Cronus's eyes as he sat with Atlas and taught him the basics of French, English and German. It was a small slice of their former existence. Instead, the only father–son activity Kreeg seemed to be engaged by was, as Rhea had stated, hunting.

Almost as soon as he could formulate sentences, Atlas began to ask about his mother, and where she was. It was a moment Lapetus had been dreading, but was well prepared for. He took his son in his arms and carried him outside, to look up at the glistening night sky.

'She is up amongst the stars, Atlas.'

'Why?' he asked.

'Because that's where people go when they leave their bodies. They become...stardust.'

His son stared at the vast heavens, eyes wide with wonder. 'Can I see Mummy?'

'Maybe, if you look very hard.' Lapetus pointed upwards. 'I think you might see her among the Seven Sisters of the Pleiades.'

'Seven Sisters?' Atlas asked.

'That's right. Do you see those stars there, that are a little brighter than the rest?' Atlas nodded, and his father smiled. 'Let me tell you their story...'

From that moment, Atlas Tanit had been captivated by the heavens and their contents. His father exhausted his knowledge of the Greek myths and legends which many believed led to their formation, as well as the physical astronomy behind the shining wonders.

'You can never be lost as long as you can see the stars, Atlas.'

'Really?'

'Yes. The North Star moves in a small circle around the

celestial pole. Because it appears stationary in the night sky, you will always be able to find your way.' He showed his son charts and maps, which he had purchased at discounted rates from his friends in the market. Atlas's fascination with the globe at such an early age was remarkable. Lapetus loved his son more than life itself, and dedicated every spare hour he had to his passions and development.

Those hours increased in 1922, when the Great Famine had devastated the country. The markets were empty, and suddenly no one had any extra money to buy bone carvings or pay for music lessons. Things became harder and harder in the household. Cronus in particular had begun to decline, often foregoing meals altogether so the others could eat more. It was now Kreeg's sole responsibility to lay the traps.

Lapetus Tanit began to think of the diamond which his wife had sequestered in the lining of her skirt. How different life might have been if it had remained in their possession… The one chance they had of escape from the horror of Russia had left with his wife and was now almost certainly in Bolshevik hands.

By the winter of 1923, the situation had become dire. With Atlas now five, and Kreeg nine, their bellies were only getting bigger. 'This is not sustainable, Lapetus. We're going to die here,' Cronus told his friend after collapsing into a chair.

'I won't let it happen, Cronus. We've come too far.'

'We need a plan for the boys. The day is coming when we'll all be too weak to feed them. We have to take action now.'

'What action do you suggest, Cronus?'

'You have told me of your wealthy family.'

'It's true, my parents have money. But they're in Switzerland. I've written to them several times to tell them I am alive, and that they have a grandson. Who knows if the letters ever made it?'

Cronus nodded, then stared at his friend. He wore a grave expression. 'I think, Lapetus…you need to go.'

'Go where?'

'You need to make your way to Switzerland. Get help. It's the only way I can see us all surviving.'

Lapetus was taken aback. 'My friend, there is nothing I

wouldn't do to improve our chances. But surely, you would agree that I would die on the journey?'

Cronus put a frail hand to his brow. 'I admit that the probability of success is…limited. But what *is* certain is that we will all perish here if we do nothing. Your boy. Kreeg, Rhea…we must do everything within our power to save them.'

Lapetus stared at the fire burning in the iron grate. 'Of course,' he replied.

'I wish I could accompany you. But I do not believe I possess the strength.'

'No,' Lapetus concurred. 'I am the only one that could attempt the journey.' Tears began to fill his eyes. 'Please look after Atlas. He is a very special child.'

'We will, Lapetus. We will.' Cronus hauled himself to his feet, and just about managed to put his arms around his old friend. 'Believe that you will see him again.'

The next morning, at first light, Lapetus woke his son, and explained to him that he was leaving to seek assistance.

'Why, Papa?' Atlas asked, a look of fear in his young eyes.

'My son… I fear the moment has come when I do not have a choice about whether to stay or go. Our situation is not sustainable. I must try and find help.'

Atlas's heart sank and he was consumed by an urgent anxiety. 'Please, Papa. You can't go. What will we do without you?'

'You are strong, my child. Perhaps not in your body, but in your mind. It is that which will keep you safe whilst I am gone.' Atlas threw himself into his father's arms, feeling their warmth for what would be the final time.

'How long will it take?' Atlas managed to ask, through ever-increasing sobs.

'I do not know. Many months.'

'We will not survive without you.'

'That is where you are wrong. If I do not leave, I do not think any of us have a future. I promise on your beloved mother's life that I shall return for you… Pray for me, wait for me.'

The boy nodded meekly.

'Remember the words of Laozi. "If you do not change direction, you may end up where you are going."'

'Please come back,' Atlas whispered.

'My precious boy, I have taught you how to navigate by the stars. If you ever need to find me, use the Seven Sisters of the Pleiades as your guides. Maia, Alcyone, Asterope, Celaeno, Taygete and Electra will protect you. And of course, Merope, whose star is special, as you can only see it sometimes. When you see her, you will know you are on your way home.'

58

Tobolsk, 1926

Kreeg Eszu moved his Knight to F3. 'Checkmate,' he grinned.

'What?' replied a baffled Atlas. 'How did you manage that?!'

'It's called a hippopotamus mate. It allows you to win in six moves.' He shrugged. 'Sorry about that.'

'Can you teach me how to do it?' Atlas asked pleadingly.

'Now, why would I give you all my secrets?' Kreeg sneered. 'What's the fun in playing chess against you if I can't win?'

'Come on, Kreeg! I want to know!'

'I'll consider it... Maybe if you go and chop my firewood for me.'

Atlas rolled his eyes. 'Fine.'

'Boys,' Rhea called, staggering into the living room. 'Maxim is coming here in half an hour. You need to clear up the chess set. You know he doesn't like a mess.'

Kreeg shot his mother a glare. 'Does Maxim have to come today? He's always here now,' he moaned.

'He does if you want to eat,' Rhea slurred under her breath.

'What?' asked Kreeg.

'Nothing. Yes, Maxim does have to come. Maybe you two could make yourselves scarce. You haven't visited your father in a while, Kreeg. Go and pay your respects.'

The elder of the boys looked downcast. 'But it makes me sad.'

'Well, Atlas will cheer you up. He's very good at that, aren't you?' She approached him and ruffled his hair. 'Take your fiddle or something, Atlas.' She took a swig from the near-empty vodka bottle in her hand.

Cronus Eszu had died approximately four months after Lapetus Tanit had begun his journey to Switzerland. Malnourished and weak, he had simply collapsed in the snow whilst checking one of the traps for rabbits or rats. It had been Atlas who had found him. He would never forget the shrill scream Kreeg let out when he ran back into the house to ask for help.

As for Lapetus, there had been no word from him since the day he had walked out into the snow in 1923. Atlas missed him terribly. Although the three that remained in Siberia talked as if he might return any day, deep down, they all knew the fate that had befallen him.

Not long after Cronus's death the outlook improved, as Rhea had taken a Bolshevik lover named Maxim, who provided the house with food on the table (however meagre) and, more importantly to Rhea, the vodka she had begun to rely on to get her through the days.

Kreeg and Atlas put on their fur boots, scarves, hats and gloves, and began the walk up the hill on which they had buried Kreeg's father.

Atlas knew how difficult his de facto brother found these trips, and tried to make conversation. 'What do you think you will be when you grow up, Kreeg?' he asked.

Kreeg sniffed. 'I don't care what I do, as long as I earn lots and lots of money. I want a big, warm house, and for all my cupboards to be full of food.'

'That would be good,' replied Atlas. 'I think I'd like to be a ship's captain. I could sail us all over the world.'

'I thought you wanted to be a musician?'

'I do!' Atlas enthused. 'Maybe I can be both!'

This produced a small chuckle from Kreeg, which pleased the younger boy. 'Maybe you can. They say that when the *Titanic* was sinking, the string quartet kept playing. So, when your boat sinks, you can play the passengers a tune.'

'My boat won't ever sink,' asserted a proud Atlas.

'That's what they said about the *Titanic*…'

'Yes, but I'll be much more careful than Captain Smith was.'

'Whatever you say, Atlas.'

The boys kept walking, and eventually reached Cronus's grave, which Kreeg had marked with a large piece of timber he had found. They stood in silence for a while, Kreeg awkwardly shuffling his feet. 'I never know what to say,' he admitted.

'Do you miss him?' Atlas asked.

'Of course,' Kreeg replied.

'Well,' Atlas soothed, 'just say that then.'

Kreeg coughed. 'I miss you, Dad.' He turned to Atlas. 'You know, I've heard you talking to your father outside the house,' he went on quietly. 'Sometimes it sounds like you're having a conversation with him.'

'It feels like I am.'

Kreeg nodded. 'Lucky you. Anyway, let's go.' He began to walk down the hill.

Atlas hurried to catch him. 'I thought you hated Maxim?'

'I do, but it's better than being up here.'

'You know that your mother doesn't love him, don't you?' Atlas said, and Kreeg shrugged. 'She does it for the bread.'

'I wish the bread was better then.' He smiled.

When the boys walked back into the house, Maxim had Rhea pushed up against the wall, and was kissing her forcefully.

'Boys, I thought I told you to go out,' Rhea said, smoothing her skirt.

'We live here,' Kreeg replied. 'You can't make us leave.'

'Did you just speak disrespectfully to your mother?' Maxim asked, turning towards Kreeg.

'I would never speak disrespectfully to my mother. I just do not like the company she keeps.'

'Kreeg…' Rhea pleaded.

Maxim slowly crossed the kitchen, until he was face to face with the boy. 'Now tell me, child. Why is that?'

'Because they are like warthogs at a watering hole.'

After a tense pause, Maxim threw back his head in laughter. 'I am a warthog?! Did you hear, Rhea? Your son called me a common pig!' Then, quick as a flash, Maxim slapped Kreeg across the face with such force he fell to the floor.

'Kreeg!' Rhea cried.

'Now, now, Rhea, the children have to learn that they must be polite to their elders.' He spun round to face her. 'Mustn't they?'

'Yes, Maxim,' Rhea said, lowering her eyes. 'Kreeg. Take note from Atlas. Now, boys, get yourselves into bed.'

Atlas ran over to Kreeg and helped him stand up. Unusually, tears were running down his face. Atlas had only seen this once before, on the day his father died. The boys scurried into their shared room, which was no more than a converted storage cupboard. Maxim had procured an ancient double mattress for them to share. Kreeg threw himself onto it, and continued to cry quietly.

Atlas perched on the other end of the mattress and gripped his knees. 'Are you all right, Kreeg? That was very hard.'

'I'm fine,' he replied.

'You were so brave. In fact,' Atlas said, 'I don't think I've ever seen anyone be as brave as that.'

Kreeg rolled over. 'Really?'

'Yes! You called Maxim a warthog!' Atlas said, grinning.

Kreeg wiped his nose on his sleeve. 'I did, didn't I?'

'It was amazing!'

Kreeg shrugged. 'It was nothing.'

'I think,' Atlas said cautiously, 'your Papa would be very proud of you.'

Kreeg cast his eyes downward, and was quiet for a while. 'Perhaps I'll teach you the hippopotamus mate tomorrow.'

'That would be brilliant!'

'All right. Anyway, I'm tired. Let's get some sleep.'

The boys sourced their blankets from the small space at the end of the mattress, and lay their heads on their pillows.

When Kreeg awoke, his mouth was dry and his tongue felt thick. As he stretched, it occurred to him that he had not drunk any water since before his game of chess with Atlas, and he was desperately thirsty. Kreeg yawned and resolved to make his way to the pitcher that was kept in the makeshift kitchen. Their tiny room was pitch black, but Kreeg was guided by a flicker of light from behind the door. He stood, and gently manoeuvred himself over Atlas, being careful not wake him. Just as he was about to turn the handle, he heard his mother's hushed voice. Kreeg frowned. He was *not* going to risk another encounter with Maxim. Instead, he put his ear to the wood and listened.

'So, would you do it for me, Maxim?' Rhea's speech was more slurred than Kreeg had ever heard it. Clearly, she was very drunk.

'Explain again. You want me to sell something?' Maxim's speech was also heavy and stilted. Both had obviously been enjoying the vodka since the boys had gone to bed.

'A Romanov diamond, Maxim. Bigger than any I've ever seen!'

'Bah. Sell it yourself.'

'You know I cannot. If I try to sell it in Tobolsk, it will link me to the Whites. They'll know about my connection to the Romanovs. But if you sell it, as a Red, they'll just...assume that you stole it.'

'Tell me, Rhea, how did you come to be in possession of a Romanov diamond?'

'I saw an opportunity and I took it.'

'Elaborate.'

'When the tsar and tsarina were taken, they left some of us behind to rot in a carriage, including a heavily pregnant woman. That night she went into labour, and I delivered the child—Atlas.'

Maxim seemed to let out a burp. 'Go on.'

'As I was delivering the child, I felt a hard lump in the lining of his mother's skirt. I grabbed it, saw what it was and placed it in my pocket.'

'You stole it?'

Rhea sighed. 'Yes.'

'Did you not fear repercussions?'

'I live in Russia. I fear repercussions for everything. I was merely doing what I thought I had to do to survive. Plus, the mother was bleeding very heavily. She was going to die.'

'What happened to the boy's father?'

'I told you, he left us to seek help. He had family in Switzerland.'

'A fool's errand. He wouldn't have lasted three days out there.'

Rhea continued. 'I considered giving the diamond back to Lapetus. But I wagered that if Clymene *had* told her husband about it, he would assume that it left with her when she was marched out of the carriage the night after giving birth.'

'If you returned it to him, he would know you had stolen it.'

'Yes.'

'So, where is it?'

'That is a secret which will only be revealed to you when you agree to sell it for me. Of course, I will give you a handsome commission. Plus, all the…extras you want.'

'Show it to me.'

'Maxim, I can't just—'

'Tell me where it is, Rhea.'

'Do you not believe me?'

'I would just like to see it.'

'It's not here.'

'No?'

'No. I have it placed somewhere else for safekeeping.'

'A pity. I would have liked to observe it. Anyway. It is late. I must be going.' Kreeg heard him stand.

'Maxim…this will stay our little secret, won't it? You won't tell anyone else of the diamond?'

'Of course not. I will see you soon.' After a few footsteps, the door to the house was slammed firmly.

Deciding against the glass of water, Kreeg crept back into bed, his head swimming with what he had just learnt. Suddenly he was aware that escape from this life was possible and, indeed, likely, if what his mother said had been true. He stared at the face of the sleeping boy he regarded as his little brother, whose chest rose and fell slowly and rhythmically.

Although thoughts dashed around his head like rats in a run, he was clear on one thing above all else.

Under no circumstances could Atlas find out what Rhea had done.

59

The Olympus, June 2007

After Kreeg had finished his story, we both sat in silence, staring out at the blue Aegean which quietly lapped against the hull of the *Olympus*.

'My father had always told me that my mother died giving birth to me,' I eventually managed.

'He lied to you,' Kreeg confirmed.

'To protect me.' I was choked. 'Do you remember the moment that the Bolsheviks took her away?' Kreeg nodded. 'Was she scared?'

Kreeg hesitated. 'Would you not be?'

'Yes,' I whispered. There was another long pause, and my eyes drifted across to the enormous gem that lay on the table. 'All these years I've had the diamond, believing it to be Rhea's. But…it belonged to my mother all along.'

'It *belonged* to the tsarina.'

'Given willingly. But then taken surreptitiously by your mother.'

'And then taken forcibly by you,' Kreeg snapped back.

'You still contest that my father knew Rhea had taken the diamond from my mother, and had charged me with stealing it back?!'

'I do.'

'Surely if he *had* known Rhea had taken it from my mother's skirt during her labour, he would have stolen it back from your mother long before?'

Kreeg frowned and shook his head. 'Semantics…it was all so long ago. After that night, when I heard my mother talk of the diamond, I asked her about it when you were out of earshot. She told me that she was keeping it for our future, for the day we left Russia. She could not sell it in Tobolsk. I…'

During the retelling of his tale a flicker of uncertainty had crept onto his face at several points.

'Kreeg,' I said gently. 'I have a request. Will you grant me a last supper, perhaps aboard the *Titan*? We can eat together like we used to do. I have no chef, as I came here alone, but there is the caviar we both used to dream of eating in the refrigerator, and a bottle of the best vodka in the pantry.'

Eszu considered it. 'Why not? As you say, we grew up as brothers and broke bread together every night—if we had it!' Kreeg uttered a grim chuckle. 'You can tell me of your life, and how it was that you came to collect your daughters from the four corners of the earth…as though you were collecting stamps.'

His words failed to wound me. 'May I stand up? And lead you aboard the *Titan*?' Eszu gave a nod. I stood and slowly made my way along to the gangplank that Kreeg had placed between the two superyachts. I crawled across on my hands and knees, before lowering myself onto the deck of the *Titan*. Kreeg, however, hesitated, unsure of what to do with the pistol.

'Here. Pass it to me,' I said.

'You must think me mad!' Kreeg replied.

'Understood. But if you won't pass it to me, then leave it onboard the *Olympus*. I swear that I am no threat to you. I never was, and I never have been.'

Kreeg eyed me, before gently placing the gun in his back pocket. Then, he hauled himself up onto the gangplank, clearly finding the task physically demanding. As he crawled across the gap between the yachts, his hands began to tremble, perhaps due to the pressure he was exerting on them. This had the effect of wobbling the plank, and Kreeg lost his balance. Unthinkingly, he put his hand out, but found that there was nothing to hold on to. Quick as a flash, I had grabbed it and pulled him towards the *Titan*.

'Are you all right?' I asked, as I helped Kreeg down onto the deck.

'Fine,' he replied, whipping his hand away and straightening himself up. 'It's a nice boat you have here. The decor is perhaps a little…old-fashioned for my tastes, but it suits you down to the ground.'

I put my hands in my pockets, and gave a nonchalant shrug. 'I've tried to fuse the past and the present.'

'Exactly what I meant.'

I produced a small laugh. 'Please, follow me.' I led Kreeg to the dining table on the main deck on the aft of the *Titan*.

'Please, have a seat. I'll bring some food up.'

I took myself to the kitchen, and on a tray, arranged a selection of caviar, smoked salmon, cheese and cured meats, along with a bottle of Russo-Baltique vodka, which I had been saving for a special occasion. When I returned to the table, the pistol had once again been placed next to Kreeg.

'I see you've developed a taste for the finer things,' Kreeg quipped.

'Says the man whose multimillion euro yacht we've just stepped off.'

Kreeg poured us both a shot of the Russo-Baltique. '*Vashee zda-ró-vye*,' he said, and raised his glass.

'*Vashee zda-ró-vye*,' I replied. Kreeg held still, watching me empty my glass before following suit.

'Kreeg, if I were to attempt a poisoning, you can rest assured the vodka I'd use would be far cheaper.'

This elicited a chuckle. 'A man after my own heart.' Together we enjoyed the caviar, and slowly began to drain the bottle that sat between us. 'Tell me, Atlas,' Kreeg continued. 'You said that certain events in your life have made you question the simplicity of the reality around us. Please elaborate.'

I swallowed my mouthful, and wiped my lips with one of the *Titan*'s white linen napkins. 'On my travels across earth as I ran to escape you, I found myself in Granada, Spain. At the time I was broken—at the point of giving up. There, in the great square in front of the cathedral, I met Angelina, a young Gypsy girl, who read my palm and told me my future. She was…

astonishing. She told me things about my life she simply could not know. She knew about you, and your relentless pursuit of me across the globe. Then she told me that I would one day be a father to seven daughters…and that one of them was already waiting for me to find her. I…' My voice cracked. 'But enough of that.'

Kreeg poured us both another shot, which we gulped down. 'Did you ever find your father?' he asked.

I shook my head. 'No… Although I spent many years searching for him. I was eventually informed he died on his journey home. He made it as far as Georgia. I did, however, hear from my grandmother in Switzerland. When she died, she left me all she had, including the land on the shores of Lake Geneva that Atlantis was built on. From there I amassed my fortune.' I smiled sadly. 'Everything I touched seemed to turn to gold, yet it meant nothing to me.'

Kreeg finished lathering a blini in cream cheese, then delicately placed his knife on the table. 'And I had to stand by and watch you do it.'

I shifted in my seat. 'Anyway. Tell me about your wife.'

Kreeg paused. 'You mean Ira?'

'Who else?' I replied.

'We met soon after her husband's funeral. She was grieving. I was there for her. What more is there to say?' He stuffed the smoked salmon-topped blini into his mouth.

'You married her for money?'

Kreeg swallowed and shook his head. 'No. I loved her.'

'Then I am deeply, deeply sorry. You endured the hardest pain a human can.'

He poured himself another shot of vodka. 'Perhaps. But my mother's death provided a shield that protected me from most of life's barbs. I suppose I should thank you for that. Anyway, I digress. Tell me how you found your daughters.'

Over the next two hours, I told Kreeg everything that had led to the adoption of the sisters, from being found by Bel under Landowski's hedge, to the business card which had been kept by Cecily Huntley-Morgan as a good luck token.

'Even though you pursued me throughout my early life, I

realise now that my continued flight from you gave me my greatest gift—my daughters. And now, I thank you for it.' I raised my glass and toasted Kreeg, but he failed to reciprocate the gesture. For some reason, the story of how I had found my girls seemed to have unsettled him. If I didn't know better, I would have said that my former brother was...rattled. 'I only have one regret,' I continued.

'What is that?' he said slowly.

'I never found my precious seventh child. My own flesh and blood... I don't know,' I mused, wistfully. 'Perhaps Angelina was wrong, and she never made it into the world.' Kreeg remained silent, slowly topping up his glass and eyeing me. 'I met my beloved Elle in Paris when we were only children. You might remember you saw her once when we were drinking with friends in a cafe in Leipzig. You came in and I knew you'd recognised me. I told Elle that we must leave immediately, but as you know, we did not, and you set my lodgings on fire. I had to jump out of the window to escape. I broke my arm and never played my beloved cello again.'

'I apologise,' Kreeg said. 'You were very talented with a bow. But no matter, you still managed to escape.'

Spurred on by the vodka, I spoke boldly. 'Of course, I knew your father was Prussian, but the shock I felt seeing you in your SS uniform...my old friend, my brother...a Nazi!'

'Poverty and starvation fuelled by bitterness can remove the heart, Atlas.'

I stared at him. 'It did not remove mine.'

Kreeg folded his arms. 'Elle was very beautiful.'

'That, we may both agree on.' I sipped my vodka. 'How did you escape Germany after the war?'

'I saw what was coming in nineteen forty-three and escaped to the one place where Hitler's mighty hands could not reach— London. I posed as a Russian émigré—my years growing up at court had given me the perfect cover. By chance, I met a White Princess who had fled to London in 1917. She was old and rich and I flattered her ego. I moved into her apartment, which stank of the many cats she petted like children. It wasn't long before she took me into her bed. I would escape to the bars of Soho whenever I could, which is when I got talking to that awful man Teddy. You can imagine my surprise when I heard the name "Tanit" crop up.'

'And our paths crossed once more.'

'I will never forget the fear in your eyes when you saw me across the street.' Kreeg flashed me the oiliest of smiles. 'It gave me a great deal of pleasure.'

'After your appearance at the bookshop, we took the decision to leave Europe's shores forever and forge a new life together on the other side of the world—to disappear into the vastness of Australia with the rest of the immigrants. We wanted—needed—peace.'

Kreeg gave a snort and took another shot of vodka. '*You* needed peace when you denied me mine?'

I continued. 'We had arranged our passage via steamship, and agreed to meet on board. But…she never came. By the time I'd searched the ship and discovered she was not present, we had set sail.' The energy suddenly left my body. 'Out of all my dark times, that voyage to Australia was the lowest point of my life. Even the long journey from Siberia to France did not compare to the desolation I felt. I…had finally lost hope.' Kreeg stayed silent, but the intensity of his stare had increased significantly. 'And yet,' I continued, 'my life was again saved by a young orphan girl. She made me remember the innate goodness of humanity. If it had not been for the kindness of strangers, we would not be sitting here now, enjoying our last supper together.'

'I lost faith in human nature long ago…'

'And I have had my own faith *restored* by people…but we were always different.'

'Oh yes!' Kreeg suddenly slammed his vodka glass hard onto the table. *You*, the perfect, kind son. Me—my mother's own flesh and blood—the troublemaker. The angry young man. It was obvious from the start she loved you more—the quiet, intelligent, sweet boy… She fussed over you, gave you the best of whatever she could find to eat… Even trusted *you* above her own son to be the messenger who would take the diamond to Gustav!'

I was genuinely shocked by Kreeg's interpretation of the past. 'Your perception of reality is warped. What you have said is simply not true. I've already explained that Rhea chose me to be the messenger to protect you. For God's sake, you were the one that was sent to tutoring!'

'So she could spend more time with you!'

Kreeg grabbed the vodka bottle and took five enormous gulps. For the first time, I saw clearly the resentment that stemmed back across the years to our childhood. He truly resented me.

'We were different, Kreeg, that is all. Neither one better than the other.'

'I hated you for your unerring belief in the goodness of humanity. Then…and now.'

I shook my head. 'It is the one thing you could never take from me. That, and my beloved Elle. I admit, I would have killed you before I allowed harm to come to her.' Kreeg muttered something into his vodka glass. 'What did you say?'

Kreeg looked up at me, leeringly. He was obviously very drunk. 'I said, I took her as well.'

'What?'

Kreeg took a moment to gather his thoughts. When he spoke again, his voice was deeper, growling. 'I took her, Atlas. From you.'

My blood pressure had begun to rise, and I fought to remain calm. 'Tell me what you mean. Now.'

'She didn't join you on the ship to Australia because I stole her away.' I tried to speak, but found I could not. 'I followed you from the bookshop to the port. You shouldn't have left her side, Atlas. That was your mistake.'

I clutched at my racing heart . 'You're…you're…lying.'

Kreeg put a finger in the air, remembering something. 'Would you like to see a photograph of us on our wedding day? I'm sure I have one somewhere…'

'Please, no. Please, God, no…'

Kreeg reached into his pocket, and produced a faded black and white photograph from his wallet. There was a young, unsmiling Kreeg, and…sure enough, the face I had not seen for sixty years. To my utter disbelief and devastation, she was wearing a wedding dress. I felt like I might pass out.

'How?! My Elle knew what you were, what you had done to me... She would never agree to marry you. I...'

Kreeg leant over to me and spoke softly. 'I simply explained to her that if she did not agree to come with me, I would climb aboard the ship and shoot you where you stood. I knew, you see, all about your intended departure...'

60

It had been a long night for Kreeg Eszu. Having followed Rupert Forbes's car down from London, he surreptitiously observed Atlas Tanit and his pretty girlfriend check in to the Voyager Hotel, then enjoy a shopping trip around the town. He watched the couple as they sat together on the dock, and Atlas had carefully drawn the girl, clearly suffused with love. Afterwards, the pair had returned to the hotel, and Kreeg positioned himself on a bench by the seafront, no more than five hundred feet from the Voyager's entrance.

He had sat there all night.

It was clear that the pair were planning to take a passage to Australia when the RMS *Orient* departed in a few hours' time. The long night had given Eszu time to consider his options. In truth, he had not expected to come across Tanit so easily. For one thing, he hadn't bothered to use an alias for his surname. How oddly careless of him.

In truth, Kreeg hadn't even been actively searching for his foe, instead dedicating his time to wooing the White Princess and blending into his new city. But fate had played its part—as it always seemed to when it came to Atlas—and their paths had crossed again sooner than expected.

For so many years, Kreeg had dreamt of seeing the light leave Atlas's eyes, his own face reflected in them. But during the war, he had witnessed so much death. Life after life had simply been extinguished in front of him, with men falling like dominos. At times, he had been jealous of those who had perished. They were at least free of the devastation that surrounded them.

As a result, Kreeg had concluded that, for Atlas, death would not be enough. No, for Tanit, the punishment had to be *living*. He now longed for his brother to experience the devastation he had endured when his brother had taken his precious mother away. The pain had been...*was*...excruciating. And he wanted Atlas to feel it too.

He only hoped that he would have his chance to exact his revenge before Tanit and his woman boarded the RMS *Orient*... If not, he too would be forced to get on the ship and follow them to Australia. He shuddered at the thought.

Tilbury Port began to bustle at approximately nine a.m., at which point Kreeg removed himself from the bench, purchased a newspaper, and positioned himself on a street corner parallel with the hotel. His heart had begun to pound a little faster in anticipation of how events might play out, and he tried to calm himself. All he required was a moment when they were separated. Yes...that was all it would take. At 9.25, Kreeg spotted the tall, muscular figure of Atlas leaving the hotel with his suitcase. He held his gaze, and to his delight, the blonde woman did not follow him. Tanit walked up the gangplank and boarded the ship.

Five minutes later, the blonde woman emerged with a suitcase and a light blue paper bag. This was his chance. Kreeg advanced towards her at a rapid pace. Using the newspaper as a shield, he reached inside his overcoat pocket and produced his Korovin pistol. With the gun firmly in his grasp, Kreeg rebalanced the folded newspaper so that it hid the weapon perfectly. He got closer and closer until the blonde woman was within touching distance.

He'd had the whole night to plan his move, and Kreeg executed his plan precisely. He grabbed the woman's shoulder and jammed the nose of the pistol into the small of her back. She gasped.

'Scream and I will shoot you,' he whispered into her ear. The woman nodded. 'Follow my lead.' Kreeg spun her round, and gazed into her terrified blue eyes. 'Hello, my darling!' he cried. 'Fancy seeing you here?' Then he embraced her, keeping the gun pointed at her chest.

'Please, don't do this,' Elle said quietly.

'Too late for that,' Kreeg whispered. He turned her around once again, so that she was facing the ship, keeping a firm grasp on her arm. 'You're going to come with me.'

'Where, Kreeg?'

'I will explain later.'

'What if I just scream now? We're in the middle of all these people.'

'That would be unwise. Before you finish your wail, I will have made my way up that gangplank and put a bullet in Atlas's head. Not to mention the one that would be embedded in your spine.'

'And if I simply refuse to accompany you?'

'Again, I will climb aboard the ship and shoot him where he stands.'

'Wherever you plan on taking me, he'll find you. I know he will.'

'Let him try. Now, come along, my dear.'

'Wait. Let me write him a note.'

Kreeg scoffed. 'A note?! To explain what has happened to you? Has he told you that I'm stupid? It wouldn't surprise me.'

'No. You wish to cause him pain, don't you? That is the purpose of stopping me from boarding that ship.'

Kreeg raised an eyebrow. 'How astute of you.'

'What could be more painful to him than believing that I have left him by choice? I will write him a goodbye note. Then, at least, I will have emotional closure…and my fiancé's agony will be doubled.' Kreeg considered her proposal. 'You can call it a last request.'

'You think I am going to kill you?'

'You have a gun in my back.'

Kreeg chuckled grimly. 'Write your damn note.' Elle leant down to open her bag, and pulled out a piece of paper she had taken from the hotel, alongside a pen. Kreeg watched her write each word over her shoulder. 'There. Is that to your satisfaction?'

Kreeg read the note.

Knowing you was the privilege of my life.
Rest easy without the burden of having to keep me safe.
Ever yours,
Elle xx
(Go and live your life, as I must live mine.)

Eszu nodded.

'Good, now let me find someone to hand it to him.'

'What? No. Come on. We're leaving now. It was a pointless idea anyway.' He gripped her arm more tightly and began to pull her away.'

'Ouch!' Elle dropped the light blue paper bag with the satin dress, but not before she had an opportunity to slip the note inside. As Eszu pulled her away from the crowd, Elle looked up at the ship. There, she caught a final glimpse of the man she loved, who was eagerly looking out onto the port below.

'Goodbye, my love,' she whispered. 'Find me.'

Kreeg led her several streets away, where he forced Elle to enter a black Rolls Royce.

'Sit in the front with me.' Elle followed his instructions, and as soon as she had shut the door, Kreeg removed the newspaper from the top of the pistol. 'If you try to run, I'll shoot you.'

The woman was breathing heavily, but resolute. 'Can I ask where we're going now?'

Kreeg sniggered. 'Would it surprise you to learn that I have not thought that far ahead?'

'Actually, it would,' replied the woman. Kreeg started the car and began to drive, the pistol sitting in his lap. 'He didn't do what you think he did, Kreeg. He is a good man. The kindest.'

Kreeg shot her a look. 'Oh, so he's told you about who I am, and why I am pursuing him?'

'Of course. We have known each other since we were children.'

'Really?' Kreeg said. 'So you too know what an arrogant,

scheming little boy he was.'

The woman thought of something. 'You know he still has the diamond. He wants to return it to you. If you stop the car, we can go and get it from him now.'

Kreeg raised an eyebrow. 'The diamond is still in his possession?'

'I swear it on my life.'

Kreeg seemed to waver for a moment before strengthening his grip on the wheel. 'The fact he has not sold it does not exonerate him for the crime of murder.'

'He did not murder your mother, Kreeg, it was the Bolshevik soldiers…'

'Silence!' Kreeg snarled. 'I see he has corrupted your brain with his lies. Atlas Tanit is no more innocent than you are ugly.'

'What are you going to do with me?' Kreeg remained silent. 'If you are going to kill me, I request that you make it quick.'

Eszu shook his head. 'I have seen enough death now. There is no point in slaughter if it is needless.'

'Then what's your plan?'

'You mentioned earlier that my aim is to cause as much harm as possible to Atlas.'

'Yes?'

'I am not going to kill you. I'm going to keep you.'

61

The Titan
June 2007

I am not ashamed to admit that I was openly weeping. 'Kreeg. You have succeeded in your life's work. You have taken everything from me.'

'I know,' he replied coldly.

'Did she not see that by leaving with you, she killed me where I stood anyway?'

'Perhaps. But it was her choice to make. I swore that, if she married me, I would no longer pursue you. I kept my word, as you know.'

'Your son did not!' I spat. 'He has stalked my daughters as if they were game on a grouse shoot…' A horrifying thought entered my head. 'God! Tell me your son is not related to me?'

'No. Zed is Ira's child.'

My head was spinning. 'The note from Elle… I've always kept it with me.' With shaking hands, I reached into my pocket and produced the piece of paper.

Kreeg looked surprised. 'What? How did you get that? As I told you, she dropped it on the dock.'

'I recognised the blue paper bag. A boy threw it aboard the ship as it was departing.'

Kreeg snatched the note from me and examined it, his eyes

straining in the fading light of the day. After a moment or two, his thin lips curled into a smile. 'I think I have given you too much credit over the years, Atlas. The note is a message. "Knowing, Rest, Ever, Elle, Go…" Take the first letter of each and you get…'

My stomach churned. 'Kreeg.' He nodded. 'But that means… She sent a letter to Horst and Astrid. 'Was that coded too? Oh God, what else have I missed over the years…' I clenched my fists and banged them against my knees. 'I beg of you, tell me what happened to Elle.'

Kreeg leant back in his chair. 'She died, about three years after we married.'

A deep pain shot through my core. 'How?!' I cried. 'Tell me everything. I must know.'

Kreeg grimaced. 'She was never the same after…the birth. She became weak. In the end, it was the flu which took her. The doctor said that a sick person must have the *will* to recover. But she did not.'

'The birth? So you *did* have a child together? Oh no.' I put my head in my hands. 'This is a nightmare.'

Kreeg stayed perfectly still. 'No. We did not have a child together.'

I looked up. 'What? So…that means…'

'Yes. Soon after I took Elle from you, she discovered she was pregnant with your baby. Your Gypsy woman was correct.'

I hung on Kreeg's every word. 'What happened to our baby?'

'Elle believed that the child died during its birth. It was a messy affair—she was operated on in hospital and knew nothing. Meanwhile, I devised a plan. Understandably, I didn't want your little bastard foisted upon me.'

'Did you murder my child too? With your own bare hands?! My God, My GOD!' What kind of animal are you?'

'Please, Atlas—I do have some modicum of compassion. Even I would not murder a child in cold blood. I left it on the doorstep of a local priest. I gave her to your precious God for safekeeping.'

'It was a "she"? A girl?'

'Yes.'

'The missing sister. My precious Merope…'

'I saw a way to taunt you, too. I put the ring you'd bought Elle in the basket with the child, hoping one day you'd somehow come across it…and realise what you'd lost.'

'Elle's emerald ring? With seven points?'

'The very same.'

Moving as quickly as I could, I grabbed the gun from Kreeg's end of the table and stood up. I pointed it at his head. I am not ashamed to say that my fury knew no bounds. 'Tell me where this priest's house was or I swear I will shoot you now.'

Kreeg raised his hands in the air. His eyes were suddenly full of fear as he realised his mistake. 'I do not recall… I…' I cocked the gun, ready to shoot. 'Ireland,' Kreeg stumbled. 'West Cork. That's where I took Elle after we left Tilbury Port.'

'Why Ireland? Why take her there? TELL ME!'

He threw his arms out. 'I wanted somewhere isolated and remote. Somewhere you'd never think to come sniffing around… And where better than the very edge of Europe? West Cork in the fifties was as rural as it got, Atlas. We didn't even have electricity. It was perfect.'

'Perfect…' I whispered, as I gripped the gun hard.

'I bought a run-down house in the middle of nowhere, using money I'd stolen from the White princess.'

'Where was the house?'

'Near a town called Clonakilty.'

'Its name?'

'Argideen House.'

'You took everything… *Everything* that was mine!'

Kreeg jumped to his feet and matched my eyeline. 'You killed my mother!'

'You know in your heart I did not. You used it as an excuse, because you hated me from the start. You believed I stole the attention that should have been yours.'

Eszu's eyes reddened. 'Everyone loved you. The perfect child.'

'I loved *you*, brother. I looked up to you, protected you if you were in trouble, covered for you…'

Now it was Kreeg who sobbed. 'Atlas the hero! Atlas the

strong! Atlas the brave! And Atlas the good…'

'No.' I shook my head wearily. 'You destroyed the Atlas I once was. You have let me carry the weight of the world on my shoulders. You have punished me for all that I am. Are you not satisfied?'

'I will never be satisfied until we no longer breathe the same air. You have the gun now. Shoot me and end it!' Kreeg had begun to tremble. 'I can see now that you have every reason to do it. Surely even *you* cannot forgive what I have told you today?'

I shifted on my feet as I weighed up my options. 'I am struggling. Yes. I admit it.'

'Then DO it!' Kreeg screeched. 'Be human for once! Punish those that have sinned against you, sought to destroy you…pull the trigger!'

I held the pistol to Kreeg's head for a while, before my hand began to shake, and I dropped it back on the table. 'No. Never.'

'What? I don't understand…'

'You will not make me change. We are not the same.' I held my head in my hands for a moment, and took several deep breaths. 'It's over, Kreeg.'

'Over?'

'Yes. I…I forgive you. Now, I am going to bed. I am an old man, and I am very, very tired.'

'What are you doing?' Eszu snarled. I simply turned away and slowly strolled towards the salon.

'Come back, Atlas! This ends tonight, one way or the other!'

'It *has* ended, Kreeg. It's over. It's all over.'

I walked downstairs and collapsed onto my bed.

62

I was woken by the rising Grecian sun shining brightly onto my face. Rolling over, I realised that I had managed to fall asleep in my clothes, something I had not done since I was a little boy. I sat up tentatively, feeling a familiar straining sensation in my chest. I chastised myself for resting, as by now, at Atlantis, my plan would be in full swing. Marina would be telephoning the girls to tell them that I had died of a heart attack.

Kreeg was supposed to have taken my life.

But here I was. Breathing. I knew I needed to get in touch with Georg as quickly as possible. I hauled myself to my feet, exited my cabin, and began climbing the main set of stairs. I walked out onto the deck, but saw no sign of my adversary.

'Kreeg?' I called out. 'Hello?' I walked from the bow to the stern, and as I did so, took in the glorious sun which hovered over the horizon. Eventually, I came to the gangplank that connected the *Titan* to the *Olympus*. Satisfied he was not on board my boat, I crawled across, despite the growing pain in my chest.

'Hello, Kreeg? It's Atlas. Hello?'

There was no sign of him. I made my way down into the bowels of the yacht, continuing to call his name. I searched cabins, offices, staff quarters and the galley—all of which were empty. Finally, I climbed up to the bridge, from where the yacht is captained. As I scanned the room, something caught my eye.

Placed atop the control panel was a familiar leather pouch. I made my way over. Next to the pouch was a white envelope, addressed to *Atlas*.

I loosened the drawstrings attached to the pouch, and to my genuine surprise, the diamond was still inside. With more than a hint of trepidation, I opened the envelope, which contained a card from Kreeg's writing desk.

YOU WIN, ATLAS. I AM GONE, GIVEN TO THE OCEAN. IT IS FINALLY OVER.

I slowly placed the card in my breast pocket, and hung the diamond around my neck. Having just undertaken a thorough search of the *Olympus*, I knew Kreeg was not on the yacht. *Given to the ocean*... Had he thrown himself overboard? I made my way onto the bridge deck and looked down at the sea. But I saw no body, nor anything that looked out of the ordinary. Was this a ploy?

I sensed not.

Kreeg had left the diamond. If he had fled, he would have surely taken it with him.

'Goodbye, Kreeg. I hope that you find peace, despite it all,' I whispered.

What was I to do now? Obviously, it was my duty to contact the Hellenic Coastguard. However, I couldn't risk them finding me here with a gun somewhere on board. As panic rose inside of me, I concocted a compromise. Returning to the control panel, I punched in the appropriate frequency on the radio.

'Coastguard, this is the motoryacht *Olympus*. Our position is latitude 37.4 north and longitude 25.3 east. We have a suspected man overboard. Over.'

There was a brief pause before the reply came. 'Motoryacht *Olympus*, message received, confirm location as Delos?'

'Confirmed,' I replied.

'Do you have eyes on the man overboard?'

'Negative. The yacht is one passenger down.'

'Confirmed, *Olympus*. Assistance is on its way,' the voice buzzed.

I returned the radio to its mount and made my way back to the *Titan* as quickly as possible, taking the gangplank with me. I could not risk the authorities believing another boat had been present. Once securely back aboard my own vessel, I hurried to the bow and hauled the anchor. The exertion was proving to be a great strain on my heart, which was now aching in my chest. Nonetheless, I did my best to hastily move myself up to the *Titan*'s bridge, where I started the engines and began the process of swinging the yacht around to face the open ocean. Unexpectedly, I heard the honk of a horn coming from the starboard side. I put the throttles to idle, and rushed to the window. To my horror, I saw a small catamaran, full of young people, doing its very best to get out of my way. I waved a hand in apology, but couldn't afford to waste any time. I engaged the *Titan*'s engines once more. The catamaran moved out of my way, no doubt cursing the evil superyacht for having no respect for fellow seafarers.

As the *Titan* headed for open waters, I wondered where I should take her now. I needed somewhere quiet to moor whilst I regrouped and came up with a new plan. Sadly, a multimillion-pound superyacht does not allow for inconspicuous getaways. As I was deep in thought, the radio crackled.

'Calling the *Titan*. *Titan*, are you receiving?'

My blood ran cold. How had the coastguard known my yacht was in the vicinity? I wondered whether I should simply cut the engines and jump overboard as Kreeg had done.

'Calling the *Titan*. This is the motoryacht *Neptune*. Please come in.'

'*Neptune*...' I whispered to myself. 'Who are you?'

I took out my binoculars and scanned my port, starboard and bow. I saw nothing, so I briefly left the bridge to observe the aft. Sure enough, there was a white speck behind me. Lifting my binoculars, I identified it as a small Sunseeker yacht, which appeared to be heading towards me at some speed.

Returning to the bridge, I pushed the *Titan*'s throttles to maximum, knowing the Benetti's awesome power would be no match for the vessel that was following me. But who were they?

'I say again, *Titan*, come in. The *Neptune* has precious cargo aboard!'

'Precious cargo?' I asked myself.

'To confirm,' the radio buzzed, 'we have your daughter, Ally, on board. She wonders if you'd like to stop for tea?'

I nearly fell where I stood. *Ally? What the hell is she doing here? No, no, no, no…* Everything I had worked so hard to plan was coming apart at the seams. 'Come on old girl,' I whispered, encouraging the *Titan* to speed me away.

The radio buzzed once more. 'Pa? It's Ally! We can see you! Do you fancy an Aegean rendezvous? Over.'

Ally's voice proved to both be a tonic and a poison. It gave me such comfort to hear her, but deep pain knowing that I could not reply.

My pocket vibrated, and I removed my mobile phone. The screen displayed an unknown number. Knowing that, in all probability, the call was from Ally aboard the *Neptune*, I ignored it. Sure enough, a few moments later, the phone rang again, telling me that I had a voicemail. I hurriedly answered the call and heard my daughter's voice once more.

'Hey, Pa! it's Ally here. Listen, you won't believe this, but I'm right behind you. I'm just with a…friend…and I wondered if you fancied stopping. Maybe we could get together for lunch? Anyway, let me know what you think. I love you. Bye.'

'I love you too, Ally,' I whispered.

I ended the call, my eyes filled with tears. In truth, there was nothing I longed to do more than stop the *Titan*, give Ally the most enormous hug, and tell her everything. But I knew in my heart of hearts how foolish it would be. I had expected that I would die today, and Kreeg would live. Now the opposite was true. To protect my daughters, they *had* to believe I'd perished. If Zed ever got wind of my presence today… I shuddered to think what the consequences might be for my girls.

Having put the throttle to the metal for the best part of an hour, Ally's Sunseeker was well out of sight. Reducing the Benetti's throttle, I took my phone back out of my pocket, and rang the one man I was able to trust. Who I had *always* been able to trust—Georg Hoffman.

'Atlas?!' he answered breathlessly. 'You're alive?'

'Yes, Georg. I am alive. And as you know, that is a huge

problem.'

'What is Kreeg's status?'

'Deceased. We need to move to plan B. Immediately.'

'Understood, Atlas.'

My girls. This is where my story truly ends. With the help of Georg, Ma, Claudia, Hans Gaia and many of my 'team', the *Titan* was returned to Nice. You were informed of my heart attack, my private funeral, and given your letters, alongside your coordinates on the armillary sphere.

No doubt, your burning question is 'But where did you go, Pa?'

I returned to the island of Delos, to live out my final days in peace amidst the beauty of the Grecian coast. With Georg's assistance, I purchased a small, whitewashed house with magnificent views of the sea, and waited for my time to come. Know that, unquestionably, my final days were filled with happy memories of our lives together on the magical shores of Atlantis.

Now you know everything.

The story of Atlas.

The story of Pa Salt.

The story of you.

The greatest gifts of my extended time on earth have been the communications I have received from Georg, detailing your progress as you have each gone on your own adventures to learn about your birth families. Know this: I could not be prouder of you. Although none of you carry my own blood, I am humbled that you have inherited my passion for travel, my spirit of adventure, and above all, my deep love for humanity and a belief in its innate goodness. I am so very sorry that I have had to deceive you. Knowing the full circumstances of my situation, as you now do, I believe that you will grant me grace.

I hope, above all else, that Georg has managed to find the missing sister. I know he has worked tirelessly to track her down after I was able to provide him with the name of Argideen House, and a drawing of the ring I once gave to her mother.

I have a feeling, however, that he is going to need your help. When you find her, my girls, show her kindness. Tell her how much I love her. How much I longed to find her. That I never gave up. Tell her how humbled I am to be her father, as I am to be yours.

There is nothing left for me to say that has not already been said. But know that you all made my life worth living. Even though I have endured tragedy and pain, you each gave me more hope and happiness than you could ever possibly know. If reading my story has taught you anything, I hope it is to heed the advice which I imparted to you throughout your lives:

Seize the day!

Live for the moment!

Relish every second of life—even its most difficult moments.

With love,

Your Pa (Salt) x

The Titan

June 2008

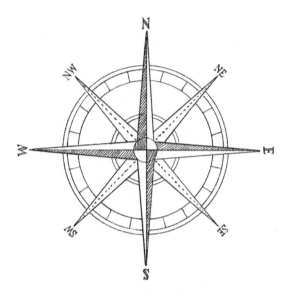

63

Star put down the final page and looked around the table. Most of her sisters were openly crying, and were being comforted by their partners. She felt Mouse's hand on her back.

'I...don't know what to say,' stuttered Ally.

'That bastard,' Electra breathed. 'He took Elle from him. All over nothing.'

'Merry...are you all right?' asked Miles, looking concerned.

She swallowed hard. 'I think so...' Her voice cracked and she let out a sob. 'Oh God, I'm sorry,' she said, waving a hand in front of her face.

'Aw, Mum, come here,' said Mary-Kate, standing up and embracing her.

'I'm so sorry, Merry. How hideous to hear what was done to your mother,' Tiggy added.

'And poor Pa. To learn all that right at the end of his life...' Maia swallowed.

'I can't even imagine,' said Ally, through snivels. 'I can't believe I got so close to him. If only Theo's boat had been a little faster.'

'He was protecting us, right until the last,' said Star. 'He wanted to sacrifice his life to ensure our safety. How very Pa.'

'Do you accept why he had to "stay dead"?' Georg asked the table. 'He was terrified that if Zed discovered that your father had been present at the time of Kreeg's death, he might have caused you harm.'

The girls all nodded. 'When did he die, Georg? Really?' Electra asked.

'Yes, how soon after he arrived on Delos did he…*go*?' sniffed CeCe.

Georg hesitated. 'I last saw him three days afterwards. I helped him with securing the property. As you may know, the island is very small, and of great mythological significance. There are only one or two houses. We offered the current owner quadruple what it was worth, and he and his goats moved out almost immediately.'

'That hasn't answered my question, Georg. When did Pa die?' Electra said firmly.

Georg shook his head, and looked pleadingly at Ally. Ally looked at Ma, who stood.

Taking a very deep breath, she began to speak. 'My little girls. It is time to be brave. Your father is not yet dead.'

The deck was silent.

Tiggy's eyes opened wide. 'I knew it…'

Electra gasped. 'No…this can't be…you're telling me Pa Salt is alive? Now?'

'Yes,' said Ma.

The ocean wind blew across the table.

'You kept this from us…' breathed Star. 'How could you be so cruel?'

'*Chérie*, I…'

'Is he still on Delos?' asked Maia.

Georg nodded. 'Yes, Maia. But he is so very weak.'

'The telephone calls…' CeCe whispered. 'Have you been talking to him, Georg?'

'Not exactly. Claudia has been with him these past few weeks. It is why she has not been present at Atlantis. She updates me regularly. He is fading fast.'

'Oh my God!' cried CeCe.

'It all makes sense now…' Star said.

'There was no way anyone could have foreseen he would survive this long, girls. We assumed that he would only be on Delos for a short number of weeks. But he has outlived every doctor's predictions.'

'How Pa,' stumbled Ally.

Georg continued. 'He has refused all medical intervention. He won't take pills or agree to any tests—he has not even been using an IV drip.'

'How is he still alive?' Electra wondered.

Georg looked to Ma, who smiled at Merry. 'I think...no, I *know* that the thought of finding the missing sister has kept him on earth.'

'The power of belief.' Tiggy nodded in understanding.

Star looked at Ally. 'How long have you known about all this?'

'Since this afternoon. I insisted that Georg tell everyone and provide Pa's final pages, which were supposed to be withheld until after his death.'

Georg's hands shook as he sipped on a glass of water. 'Believe me, girls, I have longed to share the truth with you. But you know what your father did for me. I vowed to be loyal to him until my final breath.'

'There's a difference between loyalty and cruelty, Georg,' CeCe protested.

The lawyer nodded. 'Deep down in my heart I knew that I should tell you the truth,' Georg admitted, through tears. 'And how much it would mean to him to see you all before the end.'

Nobody knew what to say.

'Why the hell aren't we moving?' Electra demanded. 'If he's dying, there's no time to lose. Get Captain Hans. I'm not waiting until morning if there's a chance we can see him again. Does everyone agree?'

'Yes. Absolutely,' said Maia, standing up. 'We have two choices now. The first is that we become angry and embittered. That is the easy choice. The second is that we accept all that has happened. We proceed with love and kindness, despite the wrongs which we might feel have been done to us. Now,' Maia asked, 'which would Pa choose?' She reached out a hand to Tiggy, who took it. Then Tiggy reached her hand across to Ally, until the Seven Sisters were joined as one.

'Georg,' said Ally. 'You heard what Electra said. Get Hans. We're going to see Pa. Now.'

Georg hurried from the dining table.

Everyone at the table was shell-shocked. The partners, in particular, were empty of words. Nothing they could say would assuage the typhoon of emotions that the sisters were currently experiencing. Eventually, it was Ally who spoke.

'Does anyone remember that I thought I heard Pa on the phone when I answered a call in his office?' she asked the others. 'Well, maybe I really did.'

This spurred a thought in Electra's mind. 'Ma?' she asked. 'When I bumped into Christian in Paris, was he doing something for Pa?'

She nodded. 'Yes, *chérie*. He was seeking out Manon Landowski—Paul's granddaughter.'

'Why was that?'

'He simply wished to thank the family that had saved him at the start of his life one final time before his death. So that their act of kindness was not forgotten as the generations continued.'

'Did Christian find her?'

Ma nodded. 'He did. She is a singer songwriter! Christian gave her the letter, and she told him that her father—Marcel—had often spoken fondly of the "silent boy".'

'Fondly!?' exclaimed Maia. 'Well. Who would have guessed?'

The rumble of the *Titan*'s engines filled the air, and Georg returned. 'Hans estimates that we will make Delos by sunrise. I will call Claudia and inform her of our arrival.' He paused. 'Girls…are we doing the right thing?'

The man who had been the source of assurance for the sisters during the past year looked utterly shaken.

'Absolutely, Georg,' affirmed Star.

'Can we speak to him on the phone, now? Just in case anything happens?' asked Ally.

Georg shook his head sadly. 'He would struggle to talk on the phone. He has hardly any strength. In fact, to save his heart, I think it is best that Claudia does not inform him of our imminent arrival.'

'Oh God. What if he doesn't last the night?' Star said.

'He will, Star. He will,' Tiggy promised.

64

As the *Titan* approached Delos, the tiny island was bathed in the gloaming of the as yet unrisen sun. It was rock-strewn, with patches of green and yellow grass that rose up towards the peak. This, combined with the ancient Grecian pillars that adorned the land, created an atmosphere of ancient wonder.

There was no hope of taking the Benetti into the tiny harbour, so Hans Gaia dropped anchor as close as he could, and organised a tender to take the sisters to shore. As Ally navigated the small boat—which also contained Georg and Ma—towards the jetty, a familiar figure came into view. One by one, Claudia helped the girls out of the tender, and embraced them all individually. She saved her longest hug for her brother, Georg. Their normally reserved housekeeper broke down in his arms.

'Girls,' she sobbed, 'your father is a guardian angel.'

'Take us to him, Claudia,' Maia said.

The housekeeper led the group up a dusty path from the harbour to the foot of a large green hill, where the walkway became so thin that the sisters had to travel in single file. Sure enough, as they neared the top, an isolated whitewashed bungalow came into view. The spectacle was as magnificent as Pa had written, offering panoramic views of the classical island and the sea that surrounded it.

'How is he, Claudia?' Ally asked.

'Even he is not invincible. Last week, he had another heart attack. Thinking it was his last day, I told him that Merry had finally been found, and that you were all coming to lay a wreath. It has kept him going. He has refused to surrender for his entire life... But now...' Claudia turned to Merry and took her hand. 'My darling, perhaps it is best if you let the girls prepare him for your arrival first. He is so very weak.'

Merry nodded. 'Of course.'

'Ma, would you go in first and tell him we are all here?' asked Maia.

'Something tells me he already knows,' whispered Tiggy.

'Of course, *chérie*,' Ma smiled sadly. 'I will go and see him first.'

Claudia led Marina through the front door of the cold, shadowy house and down the hallway to a bedroom at the back. 'Are you ready?' Claudia asked. Ma nodded, and opened the door.

On a double bed in the corner of the room, Atlas dozed, propped up by half a dozen white pillows. As Marina approached, he slowly opened his eyes, and turned to look at her. His skin was grey, and his eyes sunken. But the irises themselves contained the same brown shine which they always had.

'Bonjour, *chéri*,' she said quietly, taking his frail hand. 'It is I, Marina.'

Atlas broke into a smile. 'Hello, Ma.' She wrapped him in a gentle hug, a little unnerved by just how thin he had become. Then she pulled up a wooden chair and sat by his side. 'Marina... I...I'm so sorry. So very sorry. For everything,' he whispered.

'Shh, *chéri*,' Marina comforted him. 'There is nothing to be sorry about.'

'The girls...are they all right?'

'They are *wonderful*, Atlas.'

The news calmed him. 'Do they know I am alive?'

'Yes, Atlas, they do. And they are outside waiting to see you.'

Atlas's shoulders seemed to drop. 'The girls are here? For me?'

'Yes. *All* of them.'

'You mean...' Marina nodded. 'She...' Atlas's voice cracked. 'She is here? My first daughter?'

'Yes.'

Atlas tried to gather himself, clearly fighting his shallow breathing. 'Do they know I am near death?'

'Don't be ridiculous, *chéri*. As if you could ever do anything as normal as *dying*!'

'Ma,' he said, squeezing her hand a little tighter. 'It's all right. Do they know?'

Marina held back tears. Atlas was protecting his daughters to the last. 'Yes. They wish to say goodbye. As do I, my dear man.' She stroked his head gently. 'What troubles you have seen.'

'Troubles, Marina?' Atlas managed to shake his head. 'No. Only life and humanity—the good and the bad—played out over ninety years.'

'Before the girls come in, I want to say my own thank you, for trusting me with their upbringing. For taking me on when I had no relevant qualifications...'

'My dear Marina,' he smiled. 'I saw the way you cared for those children in Paris. I knew how much love is within you.'

'I did some dreadful things, too...things I am so ashamed of.'

He patted her hand. 'As I have told the girls so many times, never judge others on what they *do*, but on *who* they are. Now, is Georg here?' Ma nodded, and Atlas sighed. 'Do you ever wonder why he has never felt he could profess his love for you, when it has been so obvious for all these years how he feels about you?'

Ma gave a light chuckle. 'I would be lying if I said no. But, there are many things he does not know about me. I worry that he would be...*ashamed* of me.'

'I entreat you to speak to him. He and you must both lay the past to rest. Please, Marina, life is so very short...promise me you will try.' He looked at his old friend imploringly.

'I promise.' Marina took a moment to compose herself. 'Now, have you the energy to see your girls?'

A smile returned to his face. 'If I don't, I will find it. Are they going to be all right?'

'Oh, yes. We have raised some strong women.' Marina stood, took Atlas's hand again, and kissed it. 'I will send them in.'

Atlas leant back into his pillows, and summoned every last iota of strength he possessed. He took a moment to close his eyes, and send up a prayer to the heavens.

'Thank you for sending them.'

Them the door to his bedroom opened once more, and tears fell down his face as he greeted his six daughters one by one. He took each in his arms, and lightly kissed the tops of their heads, as he had done when they were children. Although every one of them cried, they were tears of joy, not pain. Though events had tried to keep the family apart, the universe had brought them together one final time.

The sisters settled themselves around their pa's bed, and he was clearly overjoyed to be surrounded by the people he loved most in the world.

'My bold, brilliant, beautiful girls. I only ever wanted to keep you safe.'

'We know, Pa, we know,' Star comforted him.

'We're just…so happy to see you again,' wept Ally.

Atlas looked up to the ceiling. 'The story is long. I did not expect to live…' He turned back to the sisters. 'But I wrote everything down, and gave it to Georg. You will all know the truth.'

'We already know, Pa,' Electra said softly. 'Georg gave us the pages before we arrived here.'

'Ah, did he now?' Atlas said, raising an eyebrow. 'Please remind me to give him the sack.' Muted chuckles punctuated the girls' tears. 'In fact,' Atlas breathed, 'where is he?'

'Outside,' said CeCe. 'Shall I fetch him?'

Atlas smiled. 'Thank you, CeCe.'

Maia leant in towards her father. 'Pa, through your "death" each of us grew up and found ourselves. We are all adults now— the people you wanted us to become.'

Atlas gave a little nod. 'I'm so proud of you. Georg has told me that each of you found your birth families.'

'Yes,' said Maia tenderly. 'But more importantly, we all found our futures. And happiness.'

'Then that,' Atlas breathed, 'is the best gift I could ever have given you.'

'Pa, just one question,' Ally said. 'Over the last year, we all at one time thought we had heard or seen you.'

'Or even smelt you,' Electra whispered.

'Did you ever come back to Atlantis?' Ally asked.

'Or were you in Bergen?' added Star. 'I thought I saw you at Ally's concert.'

Their father smiled. 'Sadly, no. Although I was following your progress. You could say I was with you in spirit, as I always will be... Just look up to the Seven Sisters of the Pleiades and I will be there, too. Atlas—your father, watching over you all.'

'You'll always be *Pa Salt* to us,' sobbed Tiggy.

He grinned. 'Of course. Do I still smell of the sea, little Maia?'

The girls laughed again. He was being so strong for them.

There was a faint knock on the bedroom door, and Georg Hoffman entered the room. 'Hello, Atlas,' said his old friend.

'Hello again, Georg. It's nice that you are here to say goodbye to me for a third time.' He gave Georg a gentle wink. 'Now, excuse me, girls, might you just make a little room?' Maia and Ally moved so that Georg could reach the bed. He took Atlas's hand, but was delicately pulled in for an embrace. The sisters watched as he whispered something to Georg, who nodded fervently before standing up. 'Thank you, my friend, for bringing everyone to me. It is the most beautiful gift.'

'Speaking of gifts,' said Georg. 'Ally? Bear has arrived.'

'Pa...would you like to meet your grandson?'

'Your boy, Ally? He is on Delos?'

She nodded. Captain Hans has just ferried him over from the *Titan.*'

Atlas's eyes glistened. 'Please, bring him in...'

Ally disappeared momentarily, and returned with her son in her arms. 'Pa, this is Bear. Bear, meet your grandpa.'

'Hello, precious one. May I hold him?' Ally hesitated a moment. 'Please, I didn't drop any of you. I don't intend to start now!' Ally smiled and gently placed her son in her father's arms. 'Bear...what a wonderful name. My goodness, Ally.' He looked up at her. 'He looks so much like you.'

The women watched their father coo and fuss over the infant, who somehow provided Atlas with a second wind of energy, as if he was taking strength from the young life—and the future—which he cradled in his arms. With his renewed vigour, Atlas was able to ask his daughters about the romantic partners that Georg had told him all about, and hear from their own lips the fates of the families he had known from long ago.

When the time felt right, Maia made eye contact with each of her sisters. They all sensed that the moment had come.

'Pa,' Maia said. 'There is someone else here to see you. She is waiting outside.'

Atlas's breathing quickened. Tiggy took his hand. 'Don't be scared, Pa. This is your reward from the universe.' The girls stood up one by one, and he blew each a kiss as they left the room.

Then, very slowly, the door opened once again, and Merry stepped inside.

'Hello, Pa,' she said with a smile. She walked towards him and gave him a gentle peck on his forehead.

Atlas's eyes were open wide. 'Elle…' he whispered.

Merry shook her head. 'I'm afraid not. Mary was the name I was given by my family in Ireland. But everyone would call me "Merry" because I was happy. Your girls say you'd be calling me "Merope" had you found me sooner.'

'Merope…Merry.' Atlas beamed at the coincidence, and stared at his daughter in wonder. 'Can it really be you?'

'It's me all right. I'm your flesh and blood.'

Atlas was too moved to speak, tears dripping down his cheeks. He reached out his hand, and Merry gripped it tightly. Soon, she began to cry too. The pair sat in silence for a while, father and daughter, taking each other in for the first time.

'You look like your mother,' Atlas managed. 'Merry, she was so beautiful. See? There she is.' Atlas pointed to the charcoal drawing from Atlantis, which now hung alongside his bed.

'I've seen the copy Georg has,' Merry replied. 'The girls have said they recognised me from it the moment I stepped on board the *Titan*.' She nodded towards the drawing. 'Everyone was wondering where the original picture had gone.'

'I asked Claudia to bring it here. It is all I have left of her, I…' Atlas stared at his daughter, choked with emotion. 'Now you are here—a part of her is with me. It is a miracle. Forgive me, my darling, that I couldn't be there to protect you. I searched for you for years, right across the world. I never expected you to be in Ireland, I…'

Merry could see Atlas becoming distressed. 'Shh, it's all right, Pa. Everything's all right now. So, tell me about her—Elle. Tell me of my mother.'

Atlas smiled widely. 'It would be my honour.'

He held Merry's hand, and told her all that he could. His eldest daughter watched the light dance in his eyes as he recalled the love of his life, and everything that she was to him. Eventually, Atlas became tired, and Merry watched him doze off, his hand still clutching hers. Slowly, his grip began to lessen, and Merry sensed her father floating away. She quickly stood up, and went to bring in the rest of the girls to say goodbye.

Each of them kissed their father in turn and sat around his bed, holding tightly to one another and weeping.

Eventually, as the sun began to rise over Delos, the light crept onto Atlas's face. He opened his eyes, and gave the room a smile which radiated warmth and love.

'I can see her,' Atlas said. 'She is waiting for me. Elle is waiting for me…'

Then, after his life of immeasurable beauty, pain and kindness, Atlas Tanit closed his eyes for the final time.

Epilogue

Atlantis
One year later

Despite it being a tight fit, the Seven Sisters just about managed to squeeze into Christian's small boat which ferried them to and from the mainland.

'You're sure you're comfortable with the controls, Ally?' he asked.

'Yes, thank you,' she replied, positioning herself at the wheel.

'Okay, Ma, we're ready,' Maia said, swivelling her torso around so that she faced the jetty. She held her two hands out.

'*Oui, chérie.*' Ma passed her the ornate brass urn which contained Atlas's ashes. When she had done so, she stepped back, and Georg placed his hands lovingly on her shoulders.

'You're sure neither of you want to come out with us? It wouldn't take Christian too long to ready a second boat,' Electra offered.

'Thank you, my darling, but no. It is only right that the seven of you lay him to rest,' replied Ma.

'We will all be here waiting for you,' Georg assured her.

Ally nodded at Christian, who untethered the line from the jetty. She put the boat into gear, and cruised slowly out into the centre of the lake. The June day was dry and bright, and warm sunlight glistened on the glassy surface. Ensuring her chosen spot was secluded, Ally killed the engines, and the women basked in the exquisite serenity of the water and the mountains.

Curiously, none of them felt any sense of sadness. Instead, each was filled with a tranquillity that they were finally able to give their father the send-off which had initially been denied to them. The boat bobbed silently on the water for a while.

'Ally, would you…?' Maia eventually managed.

Her sister nodded, and from under one of the benches, pulled out the case containing her flute. She removed it, lifted the lip plate to her mouth, and began to play. The piece the girls had chosen was 'Jupiter' from *The Planets* by Gustav Holst—one of Pa's favourites.

Ally played elegantly, as she always did, and the notes drifted back across the lake to Atlantis. Each of the sisters closed their eyes and spoke privately to their father. They thanked him for saving them from the lives they might have had, and for the unconditional love he had shown them.

'Thank you, Ally,' Star said, when her sister had finished playing.

'All right then,' Maia said, carefully prising open the urn. She took a handful of the ashes within, and gently scattered them out onto the lake. 'Bye, Pa,' she said, with stoic bravery.

The urn was passed around each of the sisters. Some spoke for a long time, others not at all. Finally, the ashes were given to Merry. 'Thank you.' She smiled, and took a deep breath. 'Pa, although I barely knew you, I am very proud to be your daughter.' She spread a final handful into the water.

After a while, Ally restarted the boat's motor, and steadily ferried her sisters back to land. On the grass beyond the jetty, a veritable throng of family and friends were gathered to toast the extraordinary life of Atlas Tanit. After Christian had tied off the line, he offered his hand to Maia, and she stepped down onto the wooden dock. Valentina hurried down the jetty, and wrapped her arms around her. Floriano followed, cradling Bel, their three-month-old daughter, who gurgled as she was placed in her mother's arms.

'Hello, my sweet,' she cooed. 'Come on, let's get out of the way so everyone else can get off.'

The sisters made their way back onto dry land, and into the

welcoming arms of their assembled loved ones. This was an auspicious day indeed, with families meeting families, and the four corners of the globe congregating at Atlantis.

'Come here, Al,' Jack said, taking his partner in his muscular arms.

After her father's (official) death, Jack had been nothing short of a rock for Ally. Never in her life had she felt so well cared for. When the dust had settled after that day on Delos, and everyone had gathered back at Atlantis, Merry had been the one to offer a toast to the couple: 'Whilst we have a glass of champagne in our hands, I'd love to say congratulations to Jack and Ally! You've, er, *emerged* over the last few days, and it's...wonderful to see you so happy.'

'Hear, hear!' Mary-Kate cheered, which led to a round of whooping from the sisters, and a red-faced Ally.

Now, Jack gave her a tender kiss. 'We heard you playing from here. It was beautiful.'

'You have to say that,' said Ally, with a small chuckle.

'No, he speaks the truth. You played magnificently. It was note-perfect,' said Ally's twin, Thom, who was next in line to embrace her.

'He means it,' confirmed Felix, who was sipping on orange juice, not Veuve Clicquot. 'Thom certainly tells me when I miss a note.' He chuckled. 'Well done indeed. You have made your Pa Salt very proud.'

'Thank you, Felix.'

'Mama!' cried Bear, who toddled at a pace towards Ally, whilst gripping on to Ma with one hand, and Georg with the other.

'You are too fast for your grandmama, *chéri*!' she exclaimed.

'And your grandpapa too, by the looks of things,' said Ally, smiling at Georg. 'Hello, Bear.' She scooped her son up in her arms.

'He's been trying to keep up with his new mate Rory,' laughed Jack. 'The boy's been racing around the place!'

'Can I get you a glass of champagne, Ally?' asked Thom.

She hesitated, and glanced at Jack. 'Actually, I think I'll stick with Felix on the orange juice just now.'

'Coming right up,' said Thom, walking in the direction of the house.

Further up the grass verge, Orlando Forbes was marvelling at the remarkable structure that was Atlantis. 'It's exquisite!' he beamed. 'Quite exquisite! And you say you've discovered it was only built in the 1960s?! I simply can't believe it, Miss Star. I have an eye for such things, and would have guessed it was eighteenth century for certain.' He put his hands on his hips. 'It is an architectural masterpiece.'

'He'd be very glad to know it has your approval, Orlando,' Star replied. 'Of course, he never would have managed it all without your grandparents.'

'Good old Grandad Rupes, eh?' Orlando replied.

'Clearly bravery and decency run in the Forbes blood,' Mouse quipped.

'Yes. What a shame it skipped a generation when it comes to you two,' Star giggled.

'Ah! You cut me to my core, Miss Star!' Orlando cried, gripping his chest dramatically.

'You know, if you behave yourself, I might even allow you to peruse Pa's libraries,' Star offered.

'How dare you insinuate that I am *ever* badly behaved,' replied Orlando.

'No insinuation is necessary when it comes to you, dear brother.' Mouse swigged his champagne.

Star glanced over his shoulder at her newest sister. 'I've just had a thought, Orlando. Have you properly met Merry yet?'

Merry turned around at the mention of her name. 'Are my ears burning?' she asked, making her way over. 'Well, well, well,' she chuckled, 'if it isn't the viscount himself! How's the wine journalism trade these days?'

Orlando seemed to physically shrink several inches. 'Ah, Merry, my humblest apologies for my little ruse. However, I'm sure you'll agree that I had the greater good in mind...' He bowed and put out his hand, which Merry shook.

Mary-Kate joined her mother in the circle. 'OMG, are you Orlando? The guy who pretended to be a viscount? You're, like, a legend in our family!'

'Oh, am I indeed?' Orlando replied, puffing up.

'Yeah! We laugh about it the whole time. If anyone ever tells a fib, we say "pulling an Orlando"!'

Mouse burst out laughing at the sight of his brother deflating like a balloon.

'Excuse me for interrupting,' said Georg. 'It has just occurred to me that I need a signature on some inheritance documentation. May I briefly borrow you?' he enquired.

'Lead on, Georg!' Merry gave a small wave to the group, and followed him inside the house.

'I am so glad you finally got to go on your world tour, Merry.'

She chuckled. 'As am I, Georg. Although it was hardly the route I was expecting to take! I only flew in from Granada last night!'

'I heard. I must say, I think it is wonderful that you decided to visit all of the places your father found himself across the years.'

Merry nodded. 'I just wanted to see it all for myself. His story was the most amazing thing I've ever read.'

'And did you manage it all?'

'Oh, yes,' Merry replied proudly. 'I saw the railway station in Tyumen, Landowski's old atelier, Bergen Harbour, Coober Pedy…the list goes on. I feel so close to him now.'

Georg put an arm on her back. 'I am sure he is with you. Speaking of which… I hear from Ally and Jack that Monsieur Peter accompanied you to a few of the European destinations?' He raised an eyebrow, and Merry tutted.

'You'll make me blush, Georg.'

'Apologies. But I am glad to hear it,' he replied sincerely.

'As am I about you and Marina!'

A smile appeared on Georg's face. 'We have loved one another for over thirty years. During that time, I observed her grace, her beauty, her patience…but never did I have the courage to say anything. As it turns out, neither did she…'

Georg led Merry into Atlas's study. She had only been in once before, and had shivered as she felt the physical and material essence of her father. Although the banks of computers and video screens were impressive, her eyes had landed on the personal treasures placed randomly on the shelves behind the desk. She smiled as she noted several of Grieg's 'lucky frogs', a battered old fiddle and a lump of opal, still encased in the rock which surrounded it.

Merry followed Georg to the desk, and he presented her with a document. 'If you could sign where I've indicated, it will officially incorporate you into Atlas's trust, as he intended.'

'It's very kind of the girls to allow it. I never had any expectations of—'

Georg interjected. 'As you know, the six girls have *insisted* that you are treated as an equal.' Merry nodded, and removed the cap from the pen. 'By the way, must you leave us tonight, Merry? We'll all miss you.'

She sighed. 'I'm afraid I have to go. It's only me that's off, though—MK is staying on with Jack and Ally. I promised I'd get over to Dublin to see Ambrose.' Merry looked dispirited. 'His health is really declining. He's done so much for me over the years that I need to be there for him now.'

Georg gave a sympathetic nod. 'I know everyone will understand.'

'Plus...' Merry finished signing, and sat herself in Atlas's deep leather chair by the window.

'Yes, Merry?'

'Do you recall that in my father's journal, he mentions Elle's brother... My uncle. He wrote that he was adopted as a baby and taken to somewhere in Europe.'

'I do recall that,' replied Georg, leaning on the desk.

'I've been trying to find out what happened to him. Doing a bit of digging and that sort of thing.'

A smile played on Georg's lips. 'Have you discovered anything?'

Merry shrugged. 'I've got a couple of little bits and pieces. I started investigating with Ambrose, just to keep his mind occupied. But now I'm totally desperate to find out what became of him. It's unlikely, of course, but...' Merry's eyes twinkled. 'It's just about possible that he's still alive.'

Georg nodded. 'I see the apple doesn't fall far from the tree, Merry. It goes without saying, but if ever you wish to enlist my services, it would be my honour to help.' He looked out at the gathering of people they had left a few moments ago. 'I also understand that Orlando Forbes is pretty useful when it comes to this sort of thing, too.'

Merry chuckled. 'Is he indeed?'

Georg nodded. Their conversation was interrupted by the voices of CeCe and Chrissie, who passed the open study door.

'Hey, I wanna know about all the secret tunnels this place has!' Chrissie exclaimed.

'We're having them sealed up, actually,' CeCe replied. 'It's time for a new start.' She noticed Georg and Merry sat together. 'Hey, you two. I don't suppose you've seen Grandpa Francis about, have you?'

Georg nodded out of the window. 'He's on the terrace, CeCe.'

'Fab, thanks!' She and Chrissie continued to the kitchen, and exited the enormous glass sliding door onto the terrace. They located Francis Abraham sitting at the antique bronze garden table, and pulled out a couple of chairs.

'Ah, girls!' he cried. 'I was beginning to wonder where you were. I just wanted to thank you again for inviting me. It is an honour to see your home and celebrate your father's life, CeCe.'

'Thank you for making the journey, Francis! I'm so happy to have you here.' She took her grandfather's hand and squeezed it tightly.

'I'd love to paint the lake. Do you think that would be possible?' he asked.

'Of course! I have canvases and palettes upstairs. We'll sort it out later.'

At the other end of the table, Zara, Charlie's daughter, was busy singing the praises of Atlantis. 'Can we just live here, guys?! It's *sick*!' She took a seat, with Charlie and Tiggy following suit.

'Oh, I don't know if you'd like it that much,' Tiggy replied. 'Every time you wanted to go to a party, you'd have to get on a boat.'

Zara laughed. '*Well*, we'd just have to have parties here!'

'I'm not sure poor old Claudia could cope with one of your famous gatherings,' said Charlie, ruffling his daughter's hair.

'Stop that, Dad,' Zara snapped.

'Yes, stop that, Charlie,' Tiggy replied, reaching up to vigorously tousle Charlie's wavy auburn hair.

'All right, all right, point taken.' A thought crossed his mind. 'Actually, would you ladies excuse me for ten minutes or so? I promised I'd have a quick chat with Ally. Can you remember where I put my big bag, Tigs?'

'It's in the kitchen, I think.'

'Smashing. Back shortly!' Charlie stood up and walked inside.

Zara looked quizzically at Tiggy, who simply shrugged and smiled.

Elsewhere, at Stella Jackson's request, Electra was walking her around one of Pa's walled gardens, with Miles joining them and listening to every word. 'I remember him talking about his flowers when he met me for dinner,' Stella reminisced. 'He was so proud of them. Now I can see why!'

'He had so many talents,' said Electra.

'No kidding. All these people, brought together by one man,' smiled Stella. 'It's quite the tribute.'

'You're right, it is,' replied Electra. 'Even though, amazingly, most of the guests here today never met him! You're in the minority, grandma.'

Stella put a hand to her heart. 'It really was my honour. He was so warm, with an ineffable quality of…decency about him. It's hard to explain.'

'And yet I know just what you mean,' Electra nodded.

'What do you think will happen to this place?' asked Miles, gesturing back at the house.

'Atlantis? We'll keep it. Forever. Whenever life gets too much, we'll always have a place of safety to come back to.'

'That's a lovely sentiment.' Stella smiled. 'Just what he'd want.'

Miles, ever the pragmatist, continued his line of questioning. 'What about Ma, Claudia and Christian? What happens to them after today?'

'Ally and Maia spoke with them. They all want to stay. Atlantis is as much their home as it is ours. Plus, with Ma and Georg now a…whatever it is they are…I definitely don't worry about her getting lonely when we're not here.'

Inside the house, Georg and Merry heard a knock on the office door. 'Come on in!' replied the lawyer. Maia poked her head in. 'Sorry, I'm not interrupting, am I?'

'Not at all, my love,' said Merry.

'I was just wondering if I could borrow Georg for a moment?'

'Of course you can!' cried Merry. 'I'm about ready for another glass of champagne anyway. We'll continue our chat later, Georg.' She crossed the room and gave Maia a gentle kiss on the cheek. 'I'll see you in a little while.'

'Thanks, Merry,' Maia said, gently shutting the door behind her. 'So.' She smoothed her dress. 'Has there been any progress?'

Georg nodded. 'I was going to speak to you later. I know this is a very emotional day...'

'It's okay, Georg. What's the news?'

'I've received a response from the parents. I'm glad to say that it is what you were hoping for. The mother and father have indeed told their son—your son—that he is adopted.'

A flutter of nerves danced through Maia's stomach. 'All right.'

'But,' Georg continued, 'they told me that they wish for him to decide if he wants your details on the occasion of his eighteenth birthday, or thereafter. He has not yet shown an interest in his birth mother, and they wisely do not want to unsettle him.'

Maia nodded. 'That sounds very sensible indeed.'

Georg put a comforting hand on Maia's shoulder. 'You are being as sagacious and cautious as he always was. He would be full of pride.'

Maia's eyes glistened. 'I hope so, Georg. I've decided that I'm going to write him a letter—when he turns eighteen—and give him the choice about whether or not he wishes to know about his past. Just like Pa did for all of us.'

'And rest assured, when you do, I will be your faithful messenger.'

'Thank you, Georg.' She wrapped her arms around him.

Two floors above them, in Ally's childhood bedroom, Dr Charlie Kinnaird looked down at the small device he had brought with him from the surgery on Ally's request.

'All done,' he confirmed.

Jack sat with Ally on the bed, squeezing her hand tightly. 'So? What do you reckon, doc?'

Charlie smiled. 'I just need a moment to know for sure.'

Ally leant her head onto Jack's shoulder. 'How's that white stag of yours doing, Charlie?' she asked.

'We rarely see him, but when we do…it's always spine-tingling. Our groundskeeper, Cal, wanted to put a tracker on the fellow, but…'—Charlie shrugged—'I thought it would ruin the magic somewhat.' The doctor recognised the nervous look in the couple's eyes. It was something he had witnessed many times before. 'How are the grapes, Jack?'

'It was a pretty good yield this year, I reckon,' he replied. 'We're due to travel back next month to take a look at the new buds.'

Charlie smiled. 'A life split between Norway and New Zealand… I'm terribly jealous!'

'We have MK to thank, really,' Ally explained. 'She does such a wonderful job of overseeing things in the winter.' She looked at Charlie in anticipation. He took the device to the window to confirm the result in the light.

'Well, it's official. Congratulations to both of you.' Jack and Ally burst out laughing, and hugged one another.

'Oh, thank you, Charlie! Thank you!' Ally stood up and crossed the room to give him a kiss.

'No need to thank me! This is wonderful news. I know how thrilled they'll all be downstairs.'

'I hope so. I wonder if…' Ally's sentence was cut short as the sound of an outboard motor approached on the lake outside.

Charlie turned around to look. 'Seems as though we have a visitor,' he said.

'Who is that?' Ally asked as she watched as the little boat grew closer and closer to the jetty. Jack joined them at the window. On the lawn below, everyone was gathering to greet the mysterious arrival. As the boat docked, the driver came into view. 'Oh no,' Ally whispered.

Outside, Tiggy stared at the jetty. 'It can't be…' she gasped.

'I'm sorry, Tiggy,' Electra said, appearing alongside her. 'I think it is.'

Dressed in a sharp grey suit, bedecked in aviator sunglasses, and with oiled, slicked-back hair, Zed Eszu tied off his boat and began to slowly make his way towards the house.

'God damn it,' said Miles, who immediately paced towards Eszu. He was soon joined by Floriano and Mouse.

'You'll stay there, thanks, old chap,' said the eldest Forbes brother.

'Who gave you permission to be here? You're trespassing!' Marina called down from the terrace.

'Such a warm welcome!' replied Zed with a greasy smile. 'I merely dropped in to see my favourite sisters, and pay my respects to their father. I saw on a mutual friend's social media that you were scattering the ashes today.'

Maia boldly made her way through the crowd to face Eszu. When she spoke, there was no hint of fear in her voice. 'You can leave, Zed. There's nothing for you here. You've come here to intimidate us. But it won't work anymore.'

'Intimidate you? Little old me? How could an ex-lover ever do such a thing, my sweet?' Floriano's fists visibly tightened. 'I just wanted to make sure you were all all right after such a…traumatic time.'

'We've been waiting to hear from you,' Electra hissed. 'But funnily enough, you've been ever so quiet since your Atlas project failed. Last I read in the papers, Lightning Communications is set to go into administration.'

Zed bristled. 'It is true to say that reimagining global internet infrastructure during the financial crisis was not my finest moment.' He sucked his teeth. 'Particularly as we were bankrolled by…Berners.'

'Who went under,' Star reminded him with relish.

'Yes. Clearly I do not possess the business nous of my father.'

'We're not afraid of you anymore,' said Tiggy, taking Maia's hand.

'Aren't you?' Zed replied, staring intensely at her.

'No. You have no power over us, Zed,' stated Maia. 'Now leave Atlantis, and never return.'

'As you wish, my dear.' Zed turned to leave, but spun back around on his heels. 'Oh, might I share something with you which you will not have read about in the papers?' His grin had become serpent-like. 'You see, I came into some good fortune when my business partner, David Rutter, died.'

'Good fortune, despite a death?' Merry shook her head.

'That's right. I wouldn't want you all to worry that Zed Eszu was going to go to rack and ruin, that's all.'

CeCe frowned. 'David Rutter... I *swear* I know that name.'

Zed snorted. 'Perhaps because you are a living, breathing human being. Everyone has heard of him. David was the CEO of Berners.'

'Oh my God, yes...' CeCe said to herself. 'He's dead?'

Zed nodded. 'He is. He had a lethal stroke not so long ago. It was the strangest thing. The man was perfectly healthy. He had a personal trainer, a dietician, and then one day...bang. Gone.'

'Just like the Eszu empire,' added Ally, who had arrived from inside.

'Not quite, my dear. Because good old David left me a little something in his will.' Zed reached into his pocket.

Somehow, CeCe already knew what he was about to produce.

Zed held up the largest pearl any of the sisters had ever seen. Its pale rose colour glistened in the sun.

'Do you know how much this little beauty is worth?' he asked.

CeCe swallowed hard. 'Well over one million euros,' she said, struggling to keep the disbelief from her face.

'Perhaps you're not as stupid as I assumed, CeCe! You are quite correct. For this is not just any pearl. This is the famous *Roseate* Pearl.' At the mention of its name, a couple of the sisters looked at each other with wide eyes. 'It was lost in Australia for many years, but David's team found it. And he left it to me when he died! Can you believe that?! I always thought the old bastard hated me. He blamed the Atlas project for the bank's collapse.'

'Wow. What a good friend,' CeCe muttered.

'Indeed! So, far from being destitute, I will remain a millionaire.' He looked lovingly at the pearl. 'I will rebuild, I assure you of that. The Atlas project will go ahead. In honour of my father.'

'It's time to go, Zed,' said Maia, stepping forward.

Zed made a sad face. 'Are you sure I'm not allowed to stay for a little glass of champagne, Maia? Just like the old times?' he said with a wink. Within a second, Floriano's fist had contacted Zed's face, producing a satisfying thudding sound which seemed to echo across the lake itself.

'You heard her. Leave!' he shouted.

Zed staggered backwards, cupping his bloody nose. 'I'll have you sued for GBH!'

'As a lawyer, I can assure you that trespassing on someone else's property and refusing to leave means that my friend here acted in self-defence. Now get your butt on that damn boat,' Miles said.

A furious Zed made his way back across the grass, onto the jetty and into the boat. He revved the engine, and sped away across the lake.

'Is everyone all right?' Ally asked. 'Maia?'

'Absolutely fine,' she said honestly, before running to Floriano. 'My hero!'

'My fist feels like it might explode,' he admitted, with a small laugh. 'I've never hit anyone before.'

'Floriano, thank you for doing what we've all wanted to do to the guy for years,' Electra said. 'I just…can't believe he turned up.'

'The pearl…' CeCe stuttered. 'He has the pearl…'

Tiggy put a hand on her sister's back. 'Are you okay, Cee?'

'It's cursed, Tigs. There's a rumour about it…some of you might remember…'

'Oh my *God*,' said Star to her sister. 'The cursed pearl you told us about? From Australia? *That* was it?'

'Yes. I can't believe it…' CeCe stumbled.

'If he *does* rebuild…whatever he throws at us…' Maia said. 'We can see to him. Can't we?'

'Yes,' confirmed Ally. 'We can.'

'You really won't have to worry about seeing him again…' CeCe whispered.

Tiggy looked out at the water. 'No, Cee. You're right. We won't.'

'Listen,' Ally interjected. 'Seeing as we're all here together…'—she peered at Jack, who nodded—'would you like some news?' She reached out a hand to her partner, and he took it.

'You might need to brace yourself for this one, Mum,' Jack said to Merry.

Ally addressed the crowd of expectant faces. 'Jack and I spoke to Charlie earlier, and he has confirmed that I'm going to have another baby.'

A cacophony of squeals and cheers filled the air, and Ally and Jack were embraced by practically everyone, led by an ecstatic Merry.

'Congratulations, congratulations, congratulations!!! Oh my Lord. I'm going to be a granny,' she said, tears quickly filling her eyes. 'If only your father had been here to see this. He'd have been so happy for you.' She looked into Ally's eyes. 'Both of them would be.'

'Oh, *mon dieu, chérie!*' Ma screeched. 'You know what this means, don't you?'

Ally nodded. 'Yes, Ma.'

'Pa and Elle's bloodline continues,' said Maia with the widest of smiles. 'How very fitting.'

'I shall go and open some more champagne!' Claudia cried. 'Not that Ally can have any…' She hurried indoors.

'This is wonderful news. Wonderful!' exclaimed Georg. 'And, I believe, the perfect moment to conduct one final piece of business… I wonder, could I borrow the Seven Sisters for just one moment?'

The women looked to one another, and started to followed Georg, who had already begun to cross the lawn. The party traversed the side of the house and eventually arrived at the collection of immaculately clipped yews which signalled the entrance to Pa's hidden garden. They passed through, and were met by the sweet scent of lavender that emanated from the well-tended flower beds. As the sisters filed in, they thought back to their childhoods. Their eyes were drawn to the set of steps that led down to a pebbled cove where they had swum in the clear, cool waters of summer.

The immaculate garden's aspect was particularly stunning today. It looked directly onto the lake, with a spectacular uninterrupted view of the sun, which was just thinking about setting between the mountains. No wonder this had been Pa's favourite place.

'So,' said Georg, 'two years later, here we are again.'

The armillary sphere shone brightly before them. The series of intricate, slender bands overlapped and shielded the small golden ball at the structure's centre—which was, in fact, a globe, skewered by a slim metal rod with an arrow at the end of it.

'There is one last thing I must show you.' Georg walked with a slow purpose towards the armillary sphere. 'I was given precise instructions from your father as to the design of the sculpture.' He reached a hand in between the bands, and clasped the central golden globe. He began to twist firmly, until his wrist started to quiver. The girls watched in shock as the globe began to loosen. Georg continued to twist, until the top half came off in his hand.

And there, sitting inside the sphere, was a huge diamond, which sent beams of reflected light dancing around the garden. The girls were silent. They each knew precisely what they were looking at.

'Wow…' Maia eventually breathed.

'It's incredible,' said Ally.

'As you now know,' Georg said, 'your pa carried this diamond everywhere with him for years. Even when he was starving. He could have sold it, but he never did.'

'We all wondered where it could have possibly gone,' laughed Tiggy. 'I just assumed that after Pa's showdown with Kreeg it was at the bottom of the Aegean.'

'Me too,' nodded Star.

'But it was here the whole time…' whispered Merry.

'That's right,' Georg continued. 'When I went to see Atlas on what transpired to be the penultimate occasion, he gave it to my keeping, and instructed me to secure it within the armillary sphere.

I was told to hand it over to you when the time seemed right. I felt today was that time.'

'One final flourish…' Maia said.

'So, what do we do with it?' Ally asked.

Georg thought for a moment. 'Your father left that to his girls to decide. He trusted your integrity.'

'How much is it worth, Georg?' asked CeCe.

'A lost diamond of the last tsarina of Russia?' he laughed. 'I am no expert, but once it is validated—which it will be—I would conservatively say ten million euros.'

'We could change lives with that money…' Maia commented.

Ally looked to her sister. 'Lots of lives,' she agreed.

'Maybe this is silly,' Star said, 'but when we were growing up, CeCe and I used to talk about how we were going to start a charity. Do you remember, Cee?'

CeCe grinned. 'You mean, The Seven Sisters charity?'

'That's right!' Star laughed. 'We…we wanted to try and help every orphan find a family as perfect as ours, no matter where they were in the world.'

The girls silently reflected on the idea, each one knowing for certain that it was *exactly* what they wanted to do.

'The Seven Sisters charity. I think that's beautiful,' said Maia. 'Here.' She took Ally's hand, who took Star's, who took CeCe's until the women encircled the sphere. Slowly and silently, Georg slipped away and out of the garden.

The sisters stood together around the armillary sphere for a while, safe in each other's company. Very slowly, the circle began to move, until it was spinning, and the garden was filled with laughter.

Merry took Christian's hand and stepped onto the boat.

'See you soon, everyone!' she cried, as they began to manoeuvre away from the jetty, which was populated by her newfound family. She returned their enthusiastic waves, and blew kisses to everyone she could. As Christian pulled the boat out onto the lake and started to head around the peninsula towards Geneva's port, Merry's sisters, and Atlantis, began to fade from view.

She allowed herself to relax on the soft leather cushions of the speedboat, closing her eyes and feeling the warm wind on her face. When she opened them again, her gaze fell on a rocky outcrop. As clear as day, she saw a tall figure in a white shirt waving to her. Without thinking, she returned the wave, and gave a wide smile. As she continued to look at the man, she realised that she knew the face.

Then a beautiful woman with blonde hair appeared next to him, and took his hand.

'Mum…' Merry whispered in a daze. 'Christian!' she shouted. 'Christian! Stop the boat! Stop it!' Without hesitation, Christian cut the engine. 'Is everything all right, Merry?'

'Please, take us over there…' Merry pointed to the couple, who were still waving to her.

'Of course.' Christian replied, and began slowly approaching the outcrop.

'I love you!' cried the man.

'I love you too,' whispered Merry.

Christian steered the boat as close as he could to the rocks. Merry held her gaze on her parents for as long as she could, but eventually, the image slowly faded away.

And she knew they had gone.

Acknowledgements

After Lucinda's death, we were faced with immediate pressure from readers over the fate of the promised eighth book. Mum had asked me to finish the series, but there was no guarantee it would be an acceptable outcome for her publishers at home and abroad.

Fortunately, my first meeting with Jeremy Trevathan and Lucy Hale from Pan Macmillan assured me that they had confidence in the plan, and the rest of the world followed suit. I am particularly grateful to the brilliant Lucy, who has continued to be enormously supportive throughout the process. In fact, the entire team at Macmillan have been phenomenal. Thanks in particular go to Jayne Osborne, Samantha Fletcher, Lorraine Green and Becky Lloyd.

To Lucinda's publishers across the globe...what can I say? Mum was in the slightly unique position of being dear friends with you all, and I know she would want to express her gratitude for your amazing contribution to the Seven Sisters legacy. Many of you began this project with her a decade ago, and *Atlas* represents the end of quite a remarkable journey together. Thank you to those who sent messages of encouragement during the writing process, specifically Claudia Negele, Grusche Juncker, Fernando Mercadante and Sander Knol. Also to Knut Gørvell, who freely admitted he had little confidence in me, but was the most enthusiastic of all after reading the manuscript! I also wish to pay tribute to the brilliant translators who have worked so diligently on the Seven Sisters series across the years. Their role is often undervalued, but never by Lucinda or myself.

I knew I needed an excellent editor, and Susan Opie has been just that. I have discovered that the life of a novelist can be a lonely one, particularly in my situation, and Susan's thoughts, reflections and catches have been invaluable. I couldn't have done it without you!

Far from *Atlas* being the end of the Seven Sisters universe, it is in fact ever-expanding. The last year has proved to be an education in the world of the screen, and I want to acknowledge

Sean Gascoine, Benjamina Mirnik-Voges, Faye Ward and Caroline Harvey for their patience and expertise.

Thank you to Jacquelyn Heslop, Nathan Moore, Charles Deane, Matthew Stallworthy, James Gamblin, Ellie Brennan, David Dunning, Cathal and Mags Dineen, Kerrie Scot, Kirsty Kennedy, Tory Hardy, Anna Evans, Martyn Weston and Richard Staples, who have all in their different ways offered me support during the past year.

June 2021–June 2022 proved to be an *annus horribilis* in which my family endured two further unexpected deaths. My grandmother (Mum's mum) Janet Edmonds died in January 2022. Granny was sweet and effervescent, and provided us with untold laughs over the years. Then, in May 2022, we lost my stepsister Olivia. Not just a wonderful sibling, Olivia acted as a personal assistant and publishing executive for Lucinda Riley Ltd for many years. She was the first point of contact for readers, and engaged with them brilliantly. She also ran the office with huge efficiency and ease. It would be remiss of me not to mention the enormous contribution she made to everything behind the scenes, including in the case of this novel. Thank you, Livi.

I owe particular thanks to my stepfather Stephen, who acts as agent and deals with aspects of the business I simply cannot. He has shouldered much of the practical responsibilities in the most testing of circumstances, and I don't know what I'd do without him. Further thanks go to Jess Kearton, who has learnt the ins and outs of her wide-ranging role at Lucinda Riley Ltd very quickly, and is completely reliable in all she does.

I am endlessly appreciative of my partner Lily, who has been a stoic pillar during the last eighteen months (apologies for the fact you've had to endure my artistic meltdowns for five years). Thanks to my cat, Tiggy, for convincing this canine fan that her species can be loving. Finally, thank you to my brother and sisters—Isabella for her superb research work early on, Leonora for her genuine enthusiasm about the book, and Kit for making me laugh like no one else. Mum would be indescribably proud of you all.

The final words must be Lucinda Riley's. I hope she won't mind me lifting them from Seven Sisters acknowledgements throughout the years:

Thanks lastly to YOU, the readers, whose love and support as I travel to the four corners of the earth and hear your stories inspire and humble me. Writing a seven-book series seemed like such a mad idea in 2012—I never guessed that my sisters would touch so many people around the world. You have taken them to your hearts, laughed, loved and cried with them as I have done when I am writing their stories.

If I have learnt one thing from the past year, it is that the moment is truly all we have. Try, if you can, to relish it, in whatever circumstances you find yourself, and never give up hope—it is the fundamental flame that keeps us human beings alive.

About Lucinda Riley

Lucinda Riley was born in Ireland and, after an early career as an actress in film, theatre and television, wrote her first book aged twenty-four. Her books have been translated into thirty-seven languages and sold forty million copies worldwide. She was a *Sunday Times* and *New York Times* number one bestseller.

Lucinda's The Seven Sisters series, which tells the story of adopted sisters and is inspired by the mythology of the famous star cluster, has become a global phenomenon. The series is a number one bestseller across the world and is currently in development with a major TV production company.

Though she brought up her four children mostly in Norfolk in England, in 2015 Lucinda fulfilled her dream of buying a remote farmhouse in West Cork, Ireland, which she always felt was her spiritual home, and indeed this was where her last five books were written. Lucinda was diagnosed with cancer in 2017 and died in June 2021.

Also from Lucinda Riley and Blue Box Press

The Missing Sister

The six D'Aplièse sisters have each been on their own incredible journey to discover their heritage, but they still have one question left unanswered: who and where is the seventh sister?

They only have one clue—an image of a star-shaped emerald ring. The search to find the missing sister will take them across the globe; from New Zealand to Canada, England, France and Ireland, uniting them all in their mission to at last complete their family.

In doing so, they will slowly unearth a story of love, strength and sacrifice that began almost one hundred years ago, as other brave young women risk everything to change the world around them.

The Missing Sister is the seventh installment in Lucinda Riley's multimillion copy epic series.

Discover yourself at the heart of history.

* * * *

The Murders at Fleat House

One dead bully. A school full of suspects.

The sudden death of a pupil in Fleat House at St Stephen's – a small private boarding school in deepest Norfolk—is a shocking event that the headmaster is very keen to call a tragic accident...

But the local police cannot rule out foul play and the case prompts the return of high-flying Detective Inspector Jazmine 'Jazz' Hunter to the force. Jazz has her own private reasons for stepping away from her police career in London, and reluctantly agrees to front the investigation as a favour to her old boss.

Reunited with her loyal sergeant Alastair Miles, she enters the closed world of the school, and as Jazz begins to probe the circumstances surrounding Charlie Cavendish's tragic death, events are soon to take another troubling turn.

Charlie is exposed as an arrogant bully, and those around him had both motive and opportunity to switch the drugs he took daily to control his epilepsy.

As staff at the school close ranks, the disappearance of young pupil Rory Millar and the death of an elderly classics master provide Jazz with important leads, but are destined to complicate the investigation further. As snow covers the landscape and another suspect goes missing, Jazz must also confront her personal demons.

Then, a particularly grim discovery at the school makes this the most challenging murder investigation of her career. Because Fleat House hides secrets darker than even Jazz could ever have imagined…

* * * *

The Butterfly Room

An emotional and beautifully English family saga, with dramatic secrets from the past. Set in the idyllic coastal town of Southwold.

Posy Montague is approaching her seventieth birthday. Her beloved childhood home—Admiral House, set in the beautiful Suffolk countryside, and where she brought up her two sons and created a magnificent garden, is crumbling around her. She knows the time has come for her to take the decision to sell it.

Then a face appears from the past—Freddie, her first love, who left her heartbroken fifty years ago when he abandoned her without a word.

Struggling to cope with her son Sam, whose business dealings have left him and his wife and children virtually destitute, and the reappearance of her other son Nick, who has arrived back in England ten years after he fled to Australia, Posy doesn't know whether she can trust to Freddie's affection.

But Freddie—and Admiral House—has kept a terrible secret

for those fifty years, and in order to move forward with Posy, Freddie knows he must also break her heart all over again.

Set in both the 40's and 50's and the present day, The Butterfly Room is a story of how a lie from the past can destroy a lifetime of belief.

* * * *

The Angel Tree

A psychological drama set in the theatres of Soho in wartime London and a country house in the Welsh mountains.

Thirty years have passed since Greta left Marchmont Hall, a grand and beautiful house nestled in the hills of rural Monmouthshire. But when she returns to the Hall for Christmas she has no recollection of her past association with it—the result of a tragic accident that has blanked out more than two decades of her life. Then, during a walk through the wintry landscape, she stumbles across a grave in the woods, and the weathered inscription on the headstone tells her that a little boy is buried there…

The poignant discovery strikes a chord in Greta's mind and soon ignites a quest to rediscover her lost memories. She begins to piece together the fragments of not only her own story, but that of her daughter, Cheska, who was the tragic victim of circumstances beyond her control. And, most definitely, not the angel she appeared to be…

* * * *

Helena's Secret / The Olive Tree

A magical house. A momentous summer. Set over two months, a summer in Cyprus reveals many secrets.

It has been twenty-four years since a young Helena spent a magical holiday in Cyprus, where she fell in love for the first time. When the now crumbling house, 'Pandora', is left to her by her godfather, she returns to spend the summer there with her family.

Yet, as soon as Helena arrives at Pandora, she knows that its idyllic beauty masks a web of secrets that she has kept from William, her husband, and Alex, her son. At the difficult age of thirteen, Alex is torn between protecting his beloved mother, and growing up. And equally, desperate to learn the truth about his real father...

When, by chance, Helena meets her childhood sweetheart, a chain of events is set in motion that threatens to make her past and present collide. Both Helena and Alex know that life will never be the same, once Pandora's secrets have been revealed...

On Behalf of Blue Box Press,

Liz Berry, M.J. Rose, and Jillian Stein would like to thank ~

Steve Berry
Doug Scofield
Benjamin Stein
Kim Guidroz
Tanaka Kangara
Asha Hossain
Chris Graham
Chelle Olson
Kasi Alexander
Jessica Saunders
Stacey Tardif
Dylan Stockton
Kate Boggs
Richard Blake
and Simon Lipskar

Made in United States
North Haven, CT
29 May 2023

37112257R00414